Ann Radcliffe (1764–1823)

Ann Radcliffe was born in London in 1764. In 1787, she married William Radcliffe, editor and proprietor of the journal *The English Chronicle*. Like many early female writers, including Jane Austen, Radcliffe had no children. Insisting on privacy, she led a reclusive life, confined to her home or traveling with her husband. Radcliffe's first two novels, *The Castles of Athlin and Dunbayne* (1789) and *A Sicilian Romance* (1790), attracted little attention. Her reputation rests primarily on her next three works, *The Romance of the Forest* (1791), *The Mysteries of Udolpho* (1794), and *The Italian* (1797), her greatest success. In the twenty-six years from the publication of *The Italian* until her death in 1823, Radcliffe published no new novels. *Gaston de Blondeville* was published posthumously in 1826.

Jane Austen (1775–1817)

Jane Austen was born in 1775 at the Steventon Rectory in Hampshire, England, to George Austen, the rector of Steventon, and his wife, Cassandra. The seventh of eight children (six boys and two girls), she led a quiet and domestic life, always living with her family. Although Austen never married, she had several suitors and accepted a marriage proposal for the brief interval of one evening. She began writing at an early age, mostly for her family's entertainment, but her work shows a worldly and wise sensibility. Austen's novels include *Sense and Sensibility* (1811), *Pride and Prejudice* (1813), *Mansfield Park* (1814), *Emma* (1816), and *Northanger Abbey* and *Persuasion* (published posthumously 1818). Austen died in 1817.

Deborah D. Rogers is Associate Professor of English at the University of Maine, and editor of *The Critical Response to Ann Radcliffe*.

TWO GOTHIC CLASSICS
BY WOMEN

The Italian
by Ann Radcliffe

AND

Northanger Abbey
by Jane Austen

*Edited and with an Introduction
by Deborah D. Rogers*

A SIGNET CLASSIC

SIGNET CLASSIC
Published by the Penguin Group
Penguin Books USA Inc., 375 Hudson Street,
New York, New York 10014, U.S.A.
Penguin Books Ltd, 27 Wrights Lane,
London W8 5TZ, England
Penguin Books Australia Ltd, Ringwood,
Victoria, Australia
Penguin Books Canada Ltd, 10 Alcorn Avenue,
Toronto, Ontario, Canada M4V 3B2
Penguin Books (N.Z.) Ltd, 182–190 Wairau Road,
Auckland 10, New Zealand

Penguin Books Ltd, Registered Offices:
Harmondsworth, Middlesex, England

Published by Signet Classic, an imprint of
a division of Penguin Books USA Inc.

First Signet Classic Printing, October, 1995
10 9 8 7 6 5 4 3 2 1

Introduction copyright © Deborah D. Rogers, 1995
All rights reserved

Ⓒ   REGISTERED TRADEMARK—MARCA REGISTRADA

Library of Congress Catalog Card Number: 95-68136

Printed in the United States of America

BOOKS ARE AVAILABLE AT QUANTITY DISCOUNTS WHEN USED TO PROMOTE PRODUCTS OR
SERVICES. FOR INFORMATION PLEASE WRITE TO PREMIUM MARKETING DIVISION, PENGUIN
BOOKS USA INC., 375 HUDSON STREET, NEW YORK, NY 10014.

INTRODUCTION

Ann Radcliffe was one of England's first popular novelists, a woman who wrote in an eerie, often bizarre, and extremely influential mode that came to be known as "Gothic." Radcliffe did not invent the genre, although she popularized it and may be said to have "reinvented" it as a metaphor for female experience. Jane Austen, writing only slightly later, acknowledged the popularity and power of Gothic novels over women when she wrote *Northanger Abbey,* a spirited satire of one young woman's bout with Gothic melodrama that leads her to the brink of romantic disaster. Both novelists anticipated and marked the special influence these exciting works would have over women readers; in different ways, both explore the powerful links between fear and sensuality, the pleasures and perils of escapism, and the many dangers awaiting unprotected women in a world of inexplicable but very real menace.

Usually set in haunted castles, ruins, wild landscapes, or other ominous atmospheres, the Gothic novels of the late eighteenth century inspire fear by exploring the supernatural and the macabre. Although Radcliffe's exuberant novels are replete with the usual fantastic details like ghosts, gloomy architecture, disembodied voices, and mysterious manuscripts, she often uses these elements to explore the problems and anxieties resulting from women's dependence, isolation, and sexuality in a patriarchal, or male-dominated, society. Radcliffe's Gothic novels follow patterns that allow their heroines to test their inner powers in the face of persecution, fight against confinement, use their innocence as a strength, and thwart male domination.

Radcliffe's works ushered in what can only be called a frenzy of Gothic romances, most evident from 1789 to 1815. During this period Radcliffe emerged as the most popular and influential novelist in Great Britain. Horace Walpole's *Castle of*

Otranto, published dramatically on Christmas Eve 1764, the year of Radcliffe's birth, pioneered the Gothic genre. *Otranto* was followed by several other Gothics including Clara Reeve's *The Champion of Virtue* (1777; republished in 1778 under the title *The Old English Baron*), Sophia Lee's *The Recess* (1783–85), and Charlotte Smith's *Emmeline* (1788). It was not, however, until Radcliffe that the Gothic may properly be said to have come of age.

Radcliffe's popular and electrifying female Gothic helped to found and sustain a vogue for the picturesque, sentimental, and sublime thriller. Radcliffe is commonly praised for her use of the unconscious, her evocation of fear and suspense, and her innovative poetic descriptions of architecture and of landscape. Not only did her work inspire plays, operas, and imitations, it also profoundly influenced Romantic and Victorian literature, the detective, psychological, and horror genres, and a whole host of individual authors including Austen, Maturin, Lewis, Hazlitt, Scott, Byron, both Shelleys, Wordsworth, Keats, Coleridge, the Brontës, Thackeray, Dickens, Hawthorne, and Poe.

Six of Radcliffe's works appeared in her lifetime, with amazing speed in the eight years from 1789 to 1797. (A seventh, *Gaston de Blondeville,* was published posthumously in 1826.) Starting when she was only twenty-five years old, Radcliffe published her first three novels in three years.

Radcliffe's initial performances, *The Castles of Athlin and Dunbayne* (1789) and *A Sicilian Romance* (1790), are considered unremarkable. Her reputation rests primarily on her next three novels: If *The Romance of the Forest* (1791) first displayed the full power of Radcliffe's poetic descriptions, *The Mysteries of Udolpho* (1794) catapulted her to fame. But it was *The Italian* (1797) that represented her supreme achievement. So great was the contemporary popularity of *The Italian* that it was immediately translated into French and German, adapted for the theater, and widely and slavishly imitated.

The plot of *The Italian* attracted much attention. In eighteenth-century Italy, the aristocratic Vivaldi falls in love with Ellena, supposedly a poor orphan. Vivaldi's parents object to their marriage for reasons of class. Vivaldi's mother, the Marchesa, conspires with her confessor, the sinister monk Schedoni, to separate the couple. They arrange to have Ellena

abducted and carried off to a convent, where she is befriended by Olivia, a nun who will turn out to be her mother.

Eventually, Vivaldi rescues Ellena. The Marchesa and
Schedoni have, however, agreed to have her murdered. As
Vivaldi and Ellena are about to be married, a band of men
carries her off to a house on the Adriatic and him to the
chambers of the Inquisition.

From the beginning, *The Italian* invited comparisons. As
might be expected, since *Udolpho* (1794) influenced *The
Monk* (1795), which in turn inspired a reaction in the form of
The Italian (1797), Matthew Gregory ("Monk") Lewis has
often been compared to Radcliffe. As she discussed in "On
the Supernatural in Poetry," Radcliffe wrote novels of terror,
which expands and awakens the spirit, whereas Lewis wrote
novels of horror, which, according to Radcliffe, constricts the
soul.

Like Lewis, most Gothic novelists explain little, attempting
to make us believe that their mysteries are real. Radcliffe,
however, employs the so-called "explained supernatural," in
which the supernatural is ultimately revealed to be the prod-
uct of an overactive imagination. This occurs in all of her
novels except *Gaston*, where the supernatural is not explained
away. Although Radcliffe's explained supernatural in *The
Italian* is far less blatant than in her previous novels, she still
uses it to dramatize the struggle between irrationality and reason, as apparently supernatural mysteries are shown to be
caused by human agency. The most notorious example,
pointed to in *Northanger Abbey*, is the image draped by the
black veil in *Udolpho*. What Emily supposed was a worm-
eaten corpse turns out to be a wax figure. Radcliffe's mun-
dane explanations of mysteries have the effect of convincing
the reader to guard against indulging in the imagination. In
this way Radcliffe may be using the female Gothic mode to
criticize classic Gothic exaggerations.

Another Radcliffe hallmark is her innovative, highly poet-
ical descriptions of landscapes, which have spiritual as well
as aesthetic dimensions. Detailed in prose that approaches poetry, Radcliffe's striking scenery not only reflects and en-
hances the plot, it also defines and summarizes character,
evoking the elevated emotions associated with "sensibility."
Picturesque scenes are related to characters' emotional and
moral awareness: only sensitive, virtuous characters experience heightened, transcendent reactions to nature. (It is, how-

ever, this same extreme sensibility that can exaggerate the terror of their situations.) In *The Italian,* which is characterized by strongly contrasted settings and variations in the use of light and darkness, the picturesque descriptions are more concise and the reflections more frequent than in Radcliffe's previous works. Powerfully communing with her surroundings, Ellena displays her spirituality.

Remarkably, Radcliffe's novels set in Italy (*A Sicilian Romance, Udolpho,* and *The Italian*) depict scenes she had never visited. Radcliffe's romantic descriptions were influenced by travel literature and by painters like Nicolas Poussin, Claude Lorrain, and Salvator Rosa. Her landscapes dramatize Edmund Burke's then highly popular and much discussed concept of the sublime, which is inspired by such sources as obscurity, privation, vastness, infinity, difficulty, and magnificence. In this aesthetic model, the soul experiences transcendence by feeling its own power confronting the unimaginable.

Radcliffe's extreme focus on the energy of the sublime scene and atmosphere to excite fear unfortunately leaves her characters somewhat undiscriminated and one-dimensional. Full of sensibility, Radcliffe's feminized heroes seem weak and ineffectual. Her villains, however, are arresting. Radcliffe's most fully elaborated character, *The Italian*'s satanically flamboyant Schedoni, anticipates the Byronic hero in his magnificent and mysterious solitude.

Because of its emphasis on the developing consciousness of Schedoni rather than that of the heroine, *The Italian* is considered Radcliffe's least female-centered novel. Nevertheless, its structure follows the pattern of the female Gothic, as Ellena experiences separation from home, fights against confinement, escapes from male domination, and reconciles with her mother.

With virtue that is beyond reproach, Radcliffe's persecuted heroines are often compared to those of Samuel Richardson. Radcliffe's female victims are conventionally beautiful, prone to tears, and sensitive to landscape. Yet they are unlike Richardson's Pamela, Burney's Evelina, or Austen's Catherine (of *Northanger Abbey*), who all seek moral guidance from male figures. Instead, Radcliffe's female characters maintain their independence in romantic relationships.

In *The Italian* Ellena is stronger and more mature than Vivaldi, whose disappearance forces her to be confined, isolated, and harassed in a Gothic environment. In this situation, interpretation becomes integral to the plot, as veils and cowls serve as images of mystification, obscurity, sexuality, concealment, enclosure, and revelation. Ellena's loneliness, confinement, and helplessness, however, are very real female anxieties.

Interestingly, Radcliffe's heroines are *not* generally rescued by their heroes. In *Udolpho* it is not Valancourt who saves Emily, and in *The Italian* it is not Vivaldi who saves Ellena.

Feminist critics have recently argued that although the traditional Gothic novel has reflected patriarchal violence, starting with Ann Radcliffe, the female Gothic has also stressed female kinship relations. Especially important is the mother-daughter bond in terms of the mother's threat to engulf her child and the daughter's quest for identification and separation. At the dramatic heart of the Radcliffean Gothic is the daughter's conflict with maternal figures from whom she cannot totally separate because of her own femaleness and because they symbolize her own fate.

Believing that her mother is dead, Ellena is unknowingly admitted into her powerless and oppressed situation when she encounters her mother, who is disguised as Sister Olivia, at the convent. Eventually Ellena escapes with Olivia's help, as she not only accepts her mother's position, but identifies with her, disguising herself with her mother's veil. Destined to repeat the pattern of her mother's life, Ellena avoids the devastating results. Ellena, like her mother, is persecuted by Schedoni, but in the end, both mother and daughter thwart patriarchal violence.

The Marchesa (the "bad mother," often compared to Lady Macbeth) in collusion with Schedoni (the "bad father") disrupts Ellena's life, but Olivia ultimately redefines her situation. Reunited with a mother whom the narrative has repressed, Ellena's value is affirmed, as she recovers the past. The discovery of her mother and, consequently, of her lineage allows for Ellena's marriage and for the possibility that she, too, may become a mother.

After achieving her greatest success with *The Italian,* at the age of thirty-four, Radcliffe stopped writing for publication. In the twenty-six years until Radcliffe's death in 1823, mysteriously, she published no new romances. During this time, many contemporaries were willing to believe—possibly because Radcliffe was the author of Gothics—that she had died or gone insane. So reticent and self-effacing was Radcliffe that she never corrected such rumors. It is known that she suffered a debilitating form of asthma during these years. Still, one reason Radcliffe stopped writing may have been the many imitations and parodies of her work. The best of these burlesques was *Northanger Abbey*.

In 1798, a year after Radcliffe published *The Italian*, Jane Austen began *Northanger Abbey*, originally entitled *Susan*, after its heroine, whose name was later changed. Austen finished her parody in 1799 and later slightly revised it before selling the anonymous manuscript to the publisher Crosby in 1803 for a measly ten pounds. (Radcliffe had received eight hundred pounds for *The Italian*.) Crosby advertised *Susan* but never issued it, perhaps because, having invested in Radcliffe's works, he feared the parody might threaten their popularity or offend their sensitive author. After all, Radcliffe was the star to be reckoned with, not the unknown author of *Susan*. In 1816 Henry Austen helped his sister buy back the copyright for the same ten pounds Crosby had originally paid for it. Apologizing for parts that were dated, Austen wrote a brief "Advertisement" for the work. Prefaced by her brother's biographical notice announcing her authorship, Austen's novel was published posthumously with *Persuasion* in December 1817 (1818 on the title page).

Exploring the relationship among female imagination, fiction, and life, *Northanger Abbey*, Austen's most self-consciously literary work, satirizes Gothic novels by contrasting their distortions with banal reality. It is, in effect, Radcliffe's explained supernatural writ large. Through dialogue and through a narrator who is more intrusive and ironic than in any of her other novels, Austen indicates at every point that the heightened perceptions of her heroine, Catherine Morland, fail to correspond to ordinary life.

The daughter of a clergyman, Catherine accompanies the Allen family to Bath, where she and Henry Tilney fall in love. Mistakenly believing that Catherine is wealthy, Henry's father, General Tilney, invites her to Northanger Abbey, the scene of the literary burlesque.

At Northanger Abbey, influenced by having read too many Gothic novels, Catherine behaves like a persecuted maiden imprisoned in a Gothic castle, even though the Tilneys' country seat is modern, fashionable, and well lit. Nevertheless, Catherine discovers a bloodstained document (which turns out to be an old laundry list) and wrongly imagines that General Tilney has murdered his wife.

Informed that Catherine has no money, General Tilney banishes her from the abbey. Henry follows and proposes to Catherine, who has learned to temper imagination with reason and good sense.

Influenced by *Sicilian Romance, Romance of the Forest, Udolpho,* and *The Italian,* Austen reinterprets Radcliffe's transformation of traditional Gothic conventions in the search for female identity. Both Radcliffe and Austen represent female powerlessness, vulnerability, and confinement (all partially the result of financial dependency on men who exercise arbitrary power) as an implied critique of patriarchal control. Austen modulates Radcliffe's female Gothic, in which heroines experience in the defeat of demonically "bad" father figures such as Montoni and Schedoni the impotence of patriarchy in general. Subversive readings of *Northanger Abbey* similarly find that Austen's heroines, like Catherine, discover in the failure of flawed fathers like General Tilney the invariable failure of patriarchy.

Austen also uses Radcliffe's model of the heroine who lacks adequate maternal guidance. Mothers in the works of both authors are useless, obtuse, or absent. In *Northanger Abbey,* Mrs. Morland is relegated to a minor role, all but ignoring Catherine as she turns her over to the care of Mrs. Allen in Bath. When Catherine goes on to Northanger Abbey, she takes leave of the vacuous Mrs. Allen, a surrogate typical of Austen's incompetent mothers, whose obsessive concern with clothes and trivial proprieties indicates their shallowness.

An unconventional heroine who loves nothing better than to roll down hills, the plain, naive, and not particularly bright Catherine may seem far removed from Radcliffe's idealized female protagonists. Yet Austen develops in Catherine one of Radcliffe's main character types: the self-deluded heroine who reforms. Like Austen's other heroines, Catherine must overcome mistaken impressions to see things as they really are and achieve a sense of her self-worth by marrying the right man.

Unlike Radcliffe's heroines, who have no male mentor, Catherine comes to prefer common sense to imaginative indulgence through the agency of Henry Tilney, who courts her by teaching her how to read both people and books judiciously. In the process Henry manipulates Catherine by mockingly providing her with a Gothic plot based on both *Romance of the Forest* and *Udolpho.* He thus increases Catherine's paranoia at Northanger Abbey.

Austen's work is, in some respects, less a satire of the Gothic than a novel about reading, as it defines characters by their reaction to literature, attacking inexperienced, uncritical readers who, like Catherine, fail to read analytically. Catherine is misled by credulously reading too many of Radcliffe's works, most recently *Udolpho,* to be followed, Catherine's friend Isabella promises, by *The Italian,* and a list of "horrid" novels. Catherine reads for cheap thrills, confusing fiction and reality as she naively superimposes elements of Gothic fiction on the trivialities of everyday life. Radcliffe's novels, which have psychological, moral, and didactic dimensions that escape her, become the barometer of literary taste. Indeed, one indication of John Thorpe's boorishness is his ignorance of Radcliffe. The more sophisticated Henry Tilney, who knows how to read correctly and has read all of Radcliffe's works, appreciates and takes pleasure in her art.

In a famous passage in Chapter 5, Austen passionately defends the novel against the many who dismissed the genre as light entertainment for bored young ladies. Not only does she protest against popular notions about the frivolity of the genre, she addresses the relationship between women and the novel and laments the undervaluing of women's writing. "There seems almost a general wish of decrying the capacity and undervaluing the labor of the novelist, and of slighting the performances which have only genius, wit, and taste to recommend them. 'I am no novel reader—I seldom look into novels—Do not imagine that *I* often read novels—It is really very well for a novel.' Such is the common cant. 'And what are you reading, Miss——?' 'Oh! It is only a novel!' replies the young lady, while she lays down her book with affected indifference, or momentary shame . . . in short, only some work in which the greatest powers of the mind are displayed, in which the most thorough knowledge of human nature, the happiest delineation of its varieties, the liveliest effusions of wit and humor, are conveyed to the world in the best-chosen language."

It is, then, not surprising that Austen's most consistently satirical work is as serious as Radcliffe's female Gothic in warning women against female paranoia and self-delusion. Following Radcliffe, Austen simultaneously demonstrates that female apprehensions do, in fact, have a basis in reality. Oppressive, domineering General Tilney may not be the Gothic murderer of Catherine's imagination. He does, however, translate the sensational evil of a Radcliffean villain into the idiom of ordinary life. He becomes representative of domestic patriarchal authority as motivated by financial considerations as the villain Montoni. In many ways Catherine's real world is as threatening to women as the fictional world of Radcliffe's works. As General Tilney drives her out of Northanger Abbey and forces her to return home unattended, Catherine contemplates "actual and natural evil" and comes to realize that "her anxiety had foundation in fact, her fears in probability. . . ." Austen's satire uses Radcliffe's female Gothic to demonstrate the difficulty of distinguishing female imaginative distortions from ordinary domestic life. Here, reality for women may indeed approximate the inexplicable, unpredictable dangers of Gothic fiction.

—*Deborah D. Rogers*

The Italian

OR THE

Confessional of the Black Penitents

A ROMANCE

Ann Radcliffe

ABOUT the year 1764, some English travellers in Italy, during one of their excursions in the environs of Naples, happened to stop before the portico of the Santa Maria del Pianto, a church belonging to a very ancient convent of the order of the Black Penitents. The magnificence of this portico, though impaired by time, excited so much admiration, that the travellers were curious to survey the structure to which it belonged, and with this intention they ascended the marble steps that led to it.

Within the shade of the portico, a person with folded arms, and eyes directed towards the ground, was pacing behind the pillars the whole extent of the pavement, and was apparently so engaged by his own thoughts, as not to observe that strangers were approaching. He turned, however, suddenly, as if startled by the sound of steps, and then, without further pausing, glided to a door that opened into the church, and disappeared.

There was something too extraordinary in the figure of this man, and too singular in his conduct, to pass unnoticed by the visitors. He was of a tall thin figure, bending forward from the shoulders; of a sallow complexion, and harsh features, and had an eye, which, as it looked up from the cloke that muffled the lower part of his countenance, seemed expressive of uncommon ferocity.

The travellers, on entering the church, looked round for the stranger, who had passed thither before them, but he was no where to be seen, and, through all the shade of the long aisles, only one other person appeared. This was a friar of the adjoining convent, who sometimes pointed out to strangers the objects in the church, which were most worthy of attention, and who now, with this design, approached the party that had just entered.

The interior of this edifice had nothing of the shewy ornament and general splendor, which distinguish the churches of Italy, and particularly those of Naples; but it exhibited a simplicity and grandeur of design, considerably more interesting to persons of taste, and a solemnity of light and shade much more suitable to promote the sublime elevation of devotion.

When the party had viewed the different shrines and whatever had been judged worthy of observation, and were returning through an obscure aisle towards the portico, they perceived the person who had appeared upon the steps, passing towards a confessional on the left, and, as he entered it, one of the party pointed him out to the friar, and enquired who he was; the friar turning to look after him, did not immediately reply, but, on the question being repeated, he inclined his head, as in a kind of obeisance, and calmly replied, "He is an assassin."

"An assassin!" exclaimed one of the Englishmen; "an assassin and at liberty!"

An Italian gentleman, who was of the party, smiled at the astonishment of his friend.

"He has sought sanctuary here," replied the friar; "within these walls he may not be hurt."

"Do your altars, then, protect the murderer?" said the Englishman.

"He could find shelter no where else," answered the friar meekly.

"This is astonishing!" said the Englishman; "of what avail are your laws, if the most atrocious criminal may thus find shelter from them? But how does he contrive to exist here! He is, at least, in danger of being starved?"

"Pardon me," replied the friar; "there are always people willing to assist those, who cannot assist themselves; and as the criminal may not leave the church in search of food, they bring it to him here."

"Is this possible!" said the Englishman, turning to his Italian friend.

"Why, the poor wretch must not starve," replied the friend; "which he inevitably would do, if food were not brought to him! But have you never, since your arrival in Italy, happened to see a person in the situation of this man? It is by no means an uncommon one."

"Never!" answered the Englishman, "and I can scarcely credit what I see now!"

"Why, my friend," observed the Italian, "if we were to shew no mercy to such unfortunate persons, assassinations are so frequent, that our cities would be half depopulated."

In notice of this profound remark, the Englishman could only gravely bow.

"But observe yonder confessional," added the Italian, "that beyond the pillars on the left of the aisle, below a painted window. Have you discovered it? The colours of the glass throw, instead of light, a shade over that part of the church, which, perhaps, prevents your distinguishing what I mean!"

The Englishman looked whither his friend pointed, and observed a confessional of oak, or some very dark wood, adjoining the wall, and remarked also, that it was the same, which the assassin had just entered. It consisted of three compartments, covered with a black canopy. In the central division was the chair of the confessor, elevated by several steps above the pavement of the church; and on either hand was a small closet, or box, with steps leading up to a grated partition, at which the penitent might kneel, and, concealed from observation, pour into the ear of the confessor, the consciousness of crimes that lay heavy on his heart.

"You observe it?" said the Italian.

"I do," replied the Englishman; "it is the same, which the assassin has passed into; and I think it one of the most gloomy spots I ever beheld; the view of it is enough to strike a criminal with despair!"

"We, in Italy, are not so apt to despair," replied the Italian smilingly.

"Well, but what of this confessional?" enquired the Englishman. "The assassin entered it!"

"He has no relation, with what I am about to mention," said the Italian; "but I wish you to mark the place, because some very extraordinary circumstances belong to it."

"What are they?" said the Englishman.

"It is now several years since the confession, which is connected with them, was made at that very confessional," added the Italian; "the view of it, and the sight of this assassin, with your surprise at the liberty which is allowed him, led me to a recollection of the story. When you return to the hotel, I will communicate it to you, if you have no pleasanter way of engaging your time."

"I have a curiosity to hear it," replied the Englishman, "cannot you relate it now?"

"It is much too long to be related now; that would occupy a week; I have it in writing, and will send you the volume. A young student of Padua, who happened to be at Naples soon after this horrible confession became public"——

"Pardon me," interrupted the Englishman, "that is surely very extraordinary? I thought confessions were always held sacred by the priest, to whom they were made."

"Your observation is reasonable," rejoined the Italian; "the faith of the priest is never broken, except by an especial command from an higher power; and the circumstances must even then be very extraordinary to justify such a departure from the law. But, when you read the narrative, your surprise on this head will cease. I was going to tell you, that it was written by a student of Padua, who, happening to be here soon after the affair became public, was so much struck with the facts, that, partly as an exercise, and partly in return for some trifling services I had rendered him, he committed them to paper for me. You will perceive from the work, that this student was very young, as to the arts of composition, but the facts are what we require, and from these he has not deviated. But come, let us leave the church."

"After I have taken another view of this solemn edifice," replied the Englishman, "and particularly of the confessional you have pointed to my notice!"

While the Englishman glanced his eye over the high roofs, and along the solemn perspectives of the Santa del Pianto, he perceived the figure of the assassin stealing from the confessional across the choir, and, shocked on again beholding him, he turned his eyes, and hastily quitted the church.

The friends then separated, and the Englishman, soon after returning to his hotel, received the volume. He read as follows:

VOLUME I

CHAPTER I

What is this secret sin; this untold tale,
That art cannot extract, nor penance cleanse?
MYSTERIOUS MOTHER

It was in the church of San Lorenzo at Naples, in the year 1758, that Vincentio di Vivaldi first saw Ellena Rosalba. The sweetness and fine expression of her voice attracted his attention to her figure, which had a distinguished air of delicacy and grace; but her face was concealed in her veil. So much indeed was he fascinated by the voice, that a most painful curiosity was excited as to her countenance, which he fancied must express all the sensibility of character that the modulation of her tones indicated. He listened to their exquisite expression with a rapt attention, and hardly withdrew his eyes from her person till the matin service had concluded; when he observed her leave the church with an aged lady, who leaned upon her arm, and who appeared to be her mother.

Vivaldi immediately followed their steps, determined to obtain, if possible, a view of Ellena's face, and to discover the home to which she should retire. They walked quickly, looking neither to the right or left, and as they turned into the Strada di Toledo he had nearly lost them; but quickening his pace, and relinquishing the cautious distance he had hitherto kept, he overtook them as they entered on the Terrazzo Nuovo, which runs along the bay of Naples, and leads towards the Gran Corso. He overtook them; but the fair unknown still held her veil close, and he knew not how to introduce himself to her notice, or to obtain a view of the features, which excited his curiosity. He was embarrassed by a respectful timidity, that mingled with his admiration, and which kept him silent, notwithstanding his wish to speak.

In descending the last steps of the *Terrazzo,* however, the foot of the elder lady faltered, and, while Vivaldi hastened to assist her, the breeze from the water caught the veil, which Ellena had no longer a hand sufficiently disengaged to confine, and, wafting it partially aside, disclosed to him a countenance more touchingly beautiful than he had dared to image. Her features were of the Grecian outline, and, though they expressed the tranquility of an elegant mind, her dark blue eyes sparkled with intelligence. She was assisting her companion so anxiously, that she did not immediately observe the admiration she had inspired; but the moment her eyes met those of Vivaldi, she became conscious of their effect, and she hastily drew her veil.

The old lady was not materially hurt by her fall, but, as she walked difficultly, Vivaldi seized the opportunity thus offered, and insisted that she should accept his arm. She refused this with many acknowledgments; but he pressed the offer so repeatedly and respectfully, that, at length, she accepted it, and they walked towards her residence together.

On the way thither, he attempted to converse with Ellena, but her replies were concise, and he arrived at the end of the walk while he was yet considering what he could say, that might interest and withdraw her from this severe reserve. From the style of their residence, he imagined that they were persons of honourable, but moderate independence. The house was small, but exhibited an air of comfort, and even of taste. It stood on an eminence, surrounded by a garden and vineyards, which commanded the city and bay of Naples, an ever-moving picture, and was canopied by a thick grove of pines and majestic date-trees; and, though the little portico and colonnade in front were of common marble, the style of architecture was elegant. While they afforded a shelter from the sun, they admitted the cooling breezes that rose from the bay below, and a prospect of the whole scope of its enchanting shores.

Vivaldi stopped at the little gate, which led into the garden, where the elder lady repeated her acknowledgments for his care, but did not invite him to enter; and he, trembling with anxiety and sinking with disappointment, remained for a moment gazing upon Ellena, unable to take leave, yet irresolute what to say that might prolong the interview, till the old lady again bade him good-day. He then summoned courage enough to request he might be allowed to enquire after her health, and, having obtained her permission, his eyes bade adieu to Ellena, who, as they were parting, ventured to thank him for the care he had taken of her aunt. The sound of her voice, and this acknowledgment of obligation, made him less willing to go than before, but at length he tore himself away. The beauty of her countenance haunting his imagination, and the touching accents of her voice still vibrating on his heart, he descended to the shore below her residence, pleasing himself with the consciousness of being near her, though he could no longer behold her; and sometimes hoping that he might again see her, however distantly, in a balcony of the house, where the silk awning seemed to invite the breeze from the sea. He lingered hour after hour, stretched beneath the umbrageous pines that waved over the shore, or traversing, regardless of the heat, the base of the cliffs that crowned it; recalling to his fancy the enchantment of her smile, and seeming still to listen to the sweetness of her accents.

In the evening he returned to his father's palace at Naples, thoughtful yet pleased, anxious yet happy; dwelling with delightful hope on the remembrance of the thanks he had received from Ellena, yet not daring to form any plan as to his future conduct. He returned time enough to attend his mother in her evening ride on the Corso, where, in every gay carriage that passed, he hoped to see the object of his constant thought; but she did not appear. His mother, the Marchesa di Vivaldi, observed his anxiety and unusual silence, and asked him some questions, which she meant should lead to an explanation of the change in his manners; but his replies only excited a stronger curiosity, and, though she forbore to press her enquiries, it was probable that she might employ a more artful means of renewing them.

Vincentio di Vivaldi was the only son of the Marchese di Vivaldi, a nobleman of one of the most ancient families of the kingdom of Naples, a favourite possessing an uncommon share of influence at Court, and a man still higher in power than in rank. His pride of birth was equal to either, but it was mingled with the justifiable pride of a principled mind; it governed his conduct in morals as well as in the jealousy of ceremonial distinctions, and elevated his practice as well as his claims. His pride was at once his vice and his virtue, his safeguard and his weakness.

The mother of Vivaldi, descended from a family as an-

cient as that of his father, was equally jealous of her importance; but her pride was that of birth and distinction, without
extending to morals. She was of violent passions, haughty,
vindictive, yet crafty and deceitful; patient in stratagem, and
indefatigable in pursuit of vengeance, on the unhappy objects who provoked her resentment. She loved her son,
rather as being the last of two illustrious houses, who was to
re-unite and support the honour of both, than with the fondness of a mother.

Vincentio inherited much of the character of his father,
and very little of that of his mother. His pride was as noble
and generous as that of the Marchese; but he had somewhat
of the fiery passions of the Marchesa, without any of her
craft, her duplicity, or vindictive thirst of revenge. Frank in
his temper, ingenuous in his sentiments, quickly offended,
but easily appeased; irritated by any appearance of disre-
spect, but melted by a concession, a high sense of honour
rendered him no more jealous of offence, than a delicate humanity made him ready for reconciliation, and anxious to
spare the feelings of others.

On the day following that, on which he had seen Ellena,
he returned to the villa Altieri, to use the permission granted
him of enquiring after the health of Signora Bianchi. The expectation of seeing Ellena agitated him with impatient joy
and trembling hope, which still encreased as he approached
her residence, till, having reached the garden-gate, he was
obliged to rest for a few moments to recover breath and
composure.

Having announced himself to an old female servant, who
came to the gate, he was soon after admitted to a small ves-
tibule, where he found Signora Bianchi winding balls of silk,
and alone; though from the position of a chair which stood
near a frame for embroidery, he judged that Ellena had but
just quitted the apartment. Signora Bianchi received him
with a reserved politeness, and seemed very cautious in her
replies to his enquiries after her niece, who, he hoped, every
moment, would appear. He lengthened his visit till there was
no longer an excuse for doing so; till he had exhausted every
topic of conversation, and till the silence of Signora Bianchi
seemed to hint, that his departure was expected. With a heart
saddened by disappointment, and having obtained only a reluctant permission to enquire after the health of that lady on
some future day, he then took leave.

On his way through the garden he often paused to look back upon the house, hoping to obtain a glimpse of Ellena at a lattice; and threw a glance around him, almost expecting to see her seated beneath the shade of the luxuriant plantains; but his search was every where vain, and he quitted the place with the slow and heavy step of despondency.

The day was employed in endeavours to obtain intelligence concerning the family of Ellena, but of this he procured little that was satisfactory. He was told, that she was an orphan, living under the care of her aunt, Signora Bianchi; that her family, which had never been illustrious, was decayed in fortune, and that her only dependence was upon this aunt. But he was ignorant of what was very true, though very secret, that she assisted to support this aged relative, whose sole property was the small estate on which they lived, and that she passed whole days in embroidering silks, which were disposed of to the nuns of a neighbouring convent, who sold them to the Neapolitan ladies, that visited their grate, at a very high advantage. He little thought, that a beautiful robe, which he had often seen his mother wear, was worked by Ellena; nor that some copies from the antique, which ornamented a cabinet of the Vivaldi palace, were drawn by her hand. If he had known these circumstances, they would only have served to encrease the passion, which, since they were proofs of a disparity of fortune, that would certainly render his family repugnant to a connection with hers, it would have been prudent to discourage.

Ellena could have endured poverty, but not contempt; and it was to protect herself from this effect of the narrow prejudices of the world around her, that she had so cautiously concealed from it a knowledge of the industry, which did honour to her character. She was not ashamed of poverty, or of the industry which overcame it, but her spirit shrunk from the senseless smile and humiliating condescension, which prosperity sometimes gives to indigence. Her mind was not yet strong enough, or her views sufficiently enlarged, to teach her a contempt of the sneer of vicious folly, and to glory in the dignity of virtuous independence. Ellena was the sole support of her aunt's declining years; was patient to her infirmities, and consoling to her sufferings; and repaid the fondness of a mother with the affection of a daughter. Her mother she had never known, having lost her while she was an infant, and from that period Signora Bianchi had performed the duties of one for her.

Thus innocent and happy in the silent performance of her duties and in the veil of retirement, lived Ellena Rosalba, when she first saw Vincentio di Vivaldi. He was not of a figure to pass unobserved when seen, and Ellena had been struck by the spirit and dignity of his air, and by his countenance, so frank, noble, and full of that kind of expression, which announces the energies of the soul. But she was cautious of admitting a sentiment more tender than admiration, and endeavoured to dismiss his image from her mind, and by engaging in her usual occupations, to recover the state of tranquillity, which his appearance had somewhat interrupted.

Vivaldi, mean while, restless from disappointment, and impatient from anxiety, having passed the greater part of the day in enquiries, which repaid him only with doubt and apprehension, determined to return to the villa Altieri, when evening should conceal his steps, consoled by the certainty of being near the object of his thoughts, and hoping, that chance might favour him once more with a view, however transient, of Ellena.

The Marchesa Vivaldi held an assembly this evening, and a suspicion concerning the impatience he betrayed, induced her to detain him about her person to a late hour, engaging him to select the music for her orchestra, and to superintend the performance of a new piece, the work of a composer whom she had brought into fashion. Her assemblies were among the most brilliant and crowded in Naples, and the nobility, who were to be at the palace this evening, were divided into two parties as to the merits of the musical genius, whom she patronized, and those of another candidate for fame. The performance of the evening, it was expected, would finally decide the victory. This, therefore, was a night of great importance and anxiety to the Marchesa, for she was as jealous of the reputation of her favourite composer as of her own, and the welfare of her son did but slightly divide her cares.

The moment he could depart unobserved, he quitted the assembly, and, muffling himself in his cloak, hastened to the villa Altieri, which lay at a short distance to the west of the city. He reached it unobserved, and, breathless with impatience, traversed the boundary of the garden; where, free from ceremonial restraint, and near the object of his affection, he experienced for the few first moments a joy as exquisite as her presence could have inspired. But this delight faded with its novelty, and in a short time he felt as forlorn as if he was separated for ever from Ellena, in whose presence he but lately almost believed himself.

The night was far advanced, and, no light appearing from the house, he concluded the inhabitants had retired to rest, and all hope of seeing her vanished from his mind. Still, however, it was sweet to be near her, and he anxiously sought to gain admittance to the gardens, that he might approach the window where it was possible she reposed. The boundary, formed of trees and thick shrubs, was not difficult to be passed, and he found himself once more in the portico of the villa.

It was nearly midnight, and the stillness that reigned was rather soothed than interrupted by the gentle dashing of the waters of the bay below, and by the hollow murmurs of Vesuvius, which threw up, at intervals its sudden flame on the horizon, and then left it to darkness. The solemnity of the scene accorded with the temper of his mind, and he listened in deep attention for the returning sounds, which broke upon the ear like distant thunder muttering imperfectly from the clouds. The pauses of silence, that succeeded each groan of the mountain, when expectation listened for the rising sound, affected the imagination of Vivaldi at this time with particular awe, and, rapt in thought, he continued to gaze upon the sublime and shadowy outline of the shores, and on the sea, just discerned beneath the twilight of a cloudless sky. Along its grey surface many vessels were pursuing their silent course, guided over the deep waters only by the polar star, which burned with steady lustre. The air was calm, and rose from the bay with most balmy and refreshing coolness; it scarcely stirred the heads of the broad pines that overspread the villa; and bore no sounds but of the waves and the groans of the far-off mountain,—till a chaunting of deep voices swelled from a distance. The solemn character of the strain engaged his attention; he perceived that it was a requiem, and he endeavoured to discover from what quarter it came. It advanced, though distantly, and then passed away on the air. The circumstance struck him; he knew it was usual in some parts of Italy to chaunt this strain over the bed of the dying; but here the mourners seemed to walk the earth, or the air. He was not doubtful as to the strain itself;—

once before he had heard it, and attended with circumstances which made it impossible that he should ever forget it. As he now listened to the choral voices softening in distance, a few pathetic notes brought full upon his remembrance the divine melody he had heard Ellena utter in the church of San Lorenzo. Overcome by the recollection, he started away, and, wandering over the garden, reached another side of the villa, where he soon heard the voice of Ellena herself, performing the midnight hymn to the Virgin, and accompanied by a lute, which she touched with most affecting and delicate expression. He stood for a moment entranced, and scarcely daring to breathe, lest he should lose any note of that meek and holy strain, which seemed to flow from a devotion almost saintly. Then, looking round to discover the object of his admiration, a light issuing from among the bowery foliage of a clematis led him to a lattice, and shewed him Ellena. The lattice had been thrown open to admit the cool air, and he had a full view of her and the apartment. She was rising from a small altar where she had concluded the service; the glow of devotion was still upon her countenance as she raised her eyes, and with a rapt earnestness fixed them on the heavens. She still held the lute, but no longer awakened it, and seemed lost to every surrounding object. Her fine hair was negligently bound up in a silk net, and some tresses that had escaped it, played on her neck, and round her beautiful countenance, which now was not even partially concealed by a veil. The light drapery of her dress, her whole figure, air, and attitude, were such as might have been copied for a Grecian nymph.

Vivaldi was perplexed and agitated between the wish of seizing an opportunity, which might never again occur, of pleading his love, and the fear of offending, by intruding upon her retirement at so sacred an hour; but, while he thus hesitated, he heard her sigh, and then with a sweetness peculiar to her accent, pronounce his name. During the trembling anxiety, with which he listened to what might follow this mention of his name, he disturbed the clematis that surrounded the lattice, and she turned her eyes towards the window; but Vivaldi was entirely concealed by the foliage. She, however, rose to close the lattice; as she approached which, Vivaldi, unable any longer to command himself, appeared before her. She stood fixed for an instant, while her countenance changed to an ashy paleness; and then, with trembling haste closing the lattice, quitted the apartment. Vivaldi felt as if all his hopes had vanished with her.

After lingering in the garden for some time without perceiving a light in any other part of the building, or hearing a sound proceed from it, he took his melancholy way to Naples. He now began to ask himself some questions, which he ought to have urged before, and to enquire wherefore he sought the dangerous pleasure of seeing Ellena, since her family was of such a condition as rendered the consent of his parents to a marriage with her unattainable.

He was lost in revery on this subject, sometimes half resolved to seek her no more, and then shrinking from a conduct, which seemed to strike him with the force of despair, when, as he emerged from the dark arch of a ruin, that extended over the road, his steps were crossed by a person in the habit of a monk, whose face was shrouded by his cowl still more than by the twilight. The stranger, addressing him by his name, said, "Signor! your steps are watched; beware how you revisit Altieri!" Having uttered this, he disappeared, before Vivaldi could return the sword he had half drawn into the scabbard, or demand an explanation of the words he had heard. He called loudly and repeatedly, conjuring the unknown person to appear, and lingered near the spot for a considerable time; but the vision came no more.

Vivaldi arrived at home with a mind occupied by this incident, and tormented by the jealousy to which it gave rise; for, after indulging various conjectures, he concluded with believing the notice, of which he had been warned, to be that of a rival, and that the danger which menaced him, was from the poniard of jealousy. This belief discovered to him at once the extent of his passion, and of the imprudence, which had thus readily admitted it; yet so far was this new prudence from overcoming his error, that, stung with a torture more exquisite than he had ever known, he resolved, at every event, to declare his love, and sue for the hand of Ellena. Unhappy young man, he knew not the fatal error, into which passion was precipitating him!

On his arrival at the Vivaldi palace, he learned, that the Marchesa had observed his absence, had repeatedly enquired for him, and had given orders that the time of his return should be mentioned to her. She had, however, retired to rest; but the Marchese, who had attended the King on an excursion to one of the royal villas on the bay, returned home

soon after Vincentio; and, before he had withdrawn to his
apartment, he met his son with looks of unusual displeasure,
but avoided saying any thing, which either explained or alluded to the subject of it; and, after a short conversation,
they separated.

Vivaldi shut himself in his apartment to deliberate, if that
may deserve the name of deliberation, in which a conflict of
passions, rather than an exertion of judgment, prevailed. For
several hours he traversed his suite of rooms, alternately tortured by the remembrance of Ellena, fired with jealousy, and
alarmed for the consequence of the imprudent step, which he
was about to take. He knew the temper of his father, and
some traits of the character of his mother, sufficiently to fear
that their displeasure would be irreconcilable concerning the
marriage he meditated; yet, when he considered that he was
their only son, he was inclined to admit a hope of forgiveness, notwithstanding the weight which the circumstance
must add to their disappointment. These reflexions were frequently interrupted by fears lest Ellena had already disposed
of her affections to this imaginary rival. He was, however,
somewhat consoled by remembering the sigh she had uttered, and the tenderness, with which she had immediately
pronounced his name. Yet, even if she were not averse to his
suit, how could he solicit her hand, and hope it would be
given him, when he should declare that this must be in secret? He scarcely dared to believe that she would condescend to enter a family who disdained to receive her; and
again despondency overcame him.

The morning found him as distracted as the night had left
him; his determination, however, was fixed; and this was, to
sacrifice what he now considered as a delusive pride of
birth, to a choice which he believed would ensure the happiness of his life. But, before he ventured to declare himself
to Ellena, it appeared necessary to ascertain whether he held
an interest in her heart, or whether she had devoted it to the
rival of his love, and who this rival really was. It was so
much easier to wish for such information than to obtain it,
that, after forming a thousand projects, either the delicacy of
his respect for Ellena, or his fear of offending her, or an apprehension of discovery from his family before he had secured an interest in her affections, constantly opposed his
views of an enquiry.

In this difficulty he opened his heart to a friend, who had

long possessed his confidence, and whose advice he solicited with somewhat more anxiety and sincerity than is usual
on such occasions. It was not a sanction of his own opinion
that he required, but the impartial judgment of another mind.
Bonarmo, however little he might be qualified for the office
of an adviser, did not scruple to give his advice. As a means
of judging whether Ellena was disposed to favour Vivaldi's
addresses, he proposed that, according to the custom of the
country, a serenade should be given; he maintained, that, if
she was not disinclined towards him, some sign of approbation would appear; and if otherwise, that she would remain
silent and invisible. Vivaldi objected to this coarse and inadequate mode of expressing a love so sacred as his, and he
had too lofty an opinion of Ellena's mind and delicacy, to
believe, that the trifling homage of a serenade would either
flatter her self-love, or interest her in his favour; nor, if it
did, could he venture to believe, that she would display any
sign of approbation.

His friend laughed at his scruples and at his opinion of
what he called such romantic delicacy, that his ignorance of
the world was his only excuse for having cherished them.
But Vivaldi interrupted this raillery, and would neither suffer
him for a moment to speak thus of Ellena, or to call such
delicacy romantic. Bonarmo, however, still urged the serenade as at least a possible means of discovering her disposition towards him before he made a formal avowal of his
suit; and Vivaldi, perplexed and distracted with apprehension and impatience to terminate his present state of suspense, was at length so far overcome by his own difficulties,
rather than by his friend's persuasion, that he consented to
make the adventure of a serenade on the approaching night.
This was adopted rather as a refuge from despondency, than
with any hope of success; for he still believed that Ellena
would not give any hint, that might terminate his uncertainty.

Beneath their cloaks they carried musical instruments,
and, muffling up their faces, so that they could not be
known, they proceeded in thoughtful silence on the way to
the villa Altieri. Already they had passed the arch, in which
Vivaldi was stopped by the stranger on the preceding night,
when he heard a sudden sound near him, and, raising his
head from the cloak, he perceived the same figure! Before
he had time for exclamation, the stranger crossed him again.

"Go not to the villa Altieri," said he in a solemn voice, "lest you meet the fate you ought to dread."

"What fate?" demanded Vivaldi, stepping back; "Speak, I conjure you!"

But the monk was gone, and the darkness of the hour baffled observation as to the way of his departure.

"Dio mi guardi!" exclaimed Bonarmo, "this is almost beyond belief! but let us return to Naples; this second warning ought to be obeyed."

"It is almost beyond endurance," exclaimed Vivaldi; "which way did he pass?"

"He glided by me," replied Bonarmo, "and he was gone before I could cross him!"

"I will tempt the worst at once," said Vivaldi; "if I have a rival, it is best to meet him. Let us go on."

Bonarmo remonstrated, and represented the serious danger that threatened from so rash a proceeding. "It is evident that you have a rival," said he, "and your courage cannot avail you against hired bravos." Vivaldi's heart swelled at the mention of a rival. "If you think it dangerous to proceed, I will go alone," said he.

Hurt by this reproof, Bonarmo accompanied his friend in silence, and they reached without interruption the boundary of the villa. Vivaldi led to the place by which he had entered on the preceding night, and they passed unmolested into the garden.

"Where are these terrible bravos of whom you warned me?" said Vivaldi, with taunting exultation.

"Speak cautiously," replied his friend; "we may, even now, be within their reach."

"They also may be within ours," observed Vivaldi.

At length, these adventurous friends came to the orangery, which was near the house, when, tired by the ascent, they rested to recover breath, and to prepare their instruments, for the serenade. The night was still, and they now heard, for the first time, murmurs as of a distant multitude; and then the sudden splendor of fireworks broke upon the sky. These arose from a villa on the western margin of the bay, and were given in honour of the birth of one of the royal princes. They soared to an immense height, and, as their lustre broke silently upon the night, it lightened on the thousand upturned faces of the gazing crowd, illumined the waters of the bay, with every little boat that skimmed its surface, and shewed distinctly the whole sweep of its rising shores, the stately city of Naples on the strand below, and, spreading far among the hills, its terraced roofs crowded with spectators, and the Corso tumultuous with carriages and blazing with torches.

While Bonarmo surveyed this magnificent scene, Vivaldi turned his eyes to the residence of Ellena, part of which looked out from among the trees, with a hope that the spectacle would draw her to a balcony; but she did not appear, nor was there any light, that might indicate her approach.

While they still rested on the turf of the orangery, they heard a sudden rustling of the leaves, as if the branches were disturbed by some person who endeavoured to make his way between them, when Vivaldi demanded who passed. No answer was returned, and a long silence followed.

"We are observed," said Bonarmo, at length, "and are even now, perhaps, almost beneath the poinard of the assassin: let us be gone."

"O that my heart were as secure from the darts of love, the assassin of my peace," exclaimed Vivaldi, "as yours is from those of bravos! My friend, you have little to interest you, since your thoughts have so much leisure for apprehension."

"My fear is that of prudence, not of weakness," retorted Bonarmo, with acrimony; "you will find, perhaps, that I have none, when you most wish me to possess it."

"I understand you," replied Vivaldi; "let us finish this business, and you shall receive reparation, since you believe yourself injured: I am as anxious to repair an offence, as jealous of receiving one."

"Yes," replied Bonarmo, "you would repair the injury you have done your friend with his blood."

"Oh! never, never!" said Vivaldi, falling on his neck. "Forgive my hasty violence; allow for the distraction of my mind."

Bonarmo returned the embrace. "It is enough," said he; "no more, no more! I hold again my friend to my heart."

While this conversation passed, they had quitted the orangery, and reached the walls of the villa, where they took their station under a balcony that overhung the lattice, through which Vivaldi had seen Ellena on the preceding night. They tuned their instruments, and opened the serenade with a duet.

Vivaldi's voice was a fine tenor, and the same susceptibility, which made him passionately fond of music, taught him to modulate its cadence with exquisite delicacy, and to give his emphasis with the most simple and pathetic expression. His soul seemed to breathe in the sounds,—so tender, so imploring, yet so energetic. On this night, enthusiasm inspired him with the highest eloquence, perhaps, which music is capable of attaining; what might be its effect on Ellena he had no means of judging, for she did not appear either at the balcony or the lattice, nor gave any hint of applause. No sounds stole on the stillness of the night, except those of the serenade, nor did any light from within the villa break upon the obscurity without; once, indeed, in a pause of the instruments, Bonarmo fancied he distinguished voices near him, as of persons who feared to be heard, and he listened attentively, but without ascertaining the truth. Sometimes they seemed to sound heavily in his ear, and then a death-like silence prevailed. Vivaldi affirmed the sound to be nothing more than the confused murmur of the distant multitude on the shore, but Bonarmo was not thus easily convinced.

The musicians, unsuccessful in their first endeavour to attract attention, removed to the opposite side of the building, and placed themselves in front of the portico, but with as little success; and, after having exercised their powers of harmony and of patience for above an hour, they resigned all further effort to win upon the obdurate Ellena. Vivaldi, notwithstanding the feebleness of his first hope of seeing her, now suffered an agony of disappointment; and Bonarmo, alarmed for the consequence of his despair, was as anxious to persuade him that he had no rival, as he had lately been pertinacious in affirming that he had one.

At length, they left the gardens, Vivaldi protesting that he would not rest till he had discovered the stranger, who so wantonly destroyed his peace, and had compelled him to explain his ambiguous warnings; and Bonarmo remonstrating on the imprudence and difficulty of the search, and representing that such conduct would probably be the means of spreading a report of his attachment, where most he dreaded it should be known.

Vivaldi refused to yield to remonstrance or considerations of any kind. "We shall see," said he, "whether this demon in the garb of a monk, will haunt me again at the accustomed place; if he does, he shall not escape my grasp; and if he does not, I will watch as vigilantly for his return, as he seems to have done for mine. I will lurk in the shade of the ruin, and wait for him, though it be till death!"

Bonarmo was particularly struck by the vehemence with which he pronounced the last words, but he no longer opposed his purpose, and only bade him consider whether he was well armed, "For," he added, "you may have need of arms there, though you had no use for them at the villa Altieri. Remember that the stranger told you that your steps were watched."

"I have my sword," replied Vivaldi, "and the dagger which I usually wear; but I ought to enquire what are your weapons of defence."

"Hush!" said Bonarmo, as they turned the foot of a rock that over-hung the road, "we are approaching the spot; yonder is the arch!" It appeared duskily in the perspective, suspended between two cliffs, where the road wound from sight, on one of which were the ruins of the Roman fort it belonged to, and on the other, shadowing pines, and thickets of oak that tufted the rock to its base.

They proceeded in silence, treading lightly, and often throwing a suspicious glance around, expecting every instant that the monk would steal out upon them from some recess of the cliffs. But they passed on unmolested to the arch-way. "We are here before him, however," said Vivaldi as they entered the darkness. "Speak low, my friend," said Bonarmo, "others besides ourselves may be shrouded in this obscurity. I like not the place."

"Who but ourselves would chuse so dismal a retreat?" whispered Vivaldi, "unless indeed, it were banditti; the savageness of the spot would, in truth, suit their humour, and it suits well also with my own."

"It would suit their purpose too, as well as their humour," observed Bonarmo. "Let us remove from this deep shade, into the more open road, where we can as closely observe who passes."

Vivaldi objected that in the road they might themselves be observed, "and if we are seen by my unknown tormentor, our design is defeated, for he comes upon us suddenly, or not at all, lest we should be prepared to detain him."

Vivaldi, as he said this, took his station within the thickest gloom of the arch, which was of considerable depth, and near a flight of steps that was cut in the rock, and ascended to the fortress. His friend stepped close to his side. After a pause of silence, during which Bonarmo was meditating, and Vivaldi was impatiently watching, "Do you really believe," said the former, "that any effort to detain him would be effectual? He glided past me with a strange facility, it was surely more than human!"

"What is it you mean?" enquired Vivaldi.

"Why, I mean that I could be superstitious. This place, perhaps, infests my mind with congenial gloom, for I find that, at this moment, there is scarcely a superstition too dark for my credulity."

Vivaldi smiled. "And you must allow," added Bonarmo, "that he has appeared under circumstances somewhat extraordinary. How should he know your name, by which, you say, he addressed you at the first meeting? How should he know from whence you came, or whether you designed to return? By what magic could he become acquainted with your plans?"

"Nor am I certain that he is acquainted with them," observed Vivaldi; "but if he is, there was no necessity for superhuman means to obtain such knowledge."

"The result of this evening surely ought to convince you that he is acquainted with your designs," said Bonarmo. "Do you believe it possible that Ellena could have been insensible to your attentions, if her heart had not been pre-engaged, and that she would not have shewn herself at a lattice?"

"You do not know Ellena," replied Vivaldi, "and therefore I once more pardon you the question. Yet had she been disposed to accept my addresses, surely some sign of approbation,"—he checked himself.

"The stranger warned you not to go to the villa Altieri," resumed Bonarmo, "he seemed to anticipate the reception, which awaited you, and to know a danger, which hitherto you have happily escaped."

"Yes, he anticipated too well that reception," said Vivaldi, losing his prudence in passionate exclamation; "and he is himself, perhaps, the rival, whom he has taught me to suspect. He has assumed a disguise only the more effectually to impose upon my credulity, and to deter me from addressing Ellena. And shall I tamely lie in wait for his approach? Shall I lurk like a guilty assassin for this rival?"

"For heaven's sake!" said Bonarmo, "moderate these transports, consider where you are. This surmise of yours is in the highest degree improbable." He gave his reasons for thinking so, and these convinced Vivaldi, who was prevailed upon to be once more patient.

They had remained watchful and still for a considerable time, when Bonarmo saw a person approach the end of the arch-way nearest to Altieri. He heard no step, but he perceived a shadowy figure station itself at the entrance of the arch, where the twilight of this brilliant climate was, for a few paces, admitted. Vivaldi's eyes were fixed on the road leading towards Naples, and he, therefore, did not perceive the object of Bonarmo's attention, who, fearful of his friend's precipitancy, forbore to point out immediately what he observed, judging it more prudent to watch the motions of this unknown person, that he might ascertain whether it really were the monk. The size of the figure, and the dark drapery in which it seemed wrapt, induced him, at length, to believe that this was the expected stranger; and he seized Vivaldi's arm to direct his attention to him, when the form gliding forward disappeared in the gloom, but not before Vivaldi had understood the occasion of his friend's gesture and significant silence. They heard no footstep pass them, and, being convinced that this person, whatever he was, had not left the arch-way, they kept their station in watchful stillness. Presently they heard a rustling, as of garments, near them, and Vivaldi, unable longer to command his patience, started from his concealment, and with arms extended to prevent any one from escaping, demanded who was there.

The sound ceased, and no reply was made. Bonarmo drew his sword, protesting he would stab the air till he found the person who lurked there; but that if the latter would discover himself, he should receive no injury. This assurance Vivaldi confirmed by his promise. Still no answer was returned; but as they listened for a voice, they thought something passed them, and the avenue was not narrow enough to have prevented such a circumstance. Vivaldi rushed forward, but did not perceive any person issue from the arch into the highway, where the stronger twilight must have discovered him.

"Somebody certainly passed," whispered Bonarmo, "and I think I hear a sound from yonder steps, that lead to the fortress."

"Let us follow," cried Vivaldi, and he began to ascend.

"Stop, for heaven's sake stop!" said Bonarmo; "consider

what you are about! Do not brave the utter darkness of these ruins; do not pursue the assassin to his den!"

"It is the monk himself!" exclaimed Vivaldi, still ascending; "he shall not escape me!"

Bonarmo paused a moment at the foot of the steps, and his friend disappeared; he hesitated what to do, till ashamed of suffering him to encounter danger alone, he sprang to the flight, and not without difficulty surmounted the rugged steps.

Having reached the summit of the rock, he found himself on a terrace, that ran along the top of the arch-way and had once been fortified; this, crossing the road, commanded the defile each way. Some remains of massy walls, that still exhibited loops for archers, were all that now hinted of its former use. It led to a watch-tower almost concealed in thick pines, that crowned the opposite cliff, and had thus served not only for a strong batter over the road, but, connecting the opposite sides of the defile, had formed a line of communication between the fort and this out-post.

Bonarmo looked round in vain for his friend, and the echoes of his own voice only, among the rocks, replied to his repeated calls. After some hesitation whether to enter the walls of the main building, or to cross to the watch-tower, he determined on the former, and entered a rugged area, the walls of which, following the declivities of the precipice, could scarcely now be traced. The citadel, a round tower, of majestic strength, with some Roman arches scattered near, was all that remained of this once important fortress; except, indeed, a mass of ruins near the edge of the cliff, the construction of which made it difficult to guess for what purpose it had been designed.

Bonarmo entered the immense walls of the citadel, but the utter darkness within checked his progress, and, contenting himself with calling loudly on Vivaldi, he returned to the open air.

As he approached the mass of ruins, whose singular form had interested his curiosity, he thought he distinguished the low accents of a human voice, and while he listened in anxiety, a person rushed forth from a doorway of the ruin, carrying a drawn sword. It was Vivaldi himself. Bonarmo sprang to meet him; he was pale and breathless, and some moments elapsed before he could speak, or appeared to hear the repeated enquiries of his friend.

"Let us go," said Vivaldi, "let us leave this place!"

"Most willingly," replied Bonarmo, "but where have you been, and who have you seen, that you are thus affected."

"Ask me no more questions, let us go," repeated Vivaldi. They descended the rock together, and when, having reached the arch-way, Bonarmo enquired, half sportively, whether they should remain any longer on the watch, his friend answered, "No!" with an emphasis that startled him. They passed hastily on the way to Naples, Bonarmo repeating enquiries which Vivaldi seemed reluctant to satisfy, and wondering no less at the cause of this sudden reserve, than anxious to know whom he had seen.

"It was the monk, then," said Bonarmo; "you secured him at last?"

"I know not what to think," replied Vivaldi, "I am more perplexed than ever."

"He escaped you then?"

"We will speak of this in future," said Vivaldi; "but be it as it may, the business rests not here. I will return in the night of to-morrow with a torch; dare you venture yourself with me?"

"I know not," replied Bonarmo, "whether I ought to do so, since I am not informed for what purpose."

"I will not press you to go," said Vivaldi; "my purpose is already known to you."

"Have you really failed to discover the stranger—have you still doubts concerning the person you pursued?"

"I have doubts, which to-morrow night, I hope, will dissipate."

"This is very strange!" said Bonarmo, "It was but now that I witnessed the horror, with which you left the fortress of Paluzzi, and already you speak of returning to it! And why at night—why not in the day, when less danger would beset you?"

"I know not as to that," replied Vivaldi, "you are to observe that day-light never pierces within the recess, to which I penetrated; we must search the place with torches at whatsoever hour we would examine it."

"Since this is necessary," said Bonarmo, "how happens it that you found your way in total darkness?"

"I was too much engaged to know how; I was led on, as by an invisible hand."

"We must, notwithstanding," observed Bonarmo, "go in

day-time, if not by day-light, provided I accompany you. It would be little less than insanity to go twice to a place, which is probably infested with robbers, and at their own hour of midnight."

"I shall watch again in the accustomed place," replied Vivaldi, "before I use my last resource, and this cannot be done during the day. Besides, it is necessary that I should go at a particular hour, the hour when the monk has usually appeared."

"He did escape you, then?" said Bonarmo, "and you are still ignorant concerning who he is?"

Vivaldi rejoined only with an enquiry whether his friend would accompany him. "If not," he added, "I must hope to find another companion."

Bonarmo said, that he must consider of the proposal, and would acquaint him with his determination before the following evening.

While this conversation concluded, they were in Naples, and at the gates of the Vivaldi palace, where they separated for the remainder of the night.

CHAPTER II

OLIVIA. Why what would you?

VIOLA.   Make me a willow cabin at your gate,
And call upon my soul within the house;
Write loyal cantos of contemned love,
And sing them loud even in the dead of night:
Halloo your name to the reverberate hills,
And make the babbling gossip of the air
Cry out, Olivia! O! you should not rest
Between the elements of air and earth,
But you should pity me.

                           TWELFTH NIGHT

SINCE Vivaldi had failed to procure an explanation of the words of the monk, he determined to relieve himself from the tortures of suspence, respecting a rival, by going to the villa Altieri, and declaring his pretensions. On the morning immediately following his late adventure, he went thither, and on enquiring for Signora Bianchi, was told that she could not be seen. With much difficulty he prevailed upon the old house-keeper to deliver a request that he might be permitted to wait upon her for a few moments. Permission was granted him, when he was conducted into the very apartment where he had formerly seen Ellena. It was unoccupied and he was told that Signora Bianchi would be there presently.

During this interval, he was agitated at one moment with quick impatience, and at another with enthusiastic pleasure, while he gazed on the altar whence he had seen Ellena rise, and where, to his fancy, she still appeared; and on every object, on which he knew her eyes had lately dwelt. These objects, so familiar to her, had in the imagination of Vivaldi acquired somewhat of the sacred character she had impressed upon his heart, and affected him in some degree as her presence would have done. He trembled as he took up the lute she had been accustomed to touch, and, when he awakened the chords, her own voice seemed to speak. A drawing, half-finished, of a dancing nymph remained on a stand, and he immediately understood that her hand had traced the lines. It was a copy from Herculaneum, and, though a copy, was touched with the spirit of original genius. The light steps appeared almost to move, and the whole figure displayed the airy lightness of exquisite grace. Vivaldi perceived this to be one of a set that ornamented the apartment, and observed with surprise, that they were the particular subjects, which adorned his father's cabinet, and which he had understood to be the only copies permitted from the originals in the royal museum.

Every object, on which his eyes rested, seemed to announce the presence of Ellena; and the very flowers that so gaily embellished the apartment, breathed forth a perfume, which fascinated his senses and affected his imagination. Before Signora Bianchi appeared, his anxiety and apprehension had encreased so much, that, believing he should be unable to support himself in her presence, he was more than once upon the point of leaving the house. At length, he heard her approaching step from the hall, and his breath almost forsook him. The figure of Signora Bianchi was not of an order to inspire admiration, and a spectator might have smiled to see the perturbation of Vivaldi, his faultering step and anxious eye, as he advanced to meet the venerable Bianchi, as he bowed upon her faded hand, and listened to her querulous voice. She received him with an air of reserve, and some moments passed before he could recollect himself sufficiently to explain the purpose of his visit; yet this, when he discovered it, did not apparently surprise her. She listened with composure, though with somewhat of a severe countenance, to his protestations of regard for her niece, and when he implored her to intercede for him in obtaining the hand of Ellena, she said, "I cannot be ignorant that a family of your rank must be averse to an union with one of mine; nor am I unacquainted that a full sense of the value of birth is a marking feature in the characters of the Marchese and Marchesa di Vivaldi. This proposal must be disagreeable or, at least, unknown to them; and I am to inform you, Signor, that, though Signora di Rosalba is their inferior in rank, she is their equal in pride."

Vivaldi disdained to prevaricate, yet was shocked to own the truth thus abruptly. The ingenuous manner, however, with which he at length did this, and the energy of a passion too eloquent to be misunderstood, somewhat soothed the anxiety of Signora Bianchi, with whom other considerations began to arise. She considered that from her own age and infirmities she must very soon, in the course of nature, leave Ellena a young and friendless orphan; still somewhat dependent upon her own industry, and entirely so on her discretion. With much beauty and little knowledge of the world, the dangers of her future situation appeared in vivid colours to the affectionate mind of Signora Bianchi; and she sometimes thought that it might be right to sacrifice considerations, which in other circumstances would be laudable, to the obtaining for her niece the protection of a husband and a man of honour. If in this instance she descended from the lofty integrity, which ought to have opposed her consent that Ellena should clandestinely enter any family, her parental anxiety may soften the censure she deserved.

But, before she determined upon this subject, it was necessary to ascertain that Vivaldi was worthy of the confidence she might repose in him. To try, also, the constancy of his affection, she gave little present encouragement to his hopes. His request to see Ellena she absolutely refused, till she should have considered further of his proposals; and his enquiry whether he had a rival, and, if he had, whether Ellena was disposed to favour him, she evaded, since she knew that a reply would give more encouragement to his hopes, than it might hereafter be proper to confirm.

Vivaldi, at length, took his leave, released, indeed, from absolute despair, but scarcely encouraged to hope; ignorant that he had a rival, yet doubtful whether Ellena honoured himself with any share of her esteem.

He had received permission to wait upon Signora Bianchi on a future day, but till that day should arrive time appeared motionless; and, since it seemed utterly impossible to endure this interval of suspence, his thoughts on the way to Naples were wholly engaged in contriving the means of concluding it, till he reached the well-known arch, and looked round, though hopelessly, for his mysterious tormentor. The stranger did not appear; and Vivaldi pursued the road, determined to re-visit the spot at night, and also to return privately to villa Altieri, where he hoped a second visit might procure for him some relief from his present anxiety.

When he reached home he found that the Marchese, his father, had left an order for him to await his arrival; which he obeyed; but the day passed without his return. The Marchesa, when she saw him, enquired, with a look that expressed much, how he had engaged himself of late, and completely frustrated his plans for the evening, by requiring him to attend her to Portici. Thus he was prevented from receiving Bonarmo's determination, from watching at Paluzzi, and from revisiting Ellena's residence.

He remained at Portici the following evening, and, on his return to Naples, the Marchese being again absent, he continued ignorant of the intended subject of the interview. A note from Bonarmo brought a refusal to accompany him to the fortress, and urged him to forbear so dangerous a visit. Being for this night unprovided with a companion for the adventure, and unwilling to go alone, Vivaldi deferred it to another evening; but no consideration could deter him from visiting the villa Altieri. Not chusing to solicit his friend to accompany him thither, since he had refused his first request, he took his solitary lute, and reached the garden at an earlier hour than usual.

The sun had been set above an hour, but the horizon still retained somewhat of a saffron brilliancy, and the whole dome of the sky had an appearance of transparency, peculiar to this enchanting climate, which seemed to diffuse a more soothing twilight over the reposing world. In the south-east the outline of Vesuvius appeared distinctly, but the mountain itself was dark and silent.

Vivaldi heard only the quick and eager voices of some Lazaroni at a distance on the shore, as they contended at the simple game of maro. From the bowery lattices of a small pavilion within the orangery, he perceived a light, and the sudden hope, which it occasioned, of seeing Ellena, almost overcame him. It was impossible to resist the opportunity of beholding her, yet he checked the impatient step he was taking, to ask himself, whether it was honorable thus to steal upon her retirement, and become an unsuspected observer of her secret thoughts. But the temptation was too powerful for this honorable hesitation; the pause was momentary; and, stepping lightly towards the pavilion, he placed himself near an open lattice, so as to be shrouded from observation by the branches of an orange-tree, while he obtained a full view of the apartment. Ellena was alone, sitting in a thoughtful attitude and holding her lute, which she did not play. She appeared lost to a consciousness of surrounding objects, and a tenderness was on her countenance, which seemed to tell him that her thoughts were engaged by some interesting subject. Recollecting that, when last he had seen her thus, she pronounced his name, his hope revived, and he was going to discover himself and appear at her feet, when she spoke, and he paused.

"Why this unreasonable pride of birth!" said she; "A visionary prejudice destroys our peace. Never would I submit to enter a family averse to receive me; they shall learn, at least, that I inherit nobility of soul. O! Vivaldi! but for this unhappy prejudice!"—

Vivaldi, while he listened to this, was immovable; he seemed as if entranced; the sound of her lute and voice recalled him, and he heard her sing the first stanza of the very air, with which he had opened the serenade on a former night, and with such sweet pathos as the composer must have felt when he was inspired with the idea.

She paused at the conclusion of the first stanza, when Vivaldi, overcome by the temptation of such an opportunity for expressing his passion, suddenly struck the chords of the lute, and replied to her in the second. The tremor of his voice, though it restrained his tones, heightened its eloquence. Ellena instantly recollected it; her colour alternately faded and returned; and, before the verse concluded, she seemed to have lost all consciousness. Vivaldi was now advancing into the pavilion, when his approach recalled her; she waved him to retire, and before he could spring to her support, she rose and would have left the place, had he not interrupted her and implored a few moments attention.

"It is impossible," said Ellena.

"Let me only hear you say that I am not hateful to you," rejoined Vivaldi; "that this intrusion has not deprived me of the regard, with which but now you acknowledged you honoured me."—

"Oh, never, never!" interrupted Ellena, impatiently; "forget that I ever made such acknowledgment; forget that you ever heard it; I know not what I said."

"Ah, beautiful Ellena! do you think it possible I ever can

forget it? It will be the solace of my solitary hours, the hope
that shall sustain me."—

"I cannot be detained Signor," interrupted Ellena, still
more embarrassed, "or forgive myself for having permitted
such a conversation;" but as she spoke the last words, an involuntary smile seemed to contradict their meaning. Vivaldi
believed the smile in spite of the words; but, before he could
express the lightning joy of conviction, she had left the pavilion; he followed through the garden—but she was gone.

From this moment Vivaldi seemed to have arisen into a
new existence; the whole world to him was Paradise; that
smile seemed impressed upon his heart for ever. In the fulness of present joy, he believed it impossible that he could
ever be unhappy again, and defied the utmost malice of future fortune. With footsteps light as air, he returned to Naples, nor once remembered to look for his old monitor on
the way.

The Marchese and his mother being from home, he was left
at his leisure to indulge the rapturous recollection, that pressed
upon his mind, and of which he was impatient of a moment's
interruption. All night he either traversed his apartment with
an agitation equal to that, which anxiety had so lately inflicted,
or composed and destroyed letters to Ellena; sometimes fearing that he had written too much, and at others feeling that he
had written too little; recollecting circumstances which he
ought to have mentioned, and lamenting the cold expression of
a passion, to which it appeared that no language could do justice.

By the hour when the domestics had risen, he had, however, completed a letter somewhat more to his satisfaction,
and he dispatched it to the villa Altieri by a confidential person; but the servant had scarcely quitted the gates, when he
recollected new arguments, which he wished to urge, and expressions to change of the utmost importance to enforce his
meaning, and he would have given half the world to have recalled the messenger.

In this state of agitation he was summoned to attend the
Marchese, who had been too much engaged of late to keep
his own appointment. Vivaldi was not long in doubt as to the
subject of this interview.

"I have wished to speak with you," said the Marchese, assuming an air of haughty severity, "upon a subject of the utmost importance to your honour and happiness; and I

wished, also, to give you an opportunity of contradicting a report, which would have occasioned me considerable uneasiness, if I could have believed it. Happily I had too much confidence in my son to credit this; and I affirmed that he understood too well what was due both to his family and himself, to take any step derogatory from the dignity of either. My motive for this conversation, therefore, is merely to afford you a moment for refuting the calumny I shall mention, and to obtain for myself authority for contradicting it to the persons who have communicated it to me."

Vivaldi waited impatiently for the conclusion of this exordium, and then begged to be informed of the subject of the report.

"It is said," resumed the Marchese, "that there is a young woman, who is called Ellena Rosalba,—I think that is the name;—do you know any person of the name?"

"Do I know!" exclaimed Vivaldi, "but pardon me, pray proceed, my Lord."

The Marchese paused, and regarded his son with sternness, but without surprize. "It is said, that a young person of this name has contrived to fascinate your affections, and"——

"It is most true, my Lord, that Signora Rosalba has won my affections," interrupted Vivaldi with honest impatience, "but without contrivance."

"I will not be interrupted," said the Marchese, interrupting in his turn. "It is said that she has so artfully adapted her temper to yours, that, with the assistance of a relation who lives with her, she has reduced you to the degrading situation of her devoted suitor."

"Signora Rosalba has, my Lord, exalted me to the honour of being her suitor," said Vivaldi, unable longer to command his feelings. He was proceeding, when the Marchese abruptly checked him, "You avow your folly then!"

"My Lord, I glory in my choice."

"Young man," rejoined his father, "as this is the arrogance and romantic enthusiasm of a boy, I am willing to forgive it for once, and observe me, only for once. If you will acknowledge your error, instantly dismiss this new favourite."——

"My Lord!"

"You must instantly dismiss her," repeated the Marchese with sterner emphasis; "and, to prove that I am more merciful than just, I am willing, on this condition, to allow her a small annuity as some reparation for the depravity, into which you have assisted to sink her."

"My Lord!" exclaimed Vivaldi aghast, and scarcely daring to trust his voice, "my Lord!—depravity?" struggling for breath. "Who has dared to pollute her spotless fame by insulting your ears with such infamous falsehood? Tell me, I conjure you, instantly tell me, that I may hasten to give him his reward. Depravity!—an annuity—an annuity! O Ellena! Ellena!" As he pronounced her name tears of tenderness mingled with those of indignation.

"Young man," said the Marchese, who had observed the violence of his emotion with strong displeasure and alarm, "I do not lightly give faith to report, and I cannot suffer myself to doubt the truth of what I have advanced. You are deceived, and your vanity will continue the delusion, unless I condescend to exert my authority, and tear the veil from your eyes. Dismiss her instantly, and I will adduce proof of her former character which will stagger even your faith, enthusiastic as it is."

"Dismiss her!" repeated Vivaldi, with calm yet stern energy, such as his father had never seen him assume; "My Lord, you have never yet doubted my word, and I now pledge you that honourable word, that Ellena is innocent. Innocent! O heavens, that it should ever be necessary to affirm so, and, above all, that it should ever be necessary for me to vindicate her!"

"I must indeed lament that it ever should," replied the Marchese coldly. "You have pledged your word, which I cannot question. I believe, therefore, that you are deceived; that you think her virtuous, notwithstanding your midnight visits to her house. And grant she is, unhappy boy! what reparation can you make her for the infatuated folly, which has thus stained her character? What"——

"By proclaiming to the world, my Lord, that she is worthy of becoming my wife," replied Vivaldi, with a glow of countenance, which announced the courage and the exultation of a virtuous mind.

"Your wife!" said the Marchese, with a look of ineffable disdain, which was instantly succeeded by one of angry alarm.—"If I believed you could so far forget what is due to the honour of your house, I would for ever disclaim you as my son."

"O! why," exclaimed Vivaldi, in an agony of conflicting passions, "why should I be in danger of forgetting what is due to a father, when I am only asserting what is due to innocence; when I am only defending her, who has no other to defend her! Why may not I be permitted to reconcile duties so congenial! But, be the event what it may, I will defend the oppressed, and glory in the virtue, which teaches me, that it is the first duty of humanity to do so. Yes, my Lord, if it must be so, I am ready to sacrifice interior duties to the grandeur of a principle, which ought to expand all hearts and impel all actions. I shall best support the honour of my house by adhering to its dictates."

"Where is the principle," said the Marchese, impatiently, "which shall teach you to disobey a father; where is the virtue which shall instruct you to degrade your family?"

"There can be no degradation, my Lord, where there is no vice," replied Vivaldi; "and there are instances, pardon me, my Lord, there are some few instances in which it is virtuous to disobey."

"This paradoxical morality," said the Marchese, with passionate displeasure, "and this romantic language, sufficiently explain to me the character of your associates, and the innocence of her, whom you defend with so chivalric an air. Are you to learn, Signor, that you belong to your family, not your family to you; that you are only a guardian of its honour, and not at liberty to dispose of yourself? My patience will endure no more!"

Nor could the patience of Vivaldi endure this repeated attack on the honour of Ellena. But, while he yet asserted her innocence, he endeavoured to do so with the temper, which was due to the presence of a father; and, though he maintained the independence of a man, he was equally anxious to preserve inviolate the duties of a son. But unfortunately the Marchese and Vivaldi differed in opinion concerning the limits of these duties; the first extending them to passive obedience, and the latter conceiving them to conclude at a point, wherein the happiness of an individual is so deeply concerned as in marriage. They parted mutually inflamed; Vivaldi unable to prevail with his father to mention the name of his infamous informant, or to acknowledge himself convinced of Ellena's innocence; and the Marchese equally unsuccessful in his endeavours to obtain from his son a promise that he would see her no more.

Here then was Vivaldi, who only a few short hours before had experienced a happiness so supreme as to efface all impressions of the past, and to annihilate every consideration of the future; a joy so full that it permitted him not to believe it possible that he could ever again taste of misery; he, who had felt as if that moment was as an eternity, rendering him independent of all others,—even he was thus soon fallen into the region of time and of suffering.

The present conflict of passion appeared endless; he loved his father, and would have been more shocked to consider the vexation he was preparing for him, had he not been resentful of the contempt he expressed for Ellena. He adored Ellena; and, while he felt the impractability of resigning his hopes, was equally indignant of the slander, which affected her name, and impatient to avenge the insult upon the original defamer.

Though the displeasure of his father concerning a marriage with Ellena had been already foreseen, the experience of it was severer and more painful than he had imagined; while the indignity offered to Ellena was as unexpected as intolerable. But this circumstance furnished him with an additional argument for addressing her; for, if it had been possible that his love could have paused, his honour seemed now engaged in her behalf; and, since he had been a means of sullying her fame, it became his duty to restore it. Willingly listening to the dictates of a duty so plausible, he determined to persevere in his original design. But his first efforts were directed to discover her slanderer, and recollecting, with surprize, those words of the Marchese, which had confessed a knowledge of his evening visits to the villa Altieri, the doubtful warnings of the monk seemed explained. He believed that this man was at once the spy of his steps, and the defamer of his love, till the inconsistency of such conduct with the seeming friendliness of his admonitions, struck Vivaldi and compelled him to believe the contrary.

Meanwhile, the heart of Ellena had been little less tranquil. It was divided by love and pride; but had she been acquainted with the circumstances of the late interview between the Marchese and Vivaldi, it would have been divided no longer, and a just regard for her own dignity would instantly have taught her to subdue, without difficulty, this infant affection.

Signora Bianchi had informed her niece of the subject of Vivaldi's visit; but she had softened the objectionable circumstances that attended his proposal, and had, at first, merely hinted that it was not to be supposed his family would approve a connection with any person so much their inferior in rank as herself. Ellena, alarmed by this suggestion, replied, that, since she believed so, she had done right to reject Vivaldi's suit; but her sigh, as she said this, did not escape the observation of Signora Bianchi, who ventured to add, that she had not *absolutely* rejected his offers.

While in this and future conversations, Ellena was pleased to perceive her secret admiration thus justified by an approbation so indisputable as that of her aunt, and was willing to believe that the circumstance, which had alarmed her just pride, was not so humiliating as she at first imagined, Bianchi was careful to conceal the real considerations, which had induced her to listen to Vivaldi, being well assured that they would have no weight with Ellena, whose generous heart and inexperienced mind would have revolted from mingling any motives of interest with an engagement so sacred as that of marriage. When, however, from further deliberation upon the advantages, which such an alliance must secure for her niece, Signora Bianchi determined to encourage his views, and to direct the mind of Ellena, whose affections were already engaged on her side, the opinions of the latter were found less ductile than had been expected. She was shocked at the idea of entering clandestinely the family of Vivaldi. But Bianchi, whose infirmities urged her wishes, was now so strongly convinced of the prudence of such an engagement for her niece, that she determined to prevail over her reluctance, though she perceived that this must be by means more gradual and persuasive than she had believed necessary. On the evening, when Vivaldi had surprised from Ellena an acknowledgment of her sentiments, her embarrassment and vexation, on her returning to the house, and relating what had occurred, sufficiently expressed to Signora Bianchi the exact situation of her heart. And when, on the following morning, his letter arrived, written with the simplicity and energy of truth, the aunt neglected not to adapt her remarks upon it, to the character of Ellena, with her usual address.

Vivaldi, after the late interview with the Marchese, passed the remainder of the day in considering various plans, which might discover to him the person, who had abused the credulity of his father; and in the evening he returned once more to the villa Altieri, not in secret, to serenade the dark balcony of his mistress, but openly, and to converse with Signora Bianchi, who now received him more courteously than on his former visit. Attributing the anxiety in his countenance to the uncertainty, concerning the disposition of her niece, she was neither surprised or offended, but ventured to relieve him from a part of it, by encouraging his hopes. Vivaldi dreaded lest she should enquire further respecting the sentiments of his family, but she spared both his delicacy and her own on this point; and, after a conversation of considerable length, he left the villa Altieri with a heart somewhat soothed by approbation, and lightened by hope, although he had not obtained a sight of Ellena. The disclosure she had made of her sentiments on the preceding evening, and the hints she had received as to those of his family, still wrought upon her mind with too much effect to permit an interview.

Soon after his return to Naples, the Marchesa, whom he was surprised to find disengaged, sent for him to her closet, where a scene passed similar to that which had occurred with his father, except that the Marchesa was more dexterous in her questions, and more subtle in her whole conduct; and that Vivaldi, never for a moment, forgot the decorum which was due to a mother. Managing his passions, rather than exasperating them, and deceiving him with respect to the degree of resentment she felt from his choice, she was less passionate than the Marchese in her observations and menaces, perhaps, only because she entertained more hope than he did of preventing the evil she contemplated.

Vivaldi quitted her, unconvinced by her arguments, unsubdued by her prophecies, and unmoved in his designs. He was not alarmed, because he did not sufficiently understand her character to apprehend her purposes. Despairing to effect these by open violence, she called in an auxiliary of no mean talents, and whose character and views well adapted him to be an instrument in her hands. It was, perhaps, the baseness of her own heart, not either depth of reflexion or keenness of penetration, which enabled her to understand the nature of his; and she determined to modulate that nature to her own views.

There lived in the Dominican convent of the Spirito Santo, at Naples, a man called father Schedoni; an Italian, as his name imported, but whose family was unknown, and from some circumstances, it appeared, that he wished to throw an impenetrable veil over his origin. For whatever reason, he was never heard to mention a relative, or the place of his nativity, and he had artfully eluded every enquiry that approached the subject, which the curiosity of his associates had occasionally prompted. There were circumstances, however, which appeared to indicate him to be a man of birth, and of fallen fortune; his spirit, as it had sometimes looked forth from under the disguise of his manners, seemed lofty; it shewed not, however, the aspirings of a generous mind, but rather the gloomy pride of a disappointed one. Some few persons in the convent, who had been interested by his appearance, believed that the peculiarities of his manners, his severe reserve and unconquerable silence, his solitary habits and frequent penances, were the effect of misfortunes preying upon a haughty and disordered spirit; while others conjectured them the consequence of some hideous crime gnawing upon an awakened conscience.

He would sometimes abstract himself from the society for whole days together, or when with such a disposition he was compelled to mingle with it, he seemed unconscious where he was, and continued shrouded in meditation and silence till he was again alone. There were times when it was unknown whither he had retired, notwithstanding that his steps had been watched, and his customary haunts examined. No one ever heard him complain. The elder brothers of the convent said that he had talents, but denied him learning; they applauded him for the profound subtlety which he occasionally discovered in argument, but observed that he seldom perceived truth when it lay on the surface; he could follow it through all the labyrinths of disquisition, but overlooked it, when it was undisguised before him. In fact he cared not for truth, nor sought it by bold and broad argument, but loved to exert the wily cunning of his nature in hunting it through artificial perplexities. At length, from a habit of intricacy and suspicion, his vitiated mind could receive nothing for truth, which was simple and easily comprehended.

Among his associates no one loved him, many disliked him, and more feared him. His figure was striking, but not so from grace; it was tall, and, though extremely thin, his limbs were large and uncouth, and as he stalked along, wrapt in the black garments of his order, there was something terrible in its air; something almost super-human. His cowl, too, as it threw a shade over the livid paleness of his face, encreased its severe character, and gave an effect to his large melancholy eye, which approached to horror. His was not the melancholy of a sensible and wounded heart, but apparently that of a gloomy and ferocious disposition. There was something in his physiognomy extremely singular, and that can not easily be defined. It bore the traces of many passions, which seemed to have fixed the features they no longer animated. An habitual gloom and severity prevailed over the deep lines of his countenance; and his eyes were so piercing that they seemed to penetrate, at a single glance, into the hearts of men, and to read their most secret thoughts; few persons could support their scrutiny, or even endure to meet them twice. Yet, notwithstanding all this gloom and austerity, some rare occasions of interest had called forth a character upon his countenance entirely different; and he could adapt himself to the tempers and passions of persons, whom he wished to conciliate, with astonishing facility, and generally with complete triumph. This monk, this Schedoni, was the confessor and secret adviser of the Marchesa di Vivaldi. In the first effervescence of pride and indignation, which the discovery of her son's intended marriage occasioned, she consulted him on the means of preventing it, and she soon perceived that his talents promised to equal her wishes. Each possessed, in a considerable degree, the power of assisting the other; Schedoni had subtlety with ambition to urge it; and the Marchesa had inexorable pride, and courtly influence; the one hoped to obtain a high benefice for his services, and the other to secure the imaginary dignity of her house, by her gifts. Prompted by such passions, and allured by such views, they concerted in private, and unknown even to the Marchese, the means of accomplishing their general end.

Vivaldi, as he quitted his mother's closet, had met Schedoni in the corridor leading thither. He knew him to be her confessor, and was not much surprised to see him, though the hour was an unusual one. Schedoni bowed his head, as he passed, and assumed a meek and holy countenance; but Vivaldi, as he eyed him with a penetrating glance, now recoiled with involuntary emotion; and it seemed as if a shuddering presentiment of what this monk was preparing for him, had crossed his mind.

CHAPTER III

—Art thou any thing?
Art thou some God, some Angel, or some Devil
That mak'st my blood cold, and my hair to stand?
Speak to me, what thou art.

JULIUS CAESAR

VIVALDI, from the period of his last visit to Altieri, was admitted a frequent visitor to Signora Bianchi, and Ellena was, at length, prevailed upon to join the party, when the conversation was always on indifferent topics. Bianchi, understanding the disposition of her niece's affections, and the accomplished mind and manners of Vivaldi, judged that he was more likely to succeed by silent attentions than by a formal declaration of his sentiments. By such declaration, Ellena, till her heart was more engaged in his cause, would, perhaps, have been alarmed into an absolute rejection of his addresses, and this was every day less likely to happen, so long as he had an opportunity of conversing with her.

Signora Bianchi had acknowledged to Vivaldi that he had no rival to apprehend; that Ellena had uniformly rejected every admirer who had hitherto discovered her within the shade of her retirement, and that her present reserve proceeded more from considerations of the sentiments of his family than from disapprobation of himself. He forbore, therefore, to press his suit, till he should have secured a stronger interest in her heart, and in this hope he was encouraged by Signora Bianchi, whose gentle remonstrances in his favour became every day more pleasing and more convincing.

Several weeks passed away in this kind of intercourse, till Ellena, yielding to the representations of Signora Bianchi, and to the pleadings of her own heart, received Vivaldi as an acknowledged admirer, and the sentiments of his family were no longer remembered, or, if remembered, it was with a hope that they might be overcome by considerations more powerful.

The lovers, with Signora Bianchi and a Signor Giotto, a distant relation of the latter, frequently made excursions in the delightful environs of Naples; for Vivaldi was no longer anxious to conceal his attachment, but wished to contradict any report injurious to his love, by the publicity of his conduct; while the consideration, that Ellena's name had suffered by his late imprudence, contributed, with the unsuspecting innocence and sweetness of her manners towards him, who had been the occasion of her injuries, to mingle a sacred pity with his love, which obliterated all family politics from his mind, and bound her irrecoverably to his heart.

These excursions sometimes led them to Puzzuoli, Baia, or the woody cliffs of Pausilippo, and as, on their return, they glided along the moon-light bay, the melodies of Italian strains seemed to give enchantment to the scenery of its shore. At this cool hour the voices of the vine-dressers were frequently heard in trio, as they reposed, after the labour of the day, on some pleasant promontory, under the shade of poplars; or the brisk music of the dance from fishermen, on the margin of the waves below. The boatmen rested on their oars, while their company listened to voices modulated by sensibility to finer eloquence, than is in the power of art alone to display; and at others, while they observed the airy natural grace, which distinguishes the dance of the fishermen and peasants of Naples. Frequently as they glided round a promontory, whose shaggy masses impended far over the sea, such magic scenes of beauty unfolded, adorned by these dancing groups on the bay beyond, as no pencil could do justice to. The deep clear waters reflected every image of the landscape, the cliffs, branching into wild forms, crowned with groves, whose rough foliage often spread down their steeps in picturesque luxuriance; the ruined villa on some bold point, peeping through the trees; peasants' cabins hanging on the precipices, and the dancing figures on the strand—all touched with the silvery tint and soft shadows of moon-light. On the other hand, the sea trembling with a long line of radiance, and shewing in the clear distance the sails of vessels stealing in every direction along its surface, presented a prospect as grand as the landscape was beautiful.

One evening that Vivaldi sat with Ellena and Signora Bianchi, in the very pavilion where he had overheard that short but interesting soliloquy, which assured him of her regard, he pleaded with more than his usual earnestness for a speedy marriage. Bianchi did not oppose his arguments; she had been unwell for some time, and, believing herself to be declining fast, was anxious to have their nuptials concluded. She surveyed with languid eyes, the scene that spread before the pavilion. The strong effulgence which a setting-sun threw over the sea, shewing innumerable gaily painted ships, and fishing-boats returning from Santa Lucia into the port of Naples, had no longer power to cheer her. Even the Roman tower that terminated the mole below, touched as it was with the slanting rays; and the various figures of fishermen, who lay smoking beneath its walls, in the long shadow, or stood in the sunshine on the beach, watching the approaching boats of their comrades, combined a picture which was no longer interesting. "Alas!" said she, breaking from meditative silence, "this sun so glorious, which lights up all the various colouring of these shores, and the glow of those majestic mountains; alas! I feel that it will not long shine for me—my eyes must soon close upon the prospect for ever!"

To Ellena's tender reproach for this melancholy suggestion Bianchi replied only by expressing an earnest wish to witness the certainty of her being protected; adding, that this must be soon, or she should not live to see it. Ellena, extremely shocked both by this presage of her aunt's fate, and by the direct reference made to her own condition in the presence of Vivaldi, burst into tears, while he, supported by the wishes of Signora Bianchi, urged his suit with encreased interest.

"This is not a time for fastidious scruples," said Bianchi, "now that a solemn truth calls out to us. My dear girl, I will not disguise my feelings; they assure me I have not long to live. Grant me then the only request I have to make, and my last hours will be comforted."

After a pause she added, as she took the hand of her niece, "This will, no doubt, be an awful separation to us both; and it must also be a mournful one, Signor," turning to Vivaldi, "for she has been as a daughter to me, and I have, I trust, fulfilled to her the duties of a mother. Judge then, what will be her feelings when I am no more. But it will be your care to soothe them."

Vivaldi looked at Ellena, and would have spoken; her aunt, however, proceeded. "My own feelings would now be little less poignant, if I did not believe that I was confiding her to a tenderness, which cannot diminish; that I should prevail with her to accept the protection of a husband. To you, Signor, I commit the legacy of my child. Watch over her future moments, guard her from inquietude as vigilantly as I have done, and, if possible, from misfortune! I have yet much to say, but my spirits are exhausted."

While he listened to this sacred charge, and recollected the injury Ellena had already sustained for his sake, by the cruel obliquy which the Marchese had thrown upon her character, he suffered a degree of generous indignation, of which he scarcely could conceal the cause, and a succeeding tenderness that almost melted him to tears; and he secretly vowed to defend her fame and protect her peace, at the sacrifice of every other consideration.

Bianchi, as she concluded her exhortation, gave Ellena's hand to Vivaldi, who received it with emotion such as his countenance, only, could express, and with solemn fervour raising his eyes to heaven, vowed that he never would betray the confidence thus reposed in him, but would watch over the happiness of Ellena with a care as tender, as anxious, and as unceasing as her own; that from this moment he considered himself bound by ties not less sacred than those which the church confers, to defend her as his wife, and would do so to the latest moment of his existence. As he said this, the truth of his feelings appeared in the energy of his manner.

Ellena, still weeping, and agitated by various considerations, spoke not, but withdrawing the handkerchief from her face, she looked at him through her tears, with a smile so meek, so affectionate, so timid, yet so confiding, as expressed all the mingled emotions of her heart, and appealed more eloquently to his, than the most energetic language could have done.

Before Vivaldi left the villa, he had some further conversation with Signora Bianchi, when it was agreed that the nuptials should be solemnized on the following week, if Ellena could be prevailed on to confirm her consent so soon; and that when he returned the next day, her determination would probably be made known to him.

He departed for Naples once more with the lightly-bounding steps of joy, which, however, when he arrived there, was somewhat alloyed by a message from the Marchese, demanding to see him in his cabinet. Vivaldi anticipated the subject of the interview, and obeyed the summons with reluctance.

He found his father so absorbed in thought, that he did not immediately perceive him. On raising his eyes from the floor, where discontent and perplexity seemed to have held them, he fixed a stern regard on Vivaldi. "I understand," said he, "that you persist in the unworthy pursuit against which I warned you. I have left you thus long to your own discretion, because I was willing to afford you an opportunity of retracting with grace the declaration, which you have dared to make me of your principles and intentions; but your conduct has not therefore been the less observed. I am informed that your visits have been as frequent at the residence of the unhappy young woman, who was the subject of our former conversation, as formerly, and that you are as much infatuated."

"If it is Signora Rosalba, whom your lordship means," said Vivaldi, "she is not unhappy; and I do not scruple to own, that I am as sincerely attached to her as ever. Why, my dear father," continued he, subduing the feelings which this degrading mention of Ellena had aroused, "why will you persist in opposing the happiness of your son; and above all, why will you continue to think unjustly of her, who deserves your admiration, as much as my love?"

"As I am not a lover," replied the Marchese, "and that the age of boyish credulity is past with me, I do not wilfully close my mind against examination, but am directed by proof and yield to conviction."

"What proof is it, my Lord, that has thus easily convinced you?" said Vivaldi; "Who is it that persists in abusing your confidence, and in destroying my peace?"

The Marchese haughtily reproved his son for such doubts and questions, and a long conversation ensued, which seemed neither to reconcile the interests or the opinions of either party. The Marchese persisted in accusation and menace; and Vivaldi in defending Ellena, and in affirming, that his affections and intentions were irrecoverable.

Not any art of persuasion could prevail with the Marchese to adduce his proofs, or deliver up the name of his informer; nor any menace awe Vivaldi into a renunciation of Ellena; and they parted mutually dissatisfied. The Marchese had failed on this occasion to act with his usual policy, for his menaces and accusations had aroused spirit and indignation, when kindness and gentle remonstrance would certainly have awakened filial affection, and might have occasioned a contest in the breast of Vivaldi. Now, no struggle of opposing duties divided his resolution. He had no hesitation on the subject of their dispute; but, regarding his father as a haughty oppressor who would rob him of his most sacred right; and as one who did not scruple to stain the name of the innocent and the defenceless, when his interest required it, upon the doubtful authority of a base informer, he suffered neither pity or remorse to mingle with the resolution of asserting the freedom of his nature; and was even more anxious than before, to conclude a marriage which he believed would secure his own happiness, and the reputation of Ellena.

He returned, therefore, on the following day to the villa Altieri, with encreased impatience to learn the result of Signora Bianchi's further conversation with her niece, and the day on which the nuptials might be solemnized. On the way thither, his thoughts were wholly occupied by Ellena, and he proceeded mechanically, and without observing where he was, till the shade which the well-known arch threw over the road recalled him to local circumstances, and a voice instantly arrested his attention. It was the voice of the monk, whose figure again passed before him. "Go not to the villa Altieri," it said solemnly, "for death is in the house!"

Before Vivaldi could recover from the dismay into which this abrupt assertion and sudden appearance had thrown him, the stranger was gone. He had escaped in the gloom of the place, and seemed to have retired into the obscurity, from which he had so suddenly emerged, for he was not seen to depart from under the archway. Vivaldi pursued him with his voice, conjuring him to appear, and demanding who was dead; but no voice replied.

Believing that the stranger could not have escaped unseen from the arch by any way, but that leading to the fortress above, Vivaldi began to ascend the steps, when, considering that the more certain means of understanding this awful assertion would be, to go immediately to the villa Altieri, he left this portentous ruin, and hastened thither.

An indifferent person would probably have understood the words of the monk to allude to Signora Bianchi, whose infirm state of health rendered her death, though sudden, not improbable; but to the affrighted fancy of Vivaldi, the dying Ellena only appeared. His fears, however probabilities might sanction, or the event justify them, were natural to ardent affection; but they were accompanied by a presentiment as extraordinary as it was horrible;—it occurred to him more than once, that Ellena was murdered. He saw her wounded, and bleeding to death; saw her ashy countenance, and her wasting eyes, from which the spirit of life was fast departing, turned piteously on himself, as if imploring him to save her from the fate that was dragging her to the grave. And, when he reached the boundary of the garden, his whole frame trembled so, with horrible apprehension, that he rested a while, unable to venture further towards the truth. At length, he summoned courage to dare it, and, unlocking a private gate, of which he had lately received the key, because it spared him a considerable distance of the road to Naples, he approached the house. Every place around it was silent and forsaken; many of the lattices were closed, and, as he endeavoured to collect from every trivial circumstance some conjecture, his spirits still sunk as he advanced, till, having arrived within a few paces of the portico, all his fears were confirmed. He heard from within a feeble sound of lamentation, and then some notes of that solemn and peculiar kind of recitative, which is in some parts of Italy the requiem of the dying. The sounds were so low and distant that they only murmured on his ear; but, without pausing for information, he rushed into the portico, and knocked loudly at the folding doors, now closed against him.

After repeated summonses, Beatrice, the old housekeeper, appeared. She did not wait for Vivaldi's enquiries. "Alas! Signor," she said, "alas-a-day! who would have thought it; who would have expected such a change as this! It was only yester-evening that you was here,—she was then as well as I am; who would have thought that she would be dead to-day?"

"She *is* dead, then!" exclaimed Vivaldi, struck to the heart; "she *is* dead!" staggering towards a pillar of the hall, and endeavouring to support himself against it. Beatrice, shocked at his condition, would have gone for assistance, but he waved her to stay. "When did she die," said he, drawing breath with difficulty, "how and where?"

"Alas! here in the villa, Signor," replied Beatrice, weeping; "who would have thought that I should live to see this day! I hoped to have laid down my old bones in peace."

"What has caused her death?" interrupted Vivaldi impatiently, "and when did she die?"

"About two of the clock this morning, Signor; about two o'clock. O miserable day, that I should live to see it!"

"I am better," said Vivaldi, raising himself; "lead me to her apartment,—I must see her. Do not hesitate, lead me on."

"Alas! Signor, it is a dismal sight; why should you wish to see her? Be persuaded; do not go, Signor; it is a woeful sight!"

"Lead me on," repeated Vivaldi sternly; "or if you refuse, I will find the way myself."

Beatrice, terrified by his look and gesture, no longer opposed him, begging only that he would wait till she had informed her lady of his arrival; but he followed her closely up the staircase and along a corridor that led round the west side of the house, which brought him to a suite of chambers darkened by the closed lattices, through which he passed towards the one where the body lay. The requiem had ceased, and no sound disturbed the awful stillness that prevailed in these deserted rooms. At the door of the last apartment, where he was compelled to stop, his agitation was such, that Beatrice, expecting every instant to see him sink to the floor, made an effort to support him with her feeble aid, but he gave a signal for her to retire. He soon recovered himself and passed into the chamber of death, the solemnity of which might have affected him in any other state of his spirits; but these were now too severely pressed upon by real suffering to feel the influence of local circumstances. Approaching the bed on which the corpse was laid, he raised his eyes to the mourner who hung weeping over it, and beheld—Ellena! who, surprised by this sudden intrusion, and still more by the agitation of Vivaldi, repeatedly demanded the occasion of it. But he had neither power or inclination to explain a circumstance, which must deeply wound the heart of Ellena, since it would have told that the same event, which excited her grief, accidentally inspired his joy.

He did not long intrude upon the sacredness of sorrow, and the short time he remained was employed in endeavours to command his own emotion and to soothe hers.

When he left Ellena, he had some conversation with

Beatrice, as to the death of Signora Bianchi, and understood that she had retired to rest on the preceding night apparently in her usual state of health. "It was about one in the morning, Signor," continued Beatrice, "I was waked out of my first sleep by a noise in my lady's chamber. It is a grievous thing to me, Signor, to be waked from my first sleep, and I, Santa Maria forgive me! was angry at being disturbed! So I would not get up, but laid my head upon the pillow again, and tried to sleep; but presently I heard the noise again; nay now, says I, somebody must be up in the house, that's certain. I had scarcely said so, Signor, when I heard my young lady's voice calling 'Beatrice! Beatrice!' Ah! poor young lady! she was indeed in a sad fright, as well she might. She was at my door in an instant, and looked as pale as death, and trembled so! 'Beatrice,' she said, 'rise this moment; my aunt is dying.' She did not stay for my answer, but was gone directly. Santa Maria protect me! I thought I should have swooned outright."

"Well, but your lady?" said Vivaldi, whose patience the tedious circumlocution of old Beatrice had exhausted.

"Ah! my poor lady! Signor, I thought I never should have been able to reach her room; and when I got there, I was scarcely more alive than herself.—There she lay on her bed! O it was a grievous sight to see! there she lay, looking so piteously; I saw she was dying. She could not speak, though she tried often, but she was sensible, for she would look so at Signora Ellena, and then try again to speak; it almost broke one's heart to see her. Something seemed to lie upon her mind, and she tried almost to the last to tell it; and as she grasped Signora Ellena's hand, she would still look up in her face with such doleful expression as no one who had not a heart of stone could bear. My poor young mistress was quite overcome by it, and cried as if her heart would break. Poor young lady! she has lost a friend indeed, such a one as she must never hope to see again."

"But she shall find one as firm and affectionate as the last!" exclaimed Vivaldi fervently.

"The good Saint grant it may prove so!" replied Beatrice, doubtingly. "All that could be done for our dear lady," she continued, "was tried, but with no avail. She could not swallow what the Doctor offered her. She grew fainter and fainter, yet would often utter such deep sighs, and then would grasp my hand so hard! At last she turned her eyes from Signora Ellena, and they grew duller and fixed, and she seemed not to see what was before her. Alas! I knew then she was going; her hand did not press mine as it had done a minute or two before, and a deadly coldness was upon it. Her face changed so too in a few minutes! This was about two o'clock, and she died before her confessor could administer."

Beatrice ceased to speak, and wept; Vivaldi almost wept with her, and it was some time before he could command his voice sufficiently to enquire, what were the symptoms of Signora Bianchi's disorder, and whether she had ever been thus suddenly attacked before.

"Never, Signor!" replied the old house-keeper; "and though, to be sure, she has long been very infirm, and going down, as one may say, yet,"—

"What is it you mean?" said Vivaldi.

"Why, Signor, I do not know what to think about my lady's death. To be sure, there is nothing certain; and I may only get scoffed at, if I speak my mind abroad, for nobody would believe me, it is so strange, yet I must have my own thoughts, for all that."

"Do speak intelligibly," said Vivaldi, "you need not apprehend censure from me."

"Not from you, Signor, but if the report should get abroad, and it was known that I had set it a-going."

"That never shall be known from me," said Vivaldi, with encreased impatience, "tell me, without fear, all that you conjecture."

"Well then, Signor, I will own, that I do not like the suddenness of my lady's death, no, nor the manner of it, nor her appearance after death!"

"Speak explicitly, and to the point," said Vivaldi.

"Nay, Signor, there are some folks that will not understand if you speak ever so plain, I am sure I speak plain enough. If I might tell my mind,—I do not believe she came fairly by her death at last!"

"How!" said Vivaldi, "your reasons?"

"Nay, Signor, I have given them already; I said I did not like the suddenness of her death, nor her appearance after, nor"—

"Good heaven!" interrupted Vivaldi, "you mean poison!"

"Hush, Signor, hush! I do not say that; but she did not seem to die naturally."

"Who has been at the villa lately?" said Vivaldi, in a tremulous voice.

"Alas! Signor, nobody has been here; she lived so privately that she saw nobody."

"Not one person?" said Vivaldi, "consider well, Beatrice, had she no visitor?"

"Not of a long while, Signor, no visitors but yourself and her cousin Signor Giotto. The only other person that has been within these walls for many weeks, to the best of my remembrance, is a sister of the Convent, who comes for the silks my young lady embroiders."

"Embroiders! What convent?"

"The Santa Maria della Pieta, yonder, Signor; if you will step this way to the window, I will shew it you. Yonder, among the woods on the hill-side, just above those gardens that stretch down to the bay. There is an olive ground close beside it, and observe, Signor, there is a red and yellowish ridge of rocks rises over the woods higher still, and looks as if it would fall down upon those old spires. Have you found it, Signor?"

"How long is it since this sister came here?" said Vivaldi.

"Three weeks at least, Signor."

"And you are certain that no other person has called within that time?"

"No other, Signor, except the fisherman and the gardener, and a man who brings maccaroni, and such sort of things; for it is such a long way to Naples, Signor, and I have so little time."

"Three weeks, say you! You said three weeks, I think? Are you certain as to this?"

"Three weeks, Signor! Santa della Pieta! Do you believe, Signor, that we could fast for three weeks! Why, they call almost every day."

"I speak of the nun," said Vivaldi.

"O yes, Signor," replied Beatrice; "it is that, at least, since she was here."

"This is strange!" said Vivaldi, musing, "but I will talk with you some other time. Meanwhile, I wish you could contrive that I should see the face of your deceased lady, without the knowledge of Signora Ellena. And, observe me, Beatrice, be strictly silent as to your surmises concerning her death: do not suffer any negligence to betray your suspicions to your young mistress. Has she any suspicions herself of the same nature?"

Beatrice replied, that she believed Signora Ellena had none; and promised faithfully to observe his injunctions.

He then left the villa, meditating on the circumstances he had just learned, and on the prophetic assertion of the monk, between whom, and the cause of Bianchi's sudden death, he could not forbear surmising there was some connection; and it now occurred to him, and for the first time, that this monk, this mysterious stranger, was no other than Schedoni, whom he had observed of late going more frequently than usual, to his mother's apartment. He almost started, in horror of the suspicion, to which this conjecture led, and precipitately rejected it, as a poison that would destroy his own peace for ever. But though he instantly dismissed the suspicion, the conjecture returned to his mind, and he endeavoured to recollect the voice and figure of the stranger, that he might compare them with those of the confessor. The voices were, he thought, of a different tone, and the persons of a different height and proportion. This comparison, however, did not forbid him to surmise that the stranger was an agent of the confessor's; that he was, at least, a secret spy upon his actions, and the defamer of Ellena; while both, if indeed there were two persons concerned, appeared to be at the command of his parents. Fired with indignation of the unworthy arts that he believed to have been employed against him, and impatient to meet the slanderer of Ellena, he determined to attempt some decisive step towards a discovery of the truth, and either to compel the confessor to reveal it to him, or to search out his agent, who, he fancied, was occasionally a resident within the ruins of Paluzzi.

The inhabitants of the convent, which Beatrice had pointed out, did not escape his consideration, but no reason appeared for supposing them the enemies of his Ellena, who, on the contrary, he understood had been for some years amicably connected with them. The embroidered silks, of which the old servant had spoken, sufficiently explained the nature of the connection, and discovering more fully the circumstances of Ellena's fortune, her conduct heightened the tender admiration, with which he had hitherto regarded her.

The hints for suspicion which Beatrice had given respecting the cause of her mistress's decease, incessantly recurred to him; and it appeared extraordinary, and sometimes in the

highest degree improbable, that any person could be sufficiently interested in the death of a woman apparently so
blameless, as to administer poison to her. What motive could
have prompted so horrible a deed, was still more inexplicable. It was true that she had long been in a declining state;
yet the suddenness of her departure and the singularity of
some circumstances preceding as well as some appearances
that had followed it, compelled Vivaldi to doubt as to the
cause. He believed, however, that, after having seen the
corpse, his doubts must vanish; and Beatrice had promised,
that, if he could return in the evening, when Ellena had retired to rest, he should be permitted to visit the chamber of
the deceased. There was something repugnant to his feelings, in going thus secretly, or, indeed, at all, to the residence of Ellena at this delicate period, yet it was necessary
he should introduce there some medical professor, on whose
judgment he could rest, respecting the occasion of Bianchi's
death; and as he believed he should so soon acquire the right
of vindicating the honour of Ellena, that consideration did
not so seriously affect him as otherwise it would have done.
The enquiry which called him thither was, besides, of a nature too solemn and important to be lightly resigned; he had,
therefore, told Beatrice he would be punctual to the hour she
appointed. His intention to search for the monk was thus
again interrupted.

CHAPTER IV

Unfold th' impenetrable mystery,
That sets your soul and you at endless discord.
                                        MYSTERIOUS MOTHER

WHEN Vivaldi returned to Naples, he enquired for the Marchesa, of whom he wished to ask some questions concerning Schedoni, which, though he scarcely expected they would be explicitly answered, might yet lead to part of the truth he sought for.

The Marchesa was in her closet, and Vivaldi found the confessor with her. "This man crosses me, like my evil genius," said he to himself as he entered, "but I will know whether he deserves my suspicions before I leave the room."

Schedoni was so deeply engaged in conversation, that he did not immediately perceive Vivaldi, who stood for a moment examining his countenance, and tracing subjects for curiosity in its deep lines. His eyes, while he spoke, were cast downward, and his features were fixed in an expression at once severe and crafty. The Marchesa was listening with deep attention, her head inclined towards him, as if to catch the lowest murmur of his voice, and her face picturing the anxiety and vexation of her mind. This was evidently a conference, not a confession.

Vivaldi advancing, the monk raised his eyes; his countenance suffered no change, as they met those of Vivaldi. He rose, but did not take leave, and returned the slight and somewhat haughty salutation of Vivaldi, with an inclination of the head, that indicated a pride without pettishness, and a firmness bordering on contempt.

The Marchesa, on perceiving her son, was somewhat embarrassed, and her brow, before slightly contracted by vexation, now frowned with severity. Yet it was an involuntary emotion, for she endeavoured to chace the expression of it with a smile. Vivaldi liked the smile still less than the frown.

Schedoni seated himself quietly, and began, with almost the ease of a man of the world, to converse on general topics. Vivaldi, however, was reserved and silent; he knew not how to begin a conversation, which might lead to the knowledge he desired, and the Marchesa did not relieve him from the difficulty. His eye and his ear assisted him to conjecture at least, if not to obtain the information he wished; and, as he listened to the deep tones of Schedoni's voice, he became almost certain, that they were not the accents of his unknown adviser, though he considered, at the same moment, that it was not difficult to disguise, or to feign a voice. His stature seemed to decide the question more reasonably; for the figure of Schedoni appeared taller than that of the stranger; and though there was something of resemblance in their air, which Vivaldi had never observed before, he again considered, that the habit of the same order, which each wore, might easily occasion an artificial resemblance. Of the likeness, as to countenance, he could not judge, since the stranger's had been so much shrouded by his cowl, that Vivaldi had never distinctly seen a single feature. Schedoni's hood was now thrown back, so that he could not compare even the air of their heads under similar circumstances; but as he remembered to have seen the confessor on a former day approaching his mother's closet with the cowl shading his face, the same gloomy severity seemed to characterize both, and nearly the same terrible portrait was drawn on his fancy. Yet this again might be only an artificial effect, a character which the cowl alone gave to the head; and any face seen imperfectly beneath its dark shade, might have appeared equally severe. Vivaldi was still extremely perplexed in his opinion. One circumstance, however, seemed to throw some light on his judgement. The stranger had appeared in the habit of a monk, and, if Vivaldi's transient observation might be trusted, he was of the very same order with that of Schedoni. Yet if he were Schedoni, or even his agent, it was not probable that he would have shewn himself in a dress that might lead to a discovery of his person. That he was anxious for concealment, his manner had strongly proved; it seemed then, that this habit of a monk was only a disguise, assumed for the purpose of misleading conjecture. Vivaldi, however, determined to put some questions to Schedoni, and at the same time to observe their effect on his countenance. He took occasion to notice some drawings of ruins, which ornamented the cabinet of the Marchesa, and to say that the fortress of Paluzzi was worthy of being added to her collection. "You have seen it lately, perhaps, reverend father," added Vivaldi, with a penetrating glance.

"It is a striking relique of antiquity," replied the confessor.

"That arch," resumed Vivaldi, his eye still fixed on Schedoni, "that arch suspended between two rocks, the one overtopped by the towers of the fortress, the other shadowed with pine and broad oak, has a fine effect. But a picture of it would want human figures. Now either the grotesque shapes of banditti lurking within the ruin, as if ready to start out upon the traveller, or a friar rolled up in his black garments, just stealing forth from under the shade of the arch, and looking like some supernatural messenger of evil, would finish the piece."

The features of Schedoni suffered no change during this speech. "Your picture is complete," said he, "and I cannot but admire the facility with which you have classed the monks together with banditti."

"Your pardon, holy father," said Vivaldi, "I did not draw a parallel between them."

"O! no offence, Signor," replied Schedoni, with a smile somewhat ghastly.

During the latter part of this conversation, if conversation it may be called, the Marchesa had followed a servant, who had brought her a letter, out of the apartment, and as the confessor appeared to await her return, Vivaldi determined to press his enquiry. "It appears, however," said he, "that Paluzzi, if not haunted by robbers, is at least frequented by ecclesiastics; for I have seldom passed it without seeing one of the order, and that one has appeared so suddenly, and vanished so suddenly, that I have been almost compelled to believe he was literally a spiritual being!"

"The convent of the Black Penitents is not far distant," observed the confessor.

"Does the dress of this convent resemble that of your order, reverend father? for I observed that the monk I speak of was habited like yourself; aye, and he was about your stature, and very much resembled you."

"That well may be, Signor," replied the confessor calmly; "there are many brethren who, no doubt, resemble each other; but the brothers of the Black Penitents are clothed in sackcloth; and the death's head on the garment, the peculiar symbol of this order, would not have escaped your observation; it could not, therefore, be a member of their society whom you have seen."

"I am not inclined to think that it was," said Vivaldi; "but be it who it may, I hope soon to be better acquainted with him, and to tell him truths so strong, that he shall not be permitted even to affect the misunderstanding of them."

"You will do right, if you have cause of complaint against him," observed Schedoni.

"And *only* if I have cause of complaint, holy father? Are strong truths to be told only when there is direct cause of complaint? Is it only when we are injured that we are to be sincere?" He believed that he had now detected Schedoni, who seemed to have betrayed a consciousness that Vivaldi had reason for complaint against the stranger.

"You will observe, reverend father, that I have not said I am injured," he added. "If you know that I am, this must be by other means than by my words; I have not even expressed resentment."

"Except by your voice and eye, Signor," replied Schedoni drily. "When a man is vehement and disordered, we usually are inclined to suppose he feels resentment, and that he has cause of complaint, either real or imaginary. As I have not the honour of being acquainted with the subject you allude to, I cannot decide to which of the two your cause belongs."

"I have never been in doubt as to that," said Vivaldi haughtily; "and if I had, you will pardon me, holy father, but I should not have requested your decision. My injuries are, alas! too real; and I now think it is also too certain to whom I may attribute them. The secret adviser, who steals into the bosom of a family only to poison its repose, the informer— the base asperser of innocence, stand revealed in one person before me."

Vivaldi delivered these words with a tempered energy, at once dignified and pointed, which seemed to strike directly to the heart of Schedoni; but, whether it was his conscience or his pride that took the alarm, did not certainly appear. Vivaldi believed the former. A dark malignity overspread the features of the monk, and at that moment Vivaldi thought he beheld a man, whose passions might impel him to the perpetration of almost any crime, how hideous soever. He recoiled from him, as if he had suddenly seen a serpent in his path, and stood gazing on his face, with an attention so wholly occupied as to be unconscious that he did so.

Schedoni almost instantly recovered himself; his features relaxed from their first expression, and that portentous darkness passed away from his countenance; but with a look that was still stern and haughty, he said, "Signor, however ignorant I may be of the subject of your discontent, I can not misunderstand that your resentment is, to some extent or other, directed against myself as the cause of it. Yet I will not suppose, Signor; I say I will not suppose," raising his voice significantly, "that you have dared to brand me with the ignominious titles you have just uttered; but"—

"I have applied them to the author of my injuries," interrupted Vivaldi; "you, father, can best inform me whether they applied to yourself."

"I have then nothing to complain of," said Schedoni, adroitly, and with a sudden calmness, that surprised Vivaldi. "If you directed them against the author of your injuries, whatever they may be, I am satisfied."

The chearful complacency, with which he spoke this, renewed the doubts of Vivaldi, who thought it nearly impossible that a man conscious of guilt could assume, under the very charge of it, the tranquil and dignified air, which the confessor now displayed. He began to accuse himself of having condemned him with passionate rashness, and gradually became shocked at the indecorum of his conduct towards a man of Schedoni's age and sacred profession. Those expressions of countenance, which had so much alarmed him, he was now inclined to think the effect of a jealous and haughty honour, and he almost forgot the malignity, which had mingled with Schedoni's pride, in sorrow for the offence that had provoked it. Thus, not less precipitate in his pity than his anger, and credulous alike to the passion of the moment, he was now as eager to apologize for his error, as he had been hasty in committing it. The frankness, with which he apologized and lamented the impropriety of his conduct, would have won an easy forgiveness from a generous heart. Schedoni listened with apparent complacency and secret contempt. He regarded Vivaldi as a rash boy, who was swayed only by his passions; but while he suffered deep resentment for the evil in his character, he felt neither respect nor kindness for the good, for the sincerity, the love of justice, the generosity, which threw a brilliancy even on his foibles. Schedoni, indeed, saw only evil in human nature.

Had the heart of Vivaldi been less generous, he would now have distrusted the satisfaction, which the confessor assumed, and have discovered the contempt and malignity, that lurked behind the smile thus imperfectly masking his countenance. The confessor perceived his power, and the character of Vivaldi lay before him as a map. He saw, or fancied he saw every line and feature of its plan, and the relative proportions of every energy and weakness of its nature. He believed, also, he could turn the very virtues of this young man against himself, and he exulted, even while the smile of good-will was yet upon his countenance, in anticipating the moment that should avenge him for the past outrage, and which, while Vivaldi was ingenuously lamenting it, he had apparently forgotten.

Schedoni was thus ruminating evil against Vivaldi, and Vivaldi was considering how he might possibly make Schedoni atonement for the affront he had offered him, when the Marchesa returned to the apartment; and perceived in the honest countenance of Vivaldi some symptoms of the agitation which had passed over it; his complexion was flushed, and his brow slightly contracted. The face of Schedoni told nothing but complacency, except that now and then when he looked at Vivaldi, it was with half-shut eyes, that indicated treachery, or, at least, cunning, trying to conceal exasperated pride.

The Marchesa, with displeasure directed against her son, enquired the reason of his emotion; but he, stung with consciousness of his conduct towards the monk, could neither endure to explain it, or to remain in her presence, and saying that he would confide his honour to the discretion of the holy father, who would speak only too favourably of his fault, he abruptly left the room.

When he had departed, Schedoni gave, with seeming reluctance, the explanation which the Marchesa required, but was cautious not to speak too favourably of Vivaldi's conduct, which, on the contrary, he represented as much more insulting than it really was; and, while he aggravated the offensive part of it, he suppressed all mention of the candour and self-reproach, which had followed the charge. Yet this he managed so artfully that he appeared to extenuate Vivaldi's errors, to lament the hastiness of his temper, and to plead for a forgiveness from his irritated mother. "He is very young," added the monk, when he perceived that he had sufficiently exasperated the Marchesa against her son; "he is very young, and youth is warm in its passions and precipitate in its judgments. He was, besides, jealous, no doubt, of the friendship, with which you are pleased to honour me; and it is natural that a son should be jealous of the attention of such a mother."

"You are too good, father," said the Marchesa; her resentment encreasing towards Vivaldi in proportion as Schedoni displayed his artificial candour and meekness.

"It is true," continued the confessor, "that I perceive all the inconveniences to which my attachment, I should say my duty to your family exposes me; but I willingly submit to these, while it is yet possible that my advice may be a means of preserving the honour of your house unsullied, and of saving this inconsiderate young man from future misery and unavailing repentance."

During the warmth of this sympathy in resentment, the Marchesa and Schedoni mutually, and sincerely, lost their remembrance of the unworthy motives, by which each knew the other to be influenced, as well as that disgust which those who act together to the same bad end, can seldom escape from feeling towards their associates. The Marchesa, while she commended the fidelity of Schedoni, forgot his views and her promises as to a rich benefice; while the confessor imputed her anxiety for the splendor of her son's condition to a real interest in his welfare, not a care of her own dignity. After mutual compliments had been exchanged, they proceeded to a long consultation concerning Vivaldi, and it was agreed, that their efforts for what they termed his preservation should no longer be confined to remonstrances.

CHAPTER V

What if it be a poison, which the friar
Subtly hath ministered?——

SHAKESPEARE

VIVALDI, when his first feelings of pity and compunction for having insulted an aged man, the member of a sacred profession, were past, and when he looked with a more deliberate eye upon some circumstances of the confessor's conduct, perceived that suspicion was again gathering on his mind. But, regarding this as a symptom of his own weakness, rather than as a hint of truth, he endeavoured, with a magnanimous disdain, to reject every surmise that boded unfavourably of Schedoni.

When evening arrived, he hastened towards the villa Altieri, and, having met without the city, according to appointment, a physician, upon whose honour and judgement he thought he might rely, they proceeded on their way together. Vivaldi had forgotten, during the confusion of his last interview with Ellena, to deliver up the key of the garden-gate, and he now entered it as usual, though he could not entirely overcome the reluctance, which he felt on thus visiting, in secret and at night, the dwelling of Ellena. Under no other circumstances, however, could the physician, whose opinion was so necessary to his peace, be introduced without betraying a suspicion, which must render her unhappy, probably for ever.

Beatrice, who had watched for them in the portico, led the way to the chamber where the corpse was laid out; and Vivaldi, though considerably affected when he entered, soon recovered composure enough to take his station on one side of the bed, while the physician placed himself on the other. Unwilling to expose his emotion to the observation of a servant, and desirous also of some private conversation with the physician, he took the lamp from Beatrice and dismissed her. As the light glared upon the livid face of the corpse, Vivaldi gazed with melancholy surprize, and an effort of reason was necessary to convince him, that this was the same countenance which only one evening preceding was animated like his own; which had looked upon him in tears, while, with anxiety the most tender, she had committed the happiness of her niece to his care, and had, alas! too justly predicted her approaching dissolution. The circumstances of that scene now appeared to him like a vision, and touched every fibre of his heart. He was fully sensible of the importance of the trust committed to him, and, as he now hung over the pale and deserted form of Bianchi, he silently renewed his solemn vows to Ellena, to deserve the confidence of her departed guardian.

Before Vivaldi had courage enough to ask the opinion of the physician, who was still viewing the face of the deceased with very earnest attention and disapproving countenance, his own suspicions strengthened from some circumstances of her appearance; and particularly from the black tint that prevailed over her complexion, it seemed to him, that her death had been by poison. He feared to break a silence, which prolonged his hope of the contrary, feeble though it was; and the physician, who probably was apprehensive for the consequence of delivering his real thought, did not speak.

"I read your opinion," said Vivaldi, at length, "it coincides with my own."

"I know not as to that, Signor," replied the physician, "though I think I perceive what is yours. Appearances are unfavourable, yet I will not take upon me to decide from them, that it is as you suspect. There are other circumstances, under which similar appearances might occur." He gave his reasons for this assertion, which were plausible even to Vivaldi, and concluded with requesting to speak with Beatrice, "for I wish to understand," said he, "what was the exact situation of this lady for some hours previous to her decease."

After a conversation of some length with Beatrice, whatever might be the opinion resulting from his enquiries, he adhered nearly to his former assertions; pronouncing that so many contradictory circumstances appeared, as rendered it impossible for him to decide, whether Bianchi had died by poison, or otherwise. He stated more fully than he had done before, the reasons, which must render the opinion of any medical person, on this subject, doubtful. But, whether it was that he feared to be responsible for a decision, which would accuse some person of murder, or that he really was inclined to believe that Bianchi died naturally, it is certain he seemed disposed to adopt the latter opinion; and that he was very anxious to quiet the suspicions of Vivaldi. He so far succeeded, indeed, as to convince him that it would be un-availing to pursue the enquiry, and almost compelled him to believe, that she had departed according to the common course of nature.

Vivaldi, having lingered awhile over the death-bed of Bianchi, and taken a last farewel of her silent form, quitted the chamber and the house as softly as he had approached, and unobserved, as he believed, by Ellena or any other person. The morning dawned over the sea, when he returned into the garden, and a few fishermen, loitering on the beach, or putting off their little boats from the shore, were the only persons visible at this early hour. The time, however, was passed for renewing the enquiry he had purposed at Paluzzi, and the brightening dawn warned him to retire. To Naples, therefore, he returned, with spirits somewhat soothed by a hope, that Bianchi had not fallen prematurely, and by the certainty that Ellena was well. On the way thither, he passed the fort without interruption, and, having parted with the physician, was admitted into his father's mansion by a confidential servant.

CHAPTER VI

—For here have been
Some six or seven, who did hide their faces
Even from darkness.

SHAKESPEARE

ELLENA, on thus suddenly losing her aunt, her only relative, the friend of her whole life, felt as if left alone in the world. But it was not in the first moments of affliction that this feeling occurred. Her own forlorn situation was not even observed, while affection, pity, and irresistible grief for Bianchi, occupied her heart.

Bianchi was to be interred in the church belonging to the convent of Santa Maria della Pieta. The body, attired according to the custom of the country, and decorated with flowers, was carried on an open bier to the place of interment, attended only by priests and torch-bearers. But Ellena could not endure thus lightly to part with the reliques of a beloved friend, and being restrained by custom from following the corpse to the grave, she repaired first to the convent, to attend the funeral service. Her sorrow did not allow her to join in the choral symphonies of the nuns, but their sacred solemnity was soothing to her spirits, and the tears she shed while she listened to the lengthening notes, assuaged the force of grief.

When the service concluded, she withdrew to the parlour of the lady Abbess, who mingled with her consolations many entreaties that Ellena would make the convent her present asylum; and her affliction required little persuasion on this subject. It was her wish to retire hither, as to a sanctuary, which was not only suitable to her particular circumstances, but especially adapted to the present state of her spirits. Here she believed that she should sooner acquire res-

ignation, and regain tranquillity, than in a place less consecrated to religion; and, before she took leave of the Abbess,
it was agreed, that she should be received as a boarder. To
acquaint Vivaldi with her intention was, indeed, her chief
motive for returning to the villa Altieri, after this her resolution had been taken. Her affection and esteem had been
gradual in their progress, and had now attained a degree of
strength, which promised to decide the happiness or misery
of her whole life. The sanction given by her aunt to this
choice, and particularly the very solemn manner in which,
on the evening preceding her death, she bequeathed Ellena
to his care, had still endeared him to her heart, and imparted
a sacredness to the engagement, which made her consider
Vivaldi as her guardian and only surviving protector. The
more tenderly she lamented her deceased relative, the more
tenderly she thought of Vivaldi; and her love for the one was
so intimately connected with her affection for the other, that
each seemed strengthened and exalted by the union.

When the funeral was over, they met at Altieri.

He was neither surprized or averse to her withdrawing
awhile to a convent; for there was a propriety in retiring,
during the period of her grief, from a home where she had
no longer a guardian, which delicacy seemed to demand. He
only stipulated, that he might be permitted to visit her in the
parlour of the convent, and to claim, when decorum should
no longer object to it, the hand, which Bianchi had resigned
to him.

Notwithstanding that he yielded to this arrangement without complaining, it was not entirely without repining; but
being assured by Ellena of the worthiness of the Abbess of
the Santa Maria della Pieta, he endeavoured to silence the
secret murmurs of his heart with the conviction of his judgment.

Meanwhile, the deep impression made by his unknown
tormentor, the monk, and especially by his prediction of the
death of Bianchi, remained upon his mind, and he once more
determined to ascertain, if possible, the true nature of this
portentous visitant, and what were the motives which induced him thus to haunt his footsteps and interrupt his
peace. He was awed by the circumstances which had attended the visitations of the monk, if monk it was; by the
suddenness of his appearance, and departure; by the truth of
his prophecies; and, above all, by the solemn event which

had verified his last warning; and his imagination, thus elevated by wonder and painful curiosity, was prepared for something above the reach of common conjecture, and beyond the accomplishment of human agency. His understanding was sufficiently clear and strong to teach him to detect many errors of opinion, that prevailed around him, as well as to despise the common superstitions of his country, and, in the usual state of his mind, he probably would not have paused for a moment on the subject before him; but his passions were now interested and his fancy awakened, and, though he was unconscious of this propensity, he would, perhaps, have been somewhat disappointed, to have descended suddenly from the region of fearful sublimity, to which he had soared—the world of terrible shadows—to the earth, on which he daily walked, and to an explanation simply natural.

He designed to visit again, at midnight, the fortress of Paluzzi, and not to watch for the appearance of the stranger, but to carry torches into every recess of the ruin, and discover, at least, whether it was haunted by other human beings than himself. The chief difficulty, which had hitherto delayed him, was that of finding a person, in whom he could confide, to accompany him in the search, since his former adventure had warned him never to renew it alone. Signor Bonarmo persisted absolutely, and, perhaps, wisely, to refuse his request on this subject; and, as Vivaldi had no other acquaintance, to whom he chose to give so much explanation of the affair as might induce compliance, he at length determined to take with him Paulo, his own servant.

On the evening, previous to the day of Ellena's departure to the Santa della Pieta, Vivaldi went to Altieri, to bid her adieu. During this interview his spirits were more than usually depressed; and, though he knew that her retirement was only for a short period, and had as much confidence in the continuance of her affection, as is, perhaps, possible to a lover, Vivaldi felt as if he was parting with her for ever. A thousand vague and fearful conjectures, such as he had never till this moment admitted, assailed him, and amongst them, it appeared probable, that the arts of the nuns might win her from the world, and sacrifice her to the cloister. In her present state of sorrow this seemed to be even more than probable, and not all the assurances which Ellena gave him, and in these parting moments she spoke with less reserve than she had hitherto done, could entirely re-assure his mind. "It should seem, Ellena, by these boding fears," said he, imprudently, "that I am parting with you for ever; I feel a weight upon my heart, which I cannot throw off. Yet I consent that you shall withdraw awhile to this convent, convinced of the propriety of the step; and I ought, also, to know that you will soon return; that I shall soon take you from its walls as my wife, never more to leave me, never more to pass from my immediate care and tenderness. I ought to feel assured of all this; yet so apt are my fears that I cannot confide in what is probable, but rather apprehend what is possible. And is it then possible that I yet may lose you; and is it only probable that you may be mine for ever? How, under such circumstances, could I weakly consent to your retirement? Why did I not urge you to bestow immediately those indissoluble bands, which no human force can burst asunder? How could I leave the destiny of all my peace within the reach of a possibility, which it was once in my power to have removed! Which it *was* in my power!—It is, perhaps, still in my power. O Ellena! let the severities of custom yield to the security of my happiness. If you do go to the Santa Maria, let it be only to visit its altar!"

Vivaldi delivered this expostulation with a rapidity, that left no pause for Ellena to interrupt him. When, at length, he concluded, she gently reproached him for doubting the continuance of her regard, and endeavoured to sooth his apprehension of misfortune, but would not listen to his request. She represented, that not only the state of her spirits required retirement, but that respect to the memory of her aunt demanded it; and added gravely, that if he had so little confidence in the steadiness of her opinions, as to doubt the constancy of her affection, and for so short a period, unless her vows were secured to him, he had done imprudently to elect her for the companion of his whole life.

Vivaldi, then ashamed of the weakness he had betrayed, besought her forgiveness, and endeavoured to appease apprehensions which passion only made plausible, and which reason reproved; notwithstanding which, he could recover neither tranquillity nor confidence; nor could Ellena, though her conduct was supported and encouraged by justness of sentiment, entirely remove the oppression of spirits she had felt from almost the first moment of this interview. They parted with many tears; and Vivaldi, before he finally took his leave, frequently returned to claim some promise, or to ascertain some explanation, till Ellena remarked with a forced smile, that these resembled eternal adieus, rather than those of only a few days; an observation which renewed all his alarm, and furnished an excuse for again delaying his departure. At length he tore himself away, and left the villa Altieri; but as the time was yet too early to suit his purposed enquiry at Paluzzi, he returned to Naples.

Ellena, meanwhile, endeavouring to dissipate melancholy recollections by employment, continued busied in preparation for her departure on the following day, till a late hour of the night. In the prospect of quitting, though only for so short a period, the home where she had passed almost every day since the dawn of her earliest remembrance, there was something melancholy, if not solemn. In leaving these well-known scenes, where, it might be said, the shade of her deceased relative seemed yet to linger, she was quitting all vestige of her late happiness, all note of former years and of present consolation; and she felt as if going forth into a new and homeless world. Her affection for the place encreased as the passing time diminished, and it seemed as if the last moment of her stay would be precisely that, in which the villa Altieri would be most valued.

In her favourite apartments she lingered for a considerable time; and in the room where she had supped on the night immediately preceding the death of Signora Bianchi, she indulged many tender and mournful recollections, and probably would have continued to indulge them much longer, had not her attention been withdrawn by a sudden rustling of the foliage that surrounded the window, when, on raising her eyes, she thought she perceived some person pass quickly from before it. The lattices had, as usual, been left open to admit the fresh breeze from the bay below, but she now rose with some alarm to close them, and had scarcely done so when she heard a distant knocking from the portico, and in the next instant the screams of Beatrice in the hall.

Alarmed for herself, Ellena had, however, the courage to advance to the assistance of her old servant, when, on entering the passage leading to the hall, three men, masked and muffled up in cloaks, appeared, advancing from the opposite extremity. While she fled, they pursued her to the apartment she had quitted. Her breath and her courage were gone, yet she struggled to sustain herself, and endeavoured to ask with calmness what was their errand. They gave no reply, but threw a veil over her face, and, seizing her arms, led her almost unresisting, but supplicating, towards the portico.

In the hall, Ellena perceived Beatrice bound to a pillar; and another ruffian, who was also masked, watching over and menacing her, not by words, but gestures. Ellena's shrieks seemed to recall the almost lifeless Beatrice, for whom she supplicated as much as for herself; but entreaty was alike unavailing for each, and Ellena was borne from the house and through the garden. All consciousness had now forsaken her. On recovering, she perceived herself in a carriage, which was driven with great rapidity, and that her arms were within the grasp of some persons, whom, when her recollection returned more fully, she believed to be the men, who had carried her from the villa. The darkness prevented her from observing their figures, and to all her questions and entreaties a death-like silence was observed.

During the whole night the carriage proceeded rapidly, stopping only while the horses were changed, when Ellena endeavoured to interest by her cries the compassion of the people at the post-houses, and by her cries only, for the blinds were closely drawn. The postilions, no doubt, imposed on the credulity of these people, for they were insensible to her distress, and her immediate companions soon overcame the only means that had remained by which she could make it known.

For the first hours, a tumult of terror and amazement occupied her mind, but, as this began to subside, and her understanding to recover its clearness, grief and despondency mingled with her fears. She saw herself separated from Vivaldi, probably for ever, for she apprehended that the strong and invisible hand which governed her course, would never relinquish its grasp till it had placed her irrecoverably beyond the reach of her lover. A conviction that she should see him no more came, at intervals, with such overwhelming force, that every other consideration and emotion disappeared before it; and at these moments she lost all anxiety as to the place of her destination, and all fear as to her personal safety.

As the morning advanced and the heat encreased, the blinds were let down a little to admit air, and Ellena then perceived, that only two of the men, who had appeared at the villa Altieri, were in the carriage, and that they were still disguised in cloaks and visors. She had no means of judging through what part of the country she was travelling, for above the small openings which the blinds left she could see only the towering tops of mountains, or sometimes the veiny precipices and tangled thickets, that closely impended over the road.

About noon, as she judged from the excessive heat, the carriage stopped at a post-house, and ice-water was handed through the window, when, as the blind was lowered to admit it, she perceived herself on a wild and solitary plain, surrounded by mountains and woods. The people at the door of the post-house seemed "unused to pity or be pitied." The lean and sallow countenance of poverty stared over their gaunt bones, and habitual discontent had fixed the furrows of their cheeks. They regarded Ellena with only a feeble curiosity, though the affliction in her looks might have interested almost any heart that was not corroded by its own sufferings; nor did the masked faces of her companions excite a much stronger attention.

Ellena accepted the cool refreshment offered her, the first she had taken on the road. Her companions having emptied their glasses drew up the blind, and, notwithstanding the almost intolerable heat of noon, the carriage proceeded. Fainting under its oppression, Ellena entreated that the windows might be open, when the men, in compliance with their own necessity rather than with her request, lowered the blinds, and she had a glimpse of the lofty region of the mountains, but of no object that could direct her conjecture concerning where she was. She saw only pinnacles and vast precipices of various-tinted marbles, intermingled with scanty vegetation, such as stunted pinasters, dwarf oak and holly, which gave dark touches to the many-coloured cliffs, and sometimes stretched in shadowy masses to the deep vallies, that, winding into obscurity, seemed to invite curiosity to explore the scenes beyond. Below these bold precipices extended the gloomy region of olive-trees, and lower still other rocky steeps sunk towards the plains, bearing terraces crowned with vines, and where often the artificial soil was propped by thickets of juniper, pomegranate and oleander.

Ellena, after having been so long shut in darkness, and brooding over her own alarming circumstances, found temporary, though feeble, relief in once more looking upon the face of nature; till, her spirits being gradually revived and elevated by the grandeur of the images around her, she said to herself, "If I am condemned to misery, surely I could endure it with more fortitude in scenes like these, than amidst the tamer landscapes of nature! Here, the objects seem to impart somewhat of their own force, their own sublimity, to the soul. It is scarcely possible to yield to the pressure of misfortune while we walk, as with the Deity, amidst his most stupendous works!"

But soon after the idea of Vivaldi glancing athwart her memory, she melted into tears; the weakness however was momentary, and during the rest of the journey she preserved a strenuous equality of mind.

It was when the heat and the light were declining that the carriage entered a rocky defile, which shewed, as through a telescope reversed, distant plains, and mountains opening beyond, lighted up with all the purple splendor of the setting sun. Along this deep and shadowy perspective a river, which was seen descending among the cliffs of a mountain, rolled with impetuous force, fretting and foaming amidst the dark rocks in its descent, and then flowing in a limpid lapse to the brink of other precipices, whence again it fell with thundering strength to the abyss, throwing its misty clouds of spray high in the air, and seeming to claim the sole empire of this solitary wild. Its bed took up the whole breadth of the chasm, which some strong convulsion of the earth seemed to have formed, not leaving space even for a road along its margin. The road, therefore, was carried high among the cliffs, that impended over the river, and seemed as if suspended in air; while the gloom and vastness of the precipices, which towered above and sunk below it, together with the amazing force and uproar of the falling waters, combined to render the pass more terrific than the pencil could describe, or language can express. Ellena ascended it, not with indifference but with calmness; she experienced somewhat of a dreadful pleasure in looking down upon the irresistible flood; but this emotion was heightened into awe, when she perceived that the road led to a slight bridge, which, thrown across the chasm at an immense height, united two opposite cliffs, between which the whole cataract of the river descended. The bridge, which was defended only by a slender railing, appeared as if hung amidst the clouds. Ellena, while she was crossing it, almost forgot her misfortunes. Having reached the opposite side of the glen, the road gradually de-

scended the precipices for about half a mile, when it opened
to extensive prospects over plains and towards distant
mountains—the sunshine landscape, which had long appeared to bound this shadowy pass. The transition was as the
passage through the vale of death to the bliss of eternity; but
the idea of its resemblance did not long remain with Ellena.
Perched high among the cliffs of a mountain, which might
be said to terminate one of the jaws of this terrific gorge,
and which was one of the loftiest of a chain that surrounded
the plains, appeared the spires and long terraces of a monastery; and she soon understood that her journey was to conclude there.

At the foot of this mountain her companions alighted, and
obliged her to do the same, for the ascent was too steep and
irregular to admit of a carriage. Ellena followed unresistingly, like a lamb to the sacrifice, up a path that wound
among the rocks, and was cooly overshadowed by thickets
of almond trees, figs, broad-leaved myrtle, and ever-green
rose bushes, intermingled with the strawberry tree, beautiful
in fruit and blossoms, the yellow jasmine, the delightful *aca-
cia mimosa,* and a variety of other fragrant plants. These
bowers frequently admitted glimpses of the glowing country
below, and sometimes opened to expansive views bounded
by the snowy mountains of Abruzzo. At every step were objects which would have afforded pleasure to a tranquil mind;
the beautifully variegated marbles, that formed the cliffs immediately above, their fractured masses embossed with
mosses and flowers of every vivid hue that paints the rain-
bow; the elegance of the shrubs that tufted, and the majestic
grace of the palms which waved over them, would have
charmed almost any other eye than Ellena's, whose spirit
was wrapt in care, or than those of her companions, whose
hearts were dead to feeling. Partial features of the vast edifice she was approaching, appeared now and then between
the trees; the tall west window of the cathedral with the
spires that overtopped it; the narrow pointed roofs of the
cloisters; angles of the insurmountable walls, which fenced
the garden from the precipices below, and the dark portal
leading into the chief court; each of these, seen at intervals
beneath the gloom of cypress and spreading cedar, seemed
as if menacing the unhappy Ellena with hints of future suffering. She passed several shrines and images half hid
among the shrubs and the cliffs; and, when she drew near

the monastery, her companions stopped at a little chapel which stood beside the path, where, after examining some papers, an act which she observed with surprise, they drew aside, as if to consult respecting herself. Their conversation was delivered in voices so low, that she could not catch a single tone distinctly, and it is probable that if she could, this would not have assisted her in conjecturing who they were; yet the profound silence they had hitherto observed had much encreased her curiosity, now that they spoke.

One of them soon after quitted the chapel and proceeded alone to the monastery, leaving Ellena in the custody of his comrade, whose pity she now made a last, though almost hopeless, effort to interest. He replied to all her entreaties only by a waving of the hand, and an averted face; and she endeavoured to meet with fortitude and to endure with patience, the evil which she could neither avoid nor subdue. The spot where she awaited the return of the ruffian, was not of a character to promote melancholy, except, indeed, that luxurious and solemn kind of melancholy, which a view of stupendous objects inspires. It overlooked the whole extent of plains, of which she had before caught partial scenes, with the vast chain of mountains, which seemed to form an insurmountable rampart to the rich landscape at their feet. Their towering and fantastic summits, crowding together into dusky air, like flames tapering to a point, exhibited images of peculiar grandeur, while each minuter line and feature withdrawing, at this evening hour, from observation, seemed to resolve itself into the more gigantic masses, to which the dubious tint, the solemn obscurity, that began to prevail over them, gave force and loftier character. The silence and deep repose of the landscape, served to impress this character more awfully on the heart, and while Ellena sat wrapt in the thoughtfulness it promoted, the vesper-service of the monks breathing softly from the cathedral above, came to her ear; it was a music which might be said to win on silence, and was in perfect unison with her feelings; solemn, deep, and full, it swelled in holy peals, and rolled away in murmurs, which attention pursued to the last faint note that melted into air. Ellena's heart owned the power of this high minstrelsy; and while she caught for a moment the sweeter voices of the nuns mingling in the chorus, she indulged a hope that they would not be wholly insensible to her sufferings, and that she should receive some consolation from sympathy as soft as these tender-breathing strains appeared to indicate.

She had rested nearly half an hour on the turfy slope before the chapel, when she perceived through the twilight, two monks descending from the monastery towards the spot where she sat. As they drew near, she distinguished their dress of grey stuff, the hood, the shaven head, where only a coronet of white hair was left, and other ensigns of their particular order. On reaching the chapel they accosted her companion, with whom they retired a few paces, and conversed. Ellena heard, for the first time, the sound of her conductor's voice, and though this was but faintly, she marked it well. The other ruffian did not yet appear, but it seemed evident that these friars had left the convent in consequence of his information; and sometimes, when she looked upon the taller of the two, she fancied she saw the person of the very man whose absence she had remarked, a conjecture which strengthened while she more accurately noticed him. The portrait had certainly much resemblance in height and bulk; and the same gaunt awkwardness, which even the cloak of the ruffian had not entirely shrouded, obtruded itself from under the folded garments of the recluse. If countenance, too, might be trusted, this same friar had a ruffian's heart, and his keen and cunning eye seemed habitually upon the watch for prey. His brother of the order shewed nothing strongly characteristic either in his face or manner.

After a private conversation of some length, the friars approached Ellena, and told her, that she must accompany them to the convent; when her disguised conductor, having resigned her to them, immediately departed and descended the mountain.

Not a word was uttered by either of the party as they pursued the steep track leading to the gates of this secluded edifice, which were opened to them by a lay-brother, and Ellena entered a spacious court. Three sides of this were enclosed to lofty buildings, lined with ranges of cloisters; the fourth opened to a garden, shaded with avenues of melancholy cypress, that extended to the cathedral, whose fretted windows and ornamented spires appeared to close the perspective. Other large and detached buildings skirted the gardens on the left, while, on the right, spacious olive-grounds and vineyards spread to the cliffs that formed a barrier to all this side of the domain of the convent.

The friar, her conductor, crossed the court to the north wing, and there ringing a bell, a door was opened by a nun, into whose hands Ellena was given. A significant look was exchanged between the devotees, but no words; the friar departed, and the nun, still silent, conducted her through many solitary passages, where not even a distant foot-fall echoed, and whose walls were roughly painted with subjects indicatory of the severe superstitions of the place, tending to inspire melancholy awe. Ellena's hope of pity vanished as her eyes glanced over these symbols of the disposition of the inhabitants, and on the countenance of the nun characterised by a gloomy malignity, which seemed ready to inflict upon others some portion of the unhappiness she herself suffered. As she glided forward with soundless step, her white drapery, floating along these solemn avenues, and her hollow features touched with the mingled light and shadow which the partial rays of a taper she held occasioned, she seemed like a spectre newly risen from the grave, rather than a living being. These passages terminated in the parlour of the Abbess, where the nun paused, and, turning to Ellena, said, "It is the hour of vespers; you will wait here till our lady of the convent leaves the church; she would speak with you."

"To what saint is the convent dedicated," said Ellena, "and who, sister, presides over it?"

The nun gave no reply, and after having eyed the forlorn stranger for a moment, with inquisitive ill-nature, quitted the room. The unhappy Ellena had not been left long to her own reflections, when the Abbess appeared; a stately lady, apparently occupied with opinions of her own importance, and prepared to receive her guest with rigour and supercilious haughtiness. This Abbess, who was herself a woman of some distinction, believed that of all possible crimes, next to that of sacrilege, offences against persons of rank were least pardonable. It is not surprising, therefore, that, supposing Ellena, a young woman of no family, to have sought clandestinely to unite herself with the noble house of Vivaldi, she should feel for her, not only disdain, but indignation, and that she should readily consent, not only to punish the offender, but at the same time, to afford means of preserving the ancient dignity of the offended.

"I understand," said the Abbess, on whose appearance the alarmed Ellena had arisen, "I understand," said she, without making any signal for her to be seated, "that you are the young person who is arrived from Naples."

"My name is Ellena di Rosalba," said her auditor, recovering some degree of courage from the manner which was designed to depress her.

"I know nothing of your name," replied the Superior; "I am informed only that you are sent here to acquire a knowledge of yourself and of your duties. Till the period shall be passed, for which you are given into my charge, I shall scrupulously observe the obligations of the troublesome office, which my regard for the honour of a noble family, has induced me to undertake."

By these words, the author and the motives of this extraordinary transaction were at once revealed to Ellena, who was for some moments almost overwhelmed by the sudden horrors that gathered on her mind, and stood silent and motionless. Fear, shame, and indignation, alternately assailed her; and the sting of offended honour, on being suspected, and thus accused of having voluntarily disturbed the tranquillity, and sought the alliance of any family, and especially of one who disdained her, struck forcibly to her heart, till the pride of conscious worth revived her courage and fortified her patience, and she demanded by whose will she had been torn from her home, and by whose authority she was now detained, as it appeared, a prisoner.

The Abbess, unaccustomed to have her power opposed, or her words questioned, was for a moment too indignant to reply, and Ellena observed, but no longer with dismay, the brooding tempest ready to burst over her head. "It is I only, who am injured," said she to herself, "and shall the guilty oppressor triumph, and the innocent sufferer sink under the shame that belongs only to guilt! Never will I yield to a weakness so contemptible. The consciousness of deserving well will recall my presence of mind, which, permitting me to estimate the characters of my oppressors by their actions, will enable me also to despise their power."

"I must remind you," said the Abbess, at length, "that the questions you make are unbecoming in your situation; and that contrition and humility are the best extenuations of error. You may withdraw."

"Most true," replied Ellena, bowing with dignity to the Superior; "and I most willingly resign them to my oppressors."

Ellena forbore to make further enquiry or remonstrance, and perceiving that reproach would not only be useless, but degrading to herself, she immediately obeyed the mandate of the Abbess, and determined, since she must suffer, to suffer, if possible, with firmness and dignity.

She was conducted from the parlour by the nun who had admitted her, and as she passed through the refectory where the nuns, just returned from vespers, were assembled, their inquisitive glances, their smiles and busy whispers, told her, that she was not only an object of curiosity, but of suspicion, and that little sympathy could be expected from hearts, which even the offices of hourly devotion had not purified from the malignant envy, that taught them to exalt themselves upon the humiliation of others.

The little room, to which Ellena was led, and where, to her great satisfaction, she was left alone, rather deserved the denomination of a cell than of a chamber; since, like those of the nuns, it had only one small lattice; and a mattress, one chair, and a table, with a crucifix and a prayer-book were all its furniture. Ellena, as she surveyed her melancholy habitation, suppressed a rising sigh, but she could not remain unaffected by recollections, which, on this view of her altered state, crowded to her mind; nor think of Vivaldi far away, perhaps for ever, and probably, even ignorant of her destination, without bitter tears. But she dried them, as the idea of the Marchesa obtruded on her thoughts, for other emotions than those of grief possessed her. It was to the Marchesa that she especially attributed her present situation; and it now appeared, that the family of Vivaldi had not only been reluctant, but absolutely averse to a connection with hers, contrary to the suggestions of Signora Bianchi, who had represented, that it might be supposed only, from their known character, that they would disapprove of the alliance, but would of course be reconciled to an event, which their haughtiest displeasure never could revoke. This discovery of their absolute rejection awakened all the proper pride, which the mistaken prudence of her aunt, and her affection for Vivaldi had lulled to rest; and she now suffered the most acute vexation and remorse, for having yielded her consent to enter clandestinely into any family. The imaginary honours of so noble an alliance vanished, when the terms of obtaining them were considered; and now, that the sound mind of Ellena was left to its own judgment, she looked with infinitely more pride and preference upon the industrious means, which had hitherto rendered her independent, than on all distinction which might be reluctantly conferred. The consciousness of innocence, which had supported her in the presence of the Superior, began to falter. "Her accusation was partly just!" said Ellena, "and I deserve punishment, since I could, even for a moment, submit to the humiliation of desiring an alliance, which I knew would be unwillingly conferred. But it is not yet too late to retrieve my own esteem by asserting my independence, and resigning Vivaldi for ever. By resigning him! by abandoning him who loves me,—abandoning him to misery! Him, whom I cannot even think of without tears,—to whom my vows have been given,—who may claim me by the sacred remembrance of my dying friend,—him, to whom my whole heart is devoted! O! miserable alternative!—that I can no longer act justly, but at the expence of all my future happiness! Justly! And would it then be just to abandon him who is willing to resign every thing for me,—abandon him to ceaseless sorrow, that the prejudices of his family may be gratified?"

Poor Ellena perceived that she could not obey the dictates of a just pride, without such opposition from her heart as she had never experienced before. Her affections were now too deeply engaged to permit her to act with firmness, at the price of long-suffering. The consideration of resigning Vivaldi was so very grievous, that she could scarcely endure to pause upon it for a moment; yet, on the other hand, when she thought of his family, it appeared that she never could consent to make a part of it. She would have blamed the erroneous judgment of Signora Bianchi, whose persuasions had so much assisted in reducing her to the present alternative, had not the tenderness with which she cherished her memory, rendered this impossible. All, that now remained for her, was to endeavour patiently to endure present evils, which she could not conquer; for, to forsake Vivaldi as the price of liberty, should liberty be offered her on such terms, or to accept him in defiance of honourable pride, should he ever effect her release, appeared to her distracted thoughts almost equally impracticable. But, as the probability of his never being able to discover her abode, returned to her consideration, the anguish she suffered told how much more she dreaded to lose than to accept Vivaldi, and that love was, after all, the most powerful affection of her heart.

CHAPTER VII

The bell then beating one!

SHAKESPEARE

VIVALDI, meanwhile, ignorant of what had occurred at villa Altieri, repaired as he had proposed, to Paluzzi, attended by his servant Paulo. It was deep night before he left Naples, and so anxious was he to conceal himself from observation, that though Paulo carried a torch, he did not permit it to be lighted, till after he should have remained some time within the arch-way, thinking it most prudent to watch a while in secret for his unknown adviser, before he proceeded to examine the fort.

His attendant, Paulo, was a true Neapolitan, shrewd, inquisitive, insinuating, adroit; possessing much of the spirit of intrigue, together with a considerable portion of humour, which displayed itself not so much in words, as in his manner and countenance, in the archness of his dark, penetrating eye, and in the exquisite adaptation of his gesture to his idea. He was a distinguished favourite with his master, who, if he had not humour himself, had a keen relish of it in others, and who certainly did possess wit, with all its lively accompaniments, in an eminent degree. Vivaldi had been won by the *naïveté* and humour of this man, to allow him an unusual degree of familiarity in conversation; and, as they now walked together towards Paluzzi, he unfolded to Paulo as much of his former adventure there as he judged necessary to interest his curiosity and excite his vigilance. The relation did both. Paulo, however, naturally courageous, was incredulous to superstition of any kind; and, having quickly perceived that his master was not altogether indisposed to attribute to a supernatural cause the extraordinary occurrences at Paluzzi, he began, in his manner, to rally him; but

Vivaldi was not in temper to endure jesting; his mood was grave, even to solemnity, and he yielded, though reluctantly, to the awe which, at intervals, returned upon him with the force of a magical spell, binding up all his faculties to sternness, and fixing them in expectation. While he was nearly regardless of defence against human agency, his servant was, however, preparing for that alone; and very properly represented the imprudence of going to Paluzzi in darkness. Vivaldi observed that they could not watch for the monk otherwise than in darkness, since the torch which lighted them would also warn him, and he had very particular reasons for watching before he proceeded to examine. He added, that after a certain time had elapsed, the torch might be lighted at a neighboring cottage. Paulo objected, that in the meanwhile, the person for whom they watched might escape; and Vivaldi compromised the affair. The torch was lighted but concealed within a hollow of the cliffs, that bordered the road, and the centinels took their station in darkness, within the deep arch, near the spot where Vivaldi had watched with Bonarmo. As they did this, the distant chime of a convent informed Vivaldi that midnight was turned. The sound recalled to his mind the words of Schedoni, concerning the vicinity of the convent of the *Black Penitents,* to Paluzzi, and he asked Paulo whether this was the chime of that convent. Paulo replied that it was, and that a remarkable circumstance had taught him to remember *the Santa del Pianto,* or *Our Lady of Tears.* "The place, Signor, would interest you," said Paulo; "for there are some odd stories told of it; and I am inclined to think, this unknown monk must be one of that society, his conduct is so strange."

"You believe then, that I am willing to give faith to wonderful stories," said Vivaldi, smiling. "But what have you heard, that is so extraordinary, respecting this convent? Speak low, or we may be discovered."

"Why, Signor, the story is not generally known," said Paulo in a whisper; "I half promised never to reveal it."

"If you are under any promise of secresy," interrupted Vivaldi, "I forbid you to tell this wonderful tale, which, however, seems somewhat too big to rest within your brain."

"The story would fain expand itself to yours, Signor," said Paulo; "and, as I did not absolutely promise to conceal it, I am very willing to reveal it."

"Proceed, then," said Vivaldi; "but let me once more caution you to speak low."

"You are obeyed, Signor. You must know, then, *Maestro*, that it was on the eve of the festival of *Santo Marco*, and about six years since"——

"Peace!" said Vivaldi. They were silent; but every thing remaining still, Paulo, after some time, ventured to proceed, though in a yet lower whisper. "It was on the eve of the *Santo Marco*, and when the last bell had rung, that a person"——He stopped again, for a rustling sound passed near him.

"You are too late," said a sudden voice beside Vivaldi, who instantly recognized the thrilling accents of the monk.—"It is past midnight; she departed an hour ago. Look to your steps!"

Though thrilled by this well-known voice, Vivaldi scarcely yielded to his feelings for a moment, but, checking the question which would have asked "who departed?" he, by a sudden spring, endeavoured to seize the intruder, while Paulo, in the first hurry of his alarm, fired a pistol, and then hastened for the torch. So certainly did Vivaldi believe himself to have leaped upon the spot whence the voice proceeded, that, on reaching it, he instantly extended his arms, and searching around, expected every moment to find his enemy in his grasp. Darkness again baffled his attempt.

"You are known," cried Vivaldi; "you shall see me at the *Santa del Pianto*! What, oh! Paulo, the torch!—the torch!"

Paulo, swift as the wind, appeared with it. "He passed up those steps in the rock, Signor; I saw the skirts of his garments ascending!"

"Follow me, then," said Vivaldi, mounting the steps. "Away, away, *Maestro*!" said Paulo, impatiently; "but, for Heaven's sake, name no more the convent of the *Santa del Pianto;* our lives may answer it!"

He followed to the terrace above, where Vivaldi, holding high the torch, looked round for the monk. The place, however, as far as his eye could penetrate, was forsaken and silent. The glare of the torch enlightened only the rude walls of the citadel, some points of the cliff below, and some tall pines that waved over them, leaving in doubtful gloom many a recess of the ruin, and many a tangled thicket, that spread among the rocks beyond.

"Do you perceive any person, Paulo?" said Vivaldi, waving the torch in the air to rouse the flame.

"Among those arches on the left, Signor, those arches that stand duskily beyond the citadel, I thought I saw a shadowy sort of a figure pass. He might be a ghost, by his silence, for aught I know, *Maestro;* but he seems to have a good mortal instinct in taking care of himself, and to have as swift a pair of heels to assist in carrying him off, as any Lazaro in Naples need desire."

"Fewer words, and more caution!" said Vivaldi, lowering the torch, and pointing it towards the quarter which Paulo had mentioned. "Be vigilant, and tread lightly."

"You are obeyed, Signor; but their eyes will inform them, though their ears refuse, while we hold a light to our own steps."

"Peace, with this buffoonery!" said Vivaldi, somewhat sternly; "follow in silence, and be on your guard."

Paulo submitted, and they proceeded towards the range of arches, which communicated with the building, whose singular structure had formerly arrested the attention of Bonarmo, and whence Vivaldi himself had returned with such unexpected precipitancy and consternation.

On perceiving the place he was approaching, he suddenly stopped, and Paulo observing his agitation, and probably not relishing the adventure, endeavoured to dissuade him from further research: "For we know not who may inhabit this gloomy place, Signor, or their numbers, and we are only two of us after all! Besides, Signor, it was through that door, yonder;" and he pointed to the very spot whence Vivaldi had so fearfully issued; "through that door, that I fancied, just now, I saw something pass,"

"Are you certain as to this?" said Vivaldi, with increased emotion. "What was its form?"

"It was so dusky thereabout, *Maestro,* that I could not distinguish."

Vivaldi's eyes were fixed upon the building, and a violent conflict of feelings seemed to shake his soul. A few seconds decided it. "I will go on," said he, "and terminate, at any hazard, this state of intolerable anxiety. Paulo, pause a moment, and consider well whether you can depend on your courage, for it may be severely tried. If you can, descend with me in silence, and I warn you to be wary; if you cannot, I will go alone."

"It is too late now, Signor, to ask myself that question," replied Paulo, with a submissive air; "and if I had not settled it long ago, I should not have followed you thus far. My courage, Signor, you never doubted before."

"Come on then," said Vivaldi. He drew his sword, and entering the narrow door-way, the torch, which he had now resigned to Paulo, shewed a stone passage, that was, however, interminable to the eye.

As they proceeded, Paulo observed, that the walls were stained in several places with what appeared to be blood, but prudently forbore to point this out to his master, observing the strict injunction of silence he had received.

Vivaldi stepped cautiously, and often paused to listen, after which he went on with a quicker pace, making signs only to Paulo to follow, and be vigilant. The passage terminated in a stair-case, that seemed to lead to vaults below. Vivaldi remembered the light which had formerly appeared there, and, as recollection of the past gathered on his mind, he faultered in his purpose.

Again he paused, looked back upon Paulo, but was going forward, when Paulo himself seized his arm. "Stop! Signor," said he in a low voice. "Do you not distinguish a figure standing yonder, in the gloom?"

Vivaldi looked onward, and perceived, indistinctly, something as of human form, but motionless and silent. It stood at the dusky extremity of the avenue, near the stair-case. Its garments, if garments they were, were dark; but its whole figure was so faintly traced to the eye, that it was impossible to ascertain whether this was the monk. Vivaldi took the light, and held it forward, endeavouring to distinguish the object before he ventured further; but the enquiry was useless, and, resigning the torch to Paulo, he rushed on. When he reached the head of the stair-case, however, the form, whatever it might be, was gone. Vivaldi had heard no footstep. Paulo pointed out the exact spot where it had stood, but no vestige of it appeared. Vivaldi called loudly upon the monk, but he heard only the lengthening echoes of his own voice revolving among the chambers below, and, after hesitating a while on the head of the stairs, he descended.

Paulo had not followed down many steps, when he called out, "It is there! Signor; I see it again! and now it flits away through the door that opens to the vaults!"

Vivaldi pursued so swiftly, that Paulo could scarcely follow fast enough with the light; and, as at length he rested to take breath, he perceived himself in the same spacious chamber to which he had formerly descended. At this moment Paulo perceived his countenance change. "You are ill, Signor," said he. "In the name of our holy Saint, let us quit this hideous place. Its inhabitants can be nothing good, and no good can come of our remaining here."

Vivaldi made no reply; he drew breath with difficulty, and his eyes remained fixed on the ground, till a noise, like the creaking of a heavy hinge, rose in a distant part of the vault. Paulo turned his eyes, at the same instant, towards the place whence it came, and they both perceived a door in the wall slowly opened, and immediately closed again, as if the person within had feared to be discovered. Each believed, from the transient view he had of it, that this was the same figure which had appeared on the stair-case, and that it was the monk himself. Reanimated by this belief, Vivaldi's nerves were instantly rebraced, and he sprang to the door, which was unfastened, and yielded immediately to his impetuous hand. "You shall not deceive me now," cried he, as he entered; "Paulo! keep guard at the door!"

He looked round the second vault, in which he now found himself, but no person appeared; he examined the place, and particularly the walls, without discovering any aperture, either of door or window, by which the figure could have quitted the chamber; a strongly-grated casement, placed near the roof, was all that admitted air, and probably light. Vivaldi was astonished! "Have you seen any thing pass?" said he to Paulo.

"Nothing, *Maestro*," replied the servant.

"This is almost incredible," exclaimed Vivaldi; " 'tis certain, this form can be nothing human!"

"If so, Signor," observed Paulo, "why should it fear us? as surely it does; or why should it have fled?"

"That is not so certain," rejoined Vivaldi; "it may have fled only to lead us into evil. But bring hither the torch; here is something in the wall which I would examine."

Paulo obeyed. It was merely a ruggedness in the stones, not the partition of a door, that had excited his curiosity. "This is inexplicable!" exclaimed Vivaldi, after a long pause. "What motive could any human being have for thus tormenting me."

"Or any being superhuman, either, my Signor?" said Paulo.

"I am warned of evils that await me," continued Vivaldi,

musing; "of events that are regularly fulfilled; the being who warns me, crosses my path perpetually, yet, with the cunning of a demon, as constantly eludes my grasp, and baffles my pursuit! It is incomprehensible, by what means he glides thus away from my eye, and fades, as if into air, at my approach! He is repeatedly in my presence, yet is never to be found!"

"It is most true, Signor," said Paulo, "that he is never to be found, and therefore let me entreat you to give up the pursuit. This place is enough to make one believe in the horrors of purgatory! Let us go, Signor."

"What but spirit could have quitted this vault so mysteriously," continued Vivaldi, not attending to Paulo; "what but spirit!"——

"I would fain prove," said the servant, "that substance can quit it as easily; I would fain evaporate through that door myself."

He had scarcely spoken the words, when the door closed, with a thundering clap that echoed through all the vaults; and Vivaldi and Paulo stood for a moment aghast! and then both hastened to open it, and to leave the place. Their consternation may be easily conceived, when they found that all their efforts at the door were ineffectual. The thick wood was inlaid with solid bars of iron; and was of such unconquerable strength, that it evidently guarded what had been designed for a prison, and appeared to be the keep or dungeon of the ancient fort.

"Ah, Signor mio!" said Paulo, "if this was a spirit, 'tis plain he knew we were not so, by his luring us hither. Would we could exchange natures with him for a moment; for I know not how, as mere mortal men, we can ever squeeze ourselves out of this scrape. You must allow, *Maestro,* that this was not one of the evils he warned you of; or, if he did, it was through my organs, for I entreated you."——

"Peace, good Signor *Buffo*!" said Vivaldi; "a truce with this nonsense, and assist in searching for some means of escape."

Vivaldi again examined the walls, and as unsuccessfully as before; but in one corner of the vault lay an object, which seemed to tell the fate of one who had been confined here, and to hint his own: it was a garment covered with blood. Vivaldi and his servant discovered it at the same instant; and a dreadful foreboding of their own destiny fixed them, for some moments, to the spot. Vivaldi first recovered himself, when instead of yielding to despondency, all his faculties were aroused to devise some means for escaping; but Paulo's hopes seemed buried beneath the dreadful vestments upon which he still gazed. "Ah, my Signor!" said he, at length, in a faultering accent, "who shall dare to raise that garment? What if it should conceal the mangled body whose blood has stained it!"

Vivaldi, shudderingly, turned to look on it again.

"It moves!" exclaimed Paulo; "I see it move!" as he said which, he started to the opposite side of the chamber. Vivaldi stepped a few paces back, and as quickly returned; when, determined to know the event at once, he raised the garment upon the point of his sword, and perceived, beneath, other remains of dress, heaped high together, while even the floor below was stained with gore.

Believing that fear had deceived the eyes of Paulo, Vivaldi watched this horrible spectacle for some time, but without perceiving the least motion; when he became convinced, that not any remains of life were shrouded beneath it, and that it contained only articles of dress, which had belonged to some unfortunate person, who had probably been decoyed hither for plunder, and afterwards murdered. This belief, and the repugnance he felt to dwell upon the spectacle, prevented him from examining further, and he turned away to a remote part of the vault. A conviction of his own fate, and of his servant's, filled his mind for a while with despair. It appeared that he had been ensnared by robbers, till, as he recollected the circumstances which had attended his entrance, and the several peculiar occurrences connected with the arch-way, this conjecture seemed highly improbable. It was unreasonable, that robbers should have taken the trouble to decoy, when they might at first have seized him; still more so, that they would have persevered so long in the attempt; and most of all, that when he had formerly been in their power, they should have neglected their opportunity, and suffered him to leave the ruin unmolested. Yet, granting that all this, improbable as it was, were, however, possible, the solemn warnings and predictions of the monk, so frequently delivered, and so faithfully fulfilled, could have no connection with the schemes of banditti. It appeared, therefore, that Vivaldi was not in the hands of robbers; or, if he were, that the monk, at least, had no connection with them;

yet it was certain that he had just heard the voice of this monk beneath the arch; that his servant had said, he saw the vestments of one ascending the steps of the fort; and that they had both reason, afterward, to believe it was his shadowy figure, which they had pursued to the very chamber where they were now confined.

As Vivaldi considered all these circumstances, his perplexity encreased, and he was more than ever inclined to believe, that the form, which had assumed the appearance of a monk, was something superhuman.

"If this being had *appeared only*," said he to himself, "I should, perhaps, have thought it the perturbed spirit of him, who doubtless has been murdered here, and that it led me hither to discover the deed, that his bones might be removed to holy ground; but this monk, or whatever it is, was neither silent, nor apparently anxious concerning himself; he spoke only of events connected with my peace, and predicted of the future, as well as reverted to the past! If he had either hinted of himself, or had been wholly silent, his appearance, and manner of eluding pursuit, is so extraordinary, that I should have yielded, for once, perhaps, to the tales of our grandfathers, and thought he was the spectre of a murdered person."

As Vivaldi expressed his incredulity, however, he returned to examine the garment once more, when, as he raised it, he observed, what had before escaped his notice, black drapery mingled with the heap beneath; and, on lifting this also on the point of his sword, he perceived part of the habiliment of a monk! He started at the discovery, as if he had seen the apparition, which had so long been tempting his credulity. Here were the vest and scapulary, rent and stained with blood! Having gazed for a moment, he let them drop upon the heap; when Paulo, who had been silently observing him, exclaimed,

"Signor! that should be the garment of the demon who led us hither. Is it a winding-sheet for us, *Maestro*? Or was it one for the body he inhabited while on earth!"

"Neither, I trust," replied Vivaldi, endeavouring to command the perturbation he suffered, and turning from the spectacle; "therefore we will try once more to regain our liberty."

This was a design, however, beyond his accomplishment; and, having again attacked the door, raised Paulo to the grated window, and vociferated for release with his utmost strength, in which he was very ably seconded by Paulo, he abandoned, for the present, all further attempts, and, weary and desponding, threw himself on the ground of the dungeon.

Paulo bitterly lamented his master's rashness in penetrating to this remote spot, and bewailed the probability of their being famished.

"For, supposing, Signor, that we were not decoyed hither for plunder and butchery, and supposing that we are not surrounded by malicious spirits, which San Januarius forbid I should take upon me to affirm is impossible! supposing all this, Signor, yet still there remains almost a certainty of our being starved to death; for how is it possible that any body can hear our cries, in a place so remote from all resort, and buried, as one may say, under ground, as this is?"

"Thou art an excellent comforter," said Vivaldi, groaning.

"You must allow, Signor, that you are even with me," replied Paulo; "and that you are as excellent a conductor."

Vivaldi gave no answer, but lay on the ground, abandoned to agonizing thought. He had now leisure to consider the late words of the monk, and to conjecture, for he was in a mood for conjecturing the worst, that they not only alluded to Ellena, but that his saying "she had departed an hour ago," was a figurative manner of telling that she had died then. This was a conjecture which dispelled almost all apprehension for himself. He started from the ground, and paced his prison with quick and unequal steps; it was now no longer a heavy despondency that oppressed him, but an acute anxiety that stung him, and, with the tortures of suspense, brought also those of passionate impatience and horror concerning the fate of Ellena. The longer he dwelt upon the possibility of her death, the more probable it appeared. This monk had already forewarned him of the death of Bianchi; and when he recollected the suspicious circumstances which had attended it, his terrors for Ellena increased. The more he yielded to his feelings, the more violent they became, till, at length, his ungovernable impatience and apprehensions arose almost to frenzy.

Paulo forgot, for a while, his own situation in the superior sufferings of his master, and now, at least, endeavoured to perform the offices of a comforter, for he tried to calm

Vivaldi's mind, by selecting the fairest circumstances for hope which the subject admitted, and he passed without noticing, or, if noticing, only lightly touched upon, the most prominent possibilities of evil. His master, however, was insensible to all he said, till he mentioned again the convent del Pianto; and this subject, as it seemed connected with the monk, who had hinted the fate of Ellena, interested the unhappy Vivaldi, who withdrew awhile from his own reflections, to listen to a recital which might assist his conjectures.

Paulo complied with his command, but not without reluctance. He looked around the empty vault, as if he feared that some person might be lurking in the obscurity, who would overhear, and even answer him.

"We are tolerably retired here too, Signor," said he, recollecting himself; "one may venture to talk secrets with little danger of being discovered. However, *Maestro,* it is best to make matters quite sure; and therefore, if you will please to take a seat on the ground, I will stand beside you and relate all I know of the convent of *Our Lady of Tears,* which is not much after all."

Vivaldi, having seated himself, and bidden Paulo do the same, the servant began in a low voice——"It was on the vigil of the *Santo Marco,* just after the last vesper-bell had tolled—You never was at the *Santo Maria del Pianto,* Signor, or you would know what a gloomy old church it has.—It was in a confessional in one of the side aisles of this church, and just after the last bell had ceased, that a person, so muffled up, that neither face nor shape could be distinguished, came and placed himself on the steps of one of the boxes adjoining the confessional chair; but if he had been as airily dressed as yourself, Signor, he might have been just as well concealed; for that dusky aisle is lighted only by one lamp, which hangs at the end next the painted window, except when the tapers at the shrine of San Antonio happen to be burning at the other extremity, and even then the place is almost as gloomy as this vault. But that is, no doubt, contrived for the purpose, that people may not blush for the sins they confess; and, in good faith, this is an accommodation which may bring more money to the poor's box, for the monks have a shrewd eye that way, and"——

"You have dropt the thread of your story," said Vivaldi.

"True, Signor, let me recollect where I lost it.—Oh! at the steps of the confessional;—the stranger knelt down upon them, and for some time poured such groans into the ear of the confessor, as were heard all along the aisle. You are to know, Signor, that the brothers of *Santa del Pianto* are of the order of *Black Penitents;* and people who have more sins than ordinary to confess, sometimes go there, to consult with the grand penitentiary what is to be done. Now it *happened,* that Father Ansaldo, the grand penitentiary himself, was in the chair, as is customary on the vigil of the *Santo Marco;* and he gently reproved the penitent for bewailing so loud, and bade him take comfort; when the other replied only by a groan deeper than before, but it was not so loud, and then proceeded to confess. But what he did confess, Signor, I know not; for the confessor, you know, never must divulge, except, indeed, on very extraordinary occasions. It was, however, something so very strange and horrible, that the grand penitentiary suddenly quitted the chair, and before he reached the cloisters he fell into strong convulsions. On recovering himself, he asked the people about him, whether the penitent, who had visited such a confessional, naming it, was gone; adding, that if he was still in the church, it was proper he should be detained. He described, at the same time, as well as he could, the sort of figure he had dimly seen approaching the confessional just before he had received the confession, at recollecting which, he seemed ready to go off again into his convulsions. One of the fathers, who had crossed the aisle, on his way to the cloisters, upon the first alarm of Ansaldo's disorder, remembered that a person, such as was described, had passed him hastily. He had seen a tall figure, muffled up in the habit of a white friar, gliding swiftly along the aisle, towards the door which opened into the outer court of the convent; but he was himself too much engaged to notice the stranger particularly. Father Ansaldo thought this must be the person; and the porter was summoned, and asked whether he had observed such an one pass. He affirmed that he had not seen any person go forth from the gate within the last quarter of an hour; which might be true enough, you know, Signor, if the rogue had been off his post. But he further said, that no one had entered, during the whole evening, habited in white, as the stranger was described to be: so the porter proved himself to be a vigilant watchman; for he must have been fast asleep too, or how could this personage have entered the convent, and left it again, without being seen by him!"

"In white, was he?" said Vivaldi; "if he had been in black, I should have thought this must have been the monk, my tormentor."

"Why, you know, Signor, that occurred to me before," observed Paulo, "and a man might easily change his dress, if that were all."

"Proceed," said Vivaldi.

"Hearing this account from the porter," continued Paulo, "the fathers believed, one and all, that the stranger must be secreted within the walls; and the convent, with every part of the precincts, was searched; but no person was found!"

"This must certainly be the monk," said Vivaldi, "notwithstanding the difference of his habit; there surely cannot be two beings in the world, who would conduct themselves in this same mysterious manner!"

He was interrupted by a low sound, which seemed, to his distracted fancy, to proceed from a dying person. Paulo also heard it; he started, and they both listened with intense and almost intolerable expectation.

"Ah!" said Paulo, at length, "it was only the wind."

"It was no more," said Vivaldi; "proceed therefore."

"From the period of this strange confession," resumed Paulo, "Father Ansaldo was never properly himself; he"——

"Doubtless the crime confessed related to himself," observed Vivaldi.

"Why, no, Signor, I never heard that that was the case; and some remarkable circumstances, which followed, seemed to prove it otherwise. About a month after the time I have mentioned, on the evening of a sultry day, when the monks were retiring from the last service"——

"Hark!" cried Vivaldi.

"I hear whispers," said Paulo, whispering himself.

"Be still!" said Vivaldi.

They listened attentively, and heard a murmuring, as of voices; but could not ascertain whether they came from the adjoining vault, or arose from beneath the one in which they were. The sound returned at intervals; and the persons who conversed, whatever they were, seemingly restrained their voices, as if they feared to be heard. Vivaldi considered whether it were better to discover himself, and call for assistance, or to remain still.

"Remember, Signor," said Paulo, "what a chance we have

of being starved, unless we venture to discover ourselves to these people, or whatever they are."

"Venture!" exclaimed Vivaldi. "What has such a wretch as I to do with fear? O, Ellena, Ellena!"

He instantly called loudly to the person whom he believed he had heard, and was seconded by Paulo; but their continued vociferations availed them nothing; no answer was returned; and even the indistinct sounds, which had awakened their attention, were heard no more.

Exhausted by their efforts, they laid down on the floor of the dungeon, abandoning all further attempts at escape till the morning light might assist them.

Vivaldi had no further spirits to enquire for the remainder of Paulo's narrative. Almost despairing for himself, he could not feel an interest concerning strangers; for he had already perceived, that it could not afford him information connected with Ellena; and Paulo, who had roared himself hoarse, was very willing to be silent.

CHAPTER VIII

Who may she be that steals through yonder cloister,
And, as the beam of evening tints her veil,
Unconsciously discloses saintly features,
Inform'd with the high soul of saintly virtue?

DURING several days after Ellena's arrival at the monastery of San Stefano, she was not permitted to leave the room. The door was locked upon her, and not any person appeared except the nun, who brought her a scanty portion of food, and who was the same, that had first admitted her into that part of the convent appropriated to the abbess.

On the fourth day, when, probably, it was believed that her spirits were subdued by confinement, and by her experience of the suffering she had to expect from resistance, she was summoned to the parlour. The abbess was alone, and the air of austerity, with which she regarded Ellena, prepared the latter to endure.

After an exordium on the heinousness of her offence, and the necessity there was for taking measures to protect the peace and dignity of a noble family, which her late conduct had nearly destroyed; the abbess informed her, that she must determine either to accept the veil, or the person whom the Marchesa di Vivaldi had, of her great goodness, selected for her husband.

"You never can be sufficiently grateful," added the abbess, "for the generosity the Marchesa displays, in allowing you a choice on the subject. After the injury you have endeavoured to inflict upon her and her family, you could not expect that any indulgence would be shewn you. It was natural to suppose, that the Marchesa would have punished you with severity; instead of which, she allows you to enter into our society; or, if you have not strength of mind sufficient to enable you to renounce a sinful world, she permits you to return into it, and gives you a suitable partner to support you through its cares and toils,—a partner much more suitable to your circumstances than him, to whom you had the temerity to lift your eye."

Ellena blushed at this coarse appeal to her pride, and persevered in a disdainful silence. Thus to give to injustice the colouring of mercy, and to acts most absolutely tyrannical the softening tints of generosity, excited her honest indignation. She was not, however, shocked by a discovery of the designs formed against her, since, from the moment of her arrival at San Stefano, she had expected something terribly severe, and had prepared her mind to meet it with fortitude; for she believed, that, so supported, she should weary the malice of her enemies, and finally triumph over misfortune. It was only when she thought of Vivaldi that her courage failed, and that the injuries she endured seemed too heavy to be long sustained.

"You are silent!" said the abbess, after a pause of expectation. "Is it possible, then, that you can be ungrateful for the generosity of the Marchesa? But, though you may at present be insensible to her goodness, I will forbear to take advantage of your indiscretion, and will still allow you liberty of choice. You may retire to your chamber, to consider and to decide. But remember, that you must abide by the determination you shall avow; and, that you will be allowed no appeal from the alternatives, which are now placed before you.—If you reject the veil, you must accept the husband who is offered you."

"It is unnecessary," said Ellena, with an air of dignified tranquillity, "that I should withdraw for the purposes of considering and deciding. My resolution is already taken, and I reject each of the offered alternatives. I will neither condemn myself to a cloister, or to the degradation, with which I am threatened on the other hand. Having said this, I am prepared to meet whatever suffering you shall inflict upon me; but be assured, that my own voice never shall sanction the evils to which I may be subjected, and that the immortal love of justice, which fills all my heart, will sustain my courage no less powerfully than the sense of what is due to my own character. You are now acquainted with my sentiments and my resolutions; I shall repeat them no more."

The abbess, whose surprise had thus long suffered Ellena to speak, still fixed upon her a stern regard, as she said,

"Where is it that you have learned these heroics, and acquired the rashness which thus prompts you to avow them!—the boldness which enables you to insult your Superior, a priestess of your holy religion, even in her sanctuary!"

"The sanctuary is prophaned," said Ellena, mildly, but with dignity: "it is become a prison. It is only when the Superior ceases to respect the precepts of that holy religion, the precepts which teach her justice and benevolence, that she herself is no longer respected. The very sentiment which bids us revere its mild and beneficent laws, bids us also reject the violators of them: when you command me to reverence my religion, you urge me to condemn yourself."

"Withdraw!" said the abbess, rising impatiently from her chair; "your admonition, so becomingly delivered, shall not be forgotten."

Ellena willingly obeyed, and was led back to her cell, where she sat down pensively, and reviewed her conduct. Her judgment approved of the frankness, with which she had asserted her rights, and of the firmness, with which she had reproved a woman, who had dared to demand respect from the very victim of her cruelty and oppression. She was the more satisfied with herself, because she had never, for an instant, forgotten her own dignity so far, as to degenerate into the vehemence of passion, or to faulter with the weakness of fear. Her conviction of the abbess's unworthy character was too clear to allow Ellena to feel abashed in her presence; for she regarded only the censure of the good, to which she had ever been as tremblingly alive, as she was obdurately insensible to that of the vicious.

Ellena, having now asserted her resolutions, determined to avoid, if possible, all repetition of scenes like the last, and to repel by silence only, whatever indignity might be offered her. She knew that she must suffer, and she resolved to endure. Of the three evils, which were placed before her, that of confinement, with all its melancholy accompaniments, appeared considerably less severe, than either the threatened marriage, or a formal renunciation of the world; either of which would devote her, during life, to misery, and that by her own act. Her choice, therefore, had been easy, and the way was plain before her. If she could endure with calmness the hardships which she could not avoid, half their weight would be unfelt; and she now most strenuously endeavoured to attain the strength of mind, which was necessary to support such equanimity.

For several days after the late interview with the abbess, she was kept a close prisoner; but on the fifth evening she was permitted to attend vespers. As she walked through the garden to the chapel, the ordinary freshness of the open air, and the verdure of the trees and shrubs were luxuries to her, who had so long been restricted from the common blessings of nature. She followed the nuns to a chapel where they usually performed their devotions, and was there seated among the novices. The solemnity of the service, and particularly of those parts, which were accompanied by music, touched all her heart, and soothed and elevated her spirit.

Among the voices of the choir, was one whose expression immediately fixed her attention; it seemed to speak a loftier sentiment of devotion than the others, and to be modulated by the melancholy of an heart, that had long since taken leave of this world. Whether it swelled with the high peal of the organ, or mingled in low and trembling accents with the sinking chorus, Ellena felt that she understood all the feelings of the breast from which it flowed; and she looked to the gallery where the nuns were assembled, to discover a countenance, that might seem to accord with the sensibility expressed in the voice. As no strangers were admitted to the chapel, some of the sisters had thrown back their veils, and she saw little that interested her in their various faces; but the figure and attitude of a nun, kneeling in a remote part of the gallery, beneath a lamp, which threw its rays aslant her head, perfectly agreed with the idea she had formed of the singer, and the sound seemed to approach immediately from that direction. Her face was concealed by a black veil, whose transparency, however, permitted the fairness of her complexion to appear; but the air of her head, and the singularity of her attitude, for she was the only person who remained kneeling, sufficiently indicated the superior degree of fervency and penitence, which the voice had expressed.

When the hymn had ceased, she rose from her knees, and Ellena, soon after, observing her throw back her veil, discovered, by the lamp, which shed its full light upon her features, a countenance, that instantly confirmed her conjecture. It was touched with a melancholy kind of resignation; yet grief seemed still to occasion the paleness, and the air of languor, that prevailed over it, and which disappeared only when the momentary energy of devotion seemed to lift her spirit above this world, and to impart to it somewhat of a seraphic grandeur. At those moments her blue eyes were raised towards Heaven, with such meek, yet fervent love, such sublime enthusiasm as the heads of Guido sometimes display, and which renewed, with Ellena, all the enchanting effects of the voice she had just heard.

While she regarded the nun with a degree of interest which rendered her insensible to every other object in the chapel, she fancied she could perceive the calmness in her countenance to be that of despair, rather than of resignation; for, when her thoughts were not elevated in prayer, there was frequently a fixedness in her look, too energetic for common suffering, or for the temper of mind, which may lead to perfect resignation. It had, however, much that attached the sympathy of Ellena, and much that seemed to speak a similarity of feeling. Ellena was not only soothed, but in some degree comforted, while she gazed upon her; a selfishness which may, perhaps, be pardoned, when it is considered, that she thus knew there was one human being, at least, in the convent, who must be capable of feeling pity, and willing to administer consolation. Ellena endeavoured to meet her eye, that she might inform her of the regard she had inspired, and express her own unhappiness; but the nun was so entirely engaged by devotion, that she did not succeed.

As they left the chapel, however, the nun passed close by Ellena, who threw back her veil, and fixed upon her a look so supplicating and expressive, that the nun paused, and in her turn regarded the novice, not with surprise only, but with a mixture of curiosity and compassion. A faint blush crossed her cheek, her spirits seemed to faulter, and she was unwilling to withdraw her eyes from Ellena: but it was necessary that she should continue in the procession, and, bidding her farewel by a smile of ineffable pity, she passed on to the court, while Ellena followed with attention still fixed upon the sister, who soon disappeared beyond the doorway of the Abbess's apartment, and Ellena had nearly reached her own, before her thoughts were sufficiently disengaged to permit her to enquire the name of the stranger.

"It is sister Olivia whom you mean, perhaps," said her conductress.

"She is very handsome," said Ellena.

"Many of the sisters are so," replied Margaritone, with an air of pique.

"Undoubtedly," said Ellena; "but she, whom I mean, has a most touching countenance; frank, noble, full of sensibility; and there is a gentle melancholy in her eye, which cannot but interest all who observe her."

Ellena was so fascinated by this interesting nun, that she forgot she was describing her to a person, whose callous heart rendered her insensible to the influence of any countenance, except, perhaps, the commanding one of the lady abbess; and to whom, therefore, a description of the fine traits, which Ellena felt, was as unintelligible as would have been an Arabic inscription.

"She is passed the bloom of youth," continued Ellena, still anxious to be understood; "but she retains all its interesting graces, and adds to them the dignity of"——

"If you mean that she is of middle age," interrupted Margaritone, peevishly, "it is sister Olivia you mention, for we are all younger than she is."

Ellena, raising her eyes almost unconsciously, as the nun spoke this, fixed them upon a face sallow, meagre, seemingly near fifty years an inhabitant of this world; and she could scarcely suppress the surprise she felt, on perceiving such wretched vanity lingering among the chilled passions of so repulsive a frame, and within the sequestered shade of a cloister. Margaritone, still jealous of the praise bestowed on Olivia, repelled all further enquiry, and, having attended Ellena to her cell, locked her up for the night.

On the following evening Ellena was again permitted to attend vespers, and, on the way to the chapel, the hope of seeing her interesting favourite reanimated her spirits. In the same part of the gallery, as on the preceding night, she again appeared, and kneeling, as before, beneath the lamp, in private orison, for the service was not begun.

Ellena endeavoured to subdue the impatience she felt to express her regard, and to be noticed by the holy sister, till she should have finished. When the nun rose, and observed Ellena, she lifted her veil, and, fixing on her the same enquiring eye, her countenance brightened into a smile so full of compassion and intelligence, that Ellena, forgetting the decorums of the place, left her seat to approach her; it seemed as if the soul, which beamed forth in that smile, had long been acquainted with hers. As she advanced, the nun dropped her veil, a reproof which she immediately understood, and she withdrew to her seat; but her attention remained fixed on the nun during the whole service.

At the conclusion, when they left the chapel, and she saw Olivia pass without noticing her, Ellena could scarcely restrain her tears; she returned in deep dejection to her room. The regard of this nun was not only delightful, but seemed necessary to her heart, and she dwelt, with fond perseverance, on the smile that had expressed so much, and which threw one gleam of comfort, even through the bars of her prison.

Her reverie was soon interrupted by a light step, that approached her cell, and in the next moment the door was unlocked, and Olivia herself appeared. Ellena rose with emotion to meet her; the nun held forth her hand to receive hers.

"You are unused to confinement," said she, curtsying mournfully, and placing on the table a little basket containing refreshment, "and our hard fare"——

"I understand you," said Ellena, with a look expressive of her gratitude; "you have a heart that can pity, though you inhabit these walls;—you have suffered too, and know the delicate generosity of softening the sorrows of others, by any attention that may tell them your sympathy. O! if I could express how much the sense of this affects me!"

Tears interrupted her. Olivia pressed her hand, looked steadily upon her face, and was somewhat agitated, but she soon recovered apparent tranquillity, and said, with a serious smile, "You judge rightly, my sister, respecting my sentiments, however you may do concerning my sufferings. My heart is not insensible to pity, nor to you, my child. You were designed for happier days than you can hope to find within these cloisters!"

She checked herself as if she had allowed too much, and then added, "But you may, perhaps, be peaceful; and since it consoles you to know that you have a friend near you, believe me that friend—but believe it in silence. I will visit you when I am permitted—but do not enquire for me; and if my visits are short, do not press me to lengthen them."

"How good this is!" said Ellena, in a faultering voice. "How sweet too it is! you will visit me, and I am pitied by you!"

"Hush!" said the nun, expressively; "no more; I may be

observed. Good night, my sister; may your slumbers be light!"

Ellena's heart sunk. She had not spirits to say, "Good night!" but her eyes, covered with tears, said more. The nun turned her own away suddenly, and, pressing her hand in silence, left the cell. Ellena, firm and tranquil under the insults of the abbess, was now melted into tears by the kindness of a friend. These gentle tears were refreshing to her long-oppressed spirits, and she indulged them. Of Vivaldi she thought with more composure than she had done since she left the villa Altieri; and something like hope began to revive in her heart, though reflection offered nothing to support it.

On the following morning, she perceived that the door of her cell had not been closed. She rose impatiently, and, not without a hope of liberty, immediately passed it. The cell, opening upon a short passage, which communicated with the main building, and which was shut up by a door, was secluded, and almost insulated from every other chamber; and this door being now secured, Ellena was as truly a prisoner as before. It appeared then, that the nun had omitted to fasten the cell only for the purpose of allowing her more space to walk in the passage, and she was grateful for the attention. Still more she was so, when, having traversed it, she perceived one extremity terminate in a narrow stair-case, that appeared to lead to other chambers.

She ascended the winding steps hastily, and found they led only to a door, opening into a small room, where nothing remarkable appeared, till she approached the windows, and beheld thence an horizon, and a landscape spread below, whose grandeur awakened all her heart. The consciousness of her prison was lost, while her eyes ranged over the wide and freely-sublime scene without. She perceived that this chamber was within a small turret, projecting from an angle of the convent over the walls, and suspended, as in air, above the vast precipices of granite, that formed part of the mountain. These precipices were broken into cliffs, which, in some places, impended far above their base, and, in others, rose, in nearly perpendicular lines, to the walls of the monastery, which they supported. Ellena, with a dreadful pleasure, looked down them, shagged as they were with larch, and frequently darkened by lines of gigantic pine bending along the rocky ledges, till her eye rested on the thick chestnut woods that extended over their winding base, and which, softening to the plains, seemed to form a gradation between the variegated cultivation there, and the awful wildness of the rocks above. Round these extensive plains were tumbled the mountains, of various shape and attitude, which Ellena had admired on her approach to San Stefano; some shaded with forests of olive and almond trees, but the greater part abandoned to the flocks, which, in summer, feed on their aromatic herbage, and on the approach of winter, descend to the sheltered plains of the *Tavogliere di Puglia.*

On the left opened the dreadful pass which she had traversed, and the thunder of whose waters now murmured at a distance. The accumulation of overtopping points, which the mountains of this dark perspective exhibited, presented an image of grandeur superior to any thing she had seen while within the pass itself.

To Ellena, whose mind was capable of being highly elevated, or sweetly soothed, by scenes of nature, the discovery of this little turret was an important circumstance. Hither she could come, and her soul, refreshed by the views it afforded, would acquire strength to bear her, with equanimity, thro' the persecutions that might await her. Here, gazing upon the stupendous imagery around her, looking, as it were, beyond the awful veil which obscures the features of the Deity, and conceals Him from the eyes of his creatures, dwelling as with a present God in the midst of his sublime works; with a mind thus elevated, how insignificant would appear to her the transactions, and the sufferings of this world! How poor the boasted power of man, when the fall of a single cliff from these mountains would with ease destroy thousands of his race assembled on the plains below! How would it avail them, that they were accoutred for battle, armed with all the instruments of destruction that human invention ever fashioned? Thus man, the giant who now held her in captivity, would shrink to the diminutiveness of a fairy; and she would experience, that his utmost force was unable to enchain her soul, or compel her to fear him, while he was destitute of virtue.

Ellena's attention was recalled from the scene without by a sound from within the gallery, and she then heard a key turning in the door of the passage. Fearing that it was sister Margaritone who approached, and who, informed by her absence of the consolatory turret she had discovered, would

perhaps debar her from ever returning to it, Ellena descended with a palpitating heart, and found that nun in the
cell. Surprise and severity were in her countenance, when
she enquired by what means Ellena had unclosed the door,
and whither she had been.

Ellena answered without any prevarication, that she had
found the door unfastened, and that she had visited the turret
above; but she forbore to express a wish to return thither,
judging that such an expression would certainly exclude her
in future. Margaritone, after sharply rebuking her for prying
beyond the passage, and setting down the breakfast she had
brought, left the room, the door of which she did not forget
to secure. Thus Ellena was at once deprived of so innocent
a means of consolation as her pleasant turret had afforded.

During several days, she saw only the austere nun, except
when she attended vespers; where, however, she was so vigilantly observed, that she feared to speak with Olivia, even
by her eyes. Olivia's were often fixed upon her face, and
with a kind of expression which Ellena, when she did venture to look at her, could not perfectly interpret. It was not
only of pity, but of anxious curiosity, and of something also
like fear. A blush would sometimes wander over her cheek,
which was succeeded by an extreme paleness, and by an air
of such universal languor as precedes a fainting fit: but the
exercises of devotion seemed frequently to recal her fleeting
spirits, and to elevate them with hope and courage.

When she left the chapel, Ellena saw Olivia no more that
night; but on the following morning she came with breakfast
to the cell. A character of peculiar sadness was on her brow.

"O! how glad I am to see you!" said Ellena; "and how
much I have regretted your long absence! I was obliged to
remember constantly what you had enjoined, to forbear
enquiring after you."

The nun replied with a melancholy smile, "I come in obedience to our lady abbess," said she, as she seated herself on
Ellena's mattress.

"And did you not wish to come?" said Ellena, mournfully.

"I did wish it," replied Olivia; "but"——and she hesitated.

"Whence then this reluctance?" enquired Ellena.

Olivia was silent a moment.

"You are a messenger of evil news!" said Ellena; "you are
only reluctant to afflict me."

"It is as you say," replied Olivia; "I am only reluctant to

afflict you; and I fear you have too many attachments to the world, to allow you to receive, without sorrow, what I have to communicate. I am ordered to prepare you for the vows, and to say, that, since you have rejected the husband which was proposed to you, you are to accept the veil; that many of the customary forms are to be dispensed with; and that the ceremony of taking the black veil, will follow without delay that of receiving the white one."

The nun paused; and Ellena said, "You are an unwilling bearer of this cruel message; and I reply only to the lady abbess, when I declare, that I never will accept either; that force may send me to the altar, but that it shall compel me to utter vows which my heart abhors; and if I am constrained to appear there, it shall be only to protest against her tyranny, and against the form intended to sanction it."

To Olivia this answer was so far from being displeasing, that it appeared to give her satisfaction.

"I dare not applaud your resolution," said she; "but I will not condemn it. You have, no doubt, connections in the world which would render a seclusion from it afflicting. You have relations, friends, from whom it would be dreadful to part?"

"I have neither," said Ellena, sighing.

"No! Can that be possible? and yet you are so unwilling to retire!"

"I have only one friend," replied Ellena, "and it is of him they would deprive me!"

"Pardon, my love, the abruptness of these enquiries," said Olivia; "yet, while I entreat your forgiveness, I am inclined to offend again, and to ask your name."

"That is a question I will readily answer. My name is Ellena di Rosalba."

"How?" said Olivia, with an air of deliberation; "Ellena di"——

"Di Rosalba," repeated her companion; "and permit me to ask your motive for the enquiry: do you know any person of my name?"

"No," replied the nun, mournfully; "but your features have some resemblance to those of a friend I once had."

As she said this, her agitation was apparent, and she rose to go. "I must not lengthen my visit, lest I should be forbidden to repeat it," said she. "What answer shall I give to the abbess? If you are determined to reject the veil, allow me to advise you to soften your refusal as much as possible; I am, perhaps, better acquainted with her character than you are; and O, my sister! I would not see you pining away your existence in this solitary cell."

"How much I am obliged by the interest you express for my welfare," said Ellena, "and by the advice you offer! I will yield my judgment in this instance to yours; you shall modulate my refusal as you think proper: but remember that it must be absolute; and beware, lest the abbess should mistake gentleness for irresolution."

"Trust me, I will be cautious in all that relates to you," said Olivia. "Farewell! I will visit you, if possible, in the evening. In the mean time the door shall be left open, that you may have more air and prospect than this cell affords. That staircase leads to a pleasant chamber."

"I have visited it already," replied Ellena, "and have to thank you for the goodness, which permitted me to do so. To go thither will greatly soothe my spirits; if I had some book, and my drawing-instruments, I could almost forget my sorrows there."

"Could you so?" said the nun, with an affectionate smile. "Adieu! I will endeavour to see you in the evening. If sister Margaritone returns, be careful not to enquire for me; nor once ask her for the little indulgence I give you."

Olivia withdrew, and Ellena retired to the chamber above, where she lost for a while all sense of sorrow amidst the great scenery, which its windows exhibited.

At noon, the step of Margaritone summoned Ellena from her retreat, and she was surprised that no reproof followed this second discovery of her absence. Margaritone only said, that the abbess had the goodness to permit Ellena to dine with the novices, and that she came to conduct her to their table.

Ellena did not rejoice in this permission, preferring to remain in her solitary turret, to the being exposed to the examining eyes of strangers; and she followed dejectedly, through the silent passages to the apartment where they were assembled. She was not less surprised than embarrassed to observe, in the manners of young people residing in a convent, an absence of that decorum, which includes beneath its modest shade every grace that ought to adorn the female character, like the veil which gives dignity to their air and softness to their features. When Ellena entered the room, the eyes of the whole company were immediately fixed upon her; the young ladies began to whisper and smile, and shewed, by various means, that she was the subject of conversation, not otherwise than censorious. No one advanced to meet and to encourage her, to welcome her to the table, or still less display one of those nameless graces, with which a generous and delicate mind delights to reanimate the modest and the unfortunate.

Ellena took a chair in silence; and, though she had at first felt forlorn and embarrassed by the impertinent manners of her companions, a consciousness of innocence gradually revived her spirits, and enabled her to resume an air of dignity, which repressed this rude presumption.

Ellena returned to her cell, for the first time, with eagerness. Margaritone did not fasten the door of it, but she was careful to secure that of the passage; and even this small indulgence she seemed to allow with a surly reluctance, as if compelled to obey the command of a superior. The moment she was gone, Ellena withdrew to her pleasant turret, where, after having suffered from the coarse manners of the novices, her gratitude was the more lively, when she perceived the delicate attention of her beloved nun. It appeared that she had visited the chamber in Ellena's absence, and had caused to be brought thither a chair and a table, on which were placed some books, and a knot of fragrant flowers. Ellena did not repress the grateful tears, which the generous feelings of Olivia excited; and she forbore, for some moments, to examine the books, that the pleasing emotions she experienced might not be interrupted.

On looking into these books, however, she perceived, that some of them treated of mystical subjects, which she laid aside with disappointment; but in others she observed a few of the best Italian poets, and a volume or two of Guicciardini's history. She was somewhat surprised, that the poets should have found their way to the library of a nun, but was too much pleased with the discovery to dwell on the enquiry.

Having arranged her books, and set her little room in order, she seated herself at a window, and, with a volume of Tasso, endeavoured to banish every painful remembrance from her mind. She continued wandering in the imaginary scenes of the poet, till the fading light recalled her to those of reality. The sun was set, but the mountain-tops were still

lighted up by his beams, and a tint of glorious purple coloured all the west, and began to change the snowy points on
the horizon. The silence and repose of the vast scene, promoted the tender melancholy that prevailed in her heart; she
thought of Vivaldi, and wept—of Vivaldi, whom she might,
perhaps, never see again, though she doubted not that he
would be indefatigable in searching for her. Every particular
of their last conversation, when he had so earnestly lamented
the approaching separation, even while he allowed of its
propriety, came to her mind; and, while she witnessed, in
imagination, the grief and distraction, which her mysterious
departure and absence must have occasioned him, the fortitude, with which she had resisted her own sufferings,
yielded to the picture of his.

The vesper-bell, at length, summoned her to prepare for
mass, and she descended to her cell to await the arrival of
her conductress. It was Margaritone, who soon appeared; but
in the chapel she, as usual, saw Olivia, who, when the service had concluded, invited her into the garden of the
convent. There, as she walked beneath the melancholy cypresses, that, ranged on either side the long walks, formed a
majestic canopy, almost excluding the evening twilight,
Olivia conversed with her on serious, but general, topics,
carefully avoiding any mention of the abbess, and of the affairs of Ellena. The latter, anxious to learn the effect of her
repeated rejection of the veil, ventured to make some enquiries, which the nun immediately discouraged, and as cautiously checked the grateful effusions of her young friend for
the attentions she had received.

Olivia accompanied Ellena to her cell, and there no longer
scrupled to relieve her from uncertainty. With a mixture of
frankness and discretion, she related as much of the conversation, that had passed between herself and the abbess, as it
appeared necessary for Ellena to know, from which it
seemed that the former was as obstinate, as the latter was
firm.

"Whatever may be your resolution," added the nun, "I
earnestly advise you, my sister, to allow the Superior some
hope of compliance, lest she proceed to extremities."

"And what extremity can be more terrible," replied
Ellena, "than either of those, to which she would now urge
me? Why should I descend to practice dissimulation?"

"To save yourself from undeserved sufferings," said Olivia mournfully.

"Yes, but I should then incur deserved ones," observed Ellena; "and forfeit such peace of mind as my oppressors never could restore to me." As she said this, she looked at the nun with an expression of gentle reproach and disappointment.

"I applaud the justness of your sentiment," replied Olivia, regarding her with tenderest compassion. "Alas! that a mind so noble should be subjected to the power of injustice and depravity!"

"Not subjected," said Ellena, "do not say subjected. I have accustomed myself to contemplate those sufferings; I have chosen the least of such as were given to my choice, and I will endure them with fortitude; and can you then say that I am subjected?"

"Alas, my sister! you know not what you promise," replied Olivia; "you do not comprehend the sufferings which may be preparing for you."

As she spoke, her eyes filled with tears, and she withdrew them from Ellena, who, surprised at the extreme concern on her countenance, entreated she would explain herself.

"I am not certain, myself, as to this point," said Olivia; "and if I were, I should not dare to explain it."

"Not dare!" repeated Ellena, mournfully. "Can benevolence like yours know fear, when courage is necessary to prevent evil?"

"Enquire no further!" said Olivia; but no blush of conscious duplicity stained her cheek. "It is sufficient that you understand the consequence of open resistance to be terrible, and that you consent to avoid it."

"But how avoid it, my beloved friend, without incurring a consequence which, in my apprehension, would be yet more dreadful? How avoid it, without either subjecting myself to a hateful marriage, or accepting the vows? Either of these events would be more terrible to me, than any thing with which I may be menaced."

"Perhaps not," said the nun. "Imagination cannot draw the horrors of— But, my sister, let me repeat, that I would save you! O, how willingly save you from the evils preparing! and that the only chance of doing so is, by prevailing with you to abandon at least the appearance of resistance."

"Your kindness deeply affects me," said Ellena; "and I am

fearful of appearing insensible of it, when I reject your advice; yet I cannot adopt it. The very dissimulation, which I should employ in self-defence, might be a means of involving me in destruction."

As Ellena concluded, and her eyes glanced upon the nun, unaccountable suspicion occurred to her, that Olivia might be insincere, and that, at this very moment, when she was advising dissimulation, she was endeavouring to draw Ellena into some snare, which the abbess had laid. She sickened at this dreadful supposition, and dismissed it without suffering herself to examine its probability. That Olivia, from whom she had received so many attentions, whose countenance and manners announced so fair a mind, and for whom she had conceived so much esteem and affection, should be cruel and treacherous, was a suspicion that gave her more pain, than the actual imprisonment in which she suffered; and when she looked again upon her face, Ellena was consoled by a clear conviction, that she was utterly incapable of perfidy.

"If it were possible that I could consent to practise deceit," resumed Ellena, after a long pause, "what could it avail me? I am entirely in the power of the abbess, who would soon put my sincerity to the proof; when a discovery of my duplicity would only provoke her vengeance, and I should be punished even for having sought to avoid injustice."

"If deceit is at any time excusable," replied Olivia, reluctantly, "it is when we practise it in self-defence. There are some rare situations, when it may be resorted to without our incurring ignominy, and yours is one of those. But I will acknowledge, that all the good I expect is from the delay which temporizing may procure you. The Superior, when she understands there is a probability of obtaining your consent to her wishes, may be willing to allow you the usual time of preparation for the veil, and meanwhile something may occur to rescue you from your present situation."

"Ah! could I but believe so!" said Ellena; "but, alas! what power can rescue me? And I have not one relative remaining even to attempt my deliverance. To what possibility do you allude?"

"The Marchesa may relent."

"Does, then, your possibility of good rest with her, my dear friend? If so, I am in despair again; for such a chance

of benefit, there would certainly be little policy in forfeiting
one's integrity."

"There are also other possibilities, my sister," said Olivia;
"but hark! what bell is that? It is the chime which assembles
the nuns in the apartment of the abbess, where she dispenses
her evening benediction. My absence will be observed.
Good night, my sister. Reflect on what I have advised; and
remember, I conjure you, to consider, that the consequence
of your decision must be solemn, and may be fatal."

The nun spoke this with a look and emphasis so extraordinary, that Ellena at once wished and dreaded to know
more; but before she had recovered from her surprise, Olivia
had left the room.

CHAPTER IX

------He, like the tenant
Of some night-haunted ruin, bore an aspect
Of horror, worn to habitude.

MYSTERIOUS MOTHER

THE adventurous Vivaldi, and his servant Paulo, after passing the night of Ellena's departure from villa Altieri in one of the subterraneous chambers of the fort of Paluzzi, and yielding, at length, to exhausted nature, awoke in terror and utter darkness, for the flambeau had expired. When a recollection of the occurrences of the preceding evening returned, they renewed their efforts for liberty with ardour. The grated window was again examined, and being found to overlook only a confined court of the fortress, no hope appeared of escaping.

The words of the monk returned with Vivaldi's first recollections, to torture him with apprehension, that Ellena was no more; and Paulo, unable either to console or to appease his master, sat down dejectedly beside him. Paulo had no longer a hope to suggest, or a joke to throw away; and he could not forbear seriously remarking, that to die of hunger was one of the most horrible means of death, or lamenting the rashness which had made them liable to so sad a probability.

He was in the midst of a very pathetic oration, of which, however, his master did not hear a single word, so wholly was his attention engaged by his own melancholy thoughts, when on a sudden he became silent, and then, starting to his feet, exclaimed, "Signor, what is yonder? Do you see nothing?"

Vivaldi looked round.

"It is certainly a ray of light," continued Paulo; "and I will soon know where it comes from."

As he said this he sprung forward, and his surprise almost equalled his joy when he discovered that the light issued through the door of the vault, which stood a little open. He could scarcely believe his senses, since the door had been strongly fastened on the preceding night, and he had not heard its ponderous bolts undrawn. He threw it widely open, but recollecting himself, stopped to look into the adjoining vault before he ventured forth; when Vivaldi darted past him, and bidding him follow instantly, ascended to the day. The courts of the fortress were silent and vacant, and Vivaldi reached the arch-way without having observed a single person, breathless with speed, and scarcely daring to believe that he had regained his liberty.

Beneath the arch he stopped to recover breath, and to consider whether he should take the road to Naples, or to the villa Altieri, for it was yet early morning, and at an hour when it appeared improbable that Ellena's family would be risen. The apprehension of her death had vanished as Vivaldi's spirits revived, which the pause of hesitation sufficiently announced: but even this was the pause only of an instant; a strong anxiety concerning her determined him to proceed to the villa Altieri, notwithstanding the unsuitableness of the hour, since he could, at least, reconnoitre her residence, and await till some sign of the family having risen should appear.

"Pray, Signor," said Paulo, while his master was deliberating, "do not let us stop here lest the enemy should appear again; and do, Signor, take the road which is nearest to some house where we may get breakfast, for the fear of starving has taken such hold upon me, that it has nearly anticipated the reality of it already."

Vivaldi immediately departed for the villa. Paulo, as he danced joyfully along, expressed all the astonishment that filled his mind, as to the cause of their late imprisonment and escape; but Vivaldi, who had now leizure to consider the subject, could not assist him in explaining it. The only certainty that appeared, was, that he had not been confined by robbers; and what interest any person could have in imprisoning him for the night, and suffering him to escape in the morning, did not appear.

On entering the garden at Altieri, he was surprised to observe that several of the lower lattices were open at this early hour, but surprise changed to terror, when, on reaching the portico, he heard a moaning of distress from the hall, and when, after loudly calling, he was answered by the piteous cries of Beatrice. The hall door was fastened, and, Beatrice being unable to open it, Vivaldi, followed by Paulo, sprang through one of the unclosed lattices; when on reaching the hall, he found the housekeeper bound to a pillar, and learned that Ellena had been carried off during the night by armed men.

For a moment he was almost stupified by the shock of this intelligence, and then asked Beatrice a thousand questions concerning the affair, without allowing her time to answer one of them. When, however, he had patience to listen, he learned that the ruffians were four in number; that they were masked; that two of them had carried Ellena through the garden, while the others, after binding Beatrice to a pillar, threatening her with death if she made any noise, and watching over her till their comrades had secured their prize, left her a prisoner. This was all the information she could give respecting Ellena.

Vivaldi, when he could think coolly, believed he had discovered the instigators and the design of the whole affair, and the cause, also, of his late confinement. It appeared that Ellena had been carried off by order of his family, to prevent the intended marriage, and that he had been decoyed into the fort of Paluzzi, and kept a prisoner there, to prevent him from intercepting the scheme, which his presence at the villa Altieri would effectually have done. He had himself spoken of his former adventure at Paluzzi; and it now appeared, that his family had taken advantage of the curiosity he had expressed, to lead him into the vaults. The event of this design was the more certain, since, as the fort lay in the direct road to the villa Altieri, Vivaldi could not go thither without being observed by the creatures of the Marchesa, who, by an artful manœuvre, might make him their prisoner, without employing violence.

As he considered these circumstances, it appeared certain, also, that father Schedoni was in truth the monk who had so long haunted his steps; that he was the secret adviser of his mother, and one of the authors of the predicted misfortunes, which, it seemed, he possessed a too certain means of fulfilling. Yet Vivaldi, while he admitted the probability of all this, reflected with new astonishment on the conduct of Schedoni, during his interview with him in the Marchesa's cabinet;—the air of dignified innocence, with which he had repressed accusation, the apparent simplicity, with which he had pointed out circumstances respecting the stranger, that seemed to make against himself; and Vivaldi's opinion of the confessor's duplicity began to waver. "Yet what other person," said he, "could be so intimately acquainted with my concerns, or have an interest sufficiently strong for thus indefatigably thwarting me, except this confessor, who is, no doubt, well rewarded for his perseverance? The monk can be no other than Schedoni, yet it is strange that he should have forborn to disguise his person, and should appear in his mysterious office in the very habit he usually wears!"

Whatever might be the truth as to Schedoni, it was evident that Ellena had been carried away by order of Vivaldi's family, and he immediately returned towards Naples with an intention of demanding her at their hands, not with any hope of their compliance, but believing that they might accidentally afford him some lights on the subject. If, however, he should fail to obtain any hint that might assist him in traceing the route she had been carried, he determined to visit Schedoni, accuse him of perfidy, urge him to a full explanation of his conduct, and, if possible, obtain from him a knowledge of Ellena's place of confinement.

When, at length, he obtained an interview with the Marchese, and, throwing himself at his feet, supplicated that Ellena might be restored to her home, the unaffected surprise of his father overwhelmed him with astonishment and despair. The look and manner of the Marchese could not be doubted; Vivaldi was convinced that he was absolutely ignorant of any step which had been taken against Ellena.

"However ungraciously you have conducted yourself," said the Marchese, "my honour has never yet been sullied by duplicity; however I may have wished to break the unworthy connection you have formed, I should disdain to employ artifice as the means. If you really design to marry this person, I shall make no other effort to prevent such a measure, than by telling you the consequence you are to expect;—from thenceforth I will disown you for my son."

The Marchese quitted the apartment when he had said this, and Vivaldi made no attempt to detain him. His words expressed little more than they had formerly done, yet Vivaldi was shocked by the absolute menace now delivered. The stronger passion of his heart, however, soon overcame their effect; and this moment, when he began to fear that he had irrecoverably lost the object of his dearest affections, was not the time, in which he could long feel remoter evils, or calculate the force of misfortunes which never might arrive. The nearer interest pressed solely upon his mind, and he was conscious only to the loss of Ellena.

The interview, which followed with his mother, was of a different character from that, which had occurred with the Marchese. The keen dart of suspicion, however, sharpened as it was by love and by despair, pierced beyond the veil of her duplicity; and Vivaldi as quickly detected her hypocrisy as he had yielded his conviction to the sincerity of the Marchese. But his power rested here; he possessed no means of awakening her pity or actuating her justice, and could not obtain even a hint, that might guide him in his search of Ellena.

Schedoni, however, yet remained to be tried; Vivaldi had no longer a doubt as to his having caballed with the Marchesa, and that he had been an agent in removing Ellena. Whether he was the person who haunted the ruins of Paluzzi, still remained to be proved, for, though several circumstances seemed to declare that he was, others, not less plausible, asserted the contrary.

On leaving the Marchesa's apartment, Vivaldi repaired to the convent of the Spirito Santo, and enquired for father Schedoni. The lay-brother who opened the gate, informed him that the father was in his cell, and Vivaldi stepped impatiently into the court requesting to be shewn thither.

"I dare not leave the gate, Signor," said the brother, "but if you cross the court, and ascend that stair-case which you see yonder beyond the door-way on your right, it will lead you to a gallery, and the third door you will come to is father Schedoni's."

Vivaldi passed on without seeing another human being, and not a sound disturbed the silence of this sanctuary, till, as he ascended the stairs, a feeble note of lamentation proceeded from the gallery, and he concluded it was uttered by some penitent at confession.

He stopped, as he had been directed, at the third door, when, as he gently knocked, the sound ceased, and the same profound silence returned. Vivaldi repeated his summons, but, receiving no answer, he ventured to open the door. In the dusky cell within no person appeared, but he still looked

round, expecting to discover some one in the dubious gloom.
The chamber contained little more than a mattress, a chair,
a table, and a crucifix; some books of devotion were upon
the table, one or two of which were written in unknown
characters; several instruments of torture lay beside them.
Vivaldi shuddered as he hastily examined these, though he
did not comprehend the manner of their application, and he
left the chamber, without noticing any other object, and returned to the court. The porter said, that since father
Schedoni was not in his cell, he was probably either in the
church or in the gardens, for that he had not passed the gates
during the morning.

"Did he pass yester-evening?" said Vivaldi, eagerly.

"Yes, he returned to vespers," replied the brother with surprise.

"Are you certain as to that, my friend?" rejoined Vivaldi,
"are you certain that he slept in the convent last night?"

"Who is it that asks the question?" said the lay-brother,
with displeasure, "and what right has he to make it? You are
ignorant of the rules of our house, Signor, or you would perceive such questions to be unnecessary; any member of our
community is liable to be severely punished if he sleep a
night without these walls, and father Schedoni would be the
last among us so to trespass. He is one of the most pious of
the brotherhood; few indeed have courage to imitate his severe example. His voluntary sufferings are sufficient for a
saint. He pass the night abroad? Go, Signor, yonder is the
church, you will find him there, perhaps."

Vivaldi did not linger to reply. "The hypocrite!" said he to
himself as he crossed to the church, which formed one side
of the quadrangle; "but I will unmask him."

The church, which he entered, was vacant and silent like
the court. "Whither can the inhabitants of this place have
withdrawn themselves?" said he; "wherever I go, I hear only
the echoes of my own footsteps; it seems as if death reigned
here over all! But, perhaps, it is one of the hours of general
meditation, and the monks have only retired to their cells."

As he paced the long aisles, he suddenly stopped to catch
the startling sound that murmured through the lofty roof; but
it seemed to be only the closing of a distant door. Yet he often looked forward into the sacred gloom, which the painted
windows threw over the remote perspective, in the expectation of perceiving a monk. He was not long disappointed; a

person appeared, standing silently in an obscure part of the cloister, cloathed in the habit of this society, and he advanced towards him.

The monk did not avoid Vivaldi, or even turn to observe who was approaching, but remained in the same attitude, fixed like a statue. This tall and gaunt figure had, at a distance, reminded him of Schedoni, and Vivaldi, as he now looked under the cowl, discovered the ghastly countenance of the confessor.

"Have I found you at last?" said Vivaldi. "I would speak with you, father, in private. This is not a proper place for such discourse as we must hold."

Schedoni made no reply, and Vivaldi, once again looking at him, observed that his features were fixed, and his eyes bent towards the ground. The words of Vivaldi seemed not to have reached his understanding, nor even to have made any impression on his senses.

He repeated them in a louder tone, but still not a single line of Schedoni's countenance acknowledged their influence. "What means this mummery?" said he, his patience exhausted, and his indignation aroused; "This wretched subterfuge shall not protect you, you are detected, your stratagems are known! Restore Ellena di Rosalba to her home, or confess where you have concealed her."

Schedoni was still silent and unmoved. A respect for his age and profession withheld Vivaldi from seizing and compelling him to answer; but the agony of impatience and indignation which he suffered, formed a striking contrast to the death-like apathy of the monk. "I now also know you," continued Vivaldi, "for my tormentor at Paluzzi, the prophet of evils, which you too well practised the means of fulfilling, the predictor of the death of Signora Bianchi." Schedoni frowned. "The forewarner of Ellena's departure; the phantom who decoyed me into the dungeons of Paluzzi; the prophet and the artificer of all my misfortunes."

The monk raised his eyes from the ground, and fixed them with terrible expression upon Vivaldi, but was still silent.

"Yes, father," added Vivaldi, "I know and will proclaim you to the world. I will strip you of the holy hypocrisy in which you shroud yourself; announce to all your society the despicable artifices you have employed, and the misery you have occasioned. Your character shall be announced aloud."

While Vivaldi spoke, the monk had withdrawn his eyes,

and fixed them again on the ground. His countenance had resumed its usual expression.

"Wretch! restore to me Ellena di Rosalba!" cried Vivaldi, with the sudden anguish of renewed despair. "Tell me at least, where she may be found, or you shall be compelled to do so. Whither, whither have you conveyed her?"

As he pronounced this in loud and passionate accents, several ecclesiastics entered the cloisters, and were passing on to the body of the church, when his voice arrested their attention. They paused, and perceiving the singular attitude of Schedoni, and the frantic gesticulations of Vivaldi, hastily advanced towards them. "Forbear!" said one of the strangers, as he seized the cloak of Vivaldi, "do you not observe!"

"I observe a hypocrite," replied Vivaldi, stepping back and disengaging himself, "I observe a destroyer of the peace, it was his duty to protect. I"——

"Forbear this desperate conduct," said the priest, "lest it provoke the just vengeance of Heaven! Do you not observe the holy office in which he is engaged?" pointing to the monk, "Leave the church while you are permitted to do so in safety; you suspect not the punishment you may provoke."

"I will not quit the spot till you answer my enquiries," said Vivaldi to Schedoni, without deigning even to look upon the priest; "Where, I repeat, is Ellena di Rosalba?"

The confessor was still silent and unmoved. "This is beyond all patience, and all belief," continued Vivaldi. "Speak! Answer me, or dread what I may unfold. Yet silent! Do you know the convent *del Pianto*? Do you know the confessional of the *Black Penitents*?"

Vivaldi thought he perceived the countenance of the monk suffer some change. "Do you remember that terrible night," he added, "when, on the steps of that confessional, a tale was told?"——

Schedoni raised his eyes, and fixing them once more on Vivaldi, with a look that seemed intended to strike him to the dust, "Avaunt!" cried he in a tremendous voice; "avaunt! sacrilegious boy! Tremble for the consequence of thy desperate impiety!"

As he concluded, he started from his position, and gliding with the silent swiftness of a shadow along the cloister, vanished in an instant. Vivaldi, when attempting to pursue him, was seized by the surrounding monks. Insensible to his sufferings, and exasperated by his assertions, they threatened, that if he did not immediately leave the convent, he should be confined, and undergo the severe punishment to which he had become liable, for having disturbed and even insulted one of their holy order while performing an act of penance.

"He has need of such acts," said Vivaldi; "but when can they restore the happiness his treachery has destroyed? Your order is disgraced by such a member, reverend fathers; your"——

"Peace!" cried a monk, "he is the pride of our house; he is severe in his devotion, and in self-punishment terrible beyond the reach of——But I am throwing away my commendations, I am talking to one who is not permitted to value or to understand the sacred mysteries of our exercises."

"Away with him to the *Padre Abbate!*" cried an enraged priest; "away with him to the dungeon!"

"Away! away!" repeated his companions, and they endeavoured to force Vivaldi through the cloisters. But with the sudden strength which pride and indignation lent him, he burst from their united hold, and, quitting the church by another door, escaped into the street.

Vivaldi returned home in a state of mind that would have engaged the pity of any heart, which prejudice or self-interest had not hardened. He avoided his father, but sought the Marchesa, who, triumphant in the success of her plan, was still insensible to the sufferings of her son.

When the Marchesa had been informed of his approaching marriage, she had, as usual, consulted with her confessor on the means of preventing it, who had advised the scheme she adopted, a scheme which was the more easily carried into effect, since the Marchesa had early in life been acquainted with the abbess of San Stefano, and knew, therefore, enough of her character and disposition to confide, without hesitation, the management of this important affair to her discretion. The answer of the abbess to her proposal, was not merely acquiescent, but zealous, and it appeared that she too faithfully justified the confidence reposed in her. After this plan had been so successfully prosecuted, it was not to be hoped that the Marchesa would be prevailed upon to relinquish it by the tears, the anguish, or all the varied sufferings of her son. Vivaldi now reproved the easiness of his own confidence in having hoped it, and quitted her cabinet with a despondency that almost reached despair.

The faithful Paulo obeyed the hasty summons of his master, but he had not succeeded in obtaining intelligence of Ellena; and Vivaldi, having dismissed him again on the same enquiry, retired to his apartment, where the excess of grief, and a feeble hope of devising some successful mode of remedy, alternately agitated and detained him.

In the evening, restless and anxious for change, though scarcely knowing whither to bend his course, he left the palace, and strolled down to the sea-beach. A few fishermen and lazzaroni only were loitering along the strand, waiting for boats from St. Lucia. Vivaldi, with folded arms, and his hat drawn over his face to shade his sorrow from observation, paced the edge of the waves, listening to their murmur, as they broke gently at his feet, and gazing upon their undulating beauty, while all consciousness was lost in melancholy reverie concerning Ellena. Her late residence appeared at a distance, rising over the shore. He remembered how often from thence they had together viewed this lovely scene! Its features had now lost their charm; they were colourless and uninteresting, or impressed only mournful ideas. The sea fluctuating beneath the setting sun, the long mole and its light-house tipped with the last rays, fishermen reposing in the shade, little boats skimming over the smooth waters, which their oars scarcely dimpled; these were images that brought to his recollection the affecting evening when he had last seen this picture from the villa Altieri, when, seated in the orangery with Ellena and Bianchi, on the night preceding the death of the latter, Ellena herself had so solemnly been given to his care, and had so affectingly consented to the dying request of her relative. The recollection of that scene came to Vivaldi with all the force of contrast, and renewed all the anguish of despair; he paced the beach with quicker steps, and long groans burst from his heart. He accused himself of indifference and inactivity, for having been thus long unable to discover a single circumstance which might direct his search; and though he knew not whither to go, he determined to leave Naples immediately, and return no more to his father's mansion till he should have rescued Ellena.

Of some fishermen who were conversing together upon the beach, he enquired whether they could accommodate him with a boat, in which he meant to coast the bay; for it appeared probable that Ellena had been conveyed from

Altieri by water, to some town or convent on the shore, the privacy and facility of such a mode of conveyance being suitable to the designs of her enemies.

"I have but one boat, Signor," said a fisherman, "and that is busy enough in going to and fro between here and Santa Lucia, but my comrade, here, perhaps can serve you. What, Carlo, can you help the Signor to your little skiff? the other, I know, has enough to do in the trade."

His comrade, however, was too much engaged with a party of three or four men, who were listening in deep attention round him, to reply; Vivaldi advancing to urge the question, was struck by the eagerness with which he delivered his narrative, as well as the uncouthness of his gesticulation; and he paused a moment in attention. One of the auditors seemed to doubt of something that had been asserted. "I tell you," replied the narrator, "I used to carry fish there, two and three times a week, and very good sort of people they were; they have laid out many a ducat with me in their time. But as I was saying, when I got there, and knocked upon the door, I heard, all of a sudden, a huge groaning, and presently I heard the voice of the old housekeeper herself, roaring out for help; but I could give her none, for the door was fastened; and, while I ran away for assistance to old Bartoli, you know old Bartoli, he lives by the road side as you go to Naples; well, while I ran to him, comes a Signor, and jumps through the window and sets her at liberty at once. So then, I heard the whole story."——

"What story?" said Vivaldi, "and of whom do you speak?"

"All in good time," *Maestro,* you shall hear," said the fisherman, who looking at him for a moment, added, "Why, Signor, it should be you I saw there, you should be the very Signor that let Beatrice loose."

Vivaldi, who had scarcely doubted before, that it was Altieri of which the man had spoken, now asked a thousand questions respecting the route the ruffians had taken Ellena, but obtained no relief to his anxiety.

"I should not wonder," said a Lazzaro who had been listening to the relation; "I should not wonder if the carriage that passed Bracelli early on the same morning, with the blinds drawn up, though it was so hot that people could scarcely breathe in the open air, should prove to be it which carried off the lady!"

This hint was sufficient to reanimate Vivaldi, who collected all the information the Lazzaro could give, which was, however, little more than that a carriage, such as he described, had been seen by him, driving furiously through Bracelli, early on the morning mentioned as that of Signora di Rosalba's departure. Vivaldi had now no doubt as to its being the one which conveyed her away, and he determined to set out immediately for that place, where he hoped to obtain from the post-master further intelligence concerning the road she had pursued.

With this intention he returned once more to his father's mansion, not to acquaint him with his purpose, or to bid him farewell, but to await the return of his servant Paulo, who he meant should accompany him in the search. Vivaldi's spirits were now animated with hope, slender as were the circumstances that supported it; and, believing his design to be wholly unsuspected by those who would be disposed to interrupt it, he did not guard either against the measures, which might impede his departure from Naples, or those which might overtake him on his journey.

CHAPTER X

What, would'st thou have a serpent sting thee twice?
SHAKESPEARE

The Marchesa, alarmed at some hints dropped by Vivaldi in the late interview between them, and by some circumstances of his latter conduct, summoned her constant adviser, Schedoni. Still suffering with the insult he had received in the church of the *Spirito Santo,* he obeyed with sullen reluctance, yet not without a malicious hope of discovering some opportunity for retaliation. That insult, which had pointed forth his hypocrisy, and ridiculed the solemn abstraction he assumed, had sunk deep in his heart, and, fermenting the direst passions of his nature, he meditated a terrible revenge. It had subjected him to mortifications of various kinds. Ambition, it has already appeared, was one of his strongest motives of action, and he had long since assumed a character of severe sanctity, chiefly for the purposes of lifting him to promotion. He was not beloved in the society of which he was a member; and many of the brotherhood, who had laboured to disappoint his views, and to detect his errors, who hated him for his pride, and envied him for his reputed sanctity, now gloried in the mortification he had received, and endeavoured to turn the circumstance to their own advantage. They had not scrupled already to display by insinuation and pointed sneers, their triumph, and to menace his reputation; and Schedoni, though he deserved contempt, was not of a temper to endure it.

But above all, some hints respecting his past life, which had fallen from Vivaldi, and which occasioned him so abruptly to leave the church, alarmed him. So much terror, indeed, had they excited, that it is not improbable that he would have sealed his secret in death, devoting Vivaldi to the grave, had he not been restrained by the dreaded vengeance of the Vivaldi family. Since that hour he had known no peace, and had never slept; he had taken scarcely any food, and was almost continually on his knees upon the steps of the high altar. The devotees who beheld him, paused and admired; such of the brothers as disliked him, sneered and passed on. Schedoni appeared alike insensible to each; lost to this world, and preparing for a higher.

The torments of his mind and the severe penance he had observed, had produced a surprising change in his appearance, so that he resembled a spectre rather than a human being. His visage was wan and wasted, his eyes were sunk and become nearly motionless, and his whole air and attitudes exhibited the wild energy of something—not of this earth.

When he was summoned by the Marchesa, his conscience whispered this to be the consequence of circumstances, which Vivaldi had revealed; and, at first, he had determined not to attend her; but, considering that if it was so, his refusal would confirm suspicion, he resolved to trust once more to the subtilty of his address for deliverance.

With these apprehensions, tempered by this hope, he entered the Marchesa's closet. She almost started on observing him, and could not immediately withdraw her eyes from his altered visage, while Schedoni was unable wholly to conceal the perturbation which such earnest observation occasioned. "Peace rest with you, daughter!" said he, and he seated himself, without lifting his eyes from the floor.

"I wished to speak with you, father, upon affairs of moment," said the Marchesa gravely, "which are probably not unknown to you." She paused, and Schedoni bowed his head, awaiting in anxious expectation what was to follow.

"You are silent, father," resumed the Marchesa. "What am I to understand by this?"

"That you have been misinformed," replied Schedoni, whose apt conscience betrayed his discretion.

"Pardon me," said the Marchesa, "I am too well informed, and should not have requested your visit if any doubt had remained upon my mind."

"Signora! be cautious of what you credit," said the confessor imprudently; "you know not the consequence of a hasty credulity."

"Would that mine were a rash credulity!" replied the Marchesa, "but—we are betrayed."

"We?" repeated the monk, beginning to revive: "What has happened?"

The Marchesa informed him of Vivaldi's absence, and inferred from its length, for it was now several days since his departure, that he had certainly discovered the place of Ellena's confinement, as well as the authors of it.

Schedoni differed from her, but hinted, that the obedience of youth was hopeless, unless severer measures were adopted.

"Severer!" exclaimed the Marchesa; "good father, is it not severe enough to confine her for life?"

"I mean severer with respect to your son, lady," replied Schedoni. "When a young man has so far overcome all reverence for an holy ordinance as publicly to insult its professors, and yet more, when that professor is in the very performance of his duties, it is time he should be controlled with a strong hand. I am not in the practice of advising such measures, but the conduct of Signor Vivaldi is such as calls aloud for them. Public decency demands it. For myself, indeed, I should have endured patiently the indignity which has been offered me, receiving it as a salutary mortification, as one of those inflictions that purify the soul from the pride which even the holiest men may unconsciously cherish. But I am no longer permitted to consider myself; the public good requires that an example should be made of the horrible impiety of which your son, it grieves me, daughter, to disclose it!—your son, unworthy of such a mother! has been guilty."

It is evident that in the style, at least, of this accusation, Schedoni suffered the force of his resentment to prevail over the usual subtilty of his address, the deep and smooth insinuation of his policy.

"To what do you allude, righteous father?" enquired the astonished Marchesa; "what indignity, what impiety has my son to answer for? I entreat you will speak explicitly, that I may prove I can lose the mother in the strict severity of the judge."

"That is spoken with the grandeur of sentiment, which has always distinguished you, my daughter! Strong minds perceive that justice is the highest of the moral attributes, mercy is only the favourite of weak ones."

Schedoni had a view in this commendation beyond that of confirming the Marchesa's present resolution against Vivaldi. He wished to prepare her for measures, which might hereafter be necessary to accomplish the revenge he meditated, and he knew that by flattering her vanity, he was most likely to succeed. He praised her, therefore, for qualities he wished her to possess, encouraged her to reject general opinions by admiring as the symptoms of a superior understanding, the convenient morality upon which she had occasionally acted; and, calling sternness justice, extolled that for strength of mind, which was only callous insensibility.

He then described to her Vivaldi's late conduct in the church of the *Spirito Santo,* exaggerated some offensive circumstances of it, invented others, and formed of the whole an instance of monstrous impiety and unprovoked insult.

The Marchesa listened to the relation with no less indignation than surprise, and her readiness to adopt the confessor's advice allowed him to depart with renovated spirits and most triumphant hopes.

Meanwhile, the Marchese remained ignorant of the subject of the conference with Schedoni. His opinions had formerly been sounded, and having been found decidedly against the dark policy it was thought expedient to practise, he was never afterwards consulted respecting Vivaldi. Parental anxiety and affection began to revive as the lengthened absence of his son was observed. Though jealous of his rank, he loved Vivaldi; and, though he had never positively believed that he designed to enter into a sacred engagement with a person, whom the Marchese considered to be so much his inferior as Ellena, he had suffered doubts, which gave him considerable uneasiness. The present extraordinary absence of Vivaldi renewed his alarm. He apprehended that if she was discovered at this moment, when the fear of losing her for ever, and the exasperation, which such complicated opposition occasioned, had awakened all the passions of his son, this rash young man might be prevailed upon to secure her for his own by the indissoluble vow. On the other hand, he dreaded the effect of Vivaldi's despair, should he fail in the pursuit; and thus, fearing at one moment that for which he wished in the next, the Marchese suffered a tumult of mind inferior only to his son's.

The instructions, which he delivered to the servants whom he sent in pursuit of Vivaldi, were given under such distraction of thought, that scarcely any person perfectly understood his commission; and, as the Marchesa had been careful

to conceal from him her knowledge of Ellena's abode, he
gave no direction concerning the route to *San Stefano.*

While the Marchese at Naples was thus employed, and
while Schedoni was forming further plans against Ellena,
Vivaldi was wandering from village to village, and from
town to town, in pursuit of her, whom all his efforts had
hitherto been unsuccessful to recover. From the people at the
post-house at Bracelli, he had obtained little information that
could direct him; they only knew that a carriage, such as had
been already described to Vivaldi, with the blinds drawn up,
changed horses there on the morning, which he remembered
to be that of Ellena's departure, and had proceeded on the
road to Morgagni.

When Vivaldi arrived thither, all trace of Ellena was lost;
the master of the post could not recollect a single circumstance connected with the travellers, and, even if he had noticed them, it would have been insufficient for Vivaldi's
purpose, unless he had also observed the road they followed;
for at this place several roads branched off into opposite
quarters of the country; Vivaldi, therefore, was reduced to
chuse one of these, as chance or fancy directed; and, as it
appeared probable that the Marchesa had conveyed Ellena to
a convent, he determined to make enquiries at every one on
his way.

He had now passed over some of the wildest tracts of the
Apennine, among scenes, which seemed abandoned by civilized society to the banditti who haunted their recesses. Yet
even here amidst wilds that were nearly inaccessible, convents, with each its small dependent hamlet, were scattered,
and, shrouded from the world by woods and mountains, enjoyed unsuspectedly many of its luxuries, and displayed, unnoticed, some of its elegance. Vivaldi, who had visited
several of these in search of Ellena, had been surprised at
the refined courtesy and hospitality, with which he was received.

It was on the seventh day of his journey, and near sun-set,
that he was bewildered in the woods of Rugieri. He had received a direction for the road he was to take at a village
some leagues distant, and had obeyed it confidently till now,
when the path was lost in several tracts that branched out
among the trees. The day was closing, and Vivaldi's spirits
began to fail, but Paulo, light of heart and ever gay, commended the shade and pleasant freshness of the woods, and

observed, that if his master did lose his way, and was obliged to remain here for the night, it could not be so very unlucky, for they could climb up among the branches of a chestnut, and find a more neat and airy lodging than any inn had yet afforded them.

While Paulo was thus endeavouring to make the best of what might happen, and his master was sunk in reverie, they suddenly heard the sound of instruments and voices from a distance. The gloom, which the trees threw around, prevented their distinguishing objects afar off, and not a single human being was visible, nor any trace of his art, beneath the shadowy scene. They listened to ascertain from what direction the sounds approached, and heard a chorus of voices, accompanied by a few instruments, performing the evening service.

"We are near a convent, Signor," said Paulo, "listen! they are at their devotions."

"It is as you say," replied Vivaldi; "and we will make the best of our way towards it."

"Well, Signor! I must say, if we find as good doings here as we had at the Capuchin's, we shall have no reason to regret our beds *al-fresco* among the chestnut branches."

"Do you perceive any walls or spires beyond the trees?" said Vivaldi, as he led the way.

"None, Signor," replied Paulo; "yet we draw nearer the sounds. Ah, Signor! do you hear that note? How it dies away! And those instruments just touched in symphony! This is not the music of peasants; a convent must be near, though we do not see it."

Still as they advanced, no walls appeared, and soon after the music ceased; but other sounds led Vivaldi forward to a pleasant part of the woods, where, the trees opening, he perceived a party of pilgrims seated on the grass. They were laughing and conversing with much gaiety, as each spread before him the supper, which he drew from his scrip; while he, who appeared to be the *Father-director* of the pilgrimage, sat with a jovial countenance in the midst of the company, dispensing jokes and merry stories, and receiving in return a tribute from every scrip. Wines of various sorts were ranged before him, of which he drank abundantly, and seemed not to refuse any dainty that was offered.

Vivaldi, whose apprehensions were now quieted, stopped to observe the groupe, as the evening rays, glancing along the skirts of the wood, threw a gleam upon their various countenances, shewing, however, in each a spirit of gaiety that might have characterized the individuals of a party of pleasure, rather than those of a pilgrimage. The *Father-director* and his flock seemed perfectly to understand each other; the Superior willingly resigned the solemn austerity of his office, and permitted the company to make themselves as happy as possible, in consideration of receiving plenty of the most delicate of their viands; yet somewhat of dignity was mingled with his condescensions, that compelled them to receive even his jokes with a degree of deference, and perhaps they laughed at them less for their spirit than because they were favours.

Addressing the Superior, Vivaldi requested to be directed how he might regain his way. The father examined him for a moment before he replied, but observing the elegance of his dress, and a certain air of distinction; and perceiving, also, that Paulo was his servant, he promised his services, and invited him to take a seat at his right hand, and partake of the supper.

Vivaldi, understanding that the party was going his road, accepted the invitation; when Paulo, having fastened the horses to a tree, soon became busy with the supper. While Vivaldi conversed with the father, Paulo engrossed all the attention of the pilgrims nearer him; they declared he was the cleverest and the merriest fellow they had ever seen, and often expressed a wish that he was going as far with them as to the shrine in a convent of Carmelites, which terminated their pilgrimage. When Vivaldi understood that this shrine was in the church of a convent, partly inhabited by nuns, and that it was a little more than a league and a half distant, he determined to accompany them, for it was as possible that Ellena was confined there as in any other cloister; and of her being imprisoned in some convent, he had less doubt, the more he considered the character and views of his mother. He set forward, therefore, with the pilgrims, and on foot, having resigned his horse to the weary *Father-director.*

Darkness closed over them long before they reached the village where they designed to pass the night; but they beguiled the way with songs and stories, now and then, only, stopping at command of the Father, to repeat some prayer or sing a hymn. But, as they drew near a village, at the base of the mountain on which the shrine stood, they halted to ar-

range themselves in procession; and the Superior having
stopped short in the midst of one of his best jokes, dis-
mounted Vivaldi's horse, placed himself at their head, and
beginning a loud strain, they proceeded in full chorus of
melancholy music.

The peasants, hearing their sonorous voices, came forth to
meet and conduct them to their cabins. The village was already crowded with devotees, but these poor peasants, looking up to them with love and reverence, made every possible
contrivance to accommodate all who came; notwithstanding
which, when Paulo soon after turned into his bed of straw,
he had more reasons than one to regret his chestnut mattress.

Vivaldi passed an anxious night, waiting impatiently for
the dawning of that day, which might possibly restore to him
Ellena. Considering that a pilgrim's habit would not only
conceal him from suspicion, but allow him opportunities for
observation, which his own dress would not permit, he employed Paulo to provide him one. The address of the servant,
assisted by a single ducat, easily procured it, and at an early
hour he set forward on his enquiry.

CHAPTER XI

Bring roses, violets, and the cold snow-drop,
Beautiful in tears, to strew the path-way
Of our saintly sister.

A FEW devotees only had begun to ascend the mountain, and Vivaldi kept aloof even from these, pursuing a lonely track, for his thoughtful mind desired solitude. The early breeze sighing among the foliage, that waved high over the path, and the hollow dashing of distant waters, he listened to with complacency, for these were sounds which soothed yet promoted his melancholy mood; and he sometimes rested to gaze upon the scenery around him, for this too was in harmony with the temper of his mind. Disappointment had subdued the wilder energy of the passions, and produced a solemn and lofty state of feeling; he viewed with pleasing sadness the dark rocks and precipices, the gloomy mountains and vast solitudes, that spread around him; nor was the convent he was approaching a less sacred feature of the scene, as its gray walks and pinnacles appeared beyond the dusky groves. "Ah! if it should enclose her!" said Vivaldi, as he caught a first glimpse of its hall. "Vain hope! I will not invite your illusions again, I will not expose myself to the agonies of new disappointment; I will search, but not expect. Yet, if she should be there!"

Having reached the gates of the convent, he passed with hasty steps into the court; where his emotion encreased as he paused a moment and looked round its silent cloisters. The porter only appeared, when Vivaldi, fearful lest he should perceive him not to be a pilgrim, drew his hood over his face, and, gathering up his garments still closer in his folded arms, passed on without speaking, though he knew not which of the avenues before him led to the shrine. He advanced, however, towards the church, a stately edifice, detached, and at some little distance, from the other parts of the convent. Its highly vaulted aisles, extending in twilight perspective, where a monk, or a pilgrim only, now and then crossed, whose dark figures, passing without sound, vanished like shadows; the universal stillness of the place, the gleam of tapers from the high altar, and of lamps, which gave a gloomy pomp to every shrine in the church:—all these circumstances conspired to impress a sacred awe upon his heart.

He followed some devotees through a side aisle to a court, that was overhung by a tremendous rock, in which was a cave, containing the shrine of *our Lady of Mount Carmel*. This court was enclosed by the rock, and by the choir of the church, except that to the south a small opening led the eye to a glimpse of the landscape below, which, seen beyond the dark jaws of the cliff, appeared free, and light, and gaily coloured, melting away into the blue and distant mountains.

Vivaldi entered the cave, where, enclosed within a filigree screen of gold, lay the image of the saint, decorated with flowers and lighted up by innumerable lamps and tapers. The steps of the shrine were thronged with kneeling pilgrims, and Vivaldi, to avoid singularity, kneeled also, till a high peal of the organ, at a distance, and the deep voices of choiristers announced that the first mass was begun. He left the cave, and, returning into the church, loitered at an extremity of the aisles, where he listened awhile to the solemn harmony pealing along the roofs, and softening away in distance. It was such full and entrancing music as frequently swells in the high festivals of the Sicilian church, and is adapted to inspire that sublime enthusiasm, which sometimes elevates its disciples. Vivaldi, unable to endure long the excess of feeling, which this harmony awakened, was leaving the church, when suddenly it ceased, and the tolling of a bell sounded in its stead. This seemed to be the knell of death, and it occurred to him, that a dying person was approaching to receive the last sacrament; when he heard remotely a warbling of female voices, mingling with the deeper tones of the monks, and with the hollow note of the bell, as it struck at intervals. So sweetly, so plaintively, did the strain grow on the air, that those, who listened, as well as those, who sung, were touched with sorrow, and seemed equally to mourn for a departing friend.

Vivaldi hastened to the choir, the pavement of which was

strewn with palm-branches and fresh flowers. A pall of black velvet lay upon the steps of the altar, where several priests were silently attending. Every where appeared the ensigns of solemn pomp and ceremony, and in every countenance the stillness and observance of expectation. Meanwhile the sounds drew nearer, and Vivaldi perceived a procession of nuns approaching from a distant aisle.

As they advanced, he distinguished the lady abbess leading the train, dressed in her pontifical robes, with the mitre on her head; and well he marked her stately step, moving in time to the slow minstrelsy, and the air of proud yet graceful dignity, with which she characterized herself. Then followed the nuns, according to their several orders, and last came the novices, carrying lighted tapers, and surrounded by other nuns, who were distinguished by a particular habit.

Having reached a part of the church appropriated for their reception, they arranged themselves in order. Vivaldi with a palpitating heart enquired the occasion of this ceremony, and was told that a nun was going to be professed.

"You are informed, no doubt, brother," added the prior who gave him this intelligence, "that on the morning of our high festival, our *lady*'s day, it is usual for such as devote themselves to heaven, to receive the veil. Stand bye a while, and you will see the ceremony."

"What is the name of the novice who is now to receive it?" said Vivaldi, in a voice whose tremulous accents betrayed his emotion.

The friar glanced an eye of scrutiny upon him, as he replied, "I know not her name, but if you will step a little this way, I will point her out to you."

Vivaldi, drawing his hood over his face, obeyed in silence.

"It is she on the right of the abbess," said the stranger, "who leans on the arm of a nun, she is covered with a white veil, and is taller than her companions."

Vivaldi observed her with a fearful eye, and, though he did not recognize the person of Ellena, yet, whether it was that his fancy was possessed with her image, or that there was truth in his surmise, he thought he perceived a resemblance of her. He enquired how long the novice had resided in the convent, and many other particulars, to which the stranger either could not or dared not reply.

With what anxious solicitude did Vivaldi endeavour to

look through the veils of the several nuns in search of Ellena, whom he believed the barbarous policy of his mother might already have devoted to the cloister! With a solicitude still stronger, he tried to catch a glimpse of the features of the novices, but their faces were shaded by hoods, and their white veils, though thrown half back, were disposed in such artful folds that they concealed them from observation, as effectually as did the pendant lawn the features of the nuns.

The ceremony began with the exhortation of the *Father-Abbot*, delivered with solemn energy; then the novice kneeling before him, made her profession, for which Vivaldi listened with intense attention, but it was delivered in such low and trembling accents, that he could not ascertain even the tone. But during the anthem that mingled with the ensuing part of the service, he thought he distinguished the voice of Ellena, that touching and well-known voice, which in the church of San Lorenzo had first attracted his attention. He listened, scarcely daring to draw breath, lest he should lose a note; and again he fancied her voice spoke in a part of the plaintive response delivered by the nuns.

Vivaldi endeavoured to command his emotion, and to await with patience some further unfolding of the truth; but when the priest prepared to withdraw the white veil from the face of the novice, and throw the black one over her, a dreadful expectation that she was Ellena seized him, and he with difficulty forbore stepping forward and discovering himself on the instant.

The veil was at length withdrawn, and a very lovely face appeared, but not Ellena's. Vivaldi breathed again, and waited with tolerable composure for the conclusion of the ceremony; till, in the solemn strain that followed the putting on of the black veil, he heard again the voice, which he was now convinced was hers. Its accents were low, and mournful, and tremulous, yet his heart acknowledged instantaneously their magic influence.

When this ceremony had concluded, another began; and he was told it was that of a noviciation. A young woman, supported by two nuns, advanced to the altar, and Vivaldi thought he beheld Ellena. The priest was beginning the customary exhortation, when she lifted her half-veil, and, shewing a countenance where meek sorrow was mingled with heavenly sweetness, raised her blue eyes, all bathed in tears, and waved her hand as if she would have spoken.—It was Ellena herself.

The priest attempted to proceed.

"I protest in the presence of this congregation," said she solemnly, "that I am brought hither to pronounce vows which my heart disclaims. I protest"——

A confusion of voices interrupted her, and at the same instant she perceived Vivaldi rushing towards the altar. Ellena gazed for a moment, and then, stretching forth her supplicating hands towards him, closed her eyes, and sunk into the arms of some persons round her, who vainly endeavoured to prevent him from approaching and assisting her. The anguish, with which he bent over her lifeless form, and called upon her name, excited the commiseration even of the nuns, and especially of Olivia, who was most assiduous in efforts to revive her young friend.

When Ellena unclosed her eyes, and looking up, once more beheld Vivaldi, the expression, with which she regarded him, told that her heart was unchanged, and that she was unconscious of the miseries of imprisonment while he was with her. She desired to withdraw, and, assisted by Vivaldi and Olivia, was leaving the church, when the abbess ordered that she should be attended by the nuns only; and, retiring from the altar, she gave directions that the young stranger should be conducted to the parlour of the convent.

Vivaldi, though he refused to obey an imperious command, yielded to the entreaties of Ellena, and to the gentle remonstrances of Olivia; and, bidding Ellena farewell for a while, he repaired to the parlour of the abbess. He was not without some hope of awakening her to a sense of justice, or of pity; but he found that her notions of right were inexorably against him, and that pride and resentment usurped the influence of every other feeling. She began her lecture with expressing the warm friendship she had so long cherished for the Marchesa, proceeded to lament that the son of a friend, whom she so highly esteemed, should have forgotten his duty to his parents, and the observance due to the dignity of his house, so far as to seek connection with a person of Ellena di Rosalba's inferior station; and concluded with a severe reprimand for having disturbed the tranquillity of her convent and the decorum of the church by his intrusion.

Vivaldi listened with submitting patience to this mention of morals and decorum from a person who, with the most

perfect self-applause, was violating some of the plainest obligations of humanity and justice; who had conspired to tear
an orphan from her home, and who designed to deprive her
for life of liberty, with all the blessings it inherits. But, when
she proceeded to speak of Ellena with the caustic of severe
reprobation, and to hint at the punishment, which her public
rejection of the vows had incurred, the patience of Vivaldi
submitted no longer; indignation and contempt rose high
against the Superior; and he exhibited a portrait of herself in
the strong colours of truth. But the mind, which compassion
could not persuade, reason could not appal; selfishness had
hardened it alike to the influence of each; her pride only was
affected, and she retaliated the mortification she suffered by
menace and denunciation.

Vivaldi, on quitting her apartment, had no other resource
than an application to the *Abate,* whose influence, at least, if
not his authority, might assuage the severity of her power. In
this Abate, a mildness of temper, and a gentleness of manner
were qualities of less value than is usually and deservedly
imputed to them; for, being connected with feebleness of
mind, they were but the pleasing merits of easy times, which
in an hour of difficulty never assumed the character of virtues, by inducing him to serve those, for whom he might
feel. And thus, with a temper and disposition directly opposite to those of the severe and violent abbess, he was equally
selfish, and almost equally culpable, since by permitting
evil, he was nearly as injurious in his conduct as those who
planned it. Indolence and timidity, a timidity the consequence of want of clear perception, deprived him of all energy of character; he was prudent rather than wise, and so
fearful of being thought to do wrong that he seldom did
right.

To Vivaldi's temperate representations and earnest entreaties that he would exert some authority towards liberating
Ellena, he listened with patience; acknowledged the hardships of her situation; lamented the unhappy divisions between Vivaldi and his family; and then declined advancing a
single step in so delicate an affair. Signora di Rosalba, he
said, was in the care of the abbess, over whom he had no
right of control in matters relative to her domestic concerns.
Vivaldi then supplicated, that, though he possessed no authority, he would, at least, intercede or remonstrate against
so unjust a procedure as that of detaining Ellena a prisoner,

and assist in restoring her to the home, from which she had been forcibly carried.

"And this, again," replied the Abate, "does not come within my jurisdiction; and I make it a rule never to encroach upon that of another person."

"And can you endure, holy father," said Vivaldi, "to witness a flagrant act of injustice and not endeavour to counteract it? not even step forward to rescue the victim when you perceive the preparation for the sacrifice?"

"I repeat, that I never interfere with the authority of others," replied the Superior; "having asserted my own, I yield to them in their sphere, the obedience which I require in mine."

"Is power then," said Vivaldi, "the infallible test of justice? Is it morality to obey where the command is criminal? The whole world have a claim upon the fortitude, the active fortitude of those who are placed as you are, between the alternative of confirming a wrong by your consent, or preventing it by your resistance. Would that your heart expanded towards that world, reverend father!"

"Would that the whole world were wrong that you might have the glory of setting it right!" said the Abate, smiling. "Young man! you are an enthusiast, and I pardon you. You are a knight of chivalry, who would go about the earth fighting with every body by way of proving your right to do good; it is unfortunate that you are born somewhat too late."

"Enthusiasm in the cause of humanity"—said Vivaldi, but he checked himself; and despairing of touching a heart so hardened by selfish prudence, and indignant at beholding an apathy so vicious in its consequence, he left the Abate without other effort. He perceived that he must now have recourse to further stratagem, a recourse which his frank and noble mind detested, but he had already tried, without success, every other possibility of rescuing the innocent victim of the Marchesa's prejudice and pride.

Ellena meanwhile had retired to her cell, agitated by a variety of considerations, and contrary emotions, of which, however, those of joy and tenderness were long predominant. Then came anxiety, apprehension, pride, and doubt, to divide and torture her heart. It was true that Vivaldi had discovered her prison, but, if it were possible, that he could release her, she must consent to quit it with him; a step from which a mind so tremblingly jealous of propriety as hers, recoiled with alarm, though it would deliver her from captivity. And how, when she considered the haughty character of the Marchese di Vivaldi, the imperious and vindictive nature of the Marchesa, and, still more, their united repugnance to a connection with her, how could she endure to think, even for a moment, of intruding herself into such a family! Pride, delicacy, good sense seemed to warn her against a conduct so humiliating and vexatious in its consequences, and to exhort her to preserve her own dignity by independence; but the esteem, the friendship, the tender affection, which she had cherished for Vivaldi, made her pause, and shrink with emotions, of little less than horror, from the eternal renunciation, which so dignified a choice required. Though the encouragement, which her deceased relative had given to this attachment, seemed to impart to it a sacred character, that considerably soothed the alarmed delicacy of Ellena, the approbation thus implied, had no power to silence her own objections, and she would have regretted the mistaken zeal, which had contributed to lead her into the present distressing situation, had she revered the memory of her aunt, or loved Vivaldi, less. Still, however, the joy, which his presence had occasioned, and which the consciousness that he was still near her had prolonged, was not subdued, though it was frequently obscured, by such anxious considerations. With jealous and indiscreet solicitude, she now recollected every look, and the accent of every word, which had told that his affection was undiminished, thus seeking, with inconsistent zeal, for a conviction of the very tenderness, which but a moment before she had thought it would be prudent to lament, and almost necessary to renounce.

She awaited with extreme anxiety the appearance of Olivia, who might probably know the result of Vivaldi's conference with the abbess, and whether he was yet in the convent.

In the evening Olivia came, a messenger of evil; and Ellena, informed of the conduct of the abbess, and the consequent departure of Vivaldi, perceived all her courage, and all the half-formed resolutions, which a consideration of his family had suggested, faulter and expire. Sensible only of grief and despondency, she ascertained, for the first time, the extent of her affection and the severity of her situation. She perceived, also, that the injustice, which his family had exercised towards her, absolved her from all consideration of their displeasure, otherwise than as it might affect herself; but this was a conviction, which it were now probably useless to admit.

Olivia not only expressed the tenderest interest in her welfare, but seemed deeply affected with her situation; and, whether it was, that the nun's misfortunes bore some resemblance to Ellena's, or from whatever cause, it is remarkable that her eyes were often filled with tears, while she regarded her young friend, and she betrayed so much emotion that Ellena noticed it with surprise. She was, however, too delicate to hint any curiosity on the subject; and too much engaged by a nearer interest, to dwell long upon the circumstance.

When Olivia withdrew, Ellena retired to her turret, to soothe her spirits with a view of serene and majestic nature, a recourse which seldom failed to elevate her mind and soften the asperities of affliction. It was to her like sweet and solemn music, breathing peace over the soul—like the oaten stop of Milton's Spirit,

> Who with his soft pipe, and smooth-dittied song,
> Well knew to still the wild winds when they roar
> And hush the waving woods.

While she sat before a window, observing the evening light beaming up the valley, and touching all the distant mountains with misty purple, a reed as sweet, though not as fanciful, sounded from among the rocks below. The instrument and the character of the strain were such as she had been unaccustomed to hear within the walls of San Stefano, and the tone diffused over her spirits pleasing melancholy, that rapt all her attention. The liquid cadence, as it trembled and sunk away, seemed to tell the dejection of no vulgar feelings, and the exquisite taste, with which the complaining notes were again swelled, almost convinced her, that the musician was Vivaldi.

On looking from the lattice, she perceived a person perched on a point of the cliff below, whither it appeared almost impracticable for any human step to have climbed, and preserved from the precipice only by some dwarf shrubs that fringed the brow. The twilight did not permit her immediately to ascertain whether it was Vivaldi, and the situation was so dangerous that she hoped it was not he. Her doubts were removed, when, looking up, he perceived Ellena, and she heard his voice.

Vivaldi had learned from a lay-brother of the convent, whom Paulo had bribed, and who, when he worked in the garden, had sometimes seen Ellena at the window, that she frequented this remote turret; and, at the hazard of his life, he had now ventured thither, with a hope of conversing with her.

Ellena, alarmed at his tremendous situation, refused to listen to him, but he would not leave the spot till he had communicated a plan concerted for her escape, and, entreating that she would confide herself to his care, assured her she would be conducted wherever she judged proper. It appeared that the brother had consented to assist his views, in consideration of an ample reward, and to admit him within the walls on this evening, when, in his pilgrim's habit, he might have an opportunity of again seeing Ellena. He conjured her to attend, if possible, in the convent parlour during supper, explaining, in a few words, the motive for this request, and the substance of the following particulars:

The Lady-abbess, in observance of the custom upon high festivals, gave a collation to the *Padre-abate,* and such of the priests as had assisted at the vesper-service. A few strangers of distinction and pilgrims were also to partake of the entertainments of this night, among which was included a concert to be performed by the nuns. At the collation was to be displayed a profusion of delicacies, arranged by the sisters, who had been busy in preparing the pastry and confectionary during several days, and who excelled in these articles no less than in embroidery and other ingenious arts. This supper was to be given in the abbess's outer parlour, while she herself, attended by some nuns of high rank, and a few favourites, was to have a table in the inner apartment, where, separated only by the grate, she could partake of the conversation of the holy fathers. The tables were to be ornamented with artificial flowers, and a variety of other fanciful devices upon which the ingenuity of the sisters had been long employed, who prepared for these festivals with as much vanity, and expected them to dissipate the gloomy monotony of their usual life, with as much eagerness of delight, as a young beauty anticipates a first ball.

On this evening, therefore, every member of the convent would be engaged either by amusement or business, and to

Vivaldi, who had been careful to inform himself of these circumstances, it would be easy, with the assistance of the brother, to obtain admittance, and mingle himself among the spectators, disguised in his pilgrim's habit. He entreated, therefore, that Ellena would contrive to be in the abbess's apartment this evening, when he would endeavour to convey to her some further particulars of the plan of escape, and would have mules in waiting at the foot of the mountain, to conduct her to the villa Altieri, or to the neighbouring convent of the Santa della Pieta. Vivaldi secretly hoped that she might be prevailed with to give him her hand on quitting San Stefano, but he forbore to mention this hope, lest it should be mistaken for a condition, and that Ellena might be either reluctant to accept his assistance, or, accepting it, might consider herself bound to grant a hasty consent.

To his mention of escape she listened with varying emotion; at one moment attending to it with hope and joy, as promising her only chance of liberation from an imprisonment, which was probably intended to last for her life, and of restoring her to Vivaldi; and at another, recoiling from the thought of departing with him, while his family was so decidedly averse to their marriage. Thus, unable to form any instant resolution on the subject, and entreating that he would leave his dangerous station before the thickening twilight should encrease the hazard of his descent, Ellena added, that she would endeavour to obtain admittance to the apartment of the abbess, and to acquaint him with her final determination. Vivaldi understood all the delicacy of her scruples, and though they afflicted him, he honoured the good sense and just pride that suggested them.

He lingered on the rock till the last moments of departing light, and then, with a heart fluttering with hopes and fears, bade Ellena farwel, and descended; while she watched his progress through the silent gloom, faintly distinguishing him gliding along ledges of the precipice, and making his adventurous way from cliff to cliff, till the winding thickets concealed him from her view. Still anxious, she remained at the lattice, but he appeared no more; no voice announced disaster; and, at length, she returned to her cell, to deliberate on the subject of her departure.

Her considerations were interrupted by Olivia, whose manner indicated something extraordinary; the usual tranquillity of her countenance was gone, and an air of grief mingled with apprehension appeared there. Before she spoke, she examined the passage and looked round the cell. "It is as I feared," said she abruptly; "my suspicions are justified, and you, my child, are sacrificed, unless it were possible for you to quit the convent this night."

"What is it that you mean?" said the alarmed Ellena.

"I have just learned," resumed the nun, "that your conduct this morning, which is understood to have thrown a premeditated insult upon the abbess, is to be punished with what they *call* imprisonment; alas! why should I soften the truth,—with what I believe is death itself, for who ever returned alive from that hideous chamber!"

"With death!" said Ellena, aghast, "Oh, heavens! how have I deserved death?"

"That is not the question, my daughter, but how you may avoid it. Within the deepest recesses of our convent, is a stone chamber, secured by doors of iron, to which such of the sisterhood as have been guilty of any heinous offence have, from time to time, been consigned. This condemnation admits of no reprieve; the unfortunate captive is left to languish in chains and darkness, receiving only an allowance of bread and water just sufficient to prolong her sufferings, till nature, at length, sinking under their intolerable pressure, obtains refuge in death. Our records relate several instances of such horrible punishment, which has generally been inflicted upon nuns, who, weary of the life which they have chosen under the first delusions of the imagination, or which they have been compelled to accept by the rigour or avarice of parents, have been detected in escaping from the convent."

The nun paused, but Ellena remaining wrapt in silent thought, she resumed: "One miserable instance of this severity has occurred within my memory. I saw the wretched victim enter that apartment—never more to quit it alive! I saw, also, her poor remains laid at rest in the convent garden! During nearly two years she languished upon a bed of straw, denied even the poor consolation of conversing through the grate with such of the sisters as pitied her; and who of us was there that did not pity her! A severe punishment was threatened to those, who should approach with any compassionate intention; thank God! I incurred it, and I endured it, also, with secret triumph."

A gleam of satisfaction passed over Olivia's countenance

as she spoke this; it was the sweetest that Ellena had ever observed there. With a sympathetic emotion, she threw herself on the bosom of the nun, and wept; for some moments they were both silent. Olivia, at length said, "Do you not believe, my child, that the officious and offended abbess will readily seize upon the circumstance of your disobedience, as a pretence for confining you in that fatal chamber? The wishes of the Marchesa will thus surely be accomplished, without the difficulty of exacting your obedience to the vows. Alas! I have received proof too absolute of her intention, and that to-morrow is assigned as the day of your sacrifice; you may, perhaps, be thankful that the business of the festival has obliged her to defer executing the sentence even till to-morrow."

Ellena replied only with a groan, as her head still drooped upon the shoulder of the nun; she was not now hesitating whether to accept the assistance of Vivaldi, but desponding lest his utmost efforts for her deliverance should be vain.

Olivia, who mistook the cause of her silence, added, "Other hints I could give, which are strong as they are dreadful, but I will forbear. Tell me how it is possible I may assist you; I am willing to incur a second punishment, in endeavouring to relieve a second sufferer."

Ellena's tears flowed fast at this new instance of the nun's generosity. "But if they should discover you in assisting me to leave the convent," she said, in a voice convulsed by her gratitude,—"O! if they should discover you!"——

"I can ascertain the punishment," Olivia replied with firmness, "and do not fear to meet it."

"How nobly generous this is!" said the weeping Elena; "I ought not to suffer you to be thus careless of yourself!"

"My conduct is not wholly disinterested," the nun modestly replied; "for I think I could endure any punishment with more fortitude than the sickening anguish of beholding such suffering as I have witnessed. What are bodily pains in comparison with the subtle, the exquisite tortures of the mind! Heaven knows I can support my own afflictions, but not the view of those of others when they are excessive. The instruments of torture I believe I could endure, if my spirit was invigorated with the consciousness of a generous purpose; but pity touches upon a nerve that vibrates instantly to the heart, and subdues resistance. Yes, my child, the agony of pity is keener than any other, except that of remorse, and even in remorse, it is, perhaps, the mingling unavailing pity, that points the sting. But, while I am indulging this egotism, I am, perhaps, increasing your danger of the suffering I deprecate."

Ellena, thus encouraged by the generous sympathy of Olivia, mentioned Vivaldi's purposed visit of this evening; and consulted with her on the probability of procuring admittance for herself to the abbess's parlour. Reanimated by this intelligence, Olivia advised her to repair not only to the supper-room, but to attend the previous concert, to which several strangers would be admitted, among whom might probably be Vivaldi. When to this, Ellena objected her dread of the abbess's observation, and of the immediate seclusion that would follow, Olivia soothed her fears of discovery, by offering her the disguise of a nun's veil, and promising not only to conduct her to the apartment, but to afford her every possible assistance towards her escape.

"Among the crowd of nuns, who will attend in that spacious apartment," Olivia added, "it is improbable you would be distinguished, even if the sisters were less occupied by amusement, and the abbess were at leisure to scrutinize. As it is, you will hazard little danger of discovery; the Superior, if she thinks of you at all, will believe that you are still a prisoner in your cell, but this is an evening of too much importance to her vanity, for any consideration, distinct from that emotion, to divide her attention. Let hope, therefore, support you, my child, and do you prepare a few lines to acquaint Vivaldi with your consent to his proposal, and with the urgency of your circumstances; you may, perhaps, find an opportunity of conveying them through the grate."

They were still conversing on this subject, when a particular chime sounded, which Olivia said summoned the nuns to the concert-room; and she immediately hastened for a black veil, while Ellena wrote the few lines that were necessary for Vivaldi.

END OF THE FIRST VOLUME

VOLUME II

CHAPTER I

> That lawn conceals her beauty
> As the thin cloud, just silver'd by the rays,
> The trembling moon: think ye 'tis shrouded from
> The curious eye?

WRAPT in Olivia's veil, Ellena descended to the music-room, and mingled with the nuns, who were assembled within the grate. Among the monks and pilgrims without it, were some strangers in the usual dress of the country, but she did not perceive any person who resembled Vivaldi; and she considered, that, if he were present, he would not venture to discover himself, while her nun's veil concealed her as effectually from him as from the lady Abbess. It would be necessary, therefore, to seek an opportunity of withdrawing it for a moment at the grate, an expedient, which must certainly expose her to the notice of strangers.

On the entrance of the lady Abbess, Ellena's fear of observation rendered her insensible to every other consideration; she fancied, that the eyes of the Superior were particularly directed upon herself. The veil seemed an insufficient protection from their penetrating glances, and she almost sunk with the terror of instant discovery.

The Abbess, however, passed on, and, having conversed for a few moments with the *padre Abate* and some visitors of distinction, took her chair; and the performance immediately opened with one of those solemn and impressive airs, which the Italian nuns know how to give with so much taste and sweetness. It rescued even Ellena for a moment from a sense of danger, and she resigned herself to the surrounding scene, of which the *coup-d'œil* was striking and grand. In a vaulted apartment of considerable extent, lighted by innumerable tapers, and where even the ornaments, though pompous, partook of the solemn character of the institution, were assembled about fifty nuns, who, in the interesting habit of their order, appeared with graceful plainness. The delicacy of their air, and their beauty, softened by the lawn that thinly veiled it, were contrasted by the severe majesty of the lady Abbess, who, seated on an elevated chair, apart from the audience, seemed the Empress of the scene, and by the venerable figures of the father *Abate* and his attendant monks, who were arranged without that screen of wire-work, extending the whole breadth of the apartment, which is called the grate. Near the holy father were placed the strangers of distinction, dressed in the splendid Neapolitan habit, whose gay colouring and airy elegance opposed well with the dark drapery of the ecclesiastics; their plumed hats loftily overtopping the half-cowled heads and grey locks of the monks. Nor was the contrast of countenances less striking; the grave, the austere, the solemn, and the gloomy, intermingling with the light, the blooming, and the debonaire, expressed all the various tempers, that render life a blessing or a burden, and, as with the spell of magic, transform this world into a transient paradise or purgatory. In the back ground of the picture stood some pilgrims, with looks less joyous and more demure than they had worn on the road the preceding day; and among them were some inferior brothers and attendants of the convent. To this part of the chamber Ellena frequently directed her attention, but did not distinguish Vivaldi; and, though she had taken a station near the grate, she had not courage indecorously to withdraw her veil before so many strangers. And thus, if he even were in the apartment, it was not probable he would venture to come forward.

The concert concluded without his having been discovered by Ellena; and she withdrew to the apartment, where the collation was spread, and where the Abbess and her guests soon after appeared. Presently, she observed a stranger, in a pilgrim's habit, station himself near the grate; his face was partly muffled in his cloak, and he seemed to be a spectator rather than a partaker of the feast.

Ellena, who understood this to be Vivaldi, was watchful for an opportunity of approaching, unseen by the Abbess, the place where he had fixed himself. Engaged in conversation with the ladies around her, the Superior soon favoured Ellena's wish, who, having reached the grate, ventured to lift her veil for one instant. The stranger, letting his cloak fall, thanked her with his eyes for her condescension, and she perceived, that he was not Vivaldi! Shocked at the interpretation, which might be given to a conduct apparently so improper, as much as by the disappointment, which Vivaldi's absence occasioned, she was hastily retiring, when another stranger approached with quick steps, whom she instantly knew, by the grace and spirit of his air, to be Vivaldi; but, determined not to expose herself a second time to the possibility of a mistake, she awaited for some further signal of his identity, before she discovered herself. His eyes were fixed upon her in earnest attention for some moments, before he drew aside the cloak from his face. But he soon did so;—and it was Vivaldi himself.

Ellena, perceiving that she was known, did not raise her veil, but advanced a few steps towards the grate. Vivaldi there deposited a small folded paper, and before she could venture to deliver her own billet, he had retired among the crowd. As she stepped forward to secure his letter, she observed a nun hastily approach the spot where he had laid it, and she paused. The garment of the Recluse wafted it from the place where it had been partly concealed; and when Ellena perceived the nun's foot rest upon the paper, she with difficulty disguised her apprehensions.

A friar, who from without the grate addressed the sister, seemed with much earnestness, yet with a certain air of secresy, communicating some important intelligence. The fears of Ellena suggested that he had observed the action of Vivaldi, and was making known his suspicions; and she expected, every instant, to see the nun lift up the paper, and deliver it to the Abbess.

From this immediate apprehension, however, she was released when the sister pushed it gently aside, without examination, a circumstance that not less surprized than relieved her. But, when the conference broke up, and the friar, hastily retreating among the crowd, disappeared from the apartment, and the nun approached and whispered to the Superior, all her terrors were renewed. She scarcely doubted, that Vivaldi was detected, and that his letter was designedly left where it had been deposited, for the purpose of alluring her to betray herself. Trembling, dismayed, and almost sinking with apprehension, she watched the countenance of the Abbess, while the nun addressed her, and thought she read her own fate in the frown that appeared there.

Whatever might be the intentions or the directions of the Superior, no active measure was at present employed; the Recluse, having received an answer, retired quietly among the sisters, and the Abbess resumed her usual manner. Ellena, however, supposing she was now observed, did not dare to seize the paper, though she believed it contained momentous information, and feared that the time was now escaping, which might facilitate her deliverance. Whenever she ventured to look round, the eyes of the Abbess seemed pointed upon her, and she judged from the position of the nun, for the veil concealed her face, that she also was vigilantly regarding her.

Above an hour had elapsed in this state of anxious suspense, when the collation concluded, and the assembly broke up; during the general bustle of which, Ellena ventured to the grate, and secured the paper. As she concealed it in her robe, she scarcely dared to enquire by a hasty glance whether she had been observed, and would have withdrawn immediately to examine the contents, had she not perceived, at the same instant, the Abbess quitting the apartment. On looking round for the nun, Ellena discovered that she was gone.

Ellena followed distantly in the Abbess's train; and, as she drew nearer to Olivia, gave a signal, and passed on to her cell. There, once more alone, and having secured the door, she sat down to read Vivaldi's billet, trying to command her impatience, and to understand the lines, over which her sight rapidly moved, when in the eagerness of turning over the paper, the lamp dropt from her trembling hand and expired. Her distress now nearly reached despair. To go forth into the convent for a light was utterly impracticable, since it would betray that she was no longer a prisoner, and not only would Olivia suffer from a discovery of the indulgence she had granted, but she herself would be immediately confined. Her only hope rested upon Olivia's arrival before it might be too late to practice the instructions of Vivaldi, if, indeed, they were still practicable; and she listened with intense solicitude for an approaching footstep, while she yet held, ignorant of its contents, the billet, that probably would decide her fate. A thousand times she turned about the eventful paper, endeavoured to trace the lines with her fingers, and to guess their import, thus enveloped in mystery; while she experienced all the various torture that the consciousness of having in her very hand the information, on a timely knowledge of which her life, perhaps, depended, without being able to understand it, could inflict.

Presently she heard advancing steps, and a light gleamed from the passage before she considered they might be some other than Olivia's; and that it was prudent to conceal the billet she held. The consideration, however, came too late to be acted upon; for, before the rustling paper was disposed of, a person entered the cell, and Ellena beheld her friend. Pale, trembling, and silent, she took the lamp from the nun, and, eagerly running over Vivaldi's note, learned, that at the time it was written, brother Jeronimo was in waiting without the gate of the nun's garden, where Vivaldi designed to join him immediately, and conduct her by a private way beyond the walls. He added, that horses were stationed at the foot of the mountain, to convey her wherever she should judge proper; and conjured her to be expeditious, since other circumstances, besides the universal engagement of the Recluses, were at that moment particularly favourable to an escape.

Ellena, desponding and appalled, gave the paper to Olivia, requesting she would read it hastily, and advise her how to act. It was now an hour and a half since Vivaldi had said, that success depended upon expedition, and that he had probably watched at the appointed place; in such an interval, how many circumstances might have occurred to destroy every possibility of a retreat, which it was certain the engagement of the Abbess and the sisters no longer favoured!

The generous Olivia, having read the billet, partook of all her young friend's distress, and was as willing, as Ellena was anxious, to dare every danger for the chance of obtaining deliverance.

Ellena could feel gratitude for such goodness even at this moment of agonizing apprehension. After a pause of deep consideration, Olivia said, "In every avenue of the convent we are now liable to meet some of the nuns; but my veil, though thin, has hitherto protected you, and we must hope it may still assist your purpose. It will be necessary, however, to pass through the refectory, where such of the sisters as did not partake of the collation, are assembled at supper, and will remain so, till the first mattin calls them to the chapel. If we wait till then, I fear it will be to no purpose to go at all."

Ellena's fears perfectly agreed with those of Olivia; and entreating that another moment might not be lost in hesitation, and that she would lead the way to the nun's garden, they quitted the cell together.

Several of the sisters passed them, as they descended to the refectory, but without particularly noticing Ellena; who, as she drew near that alarming apartment, wrapt her veil closer, and leaned with heavier pressure upon the arm of her faithful friend. At the door they were met by the Abbess, who had been overlooking the nuns assembled at supper, and missing Olivia had enquired for her. Ellena shrunk back to elude observation, and to let the Superior pass; but Olivia was obliged to answer to the summons. Having, however, unveiled herself, she was permitted to proceed; and Ellena, who had mingled with the crowd that surrounded the Abbess, and thus escaped detection, followed Olivia with faltering steps, through the refectory. The nuns were luckily too much engaged by the entertainment, at this moment, to look round them, and the fugitive reached, unsuspected, an opposite door.

In the hall, to which they descended, the adventurers were frequently crossed by servants bearing dishes from the refectory to the kitchen; and, at the very moment when they were opening the door, that led into the garden, a sister, who had observed them, demanded whether they had yet heard the mattin-bell, since they were going towards the chapel.

Terrified at this critical interruption, Ellena pressed Olivia's arm, in signal of silence, and was hastening forward, when the latter, more prudent, paused, and calmly answering the question, was then suffered to proceed.

As they crossed the garden towards the gate, Ellena's anxiety lest Vivaldi should have been compelled to leave it, encreased so much, that she had scarcely power to proceed. "O if my strength should fail before I reach it!" she said softly to Olivia, "or if I should reach it too late!"

Olivia tried to cheer her, and pointed out the gate, on which the moonlight fell; "At the end of this walk only," said Olivia, "see!—where the shadows of the trees open, is our goal."

Encouraged by the view of it, Ellena fled with lighter steps along the alley; but the gate seemed to mock her approach, and to retreat before her. Fatigue overtook her in this long alley, before she could overtake the spot so anxiously sought, and, breathless and exhausted, she was once more compelled to stop, and once more in the agony of terror exclaimed—"O, if my strength should fail before I reach it!—O, if I should drop even while it is within my view."

The pause of a moment enabled her to proceed, and she stopped not again till she arrived at the gate; when Olivia suggested the prudence of ascertaining who was without, and of receiving an answer to the signal, which Vivaldi had proposed, before they ventured to make themselves known. She then struck upon the wood, and, in the anxious pause that followed, whispering voices were distinctly heard from without, but no signal spoke in reply to the nun's.

"We are betrayed!" said Ellena softly, "but I will know the worst at once;" and she repeated the signal, when, to her unspeakable joy, it was answered by three smart raps upon the gate. Olivia, more distrustful, would have checked the sudden hope of her friend, till some further proof had appeared, that it was Vivaldi who waited without, but her precaution came too late; a key already grated in the lock; the door opened, and two persons muffled in their garments appeared at it. Ellena was hastily retreating, when a well-known voice recalled her, and she perceived, by the rays of a half-hooded lamp, which Jeronimo held, Vivaldi.

"O heavens!" he exclaimed, in a voice tremulous with joy, as he took her hand, "is it possible that you are again my own! If you could but know what I have suffered during this last hour!"—Then observing Olivia, he drew back, till Ellena expressed her deep sense of obligation to the nun.

"We have no time to lose," said Jeronimo sullenly; "we have stayed too long already, as you will find, perhaps."

"Farewel, dear Ellena!" said Olivia, "may the protection of heaven never leave you!"

The fears of Ellena now gave way to affectionate sorrow, as, weeping on the bosom of the nun, she said "farewell! O farewel, my dear, my tender friend! I must never, never see you more, but I shall always love you; and you have promised, that I shall hear from you; remember the convent della Pieta!"

"You should have settled this matter within," said Jeronimo, "we have been here these two hours already."

"Ah Ellena!" said Vivaldi, as he gently disengaged her from the nun, "do I then hold only the second place in your heart?"

Ellena, as she dismissed her tears, replied with a smile more eloquent than words; and when she had again and again bade adieu to Olivia, she gave him her hand, and quitted the gate.

"It is moonlight," observed Vivaldi to Jeronimo, "your lamp is useless, and may betray us."

"It will be necessary in the church," replied Jeronimo, "and in some circuitous avenues we must pass, for I dare not lead you out through the great gates, Signor, as you well know."

"Lead on, then," replied Vivaldi, and they reached one of the cypress walks, that extended to the church; but, before they entered it, Ellena paused and looked back to the garden gate, that she might see Olivia once again. The nun was still there, and Ellena perceived her faintly in the moonlight, waving her hand in signal of a last adieu. Ellena's heart was full; she wept, and lingered, and returned the signal, till the gentle violence of Vivaldi withdrew her from the spot.

"I envy your friend those tears," said he, "and feel jealous of the tenderness that excites them. Weep no more, my Ellena."

"If you knew her worth," replied Ellena, "and the obligations I owe her!"—Her voice was lost in sighs, and Vivaldi only pressed her hand in silence.

As they traversed the gloomy walk, that led to the church, Vivaldi said, "Are you certain, father, that not any of the brothers are doing penance at the shrines in our way?"

"Doing penance on a festival, Signor! they are more likely, by this time, to be taking down the ornaments."

"That would be equally unfortunate for us," said Vivaldi; "cannot we avoid the church, father?"

Jeronimo assured him, that this was impossible; and they immediately entered one of its lonely aisles, where he unhooded the lamp, for the tapers, which had given splendour, at an earlier hour, to the numerous shrines, had expired, except those at the high altar, which were so remote, that their rays faded into twilight long before they reached the part of the church where the fugitives passed. Here and there, indeed, a dying lamp shot a tremulous gleam upon the shrine below, and vanished again, serving to mark the distances in the long perspective of arches, rather than to enlighten the gloomy solitude; but no sound, not even of a whisper, stole along the pavement.

They crossed to a side door communicating with the court, and with the rock, which enshrined the image of *our Lady of Mount Carmel*. There, the sudden glare of tapers issuing from the cave, alarmed the fugitives, who had begun to retreat, when Jeronimo, stepping forward to examine the place, assured them, there was no symptom of any person being within, and that lights burned day and night around the shrine.

Revived by this explanation, they followed into the cave, where their conductor opened a part of the wire-work enclosing the saint, and led them to the extremity of the vault, sunk deep within which appeared a small door. While Ellena trembled with apprehension, Jeronimo applied a key, and they perceived, beyond the door, a narrow passage winding away into the rock. The monk was leading on, but Vivaldi, who had the suspicions of Ellena, paused at the entrance, and demanded whither he was conducting them.

"To the place of your *destination*," replied the brother, in a hollow voice; an answer which alarmed Ellena, and did not satisfy Vivaldi. "I have given myself to your guidance," he said, "and have confided to you what is dearer to me than existence. Your life," pointing to the short sword concealed beneath his pilgrim's vest, "your life, you may rely upon my word, shall answer for your treachery. If your purpose is evil, pause a moment, and repent, or you shall not quit this passage alive."

"Do you menace me!" replied the brother, his countenance darkening. "Of what service would be my death to you? Do you not know that every brother in the convent would rise to avenge it?"

"I know only that I will make sure of one traitor, if there be one," said Vivaldi, "and defend this lady against your host of monks; and, since you also know this, proceed accordingly."

At this instant it occurring to Ellena, that the passage in question probably led to the prison-chamber, which Olivia had described as situated within some deep recess of the convent, and that Jeronimo had certainly betrayed them, she refused to go further. "If your purpose is honest," said she, "why do you not conduct us through some direct gate of the convent; why are we brought into these subterraneous labyrinths?"

"There is no direct gate but that of the portal," Jeronimo

replied, "and this is the only other avenue leading beyond the walls." "And why can we not go out through the portal?" Vivaldi asked.

"Because it is beset with pilgrims, and lay brothers," replied Jeronimo, "and though you might pass them safely enough, what is to become of the lady? But all this you knew before, Signor; and was willing enough to trust me, then. The passage we are entering opens upon the cliffs, at some distance. I have run hazard enough already, and will waste no more time; so if you do not chuse to go forward, I will leave you, and you may act as you please."

He concluded with a laugh of derision, and was re-locking the door, when Vivaldi, alarmed for the probable consequence of his resentment, and somewhat re-assured by the indifference he discovered as to their pursuing the avenue or not, endeavoured to appease him, as well as to encourage Ellena; and he succeeded in both.

As he followed in silence through the gloomy passage, his doubts were, however, not so wholly vanquished, but that he was prepared for attack, and while he supported Ellena with one hand, he held his sword in the other.

The avenue was of considerable length, and before they reached its extremity, they heard music from a distance, winding along the rocks. "Hark!" cried Ellena, "Whence come those sounds? Listen!"

"From the cave we have left," replied Jeronimo, "and it is midnight by that; it is the last chaunt of the pilgrims at the shrine of our Lady. Make haste, Signor, I shall be called for."

The fugitives now perceived, that all retreat was cut off, and that, if they had lingered only a few moments longer in the cave, they should have been surprized by those devotees, some one of whom, however, it appeared possible might wander into this avenue, and still interrupt their escape. When Vivaldi told his apprehensions, Jeronimo, with an arch sneer, affirmed there was no danger of that, "for the passage," he added, "is known only to the brothers of the convent."

Vivaldi's doubts vanished when he further understood, that the avenue led only from the cliffs without to the cave, and was used for the purpose of conveying secretly to the shrine, such articles as were judged necessary to excite the superstitious wonder of the devotees.

While he proceeded in thoughtful silence, a distant chime sounded hollowly through the chambers of the rock. "The mattin-bell strikes!" said Jeronimo, in seeming alarm, "I am summoned. Signora quicken your steps;" an unnecessary request for Ellena already passed with her utmost speed; and she now rejoiced on perceiving a door in the remote winding of the passage, which she believed would emancipate her from the convent. But, as she advanced, the avenue appeared extending beyond it; and the door, which stood a little open allowed her a glimpse of a chamber in the cliff, duskily lighted.

Vivaldi, alarmed by the light, enquired, when he had passed, whether any person was in the chamber, and received an equivocal answer from Jeronimo, who, however, soon after pointed to an arched gate that terminated the avenue. They proceeded with lighter steps, for hope now cheared their hearts, and, on reaching the gate, all apprehension vanished. Jeronimo gave the lamp to Vivaldi, while he began to unbar and unlock the door, and Vivaldi had prepared to reward the brother for his fidelity, before they perceived that the door refused to yield. A dreadful imagination seized on Vivaldi. Jeronimo turning round, coolly said, "I fear we are betrayed; the second lock is shot! I have only the key of the first."

"We *are* betrayed," said Vivaldi, in a resolute tone, "but do not suppose that your dissimulation conceals you. I understand by whom we are betrayed. Recollect my late assertion, and consider once more, whether it is your interest to intercept us."

"My Signor," replied Jeronimo, "I do not deceive you when I protest by our holy Saint, that I have not caused this gate to be fastened, and that I would open it if I could. The lock, which holds it, was not shot an hour ago. I am the more surprized at what has happened, because this place is seldom passed, even by the holiest footstep; and I fear, whoever has passed now, has been led hither by suspicion, and comes to intercept your flight."

"Your wily explanation, brother, may serve you for an inferior occasion, but not on this," replied Vivaldi, "either, therefore, unclose the gate, or prepare for the worst. You are not now to learn, that, however slightly I may estimate my own life, I will never abandon this lady to the horrors, which your community have already prepared for her."

Ellena, summoning her fleeting spirits, endeavoured to calm the indignation of Vivaldi, and to prevent the consequence of his suspicions, as well as to prevail with Jeronimo, to unfasten the gate. Her efforts were, however, followed by a long altercation; but, at length, the art or the innocence of the brother, appeased Vivaldi, who now endeavoured to force the gate, while Jeronimo in vain represented its strength, and the certain ruin, that must fall upon himself, if it should be discovered he had concurred in destroying it.

The gate was immoveable; but, as no other chance of escaping appeared, Vivaldi was not easily prevailed with to desist; all possibility of retreating too was gone, since the church and the cave were now crowded with devotees, attending the mattin service.

Jeronimo, however, seemingly did not despair of effecting their release, but he acknowledged that they would probably be compelled to remain concealed in this gloomy avenue all night, and perhaps the next day. At length, it was agreed, that he should return to the church, to examine whether a possibility remained of the fugitives passing unobserved to the great portal; and, having conducted them back to the chamber, of which they had taken a passing glimpse, he proceeded to the shrine.

For a considerable time after his departure, they were not without hope; but, their confidence diminishing as his delay encreased, their uncertainty at length became terrible; and it was only for the sake of Vivaldi, from whom she scrupulously concealed all knowledge of the particular fate, which she was aware must await her in the convent, that Ellena appeared to endure it with calmness. Notwithstanding the plausibility of Jeronimo, suspicion of his treachery returned upon her mind. The cold and earthy air of this chamber was like that of a sepulchre; and when she looked round, it appeared exactly to correspond with the description given by Olivia of the prison where the nun had languished and expired. It was walled and vaulted with the rock, had only one small grated aperture in the roof to admit air, and contained no furniture, except one table, a bench, and the lamp, which dimly shewed the apartment. That a lamp should be found burning in a place so remote and solitary, amazed her still more when she recollected the assertion of Jeronimo,—that even holy steps seldom passed this way; and when she considered also, that he had expressed no surprize at a circumstance, according to his own assertion, so unusual. Again it appeared, that she had been betrayed into the very prison, designed for her by the Abbess; and the horror, occasioned by this supposition, was so great, that she was on the point of disclosing it to Vivaldi, but an apprehension of the distraction, into which his desperate courage might precipitate him, restrained her.

While these considerations occupied Ellena, and it appeared that any certainty would be less painful than this suspense, she frequently looked round the chamber in search of some object, which might contradict or confirm her suspicion, that this was the death-room of the unfortunate nun. No such circumstance appeared, but as her eyes glanced, with almost phrenzied eagerness, she perceived something shadowy in a remote corner of the floor; and on approaching, discovered what seemed a dreadful hieroglyphic, a mattress of straw, in which she thought she beheld the death-bed of the miserable recluse; nay more, that the impression it still retained, was that which her form had left there.

While Vivaldi was yet entreating her to explain the occasion of the horror she betrayed, the attention of each was withdrawn by a hollow sigh, that rose near them. Ellena caught unconsciously the arm of Vivaldi, and listened, aghast, for a return of the sound, but all remained still.

"It surely was not fancied!" said Vivaldi, after a long pause, "you heard it also?"

"I did!" replied Ellena.

"It was a sigh, was it not?" he added.

"O yes, and such a sigh!"

"Some person is concealed near us," observed Vivaldi, looking round; "but be not alarmed, Ellena, I have a sword."

"A sword! alas! you know not—— But hark! there, again!"

"That was very near us!" said Vivaldi. "This lamp burns so sickly!"——and he held it high, endeavouring to penetrate the furthest gloom of the chamber. "Hah! who goes there?" he cried, and stepped suddenly forward; but no person appeared, and a silence as of the tomb, returned.

"If you are in sorrow, speak!" Vivaldi, at length, said; "from fellow-sufferers you will meet with sympathy. If your designs are evil—tremble, for you shall find I am desperate."

Still no answer was returned, and he carried forward the lamp to the opposite end of the chamber, where he perceived a small door in the rock. At the same instant he heard from within, a low tremulous sound, as of a person in prayer, or in agony. He pressed against the door, which, to his surprize, yielded immediately, and discovered a figure kneeling before a crucifix, with an attention so wholly engaged, as not to observe the presence of a stranger, till Vivaldi spoke. The person then rose from his knees, and turning, shewed the silvered temples and pale features of an aged monk. The mild and sorrowful character of the countenance, and the lambent lustre of eyes, which seemed still to retain somewhat of the fire of genius, interested Vivaldi, and encouraged Ellena, who had followed him.

An unaffected surprize appeared in the air of the monk; but Vivaldi, notwithstanding the interesting benignity of his countenance, feared to answer his enquiries, till the father hinted to him, that an explanation was necessary, even to his own safety. Encouraged by his manner, rather than intimidated by this hint, and perceiving, that his situation was desperate, Vivaldi confided to the friar some partial knowledge of his embarrassment.

While he spoke, the father listened with deep attention, looked with compassion alternately upon him and Ellena; and some harassing objection seemed to contend with the pity, which urged him to assist the strangers. He enquired how long Jeronimo had been absent, and shook his head significantly when he learned that the gate of the avenue was fastened by a double lock. "You are betrayed, my children," said he, "you have trusted with the simplicity of youth, and the cunning of age has deceived you."

The terrible conviction affected Ellena to tears; and Vivaldi, scarcely able to command the indignation which a view of such treachery excited, was unable to offer her any consolation.

"You, my daughter, I remember to have seen in the church this morning," observed the friar; "I remember too, that you protested against the vows you were brought thither to seal. Alas! my child, was you aware of the consequence of such a proceeding?"

"I had only a choice of evils," Ellena replied.

"Holy father," said Vivaldi, "I will not believe, that you are one of those who either assisted in or approved the persecution of innocence. If you were acquainted with the misfortunes of this lady, you would pity, and save her; but there is now no time for detail; and I can only conjure you, by every sacred consideration, to assist her to leave the convent! If there were leisure to inform you of the unjustifiable means, which have been employed to bring her within these walls—if you knew that she was taken, an orphan, from her home at midnight—that armed ruffians brought her hither—and at the command of strangers—that she has not a single relation surviving to assert her right of independence, or reclaim her of her persecutors.—— O! holy father, if you knew all this!"——Vivaldi was unable to proceed.

The friar again regarded Ellena with compassion, but still in thoughtful silence. "All this may be very true," at length he said, "but"——and he hesitated.

"I understand you, father," said Vivaldi—"you require proof; but how can proof be adduced here? You must rely upon the honour of my word. And, if you are inclined to assist us, it must be immediately!—while you hesitate, we are lost. Even now I think I hear the footsteps of Jeronimo."

He stepped softly to the door of the chamber, but all was yet still. The friar, too, listened, but he also deliberated; while Ellena, with clasped hands and a look of eager supplication and terror, awaited his decision.

"No one is approaching," said Vivaldi, "it is not yet too late!— Good father! if you would serve us, dispatch."

"Poor innocent!" said the friar, half to himself, "in this chamber—in this fatal place!"—

"In this chamber!" exclaimed Ellena, anticipating his meaning. "It was in this chamber, then, that a nun was suffered to perish! and I, no doubt, am conducted hither to undergo a similar fate!"

"In this chamber!" re-echoed Vivaldi, in a voice of desperation. "Holy father, if you are indeed disposed to assist us, let us act this instant; the next, perhaps, may render your best intentions unavailing!"

The friar, who had regarded Ellena while she mentioned the nun, with the utmost surprize, now withdrew his attention; a few tears fell on his cheek, but he hastily dried them, and seemed struggling to overcome some grief, that was deep in his heart.

Vivaldi, finding that entreaty had no power to hasten his decision, and expecting every moment to hear the approach

of Jeronimo, paced the chamber in agonizing perturbation,
now pausing at the door to listen, and then calling, though
almost hopelessly, upon the humanity of the friar. While
Ellena, looking round the room in shuddering horror, repeatedly exclaimed, "On this very spot! in this very chamber! O
what sufferings have these walls witnessed! what are they
yet to witness!"

Vivaldi now endeavoured to soothe the spirits of Ellena,
and again urged the friar to employ this critical moment in
saving her; "O heaven!" said he, "if she is now discovered,
her fate is certain!"

"I dare not say what that fate would be," interrupted the
father, "or what my own, should I consent to assist you; but,
though I am old, I have not quite forgotten to feel for others!
They may oppress the few remaining years of my age, but
the blooming days of youth should flourish; and they shall
flourish, my children, if my power can aid you. Follow me
to the gate; we will see whether my key cannot unfasten all
the locks that hold it."

Vivaldi and Ellena immediately followed the feeble steps
of the old man, who frequently stopped to listen whether
Jeronimo, or any of the brothers, to whom the latter might
have betrayed Ellena's situation, were approaching; but not
an echo wandered along the lonely avenue, till they reached
the gate, when distant footsteps beat upon the ground.

"They are approaching, father!" whispered Ellena. "O, if
the key should not open these locks instantly, we are lost!
Hark! now I hear their voices—they call upon my name! Already they have discovered we have left the chamber."

While the friar, with trembling hands, applied the key,
Vivaldi endeavoured at once to assist him, and to encourage
Ellena.

The locks gave way, and the gate opened at once upon the
moonlight mountains. Ellena heard once more, with the joy
of liberty, the midnight breeze passing among the pensile
branches of the palms, that loftily overshadowed a rude platform before the gate, and rustling with fainter sound among
the pendent shrubs of the surrounding cliffs.

"There is no leisure for thanks, my children," said the
friar, observing they were about to speak. "I will fasten the
gate, and endeavour to delay your pursuers, that you may
have time to escape. My blessing go with you!"

Ellena and Vivaldi had scarcely a moment to bid him

"farewel!" before he closed the door, and Vivaldi, taking her arm, was hastening towards the place where he had ordered Paulo to wait with the horses, when, on turning an angle of the convent wall, they perceived a long train of pilgrims issuing forth from the portal, at a little distance.

Vivaldi drew back; yet dreading every moment, that he lingered near the monastery, to hear the voice of Jeronimo, or other persons, from the avenue, he was sometimes inclined to proceed at any hazard. The only practicable path leading to the base of the mountain, however, was now occupied by these devotees, and to mingle with them was little less than certain destruction. A bright moonlight shewed distinctly every figure, that moved in the scene, and the fugitives kept within the shadow of the walls, till, warned by an approaching footstep, they crossed to the feet of the cliffs that rose beyond some palmy hillocks on the right, whose dusky recesses promised a temporary shelter. As they passed with silent steps along the winding rocks, the tranquillity of the landscape below afforded an affecting contrast with the tumult and alarm of their minds.

Being now at some distance from the monastery, they rested under the shade of the cliffs, till the procession of devotees, which were traced descending among the thickets and hollows of the mountain, should be sufficiently remote. Often they looked back to the convent, expecting to see lights issue from the avenue, or the portal; and attended in mute anxiety for the sullen murmurs of pursuit; but none came on the breeze; nor did any gleaming lamp betray the steps of a spy.

Released, at length, from immediate apprehension, Ellena listened to the mattin-hymn of the pilgrims, as it came upon the still air and ascended towards the cloudless heavens. Not a sound mingled with the holy strain, and even in the measured pause of voices only the trembling of the foliage above was distinguished. The responses, as they softened away in distance, and swelled again on the wafting breeze, appeared like the music of spirits, watching by night upon the summits of the mountains, and answering each other in celestial airs, as they walk their high boundary, and overlook the sleeping world.

"How often, Ellena, at this hour," said Vivaldi, "have I lingered round your dwelling, consoled by the consciousness of being near you! Within those walls, I have said, she reposes; they enclose my world, all without is to me a desert. Now, I am in your presence! O Ellena! now that you are once more restored to me, suffer not the caprice of possibility again to separate us! Let me lead you to the first altar that will confirm our vows."

Vivaldi forgot, in the anxiety of a stronger interest, the delicate silence he had resolved to impose upon himself, till Ellena should be in a place of safety.

"This is not a moment," she replied, with hesitation, "for conversation; our situation is yet perilous, we tremble on the very brink of danger."

Vivaldi immediately rose; "Into what imminent danger," said he, "had my selfish folly nearly precipitated you! We are lingering in this alarming neighbourhood, when that feeble strain indicates the pilgrims to be sufficiently remote to permit us to proceed!"

As he spoke, they descended cautiously among the cliffs, often looking back to the convent, where, however, no light appeared, except what the moon shed over the spires and tall windows of its cathedral. For a moment, Ellena fancied she saw a taper in her favourite turret, and a belief, that the nuns, perhaps the Abbess herself, were searching for her there, renewed her terror and her speed. But the rays were only those of the moon, striking through opposite casements of the chamber; and the fugitives reached the base of the mountain without further alarm, where Paulo appeared with horses. "Ah! Signormio," said the servant, "I am glad to see you alive and merry; I began to fear, by the length of your stay, that the monks had clapped you up to do penance for life. How glad I am to see you, *Maestro!*"

"Not more so than I am to see you, good Paulo. But where is the pilgrim's cloak I bade you provide?"

Paulo displayed it, and Vivaldi, having wrapt it round Ellena, and placed her on horseback, they took the road towards Naples, Ellena designing to take refuge in the convent della Pieta. Vivaldi, however, apprehending that their enemies would seek them on this road, proposed leaving it as soon as practicable, and reaching the neighbourhood of villa Altieri by a circuitous way.

They soon after arrived at the tremendous pass, through which Ellena had approached the monastery, and whose horrors were considerably heightened at this dusky hour, for the moonlight fell only partially upon the deep barriers of the gorge, and frequently the precipice, with the road on its brow, was entirely shadowed by other cliffs and woody points that rose above it. But Paulo, whose spirits seldom owned the influence of local scenery, jogged merrily along, frequently congratulating himself and his master on their escape, and carolling briskly to the echoes of the rocks, till Vivaldi, apprehensive for the consequence of this loud gaiety, desired him to desist.

"Ah Signormio! I must obey you," said he, "but my heart was never so full in my life; and I would fain sing, to unburden it of some of this joy. That scrape we got into in the dungeon there, at what's the name of the place? was bad enough, but it was nothing to this, because here I was left out of it; and you, *Maestro*, might have been murdered again and again, while I, thinking of nothing at all, was quietly airing myself on the mountain by moonlight.

"But what is that yonder in the sky, Signor? It looks for all the world like a bridge; only it is perched so high, that nobody would think of building one in such an out-of-the-way place, unless to cross from cloud to cloud, much less would take the trouble of clambering up after it, for the pleasure of going over."

Vivaldi looked forward, and Ellena perceived the Alpine bridge, she had formerly crossed with so much alarm, in the moonlight perspective, airily suspended between tremendous cliffs, with the river far below, tumbling down the rocky chasm. One of the supporting cliffs, with part of the bridge, was in deep shade, but the other, feathered with foliage, and the rising surges at its foot, were strongly illumined; and many a thicket wet with the spray, sparkled in contrast to the dark rock it overhung. Beyond the arch, the long-drawn prospect faded into misty light.

"Well, to be sure!" exclaimed Paulo, "to see what curiosity will do! If there are not some people have found their way up to the bridge already."

Vivaldi now perceived figures upon the slender arch, and, as their indistinct forms glided in the moonshine, other emotions than those of wonder disturbed him, lest these might be pilgrims going to the shrine of our Lady, and who would give information of his route. No possibility, however, appeared of avoiding them, for the precipices that rose immediately above, and fell below, forbade all excursion, and the road itself was so narrow, as scarcely to admit of two horses passing each other.

"They are all off the bridge now, and without having broken their necks, perhaps!" said Paulo, "where, I wonder, will they go next! Why surely, Signor, this road does not lead to the bridge yonder; we are not going to pick our way in the air too? The roar of those waters has made my head dizzy already; and the rocks here are as dark as midnight, and seem ready to tumble upon one; they are enough to make one despair to look at them; you need not have checked my mirth, Signor."

"I would fain check your loquacity," replied Vivaldi. "Do, good Paulo, be silent and circumspect, those people may be near us, though we do not yet see them."

"The road does lead to the bridge, then, Signor!" said Paulo dolourously. "And see! there they are again; winding round that rock, and coming towards us."

"Hush! they are pilgrims," whispered Vivaldi, "we will linger under the shade of these rocks, while they pass. Remember, Paulo, that a single indiscreet word may be fatal; and that if they hail us, I alone am to answer."

"You are obeyed, Signor."

The fugitives drew up close under the cliffs, and proceeded slowly, while the words of the devotees, as they advanced, became audible.

"It gives one some comfort," said Paulo, "to hear cheerful voices, in such a place as this. Bless their merry hearts! theirs seems a pilgrimage of pleasure; but they will be demure enough, I warrant, by and bye. I wish I"——

"Paulo! have you so soon forgot?" said Vivaldi sharply.

The devotees, on perceiving the travellers, became suddenly silent; till he who appeared to be the *Father-director,* as they passed, said "Hail! in the name of *Our Lady of Mount Carmel!*" and they repeated the salutation in chorus.

"Hail!" replied Vivaldi, "the first mass is over," and he passed on.

"But if you make haste, you may come in for the second," said Paulo, jogging after.

"You have just left the shrine, then?" said one of the party, "and can tell us"——

"Poor pilgrims, like yourselves," replied Paulo, "and can tell as little. Good morrow, fathers, yonder peeps the dawn!"

He came up with his master, who had hurried forward

with Ellena, and who now severely reproved his indiscretion; while the voices of the Carmelites, singing the mattin-hymn, sunk away among the rocks, and the quietness of solitude returned.

"Thank heaven! we are quit of this adventure," said Vivaldi.

"And now we have only the bridge to get over," rejoined Paulo, "and, I hope, we shall all be safe."

They were now at the entrance of it; as they passed the trembling planks, and looked up the glen, a party of people appeared advancing on the road the fugitives had left, and a chorus of other voices than those of the Carmelites, were heard mingling with the hollow sound of the waters.

Ellena, again alarmed, hastened forward, and Vivaldi, though he endeavoured to appease her apprehension of pursuit, encouraged her speed.

"These are nothing but more pilgrims Signora," said Paulo, "or they would not send such loud shouts before them; they must needs think we can hear."

The travellers proceeded as fast as the broken road would permit; and were soon beyond the reach of the voices; but as Paulo turned to look whether the party was within sight, he perceived two persons, wrapt in cloaks, advancing under the brow of the cliffs, and within a few paces of his horse's heels. Before he could give notice to his master, they were at his side.

"Are you returning from the shrine of *our Lady*?" said one of them.

Vivaldi, startled by the voice, looked round, and demanded who asked the question?

"A brother pilgrim," replied the man, "one who has toiled up these steep rocks, till his limbs will scarcely bear him further. Would that you would take compassion on him, and give him a ride."

However compassionate Vivaldi might be to the sufferings of others, this was not a moment when he could indulge his disposition, without endangering the safety of Ellena; and he even fancied the stranger spoke in a voice of dissimulation. His suspicions strengthened when the traveller, not repulsed by a refusal, enquired the way he was going, and proposed to join his party; "For these mountains, they say, are infested with banditti," he added, "and a large company is less likely to be attacked than a small one."

"If you are so very weary, my friend," said Vivaldi, "how is it possible you can keep pace with our horses? though I acknowledge you have done wonders in overtaking them."

"The fear of these banditti," replied the stranger, "urged us on."

"You have nothing to apprehend from robbers," said Vivaldi, "if you will only moderate your pace; for a large company of pilgrims are on the road, who will soon overtake you."

He then put an end to the conversation, by clapping spurs to his horse, and the strangers were soon left far behind. The inconsistency of their complaints with their ability, and the whole of their manner, were serious subjects of alarm to the fugitives; but when they had lost sight of them, they lost also their apprehensions; and having, at length, emerged from the pass, they quitted the high road to Naples, and struck into a solitary one that led westward towards Aquila.

CHAPTER II

Thus sang th' unletter'd Swain to th' oaks and rills,
While the still morn went forth with sandals gray,
And now the sun had stretch'd out all the hills,
And now was dropt into the western bay.——

MILTON

FROM the summit of a mountain, the morning light shewed the travellers the distant lake of Celano, gleaming at the feet of other lofty mountains of the Appennine, far in the south. Thither Vivaldi judged it prudent to direct his course, for the lake lay so remote from the immediate way to Naples, and from the neighbourhood of San Stefano, that its banks promised a secure retreat. He considered, also, that among the convents scattered along those delightful banks, might easily be found a priest, who would solemnize their nuptials, should Ellena consent to an immediate marriage.

The travellers descended among olive woods, and soon after were directed by some peasants at work, into a road that leads from Aquila to the town of Celano, one of the very few roads which intrudes among the wild mountains, that on every side sequester the lake. As they approached the low grounds, the scent of orange blossoms breathed upon the morning air, and the spicy myrtle sent forth all its fragrance from among the cliffs, which it thickly tufted. Bowers of lemon and orange spread along the valley; and among the cabins of the peasants, who cultivated them, Vivaldi hoped to obtain repose and refreshment for Ellena.

The cottages, however, at which Paulo enquired were unoccupied, the owners being all gone forth to their labour: and the travellers, again ascending, found themselves soon after among mountains inhabited by the flocks, where the scent of the orange was exchanged for the aromatic perfume of the pasturage.

"My Signor!" said Paulo, "is not that a shepherd's horn sounding at a distance? If so, the Signora may yet obtain some refreshment."

While Vivaldi listened, a hautboy and a pastoral drum were heard considerably nearer.

They followed the sound over the turf, and came within view of a cabin, sheltered from the sun by a tuft of almond trees. It was a dairy-cabin belonging to some shepherds, who at a short distance were watching their flocks, and, stretched beneath the shade of chestnuts, were amusing themselves by playing upon these rural instruments; a scene of Arcadian manners frequent at this day, upon the mountains of Abruzzo. The simplicity of their appearance, approaching to wildness, was tempered by a hospitable spirit. A venerable man, the chief shepherd, advanced to meet the strangers; and, learning their wants, conducted them into his cool cabin, where cream, cheese made of goat's milk, honey extracted from the delicious herbage of the mountains, and dried figs were quickly placed before them.

Ellena, overcome with the fatigue of anxiety, rather than that of travelling, retired, when she had taken breakfast, for an hour's repose; while Vivaldi rested on the bench before the cottage, and Paulo, keeping watch, discussed his breakfast, together with the circumstances of the late alarm, under the shade of the almond trees.

When Ellena again appeared, Vivaldi proposed, that they should rest here during the intense heat of the day; and, since he now considered her to be in a place of temporary safety, he ventured to renew the subject nearest his heart; to represent the evils, that might overtake them, and to urge an immediate solemnization of their marriage.

Thoughtful and dejected, Ellena attended for some time in silence to the arguments and pleadings of Vivaldi. She secretly acknowledged the justness of his representations, but she shrunk, more than ever, from the indelicacy, the degradation of intruding herself into his family; a family, too, from whom she had not only received proofs of strong dislike, but had suffered terrible injustice, and been menaced with still severer cruelty. These latter circumstances, however, released her from all obligations of delicacy or generosity, so far as concerned only the authors of her suffering; and she had now but to consider the happiness of Vivaldi and herself. Yet she could not decide thus precipitately on a subject, which so solemnly involved the fortune of her whole life; nor forbear reminding Vivaldi, affectionately, gratefully, as she loved him, of the circumstances which with-held her decision.

"Tell me yourself," said she, "whether I ought to give my hand, while your family—your mother"—— She paused, and blushed, and burst into tears.

"Spare me the view of those tears," said Vivaldi, "and a recollection of the circumstances that excite them. O, let me not think of my mother, while I see you weep! Let me not remember, that her injustice and cruelty destined you to perpetual sorrow!"

Vivaldi's features became slightly convulsed, while he spoke; he rose, paced the room with quick steps, and then quitted it, and walked under the shade of the trees in front of the cabin.

In a few moments, however, he commanded his emotion and returned. Again he placed himself on the bench beside Ellena, and taking her hand, said solemnly, and in a voice of extreme sensibility, "Ellena, you have long witnessed how dear you are to me; you cannot doubt my love; you have long since promised—solemnly promised, in the presence of her who is now no more, but whose spirit may even at this moment look down upon us,—of her, who bequeathed you to my tenderest care, to be mine for ever. By these sacred truths, by these affecting recollections! I conjure you, abandon me not to despair, nor in the energy of a just resentment, sacrifice the son to the cruel and mistaken policy of the mother! You, nor I, can conjecture the machinations, which may be spread for us, when it shall be known that you have left San Stefano. If we delay to exchange our vows, I know, and I feel—that you are lost to me for ever!"

Ellena was affected, and for some moments unable to reply. At length, drying her tears, she said tenderly, "Resentment can have no influence on my conduct towards you; I think I feel none towards the Marchesa—for she is your mother. But pride, insulted pride, has a right to dictate, and ought to be obeyed; and the time is now, perhaps, arrived when, if I would respect myself, I must renounce you."——

"Renounce me!" interrupted Vivaldi, "renounce me! And is it, then, possible you could renounce me?" he repeated, his eyes still fixed upon her face with eagerness and consternation. "Tell me at once, Ellena, is it possible?"

"I fear it is not," she replied.

"You fear! alas! if you *fear,* it is too possible, and I have lost you already! Say, O! say but, that you *hope* it is not, and I, too, will hope again."

The anguish, with which he uttered this, awakened all her tenderness, and, forgetting the reserve she had imposed upon herself, and every half-formed resolution, she said, with a smile of ineffable sweetness, "I will neither fear nor hope in this instance; I will obey the dictates of gratitude, of affection, and will *believe* that I never can renounce you, while you are unchanged."

"Believe!" repeated Vivaldi, "only believe! And why that mention of gratitude; and why that unnecessary reservation? Yet even this assurance, feebly as it sustains my hopes, is extorted; you see my misery, and from pity, from *gratitude,* not affection, would assuage it. Besides, you will neither fear, nor hope! Ah, Ellena! did love ever yet exist without fear—and without hope? O! never, never! I fear and hope with such rapid transition; every assurance, every look of yours gives such force either to the one, or to the other, that I suffer unceasing anxiety. Why, too, that cold, that heartbreaking mention of gratitude? No, Ellena! it is too certain that you do not love me!—My mother's cruelty has estranged your heart from me!"

"How much you mistake!" said Ellena. "You have already received sacred testimonies of my regard; if you doubt their sincerity, pardon me, if I so far respect myself as to forbear entreating you will believe them."

"How calm, how indifferent, how circumspect, how prudent!" exclaimed Vivaldi in tones of mournful reproach. "But I will not distress you; forgive me for renewing this subject at this time. It was my intention to be silent till you should have reached a place of more permanent security than this; but how was it possible, with such anxiety pressing upon my heart, to persevere in that design. And what have I gained by departing from it?—increase of anxiety—of doubt—of fear!"

"Why will you persist in such self-inflictions?" said Ellena. "I cannot endure that you should doubt my affection, even for a moment. And how can you suppose it possible, that I ever can become insensible of yours; that I can ever

forget the imminent danger you have voluntarily incurred for
my release, or, remembering it, can cease to feel the warm-
est gratitude?"

"That is the very word which tortures me beyond all others!" said Vivaldi; "is it then, only a sense of obligation you
own for me? O! rather say you hate me, than suffer me to
deceive my hopes with assurances of a sentiment so cold, so
circumscribed, so dutiful as that of gratitude!"

"With me the word has a very different acceptation," replied Ellena smiling. "I understand it to imply all that is tender and generous in affection; and the sense of duty which
you say it includes, is one of the sweetest and most sacred
feelings of the human heart."

"Ah Ellena! I am too willing to be deceived, to examine
your definition rigorously; yet I believe it is your smile,
rather than the accuracy of your explanation, that persuades
me to a confidence in your affection; and I will trust, that the
gratitude *you* feel is thus tender and comprehensive. But, I
beseech you, name the word no more! Its sound is like the
touch of the Torpedo, I perceive my confidence chilled even
while I listen to my own pronunciation of it."

The entrance of Paulo interrupted the conversation, who
advancing with an air of mystery and alarm, said in a low
voice,

"Signor! as I kept watch under the almond trees, who
should I see mounting up the road from the valley yonder,
but the two barefooted Carmelites, that overtook us in the
pass of Chiari! I lost them again behind the woods, but I
dare say they are coming this way, for the moment they spy
out this dairy-hut, they will guess something good is to be
had here; and the shepherds would believe their flocks
would all die, if"——

"I see them at this moment emerging from the woods,"
said Vivaldi, "and now, they are leaving the road and crossing this way. Where is our host, Paulo!"

"He is without, at a little distance, Signor. Shall I call
him?"

"Yes," replied Vivaldi, "or, stay; I will call him myself.
Yet, if they see me"——

"Aye, Signor; or, for that matter, if they see me. But we
cannot help ourselves now; for if we call the host, we shall
betray ourselves, and, if we do not call him, he will betray
us; so they must find us out, be it as it may."

"Peace! peace! let me think a moment," said Vivaldi. While Vivaldi undertook to think, Paulo was peeping about for a hiding place, if occasion should require one.

"Call our host immediately," said Vivaldi, "I must speak with him."

"He passes the lattice at this instant," said Ellena.

Paulo obeyed, and the shepherd entered the cabin.

"My good friend," said Vivaldi, "I must entreat that you will not admit those friars, whom you see coming this way, nor suffer them to know what guests you have. They have been very troublesome to us already, on the road; I will reward you for any loss their sudden departure may occasion you."

"Nay for that matter, friend," said Paulo, "it is their visit only that can occasion you loss, begging the Signor's pardon; their departure never occasioned loss to any body. And to tell you the truth, for my master will not speak out, we were obliged to look pretty sharply about us, while they bore us company, or we have reason to think our pockets would have been the lighter. They are designing people, friend, take my word for it; banditti, perhaps, in disguise. The dress of a Carmelite would suit their purpose, at this time of the pilgrimage. So be pretty blunt with them, if they want to come in here; and you will do well, when they go, to send somebody to watch which way they take, and see them clear off, or you may lose a stray lamb, perhaps."

The old shepherd lifted up his eyes and hands. "To see how the world goes!" said he. "But thank you, *Maestro*, for your warning; they shall not come within my threshold, for all their holy seeming, and it's the first time in my life I ever said nay to one of their garb, and mine has been a pretty long one, as you may guess, perhaps, by my face. How old, Signor, should you take me to be? I warrant you will guess short of the matter tho'; for on these high mountains"——

"I will guess when you have dismissed the travellers," said Vivaldi, "after having given them some hasty refreshment without; they must be almost at the door, by this time. Dispatch, friend."

"If they should fall foul upon me, for refusing them entrance," said the shepherd, "you will come out to help me, Signor? for my lads are at some distance."

Vivaldi assured him that they would, and he left the cabin.

Paulo ventured to peep at the lattice, on what might be going forward without. "They are gone round to the door, Signor, I fancy," said he, "for I see nothing of them this way; if there was but another window! What foolish people to build a cottage with no window near the door! But I must listen."

He stepped on tip-toe to the door, and bent his head in attention.

"They are certainly spies from the monastery," said Ellena to Vivaldi, "they follow us so closely! If they were pilgrims, it is improbable, too, that their way should lie through this unfrequented region, and still more so, that they should not travel in a larger party. When my absence was discovered, these people were sent, no doubt, in pursuit of me, and having met the devotees whom we passed, they were enabled to follow our route."

"We shall do well to act upon this supposition," replied Vivaldi, "but, though I am inclined to believe them emissaries from San Stefano, it is not improbable that they are only Carmelites returning to some convent on the lake of Celano."

"I cannot hear a syllable, Signor," said Paulo. "Pray do listen yourself! and there is not a single chink in this door to afford one consolation. Well! if ever I build a cottage, there shall be a window near——"

"Listen!" said Vivaldi.

"Not a single word, Signor!" cried Paulo, after a pause, "I do not even hear a voice!— But now I hear steps, and they are coming to the door, too; they shall find it no easy matter to open it, though;" he added, placing himself against it. "Ay, ay, you may knock, friend, till your arm aches, and kick and lay about you—no matter for that."

"Silence! let us know who it is," said Vivaldi; and the old shepherd's voice was heard without. "They are gone, Signors," said he, "you may open the door."

"Which way did they go?" asked Vivaldi, when the man entered. "I cannot say, as to that, Signor, because I did not happen to see them at all; and I have been looking all about, too."

"Why, I saw them myself, crossing this way from the wood yonder," said Paulo.

"And there is nothing to shelter them from our view between the wood, and this cottage, friend," added Vivaldi; "What can they have done with themselves?"

"For that matter, gone into the wood again, perhaps," said the shepherd.

Paulo gave his master a significant look, and added, "It is likely enough, friend; and you may depend upon it they are lurking there for no good purpose. You will do well to send somebody to look after them; your flocks will suffer for it, else. Depend upon it, they design no good."

"We are not used to such sort of folks in these parts," replied the shepherd, "but if they mean any harm, they shall find we can help ourselves." As he concluded, he took down a horn from the roof, and blew a shrill blast that made the mountains echo; when immediately the younger shepherds were seen running from various quarters towards the cottage.

"Do not be alarmed, friend;" said Vivaldi, "these travellers mean you no harm, I dare say, whatever they may design against us. But, as I think them suspicious persons, and should not like to overtake them on the road, I will reward one of your lads if you will let him go a little ways towards Celano, and examine whether they are lurking on that route."

The old man consented, and, when the shepherds came up, one of them received directions from Vivaldi.

"And be sure you do not return, till you have found them," added Paulo.

"No master," replied the lad, "and I will bring them safe here, you may trust me."

"If you do, friend, you will get your head broke for your trouble. You are only to discover where they are, and to watch where they go," said Paulo.

Vivaldi, at length, made the lad comprehend what was required of him, and he departed; while the old shepherd went out to keep guard.

The time of his absence was passed in various conjectures by the party in the cabin, concerning the Carmelites. Vivaldi still inclined to believe they were honest people returning from a pilgrimage, but Paulo was decidedly against this opinion. "They are waiting for us on the road, you may depend upon it, Signor," said the latter. "You may be certain they have some *great design* in hand, or they would never have turned their steps from this dairy-house when once they had spied it, and that they did spy it, we are sure."

"But if they have in hand the great design you speak of,

Paulo," said Vivaldi, "it is probable that they have spied us also, by their taking this obscure road. Now it must have occurred to them when they saw a dairy-hut, in so solitary a region, that we might probably be found within—yet they have not examined. It appears, therefore, they have no design against us. What can you answer to this Paulo? I trust the apprehensions of Signora di Rosalba are unfounded."

"Why! do you suppose, Signor, they would attack us when we were safe housed, and had these good shepherds to lend us a helping hand? No, Signor, they would not even have shewn themselves, if they could have helped it; and being once sure we were here, they would skulk back to the woods, and lurk for us in the road they knew we must go, since, as it happens, there is only one."

"How is it possible," said Ellena, "that they can have discovered us here, since they did not approach the cabin to enquire."

"They came near enough for their purpose, Signora, I dare say; and, if the truth were known, they spied my face looking at them through the lattice."

"Come, come," said Vivaldi, "you are an ingenious tormentor, indeed, Paulo. Do you suppose they saw enough of thy face last night by moonlight, in that dusky glen, to enable them to recollect it again at a distance of forty yards? Revive, my Ellena, I think every appearance is in our favour."

"Would I could think so too!" said she, with a sigh.

"O! for that matter, Signora," rejoined Paulo, "there is nothing to be afraid of; they should find tough work of it, if they thought proper to attack us, lady."

"It is not an open attack that we have to fear," replied Ellena, "but they may surround us with their snares, and defy resistance."

However Vivaldi might accede to the truth of this remark, he would not appear to do so, but tried to laugh away her apprehensions; and Paulo was silenced for a while, by a significant look from his master.

The shepherd's boy returned much sooner than they had expected, and he probably saved his time, that he might spare his labour, for he brought no intelligence of the Carmelites. "I looked for them among the woods along the road side in the hollow, yonder, too," said the lad, "and then I mounted the hill further on, but I could see nothing of them far or near, nor of a single soul, except our goats, and some of them do stray wide enough, sometimes; they lead me a fine dance often. They sometimes, Signor, have wandered as far as Monte Nuvola, yonder, and got to the top of it, up among the clouds, and the crags, where I should break my neck if I climbed; and the rogues seemed to know it, too, for when they have seen me coming, scrambling up, puffing and blowing, they have ceased their capering, and stood peeping over a crag so sly, and so quiet, it seemed as if they were laughing at me; as much as to say, 'Catch us if you can.' "

Vivaldi, who during the latter part of this speech had been consulting with Ellena, whether they should proceed on their way immediately, asked the boy some further questions concerning the Carmelites; and becoming convinced that they had either not taken the road to Celano, or, having taken it, were at a considerable distance, he proposed setting out, and proceeding leisurely, "For I have now little apprehension of these people," he added, "and a great deal lest night should overtake us before we reach the place of our destination, since the road is mountainous and wild, and, further, we are not perfectly acquainted with it."

Ellena approving the plan, they took leave of the good shepherd, who could with difficulty be prevailed with to accept any recompence for his trouble, and who gave them some further directions as to the road; and their way was long cheered by the sound of the tabor and the sweetness of the hautboy, wafted over the wild.

When they descended into the woody hollow mentioned by the boy, Ellena sent forth many an anxious look beneath the deep shade; while Paulo, sometimes silent, and at others whistling and singing loudly, as if to overcome his fears, peeped under every bough that crossed the road, expecting to discover his friends the Carmelites lurking within its gloom.

Having emerged from this valley, the road lay over mountains covered with flocks, for it was now the season when they had quitted the plains of Apulia, to feed upon the herbage for which this region is celebrated; and it was near sunset, when, from a summit to which the travellers had long been ascending, the whole lake of Celano, with its vast circle of mountains, burst at once upon their view.

"Ah Signor!" exclaimed Paulo, "what a prospect is here! It reminds me of home; it is almost as pleasant as the bay of

Naples! I should never love it like that though, if it were an hundred times finer."

The travellers stopped to admire the scene, and to give their horses rest, after the labour of the ascent. The evening sun, shooting athwart a clear expanse of water, between eighteen and twenty leagues in circumference, lighted up all the towns and villages, and towered castles, and spiry convents, that enriched the rising shores; brought out all the various tints of cultivation, and coloured with beamy purple the mountains which on every side formed the majestic background of the landscape. Vivaldi pointed out to Ellena the gigantic Velino in the north, a barrier mountain, between the territories of Rome and Naples. Its peaked head towered far above every neighbouring summit, and its white precipices were opposed to the verdant points of the Majella, snow-crowned, and next in altitude, loved by the flocks. Westward, near woody hills, and rising immediately from the lake, appeared Monte Salviano, covered with wild sage, as its name imports, and once pompous with forests of chestnut; a branch from the Apennine extended to meet it. "See," said Vivaldi, "where Monte-Corno stands like a ruffian, huge, scarred, threatening, and horrid!—and in the south, where the sullen mountain of San Nicolo shoots up, barren and rocky! From thence, mark how other overtopping ridges of the mighty Apennine darken the horizon far along the east, and circle to approach the Velino in the north!"

"Mark too," said Ellena, "how sweetly the banks and undulating plains repose at the feet of the mountains; what an image of beauty and elegance they oppose to the awful grandeur that overlooks and guards them! Observe, too, how many a delightful valley, opening from the lake, spreads its rice and corn fields, shaded with groves of the almond, far among the winding hills; how gaily vineyards and olives alternately chequer the acclivities; and how gracefully the lofty palms bend over the higher cliffs."

"Ay, Signora!" exclaimed Paulo, "and have the goodness to observe how like are the fishing boats, that sail towards the hamlet below, to those one sees upon the bay of Naples. They are worth all the rest of the prospect, except indeed this fine sheet of water, which is almost as good as the bay, and that mountain, with its sharp head, which is almost as good as Vesuvius—if it would but throw out fire!"

"We must despair of finding a mountain in this neighbourhood, so *good* as to do that, Paulo," said Vivaldi, smiling at this stroke of nationality; "though, perhaps, many that we now see, have once been volcanic."

"I honour them for that, Signor; and look at them with double satisfaction; but *our* mountain is the only mountain in the world. O! to see it of a dark night! what a blazing it makes! and what a height it will shoot to! and what a light it throws over the sea! No other mountain can do so. It seems as if the waves were all on fire. I have seen the reflection as far off as Capri, trembling all across the gulf, and shewing every vessel as plain as at noon day; ay, and every sailor on the deck. You never saw such a sight, Signor."

"Why you do, indeed, seem to have forgotten that I ever did, Paulo, and also that a volcano can do any mischief. But let us return, Ellena, to the scene before us. Yonder, a mile or two within the shore, is the town of Celano, whither we are going."

The clearness of an Italian atmosphere permitted him to discriminate the minute though very distant features of the landscape; and on an eminence rising from the plains of a valley, opening to the west, he pointed out the modern Alba, crowned with the ruins of its ancient castle, still visible upon the splendor of the horizon, the prison and tomb of many a Prince, who, "fallen from his high estate," was sent from Imperial Rome to finish here the sad reverse of his days; to gaze from the bars of his tower upon solitudes where beauty or grandeur administered no assuaging feelings to him, whose life had passed amidst the intrigues of the world, and the feverish contentions of disappointed ambition; to him, with whom reflection brought only remorse, and anticipation despair; whom "no horizontal beam enlivened in the crimson evening of life's dusty day."

"And to such a scene as this," said Vivaldi, "a Roman Emperor came, only for the purpose of witnessing the most barbarous exhibition; to indulge the most savage delights! Here, Claudius celebrated the accomplishment of his arduous work, an aqueduct to carry the overflowing waters of the Celano to Rome, by a naval fight, in which hundreds of wretched slaves perished for his amusement! Its pure and polished surface was stained with human blood, and roughened by the plunging bodies of the slain, while the gilded gallies of the Emperor floated gaily around, and these beautiful shores were made to echo with applauding yells, worthy of the furies!"

"We scarcely dare to trust the truth of history, in some of its traits of human nature," said Ellena.

"Signor," cried Paulo, "I have been thinking that while we are taking the air, so much at our ease, here, those Carmelites may be spying at us from some hole or corner that we know nothing of, and may swoop upon us, all of a sudden, before we can help ourselves. Had we not better go on, Signor?"

"Our horses are, perhaps, sufficiently rested," replied Vivaldi, "but, if I had not long since dismissed all suspicion of the evil intention of those strangers, I should not willingly have stopped for a moment."

"But pray let us proceed," said Ellena.

"Ay, Signora, it is best to be of the safe side," observed Paulo. "Yonder, below, is Celano, and I hope we shall get safe housed there, before it is quite dark, for here we have no mountain, that will light us on our way! Ah! if we were but within twenty miles of Naples, now,—and it was an *illumination* night!"—

As they descended the mountain, Ellena, silent and dejected, abandoned herself to reflection. She was too sensible of the difficulties of her present situation, and too apprehensive of the influence, which her determination must have on all her future life, to be happy, though escaped from the prison of San Stefano, and in the presence of Vivaldi, her beloved deliverer and protector. He observed her dejection with grief, and, not understanding all the finer scruples that distressed her, interpreted her reserve into indifference towards himself. But he forbore to disturb her again with a mention of his doubts, or fears; and he determined not to urge the subject of his late entreaties, till he should have placed her in some secure asylum, where she might feel herself at perfect liberty to accept or to reject his proposal. By acting with an honour so delicate, he unconsciously adopted a certain means of increasing her esteem and gratitude, and deserved them the more, since he had to endure the apprehension of losing her by the delay thus occasioned to their nuptials.

They reached the town of Celano before the evening closed; when Vivaldi was requested by Ellena to enquire for a convent, where she might be lodged for the night. He left

her at the inn, with Paulo for her guard, and proceeded on
his search. The first gate he knocked upon belonged to a
convent of Carmelites. It appeared probable, that the pilgrims of that order, who had occasioned him so much dis-
quietude, were honest brothers of this house; but as it was
probable also, that if they were emissaries of the Abbess of
San Stefano, and came to Celano, they would take up their
lodging with a society of their own class, in preference to
that of any other, Vivaldi thought it prudent to retire from
their gates without making himself known. He passed on,
therefore, and soon after arrived at a convent of Dominicans,
where he learned, that there were only two houses of nuns in
Celano, and that these admitted no other boarders than permanent ones.

Vivaldi returned with this intelligence to Ellena, who endeavoured to reconcile herself to the necessity of remaining
where she was; but Paulo, ever active and zealous, brought
intelligence, that at a little fishing town, at some distance, on
the bank of the lake, was a convent of Ursalines, remarkable
for their hospitality to strangers. The obscurity of so remote
a place, was another reason for preferring it to Celano, and
Vivaldi proposing to remove thither, if Ellena was not too
weary to proceed, she readily assented, and they immediately set off.

"It happens to be a fine night," said Paulo, as they left
Celano, "and so, Signor, we cannot well lose our way; besides, they say, there is but one. The town we are going to
lies yonder on the edge of the lake, about a mile and a half
off. I think I can see a gray steeple or two, a little to the
right of that wood where the water gleams so."

"No, Paulo," replied Vivaldi, after looking attentively. "I
perceive what you mean; but those are not the points of stee-
ples, they are only the tops of some tall cypresses."

"Pardon me, Signor, they are too tapering for trees; that
must surely be the town. This road, however, will lead us
right, for there is no other to puzzle us, as they say."

"This cool and balmy air revives me," said Ellena; "and
what a soothing shade prevails over the scene! How softened, yet how distinct, is every near object; how sweetly dubious the more removed ones; while the mountains beyond
character themselves sublimely upon the still glowing horizon."

"Observe, too," said Vivaldi, "how their broken summits,

tipt with the beams that have set to our lower region, exhibit the portraiture of towers and castles, and embattled ramparts, which seemed designed to guard them against the enemies, that may come by the clouds."

"Yes," replied Ellena, "the mountains themselves display a sublimity, that seems to belong to a higher world; their besiegers ought not to be of this earth; they can be only spirits of the air."

"They can be nothing else, Signora," said Paulo, "for nothing of this earth can reach them. See! lady, they have some of the qualities of your spirits, too; see! how they change their shapes and colours, as the sun-beams sink. And now, how gray and dim they grow! See but how fast they vanish!"

"Every thing reposes," said Vivaldi. "Who would willingly travel in the day, when Italy has such nights as this!"

"Signor, that *is* the town before us," said Paulo, "for now I can discern, plain enough, the spires of convents; and there goes a light! Hah, hah! and there is a bell, too, chiming from one of the spires! The monks are going to mass; would we were going to supper, Signor!"

"That chime is nearer than the place you point to, Paulo, and I doubt whether it comes from the same quarter."

"Hark! Signor, the air wafts the sound! and now it is gone again."

"Yes, I believe you are right, Paulo, and that we have not far to go."

The travellers descended the gradual slopes, towards the shore; and Paulo, some time after, exclaimed, "See, Signor, where another light glides along! See! it is reflected on the lake."

"I hear the faint dashing of waves, now," said Ellena, "and the sound of oars, too. But observe, Paulo, the light is not in the town, it is in the boat that moves yonder."

"Now it retreats, and trembles in a lengthening line upon the waters," said Vivaldi. "We have been too ready to believe what we wish and have yet far to go."

The shore they were approaching formed a spacious bay for the lake, immediately below. Dark woods seemed to spread along the banks, and ascend among the cultivated slopes towards the mountains; except where, here and there, cliffs, bending over the water, were distinguished through the twilight by the whiteness of their limestone precipices.

Within the bay, the town became gradually visible; lights twinkled between the trees, appearing and vanishing, like the stars of a cloudy night; and, at length was heard the melancholy song of boatmen, who were fishing near the shore.

Other sounds soon after struck the ear. "O, what merry notes!" exclaimed Paulo, "they make my heart dance. See! Signora, there is a group, footing it away so gaily on the bank of the lake, yonder, by those trees. O, what a merry set! Would I were among them! that is, I mean, if you, *Maestro*, and the Signora were not here."

"Well corrected, Paulo."

"It is a festival, I fancy," observed Vivaldi. "These peasants of the lake can make the moments fly as gaily as the voluptuaries of the city, it seems."

"O! what merry music!" repeated Paulo. "Ah! how often I have footed it as joyously on the beach at Naples, after sun-set, of a fine night, like this; with such a pleasant fresh breeze to cool one! Ah! there are none like the fishermen of Naples for a dance by moonlight; how lightly they do trip it! O! if I was but there now! That is, I mean, if you, *Maestro*, and the Signora were there too. O! what merry notes!"

"We thank you, good Signor Paulo," said Vivaldi, "and I trust we shall all be there soon; when you shall trip it away, with as joyous an heart as the best of them."

The travellers now entered the town, which consisted of one street, straggling along the margin of the lake; and having enquired for the Ursaline convent, were directed to its gates. The portress appeared immediately upon the ringing of the bell, and carried a message to the Abbess, who as quickly returned an invitation to Ellena. She alighted, and followed the portress to the parlour, while Vivaldi remained at the gate, till he should know whether she approved of her new lodging. A second invitation induced him, also, to alight; he was admitted to the grate, and offered refreshment, which, however, he declined staying to accept, as he had yet a lodging to seek for the night. The Abbess, on learning this circumstance, courteously recommended him to a neighbouring society of Benedictines, and desired him to mention her name to the Abbot.

Vivaldi then took leave of Ellena, and though it was only for a few hours, he left her with dejection, and with some degree of apprehension for her safety, which, though circumstances could not justify him in admitting, he could not entirely subdue. She shared his dejection, but not his fears, when the door closed after him, and she found herself once more among strangers. The forlornness of her feelings could not be entirely overcome by the attentions of the Abbess; and there was a degree of curiosity, and even of scrutiny, expressed in the looks of some of the sisters, which seemed more than was due to a stranger. From such examination she eagerly escaped to the apartment allotted for her, and to the repose from which she had so long been withheld.

Vivaldi, meanwhile, had found an hospitable reception with the Benedictines, whose sequestered situation made the visit of a stranger a pleasurable novelty to them. In the eagerness of conversation, and, yielding to the satisfaction which the mind receives from exercising ideas that have long slept in dusky indolence, and to the pleasure of admitting new ones, the Abbot and a few of the brothers sat with Vivaldi to a late hour. When, at length, the traveller was suffered to retire, other subjects than those, which had interested his host, engaged his thoughts; and he revolved the means of preventing the misery that threatened him, in a serious separation from Ellena. Now, that she was received into a respectable asylum, every motive for silence upon this topic was done away. He determined, therefore, that on the following morning, he would urge all his reasons and entreaties for an immediate marriage; and among the brothers of the Benedictine, he had little doubt of prevailing with one to solemnize the nuptials, which he believed would place his happiness and Ellena's peace, beyond the influence of malignant possibilities.

CHAPTER III

> I under fair pretence of friendly ends,
> And well-placed words of glozing courtesy,
> Baited with reasons not unplausible,
> Wind me into the easy-hearted man,
> And hug him into snares.
>
> MILTON

WHILE Vivaldi and Ellena were on the way from San Stefano, the Marchese Vivaldi was suffering the utmost vexation, respecting his son; and the Marchesa felt not less apprehension, that the abode of Ellena might be discovered; yet this fear did not withhold her from mingling in all the gaieties of Naples. Her assemblies were, as usual, among the most brilliant of that voluptuous city, and she patronized, as zealously as before, the strains of her favourite composer. But, notwithstanding this perpetual dissipation, her thoughts frequently withdrew themselves from the scene, and dwelt on gloomy forebodings of disappointed pride.

A circumstance, which rendered her particularly susceptible to such disappointment at this time, was, that overtures of alliance had been lately made to the Marchese, by the father of a lady, who was held suitable, in every consideration, to become his daughter; and whose wealth rendered the union particularly desirable at a time, when the expences of such an establishment as was necessary to the vanity of the Marchesa, considerably exceeded his income, large as it was.

The Marchesa's temper had been thus irritated by the contemplation of her son's conduct in an affair, which so materially affected the fortune, and, as she believed, the honour of his family; when a courier from the Abbess of San Stefano brought intelligence of the flight of Ellena with

Vivaldi. She was in a disposition, which heightened disappointment into fury; and she forfeited, by the transports to which she yielded, the degree of pity that otherwise was due to a mother, who believed her only son to have sacrificed his family and himself to an unworthy passion. She believed, that he was now married, and irrecoverably lost. Scarcely able to endure the agony of this conviction, she sent for her ancient adviser Schedoni that he might, at least, have the relief of expressing her emotions; and of examining whether there remained a possibility of dissolving these long-dreaded nuptials. The phrenzy of passion, however, did not so far overcome her circumspection as to compel her to acquaint the Marchese with the contents of the Abbess's letter, before she had consulted with her Confessor. She knew that the principles of her husband were too just, upon the grand points of morality, to suffer him to adopt the measures she might judge necessary; and she avoided informing him of the marriage of his son, until the means of counteracting it should have been suggested and accomplished, however desperate such means might be.

Schedoni was not to be found. Trifling circumstances encrease the irritation of a mind in such a state as was hers. The delay of an opportunity for unburthening her heart to Schedoni, was hardly to be endured; another and another messenger were dispatched to her Confessor.

"My mistress has committed some great sin, truely!" said the servant, who had been twice to the convent within the last half hour. "It must lie heavy on her conscience, in good truth, since she cannot support it for one half hour. Well! the rich have this comfort, however, that, let them be ever so guilty, they can buy themselves innocent again, in the twinkling of a ducat. Now a poor man might be a month before he recovered his innocence, and that, too, not till after many a bout of hard flogging."

In the evening Schedoni came, but it was only to confirm her worst fear. He, too, had heard of the escape of Ellena, as well as that she was on the lake of Celano, and was married to Vivaldi. How he had obtained this information he did not chuse to disclose, but he mentioned so many minute circumstances in confirmation of its truth, and appeared to be so perfectly convinced of the facts he related, that the Marchesa believed them, as implicitly as himself; and her passion and despair transgressed all bounds of decorum.

Schedoni observed, with dark and silent pleasure, the turbulent excess of her feelings; and perceived that the moment was now arrived, when he might command them to his purpose, so as to render his assistance indispensable to her repose; and probably so as to accomplish the revenge he had long meditated against Vivaldi, without hazarding the favour of the Marchesa. So far was he from attempting to sooth her sufferings, that he continued to irritate her resentment, and exasperate her pride; effecting this, at the same time, with such imperceptible art, that he appeared only to be palliating the conduct of Vivaldi, and endeavouring to console his distracted mother.

"This is a rash step, certainly," said the Confessor; "but he is young, very young, and, therefore, does not foresee the consequence to which it leads. He does not perceive how seriously it will affect the dignity of his house;—how much it will depreciate his consequence with the court, with the nobles of his own rank, and even with the plebeians, with whom he has condescended to connect himself. Intoxicated with the passions of youth, he does not weigh the value of those blessings, which wisdom and the experience of maturer age know how to estimate. He neglects them *only* because he does not perceive their influence in society, and that lightly to resign them, is to degrade himself in the view of almost every mind. Unhappy young man! he is to be pitied fully as much as blamed."

"Your excuses, reverend father," said the tortured Marchesa, "prove the goodness of your heart; but they illustrate, also, the degeneracy of his mind, and detail the full extent of the effects which he has brought upon his family. It affords me no consolation to know, that this degradation proceeds from his head, rather than his heart; it is sufficient that he has incurred it, and that no possibility remains of throwing off the misfortune."

"Perhaps that is affirming too much," observed Schedoni.

"How, father!" said the Marchesa.

"Perhaps a possibility does remain," said he.

"Point it out to me, good father! I do not perceive it."

"Nay, my lady," replied the subtle Schedoni, correcting himself, "I am by no means assured, that such possibility does exist. My solicitude for your tranquillity, and for the honour of your house, makes me so unwilling to relinquish hope, that, perhaps, I only imagine a possibility in your favour. Let me consider.——Alas! the misfortune, severe as it is, must be endured;—there remain no means of escaping from it."

"It was cruel of you, father, to suggest a hope which you could not justify," observed the Marchesa.

"You must excuse my extreme solicitude, then," replied the Confessor. "But how is it possible for me to see a family of your ancient estimation brought into such circumstances; its honours blighted by the folly of a thoughtless boy, without feeling sorrow and indignation, and looking round for even some desperate means of delivering it from disgrace." He paused.

"Disgrace!" exclaimed the Marchesa, "father, you— you—Disgrace!—The word is a strong one, but——it is, alas! just. And shall we submit to this?— Is it possible we *can* submit to it?"

"There is no remedy," said Schedoni, coolly.

"Good God!" exclaimed the Marchesa, "that there should be no law to prevent, or, at least, to punish such criminal marriages!"

"It is much to be lamented," replied Schedoni.

"The woman who obtrudes herself upon a family, to dishonour it," continued the Marchesa, "deserves a punishment nearly equal to that of a state criminal, since she injures those who best support the state. She ought to suffer"——

"Not nearly, but quite equal," interrupted the Confessor, "she deserves——death!"

He paused, and there was a moment of profound silence, till he added—"for death only can obliviate the degradation she has occasioned; her death alone can restore the original splendour of the line she would have sullied."

He paused again, but the Marchesa still remaining silent, he added, "I have often marvelled that our lawgivers should have failed to perceive the justness, nay the necessity, of such punishment!"

"It is astonishing," said the Marchesa, thoughtfully, "that a regard for their own honour did not suggest it."

"Justice does not the less exist, because her laws are neglected," observed Schedoni. "A sense of what she commands lives in our breasts; and when we fail to obey that sense, it is to weakness, not to virtue, that we yield."

"Certainly," replied the Marchesa, "that truth never yet was doubted."

"Pardon me, I am not so certain as to that," said the Confessor, "when justice happens to oppose prejudice, we are apt to believe it virtuous to disobey her. For instance, though the law of justice demands the death of this girl, yet because the law of the land forbears to enforce it, you, my daughter, even you! though possessed of a man's spirit, and his clear perceptions, would think that virtue bade her live, when it was only fear!"

"Hah!" exclaimed the Marchesa, in a low voice, "What is that you mean? You shall find I have a man's courage also."

"I speak without disguise," replied Schedoni, "my meaning requires none."

The Marchesa mused, and remained silent.

"I have done my duty," resumed Schedoni, at length. "I have pointed out the only way that remains for you to escape dishonour. If my zeal is displeasing——but I have done."

"No, good father, no," said the Marchesa; "you mistake the cause of my emotion. New ideas, new prospects, open!—they confuse, they distract me! My mind has not yet attained sufficient strength to encounter them; some woman's weakness still lingers at my heart."

"Pardon my inconsiderate zeal," said Schedoni, with affected humility, "I have been to blame. If yours is a weakness, it is, at least, an amiable one, and, perhaps, deserves to be encouraged, rather than conquered."

"How, father! If it deserves encouragement, it is not a weakness, but a virtue."

"Be it so," said Schedoni, coolly, "the interest I have felt on this subject, has, perhaps, misled my judgment, and has made me unjust. Think no more of it, or, if you do, let it be only to pardon the zeal I have testified."

"It does not deserve pardon, but thanks," replied the Marchesa, "not thanks only, but reward. Good father, I hope it will some time be in my power to prove the sincerity of my words."

The Confessor bowed his head.

"I trust that the services you have rendered me, shall be gratefully repaid—rewarded, I dare not hope, for what benefit could possibly reward a service so vast, as it may, perhaps, be in your power to confer upon my family! What recompence could be balanced against the benefit of having rescued the honour of an ancient house!"

"Your goodness is beyond my thanks, or my desert," said Schedoni, and he was again silent.

The Marchesa wished him to lead her back to the point, from which she herself had deviated, and he seemed determined, that she should lead him thither. She mused, and hesitated. Her mind was not yet familiar with atrocious guilt; and the crime which Schedoni had suggested, somewhat alarmed her. She feared to think, and still more to name it; yet, so acutely susceptible was her pride, so stern her indignation, and so profound her desire of vengeance, that her mind was tossed as on a tempestuous ocean, and these terrible feelings threatened to overwhelm all the residue of humanity in her heart. Schedoni observed all its progressive movements, and, like a gaunt tyger, lurked in silence, ready to spring forward at the moment of opportunity.

"It is your advice, then, father," resumed the Marchesa, after a long pause,—"it is your opinion—that Ellena."——— She hesitated, desirous that Schedoni should anticipate her meaning; but he chose to spare his own delicacy rather than that of the Marchesa.

"You think, then, that this insidious girl deserves"——She paused again, but the Confessor, still silent, seemed to wait with submission for what the Marchesa should deliver.

"I repeat, father, that it is your opinion this girl deserves severe punishment."——

"Undoubtedly," replied Schedoni. "Is it not also your own?"

"That not any punishment can be too severe?" continued the Marchesa. "That justice, equally with necessity, demands——her life? Is not this your opinion, too?"

"O! pardon me," said Schedoni, "I may have erred; that only *was* my opinion; and when I formed it, I was probably too much under the influence of zeal to be just. When the heart is warm, how is it possible that the judgment can be cool."

"It is *not* then, your opinion, holy father," said the Marchesa with displeasure.

"I do not absolutely say that," replied the Confessor.— "But I leave it to your better judgment to decide upon its justness."

As he said this, he rose to depart. The Marchesa was agitated and perplexed, and requested he would stay; but he excused himself by alledging, that it was the hour when he must attend a particular mass.

"Well then, holy father, I will occupy no more of your valuable moments at present; but you know how highly I estimate your advice, and will not refuse, when I shall at some future time request it."

"I cannot refuse to accept an honour," replied the Confessor, with an air of meekness, "but the subject you allude to is delicate"——

"And therefore I must value, and require your opinion upon it," rejoined the Marchesa.

"I would wish you to value your own," replied Schedoni; "you cannot have a better director."

"You flatter, father."

"I only reply, my daughter."

"On the evening of to-morrow," said the Marchesa, gravely, "I shall be at vespers in the church of San Nicolo; if you should happen to be there, you will probably see me, when the service is over, and the congregation is departed, in the north cloister. We can there converse on the subject nearest my heart, and without observation.——Farewell!"

"Peace be with you, daughter! and wisdom counsel your thoughts!" said Schedoni, "I will not fail to visit San Nicolo."

He folded his hands upon his breast, bowed his head, and left the apartment with the silent footstep, that indicates weariness and conscious duplicity.

The Marchesa remained in her closet, shaken by ever-varying passions, and ever-fluctuating opinions; meditating misery for others, and inflicting it only upon herself.

CHAPTER IV

> Along the roofs sounds the low peal of Death,
> And Conscience trembles to the boding note;
> She views his dim form floating o'er the aisles,
> She hears mysterious murmurs in the air,
> And voices, strange and potent, hint the crime
> That dwells in thought, within her secret soul.

THE Marchesa repaired, according to her appointment, to the church of San Nicolo, and, ordering her servants to remain with the carriage at a side-door, entered the choir, attended only by her woman.

When vespers had concluded, she lingered till nearly every person had quitted the choir, and then walked through the solitary aisles to the north cloister. Her heart was as heavy as her step; for when is it that peace and evil passions dwell together? As she slowly paced the cloisters, she perceived a monk passing between the pillars, who, as he approached, lifted his cowl, and she knew him to be Schedoni.

He instantly observed the agitation of her spirits, and that her purpose was not yet determined, according to his hope. But, though his mind became clouded, his countenance remained unaltered; it was grave and thoughtful. The sternness of his vulture-eye was, however, somewhat softened, and its lids were contracted by subtlety.

The Marchesa bade her woman walk apart, while she conferred with her Confessor.

"This unhappy boy," said she, when the attendant was at some distance, "How much suffering does his folly inflict upon his family! My good father, I have need of all your advice and consolation. My mind is perpetually haunted by a sense of my misfortune; it has no respite; awake or in my dream, this ungrateful son alike pursues me! The only relief my heart receives is when conversing with you—my only counsellor, my only disinterested friend."

The Confessor bowed. "The Marchese is, no doubt, equally afflicted with yourself," said he; "but he is, notwithstanding, much more competent to advise you on this delicate subject than I am."

"The Marchese has prejudices, father, as you well know; he is a sensible man, but he is sometimes mistaken, and he is incorrigible in error. He has the faults of a mind that is merely well disposed; he is destitute of the discernment and the energy which would make it great. If it is necessary to adopt a conduct, that departs in the smallest degree from those common rules of morality which he has cherished, without examining them, from his infancy, he is shocked, and shrinks from action. He cannot discriminate the circumstances, that render the same action virtuous or vicious. How then, father, are we to suppose he would approve of the bold inflictions we meditate?"

"Most true!" said the artful Schedoni, with an air of admiration.

"We, therefore, must not consult him," continued the Marchesa, "lest he should now, as formerly, advance and maintain objections, to which we cannot yield. What passes in conversation with you, father, is sacred, it goes no farther."

"Sacred as a confession!" said Schedoni, crossing himself.

"I know not,"—resumed the Marchesa, and hesitated; "I know not"—she repeated in a yet lower voice, "how this girl may be disposed of; and this it is which distracts my mind."

"I marvel much at that," said Schedoni. "With opinions so singularly just, with a mind so accurate, yet so bold as you have displayed, is it possible that you can hesitate as to what is to be done! You, my daughter, will not prove yourself one of those ineffectual declaimers, who can think vigorously, but cannot act so! One way, only, remains for you to pursue, in the present instance; it is the same which your superior sagacity pointed out, and taught me to approve. Is it necessary for me to persuade *her,* by whom I am convinced! There is only one way."

"And on that I have been long meditating," replied the Marchesa, "and, shall I own my weakness? I cannot yet decide."

"My daughter! can it be possible that you should want

courage to soar above vulgar prejudice, in action, though not in opinion?" said Schedoni, who, perceiving that his assistance was necessary to fix her fluctuating mind, gradually began to steal forth from the prudent reserve, in which he had taken shelter.

"If this person was condemned by the law," he continued, "you would pronounce her sentence to be just; yet you dare not, I am humbled while I repeat it, you dare not dispense justice yourself!"

The Marchesa, after some hesitation, said, "I have not the shield of the law to protect me, father: and the boldest virtue may pause, when it reaches the utmost verge of safety."

"Never!" replied the Confessor, warmly; "virtue never trembles; it is her glory, and sublimest attribute to be superior to danger; to despise it. The best principle is not virtue till it reaches this elevation."

A philosopher might, perhaps, have been surprized to hear two persons seriously defining the limits of virtue, at the very moment in which they meditated the most atrocious crime; a man of the world would have considered it to be mere hypocrisy; a supposition which might have disclosed his general knowledge of manners, but would certainly have betrayed his ignorance of the human heart.

The Marchesa was for some time silent and thoughtful, and then repeated deliberately, "I have not the shield of the law to protect me."

"But you have the shield of the church," replied Schedoni; "you should not only have protection, but absolution."

"Absolution!— Does virtue—justice, require absolution, father?"

"When I mentioned absolution for the action which you perceive to be so just and necessary," replied Schedoni, "I accommodated my speech to vulgar prejudice, and to vulgar weakness. And, forgive me, that since you, my daughter, descended from the loftiness of your spirit to regret the shield of the law, I endeavoured to console you, by offering a shield to conscience. But enough of this; let us return to argument. This girl is put out of the way of committing more mischief, of injuring the peace and dignity of a distinguished family; she is sent to an eternal sleep, before her time.— Where is the crime, where is the evil of this? On the contrary, you perceive, and you have convinced me, that it is only strict justice, only self-defence."

The Marchesa was attentive, and the Confessor added, "She is not immortal; and the few years more, that might have been allotted her, she deserves to forfeit, since she would have employed them in cankering the honour of an illustrious house."

"Speak low, father," said the Marchesa, though he spoke almost in a whisper; "the cloister appears solitary, yet some person may lurk behind those pillars. Advise me how this business may be managed; I am ignorant of the particular means."

"There is some hazard in the accomplishment of it, I grant," replied Schedoni; "I know not whom you may confide in.—The men who make a trade of blood"——

"Hush!" said the Marchesa, looking round through the twilight—"a step!"

"It is the Friar's, yonder, who crosses to the choir," replied Schedoni.

They were watchful for a few moments, and then he resumed the subject. "Mercenaries ought not to be trusted,"—

"Yet who but mercenaries"—interrupted the Marchesa, and instantly checked herself. But the question thus implied, did not escape the Confessor.

"Pardon my astonishment," said he, "at the inconsistency, or, what shall I venture to call it? of your opinions! After the acuteness you have displayed on some points, is it possible you can doubt, that principle may both prompt and perform the deed? Why should we hesitate to do what we judge to be right?"

"Ah! reverend father," said the Marchesa, with emotion, "but where shall we find another like yourself—another, who not only can perceive with justness, but will act with energy."

Schedoni was silent.

"Such a friend is above all estimation; but where shall we seek him?"

"Daughter!" said the Monk, emphatically, "my zeal for your family is also above all calculation."

"Good father," replied the Marchesa, comprehending his full meaning. "I know not how to thank you."

"Silence is sometimes eloquence," said Schedoni, significantly.

The Marchesa mused; for her conscience also was eloquent. She tried to overcome its voice, but it would be heard; and sometimes such starts of horrible conviction came over her mind, that she felt as one who, awaking from a dream, opens his eyes only to measure the depth of the precipice on which he totters. In such moments she was astonished, that she had paused for an instant upon a subject so terrible as that of murder. The sophistry of the Confessor, together with the inconsistencies which he had betrayed, and which had not escaped the notice of the Marchesa, even at the time they were uttered, though she had been unconscious of her own, then became more strongly apparent, and she almost determined to suffer the poor Ellena to live. But returning passion, like a wave that has recoiled from the shore, afterwards came with recollected energy, and swept from her feeble mind the barriers, which reason and conscience had begun to rear.

"This confidence with which you have thought proper to honour me," said Schedoni, at length, and paused; "This affair, so momentous"———

"Ay, this affair," interrupted the Marchesa, in a hurried manner,—"but when, and where, good father? Being once convinced, I am anxious to have it settled."

"That must be as occasion offers," replied the Monk, thoughtfully.—"On the shore of the Adriatic, in the province of Apulia, not far from Manfredonia, is a house that might suit the purpose. It is a lone dwelling on the beach, and concealed from travellers, among the forests, which spread for many miles along the coast."

"And the people?" said the Marchesa.

"Ay, daughter, or why travel so far as Apulia? It is inhabited by one poor man, who sustains a miserable existence by fishing. I know him, and could unfold the reasons of his solitary life;—but no matter, it is sufficient that *I know him*."

"And would trust him, father?"

"Ay, lady, with the life of this girl———though scarcely with my own."

"How! If he is such a villain he may not be trusted! think further. But now, you objected to a mercenary, yet this man is one!"

"Daughter, he may be trusted, when it is in such a case; he is safe and sure. I have reason to know him."

"Name your reasons, father."

The Confessor was silent, and his countenance assumed a very peculiar character; it was more terrible than usual, and overspread with a dark, cadaverous hue of mingled anger and guilt. The Marchesa started involuntarily as, passing by a window, the evening gleam that fell there, discovered it; and for the first time she wished, that she had not committed herself so wholly to his power. But the die was now cast; it was too late to be prudent; and she again demanded his reasons.

"No matter," said Schedoni, in a stifled voice——"she dies!"

"By his hands?" asked the Marchesa, with strong emotion. "Think, once more, father."

They were both again silent and thoughtful. The Marchesa, at length, said, "Father, I rely upon your integrity and prudence;" and she laid a very flattering emphasis upon the word integrity. "But I conjure you to let this business be finished quickly, suspense is to me the purgatory of this world, and not to trust the accomplishment of it to a second person." She paused, and then added, "I would not willingly owe so vast a debt of obligation to any other than yourself."

"Your request, daughter, that I would not confide this business to a second person," said Schedoni, with displeasure, "cannot be accorded to. Can you suppose, that I, myself"——

"Can I doubt that principle may both prompt and perform the deed," interrupted the Marchesa with quickness, and anticipating his meaning, while she retorted upon him his former words. "Why should we hesitate to do what we judge to be right?"

The silence of Schedoni alone indicated his displeasure, which the Marchesa immediately understood.

"Consider, good father," she added significantly, "how painful it must be to me, to owe so infinite an obligation to a stranger, or to any other than so highly valued a friend as yourself."

Schedoni, while he detected her meaning, and persuaded himself that he despised the flattery, with which she so thinly veiled it, unconsciously suffered his self-love to be soothed by the compliment. He bowed his head, in signal of consent to her wish.

"Avoid violence, if that be possible," she added, immediately comprehending him, "but let her die quickly! The punishment is due to the crime."

The Marchesa happened, as she said this, to cast her eyes

upon the inscription over a Confessional, where appeared, in black letters, these awful words, "*God hears thee!*" It appeared an awful warning. Her countenance changed; it had struck upon her heart. Schedoni was too much engaged by his own thoughts to observe, or understand her silence. She soon recovered herself; and considering that this was a common inscription for Confessionals, disregarded what she had at first considered as a peculiar admonition; yet some moments elapsed, before she could renew the subject.

"You was speaking of a place, father," resumed the Marchesa——"you mentioned a"——

"Ay," muttered the Confessor, still musing,—"in a chamber of that house there is"——

"What noise is that?" said the Marchesa, interrupting him. They listened. A few low and querulous notes of the organ sounded at a distance, and stopped again.

"What mournful music is that?" said the Marchesa in a faultering voice, "It was touched by a fearful hand! Vespers were over long ago!"

"Daughter," said Schedoni, somewhat sternly, "you said you had a man's courage. Alas! you have a woman's heart."

"Excuse me, father; I know not why I feel this agitation, but I will command it. That chamber?"——

"In that chamber," resumed the Confessor, "is a secret door, constructed long ago."——

"And for what purpose constructed?" said the fearful Marchesa.

"Pardon me, daughter; 'tis sufficient that it is there; we will make a good use of it. Through that door—in the night—when she sleeps"——

"I comprehend you," said the Marchesa, "I comprehend you. But why, you have your reasons, no doubt, but why the necessity of a secret door in a house which you say is so lonely—inhabited by only one person?"

"A passage leads to the sea," continued Schedoni, without replying to the question. "There, on the shore, when darkness covers it; there, plunged amidst the waves, no stain shall hint of"——

"Hark!" interrupted the Marchesa, starting, "that note again!"

The organ sounded faintly from the choir, and paused, as before. In the next moment, a slow chaunting of voices was heard, mingling with the rising peal, in a strain particularly melancholy and solemn.

"Who is dead?" said the Marchesa, changing countenance; "it is a requiem!"

"Peace be with the departed!" exclaimed Schedoni, and crossed himself; "Peace rest with his soul!"

"Hark! to that chaunt!" said the Marchesa, in a trembling voice; "it is a first requiem; the soul has but just quitted the body!"

They listened in silence. The Marchesa was much affected; her complexion varied at every instant; her breathings were short and interrupted, and she even shed a few tears, but they were those of despair, rather than of sorrow. "That body is now cold," said she to herself, "which but an hour ago was warm and animated! Those fine senses are closed in death! And to this condition would I reduce a being like myself! Oh, wretched, wretched mother! to what has the folly of a son reduced thee!"

She turned from the Confessor, and walked alone in the cloister. Her agitation encreased; she wept without restraint, for her veil and the evening gloom concealed her, and her sighs were lost amidst the music of the choir.

Schedoni was scarcely less disturbed, but his were emotions of apprehension and contempt. "Behold, what is woman!" said he——"The slave of her passions, the dupe of her senses! When pride and revenge speak in her breast; she defies obstacles, and laughs at crimes! Assail but her senses, let music, for instance, touch some feeble chord of her heart, and echo to her fancy, and lo! all her perceptions change:— she shrinks from the act she had but an instant before believed meritorious, yields to some new emotion, and sinks—the victim of a sound! O, weak and contemptible being!"

The Marchesa, at least, seemed to justify his observations. The desperate passions, which had resisted every remonstrance of reason and humanity, were vanquished only by other passions; and, her senses touched by the mournful melody of music, and her superstitious fears awakened by the occurrence of a requiem for the dead, at the very moment when she was planning murder, she yielded, for a while, to the united influence of pity and terror. Her agitation did not subside; but she returned to the Confessor.

"We will converse on this business at some future time,"

said she; "at present, my spirits are disordered. Good night, father! Remember me in your orisons."

"Peace be with you, lady!" said the Confessor, bowing gravely, "You shall not be forgotten. Be resolute, and yourself."

The Marchesa beckoned her woman to approach, when, drawing her veil closer, and leaning upon the attendant's arm, she left the cloister. Schedoni remained for a moment on the spot, looking after her, till her figure was lost in the gloom of the long perspective; he then, with thoughtful steps, quitted the cloister by another door. He was disappointed, but he did not despair.

CHAPTER V

> The lonely mountains o'er,
> And the resounding shore,
> A voice of weeping heard, and loud lament!
> From haunted spring, and dale,
> Edg'd with poplar pale,
> The parting genius is with sighing sent;
> With flower-inwoven tresses torn
> The nymphs in twilight shade of tangled thicket mourn.
>
> MILTON

WHILE the Marchesa and the Monk were thus meditating conspiracies against Ellena, she was still in the Ursaline convent on the lake of Celano. In this obscure sanctuary, indisposition, the consequence of the long and severe anxiety she had suffered, compelled her to remain. A fever was on her spirits, and an universal lassitude prevailed over her frame; which became the more effectual, from her very solicitude to conquer it. Every approaching day she hoped she should be able to pursue her journey homeward, yet every day found her as incapable of travelling as the last, and the second week was already gone, before the fine air of Celano, and the tranquillity of her asylum, began to revive her. Vivaldi, who was her daily visitor at the grate of the convent; and who, watching over her with intense solicitude, had hitherto forbore to renew a subject, which, by agitating her spirits, might affect her health, now, that her health strengthened, ventured gradually to mention his fears lest the place of her retreat should be discovered, and lest he yet might irrecoverably lose her, unless she would approve of their speedy marriage. At every visit he now urged the subject, represented the dangers that surrounded them, and repeated his arguments and entreaties; for now, when he believed that time was pressing forward fatal evils, he could no longer attend to the delicate scruples, that bade him be sparing in entreaty. Ellena, had she obeyed the dictates of her heart, would have rewarded his attachment and his services, by a frank approbation of his proposal; but the objections which reason exhibited against such a concession, she could neither overcome or disregard.

Vivaldi, after he had again represented their present dangers, and claimed the promise of her hand, received in the presence of her deceased relative, Signora Bianchi, gently ventured to remind her, that an event as sudden as lamentable, had first deferred their nuptials, and that if Bianchi had lived, Ellena would have bestowed, long since, the vows he now solicited. Again he intreated her, by every sacred and tender recollection, to conclude the fearful uncertainty of their fate, and to bestow upon him the right to protect her, before they ventured forth from this temporary asylum.

Ellena immediately admitted the sacredness of the promise, which she had formerly given, and assured Vivaldi that she considered herself as indissolubly bound to wed him as if it had been given at the altar; but she objected to a confirmation of it, till his family should seem willing to receive her for their daughter; when, forgetting the injuries she had received from them, she would no longer refuse their alliance. She added, that Vivaldi ought to be more jealous of the dignity of the woman, whom he honoured with his esteem, than to permit her making a greater concession.

Vivaldi felt the full force of this appeal; he recollected, with anguish, circumstances of which she was happily ignorant, but which served to strengthen with him the justness of her reproof. And, as the aspersions which the Marchese had thrown upon her name, crowded to his memory, pride and indignation swelled his heart, and so far overcame apprehension of hazard, that he formed a momentary resolution to abandon every other consideration, to that of asserting the respect which was due to Ellena, and to forbear claiming her for his wife, till his family should make acknowledgment of their error, and willingly admit her in the rank of their child. But this resolution was as transient as plausible; other considerations, and former fears pressed upon him. He perceived the strong improbability, that they would ever make a voluntary sacrifice of their pride to his love; or yield mistakes, nurtured by prejudice and by willing indulgence, to truth and a sense of justice. In the mean time, the plans, which would be formed for separating him from Ellena, might succeed, and he should lose her for ever. Above all, it appeared, that the best, the only method, which remained for confuting the daring aspersions that had affected her name, was, by proving the high respect he himself felt for her, and presenting her to the world in the sacred character of his wife. These considerations quickly determined him to persevere in his suit; but it was impossible to urge them to Ellena, since the circumstances they must unfold, would not only shock her delicacy and afflict her heart, but would furnish the proper pride she cherished with new arguments against approaching a family, who had thus grossly insulted her.

While these considerations occupied him, the emotion they occasioned did not escape Ellena's observation; it encreased, as he reflected on the impossibility of urging them to her, and on the hopelessness of prevailing with her, unless he could produce new arguments in his favour. His unaffected distress awakened all her tenderness and gratitude; she asked herself whether she ought any longer to assert her own rights, when by doing so, she sacrificed the peace of him, who had incurred so much danger for her sake, who had rescued her from severe oppression, and had so long and so well proved the strength of his affection.

As she applied these questions, she appeared to herself an unjust and selfish being, unwilling to make any sacrifice for the tranquillity of him, who had given her liberty, even at the risk of his life. Her very virtues, now that they were carried to excess, seemed to her to border upon vices; her sense of dignity, appeared to be narrow pride; her delicacy weakness; her moderated affection cold ingratitude; and her circumspection, little less than prudence degenerated into meanness.

Vivaldi, as apt in admitting hope as fear, immediately perceived her resolution beginning to yield, and he urged again every argument which was likely to prevail over it. But the subject was too important for Ellena, to be immediately decided upon; he departed with only a faint assurance of encouragement; and she forbade him to return till the following day, when she would acquaint him with her final determination.

This interval was, perhaps, the most painful he had ever

experienced. Alone, and on the banks of the lake, he passed many hours in alternate hope and fear, in endeavouring to anticipate the decision, on which seemed suspended all his future peace, and abruptly recoiling from it, as often as imagination represented it to be adverse.

Of the walls, that enclosed her, he scarcely ever lost sight; the view of them seemed to cherish his hopes, and, while he gazed upon their rugged surface, Ellena alone was pictured on his fancy; till his anxiety to learn her disposition towards him arose to agony, and he would abruptly leave the spot. But an invisible spell still seemed to attract him back again, and evening found him pacing slowly beneath the shade of those melancholy boundaries that concealed his Ellena.

Her day was not more tranquil. Whenever prudence and decorous pride forbade her to become a member of the Vivaldi family, as constantly did gratitude, affection, irresistible tenderness plead the cause of Vivaldi. The memory of past times returned; and the very accents of the deceased seemed to murmur from the grave, and command her to fulfil the engagement, which had soothed the dying moments of Bianchi.

On the following morning, Vivaldi was at the gates of the convent, long before the appointed hour, and he lingered in dreadful impatience, till the clock struck the signal for his entrance.

Ellena was already in the parlour; she was alone, and rose in disorder on his approach. His steps faultered, his voice was lost, and his eyes only, which he fixed with a wild earnestness of hers, had power to enquire her resolution. She observed the paleness of his countenance, and his emotion, with a mixture of concern and approbation. At that moment, he perceived her smile, and hold out her hand to him; and fear, care, and doubt vanished at once from his mind. He was incapable of thanking her, but sighed deeply as he pressed her hand, and, overcome with joy, supported himself against the grate that separated them.

"You are, then, indeed my own!" said Vivaldi, at length recovering his voice—"We shall be no more parted—you are mine for ever! But your countenance changes! O heaven! surely I have not mistaken! Speak! I conjure you, Ellena; relieve me from these terrible doubts!"

"I am yours, Vivaldi," replied Ellena faintly, "oppression can part us no more."

She wept, and drew her veil over her eyes.

"What mean those tears?" said Vivaldi, with alarm. "Ah! Ellena," he added in a softened voice, "should tears mingle with such moments as these! Should your tears fall upon my heart now! They tell me, that your consent is given with reluctance—with grief; that your love is feeble, your heart—yes Ellena! that your whole heart is no longer mine!"

"They ought rather to tell you," replied Ellena, "that it is all your own; that my affection never was more powerful than now, when it can overcome every consideration with respect to your family, and urge me to a step which must degrade me in their eyes,—and, I fear, in my own."

"O retract that cruel assertion!" interrupted Vivaldi, "Degrade you in your own!—degrade you in their eyes!" He was much agitated; his countenance was flushed, and an air of more than usual dignity dilated his figure.

"The time shall come, my Ellena," he added with energy, "when they shall understand your worth, and acknowledge your excellence. O! that I were an Emperor, that I might shew to all the world how much I love and honour you!"

Ellena gave him her hand, and, withdrawing her veil, smiled on him through her tears, with gratitude and reviving courage.

Before Vivaldi retired to the convent, he obtained her consent to consult with an aged Benedictine, whom he had engaged in his interest, as to the hour at which the marriage might be solemnized with least observation. The priest informed him, that at the conclusion of the vesper-service, he should be disengaged for several hours; and that, as the first hour after sun-set was more solitary than almost any other, the brotherhood being then assembled in the refectory, he would meet Vivaldi and Ellena at that time, in a chapel on the edge of the lake, a short distance from the Benedictine convent, to which it belonged, and celebrate their nuptials.

With this proposal, Vivaldi immediately returned to Ellena; when it was agreed that the party should assemble at the hour mentioned by the priest. Ellena, who had thought it proper to mention her intention to the Abbess of the Ursalines, was, by her permission, to be attended by a lay-sister; and Vivaldi was to meet her without the walls, and conduct her to the altar. When the ceremony was over, the fugitives were to embark in a vessel, hired for the purpose, and, crossing the lake, proceed towards Naples. Vivaldi again withdrew to engage a boat, and Ellena to prepare for the continuance of her journey.

As the appointed hour drew near, her spirits sunk, and she watched with melancholy foreboding, the sun retiring amidst stormy clouds, and his rays fading from the highest points of the mountains, till the gloom of twilight prevailed over the scene. She then left her apartment, took a grateful leave of the hospitable Abbess, and, attended by the lay-sister, quitted the convent.

Immediately without the gate she was met by Vivaldi, whose look, as he put her arm within his, gently reproached her for the dejection of her air.

They walked in silence towards the chapel of San Sebastian. The scene appeared to sympathize with the spirits of Ellena. It was a gloomy evening, and the lake, which broke in dark waves upon the shore, mingled its hollow sounds with those of the wind, that bowed the lofty pines, and swept in gusts among the rocks. She observed with alarm the heavy thunder clouds, that rolled along the sides of the mountains, and the birds circling swiftly over the waters, and scudding away to their nests among the cliffs; and she noticed to Vivaldi, that, as a storm seemed approaching, she wished to avoid crossing the lake. He immediately ordered Paulo to dismiss the boat, and to be in waiting with a carriage, that, if the weather should become clear, they might not be detained longer than was otherwise necessary.

As they approached the chapel, Ellena fixed her eyes on the mournful cypresses which waved over it, and sighed. "Those," she said, "are funereal mementos—not such as should grace the altar of marriage! Vivaldi, I could be superstitious.—Think you not they are portentous of future misfortune? But forgive me; my spirits are weak."

Vivaldi endeavoured to soothe her mind, and tenderly reproached her for the sadness she indulged. Thus they entered the chapel. Silence, and a kind of gloomy sepulchral light, prevailed within. The venerable Benedictine, with a brother, who was to serve as guardian to the bride, were already there, but they were kneeling, and engaged in prayer.

Vivaldi led the trembling Ellena to the altar, where they waited till the Benedictines should have finished, and these were moments of great emotion. She often looked round the dusky chapel, in fearful expectation of discovering some lurking observer; and, though she knew it to be very improbable, that any person in this neighbourhood could be interested in interrupting the ceremony, her mind involuntarily admitted the possibility of it. Once, indeed, as her eyes glanced over a casement, Ellena fancied she distinguished a human face laid close to the glass, as if to watch what was passing within; but when she looked again, the apparition was gone. Notwithstanding this, she listened with anxiety to the uncertain sounds without, and sometimes started as the surges of the lake dashed over the rock below, almost believing she heard the steps and whispering voices of men in the avenues of the chapel. She tried, however, to subdue apprehension, by considering, that if this were true, an harmless curiosity might have attracted some inhabitants of the convent hither, and her spirits became more composed, till she observed a door open a little way, and a dark countenance looking from behind it. In the next instant it retreated, and the door was closed.

Vivaldi, who perceived Ellena's complexion change, as she laid her hand on his arm, followed her eyes to the door, but, no person appearing, he enquired the cause of her alarm.

"We are observed," said Ellena, "some person appeared at that door!"

"And if we are observed, my love," replied Vivaldi, "who is there in this neighbourhood whose observation we can have reason to fear? Good father, dispatch," he added, turning to the priest, "you forget that we are waiting."

The officiating priest made a signal that he had nearly concluded his orison; but the other brother rose immediately, and spoke with Vivaldi, who desired that the doors of the chapel might be fastened to prevent intrusion.

"We dare not bar the gates of this holy temple," replied the Benedictine, "it is a sanctuary, and never may be closed."

"But you will allow me to repress idle curiosity," said Vivaldi, "and to enquire who watched beyond that door? The tranquillity of this lady demands thus much."

The brother asserted, and Vivaldi stepped to the door; but perceiving no person in the obscure passage beyond it, he returned with lighter steps to the altar, from which the officiating priest now rose.

"My children," said he, "I have made you wait,—but an old man's prayers are not less important than a young man's vows, though this is not a moment when you will admit that truth."

"I will allow whatever you please, good father," replied Vivaldi, "if you will administer those vows, without further delay;——time presses."

The venerable priest took his station at the altar, and opened the book. Vivaldi placed himself on his right hand, and with looks of anxious love, endeavoured to encourage Ellena, who, with a dejected countenance, which her veil but ill concealed, and eyes fixed on the ground, leaned on her attendant sister. The figure and homely features of this sister; the tall stature and harsh visage of the brother, clothed in the gray habit of his order; the silvered head and placid physiognomy of the officiating priest, enlightened by a gleam from the lamp above, opposed to the youthful grace and spirit of Vivaldi, and the milder beauty and sweetness of Ellena, formed altogether a group worthy of the pencil.

The priest had begun the ceremony, when a noise from without again alarmed Ellena, who observed the door once more cautiously opened, and a man bend forward his gigantic figure from behind it. He carried a torch, and its glare, as the door gradually unclosed, discovered other persons in the passage beyond, looking forward over his shoulder into the chapel. The fierceness of their air, and the strange peculiarity of their dress, instantly convinced Ellena that they were not inhabitants of the Benedictine convent, but some terrible messengers of evil. Her half-stifled shriek alarmed Vivaldi, who caught her before she fell to the ground; but, as he had not faced the door, he did not understand the occasion of her terror, till the sudden rush of footsteps made him turn, when he observed several men armed, and very singularly habited, advancing towards the altar.

"Who is he that intrudes upon this sanctuary?" he demanded sternly, while he half rose from the ground where Ellena had sunk.

"What sacrilegious footsteps," cried the priest, "thus rudely violate this holy place?"

Ellena was now insensible; and the men continuing to advance, Vivaldi drew his sword to protect her.

The priest and Vivaldi now spoke together, but the words of neither could be distinguished, when a voice, tremendous from its loudness, like bursting thunder, dissipated the cloud of mystery.

"You Vincentio di Vivaldi, and of Naples," it said, "and you Ellena di Rosalba, of Villa Altieri, we summon you to surrender, in the name of the most holy Inquisition!"

"The Inquisition!" exclaimed Vivaldi, scarcely believing what he heard. "Here is some mistake!"

The official repeated the summons, without deigning to reply.

Vivaldi, yet more astonished, added, "Do not imagine you can so far impose upon my credulity, as that I can believe myself to have fallen within the cognizance of the Inquisition."

"You may believe what you please, Signor," replied the chief officer, "but you and that lady are our prisoners."

"Begone, impostor!" said Vivaldi, springing from the ground, where he had supported Ellena, "or my sword shall teach you to repent your audacity!"

"Do you insult an officer of the Inquisition!" exclaimed the ruffian. "That holy Communion will inform you what you incur by resisting its mandate."

The priest interrupted Vivaldi's retort, "If you are really officers of that tremendous tribunal," he said, "produce some proof of your office. Remember this place is sanctified, and tremble for the consequence of imposition. You do wrong to believe, that I will deliver up to you persons who have taken refuge here, without an unequivocal demand from that dread power."

"Produce your form of summons," demanded Vivaldi, with haughty impatience.

"It is here," replied the official, drawing forth a black scroll, which he delivered to the priest, "Read, and be satisfied!"

The Benedictine started the instant he beheld the scroll, but he received and deliberately examined it. The kind of parchment, the impression of the seal, the particular form of words, the private signals, understood only by the initiated— all announced this to be a true instrument of arrestation from the *Holy Office*. The scroll dropped from his hand, and he fixed his eyes, with surprize and unutterable compassion, upon Vivaldi, who stooped to reach the parchment, when it was snatched by the official.

"Unhappy young man!" said the priest, "it is too true; you are summoned by that awful power, to answer to your crime, and I am spared from the commission of a terrible offence!"

Vivaldi appeared thunderstruck. "For what crime, holy father, am I called upon to answer? This is some bold and artful imposture, since it can delude even you! What crime—what offence?"

"I did not think you had been thus hardened in guilt!" replied the priest, "Forbear! add not the audacity of falsehood, to the headlong passions of youth. you understand too well your crime."

"Falsehood!" retorted Vivaldi, "But your years, old man, and those sacred vestments, protect you. For these ruffians, who have dared to implicate that innocent victim," pointing to Ellena, "in the charge, they shall have justice from my vengeance."

"Forbear! forbear!" said the priest, seizing his arm, "have pity on yourself and on her. Know you not the punishment you incur from resistance?"

"I know nor care not," replied Vivaldi, "but I will defend Ellena di Rosalba to the last moment. Let them approach if they dare."

"It is on her, on her who lies senseless at your feet," said the priest, "that they will wreck their vengeance for these insults; on her—the partner of your guilt."

"The partner of my guilt!" exclaimed Vivaldi, with mingled astonishment and indignation——"of my guilt!"

"Rash young man! does not the very veil she wears betray it? I marvel how it could pass my observation!"

"You have stolen a nun from her convent," said the chief officer, "and must answer for the crime. When you have wearied yourself with these heroics, Signor, you must go with us; our patience is wearied already."

Vivaldi observed, for the first time, that Ellena was shrouded in a nun's veil; it was the one which Olivia had lent, to conceal her from the notice of the Abbess, on the night of her departure from San Stefano, and which, in the hurry of that departure, she had forgotten to leave with the nun. During this interval, her mind had been too entirely occupied by cares and apprehension to allow her once to notice, that the veil she wore was other than her usual one; but it had been too well observed by some of the Ursaline sisters.

Though he knew not how to account for the circumstance of the veil, Vivaldi began to perceive others which gave colour to the charge brought against him, and to ascertain the wide circumference of the snare that was spread around him. He fancied, too, that he perceived the hand of Schedoni employed upon it, and that his dark spirit was now avenging itself for the exposure he had suffered in the church of the Spirito Santo, and for all the consequent mortifications. As Vivaldi was ignorant of the ambitious hopes which the Marchesa had encouraged in father Schedoni, he did not see the improbability, that the confessor would have dared to hazard her favour by this arrest of her son; much less could he suspect, that Schedoni, having done so, had secrets in his possession, which enabled him safely to defy her resentment, and bind her in silence to his decree.

With the conviction, that Schedoni's was the master-hand that directed the present manœuvre, Vivaldi stood aghast, and gazing in silent unutterable anguish on Ellena, who, as she began to revive, stretched forth her helpless hands, and called upon him to save her. "Do not leave me," said she in accents the most supplicating, "I am safe while you are with me."

At the sound of her voice, he started from his trance, and turning fiercely upon the ruffians, who stood in sullen watchfulness around, bade them depart, or prepare for his fury. At the same instant they all drew their swords, and the shrieks of Ellena, and the supplications of the officiating priest, were lost amidst the tumult of the combatants.

Vivaldi, most unwilling to shed blood, stood merely on the defensive, till the violence of his antagonists compelled him to exert all his skill and strength. He then disabled one of the ruffians; but his skill was insufficient to repel the other two, and he was nearly overcome, when steps were heard approaching, and Paulo rushed into the chapel. Perceiving his master beset, he drew his sword, and came furiously to his aid. He fought with unconquerable audacity and fierceness, till nearly at the moment when his adversary fell, other ruffians entered the chapel, and Vivaldi with his faithful servant was wounded, and, at length, disarmed.

Ellena, who had been withheld from throwing herself between the combatants, now, on observing that Vivaldi was wounded, renewed her efforts for liberty, accompanied by such agony of supplication and complaint, as almost moved to pity the hearts of the surrounding ruffians.

Disabled by his wounds, and also held by his enemies, Vivaldi was compelled to witness her distress and danger, without a hope of rescuing her. In frantic accents he called upon the old priest to protect her.

"I dare not oppose the orders of the Inquisition," replied the Benedictine, "even if I had sufficient strength to defy its officials. Know you not, unhappy young man, that it is death to resist them?"

"Death!" exclaimed Ellena, "death!"

"Ay lady, too surely so!"

"Signor, it would have been well for you," said one of the officers, "if you had taken my advice; you will pay dearly for what you have done," pointing to the ruffian, who lay severely wounded on the ground.

"My master will not have that to pay for, friend," said Paulo, "for if you must know, that is a piece of my work; and, if my arms were now at liberty, I would try if I could not match it among one of you, though I am so slashed."

"Peace, good Paulo! the deed was mine," said Vivaldi; then addressing the official, "For myself I care not, I have done my duty—but for her!—Can you look upon her, innocent and helpless as she is, and not relent! Can you, will you, barbarians! drag her, also, to destruction, upon a charge too so daringly false?"

"Our relenting would be of no service to her," replied the official, "we must do our duty. Whether the charge is true or false, she must answer to it before her judges."

"What charge?" demanded Ellena.

"The charge of having broken your nun's vows," replied the priest.

Ellena raised her eyes to heaven; "Is it even so!" she exclaimed.

"You hear she acknowledges the crime," said one of the ruffians.

"She acknowledges no crime," replied Vivaldi; "she only perceives the extent of the malice that persecutes her. O! Ellena, must I then abandon you to their power! leave you for ever!"

The agony of this thought re-animated him with momentary strength; he burst from the grasp of the officials, and once more clasped Ellena to his bosom, who, unable to speak, wept, with the anguish of a breaking heart, as her head sunk upon his shoulder. The ruffians around them so far respected their grief, that, for a moment, they did not interrupt it.

Vivaldi's exertion was transient; faint from sorrow, and from loss of blood, he became unable to support himself, and was compelled again to relinquish Ellena.

"Is there no help?" said she, with agony; "will you suffer him to expire on the ground?"

The priest directed, that he should be conveyed to the Benedictine convent, where his wounds might be examined, and medical aid administered. The disabled ruffians were already carried thither; but Vivaldi refused to go, unless Ellena might accompany him. It was contrary to the rules of the place, that a woman should enter it, and before the priest could reply, his Benedictine brother eagerly said, that they dared not transgress the law of the convent.

Ellena's fears for Vivaldi entirely overcame those for herself, and she entreated, that he would suffer himself to be conveyed to the Benedictines; but he could not be prevailed with to leave her. The officials, however, prepared to separate them; Vivaldi in vain urged the useless cruelty of dividing him from Ellena, if, as they had hinted, she also was to be carried to the Inquisition; and as ineffectually demanded, whither they really designed to take her.

"We shall take good care of her, Signor," said an officer, "that is sufficient for you. It signifies nothing whether you are going the same way, you must not go together."

"Why, did you ever hear, Signor, of arrested persons being suffered to remain in company?" said another ruffian, "Fine plots they would lay; I warrant they would not contradict each other's evidence a tittle."

"You shall not separate me from my master, though," vociferated Paulo; "I demand to be sent to the Inquisition with him, or to the devil, but all is one for that."

"Fair and softly," replied the officer; "you shall be sent to the Inquisition first, and to the devil afterwards; you must be tried before you are condemned."

"But waste no more time," he added to his followers, and pointing to Ellena, "away with her."

As he said this, they lifted Ellena in their arms. "Let me loose!" cried Paulo, when he saw they were carrying her from the place, "let me loose, I say!" and the violence of his struggles burst asunder the cords which held him; a vain release, for he was instantly seized again.

Vivaldi, already exhausted by the loss of blood and the anguish of his mind, made, however, a last effort to save her; he tried to raise himself from the ground, but a sudden film came over his sight, and his senses forsook him, while yet the name of Ellena faultered on his lips.

As they bore her from the chapel, she continued to call upon Vivaldi, and alternately to supplicate that she might once more behold him, and take one last adieu. The ruffians were inexorable, and she heard his voice no more, for he no longer heard—no longer was able to reply to hers.

"O! once again!" she cried in agony, "One word, Vivaldi! Let me hear the sound of your voice yet once again!" But it was silent.

As she quitted the chapel, with eyes still bent towards the spot where he lay, she exclaimed, in the piercing accents of despair, "Farewel, Vivaldi!—O! for ever——ever, farewel!"

The tone, in which she pronounced the last "farewel!" was so touching, that even the cold heart of the priest could not resist it; but he impatiently wiped away the few tears, that rushed into his eyes, before they were observed. Vivaldi heard it—it seemed to arouse him from death!—he heard her mournful voice for the last time, and, turning his eyes, saw her veil floating away through the portal of the chapel. All suffering, all effort, all resistance were vain; the ruffians bound him, bleeding as he was, and conveyed him to the Benedictine convent, together with the wounded Paulo, who unceasingly vociferated on the way thither, "I demand to be sent to the Inquisition! I demand to be sent to the Inquisition!"

CHAPTER VI

> In earliest Greece to thee, with partial choice,
> The grief-full Muse address'd her infant tongue;
> The maids and matrons on her awful voice,
> Silent and pale, in wild amazement hung.
>
> COLLINS'S ODE TO FEAR

THE wounds of Vivaldi, and of his servant, were pronounced, by the Benedictine who had examined and dressed them, to be not dangerous, but those of one of the ruffians were declared doubtful. Some few of the brothers displayed much compassion and kindness towards the prisoners; but the greater part seemed fearful of expressing any degree of sympathy for persons who had fallen within the cognizance of the Holy Office, and even kept aloof from the chamber, in which they were confined. To this self-restriction, however, they were not long subjected; for Vivaldi and Paulo were compelled to begin their journey as soon as some short rest had sufficiently revived them. They were placed in the same carriage, but the presence of two officers prevented all interchange of conjecture as to the destination of Ellena, and with respect to the immediate occasion of their misfortune. Paulo, indeed, now and then hazarded a surmise, and did not scruple to affirm, that the Abbess of San Stefano was their chief enemy; that the Carmelite friars, who had overtaken them on the road, were her agents; and that, having traced their route, they had given intelligence where Vivaldi and Ellena might be found.

"I guessed we never should escape the Abbess," said Paulo, "though I would not disturb you, Signor mio, nor the poor lady Ellena, by saying so. But your Abbesses are as cunning as Inquisitors, and are so fond of governing, that they had rather, like them, send a man to the devil, than send him no where."

Vivaldi gave Paulo a significant look, which was meant to repress his imprudent loquacity, and then sunk again into silence and the abstractions of deep grief. The officers, meanwhile, never spoke, but were observant of all that Paulo said, who perceived their watchfulness, but because he despised them as spies, he thoughtlessly despised them also as enemies, and was so far from concealing opinions, which they might repeat to his prejudice, that he had a pride in exaggerating them, and in daring the worst, which the exasperated tempers of these men, shut up in the same carriage with him, and compelled to hear whatever he chose to say against the institution to which they belonged, could effect. Whenever Vivaldi, recalled from his abstractions by some bold assertion, endeavoured to check his imprudence, Paulo was contented to solace his conscience, instead of protecting himself, by saying, "It is their own fault; they would thrust themselves into my company; let them have enough of it; and, if ever they take me before their reverences, the Inquisitors, *they* shall have enough for it too. I will play up such a tune in the Inquisition as is not heard there every day. I will jingle all the bells on their fool's caps, and tell them a little honest truth, if they make me smart for it ever so."

Vivaldi, aroused once more, and seriously alarmed for the consequences which honest Paulo might be drawing upon himself, now insisted on his silence, and was obeyed.

They travelled during the whole night, stopping only to change horses. At every post house, Vivaldi looked for a carriage that might inclose Ellena, but none appeared, nor any sound of wheels told him that she followed.

With the morning light he perceived the dome of St. Peter, appearing faintly over the plains that surrounded Rome, and he understood, for the first time, that he was going to the prisons of the Inquisition in that city. The travellers descended upon the Campania, and then rested for a few hours at a small town on its borders.

When they again set forward, Vivaldi perceived that the guard was changed, the officer who had remained with him in the apartment of the inn only appearing among the new faces which surrounded him. The dress and manners of these men differed considerably from those of the other. Their conduct was more temperate, but their countenances expressed a darker cruelty, mingled with a sly demureness, and a solemn self-importance, that announced them at once as belonging to the Inquisition. They were almost invariably silent; and when they did speak, it was only in a few sententious words. To the abounding questions of Paulo, and the few earnest entreaties of his master, to be informed of the place of Ellena's destination, they made not the least reply; and listened to all the flourishing speeches of the servant against Inquisitors and the Holy Office with the most profound gravity.

Vivaldi was struck with the circumstances of the guard being changed, and still more with the appearance of the party, who now composed it. When he compared the manners of the late, with those of the present guard, he thought he discovered in the first the mere ferocity of ruffians; but in the latter, the principles of cunning and cruelty, which seemed particularly to characterize Inquisitors; he was inclined to believe, that a stratagem had enthralled him, and that now, for the first time, he was in the custody of the *Holy Office*.

It was near midnight when the prisoners entered the *Porto del Popolo,* and found themselves in the midst of the Carnival at Rome. The *Corso,* through which they were obliged to pass, was crowded with gay carriages and masks, with processions of musicians, monks, and mountebanks, was lighted up with innumerable flambeaux, and resounded with the heterogeneous rattling of wheels, the music of serenaders, and the jokes and laughter of the revellers, as they sportively threw about their sugar-plumbs. The heat of the weather made it necessary to have the windows of the coach open; and the prisoners, therefore, saw all that passed without. It was a scene, which contrasted cruelly with the feelings and circumstances of Vivaldi; torn as he was from her he most loved, in dreadful uncertainty as to her fate, and himself about to be brought before a tribunal, whose mysterious and terrible proceedings appalled even the bravest spirits. Altogether, this was one of the most striking examples, which the chequer-work of human life could shew, or human feelings endure. Vivaldi sickened as he looked upon the splendid crowd, while the carriage made its way slowly with it; but Paulo, as he gazed, was reminded of the Corso of Naples, such as it appeared at the time of Carnival, and, comparing the present scene with his native one, he found fault with every thing he beheld. The dresses were tasteless, the equipages without splendour, the people without spirit; yet, such was the propensity of his heart to sympathize with whatever was gay, that, for some moments, he forgot that he was a prisoner on his way to the Inquisition; almost forgot that he was a Neapolitan; and, while he exclaimed against the dullness of a Roman carnival, would have sprung through the carriage window to partake of its spirit, if his fetters and his wounds had not withheld him. A deep sigh from Vivaldi recalled his wandering imagination; and, when he noticed again the sorrow in his master's look, all his lightly joyous spirits fled.

"My *maestro,* my dear *maestro!*"—he said, and knew not how to finish what he wished to express.

At that moment they passed the theatre of San Carlo, the doors of which were thronged with equipages, where Roman ladies, in their gala habits, courtiers in their fantastic dresses, and masks of all descriptions, were hastening to the opera. In the midst of this gay bustle, where the carriage was unable to proceed, the officials of the Inquisition looked on in solemn silence, not a muscle of their features relaxing in sympathy, or yielding a single wrinkle of the self-importance that lifted their brows; and, while they regarded with secret contempt those, who could be thus lightly pleased, the people, in return, more wisely, perhaps, regarded with contempt the proud moroseness, that refused to partake of innocent pleasures, because they were trifling, and shrunk from countenances furrowed with the sternness of cruelty. But, when their office was distinguished, part of the crowd pressed back from the carriage in affright, while another part advanced with curiosity; though, as the majority retreated, space was left for the carriage to move on. After quitting the Corso, it proceeded for some miles through dark and deserted streets, where only here and there a lamp, hung on high before the image of a saint, shed its glimmering light, and where a melancholy and universal silence prevailed. At intervals, indeed, the moon, as the clouds passed away, shewed, for a moment, some of those mighty monuments of Rome's eternal name, those sacred ruins, those gigantic skeletons, which once enclosed a soul, whose energies governed a world! Even Vivaldi could not behold with indifference the grandeur of these reliques, as the rays fell upon the hoary walls and columns, or pass among these scenes of ancient story, without feeling a melancholy awe, a sacred enthusiasm, that withdrew him from himself. But the illusion was transient; his own misfortunes pressed too heavily upon him to be long unfelt, and his enthusiasm vanished like the moonlight.

A returning gleam lighted up, soon after, the rude and extensive area, which the carriage was crossing. It appeared, from its desolation, and the ruins scattered distantly along its skirts, to be a part of the city entirely abandoned by the modern inhabitants to the reliques of its former grandeur. Not even the shadow of a human being crossed the waste, nor any building appeared, which might be supposed to shelter one. The deep tone of a bell, however, rolling on the silence of the night, announced the haunts of man to be not far off; and Vivaldi perceived in the distance, to which he was approaching, an extent of lofty walls and towers, that, as far as the gloom would permit his eye to penetrate, bounded the horizon. He judged these to be the prisons of the Inquisition. Paulo pointed them out at the same moment. "Ah, Signor!" said he despondingly, "that is the place! what strength! If, my Lord, the Marchese were but to see where we are going! Ah!"—

He concluded with a deep sigh, and sunk again into the state of apprehension and mute expectation, which he had suffered from the moment that he quitted the Corso.

The carriage having reached the walls, followed their bendings to a considerable extent. These walls, of immense height, and strengthened by innumerable massy bulwarks, exhibited neither window or grate, but a vast and dreary blank; a small round tower only, perched here and there upon the summit, breaking their monotony.

The prisoners passed what seemed to be the principal entrance, from the grandeur of its portal, and the gigantic loftiness of the towers that rose over it; and soon after the carriage stopped at an arch-way in the walls, strongly barricadoed. One of the escort alighted, and, having struck upon the bars, a folding door within was immediately opened, and a man bearing a torch appeared behind the barricado, whose countenance, as he looked through it, might have been copied for the

"Grim-visaged comfortless Despair"

of the Poet.

No words were exchanged between him and the guard;

but on perceiving who were without, he opened the iron gate, and the prisoners, having alighted, passed with the two officials beneath the arch, the guard following with a torch. They descended a flight of broad steps, at the foot of which another iron gate admitted them to a kind of hall; such, however, it at first appeared to Vivaldi, as his eyes glanced through its gloomy extent, imperfectly ascertaining it by the lamp, which hung from the centre of the roof. No person appeared, and a death-like silence prevailed; for neither the officials nor the guard yet spoke; nor did any distant sound contradict the notion, that they were traversing the chambers of the dead. To Vivaldi it occurred, that this was one of the burial vaults of the victims, who suffered in the Inquisition, and his whole frame thrilled with horror. Several avenues, opening from the apartment, seemed to lead to distant quarters of this immense fabric, but still no footstep whispering along the pavement, or voice murmuring through the arched roofs, indicated it to be the residence of the living.

Having entered one of the passages, Vivaldi perceived a person clothed in black, and who bore a lighted taper, crossing silently in the remote perspective; and he understood too well from his habit, that he was a member of this dreadful tribunal.

The sound of footsteps seemed to reach the stranger, for he turned, and then paused, while the officers advanced. They then made signs to each other, and exchanged a few words, which neither Vivaldi or his servant could understand, when the stranger, pointing with his taper along another avenue, passed away. Vivaldi followed him with his eyes, till a door at the extremity of the passage opened, and he saw the Inquisitor enter an apartment, whence a great light proceeded, and where several other figures, habited like himself, appeared waiting to receive him. The door immediately closed; and, whether the imagination of Vivaldi was affected, or that the sounds were real, he thought, as it closed, he distinguished half-stifled groans, as of a person in agony.

The avenue, through which the prisoners passed, opened, at length, into an apartment gloomy like the first they had entered, but more extensive. The roof was supported by arches, and long arcades branched off from every side of the chamber, as from a central point, and were lost in the gloom, which the rays of the small lamps, suspended in each, but feebly penetrated.

They rested here, and a person soon after advanced, who appeared to be the jailor, into whose hands Vivaldi and Paulo were delivered. A few mysterious words having been exchanged, one of the officials crossed the hall, and ascended a wide stair-case, while the other, with the jailor and the guard, remained below, as if awaiting his return.

A long interval elapsed, during which the stillness of the place was sometimes interrupted by a closing door, and, at others, by indistinct sounds, which yet appeared to Vivaldi like lamentations and extorted groans. Inquisitors, in their long black robes, issued, from time to time, from the passages, and crossed the hall to other avenues. They eyed the prisoners with curiosity, but without pity. Their visages, with few exceptions, seemed stamped with the characters of demons. Vivaldi could not look upon the grave cruelty, or the ferocious impatience, their countenances severally expressed, without reading in them the fate of some fellow creature, the fate, which these men seemed going, even at this moment, to confirm; and, as they passed with soundless steps, he shrunk from observation, as if their very looks possessed some supernatural power, and could have struck death. But he followed their fleeting figures, as they proceeded on their work of horror, to where the last glimmering ray faded into darkness, expecting to see other doors of other chambers open to receive them. While meditating upon these horrors, Vivaldi lost every selfish consideration in astonishment and indignation of the sufferings, which the frenzied wickedness of man prepares for man, who, even at the moment of infliction, insults his victim with assertions of the justice and necessity of such procedure. "Is this possible!" said Vivaldi internally, "Can this be in human nature!—Can such horrible perversion of right be permitted! Can man, who calls himself endowed with reason, and immeasurably superior to every other created being, argue himself into the commission of such horrible folly, such inveterate cruelty, as exceeds all the acts of the most irrational and ferocious brute. Brutes do not deliberately slaughter their species; it remains for man only, man, proud of his prerogative of reason, and boasting of his sense of justice, to unite the most terrible extremes of folly and wickedness!"

Vivaldi had been no stranger to the existence of this tribunal; he had long understood the nature of the establishment, and had often received particular accounts of its customs and laws; but, though he had believed before, it was now only that conviction appeared to impress his understanding. A new view of human nature seemed to burst, at once, upon his mind, and he could not have experienced greater astonishment, if this had been the first moment, in which he had heard of the institution. But, when he thought of Ellena, considered that she was in the power of this tribunal, and that it was probable she was at this moment within the same dreadful walls, grief, indignation, and despair irritated him almost to frenzy. He seemed suddenly animated with supernatural strength, and ready to attempt impossibilities for her deliverance. It was by a strong effort for self command, that he forbore bursting the bonds, which held him, and making a desperate attempt to seek her through the vast extent of these prisons. Reflection, however, had not so entirely forsaken him, but that he saw the impossibility of succeeding in such an effort, the moment he had conceived it, and he forbore to rush upon the certain destruction, to which it must have led. His passions, thus restrained, seemed to become virtues, and to display themselves in the energy of his courage and his fortitude. His soul became stern and vigorous in despair, and his manner and countenance assumed a calm dignity, which seemed to awe, in some degree, even his guards. The pain of his wounds was no longer felt; it appeared as if the strength of his intellectual self had subdued the infirmities of the body, and, perhaps, in these moments of elevation, he could have endured the torture without shrinking.

Paulo, meanwhile, mute and grave, was watchful of all that passed; he observed the revolutions in his master's mind, with grief first, and then with surprize, but he could not imitate the noble fortitude, which now gave weight and steadiness to Vivaldi's thoughts. And when he looked on the power and gloom around him, and on the visages of the passing Inquisitors, he began to repent, that he had so freely delivered his opinion of this tribunal, in the presence of its agents, and to perceive, that if he played up the kind of tune he had threatened, it would probably be the last he should ever be permitted to perform in this world.

At length, the chief officer descended the stair-case, and

immediately bade Vivaldi follow him. Paulo was accompanying his master, but was withheld by the guard, and told he was to be disposed of in a different way. This was the moment of his severest trial; he declared he would not be separated from his master.

"What did I demand to be brought here for," he cried, "if it was not that I might go shares with the Signor in all his troubles? This is not a place to come to for pleasure, I warrant; and I can promise ye, gentlemen, I would not have come within an hundred miles of you, if it had not been for my master's sake."

The guards roughly interrupted him, and were carrying him away, when Vivaldi's commanding voice arrested them. He returned to speak a few words of consolation to his faithful servant, and, since they were to be separated, to take leave of him.

Paulo embraced his knees, and, while he wept, and his words were almost stifled by sobs, declared no force should drag him from his master, while he had life; and repeatedly appealed to the guards, with—"What did I demand to be brought here for? Did ever any body come here to seek pleasure? What right have you to prevent my going shares with my master in his troubles?"

"We do not intend to deny you that pleasure, friend," replied one of the guards.

"Don't you? Then heaven bless you!" cried Paulo, springing from his knees, and shaking the man by the hand with a violence, that would nearly have dislocated the shoulder of a person less robust.

"So come with us," added the guard, drawing him away from Vivaldi. Paulo now became outrageous, and, struggling with the guards, burst from them, and again fell at the feet of his master, who raised and embraced him, endeavouring to prevail with him to submit quietly to what was inevitable, and to encourage him with hope.

"I trust that our separation will be short," said Vivaldi, "and that we shall meet in happier circumstances. My innocence must soon appear."

"We shall never, never meet again, Signor mio, in this world," said Paulo, sobbing violently, "so don't make me hope so. That old Abbess knows what she is about too well to let us escape; or she would not have catched us up so cunningly as she did; so what signifies innocence! O! if my old lord, the Marchese, did but know where we are!"

Vivaldi interrupted him, and turning to the guards said, "I recommend my faithful servant to your compassion, he is innocent. It will some time, perhaps, be in my power to recompence you for any indulgence you may allow him, and I shall value it a thousand times more highly, than any you could shew to myself! Farewel, Paulo,——farewel! Officer, I am ready."

"O stay! Signor, for one moment—stay!" said Paulo.

"We can wait no longer," said the guard, and again drew Paulo away, who looking piteously after Vivaldi, alternately repeated, "Farewel, dear *maestro*! farewel dear, dear *maestro*!" and "What did I demand to be brought here for? What did I demand to be brought here for?—what was it for, if not to go shares with my *maestro*?" till Vivaldi was beyond the reach of sight and of hearing.

Vivaldi, having followed the officer up the stair-case, passed through a gallery to an anti-chamber, where, being delivered into the custody of some persons in waiting, his conductor disappeared beyond a folding door, that led to an inner apartment. Over this door was an inscription in Hebrew characters, traced in blood-colour. Dante's inscription on the entrance of the infernal regions, would have been suitable to a place, where every circumstance and feature seemed to say, *"Hope, that comes to all, comes not here!"*

Vivaldi conjectured, that in this chamber they were preparing for him the instruments, which were to extort a confession; and though he knew little of the regular proceedings of this tribunal, he had always understood, that the torture was inflicted, upon the accused person, till he made confession of the crime, of which he was suspected. By such a mode of proceeding, the innocent were certain of suffering longer than the guilty; for, as they had nothing to confess, the Inquisitor, mistaking innocence for obstinacy, persevered in his inflictions, and it frequently happened that he compelled the innocent to become criminal, and assert a falsehood, that they might be released from anguish, which they could no longer sustain. Vivaldi considered this circumstance undauntedly; every faculty of his soul was bent up to firmness and endurance. He believed that he understood the extent of the charge, which would be brought against him, a charge as false, as a specious confirmation of it, would be terrible in its consequence both to Ellena and himself. Yet every art would be practised to bring him to an acknowledgment of having carried off a nun, and he knew also, that, since the prosecutor and the witnesses are never confronted with the prisoner in cases of severe accusation, and since their very names are concealed from him, it would be scarcely possible for him to prove his innocence. But he did not hesitate an instant whether to sacrifice himself for Ellena, determining rather to expire beneath the merciless inflictions of the Inquisitors, than to assert a falsehood, which must involve her in destruction.

The officer, at length, appeared, and, having beckoned Vivaldi to advance, uncovered his head, and bared his arms. He then led him forward through the folding door into the chamber; having done which, he immediately withdrew, and the door, which shut out Hope, closed after him.

Vivaldi found himself in a spacious apartment, where only two persons were visible, who were seated at a large table, that occupied the centre of the room. They were both habited in black; the one, who seemed by his piercing eye, and extraordinary physiognomy, to be an Inquisitor, wore on his head a kind of black turban, which heightened the natural ferocity of his visage; the other was uncovered, and his arms bared to the elbows. A book, with some instruments of singular appearance, lay before him. Round the table were several unoccupied chairs, on the backs of which appeared figurative signs, at the upper end of the apartment, a gigantic crucifix stretched nearly to the vaulted roof; and, at the lower end, suspended from an arch in the wall, was a dark curtain, but whether it veiled a window, or shrouded some object or person, necessary to the designs of the Inquisitor, there were little means of judging. It was, however, suspended from an arch such as sometimes contains a casement, or leads to a deep recess.

The Inquisitor called on Vivaldi to advance, and, when he had reached the table, put a book into his hands, and bade him swear to reveal the truth, and keep for ever secret whatever he might see or hear in the apartment.

Vivaldi hesitated to obey so unqualified a command. The Inquisitor reminded him, by a look, not to be mistaken, that he was absolute here; but Vivaldi still hesitated. "Shall I consent to my own condemnation?" said he to himself, "The malice of demons like these may convert the most innocent circumstances into matter of accusation, for my destruction, and I must answer whatever questions they choose to ask. And shall I swear, also, to conceal whatever I may witness in this chamber, when I know that the most diabolical cruelties are hourly practised here?"

The Inquisitor, in a voice which would have made a heart less fortified than was Vivaldi's tremble, again commanded him to swear; at the same time, he made a signal to the person, who sat at the opposite end of the table, and who appeared to be an inferior officer.

Vivaldi was still silent, but he began to consider that, unconscious as he was of crime, it was scarcely possible for his words to be tortured into a self-accusation; and that, whatever he might witness, no retribution would be prevented, no evil withheld by the oath, which bound him to secresy, since his most severe denunciation could avail nothing against the supreme power of this tribunal. As he did not perceive any good, which could arise from refusing the oath; and saw much immediate evil from resistance, he consented to receive it. Notwithstanding this, when he put the book to his lips, and uttered the tremendous vow prescribed to him, hesitation and reluctance returned upon his mind, and an icy coldness struck to his heart. He was so much affected, that circumstances, apparently the most trivial, had at this moment influence upon his imagination. As he accidentally threw his eyes upon the curtain, which he had observed before without emotion, and now thought it moved, he almost started in expectation of seeing some person, an Inquisitor perhaps, as terrific as the one before him, or an Accuser as malicious as Schedoni, steal from behind it.

The Inquisitor having administered the oath, and the attendant having noted it in his book, the examination began. After demanding, as is usual, the names and titles of Vivaldi and his family, and his place of residence, to which he fully replied, the Inquisitor asked, whether he understood the nature of the accusation on which he had been arrested.

"The order for my arrestation informed me," replied Vivaldi.

"Look to your words!" said the Inquisitor, "and remember your oath. What was the ground of accusation?"

"I understood," said Vivaldi, "that I was accused of having stolen a nun from her sanctuary."

A faint degree of surprise appeared on the brow of the Inquisitor. "You confess it, then?" he said, after the pause of a moment, and making a signal to the Secretary, who immediately noted Vivaldi's words.

"I solemnly deny it," replied Vivaldi, "the accusation is false and malicious."

"Remember the oath you have taken!" repeated the Inquisitor, "learn also, that mercy is shewn to such as make full confession; but that the torture is applied to those, who have the folly and the obstinacy to withhold the truth."

"If you torture me till I acknowledge the justness of this accusation," said Vivaldi, "I must expire under your inflictions, for suffering never shall compel me to assert a falsehood. It is not the truth, which you seek; it is not the guilty, whom you punish; the innocent, having no crimes to confess, are the victims of your cruelty, or, to escape from it, become criminal, and proclaim a lie."

"Recollect yourself," said the Inquisitor, sternly. "You are not brought hither to accuse, but to answer accusation. You say you are innocent; yet acknowledge yourself to be acquainted with the subject of the charge which is to be urged against you! How could you know this, but from the voice of conscience?"

"From the words of your own summons," replied Vivaldi, "and from those of your officials who arrested me."

"How!" exclaimed the Inquisitor, "note that," pointing to the Secretary; "he says by the words of our summons; now we know, that you never read that summons. He says also by the words of our officials;—it appears, then, he is ignorant, that death would follow such a breach of confidence."

"It is true, I never did read the summons," replied Vivaldi, "and as true, that I never asserted I did; the friar, who read it, told of what it accused me, and your officials confirmed the testimony."

"No more of this equivocation!" said the Inquisitor, "Speak only to the question."

"I will not suffer my assertions to be misrepresented," replied Vivaldi, "or my words to be perverted against myself. I have sworn to speak the truth only; since you believe I violate my oath, and doubt my direct and simple words, I will speak no more."

The Inquisitor half rose from his chair, and his countenance grew paler. "Audacious heretic!" he said, "will you dispute, insult, and disobey, the commands of our most holy tribunal! You will be taught the consequence of your desperate impiety.—To the torture with him!"

A stern smile was on the features of Vivaldi; his eyes were calmly fixed on the Inquisitor, and his attitude was undaunted and firm. His courage, and the cool contempt, which his looks expressed, seemed to touch his examiner, who perceived that he had not a common mind to operate upon. He abandoned, therefore, for the present, terrific measures, and, resuming his usual manner, proceeded in the examination.

"Where were you arrested?"

"At the chapel of San Sebastian, on the lake of Celano."

"You are certain as to this?" asked the Inquisitor, "you are sure it was not at the village of Legano, on the high road between Celano and Rome?"

Vivaldi, while he confirmed his assertion, recollected with some surprise that Legano was the place where the guard had been changed, and he mentioned the circumstance. The Inquisitor, however, proceeded in his questions, without appearing to notice it. "Was any person arrested with you?"

"You cannot be ignorant," replied Vivaldi, "that Signora di Rosalba, was seized at the same time, upon the false charge of being a nun, who had broken her vows, and eloped from her convent; nor that Paulo Mendrico, my faithful servant! was also made a prisoner, though upon what pretence he was arrested I am utterly ignorant."

The Inquisitor remained for some moments in thoughtful silence, and then enquired slightly concerning the family of Ellena, and her usual place of residence. Vivaldi, fearful of making some assertion that might be prejudicial to her, referred him to herself; but the inquiry was repeated.

"She is now within these walls," replied Vivaldi, hoping to learn from the manner of his examiner, whether his fears were just, "and can answer these questions better than myself."

The Inquisitor merely bade the Notary write down her name, and then remained for a few moments meditating. At length, he said, "Do you know where you now are?"

Vivaldi, smiling at the question, replied, "I understand that I am in the prisons of the Inquisition, at Rome."

"Do you know what are the crimes that subject persons to the cognizance of the Holy Office?"

Vivaldi was silent.

"Your conscience informs *you,* and your silence confirms

me. Let me admonish you, once more, to make a full confession of your guilt; remember that this is a merciful tribunal, and shews favour to such as acknowledge their crimes."

Vivaldi smiled; but the Inquisitor proceeded.

"It does not resemble some severe, yet just courts, where immediate execution follows the confession of a criminal. No! it is merciful, and though it punishes guilt, it never applies the torture but in cases of necessity, when the obstinate silence of the prisoner requires such a measure. You see, therefore, what you may avoid, and what to expect."

"But if the prisoner has nothing to confess?" said Vivaldi,—"Can your tortures make him guilty? They may force a weak mind to be guilty of falsehood; to escape present anguish, a man may unwarily condemn himself to the death! You will find that I am not such an one."

"Young man," replied the Inquisitor, "you will understand too soon, that we never act, but upon sure authority; and will wish, too late, that you had made an honest confession. Your silence cannot keep from us a knowledge of your offences; we are in possession of facts; and your obstinacy can neither wrest from us the truth, or pervert it. Your most secret offences are already written on the tablets of the Holy Office; your conscience cannot reflect them more justly.—Tremble, therefore, and revere. But understand, that, though we have sufficient proof of your guilt, we require you to confess; and that the punishment of obstinacy is as certain, as that of any other offence."

Vivaldi made no reply, and the Inquisitor, after a momentary silence, added, "Was you ever in the church of the Spirito Santo, at Naples?"

"Before I answer the question," said Vivaldi, "I require the name of my accuser."

"You are to recollect that you have no right to demand any thing in this place," observed the Inquisitor, "nor can you be ignorant that the name of the Informer is always kept sacred from the knowledge of the Accused. Who would venture to do his duty, if his name was arbitrarily to be exposed to the vengeance of the criminal against whom he informs? It is only in a particular process that the Accuser is brought forward."

"The names of the Witnesses?" demanded Vivaldi. "The same justice conceals them also from the knowledge of the Accused," replied the Inquisitor.

"And is no justice left for the Accused?" said Vivaldi. "Is he to be tried and condemned without being confronted with either his Prosecutor, or the Witnesses!"

"Your questions are too many," said the Inquisitor, "and your answers too few. The Informer is not also the Prosecutor; the Holy Office, before which the information is laid, is the Prosecutor, and the dispenser of justice; its Public Accuser lays the circumstances, and the testimonies of the Witnesses, before the Court. But too much of this."

"How!" exclaimed Vivaldi, "is the tribunal at once the Prosecutor, Witness, and Judge! What can private malice wish for more, than such a court of *justice,* at which to arraign its enemy? The stiletto of the Assassin is not so sure, or so fatal to innocence. I now perceive, that it avails me nothing to be guiltless; a single enemy is sufficient to accomplish my destruction."

"You have an enemy then?" observed the Inquisitor.

Vivaldi was too well convinced that he had one, but there was not sufficient proof, as to the person of this enemy, to justify him in asserting that it was Schedoni. The circumstance of Ellena having been arrested, would have compelled him to suspect another person as being at least accessary to the designs of the Confessor, had not credulity started in horror from the supposition, that a mother's resentment could possibly betray her son into the prisons of the Inquisition, though this mother had exhibited a temper of remorseless cruelty towards a stranger, who had interrupted her views for that son.

"You have an enemy then?" repeated the Inquisitor.

"That I am here sufficiently proves it," replied Vivaldi. "But I am so little any man's enemy, that I know not who to call mine."

"It is evident, then, that you have no enemy," observed the subtle Inquisitor, "and that this accusation is brought against you by a respecter of truth, and a faithful servant of the Roman interest."

Vivaldi was shocked to perceive the insidious art, by which he had been betrayed into a declaration apparently so harmless, and the cruel dexterity with which it had been turned against him. A lofty and contemptuous silence was all that he opposed to the treachery of his examiner, on whose countenance appeared a smile of triumph and self-congratulation, the life of a fellow creature being, in his estimation, of no comparative importance with the self-applauses of successful art; the art, too, upon which he most valued himself—that of his profession.

The Inquisitor proceeded, "You persist, then, in withholding the truth?" He paused, but Vivaldi making no reply, he resumed.

"Since it is evident, from your own declaration, that you have no enemy, whom private resentment might have instigated to accuse you; and, from other circumstances which have occurred in your conduct, that you are conscious of more than you have confessed,—it appears, that the accusation which has been urged against you, is not a malicious slander. I exhort you, therefore, and once more conjure you, by our holy faith, to make an ingenuous confession of your offences, and to save yourself from the means, which must of necessity be enforced to obtain a confession before your trial commences. I adjure you, also, to consider, that by such open conduct only, can mercy be won to soften the justice of this most righteous tribunal!"

Vivaldi, perceiving that it was now necessary for him to reply, once more solemnly asserted his innocence of the crime alledged against him in the summons, and of the consciousness of any act, which might lawfully subject him to the notice of the Holy Office.

The Inquisitor again demanded what was the crime alledged, and, Vivaldi having repeated the accusation, he again bade the Secretary note it, as he did which, Vivaldi thought he perceived upon his features something of a malignant satisfaction, for which he knew not how to account. When the Secretary had finished, Vivaldi was ordered to subscribe his name and quality to the depositions, and he obeyed.

The Inquisitor then bade him consider of the admonition he had received, and prepare either to confess on the morrow, or to undergo the question. As he concluded, he gave a signal, and the officer, who had conducted Vivaldi into the chamber, immediately appeared.

"You know your orders," said the Inquisitor, "receive your prisoner, and see that they are obeyed."

The official bowed, and Vivaldi followed him from the apartment in melancholy silence.

CHAPTER VII

Call up the Spirit of the ocean, bid
Him raise the storm! The waves begin to heave,
To curl, to foam; the white surges run far
Upon the dark'ning waters, and mighty
Sounds of strife are heard. Wrapt in the midnight
Of the clouds, sits Terror, meditating
Woe. Her doubtful form appears and fades,
Like the shadow of Death, when he mingles
With the gloom of the sepulchre, and broods
In lonely silence. Her spirits are abroad!
They do her bidding! Hark, to that shriek!
The echoes of the shore have heard!

ELLENA, meanwhile, when she had been carried from the
chapel of San Sebastian, was placed upon a horse in waiting,
and, guarded by the two men who had seized her, commenced a journey, which continued with little interruption
during two nights and days. She had no means of judging
whither she was going, and listened in vain expectation, for
the feet of horses, and the voice of Vivaldi, who, she had
been told, was following on the same road.

The steps of travellers seldom broke upon the silence of
these regions, and, during the journey, she was met only by
some market-people passing to a neighbouring town, or now
and then by the vine-dressers or labourers in the olive
grounds; and she descended upon the vast plains of Apulia,
still ignorant of her situation. An encampment, not of war-
riors, but of shepherds, who were leading their flocks to the
mountains of Abruzzo, enlivened a small tract of these levels, which were shadowed on the north and east by the
mountainous ridge of the Garganus, stretching from the Apennine far into the Adriatic.

The appearance of the shepherds was nearly as wild and
savage as that of the men, who conducted Ellena; but their

pastoral instruments of flageolets and tabors spoke of more civilized feelings, as they sounded sweetly over the desert. Her guards rested, and refreshed themselves with goat's milk, barley cakes, and almonds, and the manners of these shepherds, like those she had formerly met with on the mountains, proved to be more hospitable than their air had indicated.

After Ellena had quitted this pastoral camp, no vestige of a human residence appeared for several leagues, except here and there the towers of a decayed fortress, perched upon the lofty acclivities she was approaching, and half concealed in the woods. The evening of the second day was drawing on, when her guards drew near the forest, which she had long observed in the distance, spreading over the many-rising steeps of the Garganus. They entered by a track, a road it could not be called, which led among oaks and gigantic chestnuts, apparently the growth of centuries, and so thickly interwoven, that their branches formed a canopy which seldom admitted the sky. The gloom which they threw around, and the thickets of cystus, juniper, and lenticus, which flourished beneath the shade, gave a character of fearful wildness to the scene.

Having reached an eminence, where the trees were more thinly scattered, Ellena perceived the forests spreading on all sides among hills and vallies, and descending towards the Adriatic, which bounded the distance in front. The coast, bending into a bay, was rocky and bold. Lofty pinnacles, wooded to their summits, rose over the shores, and cliffs of naked marble of such gigantic proportions, that they were awful even at a distance, obtruded themselves far into the waves, breasting their eternal fury. Beyond the margin of the coast, as far as the eye could reach, appeared pointed mountains, darkened with forests, rising ridge over ridge in many successions. Ellena, as she surveyed this wild scenery, felt as if she was going into eternal banishment from society. She was tranquil, but it was with the quietness of exhausted grief, not of resignation; and she looked back upon the past, and awaited the future, with a kind of out-breathed despair.

She had travelled for some miles through the forest, her guards only now and then uttering to each other a question, or an observation concerning the changes which had taken place in the bordering scenery, since they last passed it, when night began to close in upon them.

Ellena perceived her approach to the sea, only by the murmurs of its surge upon the rocky coast, till, having reached an eminence, which was, however, no more than the base of two woody mountains that towered closely over it, she saw dimly its gray surface spreading in the bay below. She now ventured to ask how much further she was to go, and whether she was to be taken on board one of the little vessels, apparently fishing smacks, that she could just discern at anchor.

"You have not far to go now," replied one of the guards, surlily; "you will soon be at the end of your journey, and at rest."

They descended to the shore, and presently came to a lonely dwelling, which stood so near the margin of the sea, as almost to be washed by the waves. No light appeared at any of the lattices; and, from the silence that reigned within, it seemed to be uninhabited. The guard had probably reason to know otherwise, for they halted at the door, and shouted with all their strength. No voice, however, answered to their call, and, while they persevered in efforts to rouse the inhabitants, Ellena anxiously examined the building, as exactly as the twilight would permit. It was of an ancient and peculiar structure, and, though scarcely important enough for a mansion, had evidently never been designed for the residence of peasants.

The walls, of unhewn marble, were high, and strengthened by bastions; and the edifice had turretted corners, which, with the porch in front, and the sloping roof, were falling fast into numerous symptoms of decay. The whole building, with its dark windows and soundless avenues, had an air strikingly forlorn and solitary. A high wall surrounded the small court in which it stood, and probably had once served as a defence to the dwelling; but the gates, which should have closed against intruders, could no longer perform their office; one of the folds had dropped from its fastenings, and lay on the ground almost concealed in a deep bed of weeds, and the other creaked on its hinges to every blast, at each swing seeming ready to follow the fate of its companion.

The repeated calls of the guard, were, at length, answered by a rough voice from within; when the door of the porch was lazily unbarred, and opened by a man, whose visage was so misery-struck, that Ellena could not look upon it with indifference, though wrapt in misery of her own. The lamp he held threw a gleam athwart it, and shewed the gaunt ferocity of famine, to which the shadow of his hollow eyes added a terrific wildness. Ellena shrunk while she gazed. She had never before seen villainy and suffering so strongly pictured on the same face, and she observed him with a degree of thrilling curiosity, which for a moment excluded from her mind all consciousness of the evils to be apprehended from him.

It was evident that this house had not been built for his reception; and she conjectured, that he was the servant of some cruel agent of the Marchesa di Vivaldi.

From the porch, she followed into an old hall, ruinous, and destitute of any kind of furniture. It was not extensive but lofty, for it seemed to ascend to the roof of the edifice, and the chambers above opened around it into a corridor.

Some half-sullen salutations were exchanged between the guard and the stranger, whom they called Spalatro, as they passed into a chamber, where, it appeared that he had been sleeping on a mattress laid in a corner. All the other furniture of the place, were two or three broken chairs and a table. He eyed Ellena with a shrewd contracted brow, and then looked significantly at the guard, but was silent, till he desired them all to sit down, adding, that he would dress some fish for supper. Ellena discovered that this man was the master of the place; it appeared also that he was the only inhabitant; and, when the guard soon after informed her their journey concluded here, her worst apprehensions were confirmed. The efforts she made to sustain her spirits, were no longer successful. It seemed that she was brought hither by ruffians to a lonely house on the sea-shore, inhabited by a man, who had "villain" engraved in every line of his face, to be the victim of inexorable pride and an insatiable desire of revenge. After considering these circumstances, and the words, which had just told her, she was to go no further, conviction struck like lightning upon her heart; and, believing she was brought hither to be assassinated, horror chilled all her frame, and her senses forsook her.

On recovering, she found herself surrounded by the guard and the stranger, and she would have supplicated for their pity, but that she feared to exasperate them by betraying her suspicions. She complained of fatigue, and requested to be shewn to her room. The men looked upon one another, hesitated, and then asked her to partake of the fish that was preparing. But Ellena having declined the invitation with as good a grace as she could assume, they consented that she should withdraw. Spalatro, taking the lamp, lighted her across the hall, to the corridor above, where he opened the door of a chamber, in which he said she was to sleep.

"Where is my bed?" said the afflicted Ellena fearfully as she looked round.

"It is there—on the floor," replied Spalatro, pointing to a miserable mattress, over which hung the tattered curtains of what had once been a canopy. "If you want the lamp," he added, "I will leave it, and come for it in a minute or two."

"Will you not let me have a lamp for the night," she said in a supplicating and timid voice.

"For the night!" said the man gruffly; "What! to set fire to the house."

Ellena still entreated that he would allow her the comfort of a light.

"Ay, ay," replied Spalatro, with a look she could not comprehend, "it would be a great comfort to you, truly! You do not know what you ask."

"What is it that you mean?" said Ellena, eagerly; "I conjure you, in the name of our holy church, to tell me!"

Spalatro stepped suddenly back, and looked upon her with surprise, but without speaking.

"Have mercy on me!" said Ellena, greatly alarmed by his manner; "I am friendless, and without help!"

"What do you fear," said the man, recovering himself; and then, without waiting her reply, added—"Is it such an unmerciful deed to take away a lamp?"

Ellena, who again feared to betray the extent of her suspicions, only replied, that it would be merciful to leave it, for that her spirits were low, and she required light to cheer them in a new abode.

"We do not stand upon such conceits here," replied Spalatro, "we have other matters to mind. Besides, it's the only lamp in the house, and the company below are in darkness while I am losing time here. I will leave it for two minutes, and no more." Ellena made a sign for him to put down the lamp; and, when he left the room, she heard the door barred upon her.

She employed these two minutes in examining the chamber, and the possibility it might afford of an escape. It was a large apartment, unfurnished and unswept of the cobwebs of many years. The only door she discovered was the one, by which she had entered, and the only window a lattice, which was grated. Such preparation for preventing escape seemed to hint how much there might be to escape from.

Having examined the chamber, without finding a single circumstance to encourage hope, tried the strength of the bars, which she could not shake, and sought in vain for an inside fastening to her door, she placed the lamp beside it, and awaited the return of Spalatro. In a few moments he came, and offered her a cup of sour wine with a slice of bread; which, being somewhat soothed by this attention, she did not think proper to reject.

Spalatro then quitted the room, and the door was again barred. Left once more alone, she tried to overcome apprehension by prayer; and after offering up her vespers with a fervent heart, she became more confiding and composed.

But it was impossible that she could so far forget the dangers of her situation, as to seek sleep, however wearied she might be, while the door of her room remained unsecured against the intrusion of the ruffians below; and, as she had no means of fastening it, she determined to watch during the whole night. Thus left to solitude and darkness, she seated herself upon the mattress to await the return of morning, and was soon lost in sad reflection; every minute occurrence of the past day, and of the conduct of her guards, moved in review before her judgment; and, combining these with the circumstances of her present situation, scarcely a doubt as to the fate designed for her remained. It seemed highly improbable, that the Marchesa di Vivaldi had sent her hither merely for imprisonment, since she might have confined her in a convent, with much less trouble; and still more so, when Ellena considered the character of the Marchesa, such as she had already experienced it. The appearance of this house, and of the man who inhabited it, with the circumstance of no woman being found residing here, each and all of these signified, that she was brought hither, not for long imprisonment, but for death. Her utmost efforts for fortitude or resignation could not overcome the cold tremblings, the sickness of heart, the faintness and universal horror, that assailed her. How often, with tears of mingled terror and grief, did she call upon Vivaldi—Vivaldi, alas! far distant—to save her; how often exclaim in agony, that she should never, never see him more!

She was spared, however, the horror of believing that he was an inhabitant of the Inquisition. Having detected the imposition, which had been practised towards herself, and that she was neither on the way to the Holy Office, nor conducted by persons belonging to it, she concluded, that the whole affair of Vivaldi's arrest, had been planned by the Marchesa, merely as a pretence for confining him, till she should be placed beyond the reach of his assistance. She hoped, therefore, that he had only been sent to some private residence belonging to his family, and that, when her fate was decided, he would be released, and she be the only victim. This was the sole consideration, that afforded any degree of assuagement to her sufferings.

The people below sat till a late hour. She listened often to their distant voices, as they were distinguishable in the pauses of the surge, that broke loud and hollow on the shore; and every time the creaking hinges of their room door moved, apprehended they were coming to her. At length, it appeared they had left the apartment, or had fallen asleep there, for a profound stillness reigned whenever the murmur of the waves sunk. Doubt did not long deceive her, for, while she yet listened, she distinguished footsteps ascending to the corridor. She heard them approach her chamber, and stop at the door; she heard, also, the low whisperings of their voices, as they seemed consulting on what was to be done, and she scarcely ventured to draw breath, while she intensely attended to them. Not a word, however, distinctly reached her, till, as one of them was departing, another called out in a half-whisper, "It is below on the table, in my girdle; make haste." The man came back, and said something in a lower voice, to which the other replied, "she sleeps," or Ellena was deceived by the hissing consonants of some other words. He then descended the stairs; and in a few minutes she perceived his comrade also pass away from the door; she listened to his retreating steps, till the roaring of the sea was alone heard in their stead.

Ellena's terrors were relieved only for a moment. Considering the import of the words, it appeared that the man who had descended, was gone for the stiletto of the other, such an instrument being usually worn in the girdle, and from the assurance, "she sleeps," he seemed to fear that his words had been overheard; and she listened again for their steps; but they came no more.

Happily for Ellena's peace, she knew not that her chamber had a door, so contrived as to open without sound, by which

assassins might enter unsuspectedly at any hour of the night.
Believing that the inhabitants of this house had now retired
to rest, her hopes and her spirits began to revive; but she
was yet sleepless and watchful. She measured the chamber
with unequal steps, often starting as the old boards shook
and groaned where she passed; and often pausing to listen
whether all was yet still in the corridor. The gleam, which a
rising moon threw between the bars of her window, now began to shew many shadowy objects in the chamber, which
she did not recollect to have observed while the lamp was
there. More than once, she fancied she saw something glide
along towards the place where the mattress was laid, and, almost congealed with terror, she stood still to watch it; but
the illusion, if such it was, disappeared where the moonlight faded, and even her fears could not give shape to it beyond. Had she not known that her chamber-door remained
strongly barred, she would have believed this was an assassin stealing to the bed where it might be supposed she slept.
Even now the thought occurred to her, and vague as it was,
had power to strike an anguish, almost deadly, through her
heart, while she considered that her immediate situation was
nearly as perilous as the one she had imagined. Again she
listened, and scarcely dared to breathe; but not the lightest
sound occurred in the pauses of the waves, and she believed
herself convinced that no person except herself was in the
room. That she was deceived in this belief, appeared from
her unwillingness to approach the mattress, while it was yet
involved in shade. Unable to overcome her reluctance, she
took her station at the window, till the strengthening rays
should allow a clearer view of the chamber, and in some degree restore her confidence; and she watched the scene without as it gradually became visible. The moon, rising over the
ocean, shewed its restless surface spreading to the wide horizon; and the waves, which broke in foam upon the rocky
beach below, retiring in long white lines far upon the waters.
She listened to their measured and solemn sound, and, somewhat soothed by the solitary grandeur of the view, remained
at the lattice till the moon had risen high into the heavens;
and even till morning began to dawn upon the sea, and purple the eastern clouds.

Re-assured, by the light that now pervaded her room, she
returned to the mattress; where anxiety at length yielded to
her weariness, and she obtained a short repose.

CHAPTER VIII

And yet I fear you; for you are fatal then,
When your eyes roll so. - - - -
- - - - - - - - - - - - - - - - - -
Alas! why gnaw you so your nether lip?
Some bloody passion shakes your very frame:
These are portents; but yet I hope, I hope,
They do not point on me.

SHAKESPEARE

ELLENA was awakened from profound sleep, by a loud noise at the door of her chamber; when, starting from her mattress, she looked around her with surprise and dismay, as imperfect recollections of the past began to gather on her mind. She distinguished the undrawing of iron bars, and then the countenance of Spalatro at her door, before she had a clear remembrance of her situation—that she was a prisoner in a house on a lonely shore, and that this man was her jailor. Such sickness of the heart returned with these convictions, such faintness and terror, that unable to support her trembling frame, she sunk again upon the mattress, without demanding the reason of this abrupt intrusion.

"I have brought you some breakfast," said Spalatro, "if you are awake to take it; but you seem to be asleep yet. Surely you have had sleep sufficient for one night; you went to rest soon enough."

Ellena made no reply, but, deeply affected with a sense of her situation, looked with beseeching eyes at the man, who advanced, holding forth an oaten cake and a bason of milk. "Where shall I set them?" said he, "you must needs be glad of them, since you had no supper."

Ellena thanked him, and desired he would place them on the floor, for there was neither table nor chair in the room.

As he did this, she was struck with the expression of his countenance, which exhibited a strange mixture of archness and malignity. He seemed congratulating himself upon his ingenuity, and anticipating some occasion of triumph; and she was so much interested, that her observation never quitted him while he remained in the room. As his eyes accidentally met hers, he turned them away, with the abruptness of a person who is conscious of evil intentions, and fears lest they should be detected; nor once looked up till he hastily left the chamber, when she heard the door secured as formerly.

The impression, which his look had left on her mind, so wholly engaged her in conjecture, that a considerable time elapsed before she remembered that he had brought the refreshment she so much required; but, as she now lifted it to her lips, a horrible suspicion arrested her hand; it was not, however, before she had swallowed a small quantity of the milk. The look of Spalatro, which occasioned her surprise, had accompanied the setting down of the breakfast, and it occurred to her, that poison was infused in this liquid. She was thus compelled to refuse the sustenance, which was become necessary to her, for she feared to taste even of the oaten cake, since Spalatro had offered it, but the little milk she had unwarily taken, was so very small that she had no apprehension concerning it.

The day, however, was passed in terror, and almost in despondency; she could neither doubt the purpose, for which she had been brought hither, nor discover any possibility of escaping from her persecutors; yet that propensity to hope, which buoys up the human heart, even in the severest hours of trial, sustained, in some degree, her fainting spirits.

During these miserable hours of solitude and suspense, the only alleviation to her suffering arose from a belief, that Vivaldi was safe, at least from danger, though not from grief; but she now understood too much of the dexterous contrivances of the Marchesa, his mother, to think it was practicable for him to escape from her designs, and again restore her to liberty.

All day Ellena either leaned against the bars of her window, lost in reverie, while her unconscious eyes were fixed upon the ocean, whose murmurs she no longer heard; or she listened for some sound from within the house, that might assist her conjectures, as to the number of persons below, or what might be passing there. The house, however, was profoundly still, except when now and then a footstep sauntered along a distant passage, or a door was heard to close; but not the hum of a single voice arose from the lower rooms, nor any symptom of there being more than one person, besides herself, in the dwelling. Though she had not heard her former guards depart, it appeared certain that they were gone, and that she was left alone in this place with Spalatro. What could be the purport of such a proceeding, Ellena could not imagine; if her death was designed, it seemed strange that one person only should be left to the hazard of the deed, when three must have rendered the completion of it certain. But this surprise vanished, when her suspicion of poison returned; for it was probable, that these men had believed their scheme to be already nearly accomplished, and had abandoned her to die alone, in a chamber from whence escape was impracticable, leaving Spalatro to dispose to her remains. All the incongruities she had separately observed in their conduct, seemed now to harmonize and unite in one plan; and her death, designed by poison, and that poison to be conveyed in the disguise of nourishment, appeared to have been the object of it. Whether it was that the strength of this conviction affected her fancy, or that the cause was real, Ellena, remembering at this moment that she had tasted the milk, was seized with an universal shuddering, and thought she felt that the poison had been sufficiently potent to affect her, even in the inconsiderable quantity she might have taken.

While she was thus agitated, she distinguished footsteps loitering near her door, and attentively listening, became convinced, that some person was in the corridor. The steps moved softly, sometimes stopping for an instant, as if to allow time for listening, and soon after passed away.

"It is Spalatro!" said Ellena; "he believes that I have taken the poison, and he comes to listen for my dying groans! Alas! he is only come somewhat too soon, perhaps!"

As this horrible supposition occurred, the shuddering returned with encreased violence, and she sunk, almost fainting, on the mattress; but the fit was not of long continuance. When it gradually left her, and recollection revived, she perceived, however, the prudence of suffering Spalatro to suppose she had taken the beverage he brought her, since such belief would at least procure some delay of further schemes, and every delay afforded some possibility for hope to rest upon. Ellena, therefore, poured through the bars of her window, the milk, which she believed Spalatro had designed should be fatal in its consequence.

It was evening, when she again fancied footsteps were lingering near her door, and the suspicion was confirmed, when, on turning her eyes, she perceived a shade on the floor, underneath it, as of some person stationed without. Presently the shadow glided away, and at the same time she distinguished departing steps treading cautiously.

"It is he!" said Ellena; "he still listens for my moans!"

This further confirmation of his designs affected her nearly as much as the first; when anxiously turning her looks towards the corridor, the shadow again appeared beneath the door, but she heard no step. Ellena now watched it with intense solicitude and expectation; fearing every instant that Spalatro would conclude her doubts by entering the room. "And O! when he discovers that I live," thought she, "what may I not expect during the first moments of his disappointment! What less than immediate death!"

The shadow, after remaining a few minutes stationary, moved a little, and then glided away as before. But it quickly returned, and a low sound followed, as of some person endeavouring to unfasten bolts without noise. Ellena heard one bar gently undrawn, and then another; she observed the door begin to move, and then to give way, till it gradually unclosed, and the face of Spalatro presented itself from behind it. Without immediately entering, he threw a glance round the chamber, as if he wished to ascertain some circumstance before he ventured further. His look was more than usually haggard as it rested upon Ellena, who apparently reposed on her mattress.

Having gazed at her for an instant, he ventured towards the bed with quick and unequal steps; his countenance expressed at once impatience, alarm, and the consciousness of guilt. When he was within a few paces, Ellena raised herself, and he started back as if a sudden spectre had crossed him. The more than usual wildness and wanness of his looks, with the whole of his conduct, seemed to confirm all her former terrors; and, when he roughly asked her how she did, Ellena had not sufficient presence of mind to answer that she was ill. For some moments, he regarded her with an earnest and sullen attention, and then a sly glance of scrutiny, which he threw round the chamber, told her that he was enquiring whether she had taken the poison. On perceiving that the bason was empty, he lifted it from the floor, and Ellena fancied a gleam of satisfaction passed over his visage.

"You have had no dinner," said he, "I forgot you; but supper will soon be ready; and you may walk up the beach till then, if you will."

Ellena, extremely surprised and perplexed by this offer of a seeming indulgence, knew not whether to accept or reject it. She suspected that some treachery lurked within it. The invitation appeared to be only a stratagem to lure her to destruction, and she determined to decline accepting it; when again she considered, that to accomplish this, it was not necessary to withdraw her from the chamber, where she was already sufficiently in the power of her persecutors. Her situation could not be more desperate than it was at present, and almost any change might make it less so.

As she descended from the corridor, and passed through the lower part of the house, no person appeared but her conductor; and she ventured to enquire, whether the men who had brought her hither were departed. Spalatro did not return an answer, but led the way in silence to the court, and, having passed the gates, he pointed toward the west, and said she might walk that way.

Ellena bent her course towards the "many-sounding waves," followed at a short distance by Spalatro, and, wrapt in thought, pursued the windings of the shore, scarcely noticing the objects around her; till, on passing the foot of a rock, she lifted her eyes to the scene that unfolded beyond, and observed some huts scattered at a considerable distance, apparently the residence of fishermen. She could just distinguish the dark sails of some skiffs turning the cliffs, and entering the little bay, where the hamlet margined the beach; but, though she saw the sails lowered, as the boats approached the shore, they were too far off to allow the figures of the men to appear. To Ellena, who had believed that no human habitation, except her prison, interrupted the vast solitudes of these forests and shores, the view of the huts, remote as they were, imparted a feeble hope, and even somewhat of joy. She looked back, to observe whether Spalatro was near; he was already within a few paces; and, casting a wistful glance forward to the remote cottages, her heart sunk again.

It was a lowering evening, and the sea was dark and swelling; the screams of the sea-birds too, as they wheeled among the clouds, and sought their high nests in the rocks, seemed to indicate an approaching storm. Ellena was not so wholly engaged by selfish sufferings, but that she could sympathise with those of others, and she rejoiced that the fishermen, whose boats she had observed, had escaped the threatening tempest, and were safely sheltered in their little homes, where, as they heard the loud waves break along the coast, they could look with keener pleasure upon the social circle, and the warm comforts around them. From such considerations however, she returned again to a sense of her own forlorn and friendless situation.

"Alas!" said she, "I have no longer a home, a circle to smile welcomes upon me! I have no longer even one friend to support, to rescue me! I—a miserable wanderer on a distant shore! tracked, perhaps, by the footsteps of the assassin, who at this instant eyes his victim with silent watchfulness, and awaits the moment of opportunity to sacrifice her!"

Ellena shuddered as she said this, and turned again to observe whether Spalatro was near. He was not within view; and, while she wondered, and congratulated herself on a possibility of escaping, she perceived a Monk walking silently beneath the dark rocks that overbrowed the beach. His black garments were folded round him; his face was inclined towards the ground, and he had the air of a man in deep meditation.

"His, no doubt, are worthy musings!" said Ellena, as she observed him, with mingled hope and surprise. "I may address myself, without fear, to one of his order. It is probably as much his wish, as it is his duty, to succour the unfortunate. Who could have hoped to find on this sequestered shore so sacred a protector! his convent cannot be far off."

He approached, his face still bent towards the ground, and Ellena advanced slowly, and with trembling steps, to meet him. As he drew near, he viewed her askance, without lifting his head; but she perceived his large eyes looking from under the shade of his cowl, and the upper part of his peculiar countenance. Her confidence in his protection began to fail, and she faultered, unable to speak, and scarcely daring to meet his eyes. The Monk stalked past her in silence, the lower part of his visage still muffled in his drapery, and as he passed her looked neither with curiosity, nor surprise.

Ellena paused, and determined, when he should be at some distance, to endeavour to make her way to the hamlet, and throw herself upon the humanity of its inhabitants, rather than solicit the pity of this forbidding stranger. But in the next moment she heard a step behind her, and, on turning, saw the Monk again approaching. He stalked by as before, surveying her, however, with a sly and scrutinizing glance from the corners of his eyes. His air and countenance were equally repulsive, and still Ellena could not summon courage enough to attempt engaging his compassion; but shrunk as from an enemy. There was something also terrific in the silent stalk of so gigantic a form; it announced both power and treachery. He passed slowly on to some distance, and disappeared among the rocks.

Ellena turned once more with an intention of hastening towards the distant hamlet, before Spalatro should observe her, whose strange absence she had scarcely time to wonder at; but she had not proceeded far, when suddenly she perceived the Monk again at her shoulder. She started, and almost shrieked; while he regarded her with more attention than before. He paused a moment, and seemed to hesitate; after which he again passed on in silence. The distress of Ellena encreased; he was gone the way she had designed to run, and she feared almost equally to follow him, and to return to her prison. Presently he turned, and passed her again, and Ellena hastened forward. But, when fearful of being pursued, she again looked back, she observed him conversing with Spalatro. They appeared to be in consultation, while they slowly advanced, till, probably observing her rapid progress, Spalatro called on her to stop, in a voice that echoed among all the rocks. It was a voice, which would not be disobeyed. She looked hopelessly at the still distant cottages, and slackened her steps. Presently the Monk again passed before her, and Spalatro had again disappeared. The frown, with which the former now regarded Ellena, was so terrific, that she shrunk trembling back, though she knew him not for her persecutor, since she had never consciously seen Schedoni. He was agitated, and his look became darker.

"Whither go you?" said he in a voice that was stifled by emotion.

"Who is it, father, that asks the question?" said Ellena, endeavouring to appear composed.

"Whither go you, and who are you?" repeated the Monk more sternly.

"I am an unhappy orphan," replied Ellena, sighing deeply, "If you are, as your habit denotes, a friend to the charities, you will regard me with compassion."

Schedoni was silent, and then said—"Who, and what is it that you fear?"

"I fear—even for my life," replied Ellena, with hesitation. She observed a darker shade pass over his countenance. "For your life!" said he, with apparent surprise, "who is there that would think it worth the taking."

Ellena was struck with these words.

"Poor insect!" added Schedoni, "who would crush thee?"

Ellena made no reply; she remained with her eyes fixed in amazement upon his face. There was something in his manner of pronouncing this, yet more extraordinary than in the words themselves. Alarmed by his manner, and awed by the encreasing gloom, and swelling surge, that broke in thunder on the beach, she at length turned away, and again walked towards the hamlet which was yet very remote.

He soon overtook her; when rudely seizing her arm, and gazing earnestly on her face, "Who is it, that you fear?" said he, "say who!"

"That is more than I dare say," replied Ellena, scarcely able to sustain herself.

"Hah! is it even so!" said the Monk, with encreasing emotion. His visage now became so terrible, that Ellena struggled to liberate her arm, and supplicated that he would not detain her. He was silent, and still gazed upon her, but his eyes, when she had ceased to struggle, assumed the fixt and vacant glare of a man, whose thoughts have retired within themselves, and who is no longer conscious to surrounding objects.

"I beseech you to release me!" repeated Ellena, "it is late, and I am far from home."

"That is true," muttered Schedoni, still grasping her arm, and seeming to reply to his own thoughts rather than to her words,—"that is very true."

"The evening is closing fast," continued Ellena, "and I shall be overtaken by the storm."

Schedoni still mused, and then muttered—"The storm, say you? Why ay, let it come."

As he spoke, he suffered her arm to drop, but still held it, and walked slowly towards the house. Ellena, thus compelled to accompany him, and yet more alarmed both by his looks, his incoherent answers, and his approach to her prison, renewed her supplications and her efforts for liberty, in a voice of piercing distress, adding, "I am far from home, father; night is coming on. See how the rocks darken! I am far from home, and shall be waited for."

"That is false!" said Schedoni, with emphasis; "and you know it to be so."

"Alas! I do," replied Ellena, with mingled shame and grief, "I have no friends to wait for me!"

"What do those deserve, who deliberately utter falsehoods," continued the Monk, "who deceive, and flatter young men to their destruction?"

"Father!" exclaimed the astonished Ellena.

"Who disturb the peace of families—who trepan, with wanton arts, the heirs of noble houses—who—hah! what do such deserve?"

Overcome with astonishment and terror, Ellena remained silent. She now understood that Schedoni, so far from being likely to prove a protector, was an agent of her worst, and as she had believed her only enemy; and an apprehension of the immediate and terrible vengeance, which such an agent seemed willing to accomplish, subdued her senses; she tottered, and sunk upon the beach. The weight, which strained the arm Schedoni held, called his attention to her situation.

As he gazed upon her helpless and faded form, he became agitated. He quitted it, and traversed the beach in short turns, and with hasty steps; came back again, and bent over it—his heart seemed sensible to some touch of pity. At one moment, he stepped towards the sea, and taking water in the hollows of his hands, threw it upon her face; at another, seeming to regret that he had done so, he would stamp with sudden fury upon the shore, and walk abruptly to a distance. The conflict between his design and his conscience was strong, or, perhaps, it was only between his passions. He, who had hitherto been insensible to every tender feeling, who, governed by ambition and resentment had contributed, by his artful instigations, to fix the baleful resolution of the Marchesa di Vivaldi, and who was come to execute her purpose,—even he could not now look upon the innocent, the wretched Ellena, without yielding to the momentary weakness, as he termed it, of compassion.

While he was yet unable to baffle the new emotion by evil passions, he despised that which conquered him. "And shall the weakness of a girl," said he, "subdue the resolution of a man! Shall the view of her transient sufferings unnerve my firm heart, and compel me to renounce the lofty plans I have so ardently, so laboriously imagined, at the very instant when they are changing into realities! Am I awake! Is one spark of the fire, which has so long smouldered within my bosom, and consumed my peace, alive! Or am I tame and abject as my fortunes? hah! as my fortunes! Shall the spirit of my family yield for ever to circumstances? The question rouses it, and I feel its energy revive within me."

He stalked with hasty steps towards Ellena, as if he feared to trust his resolution with a second pause. He had a dagger concealed beneath his Monk's habit; as he had also an assassin's heart shrouded by his garments. He had a dagger—but he hesitated to use it, the blood which it might spill, would be observed by the peasants of the neighbouring hamlet, and might lead to a discovery. It would be safer, he considered, and easier, to lay Ellena, senseless as she was, in the waves; their coldness would recal her to life, only at the moment before they would suffocate her.

As he stooped to lift her, his resolution faultered again, on beholding her innocent face, and in that moment she moved. He started back, as if she could have known his purpose, and, knowing it, could have avenged herself. The water, which he had thrown upon her face, had gradually revived her; she unclosed her eyes, and, on perceiving him, shrieked and attempted to rise. His resolution was subdued, so tremblingly fearful is guilt in the moment when it would execute its atrocities. Overcome with apprehensions, yet agitated with shame and indignation against himself for being so, he gazed at her for an instant in silence, and then abruptly turned away his eyes and left her. Ellena listened to his departing steps, and, raising herself, observed him retiring among the rocks that led towards the house. Astonished at his conduct, and surprised to find that she was alone, Ellena renewed all her efforts to sustain herself, till she should reach the hamlet so long the object of her hopes; but she had proceeded only a few paces, when Spalatro again appeared swiftly approaching. Her utmost exertion availed her nothing; her feeble steps were soon overtaken, and Ellena perceived herself again his prisoner. The look with which she resigned herself, awakened no pity in Spalatro, who uttered some taunting jest upon the swiftness of her flight, as he led her back to her prison, and proceeded in sullen watchfulness. Once again, then, she entered the gloomy walls of that fatal mansion, never more, she now believed, to quit them with life, a belief, which was strengthened when she remembered that the Monk on leaving her, had taken the way hither; for, though she knew not how to account for his late forbearance, she could not suppose that he would long be merciful. He appeared no more, however, as she passed to her chamber, where Spalatro left her again to solitude and terror, and she heard that fateful door again barred upon her. When his retreating steps had ceased to sound, a stilness, as of the grave, prevailed in the house; like the dead calm, which sometimes precedes the horrors of a tempest.

CHAPTER IX

I am settled, and bend up
Each corporal agent to this terrible feat.
SHAKSPEARE

SCHEDONI had returned from the beach to the house, in a state of perturbation, that defied the controul of even his own stern will. On the way thither he met Spalatro, whom, as he dispatched his chamber to Ellena, he strictly commanded not to approach his chamber till he should be summoned.

Having reached his apartment, he secured the door, though not any person, except himself, was in the house, nor any one expected, but those who he knew would not dare to intrude upon him. Had it been possible to have shut out all consciousness of himself, also, how willingly would he have done so! He threw himself into a chair, and remained for a considerable time motionless, and lost in thought, yet the emotions of his mind were violent and contradictory. At the very instant when his heart reproached him with the crime he had meditated, he regretted the ambitious views he must relinquish if he failed to perpetrate it, and regarded himself with some degree of contempt for having hitherto hesitated on the subject. He considered the character of his own mind with astonishment, for circumstances had drawn forth traits, of which, till now, he had no suspicion. He knew not by what doctrine to explain the inconsistencies, the contradictions, he experienced, and, perhaps, it was not one of the least that in these moments of direful and conflicting passions, his reason could still look down upon their operations, and lead him to a cool, though brief examination of his own nature. But the subtlety of self-love still eluded his enquiries, and he did not detect that pride was even at this instant of self-examination, and of critical import, the master-spring of his mind. In the earliest dawn of his character this passion had displayed its pre-dominancy, whenever occasion permitted, and its influence had led to some of the chief events of his life.

The Count di Marinella, for such had formerly been the title of the Confessor, was the younger son of an ancient family, who resided in the duchy of Milan, and near the feet of the Tyrolean Alps, on such estates of their ancestors, as the Italian wars of a former century had left them. The portion, which he had received at the death of his father, was not large, and Schedoni was not of a disposition to improve his patrimony by slow diligence, or to submit to the restraint and humiliation, which his narrow finances would have imposed. He disdained to acknowledge an inferiority of fortune to those, with whom he considered himself equal in rank; and, as he was destitute of generous feeling, and of sound judgment, he had not that loftiness of soul, which is ambitious of true grandeur. On the contrary, he was satisfied with an ostentatious display of pleasures and of power, and, thoughtless of the consequence of dissipation, was contented with the pleasures of the moment, till his exhausted resources compelled him to pause, and to reflect. He perceived, too late for his advantage, that it was necessary for him to dispose of part of his estate, and to confine himself to the income of the remainder. Incapable of submitting with grace to the reduction, which his folly had rendered expedient, he endeavoured to obtain by cunning, the luxuries that his prudence had failed to keep, and which neither his genius or his integrity could command. He withdrew, however, from the eyes of his neighbours, unwilling to submit his altered circumstances to their observation.

Concerning several years of his life, from this period, nothing was generally known; and, when he was next discovered, it was in the Spirito Santo convent at Naples, in the habit of a Monk, and under the assumed name of Schedoni. His air and countenance were as much altered as his way of life; his looks had become gloomy and severe, and the pride, which had mingled with the gaiety of their former expression, occasionally discovered itself under the disguise of humility, but more frequently in the austerity of silence, and in the barbarity of penance.

The person who discovered Schedoni, would not have recollected him, had not his remarkable eyes first fixed his attention, and then revived remembrance. As he examined his features, he traced the faint resemblance of what Marinella had been, to whom he made himself known.

The Confessor affected to have forgotten his former acquaintance, and assured him, that he was mistaken respecting himself, till the stranger so closely urged some circumstances, that the former was no longer permitted to dissemble. He retired, in some emotion, with the stranger, and, whatever might be the subject of their conference, he drew from him, before he quitted the convent, a tremendous vow, to keep secret from the brotherhood his knowledge of Schedoni's family, and never to reveal without those walls, that he had seen him. These requests he had urged in a manner, that at once surprised and awed the stranger, and which at the same time that it manifested the weight of Schedoni's fears, bade the former tremble for the consequence of disobedience; and he shuddered even while he promised to obey. Of the first part of the promise he was probably strictly observant; whether he was equally so of the second, does not appear; it is certain, that after this period, he was never more seen or heard of at Naples.

Schedoni, ever ambitious of distinction, adapted his manners to the views and prejudices of the society with whom he resided, and became one of the most exact observers of their outward forms, and almost a prodigy for self-denial and severe discipline. He was pointed out by the fathers of the convent to the juniors as a great example, who was, however, rather to be looked up to with reverential admiration, than with an hope of emulating his sublime virtues. But with such panegyrics their friendship for Schedoni concluded. They found it convenient to applaud the austerities, which they declined to practise; it procured them a character for sanctity, and saved them the necessity of earning it by mortifications of their own; but they both feared and hated Schedoni for his pride and his gloomy austerities, too much, to gratify his ambition by any thing further than empty praise. He had been several years in the society, without obtaining any considerable advancement, and with the mortification of seeing persons, who had never emulated his severity, raised to high offices in the church. Somewhat too late he discovered, that he was not to expect any substantial favour from the brotherhood, and then it was that his restless and disappointed spirit first sought preferment by other avenues. He had been some years Confessor to the Marchesa di Vivaldi, when the conduct of her son awakened his hopes, by showing him, that he might render himself not only useful but necessary to her, by his counsels. It was his custom to study the characters of those around him, with a view of adapting them to his purposes, and, having ascertained that of the Marchesa, these hopes were encouraged. He perceived that her passions were strong, her judgment weak; and he understood, that, if circumstances should ever enable him to be serviceable in promoting the end at which any one of those passions might aim, his fortune would be established.

At length, he so completely insinuated himself into her confidence, and became so necessary to her views, that he could demand his own terms, and this he had not failed to do, though with all the affected delicacy and finesse that his situation seemed to require. An office of high dignity in the church, which had long vainly excited his ambition, was promised him by the Marchesa, who had sufficient influence to obtain it; her condition was that of his preserving the honour of her family, as she delicately termed it, which she was careful to make him understand could be secured only by the death of Ellena. He acknowledged, with the Marchesa, that the death of this fascinating young woman was the only means of preserving that honour, since, if she lived, they had every evil to expect from the attachment and character of Vivaldi, who would discover and extricate her from any place of confinement, however obscure or difficult of access, to which she might be conveyed. How long and how arduously the Confessor had aimed to oblige the Marchesa, has already appeared. The last scene was now arrived, and he was on the eve of committing that atrocious act, which was to secure the pride of her house, and to satisfy at once his ambition and his desire of vengeance; when an emotion new and surprising to him, had arrested his arm, and compelled his resolution to faulter. But this emotion was transient, it disappeared almost with the object that had awakened it; and now, in the silence and retirement of his chamber, he had leisure to recollect his thoughts, to review his schemes, to re-animate his resolution, and to wonder again at the pity, which had almost won him from his purpose. The ruling passion of his nature once more resumed its authority, and he determined to earn the honour, which the Marchesa had in store for him.

After some cool, and more of tumultuous, consideration, he resolved that Ellena should be assassinated that night, while she slept, and afterwards conveyed through a passage of the house communicating with the sea, into which the body might be thrown and buried, with her sad story, beneath the waves. For his own sake, he would have avoided the danger of shedding blood, had this appeared easy; but he had too much reason to know she had suspicions of poison, to trust to a second attempt by such means; and again his indignation rose against himself, since by yielding to a momentary compassion, he had lost the opportunity afforded him of throwing her unresistingly into the surge.

Spalatro, as has already been hinted, was a former confidant of the Confessor, who knew too truly, from experience, that he could be trusted, and had, therefore, engaged him to assist on this occasion. To the hands of this man he consigned the fate of the unhappy Ellena, himself recoiling from the horrible act he had willed; and intending by such a step to involve Spalatro more deeply in the guilt, and thus more effectually to secure his secret.

The night was far advanced before Schedoni's final resolution was taken, when he summoned Spalatro to his chamber to instruct him in his office. He bolted the door, by which the man had entered, forgetting that themselves were the only persons in the house, except the poor Ellena, who, unsuspicious of what was conspiring, and her spirits worn out by the late scene, was sleeping peacefully on her mattress above. Schedoni moved softly from the door he had secured, and, beckoning Spalatro to approach, spoke in a low voice, as if he feared to be overheard. "Have you perceived any sound from her chamber lately?" said he, "Does she sleep, think you?"

"No one has moved there for this hour past, at least," replied Spalatro, "I have been watching in the corridor, till you called, and should have heard if she had stirred, the old floor shakes so with every step."

"Then hear me, Spalatro," said the Confessor. "I have tried, and found thee faithful, or I should not trust thee in a business of confidence like this. Recollect all I said to thee in the morning, and be resolute and dexterous, as I have ever found thee."

Spalatro listened in gloomy attention, and the Monk proceeded, "It is late; go, therefore, to her chamber; be certain that she sleeps. Take this," he added, "and this," giving him a dagger and a large cloak—"You know how you are to use them."

He paused, and fixed his penetrating eyes on Spalatro, who held up the dagger in silence, examined the blade, and continued to gaze upon it, with a vacant stare, as if he was unconscious of what he did.

"You know your business," repeated Schedoni, authoritatively, "dispatch! time wears; and I must set off early."

The man made no reply.

"The morning dawns already," said the Confessor, still more urgently, "Do you faulter? do you tremble? Do I not know you?"

Spalatro put up the poinard in his bosom without speaking, threw the cloak over his arm, and moved with a loitering step towards the door.

"Dispatch!" repeated the Confessor, "why do you linger?"

"I cannot say I like this business, Signor," said Spalatro surlily. "I know not why I should always do the most, and be paid the least."

"Sordid villain!" exclaimed Schedoni, "you are not satisfied then!"

"No more a villain than yourself, Signor," retorted the man, throwing down the cloak, "I only do your business; and 'tis you that are sordid, for you would take all the reward, and I would only have a poor man have his dues. Do the work yourself, or give me the greater profit."

"Peace!" said Schedoni, "dare no more to insult me with the mention of reward. Do you imagine I have sold myself! 'Tis my will that she dies; this is sufficient; and for you— the price you have asked has been granted."

"It is too little," replied Spalatro, "and besides, I do not like the work.—What harm has she done me?"

"Since when is it, that you have taken upon you to moralize?" said the Confessor, "and how long are these cowardly scruples to last? This is not the first time you have been employed; what harm had others done you! You forget that I know you, you forget the past."

"No, Signor, I remember it too well, I wish I could forget; I remember it too well.—I have never been at peace since. The bloody hand is always before me! and often of a night, when the sea roars, and storms shake the house, *they* have come, all gashed as I left them, and stood before my bed! I have got up, and ran out upon the shore for safety!"

"Peace!" repeated the Confessor, "where is this frenzy of fear to end? To what are these visions, painted in blood, to lead? I thought I was talking with a man, but find I am speaking only to a baby, possessed with his nurse's dreams! Yet I understand you,—you shall be satisfied."

Schedoni, however, had for once misunderstood this man, when he could not believe it possible that he was really averse to execute what he had undertaken. Whether the innocence and beauty of Ellena had softened his heart, or that his conscience did torture him for his past deeds, he persisted in refusing to murder her. His conscience, or his pity, was of a very peculiar kind however; for, though he refused to execute the deed himself, he consented to wait at the foot of a back stair-case, that communicated with Ellena's chamber, while Schedoni accomplished it, and afterward to assist in carrying the body to the shore. "This is a compromise between conscience and guilt, worthy of a demon," muttered Schedoni, who appeared to be insensible that he had made the same compromise with himself not an hour before; and whose extreme reluctance at this moment, to perpetrate with his own hand, what he had willingly designed for another, ought to have reminded him of that compromise.

Spalatro, released from the immediate office of an executioner, endured silently the abusive, yet half-stifled, indignation of the Confessor, who also bade him remember, that, though he now shrunk from the most active part of this transaction, he had not always been restrained, in offices of the same nature, by equal compunction; and that not only his means of subsistence, but his very life itself, was at his mercy. Spalatro readily acknowledged that it was so; and Schedoni knew, too well, the truth of what he had urged, to be restrained from his purpose, by any apprehension of the consequence of a discovery from this ruffian.

"Give me the dagger, then," said the Confessor, after a long pause, "take up the cloak, and follow to the stair-case. Let me see, whether your valour will carry you thus far."

Spalatro resigned the stiletto, and threw the cloak again over his arm. The Confessor stepped to the door, and, trying to open it, "It is fastened!" said he in alarm, "some person has got into the house,—it is fastened!"

"That well may be, Signor," replied Spalatro, calmly, "for I saw you bolt it yourself, after I came into the room."

"True," said Schedoni, recovering himself; "that is true."

He opened it, and proceeded along the silent passages, towards the private stair-case, often pausing to listen, and then stepping more lightly;—the terrific Schedoni, in this moment of meditative guilt, feared even the feeble Ellena. At the foot of the stair-case, he again stopped to listen. "Do you hear any thing?" said he in a whisper.

"I hear only the sea," replied the man.

"Hush! it is something more!" said Schedoni; "that is the murmur of voices!"

They were silent. After a pause of some length, "It is, perhaps, the voice of the spectres I told you of, Signor," said Spalatro, with a sneer. "Give me the dagger," said Schedoni.

Spalatro, instead of obeying, now grasped the arm of the Confessor, who, looking at him for an explanation of this extraordinary action, was still more surprised to observe the paleness and horror of his countenance. His starting eyes seemed to follow some object along the passage, and Schedoni, who began to partake of his feelings, looked forward to discover what occasioned this dismay, but could not perceive any thing that justified it. "What is it you fear?" said he at length.

Spalatro's eyes were still moving in horror, "Do you see nothing!" said he pointing. Schedoni looked again, but did not distinguish any object in the remote gloom of the passage, whither Spalatro's sight was now fixed.

"Come, come," said he, ashamed of his own weakness, "this is not a moment for such fancies. Awake from this idle dream."

Spalatro withdrew his eyes, but they retained all their wildness. "It was no dream," said he, in the voice of a man who is exhausted by pain, and begins to breathe somewhat more freely again. "I saw it as plainly as I now see you."

"Dotard! what did you see!" enquired the Confessor.

"It came before my eyes in a moment, and shewed itself distinctly and outspread."

"What shewed itself?" repeated Schedoni.

"And then it beckoned—yes, it beckoned me, with that blood-stained finger! and glided away down the passage, still beckoning——till it was lost in the darkness."

"This is very frenzy!" said Schedoni, excessively agitated. "Arouse yourself, and be a man!"

"Frenzy! would it were, Signor. I saw that dreadful hand—I see it now—it is there again!—there!"

Schedoni, shocked, embarrassed, and once more infected with the strange emotions of Spalatro, looked forward expecting to discover some terrific object, but still nothing was visible to him, and he soon recovered himself sufficiently to endeavour to appease the fancy of this conscience-struck ruffian. But Spalatro was insensible to all he could urge, and the Confessor, fearing that his voice, though weak and stifled, would awaken Ellena, tried to withdraw him from the spot, to the apartment they had quitted.

"The wealth of San Loretto should not make me go that way, Signor," replied he, shuddering—"that was the way *it* beckoned, it vanished that way!"

Every emotion now yielded with Schedoni, to that of apprehension lest Ellena, being awakened, should make his task more horrid by a struggle, and his embarrassment encreased at each instant, for neither command, menace, or entreaty could prevail with Spalatro to retire, till the Monk luckily remembered a door, which opened beyond the staircase, and would conduct them by another way to the opposite side of the house. The man consented so to depart, when, Schedoni unlocking a suite of rooms, of which he had always kept the keys, they passed in silence through an extent of desolate chambers, till they reached the one, which they had lately left.

Here, relieved from apprehension respecting Ellena, the Confessor expostulated more freely with Spalatro, but neither argument or menace could prevail, and the man persisted in refusing to return to the stair-case, though protesting, at the same time, that he would not remain alone in any part of the house; till the wine, with which the Confessor abundantly supplied him, began to overcome the terrors of his imagination. At length, his courage was so much re-animated, that he consented to resume his station, and await at the foot of the stairs the accomplishment of Schedoni's dreadful errand, with which agreement they returned thither by the way they had lately passed. The wine, with which Schedoni also had found it necessary to strengthen his own resolution, did not secure him from severe emotion, when he found himself again near Ellena; but he made a strenuous effort for self-subjection, as he demanded the dagger of Spalatro.

"You have it already, Signor," replied the man.

"True," said the Monk; "ascend softly, or our steps may awaken her."

"You said I was to wait at the foot of the stairs, Signor, while you"——

"True, true, true!" muttered the Confessor, and had begun to ascend, when his attendant desired him to stop. "You are not going in darkness, Signor, you have forgotten the lamp. I have another here."

Schedoni took it angrily, without speaking, and was again ascending, when he hesitated, and once more paused. "The glare will disturb her," thought he, "it is better to go in darkness.—Yet——." He considered, that he could not strike with certainty without light to direct his hand, and he kept the lamp, but returned once more to charge Spalatro not to stir from the foot of the stairs till he called, and to ascend to the chamber upon the first signal.

"I will obey, Signor, if you, on your part, will promise not to give the signal till all is over."

"I do promise," replied Schedoni. "No more!"

Again he ascended, nor stopped till he reached Ellena's door, where he listened for a sound; but all was as silent as if death already reigned in the chamber. This door was, from long disuse, difficult to be opened; formerly it would have yielded without sound, but now Schedoni was fearful of noise from every effort he made to move it. After some difficulty, however, it gave way, and he perceived, by the stillness within the apartment, that he had not disturbed Ellena. He shaded the lamp with the door for a moment, while he threw an enquiring glance forward, and when he did venture farther, held part of his dark drapery before the light, to prevent the rays from spreading through the room.

As he approached the bed, her gentle breathings informed him that she still slept, and the next moment he was at her side. She lay in deep and peaceful slumber, and seemed to have thrown herself upon the mattress, after having been wearied by her griefs; for, though sleep pressed heavily on her eyes, their lids were yet wet with tears.

While Schedoni gazed for a moment upon her innocent countenance, a faint smile stole over it. He stepped back.

"She smiles in her murderer's face!" said he, shuddering, "I must be speedy."

He searched for the dagger, and it was some time before his trembling hand could disengage it from the folds of his garment; but, having done so, he again drew near, and prepared to strike. Her dress perplexed him; it would interrupt the blow, and he stooped to examine whether he could turn her robe aside, without waking her. As the light passed over her face, her perceived that the smile had vanished—the visions of her sleep were changed, for tears stole from beneath her eye-lids, and her features suffered a slight convulsion. She spoke! Schedoni, apprehending that the light had disturbed her, suddenly drew back, and, again irresolute, shaded the lamp, and concealed himself behind the curtain, while he listened. But her words were inward and indistinct, and convinced him that she still slumbered.

His agitation and repugnance to strike encreased with every moment of delay, and, as often as he prepared to plunge the poinard in her bosom, a shuddering horror restrained him. Astonished at his own feelings, and indignant at what he termed a dastardly weakness, he found it necessary to argue with himself, and his rapid thoughts said, "Do I not feel the necessity of this act! Does not what is dearer to me than existence—does not my consequence depend on the execution of it? Is she not also beloved by the young Vivaldi?— have I already forgotten the church of the Spirito Santo?" This consideration re-animated him; vengeance nerved his arm, and drawing aside the lawn from her bosom, he once more raised it to strike; when, after gazing for an instant, some new cause of horror seemed to seize all his frame, and he stood for some moments aghast and motionless like a statue. His respiration was short and laborious, chilly drops stood on his forehead, and all his faculties of mind seemed suspended. When he recovered, he stooped to examine again the miniature, which had occasioned this revolution, and which had lain concealed beneath the lawn that he withdrew. The terrible certainty was almost confirmed, and forgetting, in his impatience to know the truth, the imprudence of suddenly discovering himself to Ellena at this hour of the night, and with a dagger at his feet, he called loudly "Awake! awake! Say, what is your name? Speak! speak quickly!"

Ellena, aroused by a man's voice, started from her mattress, when, perceiving Schedoni, and by the pale glare of the lamp, his haggard countenance, she shrieked, and sunk back on the pillow. She had not fainted; and believing that he came to murder her, she now exerted herself to plead for mercy. The energy of her feelings enabled her to rise and throw herself at his feet. "Be merciful, O father! be merciful!" said she, in a trembling voice.

"Father!" interrupted Schedoni, with earnestness; and then, seeming to restrain himself, he added, with unaffected surprise, "Why are you thus terrified?" for he had lost, in new interests and emotions, all consciousness of evil intention, and of the singularity of his situation. "What do you fear?" he repeated.

"Have pity, holy father!" exclaimed Ellena in agony.

"Why do you not say whose portrait that is?" demanded he, forgetting that he had not asked the question before.

"Whose portrait?" repeated the Confessor in a loud voice.

"Whose portrait!" said Ellena, with extreme surprise.

"Ay, how came you by it? Be quick—whose resemblance is it?"

"Why should you wish to know?" said Ellena.

"Answer my question," repeated Schedoni, with encreasing sternness.

"I cannot part with it, holy father," replied Ellena, pressing it to her bosom, "you do not wish me to part with it!"

"Is it impossible to make you answer my question!" said he, in extreme perturbation, and turning away from her, "has fear utterly confounded you!" Then, again stepping towards her, and seizing her wrist, he repeated the demand in a tone of desperation.

"Alas! he is dead! or I should not now want a protector," replied Ellena, shrinking from his grasp, and weeping.

"You trifle," said Schedoni, with a terrible look, "I once more demand an answer—whose picture?"——

Ellena lifted it, gazed upon it for a moment, and then pressing it to her lips said, "This was my father."

"Your father!" he repeated in an inward voice, "your father!" and shuddering, turned away.

Ellena looked at him with surprise. "I never knew a father's care," she said, "nor till lately did I perceive the want of it.—But now."——

"His name?" interrupted the Confessor.

"But now," continued Ellena—"if you are not as a father to me—to whom can I look for protection?"

"His name?" repeated Schedoni, with sterner emphasis.

"It is sacred," replied Ellena, "for he was unfortunate!"

"His name?" demanded the Confessor, furiously.

"I have promised to conceal it, father."

"On your life, I charge you tell it; remember, on your life!"

Ellena trembled, was silent, and with supplicating looks implored him to desist from enquiry, but he urged the question more irresistibly. "His name then," said she, "was Marinella."

Schedoni groaned and turned away; but in a few seconds, struggling to command the agitation that shattered his whole frame, he returned to Ellena, and raised her from her knees, on which she had thrown herself to implore mercy.

"The place of his residence?" said the Monk.

"It was far from hence," she replied; but he demanded an unequivocal answer, and she reluctantly gave one.

Schedoni turned away as before, groaned heavily, and paced the chamber without speaking; while Ellena, in her turn, enquired the motive of his questions, and the occasion of his agitation. But he seemed not to notice any thing she said, and, wholly given up to his feelings, was inflexibly silent, while he stalked, with measured steps, along the room, and his face, half hid by his cowl, was bent towards the ground.

Ellena's terror began to yield to astonishment, and this emotion encreased, when, Schedoni approaching her, she perceived tears swell in his eyes, which were fixt on hers, and his countenance soften from the wild disorder that had marked it. Still he could not speak. At length he yielded to the fulness of his heart, and Schedoni, the stern Schedoni, wept and sighed! He seated himself on the mattress beside Ellena, took her hand, which she affrighted attempted to withdraw, and when he could command his voice, said, "Unhappy child!——behold your more unhappy father!" As he concluded, his voice was overcome by groans, and he drew the cowl entirely over his face.

"My father!" exclaimed the astonished and doubting Ellena—"my father!" and fixed her eyes upon him. He gave no reply, but when, a moment after, he lifted his head, "Why do you reproach me with those looks!" said the conscious Schedoni.

"Reproach you!—reproach my father!" repeated Ellena, in

accents softening into tenderness, "*Why* should I reproach my father!"

"*Why!*" exclaimed Schedoni, starting from his seat, "Great God!"

As he moved, he stumbled over the dagger at his foot; at that moment it might be said to strike into his heart. He pushed it hastily from sight. Ellena had not observed it; but she observed his labouring breast, his distracted looks, and quick steps, as he walked to and fro in the chamber; and she asked, with the most soothing accents of compassion, and looks of anxious gentleness, what made him so unhappy, and tried to assuage his sufferings. They seemed to encrease with every wish she expressed to dispel them; at one moment he would pause to gaze upon her, and in the next would quit her with a frenzied start.

"Why do you look so piteously upon me, father?" Ellena said, "why are you so unhappy? Tell me, that I may comfort you."

This appeal renewed all the violence of remorse and grief, and he pressed her to his bosom, and wetted her cheek with his tears. Ellena wept to see him weep, till her doubts began to take alarm. Whatever might be the proofs, that had convinced Schedoni of the relationship between them, he had not explained these to her, and, however strong was the eloquence of nature which she witnessed, it was not sufficient to justify an entire confidence in the assertion he had made, or to allow her to permit his caresses without trembling. She shrunk, and endeavoured to disengage herself; when, immediately understanding her, he said, "Can you doubt the cause of these emotions? these signs of paternal affection?"

"Have I not reason to doubt," replied Ellena, timidly, "since I never witnessed them before?"

He withdrew his arms, and, fixing his eyes earnestly on hers, regarded her for some moments in expressive silence. "Poor Innocent!" said he, at length, "you know not how much your words convey!—It is too true, you never have known a father's tenderness till now!"

His countenance darkened while he spoke, and he rose again from his seat. Ellena, meanwhile, astonished, terrified and oppressed by a variety of emotions, had no power to demand his reasons for the belief that so much agitated him, or any explanation of his conduct; but she appealed to the portrait, and endeavoured, by tracing some resemblance

between it and Schedoni, to decide her doubts. The countenance of each was as different in character as in years. The
miniature displayed a young man rather handsome, of a gay
and smiling countenance; yet the smile expressed triumph,
rather than sweetness, and his whole air and features were
distinguished by a consciousness of superiority that rose
even to haughtiness.

Schedoni, on the contrary, advanced in years, exhibited a
severe physiognomy, furrowed by thought, no less than by
time, and darkened by the habitual indulgence of morose
passions. He looked as if he had never smiled since the portrait was drawn; and it seemed as if the painter, prophetic of
Schedoni's future disposition, had arrested and embodied
that smile, to prove hereafter that cheerfulness had once
played upon his features.

Though the expression was so different between the countenance, which Schedoni formerly owned, and that he now
wore, the same character of haughty pride was visible in
both; and Ellena did trace a resemblance in the bold outline
of the features, but not sufficient to convince her, without
farther evidence, that each belonged to the same person, and
that the Confessor had ever been the young cavalier in the
portrait. In the first tumult of her thoughts, she had not had
leisure to dwell upon the singularity of Schedoni's visiting
her at this deep hour of the night, or to urge any questions,
except vague ones, concerning the truth of her relationship
to him. But now, that her mind was somewhat recollected,
and that his looks were less terrific, she ventured to ask a
fuller explanation of these circumstances, and his reasons for
the late extraordinary assertion. "It is past midnight, father,"
said Ellena, "you may judge then how anxious I am to learn,
what motive led you to my chamber at this lonely hour?"

Schedoni made no reply.

"Did you come to warn me of danger?" she continued,
"had you discovered the cruel designs of Spalatro? Ah!
when I supplicated for your compassion on the shore this
evening, you little thought what perils surrounded me! or
you would——"

"You say true!" interrupted he, in a hurried manner, "but
name the subject no more. Why will you persist in returning
to it?"

His words surprised Ellena, who had not even alluded to
the subject till now; but the returning wildness of his coun-

tenance, made her fearful of dwelling upon the topic, even
so far as to point out his error.

Another deep pause succeeded, during which Schedoni
continued to pace the room, sometimes stopping for an instant, to fix his eyes on Ellena, and regarding her with an
earnestness that seemed to partake of frenzy, and then
gloomily withdrawing his regards, and sighing heavily, as he
turned away to a distant part of the room. She, meanwhile,
agitated with astonishment at his conduct, as well as at her
own circumstances, and with the fear of offending him by
further questions, endeavoured to summon courage to solicit
the explanation which was so important to her tranquillity.
At length she asked, how she might venture to believe a circumstance so surprising, as that of which he had just assured
her, and to remind him that he had not yet disclosed his reason for admitting the belief.

The Confessor's feelings were eloquent in reply; and,
when at length they were sufficiently subdued, to permit him
to talk coherently, he mentioned some circumstances concerning Ellena's family, that proved him at least to have
been intimately acquainted with it; and others, which she believed were known only to Bianchi and herself, that removed
every doubt of his identity.

This, however, was a period of his life too big with remorse, horror, and the first pangs of parental affection, to allow him to converse long; deep solitude was necessary for
his soul. He wished to plunge where no eye might restrain
his emotions, or observe the overflowing anguish of his
heart. Having obtained sufficient proof to convince him that
Ellena was indeed his child, and assured her that she should
be removed from this house on the following day, and be restored to her home, he abruptly left the chamber.

As he descended the stair-case, Spalatro stepped forward
to meet him, with the cloak which had been designed to
wrap the mangled form of Ellena, when it should be carried
to the shore. "Is it done?" said the ruffian, in a stifled voice,
"I am ready;" and he spread forth the cloak, and began to ascend.

"Hold! villain, hold!" said Schedoni, lifting up his head
for the first time, "Dare to enter that chamber, and your life
shall answer for it."

"What!" exclaimed the man, shrinking back astonished—
"will not *hers* satisfy you!"

He trembled for the consequence of what he had said, when he observed the changing countenance of the Confessor. But Schedoni spoke not: the tumult in his breast was too great for utterance, and he pressed hastily forward. Spalatro followed. "Be pleased to tell me what I am to do," said he, again holding forth the cloak.

"Avaunt!" exclaimed the other, turning fiercely upon him; "leave me."

"How!" said the man, whose spirit was now aroused, "has *your* courage failed too, Signor? If so, I will prove myself no dastard, though you called me one; I'll do the business myself."

"Villain! fiend!" cried Schedoni, seizing the ruffian by the throat, with a grasp that seemed intended to annihilate him; when, recollecting that the fellow was only willing to obey the very instructions he had himself but lately delivered to him, other emotions succeeded to that of rage; he slowly liberated him, and in accents broken, and softening from sternness, bade him retire to rest. "To-morrow," he added, "I will speak further with you. As for this night——I have changed my purpose. Begone!"

Spalatro was about to express the indignation, which astonishment and fear had hitherto overcome, but his employer repeated his command in a voice of thunder, and closed the door of his apartment with violence, as he shut out a man, whose presence was become hateful to him. He felt relieved by his absence, and began to breathe more freely, till, remembering that his accomplice had just boasted that he was no dastard, he dreaded lest, by way of proving the assertion, he should attempt to commit the crime, from which he had lately shrunk. Terrified at the possibility, and even apprehending that it might already have become a reality, he rushed from the room, and found Spalatro in the passage leading to the private stair-case; but, whatever might have been his purpose, the situation and looks of the latter were sufficiently alarming. At the approach of Schedoni, he turned his sullen and malignant countenance towards him, without answering the call, or the demand as to his business there; and with slow steps obeyed the order of his master, that he should withdraw to his room. Thither Schedoni followed, and, having locked him in it for the night, he repaired to the apartment of Ellena, which he secured from the possibility of intrusion. He then returned to his own, not to sleep, but to abandon himself to the agonies of remorse and horror; and he yet shuddered like a man, who has just recoiled from the brink of a precipice, but who still measures the gulf with his eye.

CHAPTER X

————But their way
Lies through the perplexed paths of this drear wood,
The nodding horror of whose shady brows
Threats the forlorn and wandering passenger.

                                                    MILTON

ELLENA, when Schedoni had left her, recollected all the particulars, which he had thought proper to reveal concerning her family, and, comparing them with such circumstances as the late Bianchi had related on the same subject, she perceived nothing that was contradictory between the two accounts. But she knew not even yet enough of her own story, to understand why Bianchi had been silent as to some particulars, which had just been disclosed. From Bianchi she had always understood, that her mother had married a nobleman of the duchy of Milan, and of the house of Marinella; that the marriage had been unfortunate; and that she herself, even before the death of the Countess, had been committed to the care of Bianchi, the only sister of that lady. Of this event, or of her mother, Ellena had no remembrance; for the kindness of Bianchi had obliterated from her mind the loss and the griefs of her early infancy; and she recollected only the accident which had discovered to her, in Bianchi's cabinet, after the death of the latter, the miniature and the name of her father. When she had enquired the reason of this injunction, Bianchi replied, that the degraded fortune of her house rendered privacy desirable; and answered her further questions concerning her father, by relating, that he had died while she was an infant. The picture, which Ellena had discovered, Bianchi had found among the trinkets of the departed Countess, and designed to present it at some future period to Ellena, when her discretion might be trusted with a knowledge of her family. This was the whole of what Signora Bianchi had judged it necessary to explain, though in her last hours it appeared that she wished to reveal more; but it was then too late.

Though Ellena perceived that many circumstances of the relations given by Schedoni, and by Signora Bianchi, coincided, and that none were contradictory, except that of his death, she could not yet subdue her amazement at this discovery, or even the doubts which occasionally recurred to her as to its truth. Schedoni, on the contrary, had not even appeared surprised, when she assured him, that she always understood her father had been dead many years; though when she asked if her mother too was living, both his distress and his assurances confirmed the relation made by Bianchi.

When Ellena's mind became more tranquil, she noticed again the singularity of Schedoni's visit to her apartment at so sacred an hour; and her thoughts glanced back involuntarily to the scene of the preceding evening on the sea-shore, and the image of her father appeared in each, in the terrific character of an agent of the Marchesa di Vivaldi. The suspicions, however, which she had formerly admitted, respecting his designs, were now impatiently rejected, for she was less anxious to discover truth, than to release herself from horrible suppositions; and she willingly believed that Schedoni, having misunderstood her character, had only designed to assist in removing her beyond the reach of Vivaldi. The ingenuity of hope suggested also, that, having just heard from her conductors, or from Spalatro, some circumstances of her story, he had been led to a suspicion of the relationship between them, and that in the first impatience of parental anxiety, he had disregarded the hour, and come, though at midnight, to her apartment to ascertain the truth.

While she soothed herself with this explanation of a circumstance, which had occasioned her considerable surprise, she perceived on the floor the point of a dagger peeping from beneath the curtains! Emotions almost too horrible to be sustained, followed this discovery; she took the instrument, and gazed upon it aghast and trembling, for a suspicion of the real motive of Schedoni's visit glanced upon her mind. But it was only for a moment; such a supposition was too terrible to be willingly endured; she again believed that Spalatro alone had meditated her destruction, and she

thanked the Confessor as her deliverer, instead of shrinking
from him as an assassin. She now understood that Schedoni,
having discovered the ruffian's design, had rushed into the
chamber to save a stranger from his murderous poniard, and
had unconsciously rescued his own daughter, when the portrait at her bosom informed him of the truth. With this conviction Ellena's eyes overflowed with gratitude, and her
heart was hushed to peace.

Schedoni, meanwhile, shut up in his chamber, was agitated by feelings of a very opposite nature. When their first
excess was exhausted, and his mind was calm enough to reflect, the images that appeared on it struck him with solemn
wonder. In pursuing Ellena at the criminal instigation of the
Marchesa di Vivaldi, it appeared that he had been persecut-
ing his own child; and in thus consenting to conspire against
the innocent, he had in the event been only punishing the
guilty, and preparing mortification for himself on the exact
subject to which he had sacrificed his conscience. Every step
that he had taken with a view of gratifying his ambition was
retrograde, and while he had been wickedly intent to serve
the Marchesa and himself, by preventing the marriage of
Vivaldi and Ellena, he had been laboriously counteracting
his own fortune. An alliance with the illustrious house of
Vivaldi, was above his loftiest hope of advancement, and
this event he had himself nearly prevented by the very
means which had been adopted, at the expence of every virtuous consideration, to obtain an inferior promotion. Thus
by a singular retribution, his own crimes had recoiled upon
himself.

Schedoni perceived the many obstacles, which lay between him and his newly awakened hopes, and that much
was to be overcome before those nuptials could be publicly
solemnized, which he was now still more anxious to promote, than he had lately been to prevent. The approbation of
the Marchesa was, at least, desirable, for she had much at
her disposal, and without it, though his daughter might be
the wife of Vivaldi, he himself would be no otherwise ben-
efited at present than by the honour of the connection. He
had some peculiar reasons for believing, that her consent
might be obtained, and, though there was hazard in delaying
the nuptials till such an experiment had been made, he resolved to encounter it, rather than forbear to solicit her con-
currence. But, if the Marchesa should prove inexorable, he

determined to bestow the hand of Ellena, without her knowledge, and in doing so, he well knew that he incurred little danger from her resentment, since he had secrets in his possession, the consciousness of which must awe her into a speedy neutrality. The consent of the Marchese, as he despaired of obtaining it, he did not mean to solicit, and the influence of the Marchesa was such, that Schedoni did not regard that as essential.

The first steps, however, to be taken, were those that might release Vivaldi from the Inquisition, the tremendous prison into which Schedoni himself, little foreseeing that he should so soon wish for his liberation, had caused him to be thrown. He had always understood, indeed, that if the Informer forbore to appear against the Accused in this Court, the latter would of course be liberated; and he also believed, that Vivaldi's freedom could be obtained whenever he should think proper to apply to a person at Naples, whom he knew to be connected with the *Holy Office* of Rome. How much the Confessor had suffered his wishes to deceive him, may appear hereafter. His motives for having thus confined Vivaldi, were partly those of self-defence. He dreaded the discovery and the vengeance, which might follow the loss of Ellena, should Vivaldi be at liberty immediately to pursue his enquiries. But he believed that all trace of her must be lost, after a few weeks had elapsed, and that Vivaldi's sufferings from confinement in the Inquisition would have given interests to his mind, which must weaken the one he felt for Ellena. Yet, though in this instance self-defence had been a principal motive with Schedoni, a desire of revenging the insult he had received in the church of the Spirito Santo, and all the consequent mortifications he experienced, had been a second; and, such was the blackness of his hatred, and the avarice of his revenge, that he had not considered the suffering, which the loss of Ellena would occasion Vivaldi, as sufficient retaliation.

In adopting a mode of punishment so extraordinary as that of imprisonment in the Inquisition, it appears, therefore, that Schedoni was influenced, partly by the difficulty of otherwise confining Vivaldi, during the period for which confinement was absolutely necessary to the success of his own schemes, and partly by a desire of inflicting the tortures of terror. He had also been encouraged by his discovery of this opportunity for conferring new obligations on the Marchesa.

The very conduct, that must have appeared to the first
glance of an honest mind fatal to his interests, he thought
might be rendered beneficial to them, and that his dexterity
could so command the business, as that the Marchesa should
eventually thank him as the deliverer of her son, instead of
discovering and execrating him as his Accuser; a scheme favoured by the unjust and cruel rule enacted by the tribunal
he approached, which permitted anonymous Informers.

To procure the arrestation of Vivaldi, it had been only
necessary to send a written accusation, without a name, to
the *Holy Office,* with a mention of the place where the accused person might be seized; but the suffering in consequence of this did not always proceed further than the
question; since, if the Informer failed to discover himself to
the Inquisitors, the prisoner, after many examinations, was
released, unless he happened unwarily to criminate himself.
Schedoni, as he did not intend to prosecute, believed, therefore, that Vivaldi would of course be discharged after a certain period, and supposing it also utterly impossible that he
could ever discover his Accuser, the Confessor determined
to appear anxious and active in effecting his release. This
character of a deliverer, he knew he should be the better enabled to support by means of a person officially connected
with the *Holy Office,* who had already unconsciously assisted his views. In the apartment of this man, Schedoni had
accidentally seen a formula of arrestation against a person
suspected of Heresy, the view of which had not only suggested to him the plan he had since adopted, but had in some
degree assisted him to carry it into effect. He had seen the
scroll only for a short time, but his observations were so
minute, and his memory so clear, that he was able to copy
it with at least sufficient exactness to impose upon the Benedictine priest, who had, perhaps, seldom or never seen a
real instrument of this kind. Schedoni had employed this artifice for the purpose of immediately securing Vivaldi, apprehending that, while the Inquisitors were slowly
deliberating upon his arrest, he might quit Celano, and elude
discovery. If the deception succeeded, it would enable him
also to seize Ellena, and to mislead Vivaldi respecting her
destination. The charge of having carried off a nun might appear to be corroborated by many circumstances, and
Schedoni would probably have made these the subject of
real denunciation, had he not foreseen the danger and the

trouble in which it might implicate himself; and that, as the charge could not be substantiated, Ellena would finally escape. As far as his plan now went, it had been successful; some of the bravoes whom he hired to personate officials, had conveyed Vivaldi to the town, where the real officers of the Inquisition were appointed to receive him; while the others carried Ellena to the shore of the Adriatic. Schedoni had much applauded his own ingenuity, in thus contriving, by the matter of the forged accusation, to throw an impenetrable veil over the fate of Ellena, and to secure himself from the suspicions or vengeance of Vivaldi, who, it appeared, would always believe that she had died, or was still confined in the unsearchable prisons of the Inquisition.

Thus he had betrayed himself in endeavouring to betray Vivaldi, whose release, however, he yet supposed could be easily obtained; but how much his policy had, in this instance, outrun his sagacity, now remained to be proved.

The subject of Schedoni's immediate perplexity was, the difficulty of conveying Ellena back to Naples; since, not chusing to appear at present in the character of her father, he could not decorously accompany her thither himself, nor could he prudently entrust her to the conduct of any person, whom he knew in this neighbourhood. It was, however, necessary to form a speedy determination, for he could neither endure to pass another day in a scene, which must continually impress him with the horrors of the preceding night, nor that Ellena should remain in it; and the morning light already gleamed upon his casements.

After some further deliberation, he resolved to be himself her conductor, as far at least as through the forests of the Garganus, and at the first town where conveniences could be procured, to throw aside his Monk's habit, and, assuming the dress of a layman, accompany her in this disguise towards Naples, till he should either discover some secure means of sending her forward to that city, or a temporary asylum for her in a convent on the way.

His mind was scarcely more tranquil, after having formed this determination, than before, and he did not attempt to repose himself even for a moment. The circumstances of the late discovery were almost perpetually recurring to his affrighted conscience, accompanied by a fear that Ellena might suspect the real purpose of his midnight visit; and he alternately formed and rejected plausible falsehoods, that might assuage her curiosity, and delude her apprehension.

The hour arrived, however, when it was necessary to prepare for departure, and found him still undecided as to the explanation he should form.

Having released Spalatro from his chamber, and given him directions to procure horses and a guide immediately from the neighbouring hamlet, he repaired to Ellena's room, to prepare her for this hasty removal. On approaching it, a remembrance of the purpose, with which he had last passed through these same passages and stair-case, appealed so powerfully to his feelings, that he was unable to proceed, and he turned back to his own apartment to recover some command over himself. A few moments restored to him his usual address, though not his tranquillity, and he again approached the chamber; it was now, however, by way of the corridor. As he unbarred the door, his hand trembled; but, when he entered the room, his countenance and manner had resumed their usual solemnity, and his voice only would have betrayed, to an attentive observer, the agitation of his mind.

Ellena was considerably affected on seeing him again, and he examined with a jealous eye the emotions he witnessed. The smile with which she met him was tender, but he perceived it pass away from her features, like the aërial colouring that illumines a mountain's brow; and the gloom of doubt and apprehension again over-spread them. As he advanced, he held forth his hand for hers, when, suddenly perceiving the dagger he had left in the chamber, he involuntarily withdrew his proffered courtesy, and his countenance changed. Ellena, whose eyes followed his to the object that attracted them, pointed to the instrument, took it up, and approaching him said, "This dagger I found last night in my chamber! O my father!"—

"That dagger!" said Schedoni, with affected surprise.

"Examine it," continued Ellena, while she held it up, "Do you know to whom it belongs? and who brought it hither?"

"What is it you mean?" asked Schedoni, betrayed by his feelings.

"Do you know, too, for what purpose it was brought?" said Ellena mournfully.

The Confessor made no reply, but irresolutely attempted to seize the instrument.

"O yes, I perceive you know too well," continued Ellena, "here, my father, while I slept"——

"Give me the dagger," interrupted Schedoni, in a frightful voice.

"Yes, my father, I will give it as an offering of my gratitude," replied Ellena, but as she raised her eyes, filled with tears, his look and fixed attitude terrified her, and she added with a still more persuasive tenderness, "Will you not accept the offering of your child, for having preserved her from the poniard of an assassin?"

Schedoni's looks became yet darker; he took the dagger in silence, and threw it with violence to the furthest end of the chamber, while his eyes remained fixed on hers. The force of the action alarmed her; "Yes, it is in vain that you would conceal the truth," she added, weeping unrestrainedly, "your goodness cannot avail; I know the whole."——

The last words aroused Schedoni again from his trance, his features became convulsed, and his look furious. "What do you know?" he demanded in a subdued voice, that seemed ready to burst in thunder.

"All that I owe you," replied Ellena, "that last night, while I slept upon this mattress, unsuspicious of what was designed against me, an assassin entered the chamber with that instrument in his hand, and——"

A stifled groan from Schedoni checked Ellena; she observed his rolling eyes, and trembled; till, believing that his agitation was occasioned by indignation against the assassin, she resumed, "Why should you think it necessary to conceal the danger which has threatened me, since it is to you that I owe my deliverance from it? O! my father, do not deny me the pleasure of shedding these tears of gratitude, do not refuse the thanks, which are due to you! While I slept upon that couch, while a ruffian stole upon my slumber—it was you, yes! can I ever forget that it was my father, who saved me from his poniard!"

Schedoni's passions were changed, but they were not less violent; he could scarcely controul them, while he said in a tremulous tone—"It is enough, say no more;" and he raised Ellena, but turned away without embracing her.

His strong emotion, as he paced in silence the furthest end of the apartment, excited her surprise, but she then attributed it to a remembrance of the perilous moment, from which he had rescued her.

Schedoni, meanwhile, to whom her thanks were daggers, was trying to subdue the feelings of remorse that tore his heart; and was so enveloped in a world of his own, as to be for some time unconscious of all around him. He continued to stalk in gloomy silence along the chamber, till the voice of Ellena, entreating him rather to rejoice that he had been permitted to save her, than so deeply to consider dangers which were past, again touched the chord that vibrated to his conscience, and recalled him to a sense of his situation. He then bade her prepare for immediate departure, and abruptly quitted the room.

Vainly hoping that in flying from the scene of his meditated crime, he should leave with it the acuteness of remembrance, and the agonizing stings of remorse, he was now more anxious than ever to leave this place. Yet he should still be accompanied by Ellena, and her innocent looks, her affectionate thanks, inflicted an anguish, which was scarcely endurable. Sometimes, thinking that her hatred, or what to him would be still severer, her contempt, must be more tolerable than this gratitude, he almost resolved to undeceive her respecting his conduct, but as constantly and impatiently repelled the thought with horror, and finally determined to suffer her to account for his late extraordinary visit in the way she had chosen.

Spalatro, at length, returned from the hamlet with horses, but without having procured a guide to conduct the travellers through a tract of the long-devolving forests of the Garganus, which it was necessary for them to pass. No person had been willing to undertake so arduous a task; and Spalatro, who was well acquainted with all the labyrinths of the way, now offered his services.

Schedoni, though he could scarcely endure the presence of this man, had no alternative but to accept him, since he had dismissed the guide who had conducted him hither. Of personal violence Schedoni had no apprehension, though he too well understood the villainy of his proposed companion; for he considered that he himself should be well armed, and he determined to ascertain that Spalatro was without weapons; he knew also, that in case of a contest, his own superior stature would easily enable him to overcome such an antagonist.

Every thing being now ready for departure, Ellena was summoned, and the Confessor led her to his own apartment, where a slight breakfast was prepared.

Her spirits being revived by the speed of this departure, she would again have expressed her thanks, but he peremptorily interrupted her, and forbade any further mention of gratitude.

On entering the court where the horses were in waiting, and perceiving Spalatro, Ellena shrunk and put her arm within Schedoni's for protection. "What recollections does the presence of that man revive!" said she, "I can scarcely venture to believe myself safe, even with you, when he is here."

Schedoni made no reply, till the remark was repeated, "You have nothing to fear from him," muttered the Confessor, while he hastened her forward, "and we have no time to lose in vague apprehension."

"How!" exclaimed Ellena, "is not he the assassin from whom you saved me! I cannot doubt, that you know him to be such, though you would spare me the pain of believing so."

"Well, well, be it so," replied the Confessor; "Spalatro, lead the horses this way."

The party were soon mounted, when, quitting this eventful mansion, and the shore of the Adriatic, as Ellena hoped for ever, they entered upon the gloomy wilderness of the Garganus. She often turned her eyes back upon the house with emotions of inexpressible awe, astonishment, and thankfulness, and gazed while a glimpse of its turretted walls could be caught beyond the dark branches, which, closing over it, at length shut it from her view. The joy of this departure, however, was considerably abated by the presence of Spalatro, and her fearful countenance enquired of Schedoni the meaning of his being suffered to accompany them. The Confessor was reluctant to speak concerning a man, of whose very existence he would willingly have ceased to think. Ellena guided her horse still closer to Schedoni's, but, forbearing to urge the enquiry otherwise than by looks, she received no reply, and endeavoured to quiet her apprehensions, by considering that he would not have permitted this man to be their guide, unless he had believed he might be trusted. This consideration, though it relieved her fears, encreased her perplexity respecting the late designs of Spalatro, and her surprise that Schedoni, if he had really understood them to be evil, should endure his presence. Every time she stole a glance at the dark countenance of this man, rendered still darker by the shade of the trees, she thought "assassin" was written in each line of it, and could scarcely doubt that he, and not the people who had conducted her to the mansion, had dropped the dagger in her chamber. Whenever she looked round through the deep glades, and on the forest-mountains that on every side closed the scene, and seemed to exclude all cheerful haunt of man, and then regarded her companions, her heart sunk, notwithstanding the reasons she had for believing herself in the protection of a father. Nay, the very looks of Schedoni himself, more than once reminding her of his appearance on the seashore, renewed the impressions of alarm and even of dismay, which she had there experienced. At such moments it was scarcely possible for her to consider him as her parent, and, in spite of every late appearance, strange and unaccountable doubts began to gather on her mind.

Schedoni, meanwhile, lost in thought, broke not, by a single word, the deep silence of the solitudes through which they passed. Spalatro was equally mute, and equally engaged by his reflections on the sudden change in Schedoni's purpose, and by wonder as to the motive, which could have induced him to lead Ellena in safety, from the very spot whither she was brought by his express command to be destroyed. He, however, was not so wholly occupied, as to be unmindful of his situation, or unwatchful of an opportunity of serving his own interests, and retaliating upon Schedoni for the treatment he had received on the preceding night.

Among the various subjects that distracted the Confessor, the difficulty of disposing of Ellena, without betraying at Naples that she was his relative, was not the least distressing. Whatever might be the reason which could justify such feelings, his fears of a premature discovery of the circumstance to the society with whom he lived, were so strong, as often to produce the most violent effect upon his countenance, and it was, perhaps, when he was occupied by this subject, that its terrific expression revived with Ellena the late scene upon the shore. His embarrassment was not less, as to the excuse to be offered the Marchesa, for having failed to fulfil his engagement, and respecting the means by which he might interest her in favour of Ellena, and even dispose her to approve the marriage, before she should be informed of the family of this unfortunate young woman. Perceiving all the necessity for ascertaining the probabilities of such consent, before he ventured to make an avowal of her origin, he determined not to reveal himself till he should be perfectly sure that the discovery would be acceptable to the Marchesa. In the mean time, as it would be necessary to say something of Ellena's birth, he meant to declare that he had discovered it to be noble, and her family worthy, in every respect, of a connection with that of the Vivaldi.

An interview with the Marchesa, was almost equally wished for and dreaded by the Confessor. He shuddered at the expectation of meeting a woman, who had instigated him to the murder of his own child, which, though he had been happily prevented from committing it, was an act that would still be wished for by the Marchesa. How could he endure her reproaches, when she should discover that he had failed to accomplish her will! How conceal the indignation of a father, and dissimulate all a father's various feelings, when, in reply to such reproaches, he must form excuses, and act humility, from which his whole soul would revolt! Never could his arts of dissimulation have been so severely tried, not even in the late scenes with Ellena, never have returned upon himself in punishment so severe, as in that which awaited him with the Marchesa. And from its approach, the cool and politic Schedoni often shrunk in such horror, that he almost determined to avoid it at any hazard, and secretly to unite Vivaldi and Ellena, without even soliciting the consent of the Marchesa.

A desire, however, of the immediate preferment, so necessary to his pride, constantly checked this scheme, and finally made him willing to subject every honest feeling, and submit to any meanness, however vicious, rather than forego the favourite object of his erroneous ambition. Never, perhaps, was the paradoxical union of pride and abjectness, more strongly exhibited than on this occasion.

While thus the travellers silently proceeded, Ellena's thoughts often turned to Vivaldi, and she considered, with trembling anxiety, the effect which the late discovery was likely to have upon their future lives. It appeared to her, that Schedoni must approve of a connection thus flattering to the pride of a father, though he would probably refuse his consent to a private marriage. And, when she further considered the revolution, which a knowledge of her family might occasion towards herself in the minds of the Vivaldi, her prospects seemed to brighten, and her cares began to dissipate.

Judging that Schedoni must be acquainted with the present situation of Vivaldi, she was continually on the point of mentioning him, but was as constantly restrained by timidity, though, had she suspected him to be an inhabitant of the Inquisition, her scruples would have vanished before an irresistible interest. As it was, believing that he, like herself, had been imposed upon by the Marchesa's agents, in the disguise of officials, she concluded, as has before appeared, that he now suffered a temporary imprisonment by order of his mother, at one of the family villas. When, however, Schedoni, awaking from his reverie, abruptly mentioned Vivaldi, her spirits fluttered with impatience to learn his exact situation, and she enquired respecting it.

"I am no stranger to your attachment," said Schedoni, evading the question, "but I wish to be informed of some circumstances relative to its commencement."

Ellena, confused, and not knowing what to reply, was for a moment silent, and then repeated her enquiry.

"Where did you first meet?" said the Confessor, still disregarding her question. Ellena related, that she had first seen Vivaldi, when attending her aunt from the church of San Lorenzo. For the present she was spared the embarrassment of further explanation by Spalatro, who, riding up to Schedoni, informed him they were approaching the town of Zanti. On looking forward, Ellena perceived houses peeping from among the forest-trees, at a short distance, and presently heard the cheerful bark of a dog, that sure herald and faithful servant of man!

Soon after the travellers entered Zanti, a small town surrounded by the forest, where, however, the poverty of the inhabitants seemed to forbid a longer stay than was absolutely necessary for repose, and a slight refreshment. Spalatro led the way to a cabin, in which the few persons, that journied this road were usually entertained. The appearance of the people, who owned it, was as wild as their country, and the interior of the dwelling was so dirty and comfortless, that Schedoni, preferring to take his repast in the open air, a table was spread under the luxuriant shade of the forest-trees, at a little distance. Here, when the host had withdrawn, and Spalatro had been dispatched to examine the post-horses, and to procure a lay-habit for the Confessor, the latter, once more alone with Ellena, began to experience again somewhat of the embarrassments of conscience; and Ellena,

whenever her eyes glanced upon him, suffered a solemnity
of fear that rose almost to terror. He, at length, terminated
this emphatic silence, by renewing his mention of Vivaldi,
and his command that Ellena should relate the history of
their affection. Not daring to refuse, she obeyed, but with as
much brevity as possible, and Schedoni did not interrupt her
by a single observation. However eligible their nuptials now
appeared to him, he forbore to give any hint of approbation,
till he should have extricated the object of her regards from
his perilous situation. But, with Ellena, this very silence implied the opinion it was meant to conceal, and, encouraged
by the hope it imparted, she ventured once more to ask, by
whose order Vivaldi had been arrested; whither he had been
conveyed, and the circumstances of his present situation.

Too politic to intrust her with a knowledge of his actual
condition, the Confessor spared her the anguish of learning
that he was a prisoner in the Inquisition. He affected ignorance of the late transaction at Celano, but ventured to believe, that both Vivaldi and herself had been arrested by
order of the Marchesa, who, he conjectured, had thrown him
into temporary confinement, a measure which she, no doubt,
had meant to enforce also towards Ellena.

"And you, my father," observed Ellena, "what brought
you to my prison,—you who was not informed with the
Marchesa's designs? What accident conducted you to that
remote solitude, just at the moment when you could save
your child!"

"Informed of the Marchesa's designs!" said Schedoni, with
embarrassment and displeasure: "Have you ever imagined that
I could be accessary—that I could consent to assist, I mean
could consent to be a confidant of such atrocious"——Schedoni, bewildered, confounded, and half betrayed, checked himself.

"Yet you have said, the Marchesa meant only to confine
me!" observed Ellena; "was that design so atrocious? Alas,
my father! I know too well that her plan was more atrocious,
and since you had too much reason to know this, why do
you say that imprisonment only was intended for me? But
your solicitude for my tranquillity leads you to"——

"What means," interrupted the suspicious Schedoni, "can
I particularly have of understanding the Marchesa's
schemes? I repeat, that I am not her confidant; how then is

it to be supposed I should know that they extended further than to imprisonment?"

"Did you not save me from the arm of the assassin!" said Ellena tenderly; "did not you wrench the very dagger from his grasp!"

"I had forgotten, I had forgotten," said the Confessor, yet more embarrassed.

"Yes, good minds are ever thus apt to forget the benefits they confer," replied Ellena. "But you shall find, my father, that a grateful heart is equally tenacious to remember them; it is the indelible register of every act that is dismissed from the memory of the benefactor."

"Mention no more of benefits," said Schedoni, impatiently; "let silence on this subject henceforth indicate your wish to oblige me."

He rose, and joined the host, who was at the door of his cabin. Schedoni wished to dismiss Spalatro as soon as possible, and he enquired for a guide to conduct him through that part of the forest, which remained to be traversed. In this poor town, a person willing to undertake that office was easily to be found, but the host went in quest of a neighbour whom he had recommended.

Meanwhile Spalatro returned, without having succeeded in his commission. Not any lay-habit could be procured, upon so short a notice, that suited Schedoni. He was obliged, therefore, to continue his journey to the next town at least, in his own dress, but the necessity was not very serious to him, since it was improbable that he should be known in this obscure region.

Presently the host appeared with his neighbour, when Schedoni, having received satisfactory answers to his questions, engaged him for the remainder of the forest-road, and dismissed Spalatro. The ruffian departed with sullen reluctance and evident ill-will, circumstances which the Confessor scarcely noticed, while occupied by the satisfaction of escaping from the presence of the atrocious partner of his conscience. But Ellena, as he passed her, observed the malignant disappointment of his look, and it served only to heighten the thankfulness his departure occasioned her.

It was afternoon before the travellers proceeded. Schedoni had calculated that they could easily reach the town, at which they designed to pass the night, before the close of evening, and he had been in no haste to depart during the heat of the day. Their track now lay through a country less savage, though scarcely less wild than that they had passed in the morning. It emerged from the interior towards the border of the forest; they were no longer enclosed by impending mountains; the withdrawing shades were no longer impenetrable to the eye, but now and then opened to gleams of sunshine-landscape, and blue distances; and in the immediate scene, many a green glade spread its bosom to the sun. The grandeur of the trees, however, did not decline; the plane, the oak, and the chestnut still threw a pomp of foliage round these smiling spots, and seemed to consecrate the mountain streams, that descended beneath their solemn shade.

To the harassed spirits of Ellena the changing scenery was refreshing, and she frequently yielded her cares to the influence of majestic nature. Over the gloom of Schedoni, no scenery had, at any moment, power; the shape and paint of external imagery gave neither impression or colour to his fancy. He contemned the sweet illusions, to which other spirits are liable, and which often confer a delight more exquisite, and not less innocent, than any, which deliberative reason can bestow.

The same thoughtful silence, that had wrapt him at the beginning of the journey, he still preserved, except when occasionally he asked a question of the guide concerning the way, and received answers too loquacious for his humour. This loquacity, however, was not easily repressed, and the peasant had already begun to relate some terrible stories of murder, committed in these forests upon people, who had been hardy enough to venture into them without a guide, before the again abstracted Schedoni even noticed that he spoke. Though Ellena did not give much credit to these narratives, they had some effect upon her fears, when soon after she entered the deep shades of a part of the forest, that lay along a narrow defile, whence every glimpse of cheerful landscape was again excluded by precipices, which towered on either side. The stillness was not less effectual than the gloom, for no sounds were heard, except such as seemed to characterize solitude, and impress its awful power more deeply on the heart,——the hollow dashing of torrents descending distantly, and the deep sighings of the wind, as it passed among trees, which threw their broad arms over the cliffs, and crowned the highest summits. Onward, through the narrowing windings of the defile, no living object appeared; but, as Ellena looked fearfully back, she thought she distinguished a human figure advancing beneath the dusky umbrage that closed the view. She communicated her suspicion to Schedoni, though not her fears, and they stopped for a moment, to observe further. The object advanced slowly, and they perceived the stature of a man, who, having continued to approach, suddenly paused, and then glided away behind the foliage that crossed the perspective, but not before Ellena fancied she discriminated the figure of Spalatro. None but a purpose the most desperate, she believed, could have urged him to follow into this pass, instead of returning, as he had pretended, to his home. Yet it appeared improbable, that he alone should be willing to attack two armed persons, for both Schedoni and the guide had weapons of defence. This consideration afforded her only a momentary respite from apprehension, since it was possible that he might not be alone, though only one person had yet been seen among the shrouding branches of the woods. "Did you not think he resembled Spalatro?" said Ellena to the Confessor, "was he not of the same stature and air? You are well armed, or I should fear for you, as well as for myself."

"I did not observe a resemblance," replied Schedoni, throwing a glance back, "but whoever he is, you have nothing to apprehend from him, for he has disappeared."

"Yes, Signor, so much the worse," observed the guide, "so much the worse, if he means us any harm, for he can steal along the rocks behind these thickets, and strike out upon us before we are aware of him. Or, if he knows the path that runs among those old oaks yonder, on the left, where the ground rises, he has us sure at the turning of the next cliff."

"Speak lower," said Schedoni, "unless you mean that he should benefit by your instructions."

Though the Confessor said this without any suspicion of evil intention from the guide, the man immediately began to justify himself, and added, "I'll give him a hint of what he may expect, however, if he attacks us." As he spoke, he fired his trombone in the air, when every rock reverberated the sound, and the faint and fainter thunder retired in murmurs through all the windings of the defile. The eagerness, with which the guide had justified himself, produced an effect upon Schedoni contrary to what he designed; and the Confessor, as he watched him suspiciously, observed, that after he had fired, he did not load his piece again. "Since you have given the enemy sufficient intimation where to find us," said Schedoni, "you will do well to prepare for his reception; load again, friend. I have arms too, and they are ready."

While the man sullenly obeyed, Ellena, again alarmed, looked back in search of the stranger, but not any person appeared beneath the gloom, and no footstep broke upon the stillness. When, however, she suddenly heard a rustling noise, she looked to the bordering thickets, almost expecting to see Spalatro break from among them, before she perceived that it was only the sounding pinions of birds, which, startled by the report of the trombone from their high nests in the cliffs, winged their way from danger.

The suspicions of the Confessor had, probably, been slight, for they were transient; and when Ellena next addressed him, he had again retired within himself. He was ruminating upon an excuse to be offered the Marchesa, which might be sufficient both to assuage her disappointment and baffle her curiosity, and he could not, at present, fabricate one that might soothe her resentment, without risk of betraying his secret.

Twilight had added its gloom to that of the rocks, before the travellers distinguished the town, at which they meant to pass the night. It terminated the defile, and its grey houses could scarcely be discerned from the precipice upon which they hung, or from the trees that embosomed them. A rapid stream rolled below, and over it a bridge conducted the wanderers to the little inn, at which they were to take up their abode. Here, quietly lodged, Ellena dismissed all present apprehensions of Spalatro, but she still believed she had seen him, and her suspicions, as to the motive of his extraordinary journey, were not appeased.

As this was a town of ampler accommodation than the one they had left, Schedoni easily procured a lay-habit, that would disguise him for the remainder of the journey; and Ellena was permitted to lay aside the nun's veil, for one of a more general fashion; but, in dismissing it, she did not forget that it had been the veil of Olivia, and she preserved it as a sacred relique of her favourite recluse.

The distance between this town and Naples was still that of several days journey, according to the usual mode of travelling; but the most dangerous part of the way was now overcome, the road having emerged from the forests; and when Schedoni, on the following morning, was departing, he would have discharged the guide, had not the host assured him, he would find one still necessary in the open, but wild, country through which he must pass. Schedoni's distrust of this guide had never been very serious, and, as the result of the preceding evening proved favourable, he had restored him so entirely to his confidence, as willingly to engage him for the present day. In this confidence, however, Ellena did not perfectly coincide; she had observed the man while he loaded the trombone, on Schedoni's order, and his evident reluctance had almost persuaded her, that he was in league with some person who designed to attack them; a conjecture, perhaps, the more readily admitted while her mind was suffering from the impression of having seen Spalatro. She now ventured to hint her distrust to the Confessor, who paid little attention to it, and reminded her, that sufficient proof of the man's honesty had appeared, in their having been permitted to pass in safety, a defile so convenient for the purpose of rapine as that of yesterday. To a reply apparently so reasonable, Ellena could oppose nothing, had she even dared to press the topic; and she recommenced the journey with gayer hopes.

END OF THE SECOND VOLUME

VOLUME III

CHAPTER I

Mark where yon ruin frowns upon the steep,
The giant-spectre of departed power!
Within those shadowy walls and silent chambers
Have stalked the crimes of days long past!

On this day, Schedoni was more communicative than on the preceding one. While they rode apart from the guide, he conversed with Ellena on various topics relative to herself, but without once alluding to Vivaldi; and even condescended to mention his design of disposing of her in a convent at some distance from Naples, till it should be convenient for him to acknowledge her for his daughter. But the difficulty of finding a suitable situation embarrassed him, and he was disconcerted by the awkwardness of introducing her himself to strangers, whose curiosity would be heightened by a sense of their interest.

These circumstances induced him the more easily to attend to the distress of Ellena, on her learning that she was again to be placed at a distance from her home, and among strangers; and the more willingly to listen to the account she gave of the convent of Santa Maria della Pieta, and to her request of returning thither. But in whatever degree he might be inclined to approve, he listened without consenting, and Ellena had only the consolation of perceiving that he was not absolutely determined to adopt his first plan.

Her thoughts were too deeply engaged upon her future prospects to permit leisure for present fears, or probably she would have suffered some return of those of yesterday, in traversing the lonely plains and rude vallies, through which the road lay. Schedoni was thankful to the landlord, who had advised him to keep the guide, the road being frequently obscured amongst the wild heaths that stretched around, and the eye often sweeping over long tracts of country, without perceiving a village, or any human dwelling. During the whole morning, they had not met one traveller, and they continued to proceed beneath the heat of noon, because Schedoni had been unable to discover even a cottage, in which shelter and repose might be obtained.

It was late in the day when the guide pointed out the grey walls of an edifice, which crowned the acclivity they were approaching. But this was so shrouded among woods, that no feature of it could be distinctly seen, and it did but slightly awaken their hopes of approaching a convent, which might receive them with hospitality.

The high banks overshadowed with thickets, between which the road ascended, soon excluded even a glimpse of the walls; but, as the travellers turned the next projection, they perceived a person on the summit of the road, crossing as if towards some place of residence, and concluded that the edifice they had seen was behind the trees, among which he had disappeared.

A few moments brought them to the spot, where, retired at a short distance among the woods that browed the hill, they discovered the extensive remains of what seemed to have been a villa, and which, from the air of desolation it exhibited, Schedoni would have judged to be wholly deserted, had he not already seen a person enter. Wearied and exhausted, he determined to ascertain whether any refreshment could be procured from the inhabitants within, and the party alighted before the portal of a deep and broad avenue of arched stone, which seemed to have been the grand approach to the villa. The entrance was obstructed by fallen fragments of columns, and by the underwood that had taken root amongst them. The travellers, however, easily overcame these interruptions: but as the avenue was of considerable extent, and as its only light proceeded from the portal, except what a few narrow loops in the walls admitted, they soon found themselves involved in an obscurity that rendered the way difficult, and Schedoni endeavoured to make himself heard by the person he had seen. The effort was unsuccessful, but, as they proceeded, a bend in the passage shewed a distant glimmering of light, which served to guide them to the opposite entrance, where an arch opened immediately into a court of the villa. Schedoni paused here in disappointment, for every object seemed to bear evidence of abandonment and desolation; and he looked, almost hopelessly, round the light colonnade which ran along three sides of the court, and to the trees that waved over the fourth, in search of the person, who had been seen from the road. No human figure stole upon the vacancy; yet the apt fears of Ellena almost imagined the form of Spalatro gliding behind the columns, and she started as the air shook over the wild plants that wreathed them, before she discovered that it was not the sound of steps. At the extravagance of her suspicions, however, and the weakness of her terrors, she blushed, and endeavoured to resist that propensity to fear, which nerves long pressed upon had occasioned in her mind.

Schedoni, meanwhile, stood in the court, like the evil spirit of the place, examining its desolation, and endeavouring to ascertain whether any person lurked in the interior of the building. Several doorways in the colonnade appeared to lead to chambers of the villa, and, after a short hesitation, Schedoni, having determined to pursue his inquiry, entered one of them, and passed through a marble hall to a suite of rooms, whose condition told how long it was since they had been inhabited. The roofs had entirely vanished, and even portions of the walls had fallen, and lay in masses amongst the woods without.

Perceiving that it was as useless as difficult to proceed, the Confessor returned to the court, where the shade of the palmetos, at least, offered an hospitable shelter to the wearied travellers. They reposed themselves beneath the branches, on some fragments of a marble fountain, whence the court opened to the extensive landscape, now mellowed by the evening beams, and partook of the remains of a repast, which had been deposited in the wallet of the guide.

"This place appears to have suffered from an earthquake, rather than from time," said Schedoni, "for the walls, though shattered, do not seem to have decayed, and much that has been strong lies in ruin, while what is comparatively slight remains uninjured; these are certainly symptoms of partial shocks of the earth. Do you know any thing of the history of this place, friend?"

"Yes, Signor," replied the guide.

"Relate it, then."

"I shall never forget the earthquake that destroyed it, Signor; for it was felt all through the Garganus. I was then about sixteen, and I remember it was near an hour before midnight that the great shock was felt. The weather had been almost stifling for several days, scarcely a breath of air had stirred, and slight tremblings of the ground were noticed by many people. I had been out all day, cutting wood in the forest with my father, and tired enough we were, when——"

"This is the history of yourself," said Schedoni, interrupting him, "Who did this place belong to?"

"Did any person suffer here?" said Ellena.

"The Baróne di Cambrusca lived here," replied the guide.

"Hah! the Baróne!" repeated Schedoni, and sunk into one of his customary fits of abstraction.

"He was a Signor little loved in the country," continued the guide, "and some people said it was a judgment upon him for——"

"Was it not rather a judgment upon the country," interrupted the Confessor, lifting up his head, and then sinking again into silence.

"I know not for that, Signor, but he had committed crimes enough to make one's hair stand on end. It was here that he——"

"Fools are always wondering at the actions of those above them," said Schedoni, testily; "Where is the Baróne now?"

"I cannot tell, Signor, but most likely where he deserves to be, for he has never been heard of since the night of the earthquake, and it is believed he was buried under the ruins."

"Did any other person suffer?" repeated Ellena.

"You shall hear, Signora," replied the peasant, "I happen to know something about the matter, because a cousin of ours lived in the family at the time, and my father has often told me all about it, as well as of the late lord's goings-on. It was near midnight when the great shock came, and the family, thinking of nothing at all, had supped, and been asleep some time. Now it happened, that the Baróne's chamber was in a tower of the old building, at which people often wondered, because, said they, why should he chuse to sleep in the old part when there are so many fine rooms in the new villa? but so it was."

"Come, dispatch your meal," said Schedoni, awaking from his deep musing, "the sun is setting, and we have yet far to go."

"I will finish the meal and the story together, Signor, with your leave," replied the guide. Schedoni did not notice what

he said, and, as the man was not forbidden, he proceeded
with his relation.

"Now it happened, that the Baróne's chamber was in that
old tower,—if you will look this way, Signora, you may see
what is left of it."

Ellena turned her attention to where the guide pointed,
and perceived the shattered remains of a tower rising beyond
the arch, through which she had entered the court.

"You see that corner of a windowcase, left in the highest
part of the wall, Signora," continued the guide, "just by that
tuft of ash, that grows out of the stone."

"I observe," said Ellena.

"Well, that was one of the windows of the very chamber,
Signora, and you see scarcely any thing else is left of it. Yes,
there is the door-case, too, but the door itself is gone; that
little stair-case, which you see beyond it, led up to another
story, which nobody now would guess had ever been; for
roof, and flooring, and all are fallen. I wonder how that little
stair-case in the corner happened to hold so fast!"

"Have you almost done?" inquired Schedoni, who had not
apparently attended to any thing the man said, and now alluded to the refreshment he was taking.

"Yes, Signor, I have not a great deal more to tell, or to eat
either, for that matter," replied the guide; "but you shall
hear. Well, yonder was the very chamber, Signora; at that
door-case, which is still in the wall, the Baróne came in; ah!
he little thought, I warrant, that he should never more go out
at it! How long he had been in the room I do not know, nor
whether he was asleep, or awake, for there is nobody that
can tell; but when the great shock came, it split the old
tower at once, before any other part of the buildings. You
see that heap of ruins, yonder, on the ground, Signora, there
lie the remains of the chamber; the Baróne, they say, was
buried under them!"

Ellena shuddered while she gazed upon this destructive
mass. A groan from Schedoni startled her, and she turned towards him, but, as he appeared shrouded in meditation, she
again directed her attention to this awful memorial. As her
eyes passed upon the neighbouring arch, she was struck with
the grandeur of its proportions, and with its singular appearance, now that the evening rays glanced upon the overhanging shrubs, and darted a line of partial light athwart the
avenue beyond. But what was her emotion, when she per-

ceived a person gliding away in the perspective of the avenue, and, as he crossed where the gleam fell, distinguished
the figure and countenance of Spalatro! She had scarcely
power faintly to exclaim, "Steps go there!" before he had
disappeared; and, when Schedoni looked round, the vacuity
and silence of solitude every where prevailed.

Ellena now did not scruple positively to affirm that she
had seen Spalatro, and Schedoni, fully sensible that, if her
imagination had not deluded her, the purpose of his thus
tracing their route must be desperate, immediately rose, and,
followed by the peasant, passed into the avenue to ascertain
the truth, leaving Ellena alone in the court. He had scarcely
disappeared before the danger of his adventuring into that
obscure passage, where an assassin might strike unseen, forcibly occurred to Ellena, and she loudly conjured him to return. She listened for his voice, but heard only his retreating
steps; when, too anxious to remain where she was, she hastened to the entrance of the avenue. But all was now hushed;
neither voice, nor steps were distinguished. Awed by the
gloom of the place, she feared to venture further, yet almost
equally dreaded to remain alone in any part of the ruin,
while a man so desperate as Spalatro was hovering about it.

As she yet listened at the entrance of the avenue, a faint
cry, which seemed to issue from the interior of the villa,
reached her. The first dreadful surmise that struck Ellena
was, that they were murdering her father, who had probably
been decoyed, by another passage, back into some chamber
of the ruin; when, instantly forgetting every fear for herself,
she hastened towards the spot whence she judged the sound
to have issued. She entered the hall, which Schedoni had noticed, and passed on through a suite of apartments beyond.
Every thing here, however, was silent, and the place apparently deserted. The suite terminated in a passage, that
seemed to lead to a distant part of the villa, and Ellena, after
a momentary hesitation, determined to follow it.

She made her way with difficulty between the half-
demolished walls, and was obliged to attend so much to her
steps, that she scarcely noticed whither she was going, till,
the deepening shade of the place recalling her attention, she
perceived herself among the ruins of the tower, whose history
had been related by the guide; and, on looking up, observed
she was at the foot of the stair-case, which still wound up the
wall, that had led to the chamber of the Baróne.

At a moment less anxious, the circumstance would have affected her; but now, she could only repeat her calls upon the name of Schedoni, and listen for some signal that he was near. Still receiving no answer, nor hearing any further sound of distress, she began to hope that her fears had deceived her, and having ascertained that the passage terminated here, she quitted the spot.

On regaining the first chamber, Ellena rested for a moment to recover breath; and, while she leaned upon what had once been a window, opening to the court, she heard a distant report of fire-arms. The sound swelled, and seemed to revolve along the avenue through which Schedoni had disappeared.—Supposing that the combatants were engaged at the farthest entrance, Ellena was preparing to go thither, when a sudden step moved near her, and, on turning, she discovered, with a degree of horror that almost deprived her of recollection, Spalatro himself stealing along the very chamber in which she was.

That part of the room which she stood in, fell into a kind of recess; and whether it was this circumstance that prevented him from immediately perceiving her, or that, his chief purpose being directed against another object, he did not chuse to pause here, he passed on with skulking steps; and, before Ellena had determined whither to go, she observed him cross the court before her, and enter the avenue. As he had passed, he looked up at the window: and it was certain he then saw her, for he instantly faultered, but in the next moment proceeded swiftly, and disappeared in the gloom.

It seemed that he had not yet encountered Schedoni, but it also occurred to Ellena, that he was gone into the avenue for the purpose of waiting to assassinate him in the darkness. While she was meditating some means of giving the Confessor a timely alarm of his danger, she once more distinguished his voice. It approached from the avenue, and Ellena immediately calling aloud that Spalatro was there, entreated him to be on his guard. In the next instant a pistol was fired there.

Among the voices that succeeded the report, Ellena thought she distinguished groans. Schedoni's voice was in the next moment heard again, but it seemed faint and low. The courage which she had before exerted was now exhausted; she remained fixed to the spot, unable to encounter the dreadful spectacle that probably awaited her in the avenue, and almost sinking beneath the expectation of it.

All was now hushed; she listened for Schedoni's voice, and even for a footstep—in vain. To endure this state of uncertainty much longer was scarcely possible, and Ellena was endeavouring to collect fortitude to meet a knowledge of the worst, when suddenly a feeble groaning was again heard. It seemed near, and to be approaching still nearer. At that moment, Ellena, on looking towards the avenue, perceived a figure covered with blood, pass into the court. A film, which drew over her eyes, prevented her noticing farther. She tottered a few paces back, and caught at the fragment of a pillar, by which she supported herself. The weakness was transient; immediate assistance appeared necessary to the wounded person, and pity soon predominating over horror, she recalled her spirits, and hastened to the court.

When, on reaching it, she looked round in search of Schedoni, he was no where to be seen; the court was again solitary and silent, till she awakened all its echoes with the name of *father*. While she repeated her calls, she hastily examined the colonnade, the separated chamber which opened immediately from it, and the shadowy ground beneath the palmetos, but without discovering any person.

As she turned towards the avenue, however, a track of blood on the ground told her too certainly where the wounded person had passed. It guided her to the entrance of a narrow passage, that seemingly led to the foot of the tower; but here she hesitated, fearing to trust the obscurity beyond. For the first time, Ellena conjectured, that not Schedoni, but Spalatro might be the person she had seen, and that, though he was wounded, vengeance might give him strength to strike his stiletto at the heart of whomsoever approached him, while the duskiness of the place would favour the deed.

She was yet at the entrance of the passage, fearful to enter, and reluctant to leave it, listening for a sound, and still hearing at intervals, swelling though feeble groans; when quick steps were suddenly heard advancing up the grand avenue, and presently her own name was repeated loudly in the voice of Schedoni. His manner was hurried as he advanced to meet her, and he threw an eager glance round the court. "We must be gone," said he, in a low tone, and taking her arm within his. "Have you seen any one pass?"

"I have seen a wounded man enter the court," replied Ellena, "and feared he was yourself."

"Where?—Which way did he go!" inquired Schedoni, eagerly, while his eyes glowed, and his countenance became fell.

Ellena, instantly comprehending his motive for the question, would not acknowledge that she knew whither Spalatro had withdrawn; and, reminding him of the danger of their situation, she entreated that they might quit the villa immediately.

"The sun is already set," she added. "I tremble at what may be the perils of this place at such an obscure hour, and even at what may be those of our road at a later!"

"You are sure he was wounded?" said the Confessor.

"Too sure," replied Ellena, faintly.

"Too sure!" sternly exclaimed Schedoni.

"Let us depart, my father; O let us go this instant!" repeated Ellena.

"What is the meaning of all this!" asked Schedoni, with anger. "You cannot, surely, have the weakness to pity this fellow!"

"It is terrible to see any one suffer," said Ellena. "Do not, by remaining here, leave me a possibility of grieving for you. What anguish it would occasion you, to see me bleed; judge, then, what must be mine, if you are wounded by the dagger of an assassin!"

Schedoni stifled the groan which swelled from his heart, and abruptly turned away.

"You trifle with me," he said, in the next moment: "you do not know that the villain is wounded. I fired at him, it is true, at the instant I saw him enter the avenue, but he has escaped me. What reason have you for your supposition?"

Ellena was going to point to the track of blood on the ground, at a little distance, but checked herself; considering that this might guide him on to Spalatro, and again she entreated they might depart, adding, "O! spare yourself, and him!"

"What! spare an assassin!" said Schedoni, impatiently.

"An assassin! He *has*, then, attempted your life?" exclaimed Ellena.

"Why no, not absolutely that," said Schedoni, recollecting himself, "but—what does the fellow do here? Let me pass, I will find him."

Ellena still hung upon his garment, while, with persuasive tenderness, she endeavoured to awaken his humanity. "O! if you had ever known what it was to expect instant death," she continued, "you would pity this man now, as he, perhaps, has sometimes pitied others! I have known such suffering, my father, and can, therefore, feel even for him!"

"Do you know for *whom* you are pleading?" said the distracted Schedoni, while every word she had uttered seemed to have penetrated his heart. The surprise which this question awakened in Ellena's countenance, recalled him to a consciousness of his imprudence; he recollected that Ellena did not certainly know the office, with which Spalatro had been commissioned against her: and when he considered that this very Spalatro, whom Ellena had with such simplicity supposed to have, at some time, spared a life through pity, had in truth spared her own, and, yet more, had been eventually a means of preventing him from destroying his own child, the Confessor turned in horror from his design; all his passions changed, and he abruptly quitted the court, nor paused till he reached the farthest extremity of the avenue, where the guide was in waiting with the horses.

A recollection of the conduct of Spalatro respecting Ellena had thus induced Schedoni to spare him; but this was all; it did not prevail with him to inquire into the condition of this man, or to mitigate his punishment; and, without remorse, he now left him to his fate.

With Ellena it was otherwise; though she was ignorant of the obligation she owed him, she could not know that any human being was left under such circumstances of suffering and solitude, without experiencing very painful emotion; but, considering how expeditiously Spalatro had been able to remove himself, she endeavoured to hope that his wound was not mortal.

The travellers, mounting their horses in silence, left the ruin, and were for some time too much engaged by the impression of the late occurrences, to converse together. When, at length, Ellena inquired the particulars of what had passed in the avenue, she understood that Schedoni, on pursuing Spalatro, had seen him there only for a moment. Spalatro had escaped by some way unknown to the Confessor, and had regained the interior of the ruin, while his pursuers were yet following the avenue. The cry, which Ellena had imagined to proceed from the interior, was uttered, as it now appeared, by the guide, who, in his haste, had fallen over some fragments of the wall that lay scattered in the avenue: the first report of arms had been from the trombone, which Schedoni had discharged on reaching the portal; and the last, when he fired a pistol, on perceiving Spalatro passing from the court.

"We have had trouble enough in running after this fellow," said the guide, "and could not catch him at last. It is strange that, if he came to look for us, he should run away so when he had found us! I do not think he meant us any harm, after all, else he might have done it easily enough in that dark passage; instead whereof he only took to his heels!"

"Silence!" said Schedoni, "fewer words, friend."

"Well, Signor, he's peppered now, however; so we need not be afraid; his wings are clipped for one while, so he cannot overtake us. We need not be in such a hurry, Signor, we shall get to the inn in good time yet. It is upon a mountain yonder, whose top you may see upon that red streak in the west. He cannot come after us; I myself saw his arm was wounded."

"Did you so?" said Schedoni, sharply: "and pray where was you when you saw so much? It was more than I saw."

"I was close at your heels, Signor, when you fired the pistol."

"I do not remember to have heard you there," observed the Confessor: "and why did you not come forward, instead of retreating? And where, also, did you hide yourself while I was searching for the fellow, instead of assisting me in the pursuit?"

The guide gave no answer, and Ellena, who had been attentively observing him during the whole of this conversation, perceived that he was now considerably embarrassed; so that her former suspicions as to his integrity began to revive, notwithstanding the several circumstances, which had occurred to render them improbable. There was, however, at present no opportunity for farther observation, Schedoni having, contrary to the advice of the guide, immediately quickened his pace, and the horses continuing on the full gallop, till a steep ascent compelled them to relax their speed.

Contrary to his usual habit, Schedoni now, while they slowly ascended, appeared desirous of conversing with this

man, and asked him several questions relative to the villa
they had left; and, whether it was that he really felt an interest on the subject, or that he wished to discover if the man
had deceived him in the circumstances he had already nar-
rated, from which he might form a judgment as to his
general character, he pressed his inquiries with a patient
minuteness, that somewhat surprised Ellena. During this
conversation, the deep twilight would no longer permit her
to notice the countenances of either Schedoni, or the guide,
but she gave much attention to the changing tones of their
voices, as different circumstances and emotions seemed to
affect them. It is to be observed, that during the whole of
this discourse, the guide rode at the side of Schedoni.

While the Confessor appeared to be musing upon something, which the peasant had related respecting the Baróne di
Cambrusca, Ellena inquired as to the fate of the other inhabitants of the villa.

"The falling of the old tower was enough for them," replied the guide; "the crash waked them all directly, and they
had time to get out of the new buildings, before the second
and third shocks laid them also in ruins. They ran out into
the woods for safety, and found it too, for they happened to
take a different road from the earthquake. Not a soul suffered, except the Baróne, and he deserved it well enough. O!
I could tell such things that I have heard of him!——"

"What became of the rest of the family?" interrupted
Schedoni.

"Why, Signor, they were scattered here and there, and every where; and they none of them ever returned to the old
spot. No! no! they had suffered enough there already, and
might have suffered to this day, if the earthquake had not
happened."

"If it had *not* happened?" repeated Ellena.

"Aye, Signora, for that put an end to the Baróne. If those
walls could but speak, they could tell strange things, for they
have looked upon sad doings: and that chamber, which I
shewed you, Signora, nobody ever went into it but himself,
except the servant, to keep it in order, and that he would
scarcely suffer, and always staid in the room the while."

"He had probably treasure secreted there," said Ellena.

"No, Signora, no treasure! He had always a lamp burning
there; and sometimes in the night he has been heard— Once,
indeed, his valet happened to—"

"Come on," said Schedoni, interrupting him; "keep pace with me. What idle dream are you relating now?"

"It is about the Baróne di Cambrusca, Signor, him that you was asking me so much about just now. I was saying what strange ways he had, and how that, on one stormy night in December, as my cousin Francisco told my father, who told me, and he lived in the family at the time it happened—"

"What happened?" said Schedoni, hastily.

"What I am going to tell, Signor. My cousin lived there at the time; so, however *unbelievable* it may seem, you may depend upon it, it is all true. My father knows I would not believe it myself till—"

"Enough of this," said Schedoni; "no more. What family had this Baróne—had he a wife at the time of this destructive shock?"

"Yes, truly, Signor, he had, as I was going to tell, if you would but condescend to have patience."

"The Baróne had more need of that, friend; I have no wife."—"The Baróne's wife had most need of it, Signor, as you shall hear. A good soul, they say, was the Baronessa! but luckily she died many years before. He had a daughter, also, and, young as she was, she had lived too long, but for the earthquake which set her free."

"How far is it to the inn?" said the Confessor, roughly.

"When we get to the top of this hill, Signor, you will see it on the next, if any light is stirring, for there will only be the hollow between us. But do not be alarmed, Signor, the fellow we left cannot overtake us. Do you know much about him, Signor?"

Schedoni inquired whether the trombone was charged; and, discovering that it was not, ordered the man to load immediately.

"Why, Signor, if you knew as much of him as I do, you could not be more afraid!" said the peasant, while he stopped to obey the order.

"I understood that he was a stranger to you!" observed the Confessor, with surprise.

"Why, Signor, he is, and he is not; I know more about him than he thinks for."

"You seem to know a vast deal too much of other persons' affairs," said Schedoni, in a tone that was meant to silence him.

"Why, that is just what he would say, Signor; but bad deeds will out, whether people like them to be known or not. This man comes to our town sometimes to market, and nobody knew where he came from for a long while; so they set themselves to work and found it out at last."

"We shall never reach the summit of this hill," said Schedoni, testily.

"And they found out, too, a great many strange things about him," continued the guide.

Ellena, who had attended to this discourse with a degree of curiosity that was painful, now listened impatiently for what might be farther mentioned concerning Spalatro, but without daring to invite, by a single question, any discovery on a subject which appeared to be so intimately connected with Schedoni.

"It was many years ago," rejoined the guide, "that this man came to live in that strange house on the sea-shore. It had been shut up ever since—"

"What are you talking of now?" interrupted the Confessor.

"Why, Signor, you never will let me tell you. You always snap me up so short at the beginning, and then ask—what am I talking about! I was going to begin the story, and it is a pretty long one. But first of all, Signor, who do you suppose this man belonged to! And what do you think the people determined to do, when the report was first set a-going? only they could not be sure it was true, and any body would be unwilling enough to believe such a shocking—"

"I have no curiosity on the subject," replied the Confessor, sternly interrupting him; "and desire to hear no more concerning it."

"I meant no harm, Signor," said the man; "I did not know it concerned you."

"And who says that it does concern me!"

"Nobody, Signor, only you seemed to be in a bit of a passion, and so I thought—— But I meant no harm, Signor, only as he happened to be your guide part of the way, I guessed you might like to know something of him."

"All that I desire to know of my guide is, that he does his duty," replied Schedoni, "that he conducts me safely, and understands when to be silent."

To this the man replied nothing, but slackened his pace, and slunk behind his reprover.

The travellers reaching, soon after, the summit of this long hill, looked out for the inn of which they had been told; but darkness now confounded every object, and no domestic light twinkling, however distantly, through the gloom, gave signal of security and comfort. They descended dejectedly into the hollow of the mountains, and found themselves once more immerged in woods. Schedoni again called the peasant to his side, and bade him keep abreast of him, but he did not discourse; and Ellena was too thoughtful to attempt conversation. The hints, which the guide had thrown out respecting Spalatro, had increased her curiosity on that subject; but the conduct of Schedoni, his impatience, his embarrassment, and the decisive manner in which he had put an end to the talk of the guide, excited a degree of surprise, that bordered on astonishment. As she had, however, no clue to lead her conjectures to any point, she was utterly bewildered in surmise, understanding only that Schedoni had been much more deeply connected with Spalatro than she had hitherto believed.

The travellers having descended into the hollow, and commenced the ascent of the opposite height, without discovering any symptom of a neighbouring town, began again to fear that their conductor had deceived them. It was now so dark that the road, though the soil was a limestone, could scarcely be discerned, the woods on either side forming a "close dungeon of innumerous boughs," that totally excluded the twilight of the stars.

While the Confessor was questioning the man, with some severity, a faint shouting was heard from a distance, and he stopped the horses to listen from what quarter it came.

"That comes the way we are going, Signor," said the guide.

"Hark!" exclaimed Schedoni, "those are strains of revelry!"

A confused sound of voices, laughter, and musical instruments, was heard, and, as the air blew stronger, tamborines and flutes were distinguished.

"Oh! Oh! we are near the end of our journey!" said the peasant; "all this comes from the town we are going to. But what makes them all so merry, I wonder!"

Ellena, revived by this intelligence, followed with alacrity the sudden speed of the Confessor; and presently reaching a point of the mountain, where the woods opened, a cluster of lights on another summit, a little higher, more certainly announced the town.

They soon after arrived at the ruinous gates, which had formerly led to a place of some strength, and passed at once from darkness and desolated walls, into a market place, blazing with light and resounding with the multitude. Booths, fantastically hung with lamps, and filled with merchandize of every kind, disposed in the gayest order, were spread on all sides, and peasants in their holiday cloaths, and parties of masks crowded every avenue. Here was a band of musicians, and there a group of dancers; on one spot the *outré* humour of a zanni provoked the never-failing laugh of an Italian rabble, in another the *improvisatore,* by the pathos of his story, and the persuasive sensibility of his strains, was holding the attention of his auditors, as in the bands of magic. Farther on was a stage raised for a display of fireworks, and near this a theatre, where a mimic opera, the "shadow of a shade," was exhibiting, whence the roar of laughter, excited by the principal *buffo* within, mingled with the heterogeneous voices of the venders of ice, maccaroni, sherbert, and diavoloni, without.

The Confessor looked upon this scene with disappointment and ill-humour, and bade the guide go before him, and shew the way to the best inn; an office which the latter undertook with great glee, though he made his way with difficulty. "To think I should not know it was the time of the fair!" said he, "though, to say truth, I never was at it but once in my life, so it is not so surprising, Signor."

"Make way through the crowd," said Schedoni.

"After jogging on so long in the dark, Signor, with nothing at all to be seen," continued the man, without attending to the direction, "then to come, all of a sudden, to such a place as this, why it is like coming out of purgatory into paradise! Well! Signor, you have forgot all your quandaries now; you think nothing now about that old ruinous place where we had such a race after the man, that would not murder us; but that shot I fired did his business."

"You fired!" said Schedoni, aroused by the assertion.

"Yes, Signor, as I was looking over your shoulder; I should have thought you must have heard it!"

"I should have thought so, too, friend."

"Aye, Signor, this fine place has put all that out of your head, I warrant, as well as what I said about the same fellow; but, indeed, Signor, I did not know he was related to you, when I talked so of him. But, perhaps, for all that, you may not know the piece of his story I was going to tell you, when you cut me off so short, though you are better acquainted with one another than I guessed for; so, when I come in from the fair, Signor, if you please, I will tell it you; and it is a pretty long history, for I happen to know the whole of it; though, where you cut me short, when you was in one of those quandaries, was only just at the beginning, but no matter for that, I can begin it again, for——"

"What is all this!" said Schedoni, again recalled from one of the thoughtful moods in which he had so habitually indulged, that even the bustle around him had failed to interrupt the course of his mind. He now bade the peasant be silent; but the man was too happy to be tractable, and proceeded to express all he felt, as they advanced slowly through the crowd. Every object here was to him new and delightful; and, nothing doubting that it must be equally so to every other person, he was continually pointing out to the proud and gloomy Confessor the trivial subjects of his own admiration. "See! Signor, there is Punchinello, see! how he eats the hot maccaroni! And look there, Signor! there is a juggler! O! good Signor, stop one minute, to look at his tricks. See! he has turned a monk into a devil already, in the twinkling of an eye!"

"Silence! and proceed," said Schedoni.

"That is what I say, Signor:—silence! for the people make such a noise that I cannot hear a word you speak.—Silence, there!"

"Considering that you could not hear, you have answered wonderfully to the purpose," said Ellena.

"Ah! Signora! is not this better than those dark woods and hills? But what have we here? Look, Signor, here is a fine sight!"

The crowd, which was assembled round a stage on which some persons grotesquely dressed, were performing, now interrupting all farther progress, the travellers were compelled to stop at the foot of the platform. The people above were acting what seemed to have been intended for a tragedy, but what their strange gestures, uncouth recitation, and incongruous countenances, had transformed into a comedy.

Schedoni, thus obliged to pause, withdrew his attention from the scene; Ellena consented to endure it, and the peasant, with gaping mouth and staring eyes, stood like a statue, yet not knowing whether he ought to laugh or cry, till suddenly turning round to the Confessor, whose horse was of necessity close to his, he seized his arm, and pointing to the stage, called out, "Look! Signor, see! Signor, what a scoundrel! what a villain! See! he had murdered his own daughter!"

At these terrible words, the indignation of Schedoni was done away by other emotions; he turned his eyes upon the stage, and perceived that the actors were performing the story of Virginia. It was at the moment when she was dying in the arms of her father, who was holding up the poniard, with which he had stabbed her. The feelings of Schedoni, at this instant, inflicted a punishment almost worthy of the crime he had meditated.

Ellena, struck with the action, and with the contrast which it seemed to offer to what she had believed to have been the late conduct of Schedoni towards herself, looked at him with most expressive tenderness, and as his glance met hers, she perceived, with surprise, the changing emotions of his soul, and the inexplicable character of his countenance. Stung to the heart, the Confessor furiously spurred his horse, that he might escape from the scene, but the poor animal was too spiritless and jaded, to force its way through the crowd; and the peasant, vexed at being hurried from a place where, almost for the first time in his life, he was suffering under the strange delights of artificial grief, and half angry, to observe an animal, of which he had the care, ill treated, loudly remonstrated, and seized the bridle of Schedoni, who, still more incensed, was applying the whip to the shoulders of the guide, when the crowd suddenly fell back and opened a way, through which the travellers passed, and arrived, with little further interruption, at the door of the inn.

Schedoni was not in a humour which rendered him fit to encounter difficulties, and still less the vulgar squabbles of a place already crowded with guests; yet it was not without much opposition that he at length obtained a lodging for the night. The peasant was not less anxious for the accommodation of his horses; and, when Ellena heard him declare, that the animal, which the Confessor had so cruelly spurred, should have a double feed, and a bed of straw as high as his head, if he himself went without one, she gave him, unnoticed by Schedoni, the only ducat she had left.

CHAPTER II

But, if you be afraid to hear the worst,
Then let the worst, unheard, fall on your head.
                                    SHAKESPEARE

SCHEDONI passed the night without sleep. The incident of
the preceding evening had not only renewed the agonies of
remorse, but excited those of pride and apprehension. There
was something in the conduct of the peasant towards him,
which he could not clearly understand, though his suspicions
were sufficient to throw his mind into a state of the utmost
perturbation. Under an air of extreme simplicity, this man
had talked of Spalatro, had discovered that he was acquainted with much of his history, and had hinted that he
knew by whom he had been employed; yet at the same time
appeared unconscious, that Schedoni's was the master-hand,
which had directed the principal actions of the ruffian. At
other times, his behaviour had seemed to contradict the supposition of his ignorance on this point; from some circumstances he had mentioned, it appeared impossible but that he
must have known who Schedoni really was, and even his
own conduct had occasionally seemed to acknowledge this,
particularly when, being interrupted in his history of
Spalatro, he attempted an apology, by saying, he did not
know it concerned Schedoni: nor could the conscious
Schedoni believe that the very pointed manner, in which the
peasant had addressed him at the representation of Virginia,
was merely accidental. He wished to dismiss the man immediately, but it was first necessary to ascertain what he knew
concerning him, and then to decide on the measures to be
taken. It was, however, a difficult matter to obtain this information, without manifesting an anxiety, which might betray
him, if the guide had, at present, only a general suspicion of

the truth; and no less difficult to determine how to proceed towards him, if it should be evident that his suspicions rested on Spalatro. To take him forward to Naples, was to bring an informer to his home; to suffer him to return with his discovery, now that he probably knew the place of Schedoni's residence, was little less hazardous. His death only could secure the secret.

After a night passed in the tumult of such considerations, the Confessor summoned the peasant to his chamber, and, with some short preface, told him he had no further occasion for his services, adding, carelessly, that he advised him to be on his guard as he re-passed the villa, lest Spalatro, who might yet lurk there, should revenge upon him the injury he had received. "According to your account of him, he is a very dangerous fellow," said Schedoni; "but your information is, perhaps, erroneous."

The guide began, testily, to justify himself for his assertions, and the Confessor then endeavoured to draw from him what he knew on the subject. But, whether the man was piqued by the treatment he had lately received, or had other reasons for reserve, he did not, at first, appear so willing to communicate as formerly.

"What you hinted of this man," said Schedoni, "has, in some degree, excited my curiosity: I have now a few moments of leisure, and you may relate, if you will, something of the wonderful history you talked of."

"It is a long story, Signor, and you would be tired before I got to the end of it," replied the peasant; "and, craving your pardon, Signor, I don't much like to be snapped up so!"

"Where did this man live?" said the Confessor. "You mentioned something of a house at the sea side."

"Aye, Signor, there is a strange history belonging to that house, too; but this man, as I was saying, came there all of a sudden, nobody knew how! and the place had been shut up ever since the Marchese——"

"The Marchese!" said Schedoni, coldly, "what Marchese, friend?"—"Why, I mean the Baróne di Cambrusca, Signor, to be sure, as I was going to have told you, of my own accord, if you would only have let me. Shut up ever since the Baróne——I left off there, I think."

"I understood that the Baróne was dead!" observed the Confessor.

"Yes, Signor," replied the peasant, fixing his eyes on

Schedoni; "but what has his death to do with what I was telling? This happened before he died."

Schedoni, somewhat disconcerted by this unexpected remark, forgot to resent the familiarity of it. "This man, then, this Spalatro, was connected with the Baróne di Cambrusca?" and he.

"It was pretty well guessed so, Signor."

"How! no more than guessed?"

"No, Signor, and that was more than enough for the Baróne's liking, I warrant. He took too much care for any thing certain to appear against him, and he was wise so to do, for if it had—it would have been worse for him. But I was going to tell you the story, Signor."

"What reasons were there for believing this was an agent of the Baróne di Cambrusca, friend?"

"I thought you wished to hear the story, Signor."

"In good time; but first what were your reasons?"

"One of them is enough, Signor, and if you would only have let me gone straight on with the story, you would have found it out by this time, Signor."

Schedoni frowned, but did not otherwise reprove the impertinence of the speech.

"It was reason enough, Signor, to my mind," continued the peasant, "that it was such a crime as nobody but the Baróne di Cambrusca could have committed; there was nobody wicked enough, in our parts, to have done it but him. Why is not this *reason* enough, Signor? What makes you look at me so? why the Baróne himself could hardly have looked worse, if I had told him as much!"

"Be less prolix," said the Confessor, in a restrained voice.

"Well then, Signor, to begin at the beginning. It is a good many years ago that Marco came first to our town. Now the story goes, that one stormy night——"

"You may spare yourself the trouble of relating the story," said Schedoni, abruptly. "Did you ever see the Baróne you was speaking of, friend?"

"Why did you bid me tell it, Signor, since you know it already! I have been here all this while, just a-going to begin it, and all for nothing!"

"It is very surprising," resumed the artful Schedoni, without having noticed what had been said, "that if this Spalatro was known to be the villain you say he is, not any step should have been taken to bring him to justice! how happened that? But, perhaps, all this story was nothing more than a report."

"Why, Signor, it was every body's business, and nobody's, as one may say; then, besides, nobody could prove what they had heard, and though every body believed the story just the same as if they had seen the whole, yet that, they said, would not do in law, but they should be made to prove it. Now, it is not one time in ten that any thing can be proved, Signor, as you well know, yet we none of us believe it the less for that!"

"So, then, you would have had this man punished for a murder, which, probably, he never committed!" said the Confessor.

"A murder!" repeated the peasant.

Schedoni was silent, but, in the next instant, said, "Did you not say it was a murder?"

"I have not told you so, Signor!"

"What was the crime, then?" resumed Schedoni, after another momentary pause, "you said it was atrocious, and what more so than—murder?" His lip quivered as he pronounced the last word.

The peasant made no reply, but remained with his eyes fixed upon the Confessor, and, at length, repeated, "Did I say it was murder, Signor?"

"If it was not that, say what it was," demanded the Confessor, haughtily; "but let it be in two words."

"As if a story could be told in two words, Signor!"

"Well, well, be brief."

"How can I, Signor, when the story is so long!"

"I will waste no more time," said Schedoni, going.

"Well, Signor, I will do my best to make it short. It was one stormy night in December, that Marco Torma had been out fishing. Marco, Signor, was an old man that lived in our town when I was a boy; I can but just remember him, but my father knew him well, and loved old Marco, and used often to say——"

"To the story!" said Schedoni.

"Why I am telling it, Signor, as fast as I can. This old Marco did not live in our town at the time it happened, but in some place, I have forgot the name of it, near the sea shore. What can the name be! it is something like——"

"Well, what happened to this old dotard?"

"You are out there, Signor, he was no old dotard; but you

shall hear. At that time, Signor, Marco lived in this place
that I have forgot the name of, and was a fisherman, but better times turned up afterwards, but that is neither here nor
there. Old Marco had been out fishing; it was a stormy
night, and he was glad enough to get on shore, I warrant. It
was quite dark, as dark, Signor, I suppose, as it was last
night, and he was making the best of his way, Signor, with
some fish along the shore, but it being so dark, he lost it notwithstanding. The rain beat, and the wind blew, and he wandered about a long while, and could see no light, nor hear
any thing but the surge near him, which sometimes seemed
as if it was coming to wash him away. He got as far off it
as he could, but he knew there were high rocks over the
beach, and he was afraid he should run his head against
them, if he went too far, I suppose. However, at last, he went
up close to them, and as he got a little shelter, he resolved
to try no further for the present. I tell it you, Signor, just as
my father told it me, and he had it from the old man himself."

"You need not be so particular," replied the Confessor:
"speak to the point."

"Well, Signor, as old Marco lay snug under the rocks, he
thought he heard somebody coming, and he lifted up his
head, I warrant, poor old soul! as if he could have seen who
it was; however, he could hear, though it was so dark, and
he heard the steps coming on; but he said nothing yet, meaning to let them come close up to him, before he discovered
himself. Presently he sees a little moving light, and it comes
nearer and nearer, till it was just opposite to him, and then
he saw the shadow of a man on the ground, and then spied
the man himself, with a dark lanthorn, passing along the
beach."

"Well, well, to the purpose," said Schedoni.

"Old Marco, Signor, my father says, was never stout-
hearted, and he took it into his head this might be a robber,
because he had the lanthorn, though, for that matter, he
would have been glad enough of a lanthorn himself, and so
he lay quiet. But, presently, he was in a rare fright, for the
man stopped to rest the load he had upon his back, on a
piece of rock near him, and old Marco saw him throw off a
heavy sack, and heard him breathe hard, as if he was hugely
tired. I tell it, Signor, just as my father does."

"What was in the sack?" said Schedoni, coolly.

"All in good time, Signor; perhaps old Marco never found out; but you shall hear. He was afraid, when he saw the sack, to stir a limb, for he thought it held booty. But, presently, the man, without saying a word, heaved it on his shoulders again, and staggered away with it along the beach, and Marco saw no more of him."

"Well! what has he to do with your story, then?" said the Confessor, "Was this Spalatro?"

"All in good time, Signor; you put me out. When the storm was down a little, Marco crept out, and, thinking there must be a village, or a hamlet, or a cottage, at no great distance, since this man had passed, he thought he would try a little further. He had better have staid where he was, for he wandered about a long while, and could see nothing, and what was worse, the storm came on louder than before, and he had no rocks to shelter him now. While he was in this quandary, he sees a light at a distance, and it came into his head this might be the lantern again, but he determined to go on notwithstanding, for if it was, he could stop short, and if it was not, he should get shelter, perhaps; so on he went, and I suppose I should have done the same, Signor."

"Well! this history never will have an end!" said Schedoni.

"Well! Signor, he had not gone far when he found out that it was no lantern, but a light at a window. When he came up to the house he knocked softly at the door, but nobody came."

"What house?" inquired the Confessor, sharply.

"The rain beat hard, Signor, and I warrant poor old Marco waited a long time before he knocked again, for he was main patient, Signor. O! how I have seen him listen to a story, let it be ever so long!"

"I have need of his patience!" said Schedoni.

"When he knocked again, Signor, the door gave way a little, and he found it was open, and so, as nobody came, he thought fit to walk in of his own accord."

"The dotard! what business had he to be so curious?" exclaimed Schedoni.

"Curious! Signor, he only sought shelter! He stumbled about in the dark, for a good while, and could find nobody, nor make nobody hear, but, at last, he came to a room where there was some fire not quite out, upon the hearth, and he went up to it, to warm himself, till somebody should come."

"What! was there nobody in the house?" said the Confessor.

"You shall hear, Signor. He had not been there, he said, no, he was sure, not above two minutes, when he heard a strange sort of a noise in the very room where he was, but the fire gave such a poor light, he could not see whether any body was there."

"What was the noise?"

"You put me out, Signor. He said he did not much like it, but what could he do! So he stirred up the fire, and tried to make it blaze a little, but it was as dusky as ever; he could see nothing. Presently, however, he heard somebody coming and saw a light, and then a man coming towards the room where he was, so he went up to him to ask shelter."

"Who was this man?" said Schedoni.

"Ask shelter. He says the man, when he came to the door of the room, turned as white as a sheet, as well he might, to see a stranger, to find a stranger there, at that time of the night. I suppose I should have done the same myself. The man did not seem very willing to let him stay, but asked what he did there, and such like; but the storm was very loud, and so Marco did not let a little matter daunt him, and, when he shewed the man what fine fish he had in his basket, and said he was welcome to it, he seemed more willing."

"Incredible!" exclaimed Schedoni, "the blockhead!"

"He had wit enough for that matter, Signor; Marco says he appeared to be main hungry——"

"Is that any proof of his wit?" said the Confessor, peevishly.

"You never will let me finish, Signor; main hungry; for he put more wood on the fire directly, to dress some of the fish. While he was doing this, Marco says his heart, somehow, misgave him, that this was the man he saw on the beach, and he looked at him pretty hard, till the other asked him, crossly, what he stared at him so for; but Marco took care not to tell. While he was busy making ready the fish, however, Marco had an opportunity of eying him the more, and every time the man looked round the room, which happened to be pretty often, he had a notion it was the same."

"Well, and if it was the same," said Schedoni.

"But when Marco happened to spy the sack, lying in a corner, he had no doubt about the matter. He says his heart then misgave him sadly, and he wished himself safe out of the house, and determined, in his own mind, to get away as soon as he could, without letting the man suspect what he thought of him. He now guessed, too, what made the man look round the room so often, and, though Marco thought before it was to find out if he had brought any body with him, he now believed it was to see whether his treasure was safe."

"Aye, likely enough," observed Schedoni.

"Well, old Marco sat not much at his ease, while the fish was preparing, and thought it was 'out of the fryingpan into the fire' with him; but what could he do?"

"Why get up and walk away, to be sure," said the Confessor, "as I shall do, if your story lasts much longer."

"You shall hear, Signor; he would have done so, if he had thought this man would have let him, but——"

"Well, this man was Spalatro, I suppose," said Schedoni, impatiently, "and this was the house on the shore you formerly mentioned."

"How well you have guessed it, Signor! though to say truth, I have been expecting you to find it out for this half hour."

Schedoni did not like the significant look, which the peasant assumed while he said this, but he bade him proceed.

"At first, Signor, Spalatro hardly spoke a word, but he came to by degrees, and by the time the fish was nearly ready, he was talkative enough."

Here the Confessor rose, with some emotion, and paced the room.

"Poor old Marco, Signor, began to think better of him, and when he heard the rain at the casements, he was loath to think of stirring. Presently Spalatro went out of the room for a plate to eat the fish on.——"

"Out of the room?" said Schedoni, and checked his steps.

"Yes, Signor, but he took care to carry the light with him. However, Marco, who had a deal of curiosity to——"

"Yes, he appears to have had a great deal, indeed!" said the Confessor, and turning away, renewed his pace.

"Nay, Signor, I am not come to that yet, he has shewn none yet;—a great deal of curiosity to know what was in the sack, before he consented to let himself stay much longer, thought this a good opportunity for looking, and as the fire was now pretty bright, he determined to see. He went up to the sack, therefore, Signor, and tried to lift it, but it was too heavy for him though it did not seem full."

Schedoni again checked his steps, and stood fixed before the peasant.

"He raised it, however, a little, Signor, but it fell from his hands, and with such a heavy weight upon the floor, that he was sure it held no common booty. Just then, he says, he thought he heard Spalatro coming, and the sound of the sack was enough to have frightened him, and so Marco quitted it; but he was mistaken, and he went to it again. But you don't seem to hear me, Signor, for you look as you do when you are in those quandaries, so busy a-thinking, and I——"

"Proceed," said Schedoni, sternly, and renewed his steps, "I hear you."

"Went to it again,"—resumed the peasant, cautiously taking up the story at the last words he had dropped. "He untied the string, Signor, that held the sack, and opened the cloth a little way, but think, Signor, what he must have thought, when he felt—cold flesh! O, Signor! and when he saw by the light of the fire, the face of a corpse within! O, Signor!"—

The peasant, in the eagerness with which he related this circumstance, had followed Schedoni to the other end of the chamber, and he now took hold of his garment, as if to secure his attention to the remainder of the story. The Confessor, however, continued his steps, and the peasant kept pace with him, still loosely holding his garment.

"Marco," he resumed, "was so terrified, as my father says, that he hardly knew where he was, and I warrant, if one could have seen him, he looked as white, Signor, as you do now."

The Confessor abruptly withdrew his garment from the peasant's grasp, and said, in an inward voice, "If I am shocked at the mere mention of such a spectacle, no wonder he was, who beheld it!" After the pause of a moment, he added,—"But what followed?"

"Marco says he had no power to tie up the cloth again, Signor, and when he came to his thoughts, his only fear was, lest Spalatro should return, though he had hardly been gone a minute, before he could get out of the house, for he cared nothing about the storm now. And sure enough he heard him coming, but he managed to get out of the room, into a passage another way from that Spalatro was in. And luckily, too, it was the same passage he had come in by, and it led him out of the house. He made no more ado, but ran straight off, without stopping to chuse which way, and many perils and dangers he got into among the woods, that night, and——"

"How happened it, that this Spalatro was not taken up, after this discovery?" said Schedoni. "What was the consequence of it?"

"Why, Signor, old Marco had like to have caught his death that night; what with the wet and what with the fright, he was laid up with a fever, and was light-headed, and raved of such strange things, that people would not believe any thing he said when he came to his senses."

"Aye," said Schedoni, "the narrative resembles a delirious dream, more than a reality; I perfectly accord with them in their opinion of this feverish old man."

"But you shall hear, Signor; after a while they began to think better of it, and there was some stir made about it; but what could poor folks do, for nothing could be proved! The house was searched, but the man was gone, and nothing could be found! From that time the place was shut up; till many years after, this Spalatro appeared, and old Marco then said he was pretty sure he was the man, but he could not swear it, and so nothing could be done."

"Then it appears, after all, that you are not certain that this long history belongs to this Spalatro!" said the Confessor; "nay, not even that the history itself is any thing more than the vision of a distempered brain!"

"I do not know, Signor, what you may call certain; but I know what we all believe. But the strangest part of the story is to come yet, and that which nobody would believe, hardly, if——"

"I have heard enough," said Schedoni, "I will hear no more!"

"Well but, Signor, I have not told you half yet; and I am sure when I heard it myself, it so terrified me."

"I have listened too long to this idle history," said the Confessor, "there seems to be no rational foundation for it. Here is what I owe you; you may depart."

"Well, Signor, 'tis plain you know the rest already, or you never would go without it. But you don't know, perhaps, Signor, what an unaccountable—I am sure it made my hair stand on end to hear of it, what an unaccountable——"

"I will hear no more of this absurdity," interrupted Schedoni, with sternness. "I reproach myself for having listened so long to such a gossip's tale, and have no further curiosity concerning it. You may withdraw; and bid the host attend me."

"Well, Signor, if you are so easily satisfied," replied the peasant, with disappointment, "there is no more to be said, but——"

"You may stay, however, while I caution you," said Schedoni, "how you pass the villa, where this Spalatro may yet linger, for, though I can only smile at the story you have related——"

"Related, Signor! why I have not told it half; and if you would only please to be patient——"

"Though I can only smile at that simple narrative,"—repeated Schedoni in a louder tone.

"Nay, Signor, for that matter, you can frown at it too, as I can testify," muttered the guide.

"Listen to me!" said the Confessor, in a yet more insisting voice. "I say, that though I give no credit to your curious history, I think this same Spalatro appears to be a desperate fellow, and, therefore, I would have you be on your guard. If you see him, you may depend upon it, that he will attempt your life in revenge of the injury I have done him. I give you, therefore, in addition to your trombone, this stiletto to defend you."

Schedoni, while he spoke, took an instrument from his bosom, but it was not the one he usually wore, or, at least, that he was seen to wear. He delivered it to the peasant, who received it with a kind of stupid surprise, and then gave him some directions as to the way in which it should be managed.

"Why, Signor," said the man, who had listened with much attention, "I am kindly obliged to you for thinking about me, but is there any thing in this stiletto different from others, that it is to be used so?"

Schedoni looked gravely at the peasant for an instant, and then replied, "Certainly not, friend, I would only instruct you to use it to the best advantage;—farewell!"

"Thank you kindly, Signor, but—but I think I have no need of it, my trombone is enough for me."

"This will defend you more adroitly," replied Schedoni, refusing to take back the stiletto, "and moreover, while you were loading the trombone, your adversary might use his poniard to advantage. Keep it, therefore, friend; it will protect you better than a dozen trombones. Put it up."

Perhaps it was Schedoni's particular look, more than his argument, that convinced the guide of the value of his gift; he received it submissively, though with a stare of stupid surprise; probably it had been better, if it had been suspicious surprise. He thanked Schedoni again, and was leaving the room, when the Confessor called out, "Send the landlord to me immediately, I shall set off for Rome without delay!"

"Yes, Signor," replied the peasant, "you are at the right place, the road parts here; but I thought you was going for Naples!"

"For Rome," said Schedoni.

"For Rome, Signor! Well, I hope you will get safe, Signor, with all my heart!" said the guide, and quitted the chamber.

While this dialogue had been passing between Schedoni and the peasant, Ellena, in solitude, was considering on the means of prevailing with the Confessor to allow her to return either to Altieri, or to the neighbouring cloister of *"Our Lady of Pity,"* instead of placing her at a distance from Naples, till he should think proper to acknowledge her. The plan, which he had mentioned, seemed to her long-harrassed mind to exile her forever from happiness, and all that was dear to her affections; it appeared like a second banishment to San Stefano, and every abbess, except that of the Santa della Pieta, came to her imagination in the portraiture of an inexorable jailor. While this subject engaged her, she was summoned to attend Schedoni, whom she found impatient to enter the carriage, which at this town they had been able to procure. Ellena, on looking out for the guide, was informed that he had already set off for his home, a circumstance, for the suddenness of which she knew not how to account.

The travellers immediately proceeded on their journey; Schedoni, reflecting on the late conversation, said little, and Ellena read not in his countenance any thing that might encourage her to introduce the subject of her own intended solicitation. Thus separately occupied, they advanced, during some hours, on the road to Naples, for thither Schedoni had designed to go, notwithstanding his late assertion to the guide, whom it appears, for whatever reason, he was anxious to deceive, as to the place of his actual residence.

They stopped to dine at a town of some consideration,

and, when Ellena heard the Confessor inquire concerning the numerous convents it contained, she perceived that it was necessary for her no longer to defer her petition. She therefore represented immediately what must be the forlornness of her state, and the anxiety of her mind, if she were placed at a distance from the scenes and the people, which affection and early habit seemed to have consecrated; especially at this time, when her spirits had scarcely recovered from the severe pressure of long-suffering, and when to soothe and renovate them, not only quiet, but the consciousness of security, were necessary; a consciousness which it was impossible, and especially so after her late experience, that she could acquire among strangers, till they should cease to be such.

To these pleadings Schedoni thoughtfully attended, but the darkness of his aspect did not indicate that his compassion was touched; and Ellena proceeded to represent, secondly, that which, had she been more artful, or less disdainful of cunning, she would have urged the first. As it was, she had begun with the mention of circumstances, which, though the least likely to prevail with Schedoni, she felt to be most important to herself; and she concluded with representing that, which was most interesting to him. Ellena suggested, that her residence in the neighbourhood of Altieri might be so managed, as that his secret would be as effectually preserved, as if she were at an hundred miles from Naples.

It may appear extraordinary, that a man of Schedoni's habitual coolness, and exact calculation, should have suffered fear, on this occasion, to obscure his perceptions; and this instance strongly proved the magnitude of the cause, which could produce so powerful an effect. While he now listened to Ellena, he began to perceive circumstances that had eluded his own observation; and he, at length, acknowledged, that it might be safer to permit her to return to the villa Altieri, and that she should from thence go, as she had formerly intended, to the Santa della Pieta, than to place her in any convent, however remote, where it would be necessary for himself to introduce her. His only remaining objection to the neighbourhood of Naples, now rested on the chance it would offer the Marchesa di Vivaldi of discovering Ellena's abode, before he should judge it convenient to disclose to her his family; and his knowledge of the Marchesa justified his most horrible suspicion, as to the consequence of such a premature discovery.

Something, however, it appeared, must be risked in any situation he might chuse for Ellena; and her residence at the Santa della Pieta, a large convent, well secured, and where, as she had been known to them from her infancy, the abbess and the sisters might be supposed to be not indifferent concerning her welfare, seemed to promise security against any actual violence from the malice of the Marchesa; against her artful duplicity every place would be almost equally insufficient. Here, as Ellena would appear in the character she had always been known in, no curiosity could be excited, or suspicion awakened, as to her family; and here, therefore, Schedoni's secret would more probably be preserved, than elsewhere. As this was, after all, the predominant subject of his anxiety, to which, however unnatural it may seem, even the safety of Ellena was secondary, he finally determined, that she should return to the Santa della Pieta; and she thanked him almost with tears, for a consent which she received as a generous indulgence, but which was in reality little more than an effect of selfish apprehension.

The remainder of the journey, which was of some days, passed without any remarkable occurrence: Schedoni, with only short intervals, was still enveloped in gloom and silence; and Ellena, with thoughts engaged by the one subject of her interest, the present situation and circumstances of Vivaldi, willingly submitted to this prolonged stillness.

As, at length, she drew near Naples, her emotions became more various and powerful; and, when she distinguished the top of Vesuvius peering over every intervening summit, she wept as her imagination charactered all the well-known country it overlooked. But when, having reached an eminence, that scenery was exhibited to her senses, when the Bay of Naples, stretching into remotest distance, was spread out before her; when every mountain of that magnificent horizon, which enclosed her native landscape, that country which she believed Vivaldi to inhabit, stood unfolded, how affecting, how overwhelming were her sensations! Every object seemed to speak of her home, of Vivaldi, and of happiness that was passed! and so exquisitely did regret mingle with hope, the tender grief of remembrance with the interest of expectation, that it were difficult to say which prevailed.

Her expressive countenance disclosed to the Confessor the

course of her thoughts and of her feelings, feelings which, while he contemned, he believed he perfectly comprehended, but of which, having never in any degree experienced them, he really understood nothing. The callous Schedoni, by a mistake not uncommon, especially to a mind of his character, substituted words for truths; not only confounding the limits of neighbouring qualities, but mistaking their very principles. Incapable of perceiving their nice distinctions, he called the persons who saw them, merely fanciful; thus making his very incapacity an argument for his superior wisdom. And, while he confounded delicacy of feeling with fatuity of mind, taste with caprice, and imagination with error, he yielded, when he most congratulated himself on his sagacity, to illusions not less egregious, because they were less brilliant, than those which are incident to sentiment and feeling.

The better to escape observation, Schedoni had contrived not to reach Naples till the close of evening, and it was entirely dark before the carriage stopped at the gate of the villa Altieri. Ellena, with a mixture of melancholy and satisfaction, viewed, once more, her long-deserted home, and while she waited till a servant should open the gate, remembered how often she had thus waited when there was a beloved friend within, to welcome her with smiles, which were now gone for ever. Beatrice, the old housekeeper, at length, however, appeared, and received her with an affection as sincere, if not as strong, as that of the relative for whom she mourned.

Here Schedoni alighted, and, having dismissed the carriage, entered the house, for the purpose of relinquishing also his disguise, and resuming his monk's habit. Before he departed, Ellena ventured to mention Vivaldi, and to express her wish to hear of his exact situation; but, though Schedoni was too well enabled to inform her of it, the policy which had hitherto kept him silent on this subject still influenced him; and he replied only, that if he should happen to learn the circumstances of his condition, she should not remain ignorant of them.

This assurance revived Ellena, for two reasons; it afforded her a hope of relief from her present uncertainty, and it also seemed to express an approbation of the object of her affection, such as the Confessor had never yet disclosed. Schedoni added, that he should see her no more, till he thought proper to acknowledge her for his daughter; but that, if circumstances made it necessary, he should, in the mean time, write to her; and he now gave her a direction by which to address him under a fictitious name, and at a place remote from his convent. Ellena, though assured of the necessity for this conduct, could not yield to such disguise, without an aversion that was strongly expressed in her manner, but of which Schedoni took no notice. He bade her, as she valued her existence, watchfully to preserve the secret of her birth; and to waste not a single day at villa Altieri, but to retire to the Santa della Pieta; and these injunctions were delivered in a manner so solemn and energetic, as not only deeply to impress upon her mind the necessity of fulfilling them, but to excite some degree of amazement.

After a short and general direction respecting her further conduct, Schedoni bade her farewell, and, privately quitting the villa, in his ecclesiastical dress, repaired to the Dominican convent, which he entered as a brother returned from a distant pilgrimage. He was received as usual by the society, and found himself, once more, the austere father Schedoni of the Spirito Santo.

The cause of his first anxiety was the necessity for justifying himself to the Marchesa di Vivaldi, for ascertaining how much he might venture to reveal of the truth, and for estimating what would be her decision, were she informed of the whole. His second step would be to obtain the release of Vivaldi; and, as his conduct in this instance would be regulated, in a great degree, by the result of his conference with the Marchesa, it would be only the second. However painful it must be to Schedoni to meet her, now that he had discovered the depth of the guilt, in which she would have involved him, he determined to seek this eventful conference on the following morning: and he passed this night partly in uneasy expectation of the approaching day, but chiefly in inventing circumstances and arranging arguments, that might bear him triumphantly towards the accomplishment of his grand design.

CHAPTER III

Beneath the silent gloom of Solitude
Tho' Peace can sit and smile, tho' meek Content
Can keep the cheerful tenor of her soul,
Ev'n in the loneliest shades, yet let not Wrath
Approach, let black Revenge keep far aloof,
Or soon they flame to madness.

ELFRIDA

SCHEDONI, on his way to the Vivaldi palace, again reviewed and arranged every argument, or rather specious circumstance, which might induce the Marchesa's consent to the nuptials he so much desired. His family was noble, though no longer wealthy, and he believed that as the seeming want of descent had hitherto been the chief objection to Ellena, the Marchesa might be prevailed with to overlook the wreck of his fortune.

At the palace he was told, that the Marchesa was at one of her villas on the bay; and he was too anxious not to follow her thither immediately. This delightful residence was situated on an airy promontory, that overhung the water, and was nearly embosomed among the woods, that spread far along the heights, and descended, with great pomp of foliage and colouring, to the very margin of the waves. It seemed scarcely possible that misery could inhabit so enchanting an abode; yet the Marchesa was wretched amidst all these luxuries of nature and art, which would have perfected the happiness of an innocent mind. Her heart was possessed by evil passions, and all her perceptions were distorted and discoloured by them, which, like a dark magician, had power to change the fairest scenes into those of gloom and desolation.

The servants had orders to admit father Schedoni at all times, and he was shewn into a saloon, in which the Marchesa was alone. Every object in this apartment announced taste, and even magnificence. The hangings were of purple and gold; the vaulted ceiling was designed by one of the first painters of the Venetian school; the marble statues that adorned the recesses were not less exquisite, and the whole symmetry and architecture, airy, yet rich; gay, yet chastened; resembled the palace of a fairy, and seemed to possess almost equal fascinations. The lattices were thrown open, to admit the prospect, as well as the air loaded with fragrance from an orangery, that spread before them. Lofty palms and plantains threw their green and refreshing tint over the windows, and on the lawn that sloped to the edge of the precipice, a shadowy perspective, beyond which appeared the ample waters of the gulf, where the light sails of feluccas, and the spreading canvas of larger vessels, glided upon the scene and passed away, as in a camera obscura. Vesuvius and the city of Naples were seen on the coast beyond, with many a bay and lofty cape of that long tract of bold and gaily-coloured scenery, which extends toward Cape Campanella, crowned by fading ranges of mountains, lighted up with all the magic of Italian sunshine. The Marchesa reclined on a sofa before an open lattice; her eyes were fixed upon the prospect without, but her attention was wholly occupied by the visions that evil passions painted to her imagination. On her still beautiful features was the languor of discontent and indisposition; and, though her manners, like her dress, displayed the elegant negligence of the graces, they concealed the movements of a careful, and even a tortured heart. On perceiving Schedoni, a faint smile lightened upon her countenance, and she held forth her hand to him; at the touch of which he shuddered.

"My good father, I rejoice to see you," said the Marchesa; "I have felt the want of your conversation much, and at this moment of indisposition especially."

She waved the attendant to withdraw; while Schedoni, stalking to a window, could with difficulty conceal the perturbation with which he now, for the first time, consciously beheld the willing destroyer of his child. Some farther compliment from the Marchesa recalled him; he soon recovered all his address, and approaching her, said,

"Daughter! you always send me away a worse Dominican than I come; I approach you with humility, but depart elated with pride, and am obliged to suffer much from self-infliction before I can descend to my proper level."

After some other flatteries had been exchanged, a silence of several moments followed, during which neither of the parties seemed to have sufficient courage to introduce the subjects that engaged their thoughts, subjects upon which their interests were now so directly and unexpectedly opposite. Had Schedoni been less occupied by his own feelings, he might have perceived the extreme agitation of the Marchesa, the tremor of her nerves, the faint flush that crossed her cheek, the wanness that succeeded, the languid movement of her eyes, and the laborious sighs that interrupted her breathing, while she wished, yet dared not ask, whether Ellena was no more, and averted her regards from him, whom she almost believed to be a murderer.

Schedoni, not less affected, though apparently tranquil, as sedulously avoided the face of the Marchesa, whom he considered with a degree of contempt almost equal to his indignation: his feelings had reversed, for the present, all his opinions on the subject of their former arguments, and had taught him, for once, to think justly. Every moment of silence now increased his embarrassment, and his reluctance even to name Ellena. He feared to tell that she lived, yet despised himself for suffering such fear, and shuddered at a recollection of the conduct, which had made any assurance concerning her life necessary. The insinuations, that he had discovered her family to be such as would not degrade that of the Marchesa, he knew not how to introduce with such delicacy of gradation as might win upon the jealousy of her pride, and soothe her disappointment; and he was still meditating how he might lead to this subject, when the Marchesa herself broke the silence.

"Father," she said, with a sigh, "I always look to you for consolation, and am seldom disappointed. You are too well acquainted with the anxiety which has long oppressed me; may I understand that the cause of it is removed?" She paused, and then added, "May I hope that my son will no longer be led from the observance of his duty?"

Schedoni, with his eyes fixed on the ground, remained silent, but, at length, said, "The chief occasion of your anxiety is certainly removed;"—and he was again silent.

"How!" exclaimed the Marchesa, with the quick-sightedness of suspicion, while all her dissimulation yielded to the urgency of her fear, "Have you failed? Is she not dead?"

In the earnestness of the question, she fixed her eyes on Schedoni's face, and, perceiving there symptoms of extraordinary emotion, added, "Relieve me from my apprehensions, good father, I entreat; tell me that you have succeeded, and that she has paid the debt of justice."

Schedoni raised his eyes to the Marchesa, but instantly averted them; indignation had lifted them, and disgust and stifled horror turned them away. Though very little of these feelings appeared, the Marchesa perceived such expression as she had never been accustomed to observe in his countenance; and, her surprise and impatience increasing, she once more repeated the question, and with a yet more decisive air than before.

"I have not failed in the grand object," replied Schedoni: "your son is no longer in danger of forming a disgraceful alliance."

"In what, then, have you failed?" asked the Marchesa; "for I perceive that you have not been completely successful."

"I ought not to say that I have failed in any respect," replied Schedoni, with emotion, "since the honour of your house is preserved, and——a life is spared."

His voice faultered as he pronounced the last words, and he seemed to experience again the horror of that moment, when, with an uplifted poniard in his grasp, he had discovered Ellena for his daughter.

"Spared!" repeated the Marchesa, doubtingly; "explain yourself, good father!"

"She lives," replied Schedoni; "but you have nothing, therefore, to apprehend."

The Marchesa, surprised no less by the tone in which he spoke, than shocked at the purport of his words, changed countenance, while she said, impatiently—"You speak in enigmas, father."

"Lady! I speak plain truth—she lives."

"I understand that sufficiently," said the Marchesa; "but when you tell me, I have nothing to apprehend——"

"I tell you truth, also," rejoined the Confessor; "and the benevolence of your nature may be permitted to rejoice, for justice no longer has forbade the exercise of mercy."

"This is all very well in its place," said the Marchesa, betrayed by the vexation she suffered; "such sentiments and such compliments are like gala suits, to be put on in fine weather. My day is cloudy; let me have a little plain strong sense: inform me of the circumstances which have occasioned this change in the course of your observations, and, good father! be brief."

Schedoni then unfolded, with his usual art, such circumstances relative to the family of Ellena as he hoped would soften the aversion of the Marchesa to the connection, and incline her, in consideration of her son's happiness, finally to approve it; with which disclosure he mingled a plausible relation of the way, in which the discovery had been made.

The Marchesa's patience would scarcely await the conclusion of his narrative, or her disappointment submit to the curb of discretion. When, at length, he had finished his history, "Is it possible," said she, with fretful displeasure, "that you have suffered yourself to be deceived by the plausibility of a girl, who might have been expected to utter any falsehood, which should appear likely to protect her! Has a man of your discernment given faith to the idle and improbable tale! Say, rather, father, that your resolution failed in the critical moment, and that you are now anxious to form excuses to yourself for a conduct so pusillanimous."

"I am not apt to give an easy faith to appearances," replied Schedoni, gravely, "and still less, to shrink from the performance of any act, which I judge to be necessary and just. To the last intimation, I make no reply; it does not become my character to vindicate myself from an implication of falsehood."

The Marchesa, perceiving that her passion had betrayed her into imprudence, condescended to apologize for that which she termed an effect of her extreme anxiety, as to what might follow from an act of such indiscreet indulgence; and Schedoni as willingly accepted the apology, each believing the assistance of the other necessary to success.

Schedoni then informed her, that he had better authority for what he had advanced than the assertion of Ellena; and he mentioned some circumstances, which proved him to be more anxious for the reputation than for the truth of his word. Believing that his origin was entirely unknown to the Marchesa, he ventured to disclose some particulars of Ellena's family, without apprehending that it could lead to a suspicion of his own.

The Marchesa, though neither appeased nor convinced, commanded her feelings so far as to appear tranquil, while the Confessor represented, with the most delicate address, the unhappiness of her son, and the satisfaction, which must finally result to herself from an acquiescence with his choice, since the object of it was known to be worthy of his alliance. He added, that, while he had believed the contrary, he had proved himself as strenuous to prevent, as he was now sincere in approving their marriage; and concluded with gently blaming her for suffering prejudice and some remains of resentment to obscure her excellent understanding. "Trusting to the natural clearness of your perceptions," he added, "I doubt not that when you have maturely considered the subject, every objection will yield to a consideration of your son's happiness."

The earnestness, with which Schedoni pleaded for Vivaldi, excited some surprise; but the Marchesa, without condescending to reply either to his argument or remonstrance, inquired whether Ellena had a suspicion of the design, with which she had been carried into the forests of the Garganus, or concerning the identity of her persecutor. Schedoni, immediately perceiving to what these questions tended, replied, with the facility with which he usually accommodated his conscience to his interest, that Ellena was totally ignorant as to who were her immediate persecutors, and equally unsuspicious of any other evil having been intended her, than that of a temporary confinement.

The last assertion was admitted by the Marchesa to be probable, till the boldness of the first made her doubt the truth of each, and occasioned her new surprize and conjecture as to the motive, which could induce Schedoni to venture these untruths. She then inquired where Ellena was now disposed of, but he had too much prudence to disclose the place of her retreat, however plausible might be the air with which the inquiry was urged; and he endeavoured to call off her attention to Vivaldi. The Confessor did not, however, venture, at present, to give a hint as to the pretended discovery of his situation in the inquisition, but reserved to a more favourable opportunity such mention, together with the zealous offer of his services to extricate the prisoner. The Marchesa, believing that her son was still engaged in pursuit of Ellena, made many inquiries concerning him, but without expressing any solicitude for his welfare; resentment appear-

ing to be the only emotion she retained towards him. While
Schedoni replied with circumspection to her questions, he
urged inquiries of his own, as to the manner in which the
Marchesa endured the long absence of Vivaldi; thus endeavouring to ascertain how far he might hereafter venture to appear in any efforts for liberating him, and how shape his
conduct respecting Ellena. It seemed that the Marchese was
not indifferent as to his son's absence; and, though he had at
first believed the search for Ellena to have occasioned it,
other apprehensions now disturbed him, and taught him the
feelings of a father. His numerous avocations and interests,
however, seemed to prevent such anxiety from preying upon
his mind; and, having dismissed persons in search of
Vivaldi, he passed his time in the usual routine of company
and the court. Of the actual situation of his son it was evident that neither he, nor the Marchesa, had the least apprehension, and this was a circumstance, which the Confessor
was very careful to ascertain.

Before he took leave, he ventured to renew the mention of
Vivaldi's attachment, and gently to plead for him. The Marchesa, however, seemed inattentive to what he represented,
till, at length, awaking from her reverie, she said—"Father,
you have judged ill——," and, before she concluded the
sentence, she relapsed again into thoughtful silence. Believing that he anticipated her meaning, Schedoni began to repeat his own justification respecting his conduct towards
Ellena.

"You have judged erroneously, father," resumed the Marchesa, with the same considering air, "in placing the girl in
such a situation; my son cannot fail to discover her there."

"Or wherever she may be," replied the Confessor, believing that he understood the Marchesa's aim. "It may not be
possible to conceal her long from his search."

"The neighbourhood of Naples ought at least to have been
avoided," observed the Marchesa.

Schedoni was silent, and she added, "So near, also, to his
own residence! How far is the Santa della Piéta from the
Vivaldi palace?"

Though Schedoni had thought that the Marchesa, while
displaying a pretended knowledge of Ellena's retreat, was
only endeavouring to obtain a real one, this mention of the
place of her actual residence shocked him; but he replied almost immediately, "I am ignorant of the distance, for, till

now, I was unacquainted that there is a convent of the name you mention. It appears, however, that this Santa della Piéta is the place, of all other, which ought to have been avoided. How could you suspect me, lady, of imprudence thus extravagant!"

While Schedoni spoke, the Marchesa regarded him attentively, and then replied, "I may be allowed, good father, to suspect your prudence in this instance, since you have just given me so unequivocal a proof of it in another."

She would then have changed the subject, but Schedoni, believing this inclination to be the consequence of her having assured herself, that she had actually discovered Ellena's asylum, and too reasonably suspecting the dreadful use she designed to make of the discovery, endeavoured to unsettle her opinion, and mislead her as to the place of Ellena's abode. He not only contradicted the fact of her present residence at the Santa della Piéta, but, without scruple, made a positive assertion, that she was at a distance from Naples, naming, at the same time, a fictitious place, whose obscurity, he added, would be the best protection from the pursuit of Vivaldi.

"Very true, father," observed the Marchesa; "I believe that my son will not readily discover the girl in the place you have named."

Whether the Marchesa believed Schedoni's assertion or not, she expressed no farther curiosity on the subject, and appeared considerably more tranquil than before. She now chatted with ease on general topics, while the Confessor dared no more to urge the subject of his secret wishes; and, having supported, for some time, a conversation most uncongenial with his temper, he took his leave, and returned to Naples. On the way thither, he reviewed, with exactness, the late behaviour of the Marchesa, and the result of this examination was a resolution—never to renew the subject of their conversation, but to solemnize, without her consent, the nuptials of Vivaldi and Ellena.

The Marchesa, meanwhile, on the departure of Schedoni, remained in the attitude in which he had left her, and absorbed by the interest, which his visit excited. The sudden change in his conduct no less astonished and perplexed, than disappointed her. She could not explain it by the supposition of any principle, or motive. Sometimes it occurred to her, that Vivaldi had bribed him with rich promises, to promote

ich he contributed to thwart; but, when she
gh expectations she had herself encouraged
e improbability of the conjecture was ap-
doni, from whatever cause, was no longer
trusted in this business, was sufficiently clear, but she
endeavoured to console herself with a hope that a more confidential person might yet be discovered. A part of Schedoni's resolution she also adopted, which was, never again
to introduce the subject of their late conversation. But, while
she should silently pursue her own plans, she determined to
conduct herself towards Schedoni in every other respect, as
usual, not suffering him to suspect that she had withdrawn
her confidence, but inducing him to believe that she had relinquished all farther design against Ellena.

CHAPTER IV

—————————We
Would learn the private virtues; how to glide
Through shades and plains, along the smoothest stream
Of rural life; or, snatch'd away by hope,
Through the dim spaces of futurity,
With earnest eye anticipate those scenes
Of happiness and wonder, where the mind,
In endless growth and infinite ascent,
Rises from state to state, and world to world.

THOMSON

ELLENA, obedient to the command of Schedoni, withdrew
from her home on the day that followed her arrival there, to
the Santa della Piéta. The Superior, who had known her
from her infancy, and, from the acquaintance which such
long observation afforded, had both esteemed and loved her,
received Ellena with a degree of satisfaction proportionate to
the concern she had suffered when informed of her disastrous removal from the villa Altieri.

Among the quiet groves of this convent, however, Ellena
vainly endeavoured to moderate her solicitude respecting the
situation of Vivaldi; for, now that she had a respite from immediate calamity, she thought with more intense anxiety as
to what might be his sufferings, and her fears and impatience
increased, as each day disappointed her expectation of intelligence from Schedoni.

If the soothings of sympathy and the delicate arts of benevolence could have restored the serenity of her mind,
Ellena would now have been peaceful; for all these were offered her by the abbess and the sisters of the Santa della
Piéta. They were not acquainted with the cause of her sorrow, but they perceived that she was unhappy, and wished
her to be otherwise. The society of Our Lady of Pity, was

such as a convent does not often shroud; to the wisdom and
virtue of the Superior, the sisterhood was principally indebted for the harmony and happiness which distinguished
them. This lady was a shining example to governesses of religious houses, and a striking instance of the influence,
which a virtuous mind may acquire over others, as well as of
the extensive good that it may thus diffuse. She was dignified without haughtiness, religious without bigotry, and
mild, though decisive and firm. She possessed penetration to
discover what was just, resolution to adhere to it, and temper
to practise it with gentleness and grace; so that even correc-
tion from her, assumed the winning air of courtesy: the person, whom she admonished, wept in sorrow for the offence,
instead of being secretly irritated by the reproof, and loved
her as a mother, rather than feared her as a judge. Whatever
might be her failings, they were effectually concealed by the
general benevolence of her heart, and the harmony of her
mind; a harmony, not the effect of torpid feelings, but the
accomplishment of correct and vigilant judgment. Her religion was neither gloomy, nor bigotted; it was the sentiment
of a grateful heart offering itself up to a Deity, who delights
in the happiness of his creatures; and she conformed to the
customs of the Roman church, without supposing a faith in
all of them to be necessary to salvation. This opinion, however, she was obliged to conceal, lest her very virtue should
draw upon her the punishment of a crime, from some fierce
ecclesiastics, who contradicted in their practise the very essential principles, which the christianity they professed
would have taught them.

In her lectures to the nuns she seldom touched upon points
of faith, but explained and enforced the moral duties, particularly such as were most practicable in the society to which she
belonged; such as tended to soften and harmonize the affections, to impart that repose of mind, which persuades to the
practise of sisterly kindness, universal charity, and the most
pure and elevated devotion. When she spoke of religion, it appeared so interesting, so beautiful, that her attentive auditors
revered and loved it as a friend, a refiner of the heart, a sublime consoler; and experienced somewhat of the meek and
holy ardour, which may belong to angelic natures.

The society appeared like a large family, of which the lady
abbess was the mother, rather than an assemblage of strangers;
and particularly when gathered around her, they listened to the

evening sermon, which she delivered with such affectionate interest, such persuasive eloquence, and sometimes with such pathetic energy, as few hearts could resist.

She encouraged in her convent every innocent and liberal pursuit, which might sweeten the austerities of confinement, and which were generally rendered instrumental to charity. The Daughters of Pity particularly excelled in music; not in those difficulties of the art, which display florid graces, and intricate execution, but in such eloquence of sound as steals upon the heart, and awakens its sweetest and best affections. It was probably the well-regulated sensibility of their own minds, that enabled these sisters to diffuse through their strains a character of such finely-tempered taste, as drew crowds of visitors, on every festival, to the church of the Santa della Piéta.

The local circumstances of this convent were scarcely less agreeable than the harmony of its society was interesting. These extensive domains included olive-grounds, vineyards, and some corn-land; a considerable tract was devoted to the pleasures of the garden, whose groves supplied walnuts, almonds, oranges, and citrons, in abundance, and almost every kind of fruit and flower, which this luxurious climate nurtured. These gardens hung upon the slope of a hill, about a mile within the shore, and afforded extensive views of the country round Naples, and of the gulf. But from the terraces, which extended along a semicircular range of rocks, that rose over the convent, and formed a part of the domain, the prospects were infinitely finer. They extended on the south to the isle of Capræa, where the gulf expands into the sea; in the west, appeared the island of Ischia, distinguished by the white pinnacles of the lofty mountain Epomeo; and near it Prosida, with its many-coloured cliffs, rose out of the waves. Overlooking many points towards Puzzuoli, the eye caught beyond other promontories, and others further still, to the north, a glimpse of the sea, that bathes the now desolate shores of Baia; with Capua, and all the towns and villas, that speckle the garden-plains between Caserta and Naples.

In the nearer scene were the rocky heights of Pausilippo, and Naples itself, with all its crowded suburbs ascending among the hills, and mingling with vineyards and overtopping cypress; the castle of San Elmo, conspicuous on its rock, overhanging the magnificent monastery of the Chartreux; while in the scene below appeared the *Castel Nuovo*, with its clustered towers, the long-extended Corso, the mole, with its tall pharos, and the harbour gay with painted shipping, and full to the brim with the blue waters of the bay. Beyond the hills of Naples, the whole horizon to the north and east was bounded by the mountains of the Apennine, an amphitheatre proportioned to the grandeur of the plain, which the gulf spread out below.

These terraces, shaded with acacias and plane-trees, were the favourite haunt of Ellena. Between the opening branches, she looked down upon villa Altieri, which brought to her remembrance the affectionate Bianchi, with all the sportive years of her childhood; and where some of her happiest hours had been passed in the society of Vivaldi. Along the windings of the coast, too, she could distinguish many places rendered sacred by affection, to which she had made excursions with her lamented relative, and Vivaldi; and, though sadness mingled with the recollections a view of them restored, they were precious to her heart. Here, alone and unobserved, she frequently yielded to the melancholy which she endeavoured to suppress in society; and at other times tried to deceive, with books and the pencil, the lingering moments of uncertainty concerning the state of Vivaldi; for day after day still elapsed without bringing any intelligence from Schedoni. Whenever the late scenes connected with the discovery of her family recurred to Ellena, she was struck with almost as much amazement as if she was gazing upon a vision, instead of recalling realities. Contrasted with the sober truth of her present life, the past appeared like romance; and there were moments when she shrunk from the relationship of Schedoni with unconquerable affright. The first emotions his appearance had excited were so opposite to those of filial tenderness, that she perceived it was now nearly impossible to love and revere him as her father, and she endeavoured, by dwelling upon all the obligations, which she believed he had lately conferred upon her, to repay him in gratitude, what was withheld in affection.

In such melancholy considerations, she often lingered under the shade of the acacias, till the sun had sunk behind the far distant promontory of Miseno, and the last bell of vespers summoned her to the convent below.

Among the nuns, Ellena had many favourites, but not one that she admired and loved equally with Olivia of San Stefano, the remembrance of whom was always accompanied with a fear lest she should have suffered from her generous compassion, and a wish that she had taken up her abode with the happy society of the Daughters of Pity, instead of being subjected to the tyranny of the abbess of San Stefano. To Ellena, the magnificent scenes of the Santa della Piéta seemed to open a secure, and, perhaps, a last asylum; for, in her present circumstances, she could not avoid perceiving how menacing and various were the objections to her marriage with Vivaldi, even should Schedoni prove propitious to it. The character of the Marchesa di Vivaldi, such as it stood unfolded by the late occurrences, struck her with dismay, for her designs appeared sufficiently atrocious, whether they had extended to the utmost limit of Ellena's suspicions, or had stopped where the affected charity of Schedoni had pointed out. In either case, the pertinacity of her aversion, and the vindictive violence of her nature, were obvious.

In this view of her character, however, it was not the inconvenience threatened to those who might become connected with her, that principally affected Ellena, but the circumstance of such a woman being the mother of Vivaldi; and, to alleviate so afflicting a consideration, she endeavoured to believe all the palliating suggestions of Schedoni, respecting the Marchesa's late intentions. But if Ellena was grieved on discovering crime in the character of Vivaldi's parent, what would have been her suffering, had she suspected the nature of Schedoni?—what, if she had been told that he was the adviser of the Marchesa's plans?—if she had known that he had been the partner of her intentional guilt? From such suffering she was yet spared, as well as from that, which a knowledge of Vivaldi's present situation, and of the result of Schedoni's efforts to procure a release from the perils, among which he had precipitated him, would have inflicted. Had she known this, it is probable that in the first despondency of her mind, she would have relinquished what is called the world, and sought a lasting asylum with the society of the holy sisters. Even as it was, she sometimes endeavoured to look with resignation upon the events which might render such a step desirable; but it was an effort that seldom soothed her even with a temporary self-delusion. Should the veil, however, prove her final refuge, it would be by her own choice; for the lady abbess of the Santa della Piéta employed no art to win a recluse, nor suffered the nuns to seduce votaries to the order.

CHAPTER V

Sullen and sad to fancy's frighted eye
Did shapes of dun and murky hue advance,
In train tumultuous, all of gesture strange,
And passing horrible.

CARACTACUS

WHILE the late events had been passing in the Garganus, and at Naples, Vivaldi and his servant Paulo remained imprisoned in distinct chambers of the Inquisition. They were again separately interrogated. From the servant no information could be obtained; he asserted only his master's innocence, without once remembering to mention his own; clamoured, with more justness than prudence, against the persons who had occasioned his arrest; seriously endeavouring to convince the inquisitors, that he himself had *no other motive* in having demanded to be brought to these prisons than that he might comfort his master, he gravely remonstrated on the injustice of separating them, adding, that he was sure when they knew the rights of the matter, they would order him to be carried to the prison of Signor Vivaldi.

"I do assure your *Serenissimo Illustrissimo*," continued Paulo, addressing the chief inquisitor with profound gravity, "that this is the last place I should have thought of coming to, on any other account; and if you will only condescend to ask your officials, who took my master up, they will tell you *as good.* They knew well enough all along, what I came here for, and if they had known it would be all in vain, it would have been but civil of them to have told me as much, and not have brought me; for this is the last place in the world I would have come to, otherwise, of my own accord."

Paulo was permitted to harangue in his own way, because

his examiners hoped that his prolixity would be a means of betraying circumstances connected with his master. By this view, however, they were misled, for Paulo, with all his simplicity of heart, was both vigilant and shrewd in Vivaldi's interest. But, when he perceived them really convinced, that his sole motive for visiting the Inquisition was that he might console his master, yet still persisting in the resolution of separately confining him, his indignation knew no bounds. He despised alike their reprehension, their thundering menaces, and their more artful exhibitions; told them of all they had to expect both here and hereafter, for their cruelty to his dear master, and said they might do what they would with him; he defied them to make him more miserable than he was.

It was not without difficulty that he was removed from the chamber; where he left his examiners in a state of astonishment at his rashness, and indignation of his honesty, such as they had, probably, never experienced before.

When Vivaldi was again called up to the table of the Holy Office, he underwent a longer examination than on a former occasion. Several inquisitors attended, and every art was employed to induce him to confess crimes, of which he was suspected, and to draw from him a discovery of others, which might have eluded even suspicion. Still the examiners cautiously avoided informing him of the subject of the accusation on which he had been arrested, and it was, therefore, only on the former assurances of the Benedictine, and the officials in the chapel of San Sebastian, that Vivaldi understood he was accused of having carried off a nun. His answers on the present occasion were concise and firm, and his whole deportment undaunted. He felt less apprehension for himself, than indignation of the general injustice and cruelty, which the tribunal was permitted to exercise upon others; and this virtuous indignation gave a loftiness, a calm heroic grandeur to his mind, which never, for a moment, forsook him, except when he conjectured what might be the sufferings of Ellena. Then, his fortitude and magnanimity failed, and his tortured spirit rose almost to frenzy.

On this, his second examination, he was urged by the same dark questions, and replied to them with the same open sincerity, as during the first. Yet the simplicity and energy of truth failed to impress conviction on minds, which, no longer possessing the virtue themselves, were not competent to understand the symptoms of it in others. Vivaldi was again threatened with the torture, and again dismissed to his prison.

On the way to this dreadful abode, a person passed him in one of the avenues, of whose air and figure he thought he had some recollection; and, as the stranger stalked away, he suddenly knew him to be the prophetic monk, who had haunted him among the ruins of Paluzzi. In the first moment of surprise, Vivaldi lost his presence of mind so far, that he made no attempt to interrupt him. In the next instant, however, he paused and looked back, with an intention of speaking; but this mysterious person was already at the extremity of the avenue. Vivaldi called, and besought him to stop. Without either speaking, or turning his head, however, he immediately disappeared beyond a door that opened at his approach. Vivaldi, on attempting to take the way of the monk, was withheld by his guards; and, when he inquired who was the stranger he had seen, the officials asked, in their turn, what stranger he alluded to.

"He who has just passed us," replied Vivaldi.

The officials seemed surprised, "Your spirits are disordered, Signor," observed one of them, "I saw no person pass!"

"He passed so closely," said Vivaldi, "that it was hardly possible you could avoid seeing him!"

"I did not even hear a footstep!" added the man.

"I do not recollect that I did," answered Vivaldi, "but I saw his figure as plainly as I now see yours; his black garments almost touched me! Was he an inquisitor?"

The official appeared astonished; and, whether his surprise was real, or affected for the purpose of concealing his knowledge of the person alluded to, his embarrassment and awe seemed natural. Vivaldi observed, with almost equal curiosity and surprise, the fear which his face expressed; but perceived also, that it would avail nothing to repeat his questions.

As they proceeded along the avenue, a kind of half-stifled groan was sometimes audible from a distance. "Whence come those sounds?" said Vivaldi, "they strike to my heart!"

"They should do so," replied the guard.

"Whence come they?" repeated Vivaldi, more impatiently, and shuddering.

"From the place of torture," said the official.

"O God! O God!" exclaimed Vivaldi, with a deep groan.

He passed with hasty steps the door of that terrible chamber, and the guard did not attempt to stop him. The officials had brought him, in obedience to the customary orders they had received, within hearing of those doleful sounds, for the purpose of impressing upon his mind the horrors of the punishment, with which he was threatened, and of inducing him to confess without incurring them.

On this same evening, Vivaldi was visited, in his prison, by a man whom he had never consciously seen before. He appeared to be between forty and fifty; was of a grave and observant physiognomy, and of manners, which, though somewhat austere, were not alarming. The account he gave of himself, and of his motive for this visit, was curious. He said that he also was a prisoner in the inquisition, but, as the ground of accusation against him was light, he had been favoured so far as to be allowed some degree of liberty within certain bounds; that, having heard of Vivaldi's situation, he had asked and obtained leave to converse with him, which he had done in compassion, and with a desire of assuaging his sufferings, so far as an expression of sympathy and commiseration might relieve them.

While he spoke, Vivaldi regarded him with deep attention, and the improbability that these pretensions should be true, did not escape him; but the suspicion which they occasioned he prudently concealed. The stranger conversed on various subjects. Vivaldi's answers were cautious and concise; but not even long pauses of silence wearied the compassionate patience of his visitor. Among other topics he, at length, introduced that of religion.

"I have, myself, been accused of heresy," said he, "and know how to pity others in the same situation."

"It is of heresy, then, that I am accused!" interrupted Vivaldi, "of heresy!"

"It availed me nothing that I asserted my innocence," continued the stranger, without noticing Vivaldi's exclamation, "I was condemned to the torture. My sufferings were too terrible to be endured! I confessed my offence———"

"Pardon me," interrupted Vivaldi, "but allow me to observe, that since your sufferings were so severe, yours, against whom the ground of accusation was light, what may be the punishment of those, whose offences are more serious?"

The stranger was somewhat embarrassed. "My offence was slight," he continued, without giving a full answer.

"Is it possible," said Vivaldi, again interrupting him, "that heresy can be considered as a slight offence before the tribunal of the Inquisition?"

"It was only of a slight degree of heresy," replied the visitor, reddening with displeasure, "that I was suspected, and——"

"Does then the Inquisition allow of degrees in heresy?" said Vivaldi.

"I confessed my offence," added the stranger with a louder emphasis, "and the consequence of this confession was a remission of punishment. After a trifling penance I shall be dismissed, and probably, in a few days, leave the prison. Before I left it, I was desirous of administering some degree of consolation to a fellow sufferer; if you have any friends whom you wish to inform of your situation, do not fear to confide their names and your message to me."

The latter part of the speech was delivered in a low voice, as if the stranger feared to be overheard. Vivaldi remained silent, while he examined, with closer attention, the countenance of his visitor. It was of the utmost importance to him, that his family should be made acquainted with his situation; yet he knew not exactly how to interpret, or to confide in this offer. Vivaldi had heard that informers sometimes visited the prisoners, and, under the affectation of kindness and sympathy, drew from them a confession of opinions, which were afterwards urged against them; and obtained discoveries relative to their connections and friends, who were, by these insidious means, frequently involved in their destruction. Vivaldi, conscious of his own innocence, had, on his first examination, acquainted the inquisitor with the names and residence of his family; he had, therefore, nothing new to apprehend from revealing them to this stranger; but he perceived that if it should be known he had attempted to convey a message, however concise and harmless, the discovery would irritate the jealous inquisitors against him, and might be urged as a new presumption of his guilt. These considerations, together with the distrust which the inconsistency of his visitor's assertions, and the occasional embarrassment of his manner, had awakened, determined Vivaldi to resist the temptation now offered to him; and the stranger, having received his thanks, reluctantly withdrew, observing,

however, that should any unforeseen circumstance detain
him in the Inquisition longer than he had reason to expect,
he should beg leave to pay him another visit. In reply to this,
Vivaldi only bowed, but he remarked that the stranger's
countenance changed, and that some dark brooding appeared
to cloud his mind, as he quitted the chamber.

Several days elapsed, during which Vivaldi heard no more
of his new acquaintance. He was then summoned to another
examination, from which he was dismissed as before; and
some weeks of solitude and of heavy uncertainty succeeded,
after which he was a fourth time called up to the table of the
Holy Office. It was then surrounded by inquisitors, and a
more than usual solemnity appeared in the proceedings.

As proofs of Vivaldi's innocence had not been obtained,
the suspicions of his examiners, of course, were not removed; and, as he persisted in denying the truth of the
charge which he understood would be exhibited against him,
and refused to make any confession of crimes, it was ordered that he should, within three hours, be put to the *question*. Till then, Vivaldi was once more dismissed to his
prison chamber. His resolution remained unshaken, but he
could not look, unmoved, upon the horrors which might be
preparing for him. The interval of expectation between the
sentence and the accomplishment of this preliminary punishment, was, indeed, dreadful. The seeming ignominy of his
situation, and his ignorance as to the degree of torture to be
applied, overcame the calmness he had before exhibited, and
as he paced his cell, cold damps, which hung upon his forehead, betrayed the agony of his mind. It was not long, however, that he suffered from a sense of ignominy; his better
judgment shewed him, that innocence cannot suffer disgrace
from any situation or circumstance, and he once more resumed the courage and the firmness which belong to virtue.

It was about midnight, that Vivaldi heard steps approaching, and a murmur of voices at the door of his cell. He understood these to be the persons come to summon him to the
torture. The door was unbarred, and two men, habited in
black, appeared at it. Without speaking, they advanced, and
throwing over him a singular kind of mantle, led him from
the chamber.

Along the galleries, and other avenues through which they
passed, not any person was seen, and, by the profound stillness that reigned, it seemed as if death had already antici-

pated his work in these regions of horror, and had condemned alike the tortured and the torturer.

They descended to the large hall, where Vivaldi had waited on the night of his entrance, and thence through an avenue, and down a long flight of steps, that led to subterranean chambers. His conductors did not utter a syllable during the whole progress; Vivaldi knew too well that questions would only subject him to greater severity, and he asked none.

The doors, through which they passed, regularly opened at the touch of an iron rod, carried by one of the officials, and without the appearance of any person. The other man bore a torch, and the passages were so dimly lighted, that the way could scarcely have been found without one. They crossed what seemed to be a burial vault, but the extent and obscurity of the place did not allow it to be ascertained; and, having reached an iron door, they stopped. One of the officials struck upon it three times with the rod, but it did not open as the others had done. While they waited, Vivaldi thought he heard, from within, low intermitting sounds, as of persons in their last extremity, but, though within, they appeared to come from a distance. His whole heart was chilled, not with fear, for at that moment he did not remember himself, but with horror.

Having waited a considerable time, during which the official did not repeat the signal, the door was partly opened by a person whom Vivaldi could not distinguish in the gloom beyond, and with whom one of his conductors communicated by signs; after which the door was closed.

Several minutes had elapsed, when tones of deep voices aroused the attention of Vivaldi. They were loud and hoarse, and spoke in a language unknown to him. At the sounds, the official immediately extinguished his torch. The voices drew nearer, and, the door again unfolding, two figures stood before Vivaldi, which, shewn by a glimmering light within, struck him with astonishment and dismay. They were cloathed, like his conductors, in black, but in a different fashion for their habits were made close to the shape. Their faces were entirely concealed beneath a very peculiar kind of cowl, which descended from the head to the feet; and their eyes only were visible through small openings contrived for the sight. It occurred to Vivaldi that these men were torturers; their appearance was worthy of demons.

Probably they were thus habited, that the persons whom they afflicted might not know them; or, perhaps, it was only for the purpose of striking terror upon the minds of the accused, and thus compelling them to confess without further difficulty. Whatever motive might have occasioned their horrific appearance, and whatever was their office, Vivaldi was delivered into their hands, and in the same moment heard the iron door shut, which enclosed him with them in a narrow passage, gloomily lighted by a lamp suspended from the arched roof. They walked in silence on each side of their prisoner, and came to a second door, which admitted them instantly into another passage. A third door, at a short distance, admitted them to a third avenue, at the end of which one of his mysterious guides struck upon a gate, and they stopped. The uncertain sounds that Vivaldi had fancied he heard, were now more audible, and he distinguished, with inexpressible horror, that they were uttered by persons suffering.

The gate was, at length, opened by a figure habited like his conductors, and two other doors of iron, placed very near each other, being also unlocked, Vivaldi found himself in a spacious chamber, the walls of which were hung with black, duskily lighted by lamps that gleamed in the lofty vault. Immediately on his entrance, a strange sound ran along the walls, and echoed among other vaults, that appeared, by the progress of the sound, to extend far beyond this.

It was not immediately that Vivaldi could sufficiently recollect himself to observe any object before him; and, even when he did so, the gloom of the place prevented his ascertaining many appearances. Shadowy countenances and uncertain forms seemed to flit through the dusk, and many instruments, the application of which he did not comprehend, struck him with horrible suspicions. Still he heard, at intervals, half-suppressed groans, and was looking round to discover the wretched people from whom they were extorted, when a voice from a remote part of the chamber, called on him to advance.

The distance, and the obscurity of the spot whence the voice issued, had prevented Vivaldi from noticing any person there, and he was now slowly obeying, when, on a second summons, his conductors seized his arms and hurried him forward.

In a remote part of this extensive chamber, he perceived

three persons seated under a black canopy, on chairs raised several steps from the floor, and who appeared to preside there in the office of either judges or examiners, or directors of the punishments. Below, at a table, sat a secretary, over whom was suspended the only lamp that could enable him to commit to paper what should occur during the examination. Vivaldi now understood that the three persons who composed the tribunal were the vicar general, or grand inquisitor, the advocate of the exchequer, and an ordinary inquisitor, who was seated between the other two, and who appeared more eagerly to engage in the duties of his cruel office. A portentous obscurity enveloped alike their persons and their proceedings.

At some distance from the tribunal stood a large iron frame, which Vivaldi conjectured to be the rack, and near it another, resembling, in shape, a coffin, but, happily, he could not distinguish through the remote obscurity, any person undergoing actual suffering. In the vaults beyond, however, the diabolical decrees of the inquisitors seemed to be fulfilling; for, whenever a distant door opened for a moment, sounds of lamentation issued forth, and men, whom he judged to be familiars, habited like those who stood beside him, were seen passing to and fro within.

Vivaldi almost believed himself in the infernal regions; the dismal aspect of this place, the horrible preparation for punishment, and, above all, the disposition and appearance of the persons that were ready to inflict it, confirmed the resemblance. That any human being should willingly afflict a fellow being who had never injured, or even offended him; that, unswayed by passion, he should deliberately become the means of torturing him, appeared to Vivaldi nearly incredible! But when he looked at the three persons who composed the tribunal, and considered that they had not only voluntarily undertaken the cruel office they fulfilled, but had probably long regarded it as the summit of their ambition, his astonishment and indignation were unbounded.

The grand inquisitor, having again called on Vivaldi by name, admonished him to confess the truth, and avoid the suffering that awaited him.

As Vivaldi had on former examinations spoken the truth, which was not believed, he had no chance of escaping present suffering, but by asserting falsehood: in doing so, to avoid such monstrous injustice and cruelty, he might, per-

haps, have been justified, had it been certain that such assertion could affect himself alone; but since he knew that the
consequence must extend to others, and, above all, believed
that Ellena di Rosalba must be involved in it, he did not hesitate for an instant to dare whatever torture his firmness
might provoke. But even if morality could have forgiven
falsehood, in such extraordinary circumstances as these, policy, after all, would have forbidden it, since a discovery of
the artifice would probably have led to the final destruction
of the accused person.

Of Ellena's situation he would now have asked, however
desperate the question; would again have asserted her innocence, and supplicated for compassion, even to inquisitors,
had he not perceived that, in doing so, he should only furnish them with a more exquisite means of torturing him than
any other they could apply; for if, when all the terrors of his
soul concerning her were understood, they should threaten to
increase her sufferings, as the punishment of what was
termed his obstinacy, they would, indeed, become the mas-
ters of his integrity, as well as of his person.

The tribunal again, and repeatedly, urged Vivaldi to confess himself guilty; and the inquisitor, at length, concluded
with saying, that the judges were innocent of whatever consequence might ensue from his obstinacy; so that, if he expired beneath his sufferings, himself only, not they, would
have occasioned his death.

"I am innocent of the charges which I understand are
urged against me," said Vivaldi, with solemnity; "I repeat,
that I am innocent! If, to escape the horrors of these moments, I could be weak enough to declare myself guilty, not
all your racks could alter truth, and make me so, except in
that assertion. The consequence of your tortures, therefore,
be upon your own heads!"

While Vivaldi spoke, the vicar general listened with attention, and, when he had ceased to speak, appeared to meditate; but the inquisitor was irritated by the boldness of his
speech, instead of being convinced by the justness of
his representation; and made a signal for the officers to prepare for the *question*. While they were obeying, Vivaldi observed, notwithstanding the agitation he suffered, a person
cross the chamber, whom he immediately knew to be the
same that had passed him in an avenue of the inquisition on
a former night, and whom he had then fancied to be the

mysterious stranger of Paluzzi. Vivaldi now fixed his eyes upon him, but his own peculiar situation prevented his feeling the interest he had formerly suffered concerning him.

The figure, air, and stalk, of this person were so striking, and so strongly resembled those of the monk of Paluzzi, that Vivaldi had no longer a doubt as to their identity. He pointed him out to one of the officials, and inquired who he was. While he spoke, the stranger was passing forward, and, before any reply was given, a door leading to the farther vaults shut him from view. Vivaldi, however, repeated the inquiry, which the official appeared unable to answer, and a reproof from the tribunal reminded him that he must not ask questions there. Vivaldi observed that it was the grand inquisitor who spoke, and that the manner of the official immediately changed.

The familiars, who were the same that had conducted Vivaldi into the chamber, having made ready the instrument of torture, approached him, and, after taking off his cloak and vest, bound him with strong cords. They threw over his head the customary black garment, which entirely enveloped his figure, and prevented his observing what was farther preparing. In this state of expectation, he was again interrogated by the inquisitor.

"Was you ever in the church of the Spirito Santo, at Naples?" said he.

"Yes," replied Vivaldi.

"Did you ever express there a contempt for the Catholic faith?"

"Never," said Vivaldi.

"Neither by word or action?" continued the inquisitor.

"Never, by either!"

"Recollect yourself," added the inquisitor. "Did you never insult there a minister of our most holy church?"

Vivaldi was silent: he began to perceive the real nature of the charge which was to be urged against him, and that it was too plausible to permit his escape from the punishment, which is adjudged for heresy. Questions so direct and minute had never been put to him here on his former examinations; they had been reserved for a moment when it was believed he could not evade them; and the real charge had been concealed from him, that he might not be prepared to elude it.

"Answer!" repeated the inquisitor.—"Did you ever insult

a minister of the Catholic faith, in the church of the Spirito Santo, at Naples?"

"Did you not insult him while he was performing an act of holy penance?" said another voice.

Vivaldi started, for he instantly recollected the well-known tones of the monk of Paluzzi. "Who asks the question?" demanded Vivaldi.

"It is you who are to answer here," resumed the inquisitor. "Answer to what I have required."

"I have offended a minister of the church," replied Vivaldi, "but never could intentionally insult our holy religion. You are not acquainted, fathers, with the injuries that provoked——"

"Enough!" interrupted the inquisitor; "speak to the question. Did you not, by insult and menace, force a pious brother to leave unperformed the act of penance in which he had engaged himself? Did you not compel him to quit the church, and fly for refuge to his convent?"

"No," replied Vivaldi. " 'Tis true, he left the church, and that in consequence of my conduct there; but the consequence was not necessary; if he had only replied to my inquiry, or promised to restore her of whom he had treacherously robbed me, he might have remained quietly in the church till this moment, had that depended upon my forbearance."

"What!" said the vicar-general, "would you have compelled him to speak, when he was engaged in silent penance? You confess, that you occasioned him to leave the church. That is enough."

"Where did you first see Ellena di Rosalba?" said the voice, which had spoken once before.

"I demand again, who gives the question," answered Vivaldi.

"Recollect yourself," said the inquisitor, "a criminal cannot make a demand."

"I do not perceive the connection between your admonition and your assertion," observed Vivaldi.

"You appear to be rather too much at your ease," said the inquisitor. "Answer to the question which was last put to you, or the familiars shall do their duty."

"Let the same person ask it," replied Vivaldi.

The question was repeated in the former voice.

"In the church of San Lorenzo, at Naples," said Vivaldi, with a heavy sigh, "I first beheld Ellena di Rosalba."

"Was she then professed?" asked the vicar-general.

"She never accepted the veil," replied Vivaldi, "nor ever intended to do so."

"Where did she reside at that period?"

"She lived with a relative at villa Altieri, and would yet reside there, had not the machinations of a monk occasioned her to be torn from her home, and confined in a convent, from which I had just assisted to release her, when she was again seized, and upon a charge most false and cruel.—O reverend fathers! I conjure, I supplicate——" Vivaldi restrained himself, for he was going to have betrayed, to the mercy of inquisitors, all the feelings of his heart.

"The name of the monk?" said the stranger, earnestly.

"If I mistake not," replied Vivaldi, "you are already acquainted with it. The monk is called father Schedoni. He is of the Dominican convent of the Spirito Santo, in Naples, and the same who accuses me of having insulted him in the church of that name."

"How did you know him for your accuser?" asked the same voice.

"Because he is my only enemy," replied Vivaldi.

"Your enemy!" observed the inquisitor; "a former deposition says, you were unconscious of having one! You are inconsistent in your replies."

"You were warned not to visit villa Altieri," said the unknown person. "Why did you not profit by the warning?"

"I was warned by yourself," answered Vivaldi. "Now I know you well."

"By me!" said the stranger, in a solemn tone.

"By you!" repeated Vivaldi: "you who also foretold the death of Signora Bianchi; and you are that enemy—that father Schedoni, by whom I am accused."

"Whence come these questions?" demanded the vicar general. "Who has been authorised thus to interrogate the prisoner?"

No reply was made. A busy hum of voices from the tribunal succeeded the silence. At length, the murmuring subsided, and the monk's voice was heard again.

"I will declare thus much," it said, addressing Vivaldi; "I am not father Schedoni."

The peculiar tone and emphasis, with which this was delivered, more than the assertion itself, persuaded Vivaldi that the stranger spoke truth; and, though he still recognized the voice of the monk of Paluzzi, he did not know it to be that of Schedoni. Vivaldi was astonished! He would have torn the veil from his eyes, and once more viewed this mysterious stranger, had his hands been at liberty. As it was, he could only conjure him to reveal his name, and the motives for his former conduct.

"Who is come amongst us?" said the vicar-general, in the voice of a person, who means to inspire in others the awe he himself suffers.

"Who is come amongst us?" he repeated, in a louder tone. Still no answer was returned; but again a confused murmur sounded from the tribunal, and a general consternation seemed to prevail. No person spoke with sufficient pre-eminence to be understood by Vivaldi; something extraordinary appeared to be passing, and he awaited the issue with all the patience he could command. Soon after he heard doors opened, and the noise of persons quitting the chamber. A deep silence followed; but he was certain that the familiars were still beside him, waiting to begin their work of torture.

After a considerable time had elapsed, Vivaldi heard footsteps advancing, and a person give orders for his release, that he might be carried back to his cell.

When the veil was removed from his eyes, he perceived that the tribunal was dissolved, and that the stranger was gone. The lamps were dying away, and the chamber appeared more gloomily terrific than before.

The familiars conducted him to the spot at which they had received him; whence the officers who had led him thither, guarded him to his prison. There, stretched upon his bed of straw, in solitude and in darkness, he had leisure enough to reflect upon what had passed, and to recollect with minute exactness every former circumstance connected with the stranger. By comparing those with the present, he endeavoured to draw a more certain conclusion as to the identity of this person, and his motives for the very extraordinary conduct he had pursued. The first appearance of this stranger, among the ruins of Paluzzi, when he had said that Vivaldi's steps were watched, and had cautioned him against returning to villa Altieri, was recalled to his mind. Vivaldi reconsidered, also, his second appearance on the same spot, and his second warning; the circumstances, which had attended his own adventures within the fortress;—the monk's prediction of Bianchi's death, and his evil tidings respecting Ellena, at the very hour when she had been seized and carried from her home. The longer he considered these several instances, as they were now connected in his mind, with the certainty of Schedoni's evil disposition towards him, the more he was inclined to believe, notwithstanding the voice of seeming truth which had just affirmed the contrary, that the unknown person was Schedoni himself, and that he had been employed by the Marchesa, to prevent Vivaldi's visits to villa Altieri. Being thus an agent in the events of which he had warned Vivaldi, he was too well enabled to predict them. Vivaldi paused upon the remembrance of Signora Bianchi's death; he considered the extraordinary and dubious circumstances that had attended it, and shuddered as a new conjecture crossed his mind.—The thought was too dreadful to be permitted, and he dismissed it instantly.

Of the conversation, however, which he had afterwards held with the Confessor in the Marchesa's cabinet, he recollected many particulars that served to renew his doubts as to the identity of the stranger; the behaviour of Schedoni when he was obliquely challenged for the monk of Paluzzi, still appeared that of a man unconscious of disguise; and above all, Vivaldi was struck with the seeming candour of his having pointed out a circumstance, which removed the probability that the stranger was a brother of the Santa del Pianto.

Some particulars, also, of the stranger's conduct did not agree with what might have been expected from Schedoni, even though the Confessor had really been Vivaldi's enemy; a circumstance which the latter was no longer permitted to doubt. Nor did those particular circumstances accord, as he was inclined to believe, with the manner of a being of this world; and, when Vivaldi considered the suddenness and mystery, with which the stranger had always appeared and retired, he felt disposed to adopt again one of his earliest conjectures, which undoubtedly the horrors of his present abode disposed his imagination to admit, as those of his former situation in the vaults of Paluzzi, together with a youthful glow of curiosity concerning the marvellous, had before contributed to impress them upon his mind.

He concluded his present reflections as he had begun

them—in doubt and perplexity; but at length found a respite from thought and from suffering in sleep.

Midnight had been passed in the vaults of the Inquisition; but it was probably not yet two o'clock, when he was imperfectly awakened by a sound, which he fancied proceeded from within his chamber. He raised himself to discover what had occasioned the noise; it was, however, impossible to discern any object, for all was dark, but he listened for a return of the sound. The wind only, was heard moaning among the inner buildings of the prison, and Vivaldi concluded, that his dream had mocked him with a mimic voice.

Satisfied with this conclusion, he again laid his head on his pillow of straw, and soon sunk into a slumber. The subject of his waking thoughts still haunted his imagination, and the stranger, whose voice he had this night recognized as that of the monk of Paluzzi, appeared before him. Vivaldi, on perceiving the figure of this unknown, felt, perhaps, nearly the same degrees of awe, curiosity, and impatience that he would have suffered, had he beheld the substance of this shadow. The monk, whose face was still shrouded, he thought advanced, till, having come within a few paces of Vivaldi, he paused, and, lifting the awful cowl that had hitherto concealed him, disclosed—not the countenance of Schedoni, but one which Vivaldi did not recollect ever having seen before! It was not less interesting to curiosity, than striking to the feelings. Vivaldi at the first glance shrunk back;—something of that strange and indescribable air, which we attach to the idea of a supernatural being, prevailed over the features; and the intense and fiery eyes resembled those of an evil spirit, rather than of a human character. He drew a poniard from beneath a fold of his garment, and, as he displayed it, pointed with a stern frown to the spots which discoloured the blade; Vivaldi perceived they were of blood! He turned away his eyes in horror, and, when he again looked round in his dream, the figure was gone.

A groan awakened him, but what were his feelings, when, on looking up, he perceived the same figure standing before him! It was not, however, immediately that he could convince himself the appearance was more than the phantom of his dream, strongly impressed upon an alarmed fancy. The voice of the monk, for his face was as usual concealed, recalled Vivaldi from his error; but his emotion cannot easily be conceived, when the stranger, slowly lifting that mysterious cowl, discovered to him the same awful countenance, which had characterized the vision in his slumber. Unable to inquire the occasion of this appearance, Vivaldi gazed in astonishment and terror, and did not immediately observe, that, instead of a dagger, the monk held a lamp, which gleamed over every deep furrow of his features, yet left their shadowy markings to hint the passions and the history of an extraordinary life.

"You are spared for this night," said the stranger, "but for to-morrow"——he paused.

"In the name of all that is most sacred," said Vivaldi, endeavouring to recollect his thoughts, "who are you, and what is your errand?"

"Ask no questions," replied the monk, solemnly;—"but answer *me*."

Vivaldi was struck by the tone, with which he said this, and dared not to urge the inquiry at the present moment.

"How long have you known father Schedoni?" continued the stranger, "Where did you first meet?"

"I have known him about a year, as my mother's confessor," replied Vivaldi. "I first saw him in a corridor of the Vivaldi palace; it was evening, and he was returning from the Marchesa's closet."

"Are you certain as to this?" said the monk, with peculiar emphasis. "It is of consequence that you should be so."

"I am certain," repeated Vivaldi.

"It is strange," observed the monk, after a pause, "that a circumstance, which must have appeared trivial to you at the moment, should have left so strong a mark on your memory! In two years we have time to forget many things!" He sighed as he spoke.

"I remember the circumstance," said Vivaldi, "because I was struck with his appearance; the evening was far advanced—it was dusk, and he came upon me suddenly. His voice startled me; as he passed he said to himself—'It is for vespers.' At the same time I heard the bell of the Spirito Santo."

"Do you know who he is?" said the stranger, solemnly.

"I know only what he appears to be," replied Vivaldi.

"Did you never hear any report of his past life?"

"Never," answered Vivaldi.

"Never any thing extraordinary concerning him," added the monk.

Vivaldi paused a moment; for he now recollected the obscure and imperfect story, which Paulo had related while they were confined in the dungeon of Paluzzi, respecting a confession made in the church of the Black Penitents; but he could not presume to affirm, that it concerned Schedoni. He remembered also the monk's garments, stained with blood, which he had discovered in the vaults of that fort. The conduct of the mysterious being, who now stood before him, with many other particulars of his own adventures there, passed like a vision over his memory. His mind resembled the glass of a magician, on which the apparitions of long-buried events arise, and as they fleet away, point portentously to shapes half-hid in the duskiness of futurity. An unusual dread seized upon him; and a superstition, such as he had never before admitted in an equal degree, usurped his judgment. He looked up to the shadowy countenance of the stranger; and almost believed he beheld an inhabitant of the world of spirits.

The monk spoke again, repeating in a severer tone, "Did you never hear any thing extraordinary concerning father Schedoni?"

"Is it reasonable," said Vivaldi, recollecting his courage, "that I should answer the questions, the minute questions, of a person who refuses to tell me even his name?"

"My name is passed away—it is no more remembered," replied the stranger, turning from Vivaldi,—"I leave you to your fate."

"What fate?" asked Vivaldi, "and what is the purpose of this visit? I conjure you, in the tremendous name of the Inquisition, to say!"

"You will know full soon; have mercy on yourself!"

"What fate?" repeated Vivaldi.

"Urge me no further," said the stranger; "but answer to what I shall demand. Schedoni——"

"I have told all that I certainly know concerning him," interrupted Vivaldi, "the rest is only conjecture."

"What is that conjecture? Does it relate to a confession made in the church of the Black Penitents of the Santa Maria del Pianto?"

"It does!" replied Vivaldi with surprise.

"What was that confession?"

"I know not," answered Vivaldi.

"Declare the truth," said the stranger, sternly.

"A confession," replied Vivaldi, "is sacred, and forever buried in the bosom of the priest to whom it is made. How, then, is it to be supposed, that I can be acquainted with the subject of this?"

"Did you never hear, that father Schedoni had been guilty of some great crimes, which he endeavours to erase from his conscience by the severity of penance?"

"Never!" said Vivaldi.

"Did you never hear that he had a wife—a brother?"

"Never!"

"Nor the means he used—no hint of—murder, of——"

The stranger paused, as if he wished Vivaldi to fill up his meaning, Vivaldi was silent and aghast.

"You know nothing then, of Schedoni," resumed the monk after a deep pause—"nothing of his past life?"

"Nothing, except what I have mentioned," replied Vivaldi.

"Then listen to what I shall unfold!" continued the monk, with solemnity. "To-morrow night you will be again carried to the place of torture; you will be taken to a chamber beyond that in which you were this night. You will there witness many extraordinary things, of which you have not now any suspicion. Be not dismayed; I shall be there, though, perhaps, not visible."

"Not visible!" exclaimed Vivaldi.

"Interrupt me not, but listen.—When you are asked of father Schedoni, say—that he has lived for fifteen years in the disguise of a monk, a member of the Dominicans of the Spirito Santo, at Naples. When you are asked who he is, reply—Ferando Count di Bruno. You will be asked the motive, for such disguise. In reply to this, refer them to the Black Penitents of the Santa Maria del Pianto, near that city; bid the inquisitors summon before their tribunal one father Ansaldo di Rovalli, the grand penitentiary of the society, and command him to divulge the crimes confessed to him in the year 1752, on the evening of the twenty-fourth of April, which was then the vigil of Santo Marco, in a confessional of the Santa del Pianto."

"It is probable he may have forgotten such confession, at this distance of time," observed Vivaldi.

"Fear not but he will remember," replied the stranger.

"But will his conscience suffer him to betray the secrets of a confession?" said Vivaldi.

"The tribunal command, and his conscience is absolved," answered the monk, "He may not refuse to obey! You are further to direct your examiners to summon father Schedoni, to answer for the crimes which Ansaldo shall reveal." The monk paused, and seemed waiting the reply of Vivaldi, who, after a momentary consideration, said,

"How can I do all this, and upon the instigation of a stranger! Neither conscience nor prudence will suffer me to assert what I cannot prove. It is true that I have reason to believe Schedoni is my bitter enemy, but I will not be unjust even to him. I have no proof that he is the Count di Bruno, nor that he is the perpetrator of the crimes you allude to, whatever those may be; and I will not be made an instrument to summon any man before a tribunal, where innocence is no protection from ignominy, and where suspicion alone may inflict death."

"You doubt, then, the truth of what I assert?" said the monk, in a haughty tone.

"Can I believe that of which I have no proof?" replied Vivaldi.

"Yes, there are cases which do not admit of proof; under your peculiar circumstances, this is one of them; you can act only upon assertion. I attest," continued the monk, raising his hollow voice to a tone of singular solemnity, "I attest the powers which are beyond this earth, to witness to the truth of what I have delivered!"

As the stranger uttered this adjuration, Vivaldi observed, with emotion, the extraordinary expression of his eyes; Vivaldi's presence of mind, however, did not forsake him, and, in the next moment, he said, "But who is he that thus attests? It is upon the assertion of a stranger that I am to rely, in defect of proof! It is a stranger who calls upon me to bring solemn charges against a man, of whose guilt I know nothing!"

"You are not required to bring charges, you are only to summon him who will."

"I should still assist in bringing forward accusations, which may be founded in error," replied Vivaldi. "If you are convinced of their truth, why do not you summon Ansaldo yourself!"

"I shall do more," said the monk.

"But why not summon also?" urged Vivaldi.

"I shall *appear*," said the stranger, with emphasis.

Vivaldi, though somewhat awed by the manner, which accompanied these words, still urged his inquiries, "As a witness?" said he.

"Aye, as a dreadful witness!" replied the monk.

"But may not a witness summon others before the tribunal of the inquisition?" continued Vivaldi, faulteringly.

"He may," said the stranger.

"Why then," observed Vivaldi, "am I, a stranger to you, called upon to do that which you could perform yourself?"

"Ask no further," said the monk, "but answer, whether you will deliver the summons?"

"The charges, which must follow," replied Vivaldi, "appear to be of a nature too solemn to justify my promoting them. I resign the task to you."

"When *I* summon," said the stranger, "*you* shall obey!"

Vivaldi, again awed by his manner, again justified his refusal, and concluded with repeating his surprise, that he should be required to assist in this mysterious affair, "Since I neither know you, father," he added, "nor the Penitentiary Ansaldo, whom you bid me admonish to appear."

"You shall know me hereafter," said the stranger, frowningly; and he drew from beneath his garment a dagger!

Vivaldi remembered his dream.

"Mark those spots," said the monk.

Vivaldi looked, and beheld blood!

"This blood," added the stranger, pointing to the blade, "would have saved yours! Here is some print of truth! Tomorrow night you will meet me in the chambers of death!"

As he spoke, he turned away; and, before Vivaldi had recovered from his consternation, the light disappeared. Vivaldi knew that the stranger had quitted the prison, only by the silence which prevailed there.

He remained sunk in thought, till, at the dawn of day, the man, on watch, unfastened the door of his cell, and brought, as usual, a jug of water, and some bread. Vivaldi inquired the name of the stranger who had visited him in the night. The centinel looked surprised, and Vivaldi repeated the question before he could obtain an answer.

"I have been on guard since the first hour," said he man, "and no person, in that time, has passed through this door!"

Vivaldi regarded the centinel with attention, while he

made this assertion, and did not perceive in his manner any consciousness of falsehood; yet he knew not how to believe what he had affirmed. "Did you hear no noise, either?" said Vivaldi. "Has all been silent during the night?"

"I have heard only the bell of San Dominico strike upon the hour," replied the man, "and the watch word of the centinels."

"This is incomprehensible!" exclaimed Vivaldi, "What! no footsteps, no voice?"

The man smiled contemptuously. "None, but of the centinels," he replied.

"How can you be certain you heard only the centinels, friend?" added Vivaldi.

"They speak only to pass the watch word, and the clash of their arms is heard at the same time."

"But their footsteps!—how are they distinguished from those of other persons?"

"By the heaviness of their tread; our sandals are braced with iron. But why these questions, Signor?"

"You have kept guard at the door of this chamber?" said Vivaldi.

"Yes, Signor."

"And you have not once heard, during the whole night, a voice from within it?"

"None, Signor."

"Fear nothing from discovery, friend; confess that you have slumbered."

"I had a comrade," replied the centinel, angrily, "has he, too, slumbered! and if he had, how could admittance be obtained without our keys?"

"And those might easily have been procured, friend, if you were overcome with sleep. You may rely upon my promise of secrecy."

"What!" said the man, "have I kept guard for three years in the Inquisition, to be suspected, by an heretic, of neglecting my duty?"

"If you were suspected by an heretic," replied Vivaldi, "you ought to console yourself by recollecting that his opinions are considered to be erroneous."

"We were watchful every minute of the night," said the centinel, going.

"This is incomprehensible!" said Vivaldi, "By what means could the stranger have entered my prison?"

"Signor, you still dream!" replied the centinel, pausing, "No person has been here."

"*Still* dream!" repeated Vivaldi, "how do you know that I have dreamt at all?" His mind deeply affected by the extraordinary circumstances of the dream, and the yet more extraordinary incident that had followed, Vivaldi gave a meaning to the words of the centinel, which did not belong to them.

"When people sleep, they are apt to dream," replied the man, dryly. "I suppose *you* had slept, Signor."

"A person, habited like a monk, came to me in the night," resumed Vivaldi, and he described the appearance of the stranger. The centinel, while he listened, became grave and thoughtful.

"Do you know any person resembling the one I have mentioned," said Vivaldi.

"No!" replied the guard.

"Though you have not seen him enter my prison," continued Vivaldi, "you may, perhaps, recollect such a person, as an inhabitant of the Inquisition."

"San Dominico forbid!"

Vivaldi, surprised at this exclamation, inquired the reason for it.

"I know him not," replied the centinel, changing countenance, and he abruptly left the prison. Whatever consideration might occasion this sudden departure, his assertion that he had been for three years a guard of the Inquisition could scarcely be credited, since he had held so long a dialogue with a prisoner, and was, apparently, insensible of the danger he incurred by so doing.

CHAPTER VI

———Is it not dead midnight?
Cold fearful drops stand on my trembling flesh,
What do I fear?

SHAKESPEARE

AT about the same hour, as on the preceding night, Vivaldi heard persons approaching his prison, and, the door unfolding, his former conductors appeared. They threw over him the same mantle as before, and, in addition, a black veil, that completely muffled his eyes; after which, they led him from the chamber. Vivaldi heard the door shut, on his departure, and the centinels followed his steps, as if their duty was finished, and he was to return thither no more. At this moment, he remembered the words of the stranger when he had displayed the poniard, and Vivaldi apprehended the worst, from having thwarted the designs of a person apparently so malignant: but he exulted in the rectitude, which had preserved him from debasement, and, with the magnanimous enthusiasm of virtue, he almost welcomed sufferings, which would prove the firmness of his justice towards an enemy; for he determined to brave every thing, rather than impute to Schedoni circumstances, the truth of which he possessed no means of ascertaining.

While Vivaldi was conducted, as on the preceding night, through many passages, he endeavoured to discover, by their length, and the abruptness of their turnings, whether they were the same he had traversed before. Suddenly, one of his conductors cried "Steps!" It was the first word Vivaldi had ever heard him utter. He immediately perceived that the ground sunk, and he began to descend; as he did which, he tried to count the number of the steps, that he might form some judgment whether this was the flight he had passed before. When he had reached the bottom, he inclined to believe that it was not so; and the care which had been observed in blinding him, seemed to indicate that he was going to some new place.

He passed through several avenues, and then ascended; soon after which, he again descended a very long stair-case, such as he had not any remembrance of, and they passed over a considerable extent of level ground. By the hollow sounds which his steps returned, he judged that he was walking over vaults. The footsteps of the centinels who had followed from the cell were no longer heard, and he seemed to be left with his conductors only. A second flight appeared to lead him into subterraneous vaults, for he perceived the air change, and felt a damp vapour wrap round him. The menace of the monk, that he should meet him in the chambers of death, frequently occurred to Vivaldi.

His conductors stopped in this vault, and seemed to hold a consultation, but they spoke in such low accents, that their words were not distinguishable, except a few unconnected ones, that hinted of more than Vivaldi could comprehend. He was, at length, again led forward; and soon after, he heard the heavy gratings of hinges, and perceived that he was passing through several doors, by the situation of which Vivaldi judged they were the same he had entered the night before, and concluded, that he was going to the hall of the tribunal.

His conductors stopped again, and Vivaldi heard the iron rod strike three times upon a door; immediately a strange voice spoke from within, and the door was unclosed. Vivaldi passed on, and imagined that he was admitted into a spacious vault; for the air was freer, and his steps sounded to a distance.

Presently, a voice, as on the preceding night, summoned him to come forward, and Vivaldi understood that he was again before the tribunal. It was the voice of the inquisitor who had been his chief examiner.

"You, Vincentio di Vivaldi," it said, "answer to your name, and to the questions which shall be put to you, without equivocation, on pain of the torture."

As the monk had predicted, Vivaldi was asked what he knew of father Schedoni, and, when he replied, as he had formerly done to his mysterious visitor, he was told that he knew more than he acknowledged.

"I *know* no more," replied Vivaldi.

"You equivocate," said the inquisitor. "Declare what you have heard, and remember that you formerly took an oath to that purpose."

Vivaldi was silent, till a tremendous voice from the tribunal commanded him to respect his oath.

"I do respect it," said Vivaldi; "and I conjure you to believe that I also respect truth, when I declare, that what I am going to relate, is a report to which I give no confidence, and concerning even the probability of which I cannot produce the smallest proof."

"Respect truth!" said another voice from the tribunal, and Vivaldi fancied he distinguished the tones of the monk. He paused a moment, and the exhortation was repeated. Vivaldi then related what the stranger had said concerning the family of Schedoni, and the disguise which the father had assumed in the convent of the Spirito Santo; but forbore even to name the penitentiary Ansaldo, and any circumstance connected with the extraordinary confession. Vivaldi concluded, with again declaring, that he had not sufficient authority to justify a belief in those reports.

"On what authority do you repeat them?" said the vicar-general.

Vivaldi was silent.

"On what authority?" inquired the inquisitor, sternly.

Vivaldi, after a momentary hesitation, said, "What I am about to declare, holy fathers, is so extraordinary——"

"Tremble!" said a voice close to his ear, which he instantly knew to be the monk's, and the suddenness of which electrified him. He was unable to conclude the sentence.

"What is your authority for the reports?" demanded the inquisitor.

"It is unknown, even to myself!" answered Vivaldi.

"Do not equivocate!" said the vicar-general.

"I solemnly protest," rejoined Vivaldi, "that I know not either the name or the condition of my informer, and that I never even beheld his face, till the period when he spoke of father Schedoni."

"Tremble!" repeated the same low, but emphatic voice in his ear. Vivaldi started, and turned involuntarily towards the sound, though his eyes could not assist his curiosity.

"You did well to say, that you had something extraordinary to add," observed the inquisitor. " 'Tis evident, also, that you expected something extraordinary from your judges, since you supposed they would credit these assertions."

Vivaldi was too proud to attempt the justifying himself against so gross an accusation, or to make any reply.

"Why do you not summon father Ansaldo?" said the voice. "Remember my words!"

Vivaldi, again awed by the voice, hesitated, for an instant, how to act, and in that instant his courage returned.

"My informer stands beside me!" said Vivaldi, boldly; "I know his voice! Detain him; it is of consequence."

"Whose voice?" demanded the inquisitor. "No person spoke but myself!"

"Whose voice?" said the vicar-general.

"The voice was close beside me," replied Vivaldi. "It spoke low, but I knew it well."

"This is either the cunning, or the frenzy of despair!" observed the vicar-general.

"Not any person is now beside you, except the familiars," said the inquisitor, "and they wait to do their office, if you shall refuse to answer the questions put to you."

"I persist in my assertion," replied Vivaldi; "and I supplicate that my eyes may be unbound, that I may know my enemy."

The tribunal, after a long private consultation, granted the request; the veil was withdrawn, and Vivaldi perceived beside him—only the familiars! Their faces, as is usual, were concealed. It appeared that one of these torturers must be the mysterious enemy, who pursued him, if, indeed, that enemy was an inhabitant of the earth! and Vivaldi requested that they might be ordered to uncover their features. He was sternly rebuked for so presumptuous a requisition, and reminded of the inviolable law and faith, which the tribunal had pledged, that persons appointed to their awful office should never be exposed to the revenge of the criminal, whom it might be their duty to punish.

"Their duty!" exclaimed Vivaldi, thrown from his guard by strong indignation. "And is faith held sacred with demons!"

Without awaiting the order of the tribunal, the familiars immediately covered Vivaldi's face with the veil, and he felt himself in their grasp. He endeavoured, however, to disentangle his hands, and, at length, shook these men from their hold, and again unveiled his eyes; but the familiars were instantly ordered to replace the veil.

The inquisitor bade Vivaldi to recollect in whose presence he then was, and to dread the punishment which his resistance had incurred, and which would be inflicted without delay, unless he could give some instance, that might tend to prove the truth of his late assertions.

"If you expect that I should say more," replied Vivaldi, "I claim, at least, protection from the unbidden violence of the men who guard me. If they are suffered, at their pleasure, to sport with the misery of their prisoner, I will be inflexibly silent; and, since I must suffer, it shall be according to the laws of the tribunal."

The vicar-general, or, as he is called, the grand inquisitor, promised Vivaldi the degree of protection he claimed, and demanded, at the same time, what were the words he had just heard.

Vivaldi considered, that, though justice bade him avoid accusing an enemy of suspicious circumstances, concerning which he had no proof, yet, that neither justice nor common sense required he should make a sacrifice of himself to the dilemma in which he was placed: he, therefore, without further scruple, acknowledged, that the voice had bidden him require of the tribunal to summon one father Ansaldo, the grand penitentiary of the Santa del Pianto, near Naples, and also father Schedoni, who was to answer to extraordinary charges, which would be brought against him by Ansaldo. Vivaldi anxiously and repeatedly declared, that he knew not the nature of the charges, nor that any just grounds for them existed.

These assertions seemed to throw the tribunal into new perplexity. Vivaldi heard their busy voices in low debate, which continued for a considerable time. In this interval, he had leisure to perceive the many improbabilities that either of the familiars should be the stranger who so mysteriously haunted him; and among these was the circumstance of his having resided so long at Naples.

The tribunal, after some time had elapsed in consultation, proceeded on the examination, and Vivaldi was asked what he knew of father Ansaldo. He immediately replied, that Ansaldo was an utter stranger to him, and that he was not even acquainted with a single person residing in the Santa del Pianto or who had any knowledge of the penitentiary.

"How!" said the grand inquisitor. "You forget that the person, who bade you require of this tribunal to summon Ansaldo, has knowledge of him."

"Pardon me, I do not forget," replied Vivaldi; "and I request it may be remembered that I am not acquainted with that person. If, therefore, he had given me any account of Ansaldo, I could not have relied upon its authenticity." Vivaldi again required of the tribunal to understand that he did not summon Ansaldo, or any other person, before them, but had merely obeyed their command, to repeat what the stranger had said.

The tribunal acknowledged the justness of this injunction, and exculpated him from any harm that should be the consequence of the summons. But this assurance of safety for himself was not sufficient to appease Vivaldi, who was alarmed lest he should be the means of bringing an innocent person under suspicion. The grand inquisitor again addressed him, after a general silence had been commanded in the court.

"The account you have given of your informer," said he, "is so extraordinary, that it would not deserve credit, but that you have discovered the utmost reluctance to reveal the charges he gave you, from which, it appears, that, on your part, at least, the summons is not malicious. But are you certain that you have not deluded yourself, and that the voice beside you was not an imaginary one, conjured up by your agitated spirits?"

"I am certain," replied Vivaldi, with firmness.

"It is true," resumed the grand inquisitor, "that several persons were near you, when you exclaimed, that you heard the voice of your informer; yet no person heard it besides yourself!"

"Where are those persons now?" demanded Vivaldi.

"They are dispersed; alarmed at your accusation."

"If you will summon them," said Vivaldi, "and order that my eyes may be uncovered, I will point out to you, without hesitation, the person of my informer, should he remain among them."

The tribunal commanded that they should appear, but new difficulties arose. It was not remembered of whom the crowd consisted; a few individuals only were recollected, and these were summoned.

Vivaldi, in solemn expectation, heard steps and the hum

of voices gathering round him, and impatiently awaited for the words that would restore him to sight, and, perhaps, release him from uncertainty. In a few moments, he heard the command given; the veil was once more removed from his eyes, and he was ordered to point out the accuser. Vivaldi threw an hasty glance upon the surrounding strangers.

"The lights burn dimly," said he, "I cannot distinguish these faces."

It was ordered that a lamp should be lowered from the roof, and that the strangers should arrange themselves on either side of Vivaldi. When this was done, and he glanced his eyes again upon the crowd, "He is not here!" said Vivaldi; "not one of these countenances resembles the monk of Paluzzi. Yet, stay; who is he that stands in the shade behind those persons on the left? Bid him lift his cowl!"

The crowd fell back, and the person, to whom Vivaldi had pointed, was left alone within the circle.

"He is an officer of the Inquisition," said a man near Vivaldi, "and he may not be compelled to discover his face, unless by an express command from the tribunal."

"I call upon the tribunal to command it!" said Vivaldi.

"Who calls!" exclaimed a voice, and Vivaldi recognized the tones of the monk, but he knew not exactly whence they came.

"I, Vincentio di Vivaldi," replied the prisoner, "I claim the privilege that has been awarded me, and bid you unveil your countenance."

There was a pause of silence in the court, except that a dull murmur ran through the tribunal. Meanwhile, the figure within the circle stood motionless, and remained veiled.

"Spare him," said the man, who had before addressed Vivaldi; "he has reasons for wishing to remain unknown, which you cannot conjecture. He is an officer of the Inquisition, and not the person you apprehend."

"Perhaps I *can* conjecture his reasons," replied Vivaldi, who, raising his voice, added, "I appeal to this tribunal, and command you, who stand alone within the circle, you in black garments, to unveil your features!"

Immediately a loud voice issued from the tribunal, and said,

"We command you, in the name of the most holy Inquisition, to reveal yourself!"

The stranger trembled, but, without presuming to hesitate,

uplifted his cowl. Vivaldi's eyes were eagerly fixed upon him; but the action disclosed, not the countenance of the monk! but of an official whom he recollected to have seen once before, though exactly on what occasion he did not now remember.

"This is not my informer!" said Vivaldi, turning from him with deep disappointment, while the stranger dropped his cowl, and the crowd closed upon him. At the assertion of Vivaldi, the members of the tribunal looked upon each other doubtingly, and were silent, till the grand inquisitor, waving his hand, as if to command attention, addressed Vivaldi.

"It appears, then, that you *have* formerly seen the face of your informer!"

"I have already declared so," replied Vivaldi.

The grand inquisitor demanded when, and where, he had seen it.

"Last night, and in my prison," answered Vivaldi.

"In your prison!" said the ordinary inquisitor, contemptuously, who had before examined him, "and in your dreams, too, no doubt!"

"In your prison!" exclaimed several members of the lower tribunal.

"He dreams still!" observed an inquisitor. "Holy fathers! he abuses your patience, and the frenzy of terror has deluded his credulity. We neglect the moments."

"We must inquire further into this," said another inquisitor. "Here is some deception. If you, Vincentio di Vivaldi, have asserted a falsehood—tremble!"

Whether Vivaldi's memory still vibrated with the voice of the monk, or that the tone in which this same word was now pronounced did resemble it, he almost started, when the inquisitor had said *tremble*! And he demanded who spoke then.

"It is ourself," answered the inquisitor.

After a short conversation among the members of the tribunal, the grand inquisitor gave orders that the centinels, who had watched on the preceding night at the prison door of Vivaldi, should be brought into the hall of justice. The persons, who had been lately summoned into the chamber, were now bidden to withdraw, and all further examination was suspended till the arrival of the centinels; Vivaldi heard only the low voices of the inquisitors, as they conversed privately together, and he remained silent, thoughtful, and amazed.

When the centinels appeared, and were asked who had entered the prison of Vivaldi during the last night, they declared, without hesitation, or confusion, that not any person had passed through the door after the hour when the prisoner had returned from examination, till the following morning, when the guard had carried in the usual allowance of bread and water. In this assertion, they persisted, without the least equivocation, notwithstanding which they were ordered into confinement, till the affair should be cleared up.

The doubts, however, which were admitted, as to the integrity of these men, did not contribute to dissipate those, which had prevailed over the opposite side of the question. On the contrary, the suspicions of the tribunal, augmenting with their perplexity, seemed to fluctuate equally over every point of the subject before them, till, instead of throwing any light upon the truth, they only served to involve the whole in deeper obscurity. More doubtful than before the honesty of Vivaldi's extraordinary assertions, the grand inquisitor informed him, that if, after further inquiry into this affair, it should appear he had been trifling with the credulity of his judges, he would be severely punished for his audacity; but that, on the other hand, should there be reason to believe that the centinels had failed in their duty, and that some person had entered his prison during the night, the tribunal would proceed in a different manner.

Vivaldi, perceiving that, to be believed, it was necessary he should be more circumstantial, described, with exactness, the person and appearance of the monk, without, however, mentioning the poniard which had been exhibited. A profound silence reigned in the chamber, while he spoke; it seemed a silence not merely of attention, but of astonishment. Vivaldi himself was awed, and, when he had concluded, almost expected to hear the voice of the monk uttering defiance, or threatening vengeance; but all remained hushed, till the inquisitor, who had first examined him, said, in a solemn tone,

"We have listened with attention to what you have delivered, and will give the case a full inquiry. Some points, on which you have touched, excite our amazement, and call for particular regard. Retire whence you came—and sleep this night without fear;—*you will soon know more.*"

Vivaldi was immediately led from the chamber, and, still blind-folded, re-conducted to the prison to which he had supposed it was designed he should return no more. When the veil was withdrawn, he perceived that his guard was changed.

Again left to the silence of his cell, he reviewed all that had passed in the chamber of justice; the questions which had been put to him; the different manners of the inquisitors; the occurrence of the monk's voice; and the similarity, which he had fancied he perceived between it and that of an inquisitor, when the latter pronounced the word *tremble;* but the consideration of all these circumstances did not in any degree relieve him from his perplexity. Sometimes he was inclined to think that the monk was an inquisitor, and the voice had more than once appeared to proceed from the tribunal; but he remembered, also, that, more than once, it had spoken close to his ear, and he knew that a member of this tribunal might not leave his station during the examination of a prisoner, and that, even if he had dared to do so, his singular dress would have pointed him out to notice, and consequently to suspicion, at the moment when Vivaldi had exclaimed, that he had heard the voice of his informer.

Vivaldi, however, could not avoid meditating, with surprise on the last words which the inquisitor, who had been his chief examiner, had addressed to him, when he was dismissed from before the tribunal. These were the more surprising, because they were the first from him that had in any degree indicated a wish to console or quiet the alarm of the prisoner; and Vivaldi even fancied that they betrayed some fore-knowledge that he would not be disturbed this night by the presence of his awful visitor. He would entirely have ceased to apprehend, though not to expect, had he been allowed a light, and any weapon of defence, if, in truth, the stranger was of a nature to fear a weapon; but, to be thus exposed to the designs of a mysterious and powerful being, whom he was conscious of having offended, to sustain such a situation, without suffering anxiety, required somewhat more than courage, or less than reason.

CHAPTER VII

—It came o'er my soul as doth the thunder,
While distant yet, with an unexpected burst,
It threats the trembling ear. Now to the trial.

CARACTACUS

In consequence of what had transpired at the last examination of Vivaldi, the grand penitentiary Ansaldo, together with the father Schedoni, were cited to appear before the table of the holy office.

Schedoni was arrested on his way to Rome, whither he was going privately to make further efforts for the liberation of Vivaldi, whose release he had found it more difficult to effect, than his imprisonment; the person upon whose assistance the Confessor relied in the first instance, having boasted of more influence than he possessed, or perhaps thought it prudent to exert. Schedoni had been the more anxious to procure an immediate release for Vivaldi, lest a report of his situation should reach his family, notwithstanding the precautions, which are usually employed to throw an impenetrable shroud over the prisoners of this dreadful tribunal, and bury them for ever from the knowledge of their friends. Such premature discovery of Vivaldi's circumstances, Schedoni apprehended might include also a discovery of the persecutor, and draw down upon himself the abhorrence and the vengeance of a family, whom it was now, more than ever, his wish and his interest to conciliate. It was still his intention, that the nuptials of Vivaldi and Ellena should be privately solemnized immediately on the release of the prisoner, who, even if he had reason to suspect Schedoni for his late persecutor, would then be interested in concealing his suspicions for ever, and from whom therefore, no evil was to be apprehended.

How little did Vivaldi foresee, that in repeating to the tribunal the stranger's summons of father Schedoni, he was deferring, or, perhaps, wholly preventing his own marriage with Ellena di Rosalba! How little, also, did he apprehend what would be the further consequences of a disclosure, which the peculiar circumstances of his situation had hardly permitted him to withhold, though, could he have understood the probable event of it, he would have braved all the terrors of the tribunal, and death itself, rather than incur the remorse of having promoted it.

The motive for his arrestation was concealed from Schedoni, who had not the remotest suspicion of its nature, but attributed the arrest, to a discovery, which the tribunal had made of his being the accuser of Vivaldi. This disclosure he attributed to his own imprudence, in having stated, as an instance of Vivaldi's contempt for the Catholic faith, that he had insulted a priest while doing penance in the church of the Spirito Santo. But by what art the tribunal had discovered that he was the priest alluded to, and the author of the accusation, Schedoni could by no means conjecture. He was willing to believe that this arrest was only for the purpose of obtaining proof of Vivaldi's guilt; and the Confessor knew that he could so conduct himself in evidence, as in all probability to exculpate the prisoner, from whom, when he should explain himself, no resentment on account of his former conduct was to be apprehended. Yet Schedoni was not perfectly at ease; for it was possible that a knowledge of Vivaldi's situation, and of the author of it, had reached his family, and had produced his own arrest. On this head, however, his fears were not powerful; since, the longer he dwelt upon the subject, the more improbable it appeared that such a disclosure, at least so far as it related to himself, could have been affected.

Vivaldi, from the night of his late examination, was not called upon, till Schedoni and father Ansaldo appeared together in the hall of the tribunal. The two latter had already been separately examined, and Ansaldo had privately stated the particulars of the confession he had received on the vigil of the Santo Marco, in the year 1752, for which disclosure he had received formal absolution. What had passed at that examination does not appear, but on this his second interrogation, he was required to repeat the subject and the circumstances of the confession. This was probably with a view of observing its effect upon Schedoni and on Vivaldi, which would direct the opinion of the tribunal as to the guilt of the Confessor, and the veracity of the young prisoner.

On this night a very exact inquiry was made, concerning every person, who had obtained admission into the hall of justice; such officials as were not immediately necessary to assist in the ceremonies of the tribunal were excluded, together with every other person belonging to the Inquisition not material to the evidence, or to the judges. When this scrutiny was over, the prisoners were brought in, and their conductors ordered to withdraw. A silence of some moments prevailed in the hall; and, however different might be the reflections of the several prisoners, the degree of anxious expectation was in each, probably, nearly the same.

The grand-vicar having spoken a few words in private to a person on his left hand, an inquisitor rose.

"If any person in this court," said he, "is known by the name of father Schedoni, belonging to the Dominican society of the Spirito Santo at Naples, let him appear!"

Schedoni answered to the summons. He came forward with a firm step, and, having crossed himself, and bowed to the tribunal, awaited in silence its commands.

The penitentiary Ansaldo was next called upon. Vivaldi observed that he faultered as he advanced; and that his obeisance to the tribunal was more profound than Schedoni's had been. Vivaldi himself was then summoned; his air was calm and dignified, and his countenance expressed the solemn energy of his feelings, but nothing of dejection.

Schedoni and Ansaldo were now, for the first time, confronted. Whatever might be the feelings of Schedoni on beholding the penitentiary of the Santa del Pianto, he effectually concealed them.

The grand-vicar himself opened the examination, "You, father Schedoni, of the Spirito Santo," he said, "answer and say, whether the person who now stands before you, bearing the title of grand penitentiary of the order of the Black Penitents, and presiding over the convent of the Santa Maria del Pianto at Naples, is known to you."

To this requisition Schedoni replied with firmness in the negative.

"You have never, to your knowledge, seen him before this hour?"

"Never!" said Schedoni.

"Let the oath be administered," added the grand-vicar. Schedoni having accepted it, the same questions were put to Ansaldo concerning the Confessor, when, to the astonishment of Vivaldi and of the greater part of the court, the penitentiary denied all knowledge of Schedoni. His negative was given, however, in a less decisive manner than that of the Confessor, and when the usual oath was offered, Ansaldo declined to accept it.

Vivaldi was next called upon to identify Schedoni: he declared, that the person who was then pointed out to him, he had never known by any other denomination than that of father Schedoni; and that he had always understood him to be a monk of the Spirito Santo; but Vivaldi was at the same time careful to repeat, that he knew nothing further relative to his life.

Schedoni was somewhat surprised at this apparent candour of Vivaldi towards himself, but accustomed to impute an evil motive to all conduct, which he could not clearly comprehend, he did not scruple to believe, that some latent mischief was directed against him in this seemingly honest declaration.

After some further preliminary forms had passed, Ansaldo was ordered to relate the particulars of the confession, which had been made to him on the eve of the Santo Marco. It must be remembered, that this was still what is called in the Inquisition, a *private* examination.

After he had taken the customary oaths to relate neither more nor less than the truth of what had passed before him, Ansaldo's depositions were written down nearly in the following words; to which Vivaldi listened with almost trembling attention, for, besides the curiosity which some previous circumstances had excited respecting them, he believed that his own fate in a great measure depended upon a discovery of the fact to which they led. What, if he had surmised how much! and that the person, whom he had been in some degree instrumental in citing before this tremendous tribunal, was the father of his Ellena di Rosalba!

Ansaldo, having again answered to his name and titles, gave his deposition as follows:

"It was on the eve of the twenty-fifth of April, and in the year 1752, that as I sat, according to my custom, in the confessional of San Marco, I was alarmed by deep groans, which came from the box on my left hand."

Vivaldi observed, that the date now mentioned agreed with that recorded by the stranger, and he was thus prepared to believe what might follow, and to give his confidence to this extraordinary and unseen personage.

Ansaldo continued, "I was the more alarmed by these sounds, because I had not been prepared for them; I knew not that any person was in the confessional, nor had even observed any one pass along the aisle—but the duskiness of the hour may account for my having failed to do so; it was after sun-set, and the tapers at the shrine of San Antonio as yet burned feebly in the twilight."

"Be brief, holy father," said the inquisitor who had formerly been most active in examining Vivaldi; "speak closely to the point."

"The groans would sometimes cease," resumed Ansaldo, "and long pauses of silence follow; they were those of a soul in agony, struggling with the consciousness of guilt, yet wanting resolution to confess it. I tried to encourage the penitent, and held forth every hope of mercy and forgiveness which my duty would allow, but for a considerable time without effect;—the enormity of the sin seemed too big for utterance, yet the penitent appeared equally unable to endure the concealment of it. His heart was bursting with the secret, and required the comfort of absolution, even at the price of the severest penance."

"Facts!" said the inquisitor, "these are only surmises."

"Facts will come full soon!" replied Ansaldo, and bowed his head, "the mention of them will petrify you, holy fathers! as they did me, though not for the same reasons. While I endeavoured to encourage the penitent, and assured him, that absolution should follow the acknowledgment of his crimes, however heinous those crimes might be, if accompanied by sincere repentance, he more than once began his confession, and abruptly dropt it. Once, indeed, he quitted the confessional; his agitated spirit required liberty; and it was then, as he walked with perturbed steps along the aisle, that I first observed his figure. He was in the habit of a white friar, and, as nearly as I can recollect, was about the stature of him, the father Schedoni, who now stands before me."

As Ansaldo delivered these words, the attention of the whole tribunal was turned upon Schedoni, who stood unmoved, and with his eyes bent towards the ground.

"His face," continued the penitentiary, "I did not see; he was, with good reason, careful to conceal it; other resemblance, therefore, than the stature, I cannot point out between them. The voice, indeed, the voice of the penitent, I think I shall never forget; I should know it again at any distance of time."

"Has it not struck your ear, since you came within these walls?" said a member of the tribunal.

"Of that hereafter," observed the inquisitor, "you wander from the point, father."

The vicar-general remarked, that the circumstances just related were important, and ought not to be passed over as irrelevant. The inquisitor submitted to this opinion, but objected that they were not pertinent to the moment; and Ansaldo was again bidden to repeat what he had heard at confession.

"When the stranger returned to the steps of the confessional, he had acquired sufficient resolution to go through with the task he had imposed upon himself, and a thrilling voice spoke through the grate the facts I am about to relate."

Father Ansaldo paused, and was somewhat agitated; he seemed endeavouring to recollect courage to go through with what he had begun. During this pause, the silence of expectation rapt the court, and the eyes of the tribunal were directed alternately to Ansaldo and Schedoni, who certainly required something more than human firmness to support unmoved the severe scrutiny, and the yet severer suspicions, to which he stood exposed. Whether, however, it was the fortitude of conscious innocence, or the hardihood of atrocious vice, that protected the Confessor, he certainly did not betray any emotion. Vivaldi, who had unceasingly observed him from the commencement of the depositions, felt inclined to believe that he was not the penitent described. Ansaldo, having, at length, recollected himself, proceeded as follows:

" 'I have been through life,' said the penitent, 'the slave of my passions, and they have led me into horrible excesses. I had once a brother!'— He stopped, and deep groans again told the agony of his soul; at length, he added—'That brother had a wife!— Now listen, father, and say, whether guilt like mine may hope for absolution! She was beautiful— I loved her; she was virtuous, and I despaired. You, father,' he continued in a frightful tone, 'never knew the fury of despair! It overcame or communicated its own

force to every other passion of my soul, and I sought to release myself from its tortures by any means. My brother
died!'—The penitent paused again," continued Ansaldo, "I
trembled while I listened; my lips were sealed. At length, I
bade him proceed, and he spoke as follows.—'My brother
died at a distance from home.'— Again the penitent paused,
and the silence continued so long, that I thought it proper to
inquire of what disorder the brother had expired. 'Father, I
was his murderer!' said the penitent in a voice which I never
can forget; it sunk into my heart."

Ansaldo appeared affected by the remembrance, and was
for a moment silent. At the last words Vivaldi had particularly noticed Schedoni, that he might judge by their effect
upon him, whether he was guilty; but he remained in his
former attitude, and his eyes were still fixed upon the
ground.

"Proceed, father!" said the inquisitor, "what was your reply to this confession?"

"I was silent," said Ansaldo; "but at length I bade the penitent go on. 'I contrived' said he, 'that my brother should die
at a distance from home, and I so conducted the affair, that his
widow never suspected the cause of his death. It was not till
long after the usual time of mourning had expired, that I ventured to solicit her hand: but she had not yet forgotten my
brother, and she rejected me. My passion would no longer be
trifled with. I caused her to be carried from her house, and she
was afterwards willing to retrieve her honour by the marriage
vow. I had sacrificed my conscience, without having found
happiness;——she did not even condescend to conceal her disdain. Mortified, exasperated by her conduct, I begun to suspect
that some other emotion than resentment occasioned this disdain; and last of all jealousy—jealousy came to crown my
misery—to light up all my passions into madness!' "

"The penitent," added Ansaldo, "appeared by the manner
in which he uttered this, to be nearly frantic at the moment,
and convulsive sobs soon stifled his words. When he resumed his confession, he said, 'I soon found an object for
my jealousy. Among the few persons, who visited us in the
retirement of our country residence, was a gentleman, who,
I fancied, loved my wife; I fancied too, that, whenever he
appeared, an air of particular satisfaction was visible on her
countenance. She seemed to have pleasure in conversing
with, and shewing him distinction. I even sometimes

thought, she had pride in displaying to me the preference she entertained for him, and that an air of triumph, and even of scorn, was addressed to me, whenever she mentioned his name. Perhaps, I mistook resentment for love, and she only wished to punish me, by exciting my jealousy. Fatal error! she punished herself also!' "

"Be less circumstantial, father," said the inquisitor.

Ansaldo bowed his head, and continued. " 'One evening,' continued the penitent, 'that I returned home unexpectedly, I was told that a visitor was with my wife! As I approached the apartment where they sat, I heard the voice of Sacchi; it seemed mournful and supplicating. I stopped to listen, and distinguished enough to fire me with vengeance. I restrained myself, however, so far as to step softly to a lattice that opened from the passage, and overlooked the apartment. The traitor was on his knee before her. Whether she had heard my step, or observed my face, through the high lattice, or that she resented his conduct, I know not, but she rose immediately from her chair. I did not pause to question her motive; but, seizing my stiletto, I rushed into the room, with intent to strike it to the villain's heart. The supposed assassin of my honour escaped into the garden, and was heard of no more.'—But your wife? said I. 'Her bosom received the poniard!' replied the penitent."

Ansaldo's voice faltered, as he repeated this part of the confession, and he was utterly unable to proceed. The tribunal, observing his condition, allowed him a chair, and, after a struggle of some moments, he added, "Think, holy fathers, O think! what must have been my feelings at that instant! I was myself the lover of the woman, whom he confessed himself to have murdered."

"Was she innocent?" said a voice; and Vivaldi, whose attention had latterly been fixed upon Ansaldo, now, on looking at Schedoni, perceived that it was he who had spoken. At the sound of his voice, the penitentiary turned instantly towards him. There was a pause of general silence, during which Ansaldo's eyes were earnestly fixed upon the accused. At length, he spoke, "She was innocent!" He replied, with solemn emphasis, "She was most virtuous!"

Schedoni had shrunk back within himself; he asked no further. A murmur ran through the tribunal, which rose by degrees, till it broke forth into audible conversation; at length, the secretary was directed to note the question of Schedoni.

"Was that the voice of the penitent, which you have just heard?" demanded the inquisitor of Ansaldo. "Remember, you have said that you should know it again!"

"I think it was," replied Ansaldo; "but I cannot swear to that."

"What infirmity of judgment is this!" said the same inquisitor, who himself was seldom troubled with the modesty of doubt, upon any subject. Ansaldo was bidden to resume the narrative.

"On this discovery of the murderer," said the penitentiary, "I quitted the confessional, and my senses forsook me before I could deliver orders for the detection of the assassin. When I recovered, it was too late; he had escaped! From that hour to the present, I have never seen him, nor dare I affirm that the person now before me is he."

The inquisitor was about to speak, but the grand-vicar waved his hand, as a signal for attention, and, addressing Ansaldo, said, "Although you may be unacquainted with Schedoni, the monk of the Spirito Santo, reverend father, can you not recollect the person of the Count di Bruno, your former friend?"

Ansaldo again looked at Schedoni, with a scrutinizing eye; he fixed it long; but the countenance of Schedoni suffered no change.

"No!" said the penitentiary, at length, "I dare not take upon me to assert, that this is the Count di Bruno. If it is he, years have wrought deeply on his features. That the penitent was the Count di Bruno I have proof; he mentioned my name as his visitor, and particular circumstances known only to the Count and myself; but that father Schedoni was the penitent, I repeat it, I dare not affirm."

"But that dare I!" said another voice; and Vivaldi, turning towards it, beheld the mysterious stranger advancing, his cowl now thrown back, and an air of menace overspreading every terrific feature. Schedoni, in the instant that he perceived him, seemed agitated; his countenance, for the first time, suffered some change.

The tribunal was profoundly silent, but surprise, and a kind of restless expectation, marked every brow. Vivaldi was about to exclaim, "That is my informer!" when the voice of the stranger checked him.

"Dost thou know me?" said he, sternly, to Schedoni, and his attitude became fixed.

Schedoni gave no reply.

"Dost thou know me?" repeated his accuser, in a steady solemn voice.

"Know thee!" uttered Schedoni, faintly.

"Dost thou know this?" cried the stranger, raising his voice, as he drew from his garment what appeared to be a dagger. "Dost thou know these indelible stains?" said he, lifting the poniard, and, with an outstretched arm, pointing it towards Schedoni.

The Confessor turned away his face; it seemed as if his heart sickened.

"With this dagger was thy brother slain!" said the terrible stranger. "Shall I declare myself?"

Schedoni's courage forsook him, and he sunk against a pillar of the hall for support.

The consternation was now general; the extraordinary appearance and conduct of the stranger seemed to strike the greater part of the tribunal, a tribunal of the inquisition itself! with dismay. Several of the members rose from their seats; others called aloud for the officials, who kept guard at the doors of the hall, and inquired who had admitted the stranger, while the vicar-general and a few inquisitors conversed privately together, during which they frequently looked at the stranger and at Schedoni, as if they were the subjects of the discourse. Meanwhile the monk remained with the dagger in his grasp, and his eyes fixed on the Confessor, whose face was still averted, and who yet supported himself against the pillar.

At length, the vicar-general called upon the members who had arisen to return to their seats, and ordered that the officials should withdraw to their posts.

"Holy brethren!" said the vicar, "we recommend to you, at this important hour, silence and deliberation. Let the examination of the accused proceed; and hereafter let us inquire as to the admittance of the accuser. For the present, suffer him also to have hearing, and the father Schedoni to reply."

"We suffer him!" answered the tribunal, and bowed their heads.

Vivaldi, who, during the tumult, had ineffectually endeavoured to make himself heard, now profited by the pause which followed the assent of the inquisitors, to claim attention: but the instant he spoke several members impatiently bade that the examination should proceed, and the grand-vicar was again obliged to command silence, before the request of Vivaldi could be understood. Permission to speak being granted him, "That person," said he, pointing to the stranger, "is the same who visited me in my prison; and the dagger the same he now displays! It was he, who commanded me to summon the penitentiary Ansaldo, and the father Schedoni. I have acquitted myself, and have nothing further to do in this struggle."

The tribunal was again agitated, and the murmurs of private conversation again prevailed. Meanwhile Schedoni appeared to have recovered some degree of self-command; he raised himself, and, bowing to the tribunal, seemed preparing to speak; but waited till the confusion of sound that filled the hall should subside. At length he could be heard, and, addressing the tribunal, he said,

"Holy fathers! the stranger who is now before you is an impostor! I will prove that my accuser was once my friend;—you may perceive how much the discovery of his perfidy affects me. The charge he brings is most false and malicious!"

"*Once* thy friend!" replied the stranger, with peculiar emphasis, "and what has made me thy enemy! View these spots," he continued, pointing to the blade of the poniard, "are they also false and malicious? are they not, on the contrary, reflected on thy conscience?"

"I know them not," replied Schedoni, "my conscience is unstained."

"A brother's blood *has* stained it!" said the stranger, in a hollow voice.

Vivaldi, whose attention was now fixed upon Schedoni, observed a livid hue overspread his complexion, and that his eyes were averted from this extraordinary person with horror: the spectre of his deceased brother could scarcely have called forth a stronger expression. It was not immediately that he could command his voice; when he could, he again appealed to the tribunal.

"Holy fathers!" said he, "suffer me to defend myself."

"Holy fathers!" said the accuser, with solemnity, "hear! hear what I shall unfold!"

Schedoni, who seemed to speak by a strong effort only,

again addressed the inquisitors; "I will prove," said he, "that this evidence is not of a nature to be trusted."

"I will bring *such* proof to the contrary!" said the monk. "And here," pointing to Ansaldo, "is sufficient testimony that the Count di Bruno did confess himself guilty of murder."

The court commanded silence, and upon the appeal of the stranger to Ansaldo, the penitentiary was asked whether he knew him. He replied, that he did not.

"Recollect yourself," said the grand inquisitor, "it is of the utmost consequence that you should be correct on this point."

The penitentiary observed the stranger with deep attention, and then repeated his assertion.

"Have you never seen him before?" said an inquisitor.

"Never, to my knowledge!" replied Ansaldo.

The inquisitors looked upon each other in silence.

"He speaks the truth," said the stranger.

This extraordinary fact did not fail to strike the tribunal, and to astonish Vivaldi. Since the accuser confirmed it, Vivaldi was at a loss to understand the means by which he could have become acquainted with the guilt of Schedoni, who, it was not to be supposed, would have acknowledged crimes of such magnitude as those contained in the accusation, to any person, except, indeed, to his confessor, and this confessor, it appeared, was so far from having betrayed his trust to the accuser, that he did not even know him. Vivaldi was no less perplexed as to what would be the nature of the testimony with which the accuser designed to support his charges: but the pause of general amazement, which had permitted Vivaldi these considerations, was now at an end; the tribunal resumed the examination, and the grand inquisitor called aloud,

"You, Vincentio di Vivaldi, answer with exactness to the questions that shall be put to you."

He was then asked some questions relative to the person, who had visited him in prison. In his answers, Vivaldi was clear and concise, constantly affirming, that the stranger was the same, who now accused Schedoni.

When the accuser was interrogated, he acknowledged, without hesitation, that Vivaldi had spoken the truth. He was then asked his motive for that extraordinary visit.

"It was," replied the monk, "that a murderer might be brought to justice."

"This," observed the grand inquisitor, "might have been accomplished by fair and open accusation. If you had known the charge to be just, it is probable that you would have appealed directly to this tribunal, instead of endeavouring insidiously to obtain an influence over the mind of a prisoner, and urging him to become the instrument of bringing the accused to punishment."

"Yet I have not shrunk from discovery," observed the stranger, calmly; "I have voluntarily appeared."

At these words, Schedoni seemed again much agitated, and even drew his hood over his eyes.

"That is just," said the grand inquisitor, addressing the stranger: "but you have neither declared your name, or whence you come!"

To this remark the monk made no reply; but Schedoni, with reviving spirit, urged the circumstance, in evidence of the malignity and falshood of the accuser.

"Wilt thou compel me to reveal my proof?" said the stranger: "Darest thou to do so?"

"Why should I fear thee?" answered Schedoni.

"Ask thy conscience!" said the stranger, with a terrible frown.

The tribunal again suspended the examination, and consulted in private together.

To the last exhortation of the monk, Schedoni was silent. Vivaldi observed, that during this short dialogue, the Confessor had never once turned his eyes towards the stranger, but apparently avoided him, as an object too affecting to be looked upon. He judged, from this circumstance, and from some other appearances in his conduct, that Schedoni was guilty; yet the consciousness of guilt alone did not perfectly account, he thought, for the strong emotion, with which he avoided the sight of his accuser—unless, indeed, he knew that accuser to have been, not only an accomplice in his crime, but the actual assassin. In this case, it appeared natural even for the stern and subtle Schedoni to betray his horror, on beholding the person of the murderer, with the very instrument of crime in his grasp. On the other hand, Vivaldi could not but perceive it to be highly improbable, that the very man who had really committed the deed should come voluntarily into a court of justice, for the purpose of accusing his employer; that he should dare publicly to accuse him, whose guilt, however enormous, was not more so than his own.

The extraordinary manner, also, in which the accuser had proceeded in the commencement of the affair, engaged Vivaldi's consideration; his apparent reluctance to be seen in this process, and the artful and mysterious plan by which he had caused Schedoni to be summoned before the tribunal, and had endeavoured that he should be there accused by Ansaldo, indicated, at least to Vivaldi's apprehension, the fearfulness of guilt, and, still more, that malice, and a thirst of vengeance, had instigated his conduct in the prosecution. If the stranger had been actuated only by a love of justice, it appeared that he would not have proceeded toward it in a way thus dark and circuitous, but have sought it by the usual process, and have produced the proofs, which he even now asserted he possessed, of Schedoni's crimes. In addition to the circumstances, which seemed to strengthen a supposition of the guiltlessness of Schedoni, was that of the accuser's avoiding to acknowledge who he was, and whence he came. But Vivaldi paused again upon this point; it appeared to be inexplicable, and he could not imagine why the accuser had adopted a style of secrecy, which, if he persisted in it, must probably defeat the very purpose of the accusation; for Vivaldi did not believe that the tribunal would condemn a prisoner upon the testimony of a person who, when called upon, should publicly refuse to reveal himself, even to them. Yet the accuser must certainly have considered this circumstance before he ventured into court; notwithstanding which, he had appeared!

These reflections led Vivaldi to various conjectures relative to the visit he had himself received from the monk, the dream that had preceded it, the extraordinary means by which he had obtained admittance to the prison, the declaration of the centinels, that not any person had passed the door, and many other unaccountable particulars; and, while Vivaldi now looked upon the wild physiognomy of the stranger, he almost fancied, as he had formerly done, that he beheld something not of this earth.

"I have heard of the spirit of the murdered," said he, to himself—"restless for justice, becoming visible in our world—" But Vivaldi checked the imperfect thought, and, though his imagination inclined him to the marvellous, and to admit ideas which, filling and expanding all the faculties of the soul, produce feelings that partake of the sublime, he now resisted the propensity, and dismissed, as absurd, a supposition, which had begun to thrill his every nerve with horror. He awaited, however, the result of the examination, and what might be the further conduct of the stranger, with intense expectation.

When the tribunal had, at length, finally determined on the method of their proceedings, Schedoni was first called upon, and examined as to his knowledge of the accuser. It was the same inquisitor who had formerly interrogated Vivaldi, that now spoke. "You, father Schedoni, a monk of the Spirito Santo convent, at Naples, otherwise Ferando Count di Bruno, answer to the questions which shall be put to you. Do you know the name of this man who now appears as your accuser?"

"I answer not to the title of Count di Bruno," replied the Confessor, "but I will declare that I know this man. His name is Nicola di Zampari."

"What is his condition?"

"He is a monk of the Dominican convent of the Spirito Santo," replied Schedoni. "Of his family I know little."

"Where have you seen him?"

"In the city of Naples, where he has resided, during some years, beneath the same roof with me, when I was of the convent of San Angiolo, and since that time, in the Spirito Santo."

"You have been a resident at the San Angiolo?" said the inquisitor.

"I have," replied Schedoni; "and it was there that we first lived together in the confidence of friendship."

"You now perceive how ill placed was that confidence," said the inquisitor, "and repent, no doubt, of your imprudence?"

The wary Schedoni was not entrapped by this observation.

"I must lament a discovery of ingratitude," he replied, calmly, "but the subjects of my confidence were too pure to give occasion for repentance."

"This Nicola di Zampari was ungrateful, then? You had rendered him services?" said the inquisitor.

"The cause of his enmity I can well explain," observed Schedoni, evading, for the present, the question.

"Explain," said the stranger, solemnly.

Schedoni hesitated; some sudden consideration seemed to occasion him perplexity.

"I call upon you, in the name of your deceased brother," said the accuser, "to reveal the cause of my enmity!"

Vivaldi, struck by the tone in which the stranger spoke this, turned his eyes upon him, but knew not how to interpret the emotion visible on his countenance.

The inquisitor commanded Schedoni to explain himself; the latter could not immediately reply, but, when he recovered a self-command, he added,

"I promised this accuser, this Nicola di Zampari, to assist his preferment with what little interest I possessed; it was but little. Some succeeding circumstances encouraged me to believe that I could more than fulfil my promise. His hopes were elevated, and, in the fulness of expectation—he was disappointed, for I was myself deceived, by the person in whom I had trusted. To the disappointment of a choleric man, I am to attribute this unjust accusation."

Schedoni paused, and an air of dissatisfaction and anxiety appeared upon his features. His accuser remained silent, but a malicious smile announced his triumph.

"You must declare, also, the services," said the inquisitor, "which merited the reward you promised."

"Those services were inestimable to me," resumed Schedoni, after a momentary hesitation; "though they cost di Zampari little: they were the consolations of sympathy, the intelligence of friendship, which he administered, and which gratitude told me never could be repaid."

"Of sympathy! of friendship!" said the grand-vicar. "Are we to believe that a man, who brings false accusation of so dreadful a nature as the one now before us, is capable of bestowing the consolations of sympathy, and of friendship? You must either acknowledge, that services of a less disinterested nature won your promises of reward; or we must conclude that your accuser's charge is just. Your assertions are inconsistent, and your explanation too trivial, to deceive for a moment."

"I have declared the truth," said Schedoni, haughtily.

"In which instance?" asked the inquisitor; "for your assertions contradict each other!"

Schedoni was silent. Vivaldi could not judge whether the pride which occasioned his silence was that of innocence, or of remorse.

"It appears, from your own testimony," said the inquisitor, "that the ingratitude was yours, not your accuser's, since he consoled you with kindness, which you have never returned him!—Have you any thing further to say?"

Schedoni was still silent.

"This, then, is your only explanation?" added the inquisitor.

Schedoni bowed his head. The inquisitor then, addressing the accuser, demanded what he had to reply.

"I have nothing to reply," said the stranger, with malicious triumph; "the accused has replied for me!"

"We are to conclude, then, that he has spoken truth, when he asserted you to be a monk of the Spirito Santo, at Naples?" said the inquisitor.

"You, holy father," said the stranger, gravely, appealing to the inquisitor, "can answer for me, whether I am."

Vivaldi listened with emotion.

The inquisitor rose from his chair, and with solemnity replied, "I answer, then, that you are not a monk of Naples."

"By that reply," said the vicar-general, in a low voice, to the inquisitor, "I perceive you think father Schedoni is guilty."

The rejoinder of the inquisitor was delivered in so low a tone, that Vivaldi could not understand it. He was perplexed to interpret the answer given to the appeal of the stranger. He thought that the inquisitor would not have ventured an assertion thus positive, if his opinion had been drawn from inference only; and that he should know the accuser, while he was conducting himself towards him as a stranger, amazed Vivaldi, no less than if he had understood the character of an inquisitor to be as artless as his own. On the other hand, he had so frequently seen the stranger at Paluzzi, and in the habit of a monk, that he could hardly question the assertion of Schedoni, as to his identity.

The inquisitor, addressing Schedoni, said, "Your evidence we know to be in part erroneous; your accuser is not a monk of Naples, but a servant of the most holy Inquisition. Judging, from this part of your evidence, we must suspect the whole."

"A servant of the Inquisition!" exclaimed Schedoni, with unaffected surprise. "Reverend father! your assertion astonishes me! You are deceived, however strange it may appear, trust me, you are deceived! You doubt the credit of my word; I, therefore, will assert no more. But inquire of Signor Vivaldi; ask him, whether he has not often, and lately, seen my accuser at Naples, and in the habit of a monk."

"I have seen him at the ruins of Paluzzi, near Naples, and in the ecclesiastical dress," replied Vivaldi, without waiting for the regular question, "and under circumstances no less extraordinary than those which have attended him here. But, in return for this frank acknowledgment, I require of you, father Schedoni, to answer some questions which I shall venture to suggest to the tribunal—By what means were you informed that I have often seen the stranger at Paluzzi—and was you interested or not in his mysterious conduct towards me there?"

To these questions, though formally delivered from the tribunal, Schedoni did not deign to reply.

"It appears, then," said the vicar-general, "that the accuser and the accused were once accomplices."

The inquisitor objected, that this did not certainly appear; and that, on the contrary, Schedoni seemed to have given his last questions in despair; an observation which Vivaldi thought extraordinary from an inquisitor.

"Be it *accomplices*, if it so please you," said Schedoni, bowing to the grand-vicar, without noticing the inquisitor: "you may call us accomplices, but I say, that we were *friends*. Since it is necessary to my own peace, that I should more fully explain some circumstances attending our intimacy, I will own that my accuser was occasionally my agent, and assisted in preserving the dignity of an illustrious family at Naples, the family of the Vivaldi. And there, holy father," added Schedoni, pointing to Vincentio, "is the son of that ancient house, for whom I have attempted so much!"

Vivaldi was almost overwhelmed by this confession of Schedoni, though he had already suspected a part of the truth. In the stranger he believed he saw the slanderer of Ellena, the base instrument of the Marchesa's policy, and of Schedoni's ambition; and the whole of his conduct at Paluzzi, at least, seemed now intelligible. In Schedoni he beheld his secret accuser, and the inexorable enemy whom he believed to have occasioned the imprisonment of Ellena. At this latter consideration, all circumspection, all prudence forsook him: he declared, with energy, that, from what Schedoni had just acknowledged to be his conduct, he knew him for his secret accuser, and the accuser, also, of Ellena di

Rosalba; and he called upon the tribunal to examine into the Confessor's motives for the accusation, and afterwards to give hearing to what he would himself unfold.

To this, the grand-vicar replied, that Vivaldi's appeal would be taken into consideration; and he then ordered that the present business should proceed.

The inquisitor, addressing Schedoni, said, "The disinterested nature of your friendship is now sufficiently explained, and the degree of credit, which is due to your late assertions understood. Of you we ask no more, but turn to father Nicola di Zampari, and demand what he has to say in support of his accusation. What are your proofs, Nicola di Zampari, that he who calls himself father Schedoni is Ferando Count di Bruno; and that he has been guilty of murder, the murder of his brother, and of his wife? Answer to our charge!"

"To your first question," said the monk, "I reply that he has himself acknowledged to me, on an occasion, which it is not necessary to mention, that he was the Count di Bruno; to the last, I produce the poniard which I received, with the dying confession of the assassin whom he employed."

"Still, these are not proofs, but assertions," observed the vicar-general, "and the first forbids our confidence in the second.—If, as you declare, Schedoni himself acknowledged to you that he was Count di Bruno, you must have been to him the intimate friend he has declared you were, or he would not have confided to you a secret so dangerous to himself. And, if you were that friend, what confidence ought we to give to your assertions respecting the dagger? since, whether your accusations be true or false, you prove yourself guilty of treachery in bringing them forward at all."

Vivaldi was surprised to hear such candour from an inquisitor.

"Here is my proof," said the stranger, who now produced a paper, containing what he asserted to be the dying confession of the assassin. It was signed by a priest of Rome, as well as by himself, and appeared from the date to have been given only a very few weeks before. The priest, he said, was living, and might be summoned. The tribunal issued an order for the apprehension of this priest, and that he should be brought to give evidence on the following evening; after which, the business of this night proceeded, without further interruption, towards its conclusion.

The vicar-general spoke again, "Nicola di Zampari, I call upon you to say, why, if your proof of Schedoni's guilt is so clear, as the confession of the assassin himself must make it,—why you thought it necessary to summon father Ansaldo to attest the criminality of the Count di Bruno? The dying confession of the assassin is certainly of more weight than any other evidence."

"I summoned the father Ansaldo," replied the stranger, "as a means of proving that Schedoni is the Count di Bruno. The confession of the assassin sufficiently proves the Count to have been the instigator of the murder, but not that Schedoni is the Count."

"But that is more than I will engage to prove," replied Ansaldo, "I know it was the Count di Bruno who confessed to me, but I do not know that the father Schedoni, who is now before me, was the person who so confessed."

"Conscientiously observed!" said the vicar-general, interrupting the stranger, who was about to reply, "but you, Nicola di Zampari, have not on this head been sufficiently explicit.— How do you know that Schedoni is the penitent who confessed to Ansaldo on the vigil of San Marco?"

"Reverend father, that is the point I was about to explain," replied the monk. "I myself accompanied Schedoni, on the eve of San Marco, to the church of the Santa Maria del Pianto, at the very hour when the confession is said to have been made. Schedoni told me he was going to confession; and, when I observed to him his unusual agitation, his behaviour implied a consciousness of extraordinary guilt; he even betrayed it by some words, which he dropt in the confusion of his mind. I parted with him at the gates of the church. He was then of an order of white friars, and habited as father Ansaldo has described. Within a few weeks after this confession, he left his convent, for what reason I never could learn, though I have often surmised it, and came to reside at the Spirito Santo, whither I also had removed."

"Here is no proof," said the vicar-general, "other friars of that order might confess at the same hour, in the same church."

"But here is strong presumption for proof," observed the inquisitor. "Holy father, we must judge from probabilities, as well as from proof."

"But probabilities themselves," replied the vicar-general, "are strongly against the evidence of a man, who would betray another by means of words dropped in the unguarded moments of powerful emotion."

"Are these the sentiments of an inquisitor!" said Vivaldi to himself, "can such glorious candour appear amidst the tribunal of an Inquisition!" Tears fell fast on Vivaldi's cheek while he gazed upon this just judge, whose candour, had it been exerted in his cause, could not have excited more powerful sensations of esteem and admiration. "An inquisitor!" he repeated to himself, "an inquisitor!"

The inferior inquisitor, however, was so far from possessing any congeniality of character with his superior, that he was evidently disappointed by the appearance of liberality, which the vicar-general discovered, and immediately said, "Has the accuser any thing further to urge in evidence, that the father Schedoni is the penitent, who confessed to the penitentiary Ansaldo?"

"I have," replied the monk, with asperity. "When I had left Schedoni in the church, I lingered without the walls for his return, according to appointment. But he appeared considerably sooner than I expected, and in a state of disorder, such as I had never witnessed in him before. In an instant he passed me, nor could my voice arrest his progress. Confusion seemed to reign within the church and the convent, and, when I would have entered, for the purpose of inquiring the occasion of it, the gates were suddenly closed, and all entrance forbidden. It has since appeared, that the monks were then searching for the penitent. A rumour afterwards reached me, that a confession had caused this disturbance; that the father-confessor, who happened at that time to be the grand penitentiary Ansaldo, had left the chair in horror of what had been divulged from the grate, and had judged it necessary that a search should be made for the penitent, who was a white friar. This report, reverend fathers, excited general attention; with me it did more—for I thought I knew the penitent. When on the following day, I questioned Schedoni as to his sudden departure from the church of the Black Penitents, his answers were dark, but emphatic, and he extorted from me a promise, thoughtless that I was! never to disclose his visit of the preceding evening to the *Santa del Pianto*. I then certainly discovered who was the penitent."

"Did he, then, confess to you also?" said the vicar-general.

"No father. I understood him to be the penitent to whom

the report alluded, but I had no suspicion of the nature of his crimes, till the assassin began his confession, the conclusion of which clearly explained the subject of Schedoni's; it explained also his motive for endeavouring ever after to attach me to his interest."

"You have now," said the vicar-general, "you have now, confessed yourself a member of the convent of the Spirito Santo at Naples, and an intimate of the father Schedoni; one whom for many years he has endeavoured to attach to him. Not an hour has passed since you denied all this; the negative to the latter circumstance was given, it is true, by implication only; but to the first a direct and absolute denial was pronounced!"

"I denied that I *am* a monk of Naples," replied the accuser, "and I appealed to the Inquisitor for the truth of my denial. He had said, that I am now a servant of the most holy Inquisition."

The vicar-general, with some surprise, looked at the inquisitor for explanation; other members of the tribunal did the same; the rest appeared to understand more than they had thought it necessary to avow. The inquisitor, who had been called upon, rose, and replied,

"Nicola di Zampari has spoken the truth. It is not many weeks since he entered the holy office. A certificate from his convent at Naples bears testimony to the truth of what I advance, and procured him admittance here."

"It is extraordinary that you should not have disclosed your knowledge of this person before!" said the vicar-general.

"Holy father, I had reasons," replied the inquisitor, "you will recollect that the accused was present, and you will understand them."

"I comprehend you," said the vicar-general, "but I do neither approve of, nor perceive any necessity for your countenancing the subterfuge of this Nicola di Zampari, relative to his identity. But more of this in private."

"I will explain all there," answered the inquisitor.

"It appears then," resumed the vicar-general, speaking aloud, "that this Nicola di Zampari was formerly the friend and confidant of father Schedoni, whom he now accuses. The accusation is evidently malicious; whether it be also false, remains to be decided. A material question naturally arises out of the subject—Why was not the accusation brought forward before this period?"

The monk's visage brightened with the satisfaction of anticipated triumph, and he immediately replied.

"Most holy father! as soon as I ascertained the crime, I prepared to prosecute the perpetrator of it. A short period only has elapsed since the assassin gave his confession. In this interval I discovered, in these prisons, Signor Vivaldi, and immediately comprehended by whose means he was confined. I knew enough both of the accuser and accused, to understand which of these was innocent, and had then a double motive for causing Schedoni to be summoned;—I wished equally to deliver the innocent and punish the criminal. The question as to the motive for my becoming the enemy of him, who was once my friend, is already answered;—it was a sense of justice, not a suggestion of malice."

The grand-vicar smiled, but asked no further; and this long examination concluded with committing Schedoni again into close custody, till full evidence should be obtained of his guilt, or his innocence should appear. Respecting the manner of his wife's death, there was yet no other evidence than that which was asserted to be his own confession, which, though perhaps sufficient to condemn a criminal before the tribunal of the Inquisition, was not enough to satisfy the present vicar-general, who gave direction that means might be employed towards obtaining proof of each article of the accusation; in order that, should Schedoni be acquitted of the charge of having murdered his brother, documents might appear for prosecuting him respecting the death of his wife.

Schedoni, when he withdrew from the hall, bowed respectfully to the tribunal, and whether, notwithstanding late appearances, he were innocent, or that subtlety enabled him to reassume his usual address, it is certain his manner no longer betrayed any symptom of conscious guilt. His countenance was firm and even tranquil, and his air dignified. Vivaldi, who, during the greater part of this examination, had been convinced of his criminality, now only doubted his innocence. Vivaldi was himself reconducted to his prison, and the sitting of the tribunal was dissolved.

CHAPTER VIII

The time shall come when Glo'ster's heart shall bleed
In life's last hours with horrors of the deed;
When dreary visions shall at last present
Thy vengeful image.——

COLLINS

WHEN the night of Schedoni's trial arrived, Vivaldi was again summoned to the hall of the tribunal. Every circumstance was now arranged according to the full ceremonies of the place; the members of the tribunal were more numerous than formerly at the examinations; the chief inquisitors wore habits of a fashion different from those, which before distinguished them, and their turbans, of a singular form and larger size, seemed to give an air of sterner ferocity to their features. The hall, as usual, was hung with black, and every person who appeared there, whether inquisitor, official, witness or prisoner, was habited in the same dismal hue, which, together with the kind of light diffused through the chamber from lamps hung high in the vaulted roof, and from torches held by parties of officials who kept watch at the several doors, and in different parts of this immense hall, gave a character of gloomy solemnity to the assembly, which was almost horrific.

Vivaldi was situated in a place, whence he beheld the whole of the tribunal, and could distinguish whatever was passing in the hall. The countenance of every member was now fully displayed to him by the torchmen, who, arranged at the steps of the platform on which the three chief inquisitors were elevated, extended in a semicircle on either hand of the place occupied by the inferior members. The red glare, which the torches threw upon the latter, certainly did not soften the expression of faces, for the most part sculptured by passions of dark malignity, or fiercer cruelty; and Vivaldi could not bear even to examine them long.

Before the bar of the tribunal, he distinguished Schedoni, and little did he suspect, that in him, a criminal brought thither to answer for the guilt of murder—the murder of a brother, and of a wife, he beheld the parent of Ellena di Rosalba!

Near Schedoni was seated the penitentiary Ansaldo; the Roman priest, who was to be a principal witness, and father Nicola di Zampari, upon whom Vivaldi could not even now look without experiencing somewhat of the awe, which had prevailed over his mind when he was inclined to consider the stranger, rather as the vision of another world, than as a being of this. The same wild and indescribable character still distinguished his air, his every look and movement, and Vivaldi could not but believe that something in the highest degree extraordinary would yet be discovered concerning him.

The witnesses being called over, Vivaldi understood that he was placed among them, though he had only repeated the words which father Nicola had spoken, and which, since Nicola himself was present as a witness against Schedoni, he did not perceive could be in the least material on the trial.

When Vivaldi had, in his turn, answered to his name, a voice, bursting forth from a distant part of the hall, exclaimed, "It is my master! my *dear* master!" and on directing his eyes whence it came, he perceived the faithful Paulo struggling with his guard. Vivaldi called to him to be patient, and to forbear resistance, an exhortation, however, which served only to increase the efforts of the servant for liberty, and in the next instant he broke from the grasp of the officials, and, darting towards Vivaldi, fell at his feet, sobbing, and clasping his knees, and exclaiming, "O my master! my master! have I found you at last?"

Vivaldi, as much affected by this meeting as Paulo, could not immediately speak. He would, however, have raised and embraced his affectionate servant, but Paulo, still clinging to his knees and sobbing, was so much agitated that he scarcely understood any thing said to him, and to the kind assurances and gentle remonstrances of Vivaldi, constantly replied as if to the officers, whom he fancied to be forcing him away.

"Remember your situation, Paulo," said Vivaldi, "consider mine also, and be governed by prudence."

"You shall not force me hence!" cried Paulo, "you can take my life only once; if I must die, it shall be here."

"Recollect yourself, Paulo, and be composed. Your life, I trust, is in no danger."

Paulo looked up, and again bursting into a passion of tears, repeated, "O! my master! my master! where have you been all this while? are you indeed alive? I thought I never should see you again! I have dreamt an hundred times that you were dead and buried! and I wished to be dead and buried with you. I thought you was gone out of this world into the next. I feared you was gone to heaven, and so believed we should never meet again. But now, I see you once more, and know that you live! O! my master! my master!"

The officers who had followed Paulo, now endeavouring to withdraw him, he became more outrageous.

"Do your worst at once," said he; "but you shall find tough work of it, if you try to force me from hence, so you had better be contented with killing me here."

The incensed officials were laying violent hands upon him, when Vivaldi interposed. "I entreat, I supplicate you," said he, "that you suffer him to remain near me."

"It is impossible," replied an officer, "we dare not."

"I will promise that he shall not even speak to me, if you will only allow him to be near," added Vivaldi.

"Not speak to you, master!" exclaimed Paulo, "but I will stay by you, and speak to you as long as I like, till my last gasp. Let them do their worst at once; I defy them all, and all the devils of inquisitors at their heels too, to force me away. I can die but once, and they ought to be satisfied with that,—so what is there to be afraid of? Not speak!"

"He knows not what he says," said Vivaldi to the officials, while he endeavoured to silence Paulo with his hand, "I am certain that he will submit to whatever I shall require of him, and will be entirely silent; or, if he does speak now and then, it shall be only in a whisper."

"A whisper!" said an officer sneeringly, "do you suppose Signor, that any person is suffered to speak in a whisper here?"

"A whisper!" shouted Paulo, "I scorn to speak in a whisper. I will speak so loud, that every word I say shall ring in the ears of all those old black devils on the benches yonder; aye, and those on that mountebank stage too, that sit there looking so grim and angry as if they longed to tear us in pieces. They"———

"Silence," said Vivaldi with emphasis, "Paulo, I command you to be silent."

"They shall know a bit of my mind," continued Paulo, without noticing Vivaldi, "I will tell them what they have to expect for all their cruel usage of my poor master. Where do they expect to go when they die, I wonder? Though for that matter, they cannot go to a worse place than they are in already, and I suppose it is, knowing that, which makes them not afraid of being ever so wicked. They shall hear a little plain truth, for once in their lives, however, they shall hear"———

During the whole of this harangue, Vivaldi, alarmed for the consequence of such imprudent, though honest indignation, had been using all possible effort to silence him, and was the more alarmed, since the officials made no further attempt to interrupt Paulo, a forbearance, which Vivaldi attributed to malignity, and to a wish that Paulo might be entrapped by his own act. At length he made himself heard.

"I *entreat*," said Vivaldi.

Paulo stopped for a moment.

"Paulo!" rejoined Vivaldi earnestly, "do you love your master?"

"Love my master!" said Paulo resentfully, without allowing Vivaldi to finish his sentence, "Have I not gone through fire and water for him? or, what is as good, have I not put myself into the Inquisition, and all on his account? and now to be asked, 'Do I love my master!' If you believe, Signor, that any thing else made me come here, into these dismal holes, you are quite entirely out; and when they have made an end of me, as I suppose they will do, before all is over, you will, perhaps, think better of me than to suspect that I came here for my own pleasure."

"All that may be as you say, Paulo," replied Vivaldi coldly, while he with difficulty commanded his tears, "but your immediate submission is the only conduct that can convince me of the sincerity of your professions. I *entreat* you to be silent."

"*Entreat* me!" said Paulo, "O my master! what have I done that it should come to this? *Entreat* me!" he repeated, sobbing.

"You will then give me this proof of your attachment?" asked Vivaldi.

"Do not use such a heart-breaking word again, master," replied Paulo, while he dashed the tears from his cheek, "such a heart-breaking word, and I will do any thing."

"You submit to what I require then, Paulo?"

"Aye, Signor, if—if it is even to kneel at the feet of that devil of an inquisitor, yonder."

"I shall only require you to be silent," replied Vivaldi, "and you may then be permitted to remain near me."

"Well, Signor, well; I will do as you bid me, then, and only just say"——

"Not a syllable! Paulo," interrupted Vivaldi.

"Only just say, master"——

"Not a word I entreat you!" added Vivaldi, "or you will be removed immediately."

"His removal does not depend on that," said one of the officials, breaking from his watchful silence, "he must go, and that without more delay."

"What! after I have promised not to open my lips!" said Paulo, "do you pretend to break your agreement?"

"There *is* no pretence, and there *was* no agreement," replied the man sharply, "so obey directly, or it will be the worse for you."

The officials were provoked, and Paulo became still more enraged and clamorous, till at length the uproar reached the tribunal at the other end of the hall, and silence having been commanded, an inquiry was made into the cause of the confusion. The consequence of this was, an order that Paulo should withdraw from Vivaldi; but as at this moment he feared no greater evil, he gave his refusal to the tribunal with as little ceremony as he had done before to the officials.

At length, after much difficulty, a sort of compromise was made, and Paulo being soothed by his master into some degree of compliance, was suffered to remain within a short distance of him.

The business of the trial soon after commenced. Ansaldo the penitentiary, and father Nicola, appeared as witnesses, as did, also, the Roman priest, who had assisted in taking the depositions of the dying assassin. He had been privately interrogated, and had given clear and satisfactory evidence as to the truth of the paper produced by Nicola. Other witnesses, also, had been subpoenaed, whom Schedoni had no expectation of meeting.

The deportment of the Confessor, on first entering the hall, was collected and firm; it remained unchanged when the Roman priest was brought forward; but, on the appearance of another witness, his courage seemed to faulter. Before this evidence was, however, called for, the depositions of the assassin were publicly read. They stated, with the closest conciseness, the chief facts, of which the following is a somewhat more dilated narrative.

It appeared, that about the year 1742, the late Count di Bruno had passed over into Greece, a journey which his brother, the present Confessor, having long expected, had meditated to take advantage of. Though a lawless passion had first suggested to the dark mind of Schedoni the atrocious act, which should destroy a brother, many circumstances and considerations had conspired to urge him towards its accomplishment. Among these was the conduct of the late Count towards himself, which, however reasonable, as it had contradicted his own selfish gratifications, and added strong reproof to opposition, had excited his most inveterate hatred. Schedoni, who, as a younger brother of his family, bore, at that time, the title of Count di Marinella, had dissipated his small patrimony at a very early age; but, though suffering might then have taught him prudence, it had only encouraged him in duplicity, and rendered him more eager to seek a temporary refuge in the same habits of extravagance which had led to it. The Count di Bruno, though his fortune was very limited, had afforded frequent supplies to his brother; till, finding that he was incorrigible, and that the sums which he himself spared with difficulty from his family were lavished, without remorse, by Marinella, instead of being applied, with economy, to his support, he refused further aid than was sufficient for his absolute necessities.

It would be difficult for a candid mind to believe how a conduct so reasonable could possibly excite hatred in any breast, or that the power of selfishness could so far warp any understanding, as to induce Marinella, whom we will, in future, again call Schedoni, to look upon his brother with detestation, because he had refused to ruin himself that his kinsman might revel! Yet it is certain that Schedoni, terming the necessary prudence of di Bruno to be meanness and cold insensibility to the comfort of others, suffered full as much resentment towards him from system, as he did from passion, though the meanness and the insensibility he imagined in his brother's character were not only real traits in his own, but were displaying themselves in the very arguments he urged against them.

The rancour thus excited was cherished by innumerable circumstances, and ripened by envy, that meanest and most malignant of the human passions; by envy of di Bruno's blessings, of an unencumbered estate, and of a beautiful wife, he was tempted to perpetrate the deed, which might transfer those blessings to himself. Spalatro, whom he employed to this purpose, was well known to him, and he did not fear to confide the conduct of the crime to this man, who was to purchase a little habitation on the remote shore of the Adriatic, and, with a certain stipend, to reside there. The ruinous dwelling, to which Ellena had been carried, as its solitary situation suited Schedoni's views, was taken for him.

Schedoni, who had good intelligence of all di Bruno's movements, acquainted Spalatro, from time to time, with his exact situation; and it was after di Bruno, on his return, had crossed the Adriatic, from Ragusi to Manfredonia, and was entering upon the woods of the Garganus, that Spalatro, with his comrade, overtook him. They fired at the Count and his attendants, who were only a valet, and a guide of the country; and, concealed among the thickets, they securely repeated the attack. The shot did not immediately succeed, and the Count, looking round to discover his enemy, prepared to defend himself, but the firing was so rapidly sustained, that, at length, both di Bruno and his servant fell, covered with wounds. The guide fled.

The unfortunate travellers were buried by their assassins on the spot; but, whether the suspicion which attends upon the consciousness of guilt, prompted Spalatro to guard against every possibility of being betrayed by the accomplice of his crime, or whatever was the motive, he returned to the forest alone; and, shrouded by night, removed the bodies to a pit, which he had prepared under the flooring of the house where he lived; thus displacing all proof, should his accomplice hereafter point out to justice the spot in which he had assisted to deposit the mangled remains of di Bruno.

Schedoni contrived a plausible history of the shipwreck of

his brother upon the Adriatic, and of the loss of the whole crew; and, as no persons but the assassins were acquainted with the real cause of his death, the guide, who had fled, and the people at the only town he had passed through, since he landed, being ignorant even of the name of di Bruno, there was not any circumstance to contradict the falsehood. It was universally credited, and even the widow of the Count had, perhaps, never doubted its truth; or if, after her compelled marriage with Schedoni, his conduct did awaken a suspicion, it was too vague to produce any serious consequence.

During the reading of Spalatro's confession, and particularly at the conclusion of it, the surprise and dismay of Schedoni were too powerful for concealment; and it was not the least considerable part of his wonder, that Spalatro should have come to Rome for the purpose of making these depositions; but further consideration gave him a conjecture of the truth.

The account, which Spalatro had given of his motive for this journey to the priest, was, that, having lately understood Schedoni to be resident at Rome, he had followed him thither, with an intention of relieving his conscience by an acknowledgment of his own crimes, and a disclosure of Schedoni's. This, however, was not exactly the fact. The design of Spalatro was to extort money from the guilty Confessor; a design, from which the latter believed he had protected himself, as well as from every other evil consequence, when he misled his late accomplice, respecting his place of residence; little foreseeing that the very artifice, which should send this man in search of him to Rome, instead of Naples, would be the means of bringing his crimes before the public.

Spalatro had followed the steps of Schedoni as far as the town at which he slept, on the first night of his journey; and, having there passed him, had reached the villa di Cambrusca, when, perceiving the Confessor approaching, he had taken shelter from observation, within the ruin. The motive, which before made him shrink from notice, had contributed, and still did so, to a suspicion that he aimed at the life of Schedoni, who, in wounding him, believed he had saved himself from an assassin. The wounds, however, of Spalatro did not so much disable him, but that he proceeded towards Rome from the town whence the parting road had conducted his master towards Naples.

The fatigue of a long journey, performed chiefly on foot, in Spalatro's wounded condition, occasioned a fever, that terminated together his journey and his life; and in his last hours he had unburdened his conscience by a full confession of his guilt. The priest, who, on this occasion, had been sent for, alarmed by the importance of the confession, since it implicated a living person, called in a friend as witness to the depositions. This witness was father Nicola, the former intimate of Schedoni, and who was of a character to rejoice in any discovery, which might punish a man from whose repeated promises he had received only severe disappointments.

Schedoni now perceived that all his designs against Spalatro had failed, and he had meditated more than have yet been fully disclosed. It may be remembered, that on parting with the peasant, his conductor, the Confessor, gave him a stiletto to defend him, as he said, from the attack of Spalatro, in case of encountering him on the road. The point of his instrument was tipped with poison; so that a scratch from it was sufficient to inflict death. Schedoni had for many years secretly carried about him such an envenomed instrument, for reasons known only to himself. He had hoped, that, should the peasant meet Spalatro, and be provoked to defend himself, this stiletto would terminate the life of his accomplice, and relieve him from all probability of discovery, since the other assassin, whom he employed, had been dead several years. The expedient failed in every respect; the peasant did not even see Spalatro; and, before he reached his home, he luckily lost the fatal stiletto, which, as he had discovered himself to be acquainted with some circumstances connected with the crimes of Schedoni, the Confessor would have wished him to keep, from the chance, that he might some time injure himself in using it. The poniard, as he had no proper means of fastening it to his dress, had fallen, and was carried away by the torrent he was crossing at that moment.

But, if Schedoni had been shocked by the confession of the assassin, his dismay was considerably greater, when a new witness was brought forward, and he perceived an ancient domestic of his house. This man identified Schedoni for Ferando Count di Bruno, with whom he had lived as a servant after the death of the Count his brother. And not only did he bear testimony to the person of Schedoni, but to the death of the Countess, his wife. Giovanni declared himself to be one of the domestics who had assisted in conveying her to her apartment, after she had been struck by the poniard of Schedoni, and who had afterwards attended her funeral in the church of the Santa del Miracoli, a convent near the late residence of di Bruno. He further affirmed, that the physicians had reported her death to be in consequence of the wound she had received, and he bore witness to the flight of his master, previous to the death of the Countess, and immediately upon the assassination, and that he had never publicly appeared upon his estate since that period.

An inquisitor asked, whether any measures had been taken by the relations of the deceased lady, toward a prosecution of the Count.

The witness replied, that a long search had been made for the Count, for such a purpose, but that he had wholly eluded discovery, and that, of course, no further step had been taken in the affair. This reply appeared to occasion dissatisfaction; the tribunal was silent, and seemed to hesitate; the vicar-general then addressed the witness.

"How can you be certain that the person now before you, calling himself father Schedoni, is the Count di Bruno, your former master, if you have never seen him during the long interval of years you mention?"

Giovanni, without hesitation, answered, that, though years had worn the features of the Count, he recollected them the moment he beheld him; and not the Count only, but the person of the penitentiary Ansaldo, whom he had seen a frequent visitor at the house of di Bruno, though his appearance, also, was considerably changed by time, and by the ecclesiastical habit which he now wore.

The vicar-general seemed still to doubt the evidence of this man, till Ansaldo himself, on being called upon, remembered him to have been a servant of the Count, though he could not identify the Count himself.

The grand-inquisitor remarked, that it was extraordinary he should recollect the face of the servant, yet forget that of the master, with whom he had lived in habits of intimacy. To this Ansaldo replied, that the stronger passions of Schedoni, together with his particular habits of life, might reasonably be supposed to have wrought a greater change upon the features of the Count than the character and circumstances of Giovanni's could have effected on his.

Schedoni, not without reason, was appalled, on the appearance of this servant, whose further testimony gave such clearness and force to some other parts of the evidence, that the tribunal pronounced sentence upon Schedoni, as the murderer of the Count his brother; and as this, the first charge, was sufficient for his condemnation to death, they did not proceed upon the second, that which related to his wife.

The emotion betrayed by Schedoni, on the appearance of the last witness, and during the delivery of the evidence, disappeared when his fate became certain; and when the dreadful sentence of the law was pronounced, it made no visible impression on his mind. From that moment, his firmness or his hardihood never forsook him.

Vivaldi, who witnessed this condemnation, appeared infinitely more affected by it than himself, and, though in revealing the circumstance of father Nicola's summons, which had eventually led to the discovery of Schedoni's crimes, he had not been left a choice in his conduct, he felt, at this moment, as miserable as if he had actually borne witness against the life of a fellow being: what, then, would have been his feelings, had he been told that this Schedoni, thus condemned, was the father of Ellena di Rosalba! But, whatever these might be, he was soon condemned to experience them. One of the most powerful of Schedoni's passions appeared even in this last scene; and as, in quitting the tribunal, he passed near Vivaldi, he uttered these few words—"In me you have murdered the father of Ellena di Rosalba!"

Not with any hope that the intercession of Vivaldi, himself also a prisoner, could in the least mitigate a sentence pronounced by the Inquisition, did he say this, but for the purpose of revenging himself for the evil, which Vivaldi's evidence had contributed to produce, and inflicting the exquisite misery such information must give. The attempt succeeded too well.

At first, indeed, Vivaldi judged this to be only the desperate assertion of a man, who believed his last chance of escaping the rigour of the law to rest with him; and, at the mention of Ellena, forgetting every precaution, he loudly demanded to know her situation. Schedoni, throwing upon him an horrible smile of triumph and derision, was passing forward without replying, but Vivaldi, unable to support this state of uncertainty, asked permission of the tribunal to converse, for a few moments, with the prisoner; a request which was granted with extreme reluctance, and only on condition that the conversation should be public.

To Vivaldi's questions, as to the situation of Ellena, Schedoni only replied, that she was his daughter, and the solemnity, which accompanied these repeated assertions, though it failed to convince Vivaldi of this truth, occasioned him agonizing doubt and apprehension: but when the Confessor, perceiving the policy of disclosing her place of residence to Vivaldi, softened from his desire of vengeance to secure the interest of his family, and named the Santa della Piéta as her present asylum, the joy of such intelligence overcame, for a time, every other consideration.

To this dialogue, however, the officials put a speedy conclusion; Schedoni was led back to his cell, and Vivaldi was soon after ordered to his former close confinement.

But Paulo became again outrageous, when he was about to be separated from his master, till the latter, having petitioned the tribunal, that his servant might accompany him to his prison, and received an absolute refusal, endeavoured to calm the violence of his despair. He fell at his master's feet, and shed tears, but he uttered no further complaints. When he rose, he turned his eyes in silence upon Vivaldi, and they seemed to say, "Dear master! I shall never see you more!" and with this sad expression, he continued to gaze on him till he had left the hall.

Vivaldi, notwithstanding the various subjects of his distress, could not bear to meet the piteous looks of this poor man, and he withdrew his eyes; yet, at every other step he took, they constantly returned to his faithful servant, till the doors folded him from sight.

When he had quitted the hall, Vivaldi pleaded, however hopelessly, to the officials, in favour of Paulo, entreating that they would speak to the persons, who kept guard over him, and prevail with them to shew him every allowable indulgence.

"No indulgence can be allowed him," replied one of the men, "except bread and water, and the liberty of walking in his cell."

"No *other*!" said Vivaldi.

"None," repeated the official. "This prisoner has been near getting one of his guards into a scrape already, for, somehow or other, he so talked him over, and won upon him, (for he is but a young one here) that the man let him have a light, and a pen and ink; but, luckily, it was found out, before any harm was done."

"And what became of this honest fellow?" inquired Vivaldi.

"Honest! he was none so honest, either, Signor, if he could not mind his duty."

"Was he punished, then?"

"No, Signor," replied the man, pausing, and looking back upon the long avenue they were passing, to inquire whether he was observed to hold this conversation with a prisoner: "no, Signor, he was a younker, so they let him off for once, and sent him to guard a man, who was not so full of his coaxing ways."

"Paulo made him merry, perhaps?" asked Vivaldi. "What were the coaxing ways you spoke of?"

"Merry, Signor! no! he made him cry, and that was as bad."

"Indeed!" said Vivaldi. "The man must have been here, then, a very short time."

"Not more than a month, or so, Signor."

"But the coaxing ways you talked of," repeated Vivaldi, "what were they?—a ducat, or so?"

"A ducat!" exclaimed the man, "no! not a *paolo!*"

"Are you *sure* of that?" cried Vivaldi, shrewdly.

"Aye, sure enough, Signor. This fellow is not worth a ducat in the world!"

"But his master is, friend," observed Vivaldi, in a very low voice, while he put some money into his hand.

The officer made no answer, but concealed the money, and nothing further was said.

Vivaldi had given this as a bribe, to procure some kindness for his servant, not from any consideration of himself, for his own critical situation had ceased at this time to be a subject of anxiety with him. His mind was at present strangely agitated between emotions the most opposite in their nature, the joy which a discovery of Ellena's safety inspired, and the horrible suspicion that Schedoni's assurances of relationship occasioned. That his Ellena was the daughter of a murderer, that the father of Ellena should be brought to ignominious death, and that he himself, however unintentionally, should have assisted to this event, were considerations almost too horrible to be sustained! Vivaldi sought refuge from them in various conjectures as to the motive,

which might have induced Schedoni to assert a falshood in
this instance; but that of revenge alone appeared plausible;
and even this surmise was weakened, when he considered
that the Confessor had assured him of Ellena's safety, an assurance which, as Vivaldi did not detect the selfish policy
connected with it, he believed Schedoni would not have
given, had his general intent towards him been malicious.
But it was possible, that this very information, on which all
his comfort reposed, might be false, and had been given only
for the purpose of inflicting the anguish a discovery of the
truth must lead to! With an anxiety so intense, as almost to
overcome his faculty of judging, he examined every minute
probability relative to this point, and concluded with believing that Schedoni had, in this last instance, at least, spoken
honestly.

Whether he had done so in his first assertion was a question, which had raised in Vivaldi's mind a tempest of conjecture and of horror; for, while the subject of it was too
astonishing to be fully believed, it was, also, too dreadful,
not to be apprehended even as a possibility.

CHAPTER IX

O holy nun! why bend the mournful head?
Why fall those tears from lids uplift in pray'r?
Why o'er thy pale cheek steals the feeble blush,
Then fades, and leaves it wan as the lily
On which a moon-beam falls?

WHILE these events were passing in the prisons of the Inquisition at Rome, Ellena, in the sanctuary of Our Lady of
Pity, remained ignorant of Schedoni's arrest, and of Vivaldi's
situation. She understood that the Confessor was preparing
to acknowledge her for his daughter, and believed that she
comprehended also the motive for his absence; but, though
he had forbidden her to expect a visit from him till his arrangement should be completed, he had promised to write in
the mean time, and inform her of all the present circumstances of Vivaldi; his unexpected silence had excited, therefore, apprehensions as various, though not so terrible, as
those which Vivaldi had suffered for her; nor did the silence
of Vivaldi himself appear less extraordinary.

"His confinement must be severe indeed," said the afflicted Ellena, "since he cannot relieve my anxiety by a single line of intelligence. Or, perhaps, harassed by unceasing
opposition, he has submitted to the command of his family,
and has consented to forget me. Ah! why did I leave the opportunity for that command to his family; why did I not enforce it myself!"

Yet, while she uttered this self-reproach, the tears she shed
contradicted the pride which had suggested it; and a conviction lurking in her heart that Vivaldi could not so resign her,
soon dissipated those tears. But other conjectures recalled
them; it was possible that he was ill—that he was dead!

In such vague and gloomy surmise her days passed away;
employment could no longer withdraw her from herself, nor

music, even for a moment, charm away the sense of sorrow; yet she regularly partook of the various occupations of the nuns; and was so far from permitting herself to indulge in any useless expression of anxiety, that she had never once disclosed the sacred subject of it; so that, though she could not assume an air of cheerfulness, she never appeared otherwise than tranquil. Her most soothing, yet perhaps most melancholy hour, was when about sun-set she could withdraw unnoticed, to the terrace among the rocks, that overlooked the convent, and formed a part of its domain. There, alone and relieved from all the ceremonial restraints of the society, her very thoughts seemed more at liberty. As, from beneath the light foliage of the acacias, or the more majestic shade of the plane-trees that waved their branches over the many-coloured cliffs of this terrace, Ellena looked down upon the magnificent scenery of the bay, it brought back to memory, in sad yet pleasing detail, the many happy days she had passed on those blue waters, or on the shores, in the society of Vivaldi and her departed relative Bianchi; and every point of the prospect marked by such remembrance, which the veiling distance stole, was rescued by imagination, and pictured by affection in tints more animated than those of brightest nature.

One evening Ellena had lingered on the terrace later than usual. She had watched the rays retiring from the highest points of the horizon, and the fading imagery of the lower scene, till, the sun having sunk into the waves, all colouring was withdrawn, except an empurpling and reposing hue, which overspread the waters and the heavens, and blended in soft confusion every feature of the landscape. The roofs and slender spires of the Santa della Pieta, with a single tower of the church rising loftily over every other part of the buildings that composed the convent, were fading fast from the eye; but the solemn tint that invested them accorded so well with their style, that Ellena was unwilling to relinquish this interesting object. Suddenly she perceived through the dubious light an unusual number of moving figures in the court of the great cloister, and listening, she fancied she could distinguish the murmuring of many voices. The white drapery of the nuns rendered them conspicuous as they moved, but it was impossible to ascertain who were the individuals engaged in this bustle. Presently the assemblage dispersed; and

Ellena, curious to understand the occasion of what she had observed, prepared to descend to the convent.

She had left the terrace, and was about to enter a long avenue of chestnuts that extended to a part of the convent, communicating immediately with the great court, when she heard approaching steps, and, on turning into the walk, perceived several persons advancing in the shady distance. Among the voices, as they drew nearer, she distinguished one whose interesting tone engaged all her attention, and began also to waken memory. She listened, wondered, doubted, hoped, and feared! It spoke again! Ellena thought she could not be deceived in those tender accents, so full of intelligence, so expressive of sensibility and refinement. She proceeded with quicker steps, yet faltered as she drew near the group, and paused to discern whether among them was any figure that might accord with the voice and justify her hopes.

The voice spoke again; it pronounced her name; pronounced it with the tremblings of tenderness and impatience, and Ellena scarcely dared to trust her senses, when she beheld Olivia, the nun of San Stefano, in the cloisters of the Della Pieta!

Ellena could find no words to express her joy and surprise on beholding her preserver in safety, and in these quiet groves; but Olivia repaid all the affectionate caresses of her young friend, and, while she promised to explain the circumstances that had led her to her present appearance here, she, in her turn, made numerous inquiries relative to Ellena's adventures after she had quitted San Stefano. They were now, however, surrounded by too many auditors to allow of unreserved conversation; Ellena, therefore, led the nun to her apartment, and Olivia then explained her reasons for having left the convent of San Stefano, which were indeed sufficient to justify, even with the most rigid devotee, her conduct as to the change. This unfortunate recluse, it appeared, persecuted by the suspicions of the abbess, who understood that she had assisted in the liberation of Ellena, had petitioned the bishop of her diocese for leave to remove to the Santa della Pieta. The abbess had not proof to proceed formally against her, as an accomplice in the escape of a novice, for though Jeronimo could have supplied the requisite evidence, he was too deeply implicated in this adventure to do so without betraying his own conduct. From his having withheld such proof, it appears, however, that accident rather than de-sign had occasioned his failure on the evening of Ellena's departure from the monastery. But, though the abbess had not testimony enough for legal punishment, she was ac-quainted with circumstances sufficient to justify suspicion, and had both the inclination and the power to render Olivia very miserable.

In her choice of the Santa della Pieta, the nun was influ-enced by many considerations, some of which were the con-sequence of conversations she had held with Ellena respecting the state of that society. Her design she had been unable to disclose to her friend, lest, by a discovery of such correspondence, the abbess of San Stefano should obtain grounds on which to proceed against her. Even in her appeal to the bishop the utmost caution and secrecy had been nec-essary, till the order for her removal, procured not without considerable delay and difficulty, arrived, and when it came, the jealous anger of the superior rendered an immediate de-parture necessary.

Olivia, during many years, had been unhappy in her local circumstances, but it is probable she would have concluded her days within the walls of San Stefano, had not the aggra-vated oppression of the abbess aroused her courage and ac-tivity, and dissipated the despondency, with which severe misfortune had obscured her views.

Ellena was particular in her inquiries whether any person of the monastery had suffered for the assistance they had given her; but learned that not one, except Olivia, had been suspected of befriending her; and then understood, that the venerable friar, who had dared to unfasten the gate which re-stored her with Vivaldi to liberty, had not been involved by his kindness.

"It is an embarrassing and rather an unusual circum-stance," concluded Olivia, "to change one's convent; but you perceive the strong reasons which determined me upon a removal. I was, however, perhaps, the more impatient of severe treatment, since you, my sister, had described to me the society of Our Lady of Pity, and since I believed it pos-sible that you might form a part of it. When, on my arrival here, I learned that my wishes had not deceived me on this point, I was impatient to see you once more, and as soon as the ceremonies attending an introduction to the superior were over, I requested to be conducted to you, and was in search of you when we met in the avenue. It is unnecessary for me to insist upon the satisfaction, which this meeting gives me; but you may not, perhaps, understand how much the manners of our lady abbess, and of the sisterhood in general, as far as a first interview will allow me to judge of them, have re-animated me. The gloom, which has long hung over my prospects, seems now to open, and a distant gleam promises to light up the evening of my stormy day."

Olivia paused and appeared to recollect herself; this was the first time she had made so direct a reference to her own misfortunes; and, while Ellena silently remarked it, and observed the dejection, which was already stealing upon the expressive countenance of the nun, she wished, yet feared to lead her back towards the subject of them.

Endeavouring to dismiss some painful remembrance, and assuming a smile of languid gaiety, Olivia said, "Now that I have related the history of my removal, and sufficiently indulged my egotism, will you let me hear what adventures have befallen you, my young friend, since the melancholy adieu you gave me in the gardens of San Stefano."

This was a task, to which Ellena's spirits, though revived by the presence of Olivia, were still unequal. Over the scenes of her past distress Time had not yet drawn his shadowing veil; the colours were all too fresh and garish for the meek dejection of her eye, and the subject was too intimately connected with that of her present anxiety, to be reviewed without very painful feelings. She therefore requested Olivia to spare her from a detail of particulars, which she could not recollect but with extreme reluctance; and, scrupulously observing the injunction of Schedoni, she merely mentioned her separation from Vivaldi upon the banks of the Celano, and that a variety of distressing circumstances had intervened before she could regain the sanctuary of the della Pieta.

Olivia understood too well the kind of feelings, from which Ellena was desirous of escaping, willingly to subject her to a renewal of them; and felt too much generous compassion for her sufferings not to endeavour to soothe the sense of them by an exertion of those delicate and nameless arts which, while they mock detection, fascinate the weary spirit as by a charm of magic!

The friends continued in conversation, till a chime from a chapel of the convent summoned them to the last vespers;

and, when the service had concluded, they separated for the night.

With the society of the Santa della Pieta, Olivia had thus found an asylum such as till lately she had never dared to hope for; but, though she frequently expressed her sense of this blessing, it was seldom without tears; and Ellena observed, with some surprise and more disappointment, within a very few days after her arrival, a cloud of melancholy spreading again over her mind.

But a nearer interest soon withdrew Ellena's attention from Olivia to fix it upon Vivaldi; and, when she saw her infirm old servant, Beatrice, enter a chamber of the convent, she anticipated that the knowledge of some extraordinary, and probably unhappy, event had brought her. She knew too well the circumspection of Schedoni to believe that Beatrice came commissioned from him; and as the uncertain situation of Vivaldi was so constantly the subject of her anxiety, she immediately concluded that her servant came to announce some evil relative to him.— His indisposition, perhaps his actual confinement in the Inquisition, which lately she had sometimes been inclined to think might not have been a mere menace to Vivaldi, though it had proved to be no more to herself;—or possibly she came to tell of his death—his death in those prisons! This last was a possibility that almost incapacitated her for inquiring what was the errand of Beatrice.

The old servant, trembling and wan, either from the fatigue of her walk, or from a consciousness of disastrous intelligence, seated herself without speaking, and some moments elapsed before she could be prevailed with to answer the repeated inquiries of Ellena.

"O Signora!" said she, at length, "you do not know what it is to walk up hill such a long way, at my age! Well! heaven protect you, I hope you never will!"

"I perceive you bring ill news," said Ellena; "I am prepared for it, and you need not fear to tell me all you know."

"Holy San Marco!" exclaimed Beatrice, "if death be ill news, you have guessed right, Signora, for I do bring news of that, it is certain. How came you, Lady, to know my errand? They have been beforehand with me, I see, though I have not walked so fast up hill this many a day, as I have now, to tell you what has happened."

She stopped on observing the changing countenance of

Ellena, who tremulously called upon her to explain what had happened—who was dead; and entreated her to relate the particulars as speedily as possible.

"You said you was prepared, Signora," said Beatrice, "but your looks tell another tale."—

"What is the event you would disclose?" said Ellena, almost breathless. "When did it happen?—be brief."

"I cannot tell exactly when it happened, Signora, but it was an own servant of the Marchese's that I had it from."

"The Marchese's?" interrupted Ellena in a faltering voice.

"Aye, Lady; you will say that is pretty good authority."

"Death! and in the Marchese's family!" exclaimed Ellena.

"Yes, Signora, I had it from his own servant. He was passing by the garden-gate just as I happened to be speaking to the maccaroni-man.—But you are ill, Lady!"—

"I am very well, if you will but proceed," replied Ellena, faintly, while her eyes were fixed upon Beatrice, as if they only had power to enforce her meaning.

" 'Well, dame,' he says to me, 'I have not seen you of a long time.' 'No,' says I, 'that is a great grievance truly! for old women now-a-days are not much thought of; out of sight out of mind with them, now-a-days!' "—

"I beseech you to the purpose," interrupted Ellena. "Whose death did he announce?" She had not courage to pronounce Vivaldi's name.

"You shall hear, Signora. I saw he looked in a sort of a bustle, so I asked him how all did at the Palazzo: so he answers, 'Bad enough, Signora Beatrice, have not you heard?' 'Heard,' says I; 'what should I have heard?' 'Why,' says he, 'of what has just happened in our family.' "

"O heavens!" exclaimed Ellena, "he is dead! Vivaldi is dead!"

"You shall hear, Signora," continued Beatrice.

"Be brief!" said Ellena, "answer me simply yes or no."

"I cannot, till I come to the right place, Signora; if you will but have a little patience, you shall hear all. But if you fluster me so, you will put me quite out."

"Grant me patience!" said Ellena, endeavouring to calm her spirits.

"With that, Signora, I asked him to walk in and rest himself, and tell me all about it. He answered, he was in a great hurry, and could not stay a moment, and he a great deal of that sort; but I, knowing that whatever happened in that family, Signora, was something to you, would not let him go off so easily; and so, when I asked him to refresh himself with a glass of lemon-ice, he forgot all his business in a minute, and we had a long chat."

And Beatrice might now have continued her circumlocution, perhaps as long as she had pleased, for Ellena had lost all power to urge inquiry, and was scarcely sensible of what was said. She neither spoke, nor shed a tear; the one image that possessed her fancy, the image of Vivaldi dead seemed to hold all her faculties, as by a spell.

"So when I asked him," added Beatrice, "again what had happened, he was ready enough to tell all about it. 'It is near a month ago,' said he, 'since she was first taken; the Marchesa had been' "——

"The Marchesa!" repeated Ellena, with whom that one word had dissolved the spell of terror—"the Marchesa!"

"Yes Signora, to be sure. Who else did I say it was!"

"Go on, Beatrice; the Marchesa?"——

"What makes you look so glad all of a sudden, Signora? I thought just now you was very sorry about it. What! I warrant you was thinking about my young lord, Vivaldi."

"Proceed," said Ellena.

"Well!" added Beatrice, " 'It was about a month ago that the Marchesa was first taken,' continued the varlet. 'She had seemed poorly a long time, but it was from a *conversazione* at the di Voglio palazzo, that she came home so ill. It is supposed she had been long in a bad state of health, but nobody thought her so near her end, till the doctors were called together; and then matters looked very bad indeed. They found out that she had been dying, or as good, for many years, though nobody else had suspected it, and the Marchesa's own physician was blamed for not finding it out before. But he,' added the rogue, 'had a regard for my lady. He was very obstinate, too, for he kept saying almost to the last, there was no danger, when every body else saw how it was going. The other doctors soon made their words good, and my lady died.' "

"And her son"—said Ellena, "was he with the Marchesa when she expired?"

"What, Signor Vivaldi, lady? No, the Signor was not there."

"That is very extraordinary!" observed Ellena with emotion. "Did the servant mention him?"

"Yes, Signora; he said what a sad thing it was that he should be out of the way at that time, and nobody know where!"

"Are his family then ignorant where he is?" asked Ellena, with increased emotion.

"To be sure they are, lady, and have been for these many weeks. They have heard nothing at all of the Signor, or one Paulo Mendrico, his servant, though the Marchesa's people have been riding post after them from one end of the kingdom to the other all the time!"

Shocked with the conviction of a circumstance, which, till lately she scarcely believed was possible, the imprisonment of Vivaldi in the Inquisition, Ellena lost for a while all power of further inquiry; but Beatrice proceeded.

"The Lady Marchesa seemed to lay something much to heart, as the man told me, and often inquired for Signor Vincentio."

"The Marchesa you are sure then was ignorant where he was?" said Ellena, with new astonishment and perplexity as to the person who, after betraying him into the Inquisition, could yet have suffered her, though arrested at the same time, to escape.

"Yes, Signora, for she wanted sadly to see him. And when she was dying, she sent for her Confessor, one father Schedoni, I think they call him, and"—

"What of him?" said Ellena incautiously.

"Nothing, Signora, for he could not be found."

"Not be found!" repeated Ellena.

"No, Signora, not just then; he was Confessor, I warrant, to other people besides the Marchesa, and I dare say they had sins enough to confess, so he could not get away in a hurry."

Ellena recollected herself sufficiently to ask no further of Schedoni; and, when she considered the probable cause of Vivaldi's arrest, she was again consoled by a belief that he had not fallen into the power of real officials, since the comrades of the men who had arrested him, had proved themselves otherwise; and she thought it highly probable, that, while undiscovered by his family, he had been, and was still engaged in searching for the place of her confinement.

"But I was saying," proceeded Beatrice, "what a bustle there was when my lady, the Marchesa was dying. As this father Schedoni was not to be found, another Confessor was sent for, and shut up with her for a long while indeed! And then my Lord Marchese was called in, and there seemed to be a deal going forward, for my Lord was heard every now and then by the attendants in the anti-chamber, talking loud, and sometimes my Lady Marchesa's voice was heard too, though she was so ill! At last all was silent, and after some time my Lord came out of the room, and he seemed very much flustered, they say, that is, very angry and yet very sorrowful. But the Confessor remained with my Lady for a long while after; and, when he departed, my Lady appeared more unhappy than ever. She lived all that night and part of the next day, and something seemed to lie very heavy at her heart, for she sometimes wept, but oftener groaned, and would look so, that it was piteous to see her. She frequently asked for the Marchese, and when he came, the attendants were sent away, and they held long conferences by themselves. The Confessor also was sent for again, just at the last, and they were all shut up together. After this, my Lady appeared more easy in her mind, and not long after she died."

Ellena, who had attended closely to this little narrative, was prevented for the present from asking the few questions which it had suggested, by the entrance of Olivia, who, on perceiving a stranger, was retiring, but Ellena, not considering these inquiries as important, prevailed with the nun to take a chair at the embroidery frame she had lately quitted.

After conversing for a few moments with Olivia, she returned to a consideration of her own interests. The absence of Schedoni still appeared to her as something more than accidental; and, though she could not urge any inquiry with Beatrice, concerning the monk of the Spirito Santo, she ventured to ask whether she had lately seen the stranger, who had restored her to Altieri, for Beatrice knew him only in the character of Ellena's deliverer.

"No, Signora," replied Beatrice rather sharply, "I have never seen his face since he attended you to the villa, though for that matter, I did not see much of it there; and then how he contrived to let himself out of the house that night without my seeing him, I cannot divine, though I have thought of it often enough since. I am sure he need not to have been ashamed to have shewn his face to me, for I should only have blessed him for bringing you safe home again!"

Ellena was somewhat surprised to find that Beatrice had

noticed a circumstance apparently so trivial, and replied, that she had herself opened the door for her protector.

While Beatrice spoke, Olivia raising her eyes from the embroidery, had fixed them upon the old servant, who respectfully withdrew hers; but, when the nun was again engaged on her work, she resumed her observation. Ellena fancied she perceived something extraordinary in this mutual examination, although the curiosity of strangers towards each other might have accounted for it.

Beatrice then received directions from Ellena as to some drawings, which she wished to have sent to the convent, and when the servant spoke in reply, Olivia again raised her eyes, and fixed them on her face with intense curiosity.

"I certainly ought to know that voice," said the nun with great emotion, "though I dare not judge from your features. Is it,—can it be possible!—is it Beatrice Olca, to whom I speak? So many years have passed"——

Beatrice with equal surprise answered, "It is, Signora; you are right in my name. But, lady, who are you that know me?"

While she earnestly regarded Olivia, there was an expression of dismay in her look, which increased Ellena's perplexity. The nun's complexion varied every instant, and her words failed when she attempted to speak. Beatrice meanwhile exclaimed, "My eyes deceive me! yet there is a strange likeness. Santa della Pieta! how it has fluttered me! my heart beats still—you are so like her, lady, yet you are very different too."

Olivia, whose regards were now entirely fixed upon Ellena, said in a voice that was scarcely articulate, while her whole frame seemed sinking beneath some irresistible feeling, "Tell me, Beatrice, I conjure you, quickly say, who is this?"—— She pointed to Ellena, and the sentence died on her lips.

Beatrice, wholly occupied by interests of her own, gave no reply, but exclaimed, "It is in truth the Lady Olivia! It is herself! In the name of all that is sacred, how came you here? O! how glad you must have been to find one another out!" She looked, still gasping with astonishment, at Olivia, while Ellena, unheard, repeatedly inquired the meaning of her words, and in the next moment found herself pressed to the bosom of the nun, who seemed better to have understood them, and who weeping, trembling, and almost fainting, held her there in silence.

Ellena, after some moments had thus passed, requested an explanation of what she witnessed, and Beatrice at the same time demanded the cause of all this emotion. "For can it be that you did not know one another?" she added.

"What new discovery is this?" said Ellena, fearfully to the nun. "It is but lately that I have found my father! O tell me by what tender name I am to call you?"

"Your father!" exclaimed Olivia.

"Your father, lady!" echoed Beatrice.

Ellena, betrayed by strong emotion into this premature mention of Schedoni, was embarrassed and remained silent.

"No, my child!" said Olivia, softening from amazement into tones of ineffable sorrow, while she again pressed Ellena to her heart—"No!—thy father is in the grave!"

Ellena no longer returned her caresses; surprise and doubt suspended every tender emotion; she gazed upon Olivia with an intenseness that partook of wildness. At length she said slowly—"It is my mother, then, whom I see! When will these discoveries end!"

"It is your mother!" replied Olivia solemnly, "a mother's blessing rests with you!"

The nun endeavoured to soothe the agitated spirits of Ellena, though she was herself nearly overwhelmed by the various and acute feelings this disclosure occasioned. For a considerable time they were unable to speak but in short sentences of affectionate exclamation, but joy was evidently a more predominant feeling with the parent than with the child. When, however, Ellena could weep, she became more tranquil, and by degrees was sensible of a degree of happiness, such as she had perhaps never experienced.

Meanwhile Beatrice seemed lost in amazement mingled with fear. She expressed no pleasure, notwithstanding the joy she witnessed, but was uniformly grave and observant.

Olivia, when she recovered some degree of composure, inquired for her sister Bianchi. The silence and sudden dejection of Ellena indicated the truth. On this mention of her late mistress, Beatrice recovered the use of speech.

"Alas! lady," said the old servant, "she is now where I believed you were! and I should as soon have expected to see my dear mistress here as yourself!"

Olivia, though affected by this intelligence, did not feel it

with the acuteness she would have done probably at any
other moment. After she had indulged her tears, she added,
that from the unusual silence of Bianchi, she had suspected
the truth, and particularly since not any answer had been returned to the letter she had sent to Altieri upon her arrival at
the Santa della Pieta.

"Alas!" said Beatrice, "I wonder much my lady abbess
failed to tell you the sad news, for she knew it too
well!—My dear mistress is buried in the church here! as for
the letter, I have brought it with me for Signora Ellena to
open."

"The lady abbess is not informed of our relationship," replied Olivia, "and I have particular reasons for wishing that
at present she should remain ignorant of it. Even you, my
Ellena, must appear only as my friend, till some inquiries
have been made, which are essential to my peace."

Olivia required an explanation of Ellena's late extraordinary assertion respecting her father, but this was a request
made with emotions very different from those which hope or
joy inspire. Ellena, believing that the same circumstances
which had deceived herself during so many years, as to his
death, had also misled Olivia, was not surprised at the incredulity her mother had shewn, but she was considerably embarrassed how to answer her inquiries. It was now too late
to observe the promise of secrecy extorted from her by
Schedoni; the first moments of surprise had betrayed her;
yet, while she trembled further to transgress his injunction, she perceived that a full explanation was now unavoid-
able. And, since Ellena considered, that as Schedoni could
not have foreseen her present peculiar situation, his command had no reference to her mother, her scruples on this
head disappeared. When, therefore, Beatrice had withdrawn,
Ellena repeated her assertion, that her father still lived;
which, though it increased the amazement of Olivia, did not
vanquish her incredulity. Olivia's tears flowed fast, while in
contradiction to this assurance, she mentioned the year in
which the Count di Bruno died, with some circumstances
relative to his death; which, however, as Ellena understood
that her mother had not witnessed it, she still believed had
not happened. To confirm her late assertion, Ellena then related a few particulars of her second interview with
Schedoni, and as some confirmation that he lived, offered to
produce the portrait, which he had claimed as his own.

Olivia, in great agitation, requested to see the miniature, and Ellena left the apartment in search of it.

Every moment of her absence was to Olivia's expectation lengthened to an hour; she paced the room; listened for a footstep; endeavoured to tranquillize her spirits, and still Ellena did not return. Some strange mystery seemed to lurk in the narrative she had just heard, which she wished, yet dreaded to develop; and when, at length, Ellena appeared with the miniature, she took it in trembling eagerness, and having gazed upon it for an instant, her complexion faded and she fainted.

Ellena had now no doubt respecting the truth of Schedoni's declaration, and blamed herself for not having more gradually prepared her mother for the knowledge of a circumstance, which she believed had overwhelmed her with joy. The usual applications, however, soon restored Olivia, who, when she was again alone with her daughter, desired to behold once more the portrait. Ellena, attributing the strong emotion, with which she still regarded it, to surprise, and fear lest she was admitting a fallacious hope, endeavoured to comfort her by renewed assurances, that not only the Count di Bruno yet existed, but that he lived at this very time in Naples, and further, that he would probably be in her presence within the hour, "When I quitted the room for the miniature," added Ellena, "I dispatched a person with a note, requesting to see my father immediately, being impatient to realize the joy, which such a meeting between my long lost parents must occasion."

In this instance Ellena had certainly suffered her generous sympathy to overcome her discretion, for, though the contents of the note to Schedoni could not positively have betrayed him, had he even been in Naples at this time, her sending it to the Spirito Santo, instead of the place which he had appointed for his letters, might have led to a premature inquiry respecting herself.

While Ellena had acquainted Olivia that Schedoni would probably be with them soon, she watched eagerly for the joyful surprise she expected would appear on her countenance; how severe then was her disappointment when only terror and dismay were expressed there! and, when, in the next moment, her mother uttered exclamations of distress and even of despair!

"If he sees me," said Olivia, "I am irrecoverably lost! O!

unhappy Ellena! your precipitancy has destroyed me. The original of this portrait is not the Count di Bruno, *my* dear lord, nor your parent, but his brother, the cruel husband"——

Olivia left the sentence unfinished, as if she was betraying more than was at present discreet; but Ellena, whom astonishment had kept silent, now entreated that she would explain her words, and the cause of her distress.

"I know not," said Olivia, "by what means that portrait has been conveyed to you; but it is the resemblance of the Count Ferando di Bruno, the brother of my lord, and my" ——second husband she should have said, but her lips refused to honour him with the title.

She paused and was much affected, but presently added—

"I cannot at present explain the subject more fully, for it is to me a very distressing one. Let me rather consider the means of avoiding an interview with di Bruno, and even of concealing, if possible, that I exist."

Olivia was, however, soothed when she understood that Ellena had not named her in the note, but had merely desired to see the Confessor upon a very particular occasion.

While they were consulting upon the excuse it would be necessary to form for this imprudent summons, the messenger returned with the note unopened, and with information, that father Schedoni was abroad on a pilgrimage, which was the explanation the brothers of the Spirito Santo chose to give of his absence; judging it prudent, for the honour of their convent, to conceal his real situation.

Olivia, thus released from her fears, consented to explain some points of the subject so interesting to Ellena; but it was not till several days after this discovery, that she could sufficiently command her spirits to relate the whole of her narrative. The first part of it agreed perfectly with the account delivered in the confession to the penitentiary Ansaldo; that which follows was known only to herself, her sister Bianchi, a physician, and one faithful servant, who had been considerably entrusted with the conduct of the plan.

It may be recollected that Schedoni left his house immediately after the act, which was designed to be fatal to the Countess his wife, and that she was carried senseless to her chamber. The wound, as appears, was not mortal. But the atrocity of the intent determined her to seize the opportunity thus offered by the absence of Schedoni, and her own peculiar circumstances, to release herself from his tyranny without having recourse to a court of justice, which would have covered with infamy the brother of her first husband. She withdrew, therefore, from his house for ever, and with the assistance of the three persons before mentioned, retired to a remote part of Italy, and sought refuge in the convent of San Stefano, while at home the report of her death was confirmed by a public funeral. Bianchi remained for some time after the departure of Olivia, in her own residence near the Villa di Bruno, having taken under her immediate care the daughter of the Countess and of the first Count di Bruno, as well as an infant daughter of the second.

After some time had elapsed, Bianchi withdrew with her young charge, but not to the neighbourhood of San Stefano. The indulgence of a mother's tenderness was denied to Olivia, for Bianchi could not reside near the convent without subjecting her to the hazard of a discovery, since Schedoni, though he now believed the report of her death, might be led to doubt it, by the conduct of Bianchi, whose steps would probably be observed by him. She chose a residence, therefore, at a distance from Olivia, though not yet at Altieri. At this period, Ellena was not two years old; the daughter of Schedoni was scarcely as many months, and she died before the year concluded. It was this his child, for whom the Confessor, who had too well concealed himself to permit Bianchi to acquaint him with her death, had mistaken Ellena, and to which mistake his own portrait, affirmed by Ellena to be that of her father, had contributed. This miniature she had found in the cabinet of Bianchi after her aunt's decease, and, observing it inscribed with the title of Count di Bruno, she had worn it with a filial fondness ever since that period.

Bianchi, when she had acquainted Ellena with the secret of her birth, was withheld, both by prudence and humanity, from intrusting her with a knowledge that her mother lived; but this, no doubt, was the circumstance she appeared so anxious to disclose on her death-bed, when the suddenness of her disorder had deprived her of the power. The abruptness of that event had thus contributed to keep the mother and daughter unknown to each other, even when they afterwards accidentally met, to which concealment the name of Rosalba, given to Ellena from her infancy by Bianchi, for the purpose of protecting her from discovery by her uncle, had assisted. Beatrice, who was not the domestic intrusted with the escape of Olivia, had believed the report of her death, and thus, though she knew Ellena to be the daughter of the Countess di Bruno, she could never have been a means of discovering them to each other, had it not happened that Olivia recognized this ancient servant of Bianchi, while Ellena was present.

When Bianchi came to reside in the neighbourhood of Naples, she was unsuspicious that Schedoni, who had never been heard of since the night of the assassination, inhabited there; and she so seldom left her house, that it is not surprising she should never happen to meet him, at least consciously; for her veil, and the monk's cowl, might easily have concealed them from each other if they had met.

It appears to have been the intention of Bianchi to disclose to Vivaldi the family of Ellena, before their nuptials were solemnized; since, on the evening of their last conversation, she had declared, when her spirits were exhausted by the exertion she had made, that much remained for her to say, which weakness obliged her to defer till another opportunity. Her unexpected death prevented any future meeting. That she had not sooner intended to make a communication, which might have removed, in a considerable degree, the objection of the Vivaldi to a connection with Ellena, appears extraordinary, till other circumstances of her family, than that of its nobility, are considered. Her present indigence, and yet more, the guilt attached to an individual of the di Bruno, it was reasonable to suppose would operate as a full antidote to the allurement of rank, however jealous of birth the Vivaldi had proved themselves.

Ferando di Bruno had contrived, even in the short interval between the death of his brother and the supposed decease of his wife, again to embarrass his affairs, and soon after his flight, the income arising from what remained of his landed property had been seized upon by his creditors, whether lawfully or not, he was then in a situation which did not permit him to contest, and Ellena was thus left wholly dependent upon her aunt. The small fortune of Bianchi had been diminished by the assistance she afforded Olivia, for whose admittance into the convent of San Stefano it had been necessary to advance a considerable sum; and her original income was afterwards reduced by the purchase of the villa Altieri. This expenditure, however, was not an imprudent one, since she preferred the comforts and independence of a pleasant home, with industry, to the indulgence of an indolence which must

have confined her to an inferior residence; and was acquainted with the means of making this industry profitable
without being dishonourable. She excelled in many elegant
and ingenious arts, and the productions of her pencil and
needle were privately disposed of to the nuns of the Santa
della Pieta. When Ellena was of an age to assist her, she resigned much of the employment and the profit to her niece,
whose genius having unfolded itself, the beauty of her designs and the elegance of her execution, both in drawings
and embroidery, were so highly valued by the purchasers at
the grate of the convent, that Bianchi committed to Ellena
altogether the exercise of her art.

Olivia meanwhile had dedicated her life to devotion in the
monastery of San Stefano, a choice which was willingly
made while her mind was yet softened by grief for the death
of her first lord, and wearied by the cruelty she had afterwards experienced. The first years of her retirement were
passed in tranquillity, except when the remembrance of her
child, whom she did not dare to see at the convent, awakened a parental pang. With Bianchi she, however, corresponded as regularly as opportunity would allow, and had at
least the consolation of knowing, that the object most dear to
her lived, till, within a short period of Ellena's arrival at the
very asylum chosen by her mother, her apprehensions were
in some degree excited by the unusual silence of Bianchi.

When Olivia had first seen Ellena in the chapel of San
Stefano, she was struck with a slight resemblance she bore to
the late Count di Bruno, and had frequently afterwards examined her features with a most painful curiosity; but, circumstanced as she was, Olivia could not reasonably suspect the
stranger to be her daughter. Once, however, a sense of this
possibility so far overcame her judgment, as to prompt an inquiry for the sirname of Ellena; but the mention of Rosalba
had checked all further conjecture. What would have been the
feelings of the nun, had she been told when her generous compassion was assisting a stranger to escape from oppression that
she was preserving her own child! It may be worthy of observation, that the virtues of Olivia, exerted in a general cause,
had thus led her unconsciously to the happiness of saving her
daughter; while the vices of Schedoni had as unconsciously
urged him nearly to destroy his niece, and had always been
preventing, by the means they prompted him to employ, the
success of his constant aim.

CHAPTER X

Those hours, which lately smil'd, where are they now?
Pallid to thought and ghastly!

YOUNG

THE Marchesa di Vivaldi, of whose death Beatrice had given an imperfect account, struck with remorse of the crime she had meditated against Ellena, and with terror of the punishment due to it, had sent, when on her death-bed, for a Confessor, to whom she unburthened her conscience, and from whom she hoped to receive, in return, an alleviation of her despair. This Confessor was a man of good sense and humanity; and, when he fully understood the story of Vivaldi and Ellena di Rosalba, he declared, that her only hope of forgiveness, both for the crime she had meditated, and the undeserved sufferings she had occasioned, rested upon her willingness to make those now happy, whom she had formerly rendered miserable. Her conscience had already given her the same lesson; and, now that she was sinking to that grave which levels all distinctions, and had her just fear of retribution no longer opposed by her pride, she became as anxious to promote the marriage of Vivaldi with Ellena as she had ever been to prevent it. She sent, therefore, for the Marchese; and, having made an avowal of the arts she had practised against the peace and reputation of Ellena, without, however, confessing the full extent of her intended crimes, she made it her last request, that he would consent to the happiness of his son.

The Marchese, however, shocked as he was at this discovery of the duplicity and cruelty of his wife, had neither her terror of the future, or remorse for the past, to overcome his objection to the rank of Ellena; and he resisted all her importunity, till the anguish of her last hours overcame every consideration but that of affording her relief; he then gave a solemn promise, in the presence of the Confessor, that he would no longer oppose the marriage of Vivaldi and Ellena, should the former persist in his attachment to her. This promise was sufficient for the Marchesa, and she died with some degree of resignation. It did not, however, appear probable, that the Marchese would soon be called upon to fulfill the engagements, into which he had so unwillingly entered, every inquiry after Vivaldi having been hitherto ineffectual.

During the progress of this fruitless search for his son, and while the Marchese was almost lamenting him as dead, the inhabitants of the Vivaldi palace were, one night, aroused from sleep by a violent knocking at the great gate of the court. The noise was so loud and incessant, that, before the porter could obey the summons, the Marchese, whose apartment looked upon the court, was alarmed, and sent an attendant from his anti-room, to inquire the occasion of it.

Presently a voice was heard from the first anti-chamber, exclaiming, "I must see my Lord Marchese directly; he will not be angry to be waked, when he knows all about it;" and, before the Marchese could order that no person, on whatever pretence, should be admitted, Paulo, haggard, ragged, and covered with dirt, was in the chamber. His wan and affrighted countenance, his disordered dress, and his very attitude, as on entering he half turned to look back upon the anti-rooms, like one, who, just escaped from bondage, listens to the fancied sounds of pursuit, were altogether so striking and terrific, that the Marchese, anticipating some dreadful news of Vivaldi, had scarcely power to inquire for him. Paulo, however, rendered questions unnecessary; for, without any circumlocution, or preface, he immediately informed the Marchese, that the Signor, his dear master, was in the prisons of the Inquisition, at Rome, if, indeed, they had not put an end to him before that time.

"Yes, my Lord," said Paulo, "I am just got out myself, for they would not let me be with the Signor, so it was of no use to stay there any longer. Yet it was a hard matter with me to go away, and leave my dear master within those dismal walls; and nothing should have persuaded me to do so, but that I hoped, when your Lordship knew where the Signor was, you might be able to get him out. But there is not a minute to be lost, my Lord, for when once a gentleman has

got within the claws of those inquisitors, there is no knowing how soon they may take it in their heads to tear him in
pieces. Shall I order horses for Rome, my Lord? I am ready
to set off again directly."

The suddenness of such intelligence, concerning an only
son, might have agitated stronger nerves than those of the
Marchese, and so much was he shocked by it, that he could
not immediately determine how to proceed, or give any answer to Paulo's repeated questions. When, however, he became sufficiently recollected to make further inquiry into the
situation of Vivaldi, he perceived the necessity of an immediate journey; but first it would be prudent to consult with
some friends, whose connections at Rome might be a means
of greatly facilitating the important purpose, which led him
thither, and this could not be done till the following morning. Yet he gave orders, that preparation should be made for
his setting out at a moment's notice; and, having listened to
as full an account as Paulo could give of the past and present
circumstances of Vivaldi, he dismissed him to repose for the
remainder of the night.

Paulo, however, though much in want of rest, was in too
great an agitation of spirits either to seek or to find it; and
the fear he had indicated, on entering the Marchese's apartment, proceeded from the hurry of his mind, rather than
from any positive apprehension of new evil. For his liberty
he was indebted to the young centinel, who had on a former
occasion been removed from the door of his prison, but who,
by means of the guard, to whom Vivaldi had given money,
as he returned one night from the tribunal, had since been
able to communicate with him. This man, of a nature too hu-
mane for his situation, was become wretched in it, and he
determined to escape from his office before the expiration of
the time, for which he had been engaged. He thought that to
be a guard over prisoners was nearly as miserable as being
a prisoner himself. "I see no difference between them," said
he, "except that the prisoner watches on one side of the
door, and the centinel on the other."

With the resolution to release himself, he conferred with
Paulo, whose good nature and feeling heart, among so many
people of a contrary character, had won his confidence and
affection, and he laid his plan of escape so well, that it was
on the point of succeeding, when Paulo's obstinacy in attempting an impossibility had nearly counteracted the whole.

It went to his heart, he said, to leave his master in prison, while he himself was to march off in safety, and he would run the risk of his neck, rather than have such a deed upon his head. He proposed, therefore, as Vivaldi's guards were of too ferocious a nature to be tampered with, to scale a wall of the court into which a grate of Vivaldi's dungeon looked. But had this lofty wall been practicable, the grate was not; and the attempt had nearly cost Paulo not only his liberty, but his life.

When, at length, he had made his way through the perilous avenues of the prison, and was fairly beyond the walls, he could hardly be prevailed upon by his companion to leave them. For near an hour, he wandered under their shade, weeping and exclaiming, and calling upon his dear master, at the evident hazard of being retaken; and probably would have remained there much longer, had not the dawn of morning rendered his companion desperate. Just, however, as the man was forcing him away, Paulo fancied he distinguished, by the strengthening light, the roof of that particular building, in whose dungeon his master was confined, and the appearance of Vivaldi himself could scarcely have occasioned a more sudden burst of joy; succeeded by one of grief. "It is the roof, it is the very roof!" exclaimed Paulo, vaulting from the ground, and clapping his hands; "it is the roof, the roof! O, my master, my master! the roof, the roof!" He continued alternately to exclaim, "My master! the roof! my master! the roof!" till his companion began to fear he was frantic, while tears streamed down his cheeks, and every look and gesture expressed the most extravagant and whimsical union of joy and sorrow. At length, the absolute terror of discovery compelled his companion to force him from the spot; when, having lost sight of the building which inclosed Vivaldi, he set off for Naples with a speed that defied all interruption, and arrived there in the condition, which has been mentioned, having taken no sleep, and scarcely any sustenance, since he left the Inquisition. Yet though in this exhausted state, the spirit of his affection remained unbroken, and when, on the following morning, the Marchese quitted Naples, neither his weariness, nor the imminent danger, to which this journey must expose him, could prevent his attending him to Rome.

The rank of the Marchese, and the influence he was known to possess at the court of Naples, were circumstances that promised to have weight with the Holy Office, and to procure Vivaldi a speedy release; but yet more than these, were the high connections which the Count di Maro, the friend of the Marchese, had in the church of Rome.

The applications, however, which were made to the inquisitors, were not so soon replied to as the wishes of the Marchese had expected, and he had been above a fortnight in that city, before he was even permitted to visit his son. In this interview, affection predominated on both sides over all remembrance of the past. The condition of Vivaldi, his faded appearance, to which the wounds he had received at Celano, and from which he was scarcely recovered, had contributed; and his situation in a melancholy and terrible prison, were circumstances that awakened all the tenderness of the father; his errors were forgiven, and the Marchese felt disposed to consent to all that might restore him to happiness, could he but be restored to liberty.

Vivaldi, when informed of his mother's death, shed bitter tears of sorrow and remorse, for having occasioned her so much uneasiness. The unreasonableness of her claims was forgotten, and her faults were extenuated; happily, indeed, for his peace, the extent of her criminal designs he had never understood; and when he learned that her dying request had been intended to promote his happiness, the cruel consciousness of having interrupted hers, occasioned him severe anguish, and he was obliged to recollect her former conduct towards Ellena at San Stefano, before he could become reconciled to himself.

CHAPTER XI

Yours in the ranks of death.
SHAKESPEARE

NEAR three weeks had elapsed since the Marchese's arrival at Rome, and not any decisive answer was returned by the Inquisition to his application, when he and Vivaldi received at the same time a summons to attend father Schedoni in his dungeon. To meet the man who had occasioned so much suffering to his family, was extremely painful to the Marchese, but he was not allowed to refuse the interview; and at the hour appointed he called at the chamber of Vivaldi; and, followed by two officials, they passed on together to that of Schedoni.

While they waited at the door of the prison-room, till the numerous bars and locks were unfastened, the agitation, which Vivaldi had suffered, on receiving the summons, returned with redoubled force, now that he was about to behold, once more, that wretched man, who had announced himself to be the parent of Ellena di Rosalba. The Marchese suffered emotions of a different nature, and with his reluctance to see Schedoni, was mingled a degree of curiosity as to the event, which had occasioned this summons.

The door being thrown open, the officials entered first, and the Marchese and Vivaldi, on following, discovered the Confessor lying on a mattress. He did not rise to receive them, but, as he lifted his head, and bowed it in obeisance, his countenance, upon which the little light admitted through the triple grate of his dungeon gleamed, seemed more than usually ghastly; his eyes were hollow, and his shrunk features appeared as if death had already touched them. Vivaldi, on perceiving him, groaned, and averted his face; but, soon recovering a command of himself, he approached the mattress.

The Marchese, suppressing every expression of resentment towards an enemy, who was reduced to this deplorable condition, inquired what he had to communicate.

"Where is father Nicola?" said Schedoni to an official, without attending to the question: "I do not see him here. Is he gone so soon, and without having heard the purport of my summons? Let him be called."

The official spoke to a centinel, who immediately left the chamber.

"Who are these that surround me?" said Schedoni. "Who is he that stands at the foot of the bed?" While he spoke, he bent his eyes on Vivaldi, who rested in deep dejection there, and was lost in thought, till, aroused by Schedoni's voice, he replied,

"It is I, Vincentio di Vivaldi; I obey your requisition, and inquire the purpose of it?"

The Marchese repeated the demand. Schedoni appeared to meditate; sometimes he fixed his eyes upon Vivaldi, for an instant, and when he withdrew them, he seemed to sink into deeper thoughtfulness. As he raised them once again, they assumed a singular expression of wildness, and then settling, as if on vacancy, a sudden glare shot from them, while he said—"Who is he, that glides there in the dusk?"

His eyes were directed beyond Vivaldi, who, on turning, perceived the monk, father Nicola, passing behind him.

"I am here," said Nicola: "what do you require of me?"

"That you will bear testimony to the truth of what I shall declare," replied Schedoni.

Nicola, and an inquisitor who had accompanied him, immediately arranged themselves on one side of the bed, while the Marchese stationed himself on the other. Vivaldi remained at its foot.

Schedoni, after a pause, began: "That which I have to make known relates to the cabal formerly carried on by him, the father Nicola, and myself, against the peace of an innocent young woman, whom, at my instigation, he has basely traduced."

At these words, Nicola attempted to interrupt the Confessor, but Vivaldi restrained him.

"Ellena di Rosalba is known to you?" continued Schedoni, addressing the Marchese.

Vivaldi's countenance changed at this abrupt mention of Ellena, but he remained silent.

"I have heard of her," replied the Marchese, coldly.

"And you have heard falsely of her," rejoined Schedoni. "Lift your eyes, my lord Marchese, and say, do you not recollect that face?" pointing to Nicola.

The Marchese regarded the monk attentively, "It is a face not easily to be forgotten," he replied; "I remember to have seen it more than once."

"Where have you seen him, my Lord?"

"In my own palace, at Naples; and you yourself introduced him to me there."

"I did," replied Schedoni.

"Why, then, do you now accuse him of falsehood," observed the Marchese, "since you acknowledge yourself to have been the instigator of his conduct?"

"O heavens!" said Vivaldi, "this monk, then, this father Nicola, is, as I suspected, the slanderer of Ellena di Rosalba!"

"Most true," rejoined Schedoni; "and it is for the purpose of vindicating——"

"And you acknowledge yourself to be the author of those infamous slanders!" passionately interrupted Vivaldi;— "you, who but lately declared yourself to be her father!"

In the instant, that Vivaldi had uttered this, he became sensible of his indiscretion, for till now he had avoided informing the Marchese, that Ellena had been declared the daughter of Schedoni. This abrupt disclosure, and at such a moment, he immediately perceived might be fatal to his hopes, and that the Marchese would not consider the promise he had given to his dying wife, however solemn, as binding, under circumstances so peculiar and unforeseen as the present. The astonishment of the Marchese, upon this discovery, cannot easily be imagined; he looked at his son for an explanation of what he had heard, and then with increased detestation at the Confessor; but Vivaldi was not in a state of mind to give any explanation at this moment, and he requested his father to suspend even his conjectures till he could converse with him alone.

The Marchese desisted for the present from further inquiry, but it was obvious that his opinion and his resolution, respecting the marriage of Vivaldi, was already formed.

"You, then, are the author of those slanders!" repeated Vivaldi.

"Hear me!" cried Schedoni, in a voice which the strength of his spirit contending with the feebleness of his condition, rendered hollow and terrible—"Hear me!"

He stopped, unable to recover immediately from the effect of the exertion he had made. At length, he resumed,

"I have declared, and I continue to declare, that Ellena di Rosalba, as she has been named for the purpose, I conjecture, of concealing her from an unworthy father, is my daughter!"

Vivaldi groaned in the excess of his despair, but made no further attempt to interrupt Schedoni. The Marchese was not equally passive. "And was it to listen to a vindication of your daughter," said he, "that I have been summoned hither? But let this Signora Rosalba, be who she may, of what importance can it be to me whether she is innocent or otherwise!"

Vivaldi, with the utmost difficulty, forebore to express the feelings, which this sentence excited. It appeared to recall all the spirit of Schedoni. "She is the daughter of a noble house," said the Confessor, haughtily, while he half raised himself from his mattress. "In me you behold the last of the Counts di Bruno."

The Marchese smiled contemptuously.

Schedoni proceeded. "I call upon you, Nicola di Zampari, who have declared yourself, on a late occasion, so strenuous for justice, I call upon you now to do justice in this instance, and to acknowledge, before these witnesses, that Ellena Rosalba is innocent of every circumstance of misconduct, which you have formerly related to the Marchese di Vivaldi!"

"Villain! do you hesitate," said Vivaldi to Nicola, "to retract the cruel slanders which you have thrown upon her name, and which have been the means of destroying her peace, perhaps for ever? Do you persist——"

The Marchese interrupted his son:—"Let me put an end to the difficulty, by concluding the interview; I perceive that my presence has been required for a purpose that does not concern me."

Before the Confessor could reply, the Marchese had turned from him to quit the chamber; but the vehemence of Vivaldi's distress prevailed with him to pause, and thus allowed him to understand from Schedoni, that the justification of the innocent Ellena, though it had been mentioned first, as being the object nearest to his heart, was not the only one that had urged him to require this meeting.

"If you consent," added Schedoni, "to listen to the vindication of my child, you shall afterwards perceive, Signor, that I, fallen though I am, have still been desirous of counteracting, as far as remains for me, the evil I have occasioned. You shall acknowledge, that what I then make known is of the utmost consequence to the repose of the Marchese di Vivaldi, high in influence, and haughty in prosperity as he now appears."

The latter part of this assurance threatened to overcome the effect of the first; the pride of the Marchese swelled high; he took some steps towards the door, but then stopped, and, conjecturing that the subject, to which Schedoni alluded, concerned the liberation of his son, he consented to attend to what Nicola should disclose.

This monk, meanwhile, had been balancing the necessity for acknowledging himself a slanderer, against the possibility of avoiding it; and it was the resolute manner of Vivaldi, who appeared to have no doubt as to his guilt in this instance, that made him apprehend the consequence of persisting in falsehood, not either remorse of conscience, or the appeal of Schedoni. He acknowledged then, after considerable circumlocution, in which he contrived to defend himself, by throwing all the odium of the original design upon the Confessor, that he had been prevailed upon by his arts to impose on the credulity of the Marchese, respecting the conduct of Ellena di Rosalba. This avowal was made upon oath, and Schedoni, by the questions he put to him, was careful it should be so full and circumstantial that even the most prejudiced hearer must have been convinced of its truth; while the most unfeeling must have yielded for once to indignation against the asperser, and pity of the aspersed. Its effect upon the present auditors was various. The Marchese had listened to the whole explanation with an unmoved countenance, but with profound attention. Vivaldi had remained in a fixed attitude, with eyes bent on father Nicola, in such eager and stern regard, as seemed to search into his very soul; and, when the monk concluded, a smile of triumphant joy lighted up his features, as he looked upon the Marchese, and claimed an acknowledgment of his conviction, that Ellena had been calumniated. The cold glance, which the Marchese returned, struck the impassioned and generous Vivaldi to the heart, who perceived that he was not only totally indifferent as to the injustice, which an innocent and helpless young woman had suffered, but fancied that he was unwilling to admit the truth, which his judgment would no longer allow him to reject.

Schedoni, meanwhile, appeared almost to writhe under the agony, which his mind inflicted upon him, and it was only by strong effort, that he sustained his spirit so far as to go through with the interrogations he had judged it necessary to put to Nicola. When the subject was finished, he sunk back on his pillow, and, closing his eyes, a hue so pallid, succeeded by one so livid, overspread his features, that Vivaldi for an instant believed he was dying; and in this supposition he was not singular, for even an official was touched with the Confessor's condition, and had advanced to assist him, when he unclosed his eyes, and seemed to revive.

The Marchese, without making any comment upon the avowal of father Nicola, demanded, on its conclusion, the disclosure, which Schedoni had asserted to be intimately connected with his peace; and the latter now inquired of a person near him, whether a secretary of the Inquisition was in the chamber, who he had requested might attend, to take a formal deposition of what he should declare. He was answered, that such an one was already in waiting. He then asked, what other persons were in the room, adding, that he should require inquisitorial witnesses to his deposition; and was answered, that an inquisitor and two officials were present, and that their evidence was more than sufficient for his purpose.

A lamp was then called for by the secretary; but, as that could not immediately be procured, the torch of one of the centinels, who watched in the dark avenue without, was brought in its stead, and this discovered to Schedoni the various figures assembled in his dusky chamber, and to them the emaciated form and ghastly visage of the Confessor. As Vivaldi now beheld him by the stronger light of the torch, he again fancied that death was in his aspect.

Every person was now ready for the declaration of Schedoni; but he himself seemed not fully prepared. He remained for some moments reclining on his pillow in silence, with his eyes shut, while the changes in his features indicated the strong emotion of his mind. Then, as if by a violent effort, he half raised himself, and made an ample confession of the arts he had practised against Vivaldi. He declared himself to be the anonymous accuser, who had caused him to be arrested by the Holy Office, and that the charge of heresy, which he had brought against him, was false and malicious.

At the moment when Vivaldi received this confirmation of his suspicions, as to the identity of his accuser, he discovered more fully that the charge was not what had been stated to him at the chapel of San Sebastian, in which Ellena was implicated; and he demanded an explanation of this circumstance. Schedoni acknowledged, that the persons, who had there arrested him, were not officers of the Inquisition, and that the instrument of arrest, containing the charge of elopement with a nun, was forged by himself, for the purpose of empowering the ruffians to carry off Ellena, without opposition from the inhabitants of the convent, in which she was then lodged.

To Vivaldi's inquiry, why it had been thought necessary to employ stratagem in the removal of Ellena, since, if Schedoni had only claimed her for his daughter, he might have removed her without any, the Confessor replied, that he was then ignorant of the relationship which existed between them. But to the further inquiries, with what design, and whither Ellena had been removed, and the means by which he had discovered her to be his daughter, Schedoni was silent; and he sunk back, overwhelmed by the recollections they awakened.

The depositions of Schedoni having been taken down by the secretary, were formally signed by the inquisitor and the officials present; and Vivaldi thus saw his innocence vindicated by the very man who had thrown him among the perils of the Inquisition. But the near prospect of release now before him failed to affect him with joy, while he understood that Ellena was the daughter of Schedoni, the child of a murderer, whom he himself had been in some degree instrumental in bringing to a dreadful and ignominious death. Still, however, willing to hope, that Schedoni had not spoken the truth concerning his relationship to Ellena, he claimed, in consideration of the affection he had so long cherished for her, a full explanation of the circumstances connected with the discovery of her family.

At this public avowal of his attachment, a haughty impatience appeared on the countenance of the Marchese, who forbade him to make further inquiry on the subject, and was immediately retiring from the chamber.

"My presence is no longer necessary," he added: "the

prisoner has concluded the only detail which I could be interested to hear from him; and, in consideration of the confession he has made as to the innocence of my son, I pardon him the suffering, which his false charge has occasioned to me and my family. The paper containing his depositions is given to your responsibility, holy father," addressing the inquisitor; "and you are required to lay it upon the table of the Holy Office, that the innocence of Vincentio di Vivaldi may appear, and that he may be released from these prisons without further delay. But first, I demand a copy of those declarations, and that the copy also shall be signed by the present witnesses."

The secretary was now bidden to copy them, and, while the Marchese waited to receive the paper, (for he would not leave the chamber till he had secured it) Vivaldi was urging his claim for an explanation respecting the family of Ellena, with unconquerable perseverance. Schedoni, no longer permitted to evade the inquiry, could not, however, give a circumstantial explanation, without partly disclosing, also, the fatal designs which had been meditated by him and the late Marchesa di Vivaldi, of whose death he was ignorant; he related, therefore, little more respecting Ellena than that a portrait, which she wore as being her father's, had first led to the discovery of her family.

While the Confessor had been giving this brief explanation, Nicola, who was somewhat withdrawn from the circle, stood gazing at him with the malignity of a demon. His glowing eyes just appeared under the edge of his cowl, while, rolled up in his dark drapery, the lower features of his face were muffled; but the intermediate part of his countenance, receiving the full glare of the torch, displayed all its speaking and terrific lines. Vivaldi, as his eye glanced upon him, saw again the very monk of Paluzzi, and he thought he beheld also a man capable of the very crimes of which he had accused Schedoni. At this instant, he remembered the dreadful garment that had been discovered in a dungeon of the fortress; and, yet more, he remembered the extraordinary circumstances attending the death of Bianchi, together with the immediate knowledge which the monk had displayed of that event. Vivaldi's suspicions respecting the cause of her death being thus revived, he determined to obtain, if possible, either a relief from, or a confirmation of them; and he solemnly called upon Schedoni, who, already condemned to die, had no longer any thing to fear from a disclosure of the truth, whatever it might be, to declare all that he knew on the subject. As he did so, he looked at Nicola, to observe the effect of this demand, whose countenance was, however, so much shrouded, that little of its expression could be seen; but Vivaldi remarked, that, while he had spoken, the monk drew his garment closer over the lower part of his face, and that he had immediately turned his eyes from him upon the Confessor.

With most solemn protestations, Schedoni declared himself to be both innocent and ignorant of the cause of Bianchi's death.

Vivaldi then demanded by what means his agent, Nicola, had obtained such immediate information, as the warning he had delivered at Paluzzi proved him to have, of an event, in which it appeared that he could be so little interested; and why that warning had been given.

Nicola did not attempt to anticipate the reply of Schedoni, who, after a momentary silence, said, "That warning, young man, was given to deter you from visiting Altieri, as was every circumstance of advice or intelligence, which you received beneath the arch of Paluzzi."

"Father," replied Vivaldi, "you have never loved, or you would have spared yourself the practice of artifices so ineffectual to mislead or to conquer a lover. Did you believe that an anonymous adviser could have more influence with me than my affection, or that I could be terrified by such stratagems into a renunciation of its object?"

"I believed," rejoined the Confessor, "that the disinterested advice of a stranger might have some weight with you; but I trusted more to the impression of awe, which the conduct and seeming foreknowledge of that stranger were adapted to inspire in a mind like yours; and I thus endeavoured to avail myself of your prevailing weakness."

"And what do you term my prevailing weakness," said Vivaldi, blushing.

"A susceptibility which renders you especially liable to superstition," replied Schedoni.

"What! does a monk call superstition a weakness!" rejoined Vivaldi. "But grant he does, on what occasion have I betrayed such weakness?"

"Have you forgotten a conversation which I once held with you on invisible spirits?" said Schedoni.

As he asked this, Vivaldi was struck with the tone of his voice; he thought it was different from what he had remembered ever to have heard from him; and he looked at Schedoni more intently, that he might be certain it was he who had spoken. The Confessor's eyes were fixed upon him, and he repeated slowly in the same tone, "Have you forgotten?"

"I have not forgotten the conversation to which you allude," replied Vivaldi, "and I do not recollect that I then disclosed any opinion that may justify your assertion."

"The opinions you avowed were rational," said Schedoni, "but the ardour of your imagination was apparent, and what ardent imagination ever was contented to trust to plain reasoning, or to the evidence of the senses? It may not willing confine itself to the dull truths of this earth, but, eager to expand its faculties, to fill its capacity, and to experience its own peculiar delights, soars after new wonders into a world of its own!"

Vivaldi blushed at this reproof, now conscious of its justness; and was surprised that Schedoni should so well have understood the nature of his mind, while he himself, with whom conjecture had never assumed the stability of opinion, on the subject to which the Confessor alluded, had been ignorant even of its propensities.

"I acknowledge the truth of your remark," said Vivaldi, "as far as it concerns myself. I have, however, inquiries to make on a point less abstracted, and towards explaining which the evidence of my senses themselves have done little. To whom belonged the bloody garments I found in the dungeon of Paluzzi, and what became of the person to whom they had pertained?"

Consternation appeared for an instant on the features of Schedoni. "What garments?" said he.

"They appeared to be those of a person who had died by violence," replied Vivaldi, "and they were discovered in a place frequented by your avowed agent, Nicola, the monk."

As he concluded the sentence, Vivaldi looked at Nicola, upon whom the attention of every person present was now directed.

"They were my own," said this monk.

"Your own! and in that condition!" exclaimed Vivaldi. "They were covered with gore!"

"They were my own," repeated Nicola. "For their condition, I have to thank you,—the wound your pistol gave me occasioned it."

Vivaldi was astonished by this apparent subterfuge, "I had no pistol," he rejoined, "my sword was my only weapon!"

"Pause a moment," said the monk.

"I repeat that I had no fire-arms," replied Vivaldi.

"I appeal to father Schedoni," rejoined Nicola, "whether I was not wounded by a pistol shot."

"To me you have no longer any right of appeal," said Schedoni. "Why should I save you from suspicions, that may bring you to a state like this, to which you have reduced me!"

"Your crimes have reduced you to it," replied Nicola, "I have only done my duty, and that which another person could have effected without my aid—the priest to whom Spalatro made his last confession."

"It is, however, a duty of such a kind," observed Vivaldi, "as I would not willingly have upon my conscience. You have betrayed the life of your former friend, and have compelled me to assist in the destruction of a fellow being."

"You, like me, have assisted to destroy a destroyer," replied the monk. "He has taken life, and deserves, therefore, to lose it. If, however, it will afford you consolation to know that you have not materially assisted in his destruction, I will hereafter give you proof for this assurance. There were other means of shewing that Schedoni was the Count di Bruno, than the testimony of Ansaldo, though I was ignorant of them when I bade you summon the penitentiary."

"If you had sooner avowed this," said Vivaldi, "the assertion would have been more plausible. Now, I can only understand that it is designed to win my silence, and prevent my retorting upon you your own maxim—that he who has taken the life of another, deserves to lose his own.—To whom did those bloody garments belong?"

"To myself, I repeat," replied Nicola, "Schedoni can bear testimony that I received at Paluzzi a pistol wound."

"Impossible," said Vivaldi, "I was armed only with my sword!"

"You had a companion," observed the monk, "had not he firearms?"

Vivaldi, after a momentary consideration, recollected that Paulo had pistols, and that he had fired one beneath the arch of Paluzzi, on the first alarm occasioned by the stranger's voice. He immediately acknowledged the recollection. "But I heard no groan, no symptom of distress!" he added. "Besides, the garments were at a considerable distance from the spot where the pistol was fired! How could a person, so severely wounded as those garments indicated, have silently withdrawn to a remote dungeon, or, having done so, is it probable he would have thrown aside his dress!"

"All that is nevertheless true," replied Nicola. "My resolution enabled me to stifle the expression of my anguish; I withdrew to the interior of the ruin, to escape from you, but you pursued me even to the dungeon, where I threw off my discoloured vestments, in which I dared not return to my convent, and departed by a way which all your ingenuity failed to discover. The people who were already in the fort, for the purpose of assisting to confine you and your servant during the night on which Signora Rosalba was taken from Altieri, procured me another habit, and relief for my wound. But, though I was unseen by you during the night, I was not entirely unheard, for my groans reached you more than once from an adjoining chamber, and my companions were entertained with the alarm which your servant testified.—Are you now convinced?"

The groans were clearly remembered by Vivaldi, and many other circumstances of Nicola's narration accorded so well with others, which he recollected to have occurred on the night alluded to, that he had no longer a doubt of its veracity. The suddenness of Bianchi's death, however, still occasioned him suspicions as to its cause; yet Schedoni had declared not only that he was innocent, but ignorant of this cause, which it appeared from his unwillingness to give testimony in favour of his agent, he would not have affirmed, had he been conscious that the monk was in any degree guilty in this instance. That Nicola could have no inducement for attempting the life of Bianchi other than a reward offered him by Schedoni, was clear; and Vivaldi, after more fully considering these circumstances, became convinced that her death was in consequence of some incident of natural decay.

While this conversation was passing, the Marchese, impatient to put a conclusion to it, and to leave the chamber, repeatedly urged the secretary to dispatch; and, while he now earnestly renewed his request, another voice answered for the secretary, that he had nearly concluded. Vivaldi thought that he had heard the voice on some former occasion, and on turning his eyes upon the person who had spoken, discovered the stranger to be the same who had first visited him in prison. Perceiving by his dress, that he was an officer of the Inquisition, Vivaldi now understood too well the purport of his former visit, and that he had come with a design to betray him by affected sympathy into a confession of some heretical opinions. Similar instances of treachery Vivaldi had heard were frequently practised upon accused persons, but he had never fully believed such cruelty possible till now, that it had been attempted towards himself.

The visit of this person bringing to his recollection the subsequent one he had received from Nicola, Vivaldi inquired whether the centinels had really admitted him to his cell, or he had entered it by other means; a question to which the monk was silent, but the smile on his features, if so strange an expression deserved to be called a smile, seemed to reply, "Do you believe that I, a servant of the Inquisition, will betray its secrets?"

Vivaldi, however, urged the inquiry, for he wished to know whether the guard, who appeared to be faithful to their office, had escaped the punishment that was threatened.

"They were honest," replied Nicola, "seek no further."

"Are the tribunal convinced of their integrity?"

Nicola smiled again in derision, and replied, "They never doubted it."

"How!" said Vivaldi. "Why were these men put under arrest, if their faithfulness was not even suspected?"

"Be satisfied with the knowledge, which experience has given you of the secrets of the Inquisition," replied Nicola solemnly, "seek to know no more!"

"It has terrible secrets!" said Schedoni, who had been long silent. "Know, young man, that almost every cell of every prisoner has a concealed entrance, by which the ministers of death may pass unnoticed to their victims. This Nicola is now one of those dreadful summoners, and is acquainted with all the secret avenues, that lead to murder."

Vivaldi shrunk from Nicola in horror, and Schedoni paused; but while he had spoken, Vivaldi had again noticed the extraordinary change in his voice, and shuddered at its sound no less than at the information it had given. Nicola was silent; but his terrible eyes were fixed in vengeance on Schedoni.

"His office has been short," resumed the Confessor, turning his heavy eyes upon Nicola, "and his task is almost done!" As he pronounced the last words his voice faltered, but they were heard by the monk, who drawing nearer to the bed, demanded an explanation of them. A ghastly smile triumphed in the features of Schedoni; "Fear not but that an explanation will come full soon," said he.

Nicola fixed himself before the Confessor, and bent his brows upon him as if he would have searched into his very soul. When Vivaldi again looked at Schedoni, he was shocked on observing the sudden alteration in his countenance, yet still a faint smile of triumph lingered there. But, while Vivaldi gazed, the features suddenly became agitated; in the next instant his whole frame was convulsed, and heavy groans laboured from his breast. Schedoni was now evidently dying.

The horror of Vivaldi, and of the Marchese, who endeavoured to leave the chamber, was equalled only by the general confusion that reigned there; every person present seemed to feel at least a momentary compassion, except Nicola, who stood unmoved beside Schedoni, and looked steadfastly upon his pangs, while a smile of derision marked his countenance. As Vivaldi observed, with detestation, this expression, a slight spasm darted over Nicola's face, and his muscles also seemed to labour with sudden contraction; but the affection was transient, and vanished as abruptly as it had appeared. The monk, however, turned from the miserable spectacle before him, and as he turned he caught involuntarily at the arm of a person near him, and leaned on his shoulder for support. His manner appeared to betray that he had not been permitted to triumph in the sufferings of his enemy, without participating at least in their horror.

Schedoni's struggles now began to abate, and in a short time he lay motionless. When he unclosed his eyes, death was in them. He was yet nearly insensible; but presently a faint gleam of recollection shot from them, and gradually lighting them up, the character of his soul appeared there; the expression was indeed feeble, but it was true. He moved his lips as if he would have spoken, and looked languidly round the chamber, seemingly in search of some person. At length, he uttered a sound, but he had not yet sufficient command of his muscles, to modulate that sound into a word, till by repeated efforts the name of Nicola became intelligible. At the call, the monk raised his head from the shoulder of the person on whom he had reclined, and turning round, Schedoni, as was evident from the sudden change of expression in his countenance, discovered him; his eyes, as they settled on Nicola seemed to recollect all their wonted fire, and the malignant triumph, lately so prevalent in his physiognomy, again appeared as in the next moment, he pointed to him. His glance seemed suddenly impowered with the destructive fascination attributed to that of the basilisk, for while it now met Nicola's, that monk seemed as if transfixed to the spot, and unable to withdraw his eyes from the glare of Schedoni's; in their expression he read the dreadful sentence of his fate, the triumph of revenge and cunning. Struck with this terrible conviction a pallid hue overspread his face; at the same time an involuntary motion convulsed his features, cold trembling seized upon his frame, and, uttering a deep groan, he fell back, and was caught in the arms of the people near him. At the instant of his fall, Schedoni uttered a sound so strange and horrible, so convulsed, yet so loud, so exulting, yet so unlike any human voice, that every person in the chamber, except those who were assisting Nicola, struck with irresistible terror, endeavoured to make their way out of it. This, however, was impracticable, for the door was fastened, until a physician, who had been sent for, should arrive, and some investigation could be made into this mysterious affair. The consternation of the Marchese and of Vivaldi, compelled to witness this scene of horror, cannot easily be imagined.

Schedoni, having uttered that demoniacal sound of exultation, was not permitted to repeat it, for the pangs he had lately suffered returned upon him, and he was again in strong convulsions, when the physician entered the chamber. The moment he beheld Schedoni, he declared him to be poisoned; and he pronounced a similar opinion on father Nicola; affirming, also, that the drug, as appeared from the violence of the effect, was of too subtle and inveterate a nature to allow of antidote. He was, however, willing to administer the medicine usual in such cases.

While he was giving orders to an attendant, with respect to this, the violence of Schedoni's convulsions once more relaxed; but Nicola appeared in the last extremity. His sufferings were incessant, his senses never for a moment returned, and he expired, before the medicine, which had been sent for, could be brought. When it came, however, it was administered with some success to Schedoni, who recovered not only his recollection, but his voice; and the first word he uttered was, as formerly, the name of Nicola.

"Does he live?" added the Confessor with the utmost difficulty, and after a long pause. The persons around him were silent, but the truth, which this silence indicated, seemed to revive him.

The inquisitor, who had attended, perceiving that Schedoni had recovered the use of his intellects, now judged it prudent to ask some questions relative to his present condition, and to the cause of Nicola's death.

"Poison," replied Schedoni readily.

"By whom administered?" said the inquisitor, "consider that, while you answer, you are on your death-bed."

"I have no wish to conceal the truth," rejoined Schedoni, "nor the satisfaction"—he was obliged to pause, but presently added, "I have destroyed him, who would have destroyed me, and—and I have escaped an ignominious death."

He paused again; it was with difficulty that he had said thus much, and he was now overcome by the exertion he had made. The secretary, who had not been permitted to leave the chamber, was ordered to note Schedoni's words.

"You avow then," continued the inquisitor, "that the poison was administered, both in the case of father Nicola and in your own, by yourself?"

Schedoni could not immediately reply; but when he did, he said, "I avow it."

He was asked by what means he had contrived to procure the poison, and was bidden to name his accomplice.

"I had no accomplice," replied Schedoni.

"How did you procure the poison, then?"

Schedoni, slowly and with difficulty, replied, "It was concealed in my vest."

"Consider that you are dying," said the inquisitor, "and confess the truth. We cannot believe what you have last asserted. It is improbable that you should have had an opportunity of providing yourself with poison after your arrest, and equally improbable that you should have thought such provision necessary before that period. Confess who is your accomplice."

This accusation of falsehood recalled the spirit of Schedoni, which, contending with, and conquering, for a moment, corporeal suffering, he said in a firmer tone, "It was the poison, on which I dip my poniard, the better to defend me."

The inquisitor smiled in contempt of this explanation, and

Schedoni, observing him, desired a particular part of his vest might be examined, where would be found some remains of the drug concealed as he had affirmed. He was indulged in his request, and the poison was discovered within a broad hem of his garment.

Still it was inconceivable how he had contrived to administer it to Nicola, who, though he had been for some time alone with him on this day, would scarcely have so far confided in an enemy, as to have accepted any seeming sustenance that might have been offered by him. The inquisitor, still anxious to discover an accomplice, asked Schedoni who had assisted to administer the drug to Nicola, but the Confessor was no longer in a condition to reply. Life was now sinking apace; the gleam of spirit and of character that had returned to his eyes, was departed, and left them haggard and fixed; and presently a livid corse was all that remained of the once terrible Schedoni!

While this awful event had been accomplishing, the Marchese, suffering under the utmost perturbation, had withdrawn to the distant grate of the dungeon, where he conversed with an official as to what might be the probable consequence of his present situation to himself; but Vivaldi, in an agony of horror, had been calling incessantly for the medicine, which might possibly afford some relief to the anguish he witnessed; and when it was brought, he had assisted to support the sufferers.

At length, now that the worst was over, and when the several witnesses had signed to the last avowal of Schedoni, every person in the chamber was suffered to depart; and Vivaldi was re-conducted to his prison, accompanied by the Marchese, where he was to remain till the decision of the holy office respecting his innocence, as asserted by the deposition of Schedoni, should be known. He was too much affected by the late scene to give the Marchese any explanation at present, respecting the family of Ellena di Rosalba, and the Marchese, having remained for some time with his son, withdrew to the residence of his friend.

CHAPTER XII

Master, go on, and I will follow thee
To the last gasp, with truth and loyalty.
                                        SHAKESPEARE

In consequence of the dying confession of Schedoni, an order was sent from the holy office for the release of Vivaldi, within a few days after the death of the Confessor; and the Marchese conducted his son from the prisons of the Inquisition to the mansion of his friend the Count di Maro, with whom he had resided since his arrival at Rome.

While they were receiving the ceremonious congratulations of the Count, and of some nobles assembled to welcome the emancipated prisoner, a loud voice was heard from the anti-chamber exclaiming, "Let me pass! It is my master, let me pass! May all those who attempt to stop me, be sent to the Inquisition themselves!"

In the next instant Paulo burst into the saloon, followed by a group of lacqueys, who, however, paused at the door, fearful of the displeasure of their lord, yet scarcely able to stifle a laugh; while Paulo, springing forward, had nearly overset some of the company, who happened at that moment to be bowing with profound joy to Vivaldi.

"It is my master! it is my dear master!" cried Paulo, and, sending off a nobleman with each elbow, as he made his way between them, he hugged Vivaldi in his arms, repeating, "O, my master! my master!" till a passion of joy and affection overcame his voice, and he fell at his master's feet and wept.

This was a moment of finer joy to Vivaldi, than he had known since his meeting with his father, and he was too much interested by his faithful servant, to have leisure to apologize to the astonished company for his rudeness. While the lacqueys were repairing the mischief Paulo had occasioned, were picking up the rolling snuff-boxes he had jerked away in his passage, and wiping the snuff from the soiled clothes, Vivaldi was participating in all the delight, and returning all the affection of his servant, and was so wholly occupied by these pleasurable feelings as scarcely to be sensible that any persons besides themselves were in the room. The Marchese, meanwhile was making a thousand apologies for the disasters Paulo had occasioned; was alternately calling upon him to recollect in whose presence he was, and to quit the apartment immediately; explaining to the company that he had not seen Vivaldi since they were together in the Inquisition, and remarking profoundly, that he was much attached to his master. But Paulo, insensible to the repeated commands of the Marchese, and to the endeavours of Vivaldi to raise him, was still pouring forth his whole heart at his master's feet. "Ah! my Signor," said he, "if you could but know how miserable I was when I got out of the Inquisition!"—

"He raves!" observed the Count to the Marchese, "you perceive that joy has rendered him delirious!"

"How I wandered about the walls half the night, and what it cost me to leave them! But when I lost sight of them, Signor, O! San Dominico! I thought my heart would have broke. I had a great mind to have gone back again and given myself up; and, perhaps, I should too, if it had not been for my friend, the centinel, who escaped with me, and I would not do him an injury, poor fellow! for he meant nothing but kindness when he let me out. And sure enough, as it has proved, it was all for the best, for now I am here, too, Signor, as well as you; and can tell you all I felt when I believe I should never see you again."

The contrast of his present joy to his remembered grief again brought tears into Paulo's eyes; he smiled and wept, and sobbed and laughed with such rapid transition, that Vivaldi began to be alarmed for him; when, suddenly becoming calm, he looked up in his master's face and said gravely, but with eagerness, "Pray Signor, was not the roof of your little prison peaked, and was there not a little turret stuck up at one corner of it? and was there not a battlement round the turret? and was there not"——Vivaldi, after regarding him for a moment, replied smilingly, "Why truly, my good Paulo, my dungeon was so far from the roof, that I never had an opportunity of observing it."

"That is very true, Signor," replied Paulo, "very true indeed; but I did not happen to think of that. I am certain, though, it was as I say, and I was sure of it at the time. O Signor! I thought that roof would have broke my heart, O how I did look at it! and now to think that I am here, with my dear master once again!"

As Paulo concluded, his tears and sobs returned with more violence than before; and Vivaldi, who could not perceive any necessary connection between this mention of the roof of his late prison, and the joy his servant expressed on seeing him again, began to fear that his senses were bewildered, and desired an explanation of his words. Paulo's account, rude and simple as it was, soon discovered to him the relation of these apparently heterogeneous circumstances to each other; when Vivaldi, overcome by this new instance of the power of Paulo's affection, embraced him with his whole heart, and, compelling him to rise, presented him to the assembly as his faithful friend, and chief deliverer.

The Marchese, affected by the scene he had witnessed, and with the truth of Vivaldi's words, condescended to give Paulo a hearty shake by the hand, and to thank him warmly for the bravery and fidelity he had displayed in his master's interest. "I never can fully reward your attachment," added the Marchese, "but what remains for me to do, shall be done. From this moment I make you independent, and promise, in the presence of this noble company, to give you a thousand sequins, as some acknowledgement of your services."

Paulo did not express all the gratitude for this gift which the Marchese expected. He stammered, and bowed and blushed, and at length burst into tears; and when Vivaldi inquired what distressed him, he replied, "Why, Signor, of what use are the thousand sequins to me, if I am to be independent! what use if I am not to stay with you?"

Vivaldi cordially assured Paulo, that he should always remain with him, and that he should consider it as his duty to render his future life happy. "You shall henceforth," added Vivaldi, "be placed at the head of my houshold; the management of my servants, and the whole conduct of my domestic concerns shall be committed to you, as a proof of my entire confidence in your integrity and attachment; and because this is a situation which will allow you to be always near me."

"Thank you, my Signor," replied Paulo, in a voice rendered almost inarticulate by his gratitude, "Thank you with my whole heart! if I stay with you, that is enough for me, I ask no more. But I hope my Lord Marchese will not think me ungrateful for refusing to accept of the thousand sequins he was so kind as to offer me, if I would but be independent, for I thank him as much as if I had received them, and a great deal more too."

The Marchese, smiling at Paulo's mistake, rejoined, "As I do not perceive, my good friend, how your remaining with your master can be a circumstance to disqualify you from accepting a thousand sequins, I command you, on pain of my displeasure, to receive them; and whenever you marry, I shall expect that you will shew your obedience to me again, by accepting another thousand from me with your wife, as her dower."

"This is too much, Signor," said Paulo sobbing—"too much to be borne!" and ran out of the saloon. But amidst the murmur of applause which his conduct drew from the noble spectators, for Paulo's warm heart had subdued even the coldness of their pride, a convulsive sound from the anti-chamber betrayed the excess of emotion, which he had thus abruptly withdrawn himself to conceal.

In a few hours, the Marchese and Vivaldi took leave of their friends, and set out for Naples, where they arrived, without any interruption, on the fourth day. But it was a melancholy journey to Vivaldi, notwithstanding the joy of his late escape; for the Marchese, having introduced the mention of his attachment to Ellena di Rosalba, informed him, that, under the present unforeseen circumstances, he could not consider his late engagement to the Marchesa on that subject as binding, and that Vivaldi must relinquish Ellena, if it should appear that she really was the daughter of the late Schedoni.

Immediately on his arrival at Naples, however, Vivaldi, with a degree of impatience, to which his utmost speed was inadequate, and with a revived joy so powerful as to overcome every fear, and every melancholy consideration, which the late conversation with his father had occasioned, hastened to the Santa della Piéta.

Ellena heard his voice from the grate, inquiring for her of a nun, who was in the parlour, and in the next instant they beheld each other yet once again.

In such a meeting, after the long uncertainty of terror, which each had suffered for the fate of the other, and the dangers and hardships they had really incurred, joy was exalted almost to agony. Ellena wept, and some minutes passed before she could answer to Vivaldi's few words of tender exclamation: it was long ere she was tranquil enough to observe the alteration, which severe confinement had given to his appearance. The animated expression of his countenance was unchanged; yet, when the first glow of joy had faded from it, and Ellena had leisure to observe its wanness, she understood, too certainly, that he had been a prisoner in the Inquisition.

During this interview, he related, at Ellena's request, the particulars of his adventures, since he had been separated from her in the chapel of San Sebastian; but, when he came to that part of the narration where it was necessary to mention Schedoni, he paused in unconquerable embarrassment and a distress not unmingled with horror. Vivaldi could scarcely endure even to hint to Ellena any part of the unjust conduct, which the Confessor had practised towards him, yet it was impossible to conclude his account, without expressing much more than hints; nor could he bear to afflict her with a knowledge of the death of him who he believed to be her parent, however the dreadful circumstances of that event might be concealed. His embarrassment became obvious, and was still increased by Ellena's inquiries.

At length, as an introduction to the information it was necessary to give, and to the fuller explanation he wished to receive upon a subject, which, though it was the one that pressed most anxiously upon his mind, he had not yet dared to mention, Vivaldi ventured to declare his knowledge of her having discovered her parent to be living. The satisfaction immediately apparent upon Ellena's countenance heightened his distress, and his reluctance to proceed; believing, as he did, that the event he had to communicate must change her gladness to grief.

Ellena, however, upon this mention of a topic so interesting to them both, proceeded to express the happiness she had received from the discovery of a parent, whose virtues had even won her affection long before she understood her own interest in them. It was with some difficulty, that Vivaldi could conceal his surprise at such an avowal of prepossession; the manners of Schedoni, of whom he believed her to speak, having certainly never been adapted to inspire tenderness. But his surprise soon changed its subject, when Olivia, who had heard that a stranger was at the grate, entered the parlour, and was announced as the mother of Ellena di Rosalba.

Before Vivaldi left the convent, a full explanation, as to family, was given on both sides, when he had the infinite joy of learning, that Ellena was not the daughter of Schedoni; and Olivia had the satisfaction to know that she had no future evil to apprehend from him who had hitherto been her worst enemy. The manner of his death, however, with all the circumstances of his character, as unfolded by his late trial, Vivaldi was careful to conceal.

When Ellena had withdrawn from the room, Vivaldi made a full acknowledgment to Olivia of his long attachment to her daughter, and supplicated for her consent to their marriage. To this application, however, Olivia replied, that, though she had long been no stranger to their mutual affection, or to the several circumstances which had both proved its durability, and tried their fortitude, she never could consent that her daughter should become a member of any family, whose principal was either insensible of her value, or unwilling to acknowledge it; and that in this instance it would be necessary to Vivaldi's success, not only that he, but that his father should be a suitor; on which condition only, she allowed him to hope for her acquiescence.

Such a stipulation scarcely chilled the hopes of Vivaldi, now that Ellena was proved to be the daughter not of the murderer Schedoni, but of a Count di Bruno, who had been no less respectable in character than in rank; and he had little doubt that his father would consent to fulfil the promise he had given to the dying Marchesa.

In this belief he was not mistaken. The Marchese, having attended to Vivaldi's account of Ellena's family, promised, that if it should appear there was no second mistake on the subject, he would not longer oppose the wishes of his son.

The Marchese immediately caused a private inquiry to be made as to the identity of Olivia, the present Countess di Bruno; and, though this was not pursued without difficulty, the physician, who had assisted in the plan of her escape from the cruelty of Ferando di Bruno, and who was living, as well as Beatrice, who clearly remembered the sister of her late mistress, at length rendered Olivia's identity unquestionable. Now, therefore, that the Marchese's every doubt was removed, he paid a visit to the Santa della Piéta, and solicited, in due form, Olivia's consent to the nuptials of Vivaldi with Ellena; which she granted him with an entire satisfaction. In this interview, the Marchese was so much fascinated by the manners of the Countess, and pleased with the delicacy and sweetness, which appeared in those of Ellena, that his consent was no longer a constrained one, and he willingly relinquished the views of superior rank and fortune, which he had formerly looked to for his son, for those of virtue and permanent happiness that were now unfolded to him.

On the twentieth of May, the day on which Ellena completed her eighteenth year, her nuptials with Vivaldi were solemnized in the church of the Santa Maria della Piéta, in the presence of the Marchese and of the Countess di Bruno. As Ellena advanced through the church, she recollected, when on a former occasion she had met Vivaldi at the altar, and, the scenes of San Sebastian rising to her memory, the happy character of those, which her present situation opposed to them, drew tears of tender joy and gratitude to her eyes. Then, irresolute, desolate, surrounded by strangers, and ensnared by enemies, she had believed she saw Vivaldi for the last time; now, supported by the presence of a beloved parent, and by the willing approbation of the person, who had hitherto so strenuously opposed her, they were met to part no more; and, as a recollection of the moment when she had been carried from the chapel glanced upon her mind, that moment when she had called upon him for succour, supplicated even to hear his voice once more, and when a blank silence, which, as she believed, was that of death, had succeeded; as the anguish of that moment was now remembered, Ellena became more than ever sensible of the happiness of the present.

Olivia, in thus relinquishing her daughter so soon after she had found her, suffered some pain, but she was consoled by the fair prospect of happiness, that opened to Ellena, and cheered, by considering, that, though she relinquished, she should not lose her, since the vicinity of Vivaldi's residence to La Piéta, would permit a frequent intercourse with the convent.

As a testimony of singular esteem, Paulo was permitted to be present at the marriage of his master, when, as perched in a high gallery of the church, he looked down upon the ceremony, and witnessed the delight in Vivaldi's countenance, the satisfaction in that of my "old Lord Marchese," the pensive happiness in the Countess di Bruno's, and the tender complacency of Ellena's, which her veil, partly undrawn, allowed him to observe, he could scarcely refrain from expressing the joy he felt, and shouting aloud, *"O! giorno felíce! O! giorno felíce!"**

*O happy day! O happy day!

CHAPTER XIII

Ah! where shall I so sweet a dwelling find!
For all around, without, and all within,
Nothing save what delightful was and kind,
Of goodness favouring and a tender mind,
E'er rose to view.

THOMSON

The fête which, some time after the nuptials, was given by the Marchese, in celebration of them, was held at a delightful villa, belonging to Vivaldi, a few miles distant from Naples, upon the border of the gulf, and on the opposite shore to that which had been the frequent abode of the Marchesa. The beauty of its situation and its interior elegance induced Vivaldi and Ellena to select it as their chief residence. It was, in truth, a scene of fairy-land. The pleasure-grounds extended over a valley, which opened to the bay, and the house stood at the entrance of this valley, upon a gentle slope that margined the water, and commanded the whole extent of its luxuriant shores, from the lofty cape of Miseno to the bold mountains of the south, which, stretching across the distance, appeared to rise out of the sea, and divided the gulf of Naples from that of Salerno.

The marble porticoes and arcades of the villa were shadowed by groves of the beautiful magnolia, flowering ash, cedrati, camellias, and majestic palms; and the cool and airy halls, opening on two opposite sides to a colonade, admitted beyond the rich foliage all the seas and shores of Naples, from the west; and to the east, views of the valley of the domain, withdrawing among winding hills wooded to their summits, except where cliffs of various-coloured granites, yellow, green, and purple, lifted their tall heads, and threw gay gleams of light amidst the umbrageous landscape.

The style of the gardens, where lawns and groves, and woods varied the undulating surface, was that of England, and of the present day, rather than of Italy; except "Where a long alley peeping on the main," exhibited such gigantic loftiness of shade, and grandeur of perspective, as characterize the Italian taste.

On this jubilee, every avenue and grove, and pavilion was richly illuminated. The villa itself, where each airy hall and arcade was resplendent with lights, and lavishly decorated with flowers and the most beautiful shrubs, whose buds seemed to pour all Arabia's perfumes upon the air, this villa resembled a fabric called up by enchantment, rather than a structure of human art.

The dresses of the higher rank of visitors were as splendid as the scenery, of which Ellena was, in every respect, the queen. But this entertainment was not given to persons of distinction only, for both Vivaldi and Ellena had wished that all the tenants of the domain should partake of it, and share the abundant happiness which themselves possessed; so that the grounds, which were extensive enough to accommodate each rank, were relinquished to a general gaiety. Paulo was, on this occasion, a sort of master of the revels; and, surrounded by a party of his own particular associates, danced once more, as he had so often wished, upon the moon-light shore of Naples.

As Vivaldi and Ellena were passing the spot, which Paulo had chosen for the scene of his festivity, they paused to observe his strange capers and extravagant gesticulation, as he mingled in the dance, while every now-and-then he shouted forth, though half breathless with the heartiness of the exercise, *"O! giorno felíce! O! giorno felíce!"*

On perceiving Vivaldi, and the smiles with which he and Ellena regarded him, he quitted his sports, and advancing, "Ah! my dear master," said he, "do you remember the night, when we were travelling on the banks of the Celano, before that diabolical accident happened in the chapel of San Sebastian; don't you remember how those people, who were tripping it away so joyously, by moon-light, reminded me of Naples and the many merry dances I had footed on the beach here?"

"I remember it well," replied Vivaldi.

"Ah! Signor *mio,* you said at the time, that you hoped we should soon be here, and that then I should frisk it away with as glad a heart as the best of them. The first part of your hope, my dear master, you was out in, for, as it happened, we had to go through purgatory before we could reach paradise; but the second part is come at last;—for here I am, sure enough! dancing my moonlight, in my own dear bay of Naples, with my own dear master and mistress, in safety, and as happy *almost* as myself; and with that old mountain yonder, Vesuvius, which I, forsooth! thought I was never to see again, spouting up fire, just as it used to do before we got ourselves put into the Inquisition! O! who could have foreseen all this! *O! giorno felíce! O! giorno felíce!*"

"I rejoice in your happiness, my good Paulo," said Vivaldi, "almost as much as in my own; though I do not entirely agree with you as to the comparative proportion of each."

"Paulo!" said Ellena, "I am indebted to you beyond any ability to repay; for to your intrepid affection your master owes his present safety. I will not attempt to thank you for your attachment to him; my care of your welfare shall prove how well I know it; but I wish to give to all your friends this acknowledgment of your worth, and of my sense of it."

Paulo bowed, and stammered, and writhed and blushed, and was unable to reply; till, at length, giving a sudden and lofty spring from the ground, the emotion which had nearly stifled him burst forth in words, and *"O! giorno felíce! O! giorno felíce!"* flew from his lips with the force of an electric shock. They communicated his enthusiasm to the whole company, the words passed like lightning from one individual to another, till Vivaldi and Ellena withdrew amidst a choral shout, and all the woods and strands of Naples re-echoed with—*"O! giorno felíce! O! giorno felíce!"*

"You see," said Paulo, when they had departed, and he came to himself again, "you see how people get through their misfortunes, if they have but a heart to bear up against them, and do nothing that can lie on their conscience afterwards; and how suddenly one comes to be happy, just when one is beginning to think one never is to be happy again! Who would have guessed that my dear master and I, when we were clapped up in that diabolical place, the Inquisition, should ever come out again into this world! Who would have guessed when we were taken before those old devils of Inquisitors, sitting there all of a row in a place under ground, hung with black, and nothing but torches all around, and faces grinning at us, that looked as black as the gentry aforesaid; and when I was not so much as suffered to open my mouth, no! they would not let me open my mouth to my master!—who, I say, would have guessed we should ever be let loose again! who would have thought we should ever know what it is to be happy! Yet here we are all abroad once more! All at liberty! And may run, if we will, straight forward, from one end of the earth to the other, and back again without being stopped! May fly in the sea, or swim in the sky, or tumble over head and heels into the moon! For remember, my good friends, we have no lead in our consciences to keep us down!"

"You mean swim in the sea, and fly in the sky, I suppose," observed a grave personage near him, "but as for tumbling over head and heels into the moon! I don't know what you mean by that!"

"Pshaw!" replied Paulo, "who can stop, at such a time as this, to think about what he means! I wish that all those, who on this night are not merry enough to speak before they think, may ever after be grave enough to think before they speak! But you, none of you, no! not one of you! I warrant, ever saw the roof of a prison, when your master happened to be below in the dungeon, nor know what it is to be forced to run away, and leave him behind to die by himself. Poor souls! But no matter for that, you can be tolerably happy, perhaps, notwithstanding; but as for guessing how happy I am, or knowing any thing about the matter.—O! it's quite beyond what you can understand. *O! giorno felíce! O! giorno felíce!*" repeated Paulo, as he bounded forward to mingle in the dance, and *"O! giorno felíce!"* was again shouted in chorus by his joyful companions.

THE END

Northanger
Abbey

Jane Austen

ADVERTISEMENT
by the authoress
to
Northanger Abbey

THIS little work was finished in the year 1803, and intended for immediate publication. It was disposed of to a bookseller, it was even advertised, and why the business proceeded no farther, the author has never been able to learn. That any bookseller should think it worth-while to purchase what he did not think it worth-while to publish seems extraordinary. But with this, neither the author nor the public have any other concern than as some observation is necessary upon those parts of the work which thirteen years have made comparatively obsolete. The public are entreated to bear in mind that thirteen years have passed since it was finished, many more since it was begun, and that during that period, places, manners, books, and opinions have undergone considerable changes.

CHAPTER I

No one who had ever seen Catherine Morland in her infancy would have supposed her born to be an heroine. Her situation in life, the character of her father and mother, her own person and disposition, were all equally against her. Her father was a clergyman, without being neglected, or poor, and a very respectable man, though his name was Richard—and he had never been handsome. He had a considerable independence besides two good livings—and he was not in the least addicted to locking up his daughters. Her mother was a woman of useful plain sense, with a good temper, and, what is more remarkable, with a good constitution. She had three sons before Catherine was born; and instead of dying in bringing the latter into the world, as anybody might expect, she still lived on—lived to have six children more—to see them growing up around her, and to enjoy excellent health herself. A family of ten children will be always called a fine family, where there are heads and arms and legs enough for the number; but the Morlands had little other right to the word, for they were in general very plain, and Catherine, for many years of her life, as plain as any. She had a thin awkward figure, a sallow skin without colour, dark lank hair, and strong features—so much for her person; and not less unpropitious for heroism seemed her mind. She was fond of all boy's plays, and greatly preferred cricket not merely to dolls, but to the more heroic enjoyments of infancy, nursing a dormouse, feeding a canary-bird, or watering a rose-bush. Indeed she had no taste for a garden; and if she gathered flowers at all, it was chiefly for the pleasure of mischief—at least so it was conjectured from her always preferring those which she was forbidden to take. Such were her propensities—her abilities were quite as extraordinary. She never could learn or understand anything before she was taught; and sometimes not even then, for she was often inattentive, and occasionally stupid. Her mother was three months in teaching her only to repeat the "Beggar's Petition"; and after all, her next sister, Sally, could say it better than she did. Not that Catherine was always stupid—by no means; she learnt the fable of "The Hare and Many Friends" as quickly as any girl in England. Her mother wished her to learn music; and Catherine was sure she should like it, for she was very fond of tinkling the keys of the old forlorn spinnet; so, at eight years old she began. She learnt a year, and could not bear it; and Mrs. Morland, who did not insist on her daughters being accomplished in spite of incapacity or distaste, allowed her to leave off. The day which dismissed the music-master was one of the happiest of Catherine's life. Her taste for drawing was not superior; though whenever she could obtain the outside of a letter from her mother or seize upon any other odd piece of paper, she did what she could in that way, by drawing houses and trees, hens and chickens, all very much like one another. Writing and accounts she was taught by her father; French by her mother: her proficiency in either was not remarkable, and she shirked her lessons in both whenever she could. What a strange, unaccountable character!—for with all these symptoms of profligacy at ten years old, she had neither a bad heart nor a bad temper, was seldom stubborn, scarcely ever quarrelsome, and very kind to the little ones, with few interruptions of tyranny; she was moreover noisy and wild, hated confinement and cleanliness, and loved nothing so well in the world as rolling down the green slope at the back of the house.

Such was Catherine Morland at ten. At fifteen, appearances were mending; she began to curl her hair and long for balls; her complexion improved, her features were softened by plumpness and colour, her eyes gained more animation, and her figure more consequence. Her love of dirt gave way to an inclination for finery, and she grew clean as she grew smart; she had now the pleasure of sometimes hearing her father and mother remark on her personal improvement. "Catherine grows quite a good-looking girl—she is almost pretty today," were words which caught her ears now and then; and how welcome were the sounds! To look *almost* pretty is an acquisition of higher delight to a girl who has been looking plain the first fifteen years of her life than a beauty from her cradle can ever receive.

Mrs. Morland was a very good woman, and wished to see her children everything they ought to be; but her time was so much occupied in lying-in and teaching the little ones, that her elder daughters were inevitably left to shift for themselves; and it was not very wonderful that Catherine, who had by nature nothing heroic about her, should prefer cricket, baseball, riding on horseback, and running about the country at the age of fourteen, to books—or at least books of information—for, provided that nothing like useful knowledge could be gained from them, provided they were all story and no reflection, she had never any objection to books at all. But from fifteen to seventeen she was in training for a heroine; she read all such works as heroines must read to supply their memories with those quotations which are so serviceable and so soothing in the vicissitudes of their eventful lives.

From Pope, she learnt to censure those who

"bear about the mockery of woe."

From Gray, that

"Many a flower is born to blush unseen,
And waste its fragrance on the desert air."

From Thompson, that

"It is a delightful task
To teach the young idea how to shoot."

And from Shakespeare she gained a great store of information—amongst the rest, that

"Trifles light as air,
Are, to the jealous, confirmation strong,
As proofs of Holy Writ."

That

"The poor beetle, which we tread upon,
In corporal sufferance feels a pang as great
As when a giant dies."

And that a young woman in love always looks

> "like Patience on a monument
> Smiling at Grief."

So far her improvement was sufficient—and in many
other points she came on exceedingly well; for though she
could not write sonnets, she brought herself to read them;
and though there seemed no chance of her throwing a whole
party into raptures by a prelude on the pianoforte, of her
own composition, she could listen to other people's performance with very little fatigue. Her greatest deficiency was in
the pencil—she had no notion of drawing—not enough even
to attempt a sketch of her lover's profile, that she might be
detected in the design. There she fell miserably short of the
true heroic height. At present she did not know her own poverty, for she had no lover to portray. She had reached the age
of seventeen, without having seen one amiable youth who
could call forth her sensibility, without having inspired one
real passion, and without having excited even any admiration but what was very moderate and very transient. This
was strange indeed! But strange things may be generally accounted for if their cause be fairly searched out. There was
not one lord in the neighbourhood; no—not even a baronet.
There was not one family among their acquaintance who had
reared and supported a boy accidentally found at their
door—not one young man whose origin was unknown. Her
father had no ward, and the squire of the parish no children.

But when a young lady is to be a heroine, the perverse-
ness of forty surrounding families cannot prevent her. Something must and will happen to throw a hero in her way.

Mr. Allen, who owned the chief of the property about
Fullerton, the village in Wiltshire where the Morlands lived,
was ordered to Bath for the benefit of a gouty constitution—
and his lady, a good-humoured woman, fond of Miss
Morland, and probably aware that if adventures will not be-
fall a young lady in her own village, she must seek them
abroad, invited her to go with them. Mr. and Mrs. Morland
were all compliance, and Catherine all happiness.

CHAPTER II

In addition to what has been already said of Catherine Morland's personal and mental endowments, when about to be launched into all the difficulties and dangers of a six weeks' residence in Bath, it may be stated, for the reader's more certain information, lest the following pages should otherwise fail of giving any idea of what her character is meant to be, that her heart was affectionate; her disposition cheerful and open, without conceit or affectation of any kind—her manners just removed from the awkwardness and shyness of a girl; her person pleasing, and, when in good looks, pretty—and her mind about as ignorant and uninformed as the female mind at seventeen usually is.

When the hour of departure drew near, the maternal anxiety of Mrs. Morland will be naturally supposed to be most severe. A thousand alarming presentiments of evil to her beloved Catherine from this terrific separation must oppress her heart with sadness, and drown her in tears for the last day or two of their being together; and advice of the most important and applicable nature must of course flow from her wise lips in their parting conference in her closet. Cautions against the violence of such noblemen and baronets as delight in forcing young ladies away to some remote farmhouse, must, at such a moment, relieve the fulness of her heart. Who would not think so? But Mrs. Morland knew so little of lords and baronets, that she entertained no notion of their general mischievousness, and was wholly unsuspicious of danger to her daughter from their machinations. Her cautions were confined to the following points. "I beg, Catherine, you will always wrap yourself up very warm about the throat, when you come from the rooms at night; and I wish you would try to keep some account of the money you spend; I will give you this little book on purpose."

Sally, or rather Sarah (for what young lady of common

gentility will reach the age of sixteen without altering her name as far as she can?), must from situation be at this time the intimate friend and confidante of her sister. It is remarkable, however, that she neither insisted on Catherine's writing by every post, nor exacted her promise of transmitting the character of every new acquaintance, nor a detail of every interesting conversation that Bath might produce. Everything indeed relative to this important journey was done, on the part of the Morlands, with a degree of moderation and composure, which seemed rather consistent with the common feelings of common life, than with the refined susceptibilities, the tender emotions which the first separation of a heroine from her family ought always to excite. Her father, instead of giving her an unlimited order on his banker, or even putting an hundred pounds bank-bill into her hands, gave her only ten guineas, and promised her more when she wanted it.

Under these unpromising auspices, the parting took place, and the journey began. It was performed with suitable quietness and uneventful safety. Neither robbers nor tempests befriended them, nor one lucky overturn to introduce them to the hero. Nothing more alarming occurred than a fear, on Mrs. Allen's side, of having once left her clogs behind her at an inn, and that fortunately proved to be groundless.

They arrived at Bath. Catherine was all eager delight—her eyes were here, there, everywhere, as they approached its fine and striking environs, and afterwards drove through those streets which conducted them to the hotel. She was come to be happy, and she felt happy already.

They were soon settled in comfortable lodgings in Pulteney Street.

It is now expedient to give some description of Mrs. Allen, that the reader may be able to judge in what manner her actions will hereafter tend to promote the general distress of the work, and how she will, probably, contribute to reduce poor Catherine to all the desperate wretchedness of which a last volume is capable—whether by her imprudence, vulgarity, or jealousy—whether by intercepting her letters, ruining her character, or turning her out of doors.

Mrs. Allen was one of that numerous class of females, whose society can raise no other emotion than surprise at there being any men in the world who could like them well enough to marry them. She had neither beauty, genius, accomplishment, nor manner. The air of a gentlewoman, a great deal of quiet, inactive good temper, and a trifling turn of mind were all that could account for her being the choice of a sensible, intelligent man like Mr. Allen. In one respect she was admirably fitted to introduce a young lady into public, being as fond of going everywhere and seeing everything herself as any young lady could be. Dress was her passion. She had a most harmless delight in being fine; and our heroine's entrée into life could not take place till after three or four days had been spent in learning what was mostly worn, and her chaperone was provided with a dress of the newest fashion. Catherine too made some purchases herself, and when all these matters were arranged, the important evening came which was to usher her into the Upper Rooms. Her hair was cut and dressed by the best hand, her clothes put on with care, and both Mrs. Allen and her maid declared she looked quite as she should do. With such encouragement, Catherine hoped at least to pass uncensured through the crowd. As for admiration, it was always very welcome when it came, but she did not depend on it.

Mrs. Allen was so long in dressing that they did not enter the ballroom till late. The season was full, the room crowded, and the ladies squeezed in as well as they could. As for Mr. Allen, he repaired directly to the card-room, and left them to enjoy a mob by themselves. With more care for the safety of her new gown than for the comfort of her protégée, Mrs. Allen made her way through the throng of men by the door, as swiftly as the necessary caution would allow; Catherine, however, kept close at her side, and linked her arm too firmly within her friend's to be torn asunder by any common effort of a struggling assembly. But to her utter amazement she found that to proceed along the room was by no means the way to disengage themselves from the crowd; it seemed rather to increase as they went on, whereas she had imagined that when once fairly within the door, they should easily find seats and be able to watch the dances with perfect convenience. But this was far from being the case, and though by unwearied diligence they gained even the top of the room, their situation was just the same; they saw nothing of the dancers but the high feathers of some of the ladies. Still they moved on—something better was yet in view; and by a continued exertion of strength and ingenuity they found themselves at last in the passage behind the high-

est bench. Here there was something less of crowd than below; and hence Miss Morland had a comprehensive view of
all the company beneath her, and of all the dangers of her
late passage through them. It was a splendid sight, and she
began, for the first time that evening, to feel herself at a ball:
she longed to dance, but she had not an acquaintance in the
room. Mrs. Allen did all that she could do in such a case by
saying very placidly, every now and then, "I wish you could
dance, my dear—I wish you could get a partner." For some
time her young friend felt obliged to her for these wishes;
but they were repeated so often, and proved so totally ineffectual, that Catherine grew tired at last, and would thank
her no more.

They were not long able, however, to enjoy the repose of
the eminence they had so laboriously gained. Everybody was
shortly in motion for tea, and they must squeeze out like the
rest. Catherine began to feel something of disappointment—
she was tired of being continually pressed against by people,
the generality of whose faces possessed nothing to interest,
and with all of whom she was so wholly unacquainted that
she could not relieve the irksomeness of imprisonment by
the exchange of a syllable with any of her fellow captives;
and when at last arrived in the tea-room, she felt yet more
the awkwardness of having no party to join, no acquaintance
to claim, no gentleman to assist them. They saw nothing of
Mr. Allen; and after looking about them in vain for a more
eligible situation, were obliged to sit down at the end of a table, at which a large party were already placed, without having anything to do there, or anybody to speak to, except each
other.

Mrs. Allen congratulated herself, as soon as they were
seated, on having preserved her gown from injury. "It would
have been very shocking to have it torn," said she, "would
not it? It is such a delicate muslin. For my part I have not
seen anything I like so well in the whole room, I assure
you."

"How uncomfortable it is," whispered Catherine, "not to
have a single acquaintance here!"

"Yes, my dear," replied Mrs. Allen, with perfect serenity,
"it is very uncomfortable indeed."

"What shall we do? The gentlemen and ladies at this table
look as if they wondered why we came here—we seem
forcing ourselves into their party."

"Aye, so we do. That is very disagreeable. I wish we had a large acquaintance here."

"I wish we had *any*—it would be somebody to go to."

"Very true, my dear; and if we knew anybody we would join them directly. The Skinners were here last year—I wish they were here now."

"Had not we better go away as it is? Here are no tea-things for us, you see."

"No more there are, indeed. How very provoking! But I think we had better sit still, for one gets so tumbled in such a crowd! How is my head, my dear? Somebody gave me a push that has hurt it, I am afraid."

"No, indeed, it looks very nice. But, dear Mrs. Allen, are you sure there is nobody you know in all this multitude of people? I think you *must* know somebody."

"I don't, upon my word—I wish I did. I wish I had a large acquaintance here with all my heart, and then I should get you a partner. I should be so glad to have you dance. There goes a strange-looking woman! What an odd gown she has got on! How old-fashioned it is! Look at the back."

After some time they received an offer of tea from one of their neighbours; it was thankfully accepted, and this introduced a light conversation with the gentleman who offered it, which was the only time that anybody spoke to them during the evening, till they were discovered and joined by Mr. Allen when the dance was over.

"Well, Miss Morland," said he, directly, "I hope you have had an agreeable ball."

"Very agreeable indeed," she replied, vainly endeavouring to hide a great yawn.

"I wish she had been able to dance," said his wife; "I wish we could have got a partner for her. I have been saying how glad I should be if the Skinners were here this winter instead of last; or if the Parrys had come, as they talked of once, she might have danced with George Parry. I am sorry she has not had a partner!"

"We shall do better another evening I hope," was Mr. Allen's consolation.

The company began to disperse when the dancing was over—enough to leave space for the remainder to walk about in some comfort; and now was the time for a heroine, who had not yet played a very distinguished part in the events of the evening, to be noticed and admired. Every five minutes, by removing some of the crowd, gave greater openings for her charms. She was now seen by many young men who had not been near her before. Not one, however, started with rapturous wonder on beholding her, no whisper of eager inquiry ran round the room, nor was she once called a divinity by anybody. Yet Catherine was in very good looks, and had the company only seen her three years before, they would *now* have thought her exceedingly handsome.

She *was* looked at, however, and with some admiration; for, in her own hearing, two gentlemen pronounced her to be a pretty girl. Such words had their due effect; she immediately thought the evening pleasanter than she had found it before—her humble vanity was contented—she felt more obliged to the two young men for this simple praise than a true-quality heroine would have been for fifteen sonnets in celebration of her charms, and went to her chair in good humour with everybody, and perfectly satisfied with her share of public attention.

CHAPTER III

EVERY morning now brought its regular duties—shops were to be visited; some new part of the town to be looked at; and the pump-room to be attended, where they paraded up and down for an hour, looking at everybody and speaking to no one. The wish of a numerous acquaintance in Bath was still uppermost with Mrs. Allen, and she repeated it after every fresh proof, which every morning brought, of her knowing nobody at all.

They made their appearance in the Lower Rooms; and here fortune was more favourable to our heroine. The master of the ceremonies introduced to her a very gentlemanlike young man as a partner; his name was Tilney. He seemed to be about four or five and twenty, was rather tall, had a pleasing countenance, a very intelligent and lively eye, and, if not quite handsome, was very near it. His address was good, and Catherine felt herself in high luck. There was little leisure for speaking while they danced; but when they were seated at tea, she found him as agreeable as she had already given him credit for being. He talked with fluency and spirit—and there was an archness and pleasantry in his manner which interested, though it was hardly understood by her. After chatting some time on such matters as naturally arose from the objects around them, he suddenly addressed her with—"I have hitherto been very remiss, madam, in the proper attentions of a partner here; I have not yet asked you how long you have been in Bath; whether you were ever here before; whether you have been at the Upper Rooms, the theatre, and the concert; and how you like the place altogether. I have been very negligent—but are you now at leisure to satisfy me in these particulars? If you are I will begin directly."

"You need not give yourself that trouble, sir."

"No trouble, I assure you, madam." Then forming his features into a set smile, and affectedly softening his voice, he added, with a simpering air, "Have you been long in Bath, madam?"

"About a week, sir," replied Catherine, trying not to laugh.

"Really!" with affected astonishment.

"Why should you be surprised, sir?"

"Why, indeed!" said he, in his natural tone. "But some emotion must appear to be raised by your reply, and surprise is more easily assumed, and not less reasonable than any other. Now let us go on. Were you never here before, madam?"

"Never, sir."

"Indeed! Have you yet honoured the Upper Rooms?"

"Yes, sir, I was there last Monday."

"Have you been to the theatre?"

"Yes, sir, I was at the play on Tuesday."

"To the concert?"

"Yes, sir, on Wednesday."

"And are you altogether pleased with Bath?"

"Yes—I like it very well."

"Now I must give one smirk, and then we may be rational again."

Catherine turned away her head, not knowing whether she might venture to laugh.

"I see what you think of me," said he gravely—"I shall make but a poor figure in your journal tomorrow."

"My journal!"

"Yes, I know exactly what you will say: Friday, went to the Lower Rooms; wore my sprigged muslin robe with blue trimmings—plain black shoes—appeared to much advantage; but was strangely harassed by a queer, half-witted man, who would make me dance with him, and distressed me by his nonsense."

"Indeed I shall say no such thing."

"Shall I tell you what you ought to say?"

"If you please."

"I danced with a very agreeable young man, introduced by Mr. King; had a great deal of conversation with him—seems a most extraordinary genius—hope I may know more of him. *That,* madam, is what I *wish* you to say."

"But, perhaps, I keep no journal."

"Perhaps you are not sitting in this room, and I am not sitting by you. These are points in which a doubt is equally possible. Not keep a journal! How are your absent cousins to understand the tenour of your life in Bath without one? How are the civilities and compliments of every day to be related as they ought to be, unless noted down every evening in a journal? How are your various dresses to be remembered, and the particular state of your complexion, and curl of your hair to be described in all their diversities, without having constant recourse to a journal? My dear madam, I am not so ignorant of young ladies' ways as you wish to believe me; it is this delightful habit of journalizing which largely contributes to form the easy style of writing for which ladies are so generally celebrated. Everybody allows that the talent of writing agreeable letters is peculiarly female. Nature may have done something, but I am sure it must be essentially assisted by the practice of keeping a journal."

"I have sometimes thought," said Catherine, doubtingly, "whether ladies do write so much better letters than gentlemen! That is—I should not think the superiority was always on our side."

"As far as I have had opportunity of judging, it appears to me that the usual style of letter-writing among women is faultless, except in three particulars."

"And what are they?"

"A general deficiency of subject, a total inattention to stops, and a very frequent ignorance of grammar."

"Upon my word! I need not have been afraid of disclaiming the compliment. You do not think too highly of us in that way."

"I should no more lay it down as a general rule that women write better letters than men, than that they sing better duets, or draw better landscapes. In every power, of which taste is the foundation, excellence is pretty fairly divided between the sexes."

They were interrupted by Mrs. Allen: "My dear Catherine," said she, "do take this pin out of my sleeve; I am afraid it has torn a hole already; I shall be quite sorry if it has, for this is a favourite gown, though it cost but nine shillings a yard."

"That is exactly what I should have guessed it, madam," said Mr. Tilney, looking at the muslin.

"Do you understand muslins, sir?"

"Particularly well; I always buy my own cravats, and am allowed to be an excellent judge; and my sister has often trusted me in the choice of a gown. I bought one for her the other day, and it was pronounced to be a prodigious bargain by every lady who saw it. I gave but five shillings a yard for it, and a true Indian muslin."

Mrs. Allen was quite struck by his genius. "Men commonly take so little notice of those things," said she; "I can never get Mr. Allen to know one of my gowns from another. You must be a great comfort to your sister, sir."

"I hope I am, madam."

"And pray, sir, what do you think of Miss Morland's gown?"

"It is very pretty, madam," said he, gravely examining it; "but I do not think it will wash well; I am afraid it will fray."

"How can you," said Catherine, laughing, "be so—" She had almost said "strange."

"I am quite of your opinion, sir," replied Mrs. Allen; "and so I told Miss Morland when she bought it."

"But then you know, madam, muslin always turns to some account or other; Miss Morland will get enough out of it for a handkerchief, or a cap, or a cloak. Muslin can never be said to be wasted. I have heard my sister say so forty times, when she has been extravagant in buying more than she wanted, or careless in cutting it to pieces."

"Bath is a charming place, sir; there are so many good shops here. We are sadly off in the country; not but what we have very good shops in Salisbury, but it is so far to go—eight miles is a long way; Mr. Allen says it is nine, measured nine; but I am sure it cannot be more than eight; and it is such a fag—I come back tired to death. Now, here one can step out of doors and get a thing in five minutes."

Mr. Tilney was polite enough to seem interested in what she said; and she kept him on the subject of muslins till the dancing recommenced. Catherine feared, as she listened to their discourse, that he indulged himself a little too much with the foibles of others. "What are you thinking of so earnestly?" said he, as they walked back to the ballroom; "not of your partner, I hope, for, by that shake of the head, your meditations are not satisfactory."

Catherine coloured, and said, "I was not thinking of anything."

"That is artful and deep, to be sure; but I had rather be told at once that you will not tell me."

"Well then, I will not."

"Thank you; for now we shall soon be acquainted, as I am authorized to tease you on this subject whenever we meet, and nothing in the world advances intimacy so much."

They danced again; and, when the assembly closed, parted, on the lady's side at least, with a strong inclination for continuing the acquaintance. Whether she thought of him so much, while she drank her warm wine and water, and prepared herself for bed, as to dream of him when there, cannot be ascertained; but I hope it was no more than in a slight slumber, or a morning doze at most; for if it be true, as a celebrated writer has maintained, that no young lady can be justified in falling in love before the gentleman's love is declared,* it must be very improper that a young lady should dream of a gentleman before the gentleman is first known to have dreamt of her. How proper Mr. Tilney might be as a dreamer or a lover had not yet perhaps entered Mr. Allen's head, but that he was not objectionable as a common acquaintance for his young charge he was on inquiry satisfied; for he had early in the evening taken pains to know who her partner was, and had been assured of Mr. Tilney's being a clergyman, and of a very respectable family in Gloucestershire.

---

*Vide a letter from Mr. Richardson, No. 97, Vol. II, Rambler.

CHAPTER IV

WITH more than usual eagerness did Catherine hasten to the pump-room the next day, secure within herself of seeing Mr. Tilney there before the morning were over, and ready to meet him with a smile; but no smile was demanded—Mr. Tilney did not appear. Every creature in Bath, except himself, was to be seen in the room at different periods of the fashionable hours; crowds of people were every moment passing in and out, up the steps and down; people whom nobody cared about, and nobody wanted to see; and he only was absent. "What a delightful place Bath is," said Mrs. Allen as they sat down near the great clock, after parading the room till they were tired; "and how pleasant it would be if we had any acquaintance here."

This sentiment had been uttered so often in vain that Mrs. Allen had no particular reason to hope it would be followed with more advantage now; but we are told to "despair of nothing we would attain," as "unwearied diligence our point would gain"; and the unwearied diligence with which she had every day wished for the same thing was at length to have its just reward, for hardly had she been seated ten minutes before a lady of about her own age, who was sitting by her, and had been looking at her attentively for several minutes, addressed her with great complaisance in these words: "I think, madam, I cannot be mistaken; it is a long time since I had the pleasure of seeing you, but is not your name Allen?" This question answered, as it readily was, the stranger pronounced hers to be Thorpe; and Mrs. Allen immediately recognized the features of a former schoolfellow and intimate, whom she had seen only once since their respective marriages, and that many years ago. Their joy on this meeting was very great, as well it might, since they had been contented to know nothing of each other for the last fifteen years. Compliments on good looks now passed; and, after observing how time had slipped away since they were last together, how little they had thought of meeting in Bath, and what a pleasure it was to see an old friend, they proceeded to make inquiries and give intelligence as to their families, sisters, and cousins, talking both together, far more ready to give than to receive information, and each hearing very little of what the other said. Mrs. Thorpe, however, had one great advantage as a talker, over Mrs. Allen, in a family of children; and when she expatiated on the talents of her sons, and the beauty of her daughters, when she related their different situations and views—that John was at Oxford, Edward at Merchant Taylors', and William at sea—and all of them more beloved and respected in their different station than any other three beings ever were, Mrs. Allen had no similar information to give, no similar triumphs to press on the unwilling and unbelieving ear of her friend, and was forced to sit and appear to listen to all these maternal effusions, consoling herself, however, with the discovery, which her keen eye soon made, that the lace on Mrs. Thorpe's pelisse was not half so handsome as that on her own.

"Here come my dear girls," cried Mrs. Thorpe, pointing at three smart-looking females who, arm in arm, were then moving towards her. "My dear Mrs. Allen, I long to introduce them; they will be so delighted to see you: the tallest is Isabella, my eldest; is not she a fine young woman? The others are very much admired too, but I believe Isabella is the handsomest."

The Miss Thorpes were introduced; and Miss Morland, who had been for a short time forgotten, was introduced likewise. The name seemed to strike them all; and, after speaking to her with great civility, the eldest young lady observed aloud to the rest, "How excessively like her brother Miss Morland is!"

"The very picture of him indeed!" cried the mother—and "I should have known her anywhere for his sister!" was repeated by them all, two or three times over. For a moment Catherine was surprised; but Mrs. Thorpe and her daughters had scarcely begun the history of their acquaintance with Mr. James Morland, before she remembered that her eldest brother had lately formed an intimacy with a young man of his own college, of the name of Thorpe; and that he had spent the last week of the Christmas vacation with his family, near London.

The whole being explained, many obliging things were said by the Miss Thorpes of their wish of being better acquainted with her; of being considered as already friends, through the friendship of their brothers, etc., which Catherine heard with pleasure, and answered with all the pretty expressions she could command; and, as the first proof of amity, she was soon invited to accept an arm of the eldest Miss Thorpe, and take a turn with her about the room. Catherine was delighted with this extension of her Bath acquaintance, and almost forgot Mr. Tilney while she talked to Miss Thorpe. Friendship is certainly the finest balm for the pangs of disappointed love.

Their conversation turned upon those subjects, of which the free discussion was generally much to do in perfecting a sudden intimacy between two young ladies: such as dress, balls, flirtations, and quizzes. Miss Thorpe, however, being four years older than Miss Morland, and at least four years better informed, had a very decided advantage in discussing such points; she could compare the balls of Bath with those of Tunbridge, its fashions with the fashions of London; could rectify the opinions of her new friend in many articles of tasteful attire; could discover a flirtation between any gentleman and lady who only smiled on each other; and point out a quiz through the thickness of a crowd. These powers received due admiration from Catherine, to whom they were entirely new; and the respect which they naturally inspired might have been too great for familiarity, had not the easy gaiety of Miss Thorpe's manners, and her frequent expressions of delight on this acquaintance with her, softened down every feeling of awe, and left nothing but tender affection. Their increasing attachment was not to be satisfied with half a dozen turns in the pump-room, but required, when they all quitted it together, that Miss Thorpe should accompany Miss Morland to the very door of Mr. Allen's house; and that they should there part with a most affectionate and lengthened shake of hands, after learning, to their mutual relief, that they should see each other across the theatre at night, and say their prayers in the same chapel the next morning. Catherine then ran directly upstairs, and watched Miss Thorpe's progress down the street from the drawing-room window; admired the graceful spirit of her walk, the fashionable air of her figure and dress; and felt grateful, as well she might, for the chance which had procured her such a friend.

Mrs. Thorpe was a widow, and not a very rich one; she was a good-humoured, well-meaning woman, and a very indulgent mother. Her eldest daughter had great personal beauty, and the younger ones, by pretending to be as handsome as their sister, imitating her air, and dressing in the same style, did very well.

This brief account of the family is intended to supersede the necessity of a long and minute detail from Mrs. Thorpe herself, of her past adventures and sufferings, which might otherwise be expected to occupy the three or four following chapters; in which the worthlessness of lords and attornies might be set forth, and conversations, which had passed twenty years before, be minutely repeated.

CHAPTER V

CATHERINE was not so much engaged at the theatre that evening, in returning the nods and smiles of Miss Thorpe, though they certainly claimed much of her leisure, as to forget to look with an inquiring eye for Mr. Tilney in every box which her eye could reach; but she looked in vain. Mr. Tilney was no fonder of the play than the pump-room. She hoped to be more fortunate the next day; and when her wishes for fine weather were answered by seeing a beautiful morning, she hardly felt a doubt of it; for a fine Sunday in Bath empties every house of its inhabitants, and all the world appears on such an occasion to walk about and tell their acquaintance what a charming day it is.

As soon as divine service was over, the Thorpes and Allens eagerly joined each other; and after staying long enough in the pump-room to discover that the crowd was insupportable, and that there was not a genteel face to be seen, which everybody discovers every Sunday throughout the season, they hastened away to the Crescent, to breathe the fresh air of better company. Here Catherine and Isabella, arm in arm, again tasted the sweets of friendship in an unreserved conversation; they talked much, and with much enjoyment; but again was Catherine disappointed in her hope of reseeing her partner. He was nowhere to be met with; every search for him was equally unsuccessful, in morning lounges or evening assemblies; neither at the upper nor lower rooms, at dressed or undressed balls, was he perceivable; nor among the walkers, the horsemen, or the curricle-drivers of the morning. His name was not in the pump-room book, and curiosity could do no more. He must be gone from Bath. Yet he had not mentioned that his stay would be so short! This sort of mysteriousness, which is always so becoming in a hero, threw a fresh grace in Catherine's imagination around his person and manners, and increased her anxiety to know more of him. From the Thorpes she could learn nothing, for they had been only two days in Bath before they met with Mrs. Allen. It was a subject, however, in which she often indulged with her fair friend, from whom she received every possible encouragement to continue to think of him; and his impression on her fancy was not suffered therefore to weaken. Isabella was very sure that he must be a charming young man, and was equally sure that he must have been delighted with her dear Catherine, and would therefore shortly return. She liked him the better for being a clergyman, "for she must confess herself very partial to the profession"; and something like a sigh escaped her as she said it. Perhaps Catherine was wrong in not demanding the cause of that gentle emotion—but she was not experienced enough in the finesse of love, or the duties of friendship, to know when delicate raillery was properly called for, or when a confidence should be forced.

Mrs. Allen was now quite happy—quite satisfied with Bath. She had found some acquaintance, had been so lucky too as to find in them the family of a most worthy old friend; and, as the completion of good fortune, had found these friends by no means so expensively dressed as herself. Her daily expressions were no longer, "I wish we had some acquaintance in Bath!" They were changed into, "How glad I am we have met with Mrs. Thorpe!" and she was as eager in promoting the intercourse of the two families, as her young charge and Isabella themselves could be; never satisfied with the day unless she spent the chief of it by the side of Mrs. Thorpe, in what they called conversation, but in which there was scarcely ever any exchange of opinion, and not often any resemblance of subject, for Mrs. Thorpe talked chiefly of her children, and Mrs. Allen of her gowns.

The progress of the friendship between Catherine and Isabella was quick as its beginning had been warm, and they passed so rapidly through every gradation of increasing tenderness that there was shortly no fresh proof of it to be given to their friends or themselves. They called each other by their Christian name, were always arm in arm when they walked, pinned up each other's train for the dance, and were not to be divided in the set; and if a rainy morning deprived them of other enjoyments, they were still resolute in meeting in defiance of wet and dirt, and shut themselves up, to read novels together. Yes, novels; for I will not adopt that ungenerous and impolitic custom so common with novel-writers, of degrading by their contemptuous censure the very performances, to the number of which they are themselves adding—joining with their greatest enemies in bestowing the harshest epithets on such works, and scarcely ever permitting them to be read by their own heroine, who, if she accidentally take up a novel, is sure to turn over its insipid pages with disgust. Alas! If the heroine of one novel be not patronized by the heroine of another, from whom can she expect protection and regard? I cannot approve of it. Let us leave it to the reviewers to abuse such effusions of fancy at their leisure, and over every new novel to talk in threadbare strains of the trash with which the press now groans. Let us not desert one another; we are an injured body. Although our productions have afforded more extensive and unaffected pleasure than those of any other literary corporation in the world, no species of composition has been so much decried. From pride, ignorance, or fashion, our foes are almost as many as our readers. And while the abilities of the nine-hundredth abridger of the *History of England,* or of the man who collects and publishes in a volume some dozen lines of Milton, Pope, and Prior, with a paper from the *Spectator,* and a chapter from Sterne, are eulogized by a thousand pens— there seems almost a general wish of decrying the capacity and undervaluing the labour of the novelist, and of slighting the performances which have only genius, wit, and taste to recommend them. "I am no novel-reader—I seldom look into novels—Do not imagine that *I* often read novels—It is really very well for a novel." Such is the common cant. "And what are you reading, Miss—?" "Oh! It is only a novel!" replies the young lady, while she lays down her book with affected indifference, or momentary shame. "It is only *Cecilia,* or *Camilla,* or *Belinda*"; or, in short, only some work in which the greatest powers of the mind are displayed, in which the most thorough knowledge of human nature, the happiest delineation of its varieties, the liveliest effusions of wit and humour, are conveyed to the world in the best-chosen language. Now, had the same young lady been engaged with a volume of the *Spectator,* instead of such a work, how proudly would she have produced the book, and told its name; though the chances must be against her being occupied by any part of that voluminous publication, of which either the matter or manner would not disgust a young person of taste: the substance of its papers so often consisting in the statement of improbable circumstances, unnatural characters, and topics of conversation which no longer concern anyone living; and their language, too, frequently so coarse as to give no very favourable idea of the age that could endure it.

CHAPTER VI

THE following conversation, which took place between the two friends in the pump-room one morning, after an acquaintance of eight or nine days, is given as a specimen of their very warm attachment, and of the delicacy, discretion, originality of thought, and literary taste which marked the reasonableness of that attachment.

They met by appointment; and as Isabella had arrived nearly five minutes before her friend, her first address naturally was, "My dearest creature, what can have made you so late? I have been waiting for you at least this age!"

"Have you, indeed! I am very sorry for it; but really I thought I was in very good time. It is but just one. I hope you have not been here long?"

"Oh! These ten ages at least. I am sure I have been here this half hour. But now, let us go and sit down at the other end of the room, and enjoy ourselves. I have an hundred things to say to you. In the first place, I was so afraid it would rain this morning, just as I wanted to set off; it looked very showery, and that would have thrown me into agonies! Do you know, I saw the prettiest hat you can imagine, in a shop window in Milsom Street just now—very like yours, only with coquelicot ribbons instead of green; I quite longed for it. But, my dearest Catherine, what have you been doing with yourself all this morning? Have you gone on with *Udolpho*?"

"Yes, I have been reading it ever since I woke; and I am got to the black veil."

"Are you, indeed? How delightful! Oh! I would not tell you what is behind the black veil for the world! Are not you wild to know?"

"Oh! Yes, quite; what can it be? But do not tell me—I would not be told upon any account. I know it must be a skeleton, I am sure it is Laurentina's skeleton. Oh! I am delighted with the book! I should like to spend my whole life in reading it. I assure you, if it had not been to meet you, I would not have come away from it for all the world."

"Dear creature! How much I am obliged to you; and when you have finished *Udolpho*, we will read the Italian together; and I have made out a list of ten or twelve more of the same kind for you."

"Have you, indeed! How glad I am! What are they all?"

"I will read you their names directly; here they are, in my pocketbook. *Castle of Wolfenbach, Clermont, Mysterious Warnings, Necromancer of the Black Forest, Midnight Bell, Orphan of the Rhine,* and *Horrid Mysteries.* Those will last us some time."

"Yes, pretty well; but are they all horrid, are you sure they are all horrid?"

"Yes, quite sure; for a particular friend of mine, a Miss Andrews, a sweet girl, one of the sweetest creatures in the world, has read every one of them. I wish you knew Miss Andrews, you would be delighted with her. She is netting herself the sweetest cloak you can conceive. I think her as beautiful as an angel, and I am so vexed with the men for not admiring her! I scold them all amazingly about it."

"Scold them! Do you scold them for not admiring her?"

"Yes, that I do. There is nothing I would not do for those who are really my friends. I have no notion of loving people by halves; it is not my nature. My attachments are always excessively strong. I told Captain Hunt at one of our assemblies this winter that if he was to tease me all night, I would not dance with him, unless he would allow Miss Andrews to be as beautiful as an angel. The men think us incapable of real friendship, you know, and I am determined to show them the difference. Now, if I were to hear anybody speak slightingly of you, I should fire up in a moment: but that is not at all likely, for *you* are just the kind of girl to be a great favourite with the men."

"Oh, dear!" cried Catherine, colouring. "How can you say so?"

"I know you very well; you have so much animation, which is exactly what Miss Andrews wants, for I must confess there is something amazingly insipid about her. Oh! I must tell you, that just after we parted yesterday, I saw a young man looking at you so earnestly—I am sure he is in love with you." Catherine coloured, and disclaimed again.

Isabella laughed. "It is very true, upon my honour, but I see how it is; you are indifferent to everybody's admiration, except that of one gentleman, who shall be nameless. Nay, I cannot blame you"—speaking more seriously—"your feelings are easily understood. Where the heart is really attached, I know very well how little one can be pleased with the attention of anybody else. Everything is so insipid, so uninteresting, that does not relate to the beloved object! I can perfectly comprehend your feelings."

"But you should not persuade me that I think so very much about Mr. Tilney, for perhaps I may never see him again."

"Not see him again! My dearest creature, do not talk of it. I am sure you would be miserable if you thought so."

"No, indeed, I should not. I do not pretend to say that I was not very much pleased with him; but while I have *Udolpho* to read, I feel as if nobody could make me miserable. Oh! The dreadful black veil! My dear Isabella, I am sure there must be Laurentina's skeleton behind it."

"It is so odd to me, that you should never have read *Udolpho* before; but I suppose Mrs. Morland objects to novels."

"No, she does not. She very often reads Sir Charles Grandison herself; but new books do not fall in our way."

"Sir Charles Grandison! That is an amazing horrid book, is it not? I remember Miss Andrews could not get through the first volume."

"It is not like *Udolpho* at all; but yet I think it is very entertaining."

"Do you indeed! You surprise me; I thought it had not been readable. But, my dearest Catherine, have you settled what to wear on your head tonight? I am determined at all events to be dressed exactly like you. The men take notice of *that* sometimes, you know."

"But it does not signify if they do," said Catherine, very innocently.

"Signify! Oh, heavens! I make it a rule never to mind what they say. They are very often amazingly impertinent if you do not treat them with spirit, and make them keep their distance."

"Are they? Well, I never observed *that*. They always behave very well to me."

"Oh! They give themselves such airs. They are the most

conceited creatures in the world, and think themselves of so much importance! By the by, though I have thought of it a hundred times, I have always forgot to ask you what is your favourite complexion in a man. Do you like them best dark or fair?"

"I hardly know. I never much thought about it. Something between both, I think. Brown—not fair, and—and not very dark."

"Very well, Catherine. That is exactly he. I have not forgot your description of Mr. Tilney—'a brown skin, with dark eyes, and rather dark hair.' Well, my taste is different. I prefer light eyes, and as to complexion—do you know—I like a sallow better than any other. You must not betray me, if you should ever meet with one of your acquaintance answering that description."

"Betray you! What do you mean?"

"Nay, do not distress me. I believe I have said too much. Let us drop the subject."

Catherine, in some amazement, complied, and after remaining a few moments silent, was on the point of reverting to what interested her at that time rather more than anything else in the world, Laurentina's skeleton, when her friend prevented her, by saying, "For heaven's sake! Let us move away from this end of the room. Do you know, there are two odious young men who have been staring at me this half hour. They really put me quite out of countenance. Let us go and look at the arrivals. They will hardly follow us there."

Away they walked to the book; and while Isabella examined the names, it was Catherine's employment to watch the proceedings of these alarming young men.

"They are not coming this way, are they? I hope they are not so impertinent as to follow us. Pray let me know if they are coming. I am determined I will not look up."

In a few moments Catherine, with unaffected pleasure, assured her that she need not be longer uneasy, as the gentlemen had just left the pump-room.

"And which way are they gone?" said Isabella, turning hastily round. "One was a very good-looking young man."

"They went towards the church-yard."

"Well, I am amazingly glad I have got rid of them! And now, what say you to going to Edgar's Buildings with me, and looking at my new hat? You said you should like to see it."

Catherine readily agreed. "Only," she added, "perhaps we may overtake the two young men."

"Oh! Never mind that. If we make haste, we shall pass by them presently, and I am dying to show you my hat."

"But if we only wait a few minutes, there will be no danger of our seeing them at all."

"I shall not pay them any such compliment, I assure you. I have no notion of treating men with such respect. *That* is the way to spoil them."

Catherine had nothing to oppose against such reasoning; and therefore, to show the independence of Miss Thorpe, and her resolution of humbling the sex, they set off immediately as fast as they could walk, in pursuit of the two young men.

CHAPTER VII

HALF a minute conducted them through the pump-yard to the archway, opposite Union Passage; but here they were stopped. Everybody acquainted with Bath may remember the difficulties of crossing Cheap Street at this point; it is indeed a street of so impertinent a nature, so unfortunately connected with the great London and Oxford roads, and the principal inn of the city, that a day never passes in which parties of ladies, however important their business, whether in quest of pastry, millinery, or even (as in the present case) of young men, are not detained on one side or other by carriages, horsemen, or carts. This evil had been felt and lamented, at least three times a day, by Isabella since her residence in Bath; and she was now fated to feel and lament it once more, for at the very moment of coming opposite to Union Passage, and within view of the two gentlemen who were proceeding through the crowds, and threading the gutters of that interesting alley, they were prevented crossing by the approach of a gig, driven along on bad pavement by a most knowing-looking coachman with all the vehemence that could most fitly endanger the lives of himself, his companion, and his horse.

"Oh, these odious gigs!" said Isabella, looking up. "How I detest them." But this detestation, though so just, was of short duration, for she looked again and exclaimed, "Delightful! Mr. Morland and my brother!"

"Good heaven! 'Tis James!" was uttered at the same moment by Catherine; and, on catching the young men's eyes, the horse was immediately checked with a violence which almost threw him on his haunches, and the servant having now scampered up, the gentlemen jumped out, and the equipage was delivered to his care.

Catherine, by whom this meeting was wholly unexpected, received her brother with the liveliest pleasure; and he, being of a very amiable disposition, and sincerely attached to her, gave every proof on his side of equal satisfaction, which he could have leisure to do, while the bright eyes of Miss Thorpe were incessantly challenging his notice; and to her his devoirs were speedily paid, with a mixture of joy and embarrassment which might have informed Catherine, had she been more expert in the development of other people's feelings, and less simply engrossed by her own, that her brother thought her friend quite as pretty as she could do herself.

John Thorpe, who in the meantime had been giving orders about the horses, soon joined them, and from him she directly received the amends which were her due; for while he slightly and carelessly touched the hand of Isabella, on her he bestowed a whole scrape and half a short bow. He was a stout young man of middling height, who, with a plain face and ungraceful form, seemed fearful of being too handsome unless he wore the dress of a groom, and too much like a gentleman unless he were easy where he ought to be civil, and impudent where he might be allowed to be easy. He took out his watch: "How long do you think we have been running it from Tetbury, Miss Morland?"

"I do not know the distance." Her brother told her that it was twenty-three miles.

"*Three* and twenty!" cried Thorpe. "Five and twenty if it is an inch." Morland remonstrated, pleaded the authority of road-books, innkeepers, and milestones; but his friend disregarded them all; he had a surer test of distance. "I know it must be five and twenty," said he, "by the time we have been doing it. It is now half after one; we drove out of the inn-yard at Tetbury as the town clock struck eleven; and I defy any man in England to make my horse go less than ten miles an hour in harness; that makes it exactly twenty-five."

"You have lost an hour," said Morland; "it was only ten o'clock when we came from Tetbury."

"Ten o'clock! It was eleven, upon my soul! I counted every stroke. This brother of yours would persuade me out of my senses, Miss Morland; do but look at my horse; did you ever see an animal so made for speed in your life?" (The servant had just mounted the carriage and was driving off.) "Such true blood! Three hours and a half indeed coming only three and twenty miles! Look at that creature, and suppose it possible if you can."

"He *does* look very hot, to be sure."

"Hot! He had not turned a hair till we came to Walcot Church; but look at his forehand; look at his loins; only see how he moves; that horse *cannot* go less than ten miles an hour: tie his legs and he will get on. What do you think of my gig, Miss Morland? A neat one, is not it? Well hung; town-built; I have not had it a month. It was built for a Christchurch man, a friend of mine, a very good sort of fellow; he ran it a few weeks, till, I believe, it was convenient to have done with it. I happened just then to be looking out for some light thing of the kind, though I had pretty well determined on a curricle too; but I chanced to meet him on Magdalen Bridge, as he was driving into Oxford, last term: 'Ah! Thorpe,' said he, 'do you happen to want such a little thing as this? It is a capital one of the kind, but I am cursed tired of it.' 'Oh! D—,' said I; 'I am your man; what do you ask?' And how much do you think he did, Miss Morland?"

"I am sure I cannot guess at all."

"Curricle-hung, you see; seat, trunk, sword-case, splashing-board, lamps, silver moulding, all you see complete; the iron-work as good as new, or better. He asked fifty guineas; I closed with him directly, threw down the money, and the carriage was mine."

"And I am sure," said Catherine, "I know so little of such things that I cannot judge whether it was cheap or dear."

"Neither one nor t'other; I might have got it for less, I dare say; but I hate haggling, and poor Freeman wanted cash."

"That was very good-natured of you," said Catherine, quite pleased.

"Oh! D— it, when one has the means of doing a kind thing by a friend, I hate to be pitiful."

An inquiry now took place into the intended movements of the young ladies; and, on finding whither they were going, it was decided that the gentlemen should accompany them to Edgar's Buildings, and pay their respects to Mrs. Thorpe. James and Isabella led the way; and so well satisfied was the latter with her lot, so contentedly was she endeavouring to ensure a pleasant walk to him who brought the double recommendation of being her brother's friend, and her friend's brother, so pure and uncoquettish were her feelings, that, though they overtook and passed the two offending young men in Milsom Street, she was so far from seeking to attract their notice, that she looked back at them only three times.

John Thorpe kept of course with Catherine, and, after a few minutes' silence, renewed the conversation about his gig. "You will find, however, Miss Morland, it would be reckoned a cheap thing by some people, for I might have sold it for ten guineas more the next day; Jackson, of Oriel, bid me sixty at once; Morland was with me at the time."

"Yes," said Morland, who overheard this; "but you forget that your horse was included."

"My horse! Oh, d— it! I would not sell my horse for a hundred. Are you fond of an open carriage, Miss Morland?"

"Yes, very; I have hardly ever an opportunity of being in one; but I am particularly fond of it."

"I am glad of it; I will drive you out in mine every day."

"Thank you," said Catherine, in some distress, from a doubt of the propriety of accepting such an offer.

"I will drive you up Lansdown Hill tomorrow."

"Thank you; but will not your horse want rest?"

"Rest! He has only come three and twenty miles today; all nonsense; nothing ruins horses so much as rest; nothing knocks them up so soon. No, no; I shall exercise mine at the average of four hours every day while I am here."

"Shall you indeed!" said Catherine very seriously. "That will be forty miles a day."

"Forty! Aye, fifty, for what I care. Well, I will drive you up Lansdown tomorrow; mind, I am engaged."

"How delightful that will be!" cried Isabella, turning round. "My dearest Catherine, I quite envy you; but I am afraid, brother, you will not have room for a third."

"A third indeed! No, no; I did not come to Bath to drive my sisters about; that would be a good joke, faith! Morland must take care of you."

This brought on a dialogue of civilities between the other two; but Catherine heard neither the particulars nor the result. Her companion's discourse now sunk from its hitherto animated pitch to nothing more than a short decisive sentence of praise or condemnation on the face of every woman they met; and Catherine, after listening and agreeing as long as she could, with all the civility and deference of the youthful female mind, fearful of hazarding an opinion of its own in opposition to that of a self-assured man, especially where the beauty of her own sex is concerned, ventured at length to vary the subject by a question which had been long uppermost in her thoughts; it was, "Have you ever read *Udolpho,* Mr. Thorpe?"

"*Udolpho!* Oh, Lord! Not I; I never read novels; I have something else to do."

Catherine, humbled and ashamed, was going to apologize for her question, but he prevented her by saying, "Novels are all so full of nonsense and stuff; there has not been a tolerably decent one come out since *Tom Jones,* except *The Monk;* I read that t'other day; but as for all the others, they are the stupidest things in creation."

"I think you must like *Udolpho,* if you were to read it; it is so very interesting."

"Not I, faith! No, if I read any, it shall be Mrs. Radcliffe's; her novels are amusing enough; they are worth reading; some fun and nature in *them.*"

"*Udolpho* was written by Mrs. Radcliffe," said Catherine, with some hesitation, from the fear of mortifying him.

"No sure; was it? Aye, I remember, so it was; I was thinking of that other stupid book, written by that woman they make such a fuss about, she who married the French emigrant."

"I suppose you mean *Camilla*?"

"Yes, that's the book; such unnatural stuff! An old man playing at see-saw! I took up the first volume once and looked it over, but I soon found it would not do; indeed I guessed what sort of stuff it must be before I saw it: as soon as I heard she had married an emigrant, I was sure I should never be able to get through it."

"I have never read it."

"You had no loss, I assure you; it is the horridest nonsense you can imagine; there is nothing in the world in it but an old man's playing at see-saw and learning Latin; upon my soul there is not."

This critique, the justness of which was unfortunately lost on poor Catherine, brought them to the door of Mrs. Thorpe's lodgings, and the feelings of the discerning and unprejudiced reader of *Camilla* gave way to the feelings of the dutiful and affectionate son, as they met Mrs. Thorpe, who had descried them from above, in the passage. "Ah, Mother! How do you do?" said he, giving her a hearty shake of the hand. "Where did you get that quiz of a hat? It makes you look like an old witch. Here is Morland and I come to stay a few days with you, so you must look out for a couple of good beds somewhere near." And this address seemed to satisfy all the fondest wishes of the mother's heart, for she received him with the most delighted and exulting affection. On his two younger sisters he then bestowed an equal portion of his fraternal tenderness, for he asked each of them how they did, and observed that they both looked very ugly.

These manners did not please Catherine; but he was James's friend and Isabella's brother; and her judgment was further bought off by Isabella's assuring her, when they withdrew to see the new hat, that John thought her the most charming girl in the world, and by John's engaging her before they parted to dance with him that evening. Had she been older or vainer, such attacks might have done little; but, where youth and diffidence are united, it requires uncommon steadiness of reason to resist the attraction of being called the most charming girl in the world, and of being so very early engaged as a partner; and the consequence was that, when the two Morlands, after sitting an hour with the Thorpes, set off to walk together to Mr. Allen's, and James, as the door was closed on them, said, "Well, Catherine, how do you like my friend Thorpe?" instead of answering, as she probably would have done, had there been no friendship and no flattery in the case, "I do not like him at all," she directly replied, "I like him very much; he seems very agreeable."

"He is as good-natured a fellow as ever lived; a little of a rattle; but that will recommend him to your sex, I believe: and how do you like the rest of the family?"

"Very, very much indeed: Isabella particularly."

"I am very glad to hear you say so; she is just the kind of young woman I could wish to see you attached to; she has so much good sense, and is so thoroughly unaffected and amiable; I always wanted you to know her; and she seems very fond of you. She said the highest things in your praise that could possibly be; and the praise of such a girl as Miss Thorpe even you, Catherine," taking her hand with affection, "may be proud of."

"Indeed I am," she replied; "I love her exceedingly, and am delighted to find that you like her too. You hardly mentioned anything of her when you wrote to me after your visit there."

"Because I thought I should soon see you myself. I hope you will be a great deal together while you are in Bath. She is a most amiable girl; such a superior understanding! How fond all the family are of her; she is evidently the general favourite; and how much she must be admired in such a place as this—is not she?"

"Yes, very much indeed, I fancy; Mr. Allen thinks her the prettiest girl in Bath."

"I dare say he does; and I do not know any man who is a better judge of beauty than Mr. Allen. I need not ask you whether you are happy here, my dear Catherine; with such a companion and friend as Isabella Thorpe, it would be impossible for you to be otherwise; and the Allens, I am sure, are very kind to you?"

"Yes, very kind; I never was so happy before; and now you are come it will be more delightful than ever; how good it is of you to come so far on purpose to see *me*."

James accepted this tribute of gratitude, and qualified his conscience for accepting it too, by saying with perfect sincerity, "Indeed, Catherine, I love you dearly."

Inquiries and communications concerning brothers and sisters, the situation of some, the growth of the rest, and other family matters now passed between them, and continued, with only one small digression on James's part, in praise of Miss Thorpe, till they reached Pulteney Street, where he was welcomed with great kindness by Mr. and Mrs. Allen, invited by the former to dine with them, and summoned by the latter to guess the price and weigh the merits of a new muff and tippet. A pre-engagement in Edgar's Buildings prevented his accepting the invitation of one friend, and obliged him to hurry away as soon as he had satisfied the demands of the other. The time of the two parties uniting in the Octagon Room being correctly adjusted, Catherine was then left to the luxury of a raised, restless, and frightened imagination over the pages of *Udolpho*, lost from all worldly concerns of dressing and dinner, incapable of soothing Mrs. Allen's fears on the delay of an expected dressmaker, and having only one minute in sixty to bestow even on the reflection of her own felicity, in being already engaged for the evening.

CHAPTER VIII

IN spite of *Udolpho* and the dressmaker, however, the party from Pulteney Street reached the Upper Rooms in very good time. The Thorpes and James Morland were there only two minutes before them; and Isabella having gone through the usual ceremonial of meeting her friend with the most smiling and affectionate haste, of admiring the set of her gown, and envying the curl of her hair, they followed their chaperones, arm in arm, into the ballroom, whispering to each other whenever a thought occurred, and supplying the place of many ideas by a squeeze of the hand or a smile of affection.

The dancing began within a few minutes after they were seated; and James, who had been engaged quite as long as his sister, was very importunate with Isabella to stand up; but John was gone into the card-room to speak to a friend, and nothing, she declared, should induce her to join the set before her dear Catherine could join it too. "I assure you," said she, "I would not stand up without your dear sister for all the world; for if I did we should certainly be separated the whole evening." Catherine accepted this kindness with gratitude, and they continued as they were for three minutes longer, when Isabella, who had been talking to James on the other side of her, turned again to his sister and whispered, "My dear creature, I am afraid I must leave you, your brother is so amazingly impatient to begin; I know you will not mind my going away, and I dare say John will be back in a moment, and then you may easily find me out." Catherine, though a little disappointed, had too much good nature to make any opposition, and the others rising up, Isabella had only time to press her friend's hand and say, "Good-bye, my dear love," before they hurried off. The younger Miss Thorpes being also dancing, Catherine was left to the mercy of Mrs. Thorpe and Mrs. Allen, between whom she now remained. She could not help being vexed at the non-appearance of Mr. Thorpe, for she not only longed to be dancing, but was likewise aware that, as the real dignity of her situation could not be known, she was sharing with the scores of other young ladies still sitting down all the discredit of wanting a partner. To be disgraced in the eye of the world, to wear the appearance of infamy while her heart is all purity, her actions all innocence, and the misconduct of another the true source of her debasement, is one of those circumstances which peculiarly belong to the heroine's life, and her fortitude under it what particularly dignifies her character. Catherine had fortitude too; she suffered, but no murmur passed her lips.

From this state of humiliation, she was roused, at the end of ten minutes, to a pleasanter feeling, by seeing, not Mr. Thorpe, but Mr. Tilney, within three yards of the place where they sat; he seemed to be moving that way, but he did not see her, and therefore the smile and the blush, which his sudden reappearance raised in Catherine, passed away without sullying her heroic importance. He looked as handsome and as lively as ever, and was talking with interest to a fashionable and pleasing-looking young woman, who leant on his arm, and whom Catherine immediately guessed to be his sister; thus unthinkingly throwing away a fair opportunity of considering him lost to her forever, by being married already. But guided only by what was simple and probable, it had never entered her head that Mr. Tilney could be married; he had not behaved, he had not talked, like the married men to whom she had been used; he had never mentioned a wife, and he had acknowledged a sister. From these circumstances sprang the instant conclusion of his sister's now being by his side; and therefore, instead of turning of a deathlike paleness and falling in a fit on Mrs. Allen's bosom, Catherine sat erect, in the perfect use of her senses, and with cheeks only a little redder than usual.

Mr. Tilney and his companion, who continued, though slowly, to approach, were immediately preceded by a lady, an acquaintance of Mrs. Thorpe; and this lady stopping to speak to her, they, as belonging to her, stopped likewise, and Catherine, catching Mr. Tilney's eye, instantly received from him the smiling tribute of recognition. She returned it with pleasure, and then advancing still nearer, he spoke both to her and Mrs. Allen, by whom he was very civilly acknowledged. "I am very happy to see you again, sir, indeed; I was afraid you had left Bath." He thanked her for her fears, and said that he had quitted it for a week, on the very morning after his having had the pleasure of seeing her.

"Well, sir, and I dare say you are not sorry to be back again, for it is just the place for young people—and indeed for everybody else too. I tell Mr. Allen, when he talks of being sick of it, that I am sure he should not complain, for it is so very agreeable a place, that it is much better to be here than at home at this dull time of year. I tell him he is quite in luck to be sent here for his health."

"And I hope, madam, that Mr. Allen will be obliged to like the place, from finding it of service to him."

"Thank you, sir. I have no doubt that he will. A neighbour of ours, Dr. Skinner, was here for his health last winter, and came away quite stout."

"That circumstance must give great encouragement."

"Yes, sir—and Dr. Skinner and his family were here three months; so I tell Mr. Allen he must not be in a hurry to get away."

Here they were interrupted by a request from Mrs. Thorpe to Mrs. Allen, that she would move a little to accommodate Mrs. Hughes and Miss Tilney with seats, as they had agreed to join their party. This was accordingly done, Mr. Tilney still continuing standing before them; and after a few minutes' consideration, he asked Catherine to dance with him. This compliment, delightful as it was, produced severe mortification to the lady; and in giving her denial, she expressed her sorrow on the occasion so very much as if she really felt it that had Thorpe, who joined her just afterwards, been half a minute earlier, he might have thought her sufferings rather too acute. The very easy manner in which he then told her that he had kept her waiting did not by any means reconcile her more to her lot; nor did the particulars which he entered into while they were standing up, of the horses and dogs of the friend whom he had just left, and of a proposed exchange of terriers between them, interest her so much as to prevent her looking very often towards that part of the room where she had left Mr. Tilney. Of her dear Isabella, to whom she particularly longed to point out that gentleman, she could see nothing. They were in different sets. She was separated from all her party, and away from all her acquaintance; one mortification succeeded another, and from the whole she deduced this useful lesson, that to go previously engaged to a ball does not necessarily increase either the dignity or enjoyment of a young lady. From such a moralizing strain as this, she was suddenly roused by a touch on the shoulder, and turning round, perceived Mrs. Hughes directly behind her, attended by Miss Tilney and a gentleman. "I beg your pardon, Miss Morland," said she, "for this liberty—but I cannot anyhow get to Miss Thorpe, and Mrs. Thorpe said she was sure you would not have the least objection to letting in this young lady by you." Mrs. Hughes could not have applied to any creature in the room more happy to oblige her than Catherine. The young ladies were introduced to each other, Miss Tilney expressing a proper sense of such goodness, Miss Morland with the real delicacy of a generous mind making light of the obligation; and Mrs. Hughes, satisfied with having so respectably settled her young charge, returned to her party.

Miss Tilney had a good figure, a pretty face, and a very agreeable countenance; and her air, though it had not all the decided pretension, the resolute stylishness of Miss Thorpe's, had more real elegance. Her manners showed good sense and good breeding; they were neither shy nor affectedly open; and she seemed capable of being young, attractive, and at a ball without wanting to fix the attention of every man near her, and without exaggerated feelings of ecstatic delight or inconceivable vexation on every little trifling occurrence. Catherine, interested at once by her appearance and her relationship to Mr. Tilney, was desirous of being acquainted with her, and readily talked therefore whenever she could think of anything to say, and had courage and leisure for saying it. But the hindrance thrown in the way of a very speedy intimacy, by the frequent want of one or more of these requisites, prevented their doing more than going through the first rudiments of an acquaintance, by informing themselves how well the other liked Bath, how much she admired its buildings and surrounding country, whether she drew, or played, or sang, and whether she was fond of riding on horseback.

The two dances were scarcely concluded before Catherine found her arm gently seized by her faithful Isabella, who in great spirits exclaimed, "At last I have got you. My dearest creature, I have been looking for you this hour. What could induce you to come into this set, when you knew I was in the other? I have been quite wretched without you."

"My dear Isabella, how was it possible for me to get at you? I could not even see where you were."

"So I told your brother all the time—but he would not believe me. Do go and see for her, Mr. Morland, said I—but all in vain—he would not stir an inch. Was not it so, Mr. Morland? But you men are all so immoderately lazy! I have been scolding him to such a degree, my dear Catherine, you would be quite amazed. You know I never stand upon ceremony with such people."

"Look at that young lady with the white beads round her head," whispered Catherine, detaching her friend from James. "It is Mr. Tilney's sister."

"Oh! Heavens! You don't say so! Let me look at her this moment. What a delightful girl! I never saw anything half so beautiful! But where is her all-conquering brother? Is he in the room? Point him out to me this instant, if he is. I die to see him. Mr. Morland, you are not to listen. We are not talking about you."

"But what is all this whispering about? What is going on?"

"There now, I knew how it would be. You men have such restless curiosity! Talk of the curiosity of women, indeed! 'Tis nothing. But be satisfied, for you are not to know anything at all of the matter."

"And is that likely to satisfy me, do you think?"

"Well, I declare I never knew anything like you. What can it signify to you, what we are talking of? Perhaps we are talking about you; therefore I would advise you not to listen, or you may happen to hear something not very agreeable."

In this commonplace chatter, which lasted some time, the original subject seemed entirely forgotten; and though Catherine was very well pleased to have it dropped for a while, she could not avoid a little suspicion at the total suspension of all Isabella's impatient desire to see Mr. Tilney. When the orchestra struck up a fresh dance, James would have led his fair partner away, but she resisted. "I tell you, Mr. Morland," she cried, "I would not do such a thing for all the world. How can you be so teasing; only conceive, my dear Catherine, what your brother wants me to do. He wants me to dance with him again, though I tell him that it is a most improper thing, and entirely against the rules. It would make us the talk of the place, if we were not to change partners."

"Upon my honour," said James, "in these public assemblies, it is as often done as not."

"Nonsense, how can you say so? But when you men have a point to carry, you never stick at anything. My sweet Catherine, do support me; persuade your brother how impossible it is. Tell him that it would quite shock you to see me do such a thing; now would not it?"

"No, not at all; but if you think it wrong, you had much better change."

"There," cried Isabella, "you hear what your sister says, and yet you will not mind her. Well, remember that it is not my fault, if we set all the old ladies in Bath in a bustle. Come along, my dearest Catherine, for heaven's sake, and stand by me." And off they went, to regain their former place. John Thorpe, in the meanwhile, had walked away; and Catherine, ever willing to give Mr. Tilney an opportunity of repeating the agreeable request which had already flattered her once, made her way to Mrs. Allen and Mrs. Thorpe as fast as she could, in the hope of finding him still with them—a hope which, when it proved to be fruitless, she felt to have been highly unreasonable. "Well, my dear," said Mrs. Thorpe, impatient for praise of her son, "I hope you have had an agreeable partner."

"Very agreeable, madam."

"I am glad of it. John has charming spirits, has not he?"

"Did you meet Mr. Tilney, my dear?" said Mrs. Allen.

"No, where is he?"

"He was with us just now, and said he was so tired of lounging about, that he was resolved to go and dance; so I thought perhaps he would ask you, if he met with you."

"Where can he be?" said Catherine, looking round; but she had not looked round long before she saw him leading a young lady to the dance.

"Ah! He has got a partner; I wish he had asked *you,*" said Mrs. Allen; and after a short silence, she added, "he is a very agreeable young man."

"Indeed he is, Mrs. Allen," said Mrs. Thorpe, smiling complacently; "I must say it, though I *am* his mother, that there is not a more agreeable young man in the world."

This inapplicable answer might have been too much for the comprehension of many; but it did not puzzle Mrs. Allen, for after only a moment's consideration, she said, in a whisper to Catherine, "I dare say she thought I was speaking of her son."

Catherine was disappointed and vexed. She seemed to have missed by so little the very object she had had in view; and this persuasion did not incline her to a very gracious reply, when John Thorpe came up to her soon afterwards and said, "Well, Miss Morland, I suppose you and I are to stand up and jig it together again."

"Oh, no; I am much obliged to you, our two dances are over; and, besides, I am tired, and do not mean to dance any more."

"Do not you? Then let us walk about and quiz people. Come along with me, and I will show you the four greatest quizzers in the room; my two younger sisters and their partners. I have been laughing at them this half hour."

Again Catherine excused herself; and at last he walked off to quiz his sisters by himself. The rest of the evening she found very dull; Mr. Tilney was drawn away from their party at tea, to attend that of his partner; Miss Tilney, though belonging to it, did not sit near her, and James and Isabella were so much engaged in conversing together that the latter had no leisure to bestow more on her friend than one smile, one squeeze, and one "dearest Catherine."

CHAPTER IX

THE progress of Catherine's unhappiness from the events of the evening was as follows. It appeared first in a general dissatisfaction with everybody about her, while she remained in the rooms, which speedily brought on considerable weariness and a violent desire to go home. This, on arriving in Pulteney Street, took the direction of extraordinary hunger, and when that was appeased, changed into an earnest longing to be in bed; such was the extreme point of her distress; for when there she immediately fell into a sound sleep which lasted nine hours, and from which she awoke perfectly revived, in excellent spirits, with fresh hopes and fresh schemes. The first wish of her heart was to improve her acquaintance with Miss Tilney, and almost her first resolution, to seek her for that purpose, in the pump-room at noon. In the pump-room, one so newly arrived in Bath must be met with, and that building she had already found so favourable for the discovery of female excellence, and the completion of female intimacy, so admirably adapted for secret discourses and unlimited confidence, that she was most reasonably encouraged to expect another friend from within its walls. Her plan for the morning thus settled, she sat quietly down to her book after breakfast, resolving to remain in the same place and the same employment till the clock struck one; and from habitude very little incommoded by the remarks and ejaculations of Mrs. Allen, whose vacancy of mind and incapacity for thinking were such, that as she never talked a great deal, so she could never be entirely silent; and, therefore, while she sat at her work, if she lost her needle or broke her thread, if she heard a carriage in the street, or saw a speck upon her gown, she must observe it aloud, whether there were anyone at leisure to answer her or not. At about half past twelve, a remarkably loud rap drew her in haste to the window, and scarcely had she time to in-

form Catherine of there being two open carriages at the
door, in the first only a servant, her brother driving Miss
Thorpe in the second, before John Thorpe came running upstairs, calling out, "Well, Miss Morland, here I am. Have
you been waiting long? We could not come before; the old
devil of a coachmaker was such an eternity finding out a
thing fit to be got into, and now it is ten thousand to one but
they break down before we are out of the street. How do you
do, Mrs. Allen? A famous ball last night, was not it? Come,
Miss Morland, be quick, for the others are in a confounded
hurry to be off. They want to get their tumble over."

"What do you mean?" said Catherine. "Where are you all
going to?"

"Going to? Why, you have not forgot our engagement!
Did not we agree together to take a drive this morning?
What a head you have! We are going up Claverton Down."

"Something was said about it, I remember," said Catherine, looking at Mrs. Allen for her opinion; "but really I did
not expect you."

"Not expect me! That's a good one! And what a dust you
would have made, if I had not come."

Catherine's silent appeal to her friend, meanwhile, was
entirely thrown away, for Mrs. Allen, not being at all in the
habit of conveying any expression herself by a look, was not
aware of its being ever intended by anybody else; and Catherine, whose desire of seeing Miss Tilney again could at that
moment bear a short delay in favour of a drive, and who
thought there could be no impropriety in her going with Mr.
Thorpe, as Isabella was going at the same time with James,
was therefore obliged to speak plainer. "Well, ma'am, what
do you say to it? Can you spare me for an hour or two? Shall
I go?"

"Do just as you please, my dear," replied Mrs. Allen, with
the most placid indifference. Catherine took the advice, and
ran off to get ready. In a very few minutes she reappeared,
having scarcely allowed the two others time enough to get
through a few short sentences in her praise, after Thorpe had
procured Mrs. Allen's admiration of his gig; and then receiving her friend's parting good wishes, they both hurried
downstairs. "My dearest creature," cried Isabella, to whom
the duty of friendship immediately called her before she
could get into the carriage, "you have been at least three
hours getting ready. I was afraid you were ill. What a de-

lightful ball we had last night. I have a thousand things to say to you; but make haste and get in, for I long to be off."

Catherine followed her orders and turned away, but not too soon to hear her friend exclaim aloud to James, "What a sweet girl she is! I quite dote on her."

"You will not be frightened, Miss Morland," said Thorpe, as he handed her in, "if my horse should dance about a little at first setting off. He will, most likely, give a plunge or two, and perhaps take the rest for a minute; but he will soon know his master. He is full of spirits, playful as can be, but there is no vice in him."

Catherine did not think the portrait a very inviting one, but it was too late to retreat, and she was too young to own herself frightened; so, resigning herself to her fate, and trusting to the animal's boasted knowledge of its owner, she sat peaceably down, and saw Thorpe sit down by her. Everything being then arranged, the servant who stood at the horse's head was bid in an important voice "to let him go," and off they went in the quietest manner imaginable, without a plunge or a caper, or anything like one. Catherine, delighted at so happy an escape, spoke her pleasure aloud with grateful surprise; and her companion immediately made the matter perfectly simple by assuring her that it was entirely owing to the peculiarly judicious manner in which he had then held the reins, and the singular discernment and dexterity with which he had directed his whip. Catherine, though she could not help wondering that with such perfect command of his horse, he should think it necessary to alarm her with a relation of its tricks, congratulated herself sincerely on being under the care of so excellent a coachman; and perceiving that the animal continued to go on in the same quiet manner, without showing the smallest propensity towards any unpleasant vivacity, and (considering its inevitable pace was ten miles an hour) by no means alarmingly fast, gave herself up to all the enjoyment of air and exercise of the most invigorating kind, in a fine mild day of February, with the consciousness of safety. A silence of several minutes succeeded their first short dialogue; it was broken by Thorpe's saying very abruptly, "Old Allen is as rich as a Jew—is not he?" Catherine did not understand him—and he repeated his question, adding in explanation, "Old Allen, the man you are with."

"Oh! Mr. Allen, you mean. Yes, I believe, he is very rich."

"And no children at all?"

"No—not any."

"A famous thing for his next heirs. He is *your* godfather, is not he?"

"My godfather! No."

"But you are always very much with them."

"Yes, very much."

"Aye, that is what I meant. He seems a good kind of old fellow enough, and has lived very well in his time, I dare say; he is not gouty for nothing. Does he drink his bottle a day now?"

"His bottle a day! No. Why should you think of such a thing? He is a very temperate man, and you could not fancy him in liquor last night?"

"Lord help you! You women are always thinking of men's being in liquor. Why, you do not suppose a man is overset by a bottle? I am sure of *this*—that if everybody was to drink their bottle a day, there would not be half the disorders in the world there are now. It would be a famous good thing for us all."

"I cannot believe it."

"Oh! Lord, it would be the saving of thousands. There is not the hundredth part of the wine consumed in this kingdom that there ought to be. Our foggy climate wants help."

"And yet I have heard that there is a great deal of wine drunk in Oxford."

"Oxford! There is no drinking at Oxford now, I assure you. Nobody drinks there. You would hardly meet with a man who goes beyond his four pints at the utmost. Now, for instance, it was reckoned a remarkable thing at the last party in my rooms, that upon an average we cleared about five pints a head. It was looked upon as something out of the common way. *Mine* is famous good stuff, to be sure. You would not often meet with anything like it in Oxford—and that may account for it. But this will just give you a notion of the general rate of drinking there."

"Yes, it does give a notion," said Catherine warmly, "and that is, that you all drink a great deal more wine than I thought you did. However, I am sure James does not drink so much."

This declaration brought on a loud and overpowering reply, of which no part was very distinct, except the frequent exclamations, amounting almost to oaths, which adorned it, and Catherine was left, when it ended, with rather a strengthened belief of there being a great deal of wine drunk in Oxford, and the same happy conviction of her brother's comparative sobriety.

Thorpe's ideas then all reverted to the merits of his own equipage, and she was called on to admire the spirit and freedom with which his horse moved along, and the ease which his paces, as well as the excellence of the springs, gave the motion of the carriage. She followed him in all his admiration as well as she could. To go before or beyond him was impossible. His knowledge and her ignorance of the subject, his rapidity of expression, and her diffidence of herself put that out of her power; she could strike out nothing new in commendation, but she readily echoed whatever he chose to assert, and it was finally settled between them without any difficulty that his equipage was altogether the most complete of its kind in England, his carriage the neatest, his horse the best goer, and himself the best coachman. "You do not really think, Mr. Thorpe," said Catherine, venturing after some time to consider the matter as entirely decided, and to offer some little variation on the subject, "that James's gig will break down?"

"Break down! Oh! Lord! Did you ever see such a little tit-tuppy thing in your life? There is not a sound piece of iron about it. The wheels have been fairly worn out these ten years at least—and as for the body! Upon my soul, you might shake it to pieces yourself with a touch. It is the most devilish little rickety business I ever beheld! Thank God! we have got a better. I would not be bound to go two miles in it for fifty thousand pounds."

"Good heavens!" cried Catherine, quite frightened. "Then pray let us turn back; they will certainly meet with an accident if we go on. Do let us turn back, Mr. Thorpe; stop and speak to my brother, and tell him how very unsafe it is."

"Unsafe! Oh, lord! What is there in that? They will only get a roll if it does break down; and there is plenty of dirt; it will be excellent falling. Oh, curse it! The carriage is safe enough, if a man knows how to drive it; a thing of that sort in good hands will last above twenty years after it is fairly worn out. Lord bless you! I would undertake for five pounds to drive it to York and back again, without losing a nail."

Catherine listened with astonishment; she knew not how to reconcile two such very different accounts of the same thing; for she had not been brought up to understand the propensities of a rattle, nor to know to how many idle assertions and impudent falsehoods the excess of vanity will lead. Her own family were plain, matter-of-fact people who seldom aimed at wit of any kind; her father, at the utmost, being contented with a pun, and her mother with a proverb; they were not in the habit therefore of telling lies to increase their importance, or of asserting at one moment what they would contradict the next. She reflected on the affair for some time in much perplexity, and was more than once on the point of requesting from Mr. Thorpe a clearer insight into his real opinion on the subject; but she checked herself, because it appeared to her that he did not excel in giving those clearer insights, in making those things plain which he had before made ambiguous; and, joining to this, the consideration that he would not really suffer his sister and his friend to be exposed to a danger from which he might easily preserve them, she concluded at last that he must know the carriage to be in fact perfectly safe, and therefore would alarm herself no longer. By him the whole matter seemed entirely forgotten; and all the rest of his conversation, or rather talk, began and ended with himself and his own concerns. He told her of horses which he had bought for a trifle and sold for incredible sums; of racing matches, in which his judgment had infallibly foretold the winner; of shooting parties, in which he had killed more birds (though without having one good shot) than all his companions together; and described to her some famous day's sport, with the fox-hounds, in which his foresight and skill in directing the dogs had repaired the mistakes of the most experienced huntsman, and in which the boldness of his riding, though it had never endangered his own life for a moment, had been constantly leading others into difficulties, which he calmly concluded had broken the necks of many.

Little as Catherine was in the habit of judging for herself, and unfixed as were her general notions of what men ought to be, she could not entirely repress a doubt, while she bore with the effusions of his endless conceit, of his being altogether completely agreeable. It was a bold surmise, for he was Isabella's brother; and she had been assured by James that his manners would recommend him to all her sex; but in spite of this, the extreme weariness of his company, which crept over her before they had been out an hour, and which continued unceasingly to increase till they stopped in Pulteney Street again, induced her, in some small degree, to resist such high authority, and to distrust his powers of giving universal pleasure.

When they arrived at Mrs. Allen's door, the astonishment of Isabella was hardly to be expressed, on finding that it was too late in the day for them to attend her friend into the house: "Past three o'clock!" It was inconceivable, incredible, impossible! And she would neither believe her own watch, nor her brother's, nor the servant's; she would believe no assurance of it founded on reason or reality, till Morland produced his watch, and ascertained the fact; to have doubted a moment longer *then* would have been equally inconceivable, incredible, and impossible; and she could only protest, over and over again, that no two hours and a half had ever gone off so swiftly before, as Catherine was called on to confirm; Catherine could not tell a falsehood even to please Isabella; but the latter was spared the misery of her friend's dissenting voice, by not waiting for her answer. Her own feelings entirely engrossed her; her wretchedness was most acute on finding herself obliged to go directly home. It was ages since she had had a moment's conversation with her dearest Catherine; and, though she had such thousands of things to say to her, it appeared as if they were never to be together again; so, with smiles of most exquisite misery, and the laughing eye of utter despondency, she bade her friend adieu and went on.

Catherine found Mrs. Allen just returned from all the busy idleness of the morning, and was immediately greeted with, "Well, my dear, here you are," a truth which she had no greater inclination than power to dispute; "and I hope you have had a pleasant airing?"

"Yes, ma'am, I thank you; we could not have had a nicer day."

"So Mrs. Thorpe said; she was vastly pleased at your all going."

"You have seen Mrs. Thorpe, then?"

"Yes, I went to the pump-room as soon as you were gone, and there I met her, and we had a great deal of talk together. She says there was hardly any veal to be got at market this morning, it is so uncommonly scarce."

"Did you see anybody else of our acquaintance?"

"Yes; we agreed to take a turn in the Crescent, and there we met Mrs. Hughes, and Mr. and Miss Tilney walking with her."

"Did you indeed? And did they speak to you?"

"Yes, we walked along the Crescent together for half an hour. They seem very agreeable people. Miss Tilney was in a very pretty spotted muslin, and I fancy, by what I can learn, that she always dresses very handsomely. Mrs. Hughes talked to me a great deal about the family."

"And what did she tell you of them?"

"Oh! A vast deal indeed; she hardly talked of anything else."

"Did she tell you what part of Gloucestershire they come from?"

"Yes, she did; but I cannot recollect now. But they are very good kind of people, and very rich. Mrs. Tilney was a Miss Drummond, and she and Mrs. Hughes were schoolfellows; and Miss Drummond had a very large fortune; and, when she married, her father gave her twenty thousand pounds, and five hundred to buy wedding-clothes. Mrs. Hughes saw all the clothes after they came from the warehouse."

"And are Mr. and Mrs. Tilney in Bath?"

"Yes, I fancy they are, but I am not quite certain. Upon recollection, however, I have a notion they are both dead; at least the mother is; yes, I am sure Mrs. Tilney is dead, because Mrs. Hughes told me there was a very beautiful set of pearls that Mr. Drummond gave his daughter on her wedding-day and that Miss Tilney has got now, for they were put by for her when her mother died."

"And is Mr. Tilney, my partner, the only son?"

"I cannot be quite positive about that, my dear; I have some idea he is; but, however, he is a very fine young man, Mrs. Hughes says, and likely to do very well."

Catherine inquired no further; she had heard enough to feel that Mrs. Allen had no real intelligence to give, and that she was most particularly unfortunate herself in having missed such a meeting with both brother and sister. Could she have foreseen such a circumstance, nothing should have persuaded her to go out with the others; and, as it was, she could only lament her ill luck, and think over what she had lost, till it was clear to her that the drive had by no means been very pleasant and that John Thorpe himself was quite disagreeable.

CHAPTER X

THE Allens, Thorpes, and Morlands all met in the evening at the theatre; and, as Catherine and Isabella sat together, there was then an opportunity for the latter to utter some few of the many thousand things which had been collecting within her for communication in the immeasurable length of time which had divided them. "Oh, heavens! My beloved Catherine, have I got you at last?" was her address on Catherine's entering the box and sitting by her. "Now, Mr. Morland," for he was close to her on the other side, "I shall not speak another word to you all the rest of the evening; so I charge you not to expect it. My sweetest Catherine, how have you been this long age? But I need not ask you, for you look delightfully. You really have done your hair in a more heavenly style than ever; you mischievous creature, do you want to attract everybody? I assure you, my brother is quite in love with you already; and as for Mr. Tilney—but *that* is a settled thing—even *your* modesty cannot doubt his attachment now; his coming back to Bath makes it too plain. Oh! What would not I give to see him! I really am quite wild with impatience. My mother says he is the most delightful young man in the world; she saw him this morning, you know; you must introduce him to me. Is he in the house now? Look about, for heaven's sake! I assure you, I can hardly exist till I see him."

"No," said Catherine, "he is not here; I cannot see him anywhere."

"Oh, horrid! Am I never to be acquainted with him? How do you like my gown? I think it does not look amiss; the sleeves were entirely my own thought. Do you know, I get so immoderately sick of Bath; your brother and I were agreeing this morning that, though it is vastly well to be here for a few weeks, we would not live here for millions. We soon found out that our tastes were exactly alike in preferring the country to every other place; really, our opinions were so exactly the same, it was quite ridiculous! There was not a single point in which we differed; I would not have had you by for the world; you are such a sly thing, I am sure you would have made some droll remark or other about it."

"No, indeed I should not."

"Oh, yes you would indeed; I know you better than you know yourself. You would have told us that we seemed born for each other, or some nonsense of that kind, which would have distressed me beyond conception; my cheeks would have been as red as your roses; I would not have had you by for the world."

"Indeed you do me injustice; I would not have made so improper a remark upon any account; and besides, I am sure it would never have entered my head."

Isabella smiled incredulously and talked the rest of the evening to James.

Catherine's resolution of endeavouring to meet Miss Tilney again continued in full force the next morning; and till the usual moment of going to the pump-room, she felt some alarm from the dread of a second prevention. But nothing of that kind occurred, no visitors appeared to delay them, and they all three set off in good time for the pump-room, where the ordinary course of events and conversation took place; Mr. Allen, after drinking his glass of water, joined some gentlemen to talk over the politics of the day and compare the account of their newspapers; and the ladies walked about together, noticing every new face, and almost every new bonnet in the room. The female part of the Thorpe family, attended by James Morland, appeared among the crowd in less than a quarter of an hour, and Catherine immediately took her usual place by the side of her friend. James, who was now in constant attendance, maintained a similar position, and separating themselves from the rest of their party, they walked in that manner for some time, till Catherine began to doubt the happiness of a situation which, confining her entirely to her friend and brother, gave her very little share in the notice of either. They were always engaged in some sentimental discussion or lively dispute, but their sentiment was conveyed in such whispering voices, and their vivacity attended with so much laughter, that though Catherine's supporting opinion was not unfrequently called for by one or the other, she was never able to give any, from not having heard a word of the subject. At length however she was empowered to disengage herself from her friend, by the avowed necessity of speaking to Miss Tilney, whom she most joyfully saw just entering the room with Mrs. Hughes, and whom she instantly joined, with a firmer determination to be acquainted, than she might have had courage to command, had she not been urged by the disappointment of the day before. Miss Tilney met her with great civility, returned her advances with equal goodwill, and they continued talking together as long as both parties remained in the room; and though in all probability not an observation was made, nor an expression used by either which had not been made and used some thousands of times before, under that roof, in every Bath season, yet the merit of their being spoken with simplicity and truth, and without personal conceit, might be something uncommon.

"How well your brother dances!" was an artless exclamation of Catherine's towards the close of their conversation, which at once surprised and amused her companion.

"Henry!" she replied with a smile. "Yes, he does dance very well."

"He must have thought it very odd to hear me say I was engaged the other evening, when he saw me sitting down. But I really had been engaged the whole day to Mr. Thorpe." Miss Tilney could only bow. "You cannot think," added Catherine after a moment's silence, "how surprised I was to see him again. I felt so sure of his being quite gone away."

"When Henry had the pleasure of seeing you before, he was in Bath but for a couple of days. He came only to engage lodgings for us."

"*That* never occurred to me; and of course, not seeing him anywhere, I thought he must be gone. Was not the young lady he danced with on Monday a Miss Smith?"

"Yes, an acquaintance of Mrs. Hughes."

"I dare say she was very glad to dance. Do you think her pretty?"

"Not very."

"He never comes to the pump-room, I suppose?"

"Yes, sometimes; but he has rid out this morning with my father."

Mrs. Hughes now joined them, and asked Miss Tilney if she was ready to go. "I hope I shall have the pleasure of seeing you again soon," said Catherine. "Shall you be at the cotillion ball tomorrow?"

"Perhaps we— Yes, I think we certainly shall."

"I am glad of it, for we shall all be there." This civility was duly returned; and they parted—on Miss Tilney's side with some knowledge of her new acquaintance's feelings, and on Catherine's, without the smallest consciousness of having explained them.

She went home very happy. The morning had answered all her hopes, and the evening of the following day was now the object of expectation, the future good. What gown and what head-dress she should wear on the occasion became her chief concern. She cannot be justified in it. Dress is at all times a frivolous distinction, and excessive solicitude about it often destroys its own aim. Catherine knew all this very well; her great aunt had read her a lecture on the subject only the Christmas before; and yet she lay awake ten minutes on Wednesday night debating between her spotted and her tamboured muslin, and nothing but the shortness of the time prevented her buying a new one for the evening. This would have been an error in judgment, great though not uncommon, from which one of the other sex rather than her own, a brother rather than a great aunt, might have warned her, for man only can be aware of the insensibility of man towards a new gown. It would be mortifying to the feelings of many ladies, could they be made to understand how little the heart of man is affected by what is costly or new in their attire; how little it is biased by the texture of their muslin, and how unsusceptible of peculiar tenderness towards the spotted, the sprigged, the mull, or the jackonet. Woman is fine for her own satisfaction alone. No man will admire her the more, no woman will like her the better for it. Neatness and fashion are enough for the former, and a something of shabbiness or impropriety will be most endearing to the latter. But not one of these grave reflections troubled the tranquillity of Catherine.

She entered the rooms on Thursday evening with feelings very different from what had attended her thither the Monday before. She had then been exulting in her engagement to Thorpe, and was now chiefly anxious to avoid his sight, lest he should engage her again; for though she could not, dared not expect that Mr. Tilney should ask her a third time to dance, her wishes, hopes, and plans all centred in nothing less. Every young lady may feel for my heroine in this critical moment, for every young lady has at some time or other known the same agitation. All have been, or at least all have believed themselves to be, in danger from the pursuit of someone whom they wished to avoid; and all have been anxious for the attentions of someone whom they wished to please. As soon as they were joined by the Thorpes, Catherine's agony began; she fidgeted about if John Thorpe came towards her, hid herself as much as possible from his view, and when he spoke to her pretended not to hear him. The cotillions were over, the country-dancing beginning, and she saw nothing of the Tilneys.

"Do not be frightened, my dear Catherine," whispered Isabella, "but I am really going to dance with your brother again. I declare positively it is quite shocking. I tell him he ought to be ashamed of himself, but you and John must keep us in countenance. Make haste, my dear creature, and come to us. John is just walked off, but he will be back in a moment."

Catherine had neither time nor inclination to answer. The others walked away, John Thorpe was still in view, and she gave herself up for lost. That she might not appear, however, to observe or expect him, she kept her eyes intently fixed on her fan; and a self-condemnation for her folly, in supposing that among such a crowd they should even meet with the Tilneys in any reasonable time, had just passed through her mind, when she suddenly found herself addressed and again solicited to dance, by Mr. Tilney himself. With what sparkling eyes and ready motion she granted his request, and with how pleasing a flutter of heart she went with him to the set, may be easily imagined. To escape, and, as she believed, so narrowly escape John Thorpe, and to be asked, so immediately on his joining her, asked by Mr. Tilney, as if he had sought her on purpose!—it did not appear to her that life could supply any greater felicity.

Scarcely had they worked themselves into the quiet possession of a place, however, when her attention was claimed by John Thorpe, who stood behind her. "Heyday, Miss Morland!" said he. "What is the meaning of this? I thought you and I were to dance together."

"I wonder you should think so, for you never asked me."

"That is a good one, by Jove! I asked you as soon as I came into the room, and I was just going to ask you again, but when I turned round, you were gone! This is a cursed shabby trick! I only came for the sake of dancing with *you*, and I firmly believe you were engaged to me ever since Monday. Yes; I remember, I asked you while you were waiting in the lobby for your cloak. And here have I been telling all my acquaintance that I was going to dance with the prettiest girl in the room; and when they see you standing up with somebody else, they will quiz me famously."

"Oh, no; they will never think of *me,* after such a description as that."

"By heavens, if they do not, I will kick them out of the room for blockheads. What chap have you there?" Catherine satisfied his curiosity. "Tilney," he repeated. "Hum—I do not know him. A good figure of a man; well put together. Does he want a horse? Here is a friend of mine, Sam Fletcher, has got one to sell that would suit anybody. A famous clever animal for the road—only forty guineas. I had fifty minds to buy it myself, for it is one of my maxims always to buy a good horse when I meet with one; but it would not answer my purpose, it would not do for the field. I would give any money for a real good hunter. I have three now, the best that ever were backed. I would not take eight hundred guineas for them. Fletcher and I mean to get a house in Leicestershire, against the next season. It is so d— uncomfortable, living at an inn."

This was the last sentence by which he could weary Catherine's attention, for he was just then borne off by the resistless pressure of a long string of passing ladies. Her partner now drew near, and said, "That gentleman would have put me out of patience, had he stayed with you half a minute longer. He has no business to withdraw the attention of my partner from me. We have entered into a contract of mutual agreeableness for the space of an evening, and all our agreeableness belongs solely to each other for that time. Nobody can fasten themselves on the notice of one, without injuring the rights of the other. I consider a country-dance as an emblem of marriage. Fidelity and complaisance are the principal duties of both; and those men who do not choose to dance or marry themselves, have no business with the partners or wives of their neighbours."

"But they are such very different things!"

"—That you think they cannot be compared together."

"To be sure not. People that marry can never part, but must go and keep house together. People that dance only stand opposite each other in a long room for half an hour."

"And such is your definition of matrimony and dancing. Taken in that light certainly, their resemblance is not striking; but I think I could place them in such a view. You will allow, that in both, man has the advantage of choice, woman only the power of refusal; that in both, it is an engagement between man and woman, formed for the advantage of each; and that when once entered into, they belong exclusively to each other till the moment of its dissolution; that it is their duty, each to endeavour to give the other no cause for wishing that he or she had bestowed themselves elsewhere, and their best interest to keep their own imaginations from wandering towards the perfections of their neighbours, or fancying that they should have been better off with anyone else. You will allow all this?"

"Yes, to be sure, as you state it, all this sounds very well; but still they are so very different. I cannot look upon them at all in the same light, nor think the same duties belong to them."

"In one respect, there certainly is a difference. In marriage, the man is supposed to provide for the support of the woman, the woman to make the home agreeable to the man; he is to purvey, and she is to smile. But in dancing, their duties are exactly changed; the agreeableness, the compliance are expected from him, while she furnishes the fan and the lavender water. *That,* I suppose, was the difference of duties which struck you, as rendering the conditions incapable of comparison."

"No, indeed, I never thought of that."

"Then I am quite at a loss. One thing, however, I must observe. This disposition on your side is rather alarming. You totally disallow any similarity in the obligations; and may I not thence infer that your notions of the duties of the dancing state are not so strict as your partner might wish? Have I not reason to fear that if the gentleman who spoke to you just now were to return, or if any other gentleman were to address you, there would be nothing to restrain you from conversing with him as long as you chose?"

"Mr. Thorpe is such a very particular friend of my brother's, that if he talks to me, I must talk to him again; but there are hardly three young men in the room besides him that I have any acquaintance with."

"And is that to be my only security? Alas, alas!"

"Nay, I am sure you cannot have a better; for if I do not

know anybody, it is impossible for me to talk to them; and, besides, I do not *want* to talk to anybody."

"Now you have given me a security worth having; and I shall proceed with courage. Do you find Bath as agreeable as when I had the honour of making the inquiry before?"

"Yes, quite—more so, indeed."

"More so! Take care, or you will forget to be tired of it at the proper time. You ought to be tired at the end of six weeks."

"I do not think I should be tired, if I were to stay here six months."

"Bath, compared with London, has little variety, and so everybody finds out every year. 'For six weeks, I allow Bath is pleasant enough; but beyond *that,* it is the most tiresome place in the world.' You would be told so by people of all descriptions, who come regularly every winter, lengthen their six weeks into ten or twelve, and go away at last because they can afford to stay no longer."

"Well, other people must judge for themselves, and those who go to London may think nothing of Bath. But I, who live in a small retired village in the country, can never find greater sameness in such a place as this than in my own home; for here are a variety of amusements, a variety of things to be seen and done all day long, which I can know nothing of there."

"You are not fond of the country."

"Yes, I am. I have always lived there, and always been very happy. But certainly there is much more sameness in a country life than in a Bath life. One day in the country is exactly like another."

"But then you spend your time so much more rationally in the country."

"Do I?"

"Do you not?"

"I do not believe there is much difference."

"Here you are in pursuit only of amusement all day long."

"And so I am at home—only I do not find so much of it. I walk about here, and so I do there; but here I see a variety of people in every street, and there I can only go and call on Mrs. Allen."

Mr. Tilney was very much amused.

"Only go and call on Mrs. Allen!" he repeated. "What a picture of intellectual poverty! However, when you sink into this abyss again, you will have more to say. You will be able to talk of Bath, and of all that you did here."

"Oh! Yes. I shall never be in want of something to talk of again to Mrs. Allen, or anybody else. I really believe I shall always be talking of Bath, when I am at home again—I *do* like it so very much. If I could but have Papa and Mamma, and the rest of them here, I suppose I should be too happy! James's coming (my eldest brother) is quite delightful—and especially as it turns out that the very family we are just got so intimate with are his intimate friends already. Oh! Who can ever be tired of Bath?"

"Not those who bring such fresh feelings of every sort to it as you do. But papas and mammas, and brothers, and intimate friends are a good deal gone by, to most of the frequenters of Bath—and the honest relish of balls and plays, and everyday sights, is past with them."

Here their conversation closed, the demands of the dance becoming now too importunate for a divided attention.

Soon after their reaching the bottom of the set, Catherine perceived herself to be earnestly regarded by a gentleman who stood among the lookers-on, immediately behind her partner. He was a very handsome man, of a commanding aspect, past the bloom, but not past the vigour of life; and with his eye still directed towards her, she saw him presently address Mr. Tilney in a familiar whisper. Confused by his notice, and blushing from the fear of its being excited by something wrong in her appearance, she turned away her head. But while she did so, the gentleman retreated, and her partner, coming nearer, said, "I see that you guess what I have just been asked. That gentleman knows your name, and you have a right to know his. It is General Tilney, my father."

Catherine's answer was only "Oh!"—but it was an "Oh!" expressing everything needful: attention to his words, and perfect reliance on their truth. With real interest and strong admiration did her eye now follow the general, as he moved through the crowd, and "How handsome a family they are!" was her secret remark.

In chatting with Miss Tilney before the evening concluded, a new source of felicity arose to her. She had never taken a country walk since her arrival in Bath. Miss Tilney, to whom all the commonly frequented environs were familiar, spoke of them in terms which made her all eagerness to

know them too; and on her openly fearing that she might
find nobody to go with her, it was proposed by the brother
and sister that they should join in a walk, some morning or
other. "I shall like it," she cried, "beyond anything in the
world; and do not let us put it off—let us go tomorrow."
This was readily agreed to, with only a proviso of Miss
Tilney's, that it did not rain, which Catherine was sure it
would not. At twelve o'clock, they were to call for her in
Pulteney Street; and "Remember—twelve o'clock," was her
parting speech to her new friend. Of her other, her older, her
more established friend, Isabella, of whose fidelity and
worth she had enjoyed a fortnight's experience, she scarcely
saw anything during the evening. Yet, though longing to
make her acquainted with her happiness, she cheerfully submitted to the wish of Mr. Allen, which took them rather
early away, and her spirits danced within her, as she danced
in her chair all the way home.

CHAPTER XI

The morrow brought a very sober-looking morning, the sun making only a few efforts to appear, and Catherine augured from it everything most favourable to her wishes. A bright morning so early in the year, she allowed, would generally turn to rain, but a cloudy one foretold improvement as the day advanced. She applied to Mr. Allen for confirmation of her hopes, but Mr. Allen, not having his own skies and barometer about him, declined giving any absolute promise of sunshine. She applied to Mrs. Allen, and Mrs. Allen's opinion was more positive. "She had no doubt in the world of its being a very fine day, if the clouds would only go off, and the sun keep out."

At about eleven o'clock, however, a few specks of small rain upon the windows caught Catherine's watchful eye, and "Oh! dear, I do believe it will be wet," broke from her in a most desponding tone.

"I thought how it would be," said Mrs. Allen.

"No walk for me today," sighed Catherine; "but perhaps it may come to nothing, or it may hold up before twelve."

"Perhaps it may, but then, my dear, it will be so dirty."

"Oh! That will not signify; I never mind dirt."

"No," replied her friend very placidly, "I know you never mind dirt."

After a short pause, "It comes on faster and faster!" said Catherine, as she stood watching at a window.

"So it does indeed. If it keeps raining, the streets will be very wet."

"There are four umbrellas up already. How I hate the sight of an umbrella!"

"They are disagreeable things to carry. I would much rather take a chair at any time."

"It was such a nice-looking morning! I felt so convinced it would be dry!"

"Anybody would have thought so indeed. There will be very few people in the pump-room, if it rains all the morning. I hope Mr. Allen will put on his greatcoat when he goes, but I dare say he will not, for he had rather do anything in the world than walk out in a greatcoat; I wonder he should dislike it, it must be so comfortable."

The rain continued—fast, though not heavy. Catherine went every five minutes to the clock, threatening on each return that, if it still kept on raining another five minutes, she would give up the matter as hopeless. The clock struck twelve, and it still rained. "You will not be able to go, my dear."

"I do not quite despair yet. I shall not give it up till a quarter after twelve. This is just the time of day for it to clear up, and I do think it looks a little lighter. There, it is twenty minutes after twelve, and now I *shall* give it up entirely. Oh! That we had such weather here as they had at Udolpho, or at least in Tuscany and the south of France!——the night that poor St. Aubin died!—such beautiful weather!"

At half past twelve, when Catherine's anxious attention to the weather was over and she could no longer claim any merit from its amendment, the sky began voluntarily to clear. A gleam of sunshine took her quite by surprise; she looked round; the clouds were parting, and she instantly returned to the window to watch over and encourage the happy appearance. Ten minutes more made it certain that a bright afternoon would succeed, and justified the opinion of Mrs. Allen, who had "always thought it would clear up." But whether Catherine might still expect her friends, whether there had not been too much rain for Miss Tilney to venture, must yet be a question.

It was too dirty for Mrs. Allen to accompany her husband to the pump-room; he accordingly set off by himself, and Catherine had barely watched him down the street when her notice was claimed by the approach of the same two open carriages, containing the same three people that had surprised her so much a few mornings back.

"Isabella, my brother, and Mr. Thorpe, I declare! They are coming for me perhaps—but I shall not go—I cannot go indeed, for you know Miss Tilney may still call." Mrs. Allen agreed to it. John Thorpe was soon with them, and his voice was with them yet sooner, for on the stairs he was calling out to Miss Morland to be quick. "Make haste! Make haste!" as he threw open the door. "Put on your hat this moment—there is no time to be lost—we are going to Bristol. How d'ye do, Mrs. Allen?"

"To Bristol! Is not that a great way off? But, however, I cannot go with you today, because I am engaged; I expect some friends every moment." This was of course vehemently talked down as no reason at all; Mrs. Allen was called on to second him, and the two others walked in, to give their assistance. "My sweetest Catherine, is not this delightful? We shall have a most heavenly drive. You are to thank your brother and me for the scheme; it darted into our heads at breakfast-time, I verily believe at the same instant; and we should have been off two hours ago if it had not been for this detestable rain. But it does not signify, the nights are moonlight, and we shall do delightfully. Oh! I am in such ecstasies at the thoughts of a little country air and quiet! So much better than going to the Lower Rooms. We shall drive directly to Clifton and dine there; and, as soon as dinner is over, if there is time for it, go on to Kingsweston."

"I doubt our being able to do so much," said Morland.

"You croaking fellow!" cried Thorpe. "We shall be able to do ten times more. Kingsweston! Aye, and Blaize Castle too, and anything else we can hear of; but here is your sister says she will not go."

"Blaize Castle!" cried Catherine. "What is that?"

"The finest place in England—worth going fifty miles at any time to see."

"What, is it really a castle, an old castle?"

"The oldest in the kingdom."

"But is it like what one reads of?"

"Exactly—the very same."

"But now really—are there towers and long galleries?"

"By dozens."

"Then I should like to see it; but I cannot—I cannot go."

"Not go! My beloved creature, what do you mean?"

"I cannot go, because"—looking down as she spoke, fearful of Isabella's smile—"I expect Miss Tilney and her brother to call on me to take a country walk. They promised to come at twelve, only it rained; but now, as it is so fine, I dare say they will be here soon."

"Not they indeed," cried Thorpe; "for, as we turned into

Broad Street, I saw them—does he not drive a phaeton with bright chestnuts?"

"I do not know indeed."

"Yes, I know he does; I saw him. You are talking of the man you danced with last night, are not you?"

"Yes."

"Well, I saw him at that moment turn up the Lansdown Road, driving a smart-looking girl."

"Did you indeed?"

"Did upon my soul; knew him again directly, and he seemed to have got some very pretty cattle too."

"It is very odd! But I suppose they thought it would be too dirty for a walk."

"And well they might, for I never saw so much dirt in my life. Walk! You could no more walk than you could fly! It has not been so dirty the whole winter; it is ankle-deep everywhere."

Isabella corroborated it: "My dearest Catherine, you cannot form an idea of the dirt; come, you must go; you cannot refuse going now."

"I should like to see the castle; but may we go all over it? May we go up every staircase, and into every suite of rooms?"

"Yes, yes, every hole and corner."

"But then, if they should only be gone out for an hour till it is dryer, and call by and by?"

"Make yourself easy, there is no danger of that, for I heard Tilney hallooing to a man who was just passing by on horseback, that they were going as far as Wick Rocks."

"Then I will. Shall I go, Mrs. Allen?"

"Just as you please, my dear."

"Mrs. Allen, you must persuade her to go," was the general cry. Mrs. Allen was not inattentive to it: "Well, my dear," said she, "suppose you go." And in two minutes they were off.

Catherine's feelings, as she got into the carriage, were in a very unsettled state; divided between regret for the loss of one great pleasure, and the hope of soon enjoying another, almost its equal in degree, however unlike in kind. She could not think the Tilneys had acted quite well by her, in so readily giving up their engagement, without sending her any message of excuse. It was now but an hour later than the time fixed on for the beginning of their walk; and, in spite of what she had heard of the prodigious accumulation of dirt in the course of that hour, she could not from her own observation help thinking that they might have gone with very little inconvenience. To feel herself slighted by them was very painful. On the other hand, the delight of exploring an edifice like Udolpho, as her fancy represented Blaize Castle to be, was such a counterpoise of good as might console her for almost anything.

They passed briskly down Pulteney Street, and through Laura Place, without the exchange of many words. Thorpe talked to his horse, and she meditated, by turns, on broken promises and broken arches, phaetons and false hangings, Tilneys and trap-doors. As they entered Argyle Buildings, however, she was roused by this address from her companion, "Who is that girl who looked at you so hard as she went by?"

"Who? Where?"

"On the right-hand pavement—she must be almost out of sight now." Catherine looked round and saw Miss Tilney leaning on her brother's arm, walking slowly down the street. She saw them both looking back at her. "Stop, stop, Mr. Thorpe," she impatiently cried; "it is Miss Tilney; it is indeed. How could you tell me they were gone? Stop, stop, I will get out this moment and go to them." But to what purpose did she speak? Thorpe only lashed his horse into a brisker trot; the Tilneys, who had soon ceased to look after her, were in a moment out of sight round the corner of Laura Place, and in another moment she was herself whisked into the marketplace. Still, however, and during the length of another street, she entreated him to stop. "Pray, pray stop, Mr. Thorpe. I cannot go on. I will not go on. I must go back to Miss Tilney." But Mr. Thorpe only laughed, smacked his whip, encouraged his horse, made odd noises, and drove on; and Catherine, angry and vexed as she was, having no power of getting away, was obliged to give up the point and submit. Her reproaches, however, were not spared. "How could you deceive me so, Mr. Thorpe? How could you say that you saw them driving up the Lansdown Road? I would not have had it happen so for the world. They must think it so strange, so rude of me! To go by them, too, without saying a word! You do not know how vexed I am; I shall have no pleasure at Clifton, nor in anything else. I had rather, ten thousand times rather, get out now, and walk back to them.

How could you say you saw them driving out in a phaeton?"
Thorpe defended himself very stoutly, declared he had never
seen two men so much alike in his life, and would hardly
give up the point of its having been Tilney himself.

Their drive, even when this subject was over, was not
likely to be very agreeable. Catherine's complaisance was no
longer what it had been in their former airing. She listened
reluctantly, and her replies were short. Blaize Castle remained her only comfort; towards *that,* she still looked at intervals with pleasure; though rather than be disappointed of
the promised walk, and especially rather than be thought ill
of by the Tilneys, she would willingly have given up all the
happiness which its walls could supply—the happiness of a
progress through a long suite of lofty rooms, exhibiting the
remains of magnificent furniture, though now for many
years deserted—the happiness of being stopped in their way
along narrow, winding vaults, by a low, grated door; or even
of having their lamp, their only lamp, extinguished by a sudden gust of wind, and of being left in total darkness. In the
meanwhile, they proceeded on their journey without any
mischance, and were within view of the town of Keynsham,
when a halloo from Morland, who was behind them, made
his friend pull up, to know what was the matter. The others
then came close enough for conversation, and Morland said,
"We had better go back, Thorpe; it is too late to go on today;
your sister thinks so as well as I. We have been exactly an
hour coming from Pulteney Street, very little more than
seven miles; and, I suppose, we have at least eight more to
go. It will never do. We set out a great deal too late. We had
much better put it off till another day, and turn around."

"It is all one to me," replied Thorpe rather angrily; and instantly turning his horse, they were on their way back to
Bath.

"If your brother had not got such a d— beast to drive,"
said he soon afterwards, "we might have done it very well.
My horse would have trotted to Clifton within the hour, if
left to himself, and I have almost broke my arm with pulling
him in to that cursed broken-winded jade's pace. Morland is
a fool for not keeping a horse and gig of his own."

"No, he is not," said Catherine warmly, "for I am sure he
could not afford it."

"And why cannot he afford it?"

"Because he has not money enough."

"And whose fault is that?"

"Nobody's, that I know of." Thorpe then said something in the loud, incoherent way to which he had often recourse, about its being a d— thing to be miserly; and that if people who rolled in money could not afford things, he did not know who could, which Catherine did not even endeavour to understand. Disappointed of what was to have been the consolation for her first disappointment, she was less and less disposed either to be agreeable herself or to find her companion so; and they returned to Pulteney Street without her speaking twenty words.

As she entered the house, the footman told her that a gentleman and lady had called and inquired for her a few minutes after her setting off; that, when he told them she was gone out with Mr. Thorpe, the lady had asked whether any message had been left for her; and on his saying no, had felt for a card, but said she had none about her, and went away. Pondering over these heart-rending tidings, Catherine walked slowly upstairs. At the head of them she was met by Mr. Allen, who, on hearing the reason of their speedy return, said, "I am glad your brother had so much sense; I am glad you are come back. It was strange, wild scheme."

They all spent the evening together at Thorpe's. Catherine was disturbed and out of spirits; but Isabella seemed to find a pool of commerce, in the fate of which she shared, by private partnership with Morland, a very good equivalent for the quiet and country air of an inn at Clifton. Her satisfaction, too, in not being at the Lower Rooms was spoken more than once. "How I pity the poor creatures that are going there! How glad I am that I am not amongst them! I wonder whether it will be a full ball or not! They have not begun dancing yet. I would not be there for all the world. It is so delightful to have an evening now and then to oneself. I dare say it will not be a very good ball. I know the Mitchells will not be there. I am sure I pity everybody that is. But I dare say, Mr. Morland, you long to be at it, do not you? I am sure you do. Well, pray do not let anybody here be a restraint on you. I dare say we could do very well without you; but you men think yourselves of such consequence."

Catherine could almost have accused Isabella of being wanting in tenderness towards herself and her sorrows, so very little did they appear to dwell on her mind, and so very inadequate was the comfort she offered. "Do not be so dull, my dearest creature," she whispered. "You will quite break my heart. It was amazingly shocking, to be sure; but the Tilneys were entirely to blame. Why were not they more punctual? It was dirty, indeed, but what did that signify? I am sure John and I should not have minded it. I never mind going through anything, where a friend is concerned; that is my disposition, and John is just the same; he has amazing strong feelings. Good heavens! What a delightful hand you have got! Kings, I vow! I never was so happy in my life! I would fifty times rather you should have them than myself."

And now I may dismiss my heroine to the sleepless couch, which is the true heroine's portion; to a pillow strewed with thorns and wet with tears. And lucky may she think herself, if she get another good night's rest in the course of the next three months.

CHAPTER XII

"Mrs. Allen," said Catherine the next morning, "will there be any harm in my calling on Miss Tilney today? I shall not be easy till I have explained everything."

"Go, by all means, my dear; only put on a white gown; Miss Tilney always wears white."

Catherine cheerfully complied, and being properly equipped, was more impatient than ever to be at the pump-room, that she might inform herself of General Tilney's lodgings, for though she believed they were in Milsom Street, she was not certain of the house, and Mrs. Allen's wavering convictions only made it more doubtful. To Milsom Street she was directed, and having made herself perfect in the number, hastened away with eager steps and a beating heart to pay her visit, explain her conduct, and be forgiven; tripping lightly through the church-yard, and resolutely turning away her eyes, that she might not be obliged to see her beloved Isabella and her dear family, who, she had reason to believe, were in a shop hard by. She reached the house without any impediment, looked at the number, knocked at the door, and inquired for Miss Tilney. The man believed Miss Tilney to be at home, but was not quite certain. Would she be pleased to send up her name? She gave her card. In a few minutes the servant returned, and with a look which did not quite confirm his words, said he had been mistaken, for that Miss Tilney was walked out. Catherine, with a blush of mortification, left the house. She felt almost persuaded that Miss Tilney *was* at home, and too much offended to admit her; and as she retired down the street, could not withhold one glance at the drawing-room windows, in expectation of seeing her there, but no one appeared at them. At the bottom of the street, however, she looked back again, and then, not at a window, but issuing from the door, she saw Miss Tilney herself. She was fol-

lowed by a gentleman, whom Catherine believed to be her
father, and they turned up towards Edgar's Buildings. Catherine, in deep mortification, proceeded on her way. She
could almost be angry herself at such angry incivility; but
she checked the resentful sensation; she remembered her
own ignorance. She knew not how such an offence as hers
might be classed by the laws of worldly politeness, to what
a degree of unforgivingness it might with propriety lead, nor
to what rigours of rudeness in return it might justly make her
amenable.

Dejected and humbled, she had even some thoughts of not
going with the others to the theatre that night; but it must be
confessed that they were not of long continuance, for she
soon recollected, in the first place, that she was without any
excuse for staying at home; and, in the second, that it was
a play she wanted very much to see. To the theatre accordingly they all went; no Tilneys appeared to plague or please
her; she feared that, amongst the many perfections of the
family, a fondness for plays was not to be ranked; but perhaps it was because they were habituated to the finer performances of the London stage, which she knew, on
Isabella's authority, rendered everything else of the kind
"quite horrid." She was not deceived in her own expectation
of pleasure; the comedy so well suspended her care that no
one, observing her during the first four acts, would have
supposed she had any wretchedness about her. On the beginning of the fifth, however, the sudden view of Mr. Henry
Tilney and his father, joining a party in the opposite box, recalled her to anxiety and distress. The stage could no longer
excite genuine merriment—no longer keep her whole attention. Every other look upon an average was directed towards
the opposite box; and, for the space of two entire scenes, did
she thus watch Henry Tilney, without being once able to
catch his eye. No longer could he be suspected of indifference for a play; his notice was never withdrawn from the
stage during two whole scenes. At length, however, he did
look towards her, and he bowed—but such a bow! No smile,
no continued observance attended it; his eyes were immediately returned to their former direction. Catherine was
restlessly miserable; she could almost have run round to
the box in which he sat and forced him to hear her explanation. Feelings rather natural than heroic possessed her;
instead of considering her own dignity injured by this ready

condemnation—instead of proudly resolving, in conscious innocence, to show her resentment towards him who could harbour a doubt of it, to leave to him all the trouble of seeking an explanation, and to enlighten him on the past only by avoiding his sight, or flirting with somebody else—she took to herself all the shame of misconduct, or at least of its appearance, and was only eager for an opportunity of explaining its cause.

The play concluded—the curtain fell—Henry Tilney was no longer to be seen where he had hitherto sat, but his father remained, and perhaps he might be now coming round to their box. She was right; in a few minutes he appeared, and, making his way through the then thinning rows, spoke with like calm politeness to Mrs. Allen and her friend. Not with such calmness was he answered by the latter: "Oh! Mr. Tilney, I have been quite wild to speak to you, and make my apologies. You must have thought me so rude; but indeed it was not my own fault, was it, Mrs. Allen? Did not they tell me that Mr. Tilney and his sister were gone out in a phaeton together? And then what could I do? But I had ten thousand times rather have been with you; now had not I, Mrs. Allen?"

"My dear, you tumble my gown," was Mrs. Allen's reply.

Her assurance, however, standing sole as it did, was not thrown away; it brought a more cordial, more natural smile into his countenance, and he replied in a tone which retained only a little affected reserve: "We were much obliged to you at any rate for wishing us a pleasant walk after our passing you in Argyle Street: you were so kind as to look back on purpose."

"But indeed I did not wish you a pleasant walk; I never thought of such a thing; but I begged Mr. Thorpe so earnestly to stop; I called out to him as soon as ever I saw you; now, Mrs. Allen, did not— Oh! You were not there; but indeed I did; and, if Mr. Thorpe would only have stopped, I would have jumped out and run after you."

Is there a Henry in the world who could be insensible to such a declaration? Henry Tilney at least was not. With a yet sweeter smile, he said everything that need be said of his sister's concern, regret, and dependence on Catherine's honour. "Oh! Do not say Miss Tilney was not angry," cried Catherine, "because I know she was; for she would not see me this morning when I called; I saw her walk out of the house the next minute after my leaving it; I was hurt, but I was not affronted. Perhaps you did not know I had been there."

"I was not within at the time; but I heard of it from Eleanor, and she has been wishing ever since to see you, to explain the reason of such incivility; but perhaps I can do it as well. It was nothing more than that my father—they were just preparing to walk out, and he being hurried for time, and not caring to have it put off—made a point of her being denied. That was all, I do assure you. She was very much vexed, and meant to make her apology as soon as possible."

Catherine's mind was greatly eased by this information, yet a something of solicitude remained, from which sprang the following question, thoroughly artless in itself, though rather distressing to the gentleman: "But, Mr. Tilney, why were *you* less generous than your sister? If she felt such confidence in my good intentions, and could suppose it to be only a mistake, why should *you* be so ready to take offence?"

"Me! I take offence!"

"Nay, I am sure by your look, when you came into the box, you were angry."

"I angry! I could have no right."

"Well, nobody would have thought you had no right who saw your face." He replied by asking her to make room for him, and talking of the play.

He remained with them some time, and was only too agreeable for Catherine to be contented when he went away. Before they parted, however, it was agreed that the projected walk should be taken as soon as possible; and, setting aside the misery of his quitting their box, she was, upon the whole, left one of the happiest creatures in the world.

While talking to each other, she had observed with some surprise that John Thorpe, who was never in the same part of the house for ten minutes together, was engaged in conversation with General Tilney; and she felt something more than surprise when she thought she could perceive herself the object of their attention and discourse. What could they have to say of her? She feared General Tilney did not like her appearance: she found it was implied in his preventing her admittance to his daughter, rather than postpone his own walk a few minutes. "How came Mr. Thorpe to know your father?" was her anxious inquiry, as she pointed them out to her companion. He knew nothing about it; but his father, like every military man, had a very large acquaintance.

When the entertainment was over, Thorpe came to assist them in getting out. Catherine was the immediate object of his gallantry; and, while they waited in the lobby for a chair, he prevented the inquiry which had travelled from her heart almost to the tip of her tongue, by asking, in a consequential manner, whether she had seen him talking with General Tilney: "He is a fine old fellow, upon my soul! Stout, active—looks as young as his son. I have a great regard for him, I assure you: a gentleman-like, good sort of fellow as ever lived."

"But how came you to know him?"

"Know him! There are few people much about town that I do not know. I have met him forever at the Bedford; and I knew his face again today the moment he came into the billiard-room. One of the best players we have, by the by; and we had a little touch together, though I was almost afraid of him at first: the odds were five to four against me; and, if I had not made one of the cleanest strokes that perhaps ever was made in this world—I took his ball exactly— but I could not make you understand it without a table; however, I *did* beat him. A very fine fellow; as rich as a Jew. I should like to dine with him; I dare say he gives famous dinners. But what do you think we have been talking of? You. Yes, by heavens! And the general thinks you the finest girl in Bath."

"Oh! Nonsense! How can you say so?"

"And what do you think I said?"—lowering his voice— "well done, general, said I; I am quite of your mind."

Here Catherine, who was much less gratified by his admiration than by General Tilney's, was not sorry to be called away by Mr. Allen. Thorpe, however, would see her to her chair, and, till she entered it, continued the same kind of delicate flattery, in spite of her entreating him to have done.

That General Tilney, instead of disliking, should admire her, was very delightful; and she joyfully thought that there was not one of the family whom she need now fear to meet. The evening had done more, much more, for her than could have been expected.

CHAPTER XIII

MONDAY, Tuesday, Wednesday, Thursday, Friday, and Saturday have now passed in review before the reader; the events of each day, its hopes and fears, mortifications and pleasures, have been separately stated, and the pangs of Sunday only now remain to be described, and close the week. The Clifton scheme had been deferred, not relinquished, and on the afternoon's crescent of this day, it was brought forward again. In a private consultation between Isabella and James, the former of whom had particularly set her heart upon going, and the latter no less anxiously placed his upon pleasing her, it was agreed that, provided the weather were fair, the party should take place on the following morning; and they were to set off very early, in order to be at home in good time. The affair thus determined, and Thorpe's approbation secured, Catherine only remained to be apprised of it. She had left them for a few minutes to speak to Miss Tilney. In that interval the plan was completed, and as soon as she came again, her agreement was demanded; but instead of the gay acquiescence expected by Isabella, Catherine looked grave, was very sorry, but could not go. The engagement which ought to have kept her from joining in the former attempt would make it impossible for her to accompany them now. She had that moment settled with Miss Tilney to take their promised walk tomorrow; it was quite determined, and she would not, upon any account, retract. But that she *must* and *should* retract was instantly the eager cry of both the Thorpes; they must go to Clifton tomorrow, they would not go without her, it would be nothing to put off a mere walk for one day longer, and they would not hear of a refusal. Catherine was distressed, but not subdued. "Do not urge me, Isabella. I am engaged to Miss Tilney. I cannot go." This availed nothing. The same arguments assailed her again; she must go, she should go, and they would not hear of a refusal.

"It would be so easy to tell Miss Tilney that you had just been reminded of a prior engagement, and must only beg to put off the walk till Tuesday."

"No, it would not be easy. I could not do it. There has been no prior engagement." But Isabella became only more and more urgent, calling on her in the most affectionate manner, addressing her by the most endearing names. She was sure her dearest, sweetest Catherine would not seriously refuse such a trifling request to a friend who loved her so dearly. She knew her beloved Catherine to have so feeling a heart, so sweet a temper, to be so easily persuaded by those she loved. But all in vain; Catherine felt herself to be in the right, and though pained by such tender, such flattering supplication, could not allow it to influence her. Isabella then tried another method. She reproached her with having more affection for Miss Tilney, though she had known her so little a while, than for her best and oldest friends, with being grown cold and indifferent, in short, towards herself. "I cannot help being jealous, Catherine, when I see myself slighted for strangers, I, who love you so excessively! When once my affections are placed, it is not in the power of anything to change them. But I believe my feelings are stronger than anybody's; I am sure they are too strong for my own peace; and to see myself supplanted in your friendship by strangers does cut me to the quick, I own. These Tilneys seem to swallow up everything else."

Catherine thought this reproach equally strange and unkind. Was it the part of a friend thus to expose her feelings to the notice of others? Isabella appeared to her ungenerous and selfish, regardless of everything but her own gratification. These painful ideas crossed her mind, though she said nothing. Isabella, in the meanwhile, had applied her handkerchief to her eyes; and Morland, miserable at such a sight, could not help saying, "Nay, Catherine. I think you cannot standout any longer now. The sacrifice is not much; and to oblige such a friend—I shall think you quite unkind, if you still refuse."

This was the first time of her brother's openly siding against her, and anxious to avoid his displeasure, she proposed a compromise. If they would only put off their scheme till Tuesday, which they might easily do, as it depended only on themselves, she could go with them, and everybody might then be satisfied. But "No, no, no!" was the immediate answer; "that could not be, for Thorpe did not know that he might not go to town on Tuesday." Catherine was sorry, but could do no more; and a short silence ensued, which was broken by Isabella, who in a voice of cold resentment said, "Very well, then there is an end of the party. If Catherine does not go, I cannot. I cannot be the only woman. I would not, upon any account in the world, do so improper a thing."

"Catherine, you must go," said James.

"But why cannot Mr. Thorpe drive one of his other sisters? I dare say either of them would like to go."

"Thank ye," cried Thorpe, "but I did not come to Bath to drive my sisters about, and look like a fool. No, if you do not go, d— me if I do. I only go for the sake of driving you."

"That is a compliment which gives me no pleasure." But her words were lost on Thorpe, who had turned abruptly away.

The three others still continued together, walking in a most uncomfortable manner to poor Catherine; sometimes not a word was said, sometimes she was again attacked with supplications or reproaches, and her arm was still linked within Isabella's, though their hearts were at war. At one moment she was softened, at another irritated; always distressed, but always steady.

"I did not think you had been so obstinate, Catherine," said James; "you were not used to be so hard to persuade; you once were the kindest, best-tempered of my sisters."

"I hope I am not less so now," she replied, very feelingly; "but indeed I cannot go. If I am wrong, I am doing what I believe to be right."

"I suspect," said Isabella, in a low voice, "there is no great struggle."

Catherine's heart swelled; she drew away her arm, and Isabella made no opposition. Thus passed a long ten minutes, till they were again joined by Thorpe, who, coming to them with a gayer look, said, "Well, I have settled the matter, and now we may all go tomorrow with a safe conscience. I have been to Miss Tilney, and made your excuses."

"You have not!" cried Catherine.

"I have, upon my soul. Left her this moment. Told her you had sent me to say that, having just recollected a prior engagement of going to Clifton with us tomorrow, you could not have the pleasure of walking with her till Tuesday. She said very well, Tuesday was just as convenient to her; so there is an end of all our difficulties. A pretty good thought of mine—hey?"

Isabella's countenance was once more all smiles and good humour, and James too looked happy again.

"A most heavenly thought indeed! Now, my sweet Catherine, all our distresses are over; you are honourably acquitted, and we shall have a most delightful party."

"This will not do," said Catherine; "I cannot submit to this. I must run after Miss Tilney directly and set her right."

Isabella, however, caught hold of one hand, Thorpe of the other, and remonstrances poured in from all three. Even James was quite angry. When everything was settled, when Miss Tilney herself said that Tuesday would suit her as well, it was quite ridiculous, quite absurd, to make any further objection.

"I do not care. Mr. Thorpe had no business to invent any such message. If I had thought it right to put it off, I could have spoken to Miss Tilney myself. This is only doing it in a ruder way; and how do I know that Mr. Thorpe has— He may be mistaken again perhaps; he led me into one act of rudeness by his mistake on Friday. Let me go, Mr. Thorpe; Isabella, do not hold me."

Thorpe told her it would be in vain to go after the Tilneys; they were turning the corner into Brock Street, when he had overtaken them, and were at home by this time.

"Then I will go after them," said Catherine; "wherever they are I will go after them. It does not signify talking. If I could not be persuaded into doing what I thought wrong, I never will be tricked into it." And with these words she broke away and hurried off. Thorpe would have darted after her, but Morland withheld him. "Let her go, let her go, if she will go. She is as obstinate as—"

Morland never finished the simile, for it could hardly have been a proper one.

Away walked Catherine in great agitation, as fast as the crowd would permit her, fearful of being pursued, yet determined to persevere. As she walked, she reflected on what had passed. It was painful to her to disappoint and displease them, particularly to displease her brother; but she could not repent her resistance. Setting her own inclination apart, to have failed a second time in her engagement to Miss Tilney, to have retracted a promise voluntarily made only five minutes before, and on a false pretence too, must have been wrong. She had not been withstanding them on selfish principles alone, she had not consulted merely her own gratification; *that* might have been ensured in some degree by the excursion itself, by seeing Blaize Castle; no, she had attended to what was due to others, and to her own character in their opinion. Her conviction of being right, however, was not enough to restore her composure; till she had spoken to Miss Tilney she could not be at ease; and quickening her pace when she got clear of the Crescent, she almost ran over the remaining ground till she gained the top of Milsom Street. So rapid had been her movements that in spite of the Tilneys' advantage in the outset, they were but just turning into their lodgings as she came within view of them; and the servant still remaining at the open door, she used only the ceremony of saying that she must speak with Miss Tilney that moment, and hurrying by him proceeded upstairs. Then, opening the first door before her, which happened to be the right, she immediately found herself in the drawing-room with General Tilney, his son, and daughter. Her explanation, defective only in being—from her irritation of nerves and shortness of breath—no explanation at all, was instantly given. "I am come in a great hurry—It was all a mistake—I never promised to go—I told them from the first I could not go.—I ran away in a great hurry to explain it.—I did not care what you thought of me.—I would not stay for the servant."

The business, however, though not perfectly elucidated by this speech, soon ceased to be a puzzle. Catherine found that John Thorpe *had* given the message; and Miss Tilney had no scruple in owning herself greatly surprised by it. But whether her brother had still exceeded her in resentment, Catherine, though she instinctively addressed herself as much to one as to the other in her vindication, had no means of knowing. Whatever might have been felt before her arrival, her eager declarations immediately made every look and sentence as friendly as she could desire.

The affair thus happily settled, she was introduced by Miss Tilney to her father, and received by him with such ready, such solicitous politeness as recalled Thorpe's information to her mind, and made her think with pleasure that he might be sometimes depended on. To such anxious attention was the general's civility carried, that not aware of her extraordinary swiftness in entering the house, he was quite angry with the servant whose neglect had reduced her to open the door of the apartment herself. "What did William mean by it? He should make a point of inquiring into the matter." And if Catherine had not most warmly asserted his innocence, it seemed likely that William would lose the favour of his master forever, if not his place, by her rapidity.

After sitting with them a quarter of an hour, she rose to take leave, and was then most agreeably surprised by General Tilney's asking her if she would do his daughter the honour of dining and spending the rest of the day with her. Miss Tilney added her own wishes. Catherine was greatly obliged; but it was quite out of her power. Mr. and Mrs. Allen would expect her back every moment. The general declared he could say no more; the claims of Mr. and Mrs. Allen were not to be superseded; but on some other day he trusted, when longer notice could be given, they would not refuse to spare her to her friend. "Oh, no; Catherine was sure they would not have the least objection, and she should have great pleasure in coming." The general attended her himself to the street-door, saying everything gallant as they went downstairs, admiring the elasticity of her walk, which corresponded exactly with the spirit of her dancing, and making her one of the most gracious bows she had ever beheld, when they parted.

Catherine, delighted by all that had passed, proceeded gaily to Pulteney Street, walking, as she concluded, with great elasticity, though she had never thought of it before. She reached home without seeing anything more of the offended party; and now that she had been triumphant throughout, had carried her point, and was secure of her walk, she began (as the flutter of her spirits subsided) to doubt whether she had been perfectly right. A sacrifice was always noble; and if she had given way to their entreaties, she should have been spared the distressing idea of a friend displeased, a brother angry, and a scheme of great happiness to both destroyed, perhaps through her means. To ease her mind, and ascertain by the opinion of an unprejudiced person what her own conduct had really been, she took occasion to mention before Mr. Allen the half-settled scheme of her brother and the Thorpes for the following day. Mr. Allen caught at it directly. "Well," said he, "and do you think of going too?"

"No; I had just engaged myself to walk with Miss Tilney before they told me of it; and therefore you know I could not go with them, could I?"

"No, certainly not; and I am glad you do not think of it. These schemes are not at all the thing. Young men and women driving about the country in open carriages! Now and then it is very well; but going to inns and public places together! It is not right; and I wonder Mrs. Thorpe should allow it. I am glad you do not think of going; I am sure Mrs. Morland would not be pleased. Mrs. Allen, are not you of my way of thinking? Do not you think these kind of projects objectionable?"

"Yes, very much so indeed. Open carriages are nasty things. A clean gown is not five minutes' wear in them. You are splashed getting in and getting out; and the wind takes your hair and your bonnet in every direction. I hate an open carriage myself."

"I know you do; but that is not the question. Do not you think it has an odd appearance, if young ladies are frequently driven about in them by young men, to whom they are not even related?"

"Yes, my dear, a very odd appearance indeed. I cannot bear to see it."

"Dear madam," cried Catherine, "then why did not you tell me so before? I am sure if I had known it to be improper, I would not have gone with Mr. Thorpe at all; but I always hoped you would tell me, if you thought I was doing wrong."

"And so I should, my dear, you may depend on it; for as I told Mrs. Morland at parting, I would always do the best for you in my power. But one must not be over particular. Young people *will* be young people, as your good mother says herself. You know I wanted you, when we first came, not to buy that sprigged muslin, but you would. Young people do not like to be always thwarted."

"But this was something of real consequence; and I do not think you would have found me hard to persuade."

"As far as it has gone hitherto, there is no harm done," said Mr. Allen; "and I would only advise you, my dear, not to go out with Mr. Thorpe any more."

"That is just what I was going to say," added his wife.

Catherine, relieved for herself, felt uneasy for Isabella, and after a moment's thought, asked Mr. Allen whether it

would not be both proper and kind in her to write to Miss
Thorpe, and explain the indecorum of which she must be as
insensible as herself; for she considered that Isabella might
otherwise perhaps be going to Clifton the next day, in spite
of what had passed. Mr. Allen, however, discouraged her
from doing any such thing. "You had better leave her alone,
my dear; she is old enough to know what she is about, and
if not, has a mother to advise her. Mrs. Thorpe is too indulgent beyond a doubt; but, however, you had better not interfere. She and your brother choose to go, and you will be
only getting ill will."

Catherine submitted, and though sorry to think that Isabella should be doing wrong, felt greatly relieved by Mr. Allen's approbation of her own conduct, and truly rejoiced to
be preserved by his advice from the danger of falling into
such an error herself. Her escape from being one of the party
to Clifton was now an escape indeed; for what would the
Tilneys have thought of her, if she had broken her promise
to them in order to do what was wrong in itself, if she had
been guilty of one breach of propriety, only to enable her to
be guilty of another?

CHAPTER XIV

THE next morning was fair, and Catherine almost expected another attack from the assembled party. With Mr. Allen to support her, she felt no dread of the event: but she would gladly be spared a contest, where victory itself was painful, and was heartily rejoiced therefore at neither seeing nor hearing anything of them. The Tilneys called for her at the appointed time; and no new difficulty arising, no sudden recollection, no unexpected summons, no impertinent intrusion to disconcert their measures, my heroine was most unnaturally able to fulfil her engagement, though it was made with the hero himself. They determined on walking around Beechen Cliff, that noble hill whose beautiful verdure and hanging coppice render it so striking an object from almost every opening in Bath.

"I never look at it," said Catherine, as they walked along the side of the river, "without thinking of the south of France."

"You have been abroad then?" said Henry, a little surprised.

"Oh! No, I only mean what I have read about. It always puts me in mind of the country that Emily and her father travelled through, in *The Mysteries of Udolpho*. But you never read novels, I dare say?"

"Why not?"

"Because they are not clever enough for you—gentlemen read better books."

"The person, be it gentleman or lady, who has not pleasure in a good novel, must be intolerably stupid. I have read all Mrs. Radcliffe's works, and most of them with great pleasure. *The Mysteries of Udolpho*, when I had once begun it, I could not lay down again; I remember finishing it in two days—my hair standing on end the whole time."

"Yes," added Miss Tilney, "and I remember that you undertook to read it aloud to me, and that when I was called away for only five minutes to answer a note, instead of waiting for me, you took the volume into the Hermitage Walk, and I was obliged to stay till you had finished it."

"Thank you, Eleanor—a most honourable testimony. You see, Miss Morland, the injustice of your suspicions. Here was I, in my eagerness to get on, refusing to wait only five minutes for my sister, breaking the promise I had made of reading it aloud, and keeping her in suspense at a most interesting part, by running away with the volume, which, you are to observe, was her own, particularly her own. I am proud when I reflect on it, and I think it must establish me in your good opinion."

"I am very glad to hear it indeed, and now I shall never be ashamed of liking *Udolpho* myself. But I really thought before, young men despised novels amazingly."

"It is *amazingly;* it may well suggest *amazement* if they do—for they read nearly as many as women. I myself have read hundreds and hundreds. Do not imagine that you can cope with me in a knowledge of Julias and Louisas. If we proceed to particulars, and engage in the never-ceasing inquiry of 'Have you read this?' and 'Have you read that?' I shall soon leave you as far behind me as—what shall I say?—I want an appropriate simile.—as far as your friend Emily herself left poor Valancourt when she went with her aunt into Italy. Consider how many years I have had the start of you. I had entered on my studies at Oxford, while you were a good little girl working your sampler at home!"

"Not very good, I am afraid. But now really, do not you think *Udolpho* the nicest book in the world?"

"The nicest—by which I suppose you mean the neatest. That must depend upon the binding."

"Henry," said Miss Tilney, "you are very impertinent. Miss Morland, he is treating you exactly as he does his sister. He is forever finding fault with me, for some incorrectness of language, and now he is taking the same liberty with you. The word 'nicest,' as you used it, did not suit him; and you had better change it as soon as you can, or we shall be overpowered with Johnson and Blair all the rest of the way."

"I am sure," cried Catherine, "I did not mean to say anything wrong; but it *is* a nice book, and why should not I call it so?"

"Very true," said Henry, "and this is a very nice day, and

we are taking a very nice walk, and you are two very nice young ladies. Oh! It is a very nice word indeed! It does for everything. Originally perhaps it was applied only to express neatness, propriety, delicacy, or refinement—people were nice in their dress, in their sentiments, or their choice. But now every commendation on every subject is comprised in that one word."

"While, in fact," cried his sister, "it ought only to be applied to you, without any commendation at all. You are more nice than wise. Come, Miss Morland, let us leave him to meditate over our faults in the utmost propriety of diction, while we praise *Udolpho* in whatever terms we like best. It is a most interesting work. You are fond of that kind of reading?"

"To say the truth, I do not much like any other."

"Indeed!"

"That is, I can read poetry and plays, and things of that sort, and do not dislike travels. But history, real solemn history, I cannot be interested in. Can you?"

"Yes, I am fond of history."

"I wish I were too. I read it a little as a duty, but it tells me nothing that does not either vex or weary me. The quarrels of popes and kings, with wars and pestilences, in every page; the men all so good for nothing, and hardly any women at all—it is very tiresome; and yet I often think it odd that it should be so dull, for a great deal of it must be invention. The speeches that are put into the heroes' mouths, their thoughts and designs—the chief of all this must be invention, and invention is what delights me in other books."

"Historians, you think," said Miss Tilney, "are not happy in their flights of fancy. They display imagination without raising interest. I am fond of history—and am very well contented to take the false with the true. In the principal facts they have sources of intelligence in former histories and records, which may be as much depended on, I conclude, as anything that does not actually pass under one's own observation; and as for the little embellishments you speak of, they are embellishments, and I like them as such. If a speech be well drawn up, I read it with pleasure, by whomsoever it may be made—and probably with much greater, if the production of Mr. Hume or Mr. Robertson, than if the genuine words of Caractacus, Agricola, or Alfred the Great."

"You are fond of history! And so are Mr. Allen and my

father; and I have two brothers who do not dislike it. So many instances within my small circle of friends is remarkable! At this rate, I shall not pity the writers of history any longer. If people like to read their books, it is all very well, but to be at so much trouble in filling great volumes, which, as I used to think, nobody would willingly ever look into, to be labouring only for the torment of little boys and girls, always struck me as a hard fate; and though I know it is all very right and necessary, I have often wondered at the person's courage that could sit down on purpose to do it."

"That little boys and girls should be tormented," said Henry, "is what no one at all acquainted with human nature in a civilized state can deny; but in behalf of our most distinguished historians, I must observe that they might well be offended at being supposed to have no higher aim, and that by their method and style, they are perfectly well qualified to torment readers of the most advanced reason and mature time of life. I use the verb 'to torment,' as I observed to be your own method, instead of 'to instruct,' supposing them to be now admitted as synonymous."

"You think me foolish to call instruction a torment, but if you had been as much used as myself to hear poor little children first learning their letters and then learning to spell, if you had ever seen how stupid they can be for a whole morning together, and how tired my poor mother is at the end of it, as I am in the habit of seeing almost every day of my life at home, you would allow that 'to torment' and 'to instruct' might sometimes be used as synonymous words."

"Very probably. But historians are not accountable for the difficulty of learning to read; and even you yourself, who do not altogether seem particularly friendly to very severe, very intense application, may perhaps be brought to acknowledge that it is very well worth-while to be tormented for two or three years of one's life, for the sake of being able to read all the rest of it. Consider—if reading had not been taught, Mrs. Radcliffe would have written in vain—or perhaps might not have written at all."

Catherine assented—and a very warm panegyric from her on that lady's merits closed the subject. The Tilneys were soon engaged in another on which she had nothing to say. They were viewing the country with the eyes of persons accustomed to drawing, and decided on its capability of being formed into pictures, with all the eagerness of real taste.

Here Catherine was quite lost. She knew nothing of drawing—nothing of taste: and she listened to them with an attention which brought her little profit, for they talked in phrases which conveyed scarcely any idea to her. The little which she could understand, however, appeared to contradict the very few notions she had entertained on the matter before. It seemed as if a good view were no longer to be taken from the top of an high hill, and that a clear blue sky was no longer a proof of a fine day. She was heartily ashamed of her ignorance. A misplaced shame. Where people wish to attach, they should always be ignorant. To come with a well-informed mind is to come with an inability of administering to the vanity of others, which a sensible person would always wish to avoid. A woman especially, if she have the misfortune of knowing anything, should conceal it as well as she can.

The advantages of natural folly in a beautiful girl have been already set forth by the capital pen of a sister author; and to her treatment of the subject I will only add, in justice to men, that though to the larger and more trifling part of the sex, imbecility in females is a great enhancement of their personal charms, there is a portion of them too reasonable and too well informed themselves to desire anything more in woman than ignorance. But Catherine did not know her own advantages—did not know that a good-looking girl, with an affectionate heart and a very ignorant mind, cannot fail of attracting a clever young man, unless circumstances are particularly untoward. In the present instance, she confessed and lamented her want of knowledge, declared that she would give anything in the world to be able to draw; and a lecture on the picturesque immediately followed, in which his instructions were so clear that she soon began to see beauty in everything admired by him, and her attention was so earnest that he became perfectly satisfied of her having a great deal of natural taste. He talked of foregrounds, distances, and second distances—side-screens and perspectives—lights and shades; and Catherine was so hopeful a scholar that when they gained the top of Beechen Cliff, she voluntarily rejected the whole city of Bath as unworthy to make part of a landscape. Delighted with her progress, and fearful of wearying her with too much wisdom at once, Henry suffered the subject to decline, and by an easy transition from a piece of rocky fragment and the withered oak which he had placed near its summit, to oaks in general, to forests, the enclosure of them, waste lands, crown lands and government, he shortly found himself arrived at politics; and from politics, it was an easy step to silence. The general pause which succeeded his short disquisition on the state of the nation was put an end to by Catherine, who, in rather a solemn tone of voice, uttered these words, "I have heard that something very shocking indeed will soon come out in London."

Miss Tilney, to whom this was chiefly addressed, was startled, and hastily replied, "Indeed! And of what nature?"

"That I do not know, nor who is the author. I have only heard that it is to be more horrible than anything we have met with yet."

"Good heaven! Where could you hear of such a thing?"

"A particular friend of mine had an account of it in a letter from London yesterday. It is to be uncommonly dreadful. I shall expect murder and everything of the kind."

"You speak with astonishing composure! But I hope your friend's accounts have been exaggerated; and if such a design is known beforehand, proper measures will undoubtedly be taken by government to prevent its coming to effect."

"Government," said Henry, endeavouring not to smile, "neither desires nor dares to interfere in such matters. There must be murder; and government cares not how much."

The ladies stared. He laughed, and added, "Come, shall I make you understand each other, or leave you to puzzle out an explanation as you can? No—I will be noble. I will prove myself a man, no less by the generosity of my soul than the clearness of my head. I have no patience with such of my sex as disdain to let themselves sometimes down to the comprehension of yours. Perhaps the abilities of women are neither sound nor acute—neither vigorous nor keen. Perhaps they may want observation, discernment, judgment, fire, genius, and wit."

"Miss Morland, do not mind what he says; but have the goodness to satisfy me as to this dreadful riot."

"Riot! What riot?"

"My dear Eleanor, the riot is only in your own brain. The confusion there is scandalous. Miss Morland has been talking of nothing more dreadful than a new publication which is shortly to come out, in three duodecimo volumes, two hundred and seventy-six pages in each, with a frontispiece to

the first, of two tombstones and a lantern—do you understand? And you, Miss Morland—my stupid sister has mistaken all your clearest expressions. You talked of expected
horrors in London—and instead of instantly conceiving, as
any rational creature would have done, that such words
could relate only to a circulating library, she immediately
pictured to herself a mob of three thousand men assembling
in St. George's Fields, the Bank attacked, the Tower threatened, the streets of London flowing with blood, a detach-
ment of the Twelfth Light Dragoons (the hopes of the
nation) called up from Northampton to quell the insurgents,
and the gallant Captain Frederick Tilney, in the moment of
charging at the head of his troop, knocked off his horse by
a brickbat from an upper window. Forgive her stupidity. The
fears of the sister have added to the weakness of the woman;
but she is by no means a simpleton in general."

Catherine looked grave. "And now, Henry," said Miss
Tilney, "that you have made us understand each other, you
may as well make Miss Morland understand yourself—
unless you mean to have her think you intolerably rude to
your sister, and a great brute in your opinion of women in
general. Miss Morland is not used to your odd ways."

"I shall be most happy to make her better acquainted with
them."

"No doubt; but that is no explanation of the present."

"What am I to do?"

"You know what you ought to do. Clear your character
handsomely before her. Tell her that you think very highly of
the understanding of women."

"Miss Morland, I think very highly of the understanding
of all the women in the world—especially of those—
whoever they may be—with whom I happen to be in company."

"That is not enough. Be more serious."

"Miss Morland, no one can think more highly of the understanding of women than I do. In my opinion, nature has
given them so much that they never find it necessary to use
more than half."

"We shall get nothing more serious from him now, Miss
Morland. He is not in a sober mood. But I do assure you that
he must be entirely misunderstood, if he can ever appear to
say an unjust thing of any woman at all, or an unkind one of
me."

It was no effect to Catherine to believe that Henry Tilney could never be wrong. His manner might sometimes surprise, but his meaning must always be just: and what she did not understand, she was almost as ready to admire, as what she did. The whole walk was delightful, and though it ended too soon, its conclusion was delightful too; her friends attended her into the house, and Miss Tilney, before they parted, addressing herself with respectful form, as much to Mrs. Allen as to Catherine, petitioned for the pleasure of her company to dinner on the day after the next. No difficulty was made on Mrs. Allen's side, and the only difficulty on Catherine's was in concealing the excess of her pleasure.

The morning had passed away so charmingly as to banish all her friendship and natural affection, for no thought of Isabella or James had crossed her during their walk. When the Tilneys were gone, she became amiable again, but she was amiable for some time to little effect; Mrs. Allen had no intelligence to give that could relieve her anxiety; she had heard nothing of any of them. Towards the end of the morning, however, Catherine, having occasion for some indispensable yard of ribbon which must be bought without a moment's delay, walked out into the town, and in Bond Street overtook the second Miss Thorpe as she was loitering towards Edgar's Buildings between two of the sweetest girls in the world, who had been her dear friends all the morning. From her, she soon learned that the party to Clifton had taken place. "They set off at eight this morning," said Miss Anne, "and I am sure I do not envy them their drive. I think you and I are very well off to be out of the scrape. It must be the dullest thing in the world, for there is not a soul at Clifton at this time of year. Belle went with your brother, and John drove Maria."

Catherine spoke the pleasure she really felt on hearing this part of the arrangement.

"Oh! yes," rejoined the other, "Maria is gone. She was quite wild to go. She thought it would be something very fine. I cannot say I admire her taste; and for my part, I was determined from the first not to go, if they pressed me ever so much."

Catherine, a little doubtful of this, could not help answering, "I wish you could have gone too. It is a pity you could not go all go."

"Thank you; but it is quite a matter of indifference to me.

Indeed, I would not have gone on any account. I was saying so to Emily and Sophia when you overtook us."

Catherine was still unconvinced; but glad that Anne should have the friendship of an Emily and a Sophia to console her, she bade her adieu without much uneasiness, and returned home, pleased that the party had not been prevented by her refusing to join it, and very heartily wishing that it might be too pleasant to allow either James or Isabella to resent her resistance any longer.

CHAPTER XV

EARLY the next day, a note from Isabella, speaking peace and tenderness in every line, and entreating the immediate presence of her friend on a matter of the utmost importance, hastened Catherine, in the happiest state of confidence and curiosity, to Edgar's Buildings. The two youngest Miss Thorpes were by themselves in the parlour; and, on Anne's quitting it to call her sister, Catherine took the opportunity of asking the other for some particulars of their yesterday's party. Maria desired no greater pleasure than to speak of it; and Catherine immediately learnt that it had been altogether the most delightful scheme in the world, that nobody could imagine how charming it had been, and that it had been more delightful than anybody could conceive. Such was the information of the first five minutes; the second unfolded thus much in detail—that they had driven directly to the York Hotel, ate some soup, and bespoke an early dinner, walked down to the pump-room, tasted the water, and laid out some shillings in purses and spars; thence adjoined to eat ice at a pastry-cook's, and hurrying back to the hotel, swallowed their dinner in haste, to prevent being in the dark; and then had a delightful drive back, only the moon was not up, and it rained a little, and Mr. Morland's horse was so tired he could hardly get it along.

Catherine listened with heartfelt satisfaction. It appeared that Blaize Castle had never been thought of; and, as for all the rest, there was nothing to regret for half an instant. Maria's intelligence concluded with a tender effusion of pity for her sister Anne, whom she represented as insupportably cross, from being excluded the party.

"She will never forgive me, I am sure; but, you know, how could I help it? John would have me go, for he vowed he would not drive her, because she had such thick ankles. I dare say she will not be in good humour again this month;

but I am determined I will not be cross; it is not a little matter that puts me out of temper."

Isabella now entered the room with so eager a step, and a look of such happy importance, as engaged all her friend's notice. Maria was without ceremony sent away, and Isabella, embracing Catherine, thus began: "Yes, my dear Catherine, it is so indeed; your penetration has not deceived you. Oh! That arch eye of yours! It sees through everything."

Catherine replied only by a look of wondering ignorance.

"Nay, my beloved, sweetest friend," continued the other, "compose yourself. I am amazingly agitated, as you perceive. Let us sit down and talk in comfort. Well, and so you guessed it the moment you had my note? Sly creature! Oh! My dear Catherine, you alone, who know my heart, can judge of my present happiness. Your brother is the most charming of men. I only wish I were more worthy of him. But what will your excellent father and mother say? Oh! Heavens! When I think of them I am so agitated!"

Catherine's understanding began to awake: an idea of the truth suddenly darted into her mind; and, with the natural blush of so new an emotion, she cried out, "Good heaven! My dear Isabella, what do you mean? Can you—can you really be in love with James?"

This bold surmise, however, she soon learnt comprehended but half the fact. The anxious affection, which she was accused of having continually watched in Isabella's every look and action, had, in the course of their yesterday's party, received the delightful confession of an equal love. Her heart and faith were alike engaged to James. Never had Catherine listened to anything so full of interest, wonder, and joy. Her brother and her friend engaged! New to such circumstances, the importance of it appeared unspeakably great, and she contemplated it as one of those grand events, of which the ordinary course of life can hardly afford a return. The strength of her feelings she could not express; the nature of them, however, contented her friend. The happiness of having such a sister was their first effusion, and the fair ladies mingled in embraces and tears of joy.

Delighting, however, as Catherine sincerely did in the prospect of the connection, it must be acknowledged that Isabella far surpassed her in tender anticipations. "You will be so infinitely dearer to me, my Catherine, than either Anne or

Maria: I feel that I shall be so much more attached to my dear Morland's family than to my own."

This was a pitch of friendship beyond Catherine.

"You are so like your dear brother," continued Isabella, "that I quite doted on you the first moment I saw you. But so it always is with me; the first moment settles everything. The very first day that Morland came to us last Christmas— the very first moment I beheld him—my heart was irrecoverably gone. I remember I wore my yellow gown, with my hair done up in braids; and when I came into the drawing-room, and John introduced him, I thought I never saw anybody so handsome before."

Here Catherine secretly acknowledged the power of love; for, though exceedingly fond of her brother, and partial to all his endowments, she had never in her life thought him handsome.

"I remember too, Miss Andrews drank tea with us that evening, and wore her puce-coloured sarsenet; and she looked so heavenly that I thought your brother must certainly fall in love with her; I could not sleep a wink all night for thinking of it. Oh! Catherine, the many sleepless nights I have had on your brother's account! I would not have you suffer half what I have done! I am grown wretchedly thin, I know; but I will not pain you by describing my anxiety; you have seen enough of it. I feel that I have betrayed myself perpetually—so unguarded in speaking of my partiality for the church! But my secret I was always sure would be safe with *you*."

Catherine felt that nothing could have been safer; but ashamed of an ignorance little expected, she dared no longer contest the point, nor refuse to have been as full of arch penetration and affectionate sympathy as Isabella chose to consider her. Her brother, she found, was preparing to set off with all speed to Fullerton, to make known his situation and ask consent; and here was a source of some real agitation to the mind of Isabella. Catherine endeavoured to persuade her, as she was herself persuaded, that her father and mother would never oppose their son's wishes. "It is impossible," said she, "for parents to be more kind, or more desirous of their children's happiness; I have no doubt of their consenting immediately."

"Morland says exactly the same," replied Isabella; "and yet I dare not expect it; my fortune will be so small; they never can consent to it. Your brother, who might marry any-body!"

Here Catherine again discerned the force of love.

"Indeed, Isabella, you are too humble. The difference of fortune can be nothing to signify."

"Oh! My sweet Catherine, in *your* generous heart I know it would signify nothing; but we must not expect such disin-terestedness in many. As for myself, I am sure I only wish our situations were reversed. Had I the command of mil-lions, were I mistress of the whole world, your brother would be my only choice."

This charming sentiment, recommended as much by sense as novelty, gave Catherine a most pleasing remembrance of all the heroines of her acquaintance; and she thought her friend never looked more lovely than in uttering the grand idea. "I am sure they will consent," was her frequent decla-ration; "I am sure they will be delighted with you."

"For my own part," said Isabella, "my wishes are so mod-erate that the smallest income in nature would be enough for me. Where people are really attached, poverty itself is wealth; grandeur I detest: I would not settle in London for the universe. A cottage in some retired village would be ec-stasy. There are some charming little villas about Rich-mond."

"Richmond!" cried Catherine. "You must settle near Fullerton. You must be near us."

"I am sure I shall be miserable if we do not. If I can but be near *you*, I shall be satisfied. But this is idle talk-ing! I will not allow myself to think of such things, till we have your father's answer. Morland says that by sending it tonight to Salisbury, we may have it tomorrow. Tomorrow? I know I shall never have courage to open the letter. I know it will be the death of me."

A reverie succeeded his conviction—and when Isabella spoke again, it was to resolve on the quality of her wedding-gown.

Their conference was put an end to by the anxious young lover himself, who came to breathe his parting sigh before he set off for Wiltshire. Catherine wished to congratulate him, but knew not what to say, and her eloquence was only in her eyes. From them, however, the eight parts of speech shone out most expressively, and James could combine them with ease. Impatient for the realization of all that he hoped at home, his adieus were not long; and they would have been yet shorter, had he not been frequently detained by the urgent entreaties of his fair one that he would go. Twice was he called almost from the door by her eagerness to have him gone. "Indeed, Morland, I must drive you away. Consider how far you have to ride. I cannot bear to see you linger so. For heaven's sake, waste no more time. There, go, go—I insist on it."

The two friends, with hearts now more united than ever, were inseparable for the day; and in schemes of sisterly happiness the hours flew along. Mrs. Thorpe and her son, who were acquainted with everything, and who seemed only to want Mr. Morland's consent, to consider Isabella's engagement as the most fortunate circumstance imaginable for their family, were allowed to join their counsels, and add their quota of significant looks and mysterious expressions to fill up the measure of curiosity to be raised in the unprivileged younger sisters. To Catherine's simple feelings, this odd sort of reserve seemed neither kindly meant, nor consistently supported; and its unkindness she would hardly have forborne pointing out, had its inconsistency been less their friend; but Anne and Maria soon set her heart at ease by the sagacity of their "I know what"; and the evening was spent in a sort of war of wit, a display of family ingenuity, on one side in the mystery of an affected secret, on the other of undefined discovery, all equally acute.

Catherine was with her friend again the next day, endeavouring to support her spirits and while away the many tedious hours before the delivery of the letters; a needful exertion, for as the time of reasonable expectation drew near, Isabella became more and more desponding, and before the letter arrived, had worked herself into a state of real distress. But when it did come, where could distress be found? "I have had no difficulty in gaining the consent of my kind parents, and am promised that everything in their power shall be done to forward my happiness," were the first three lines, and in one moment all was joyful security. The brightest glow was instantly spread over Isabella's features, all care and anxiety seemed removed, her spirits became almost too high for control, and she called herself without scruple the happiest of mortals.

Mrs. Thorpe, with tears of joy, embraced her daughter, her son, her visitor, and could have embraced half the inhabitants of Bath with satisfaction. Her heart was overflowing with tenderness. It was "dear John" and "dear Catherine" at every word; "dear Anne and dear Maria" must immediately be made sharers in their felicity; and two "dears" at once before the name of Isabella were not more than that beloved child had now well earned. John himself was no skulker in joy. He not only bestowed on Mr. Morland the high commendation of being one of the finest fellows in the world, but swore off many sentences in his praise.

The letter, whence sprang all this felicity, was short, containing little more than this assurance of success; and every particular was deferred till James could write again. But for particulars Isabella could well afford to wait. The needful was comprised in Mr. Morland's promise; his honour was pledged to make everything easy; and by what means their income was to be formed, whether landed property were to be resigned, or funded money made over, was a matter in which her disinterested spirit took no concern. She knew enough to feel secure of an honourable and speedy establishment, and her imagination took a rapid flight over its attendant felicities. She saw herself at the end of a few weeks, the gaze and admiration of every new acquaintance at Fullerton, the envy of every valued old friend in Putney, with a carriage at her command, a new name on her tickets, and a brilliant exhibition of hoop rings on her finger.

When the contents of the letter were ascertained, John Thorpe, who had only waited its arrival to begin his journey to London, prepared to set off. "Well, Miss Morland," said he, on finding her alone in the parlour, "I am come to bid you good-bye." Catherine wished him a good journey. Without appearing to hear her, he walked to the window, fidgeted about, hummed a tune, and seemed wholly self-occupied.

"Shall not you be late at Devises?" said Catherine. He made no answer; but after a minute's silence burst out with, "A famous good thing this marrying scheme, upon my soul! A clever fancy of Morland's and Belle's. What do you think of it, Miss Morland? *I* say it is no bad notion."

"I am sure I think it a very good one."

"Do you? That's honest, by heavens! I am glad you are no enemy to matrimony, however. Did you ever hear the old song 'Going to One Wedding Brings on Another?' I say, you will come to Belle's wedding, I hope."

"Yes; I have promised your sister to be with her, if possible."

"And then you know"—twisting himself about and forcing a foolish laugh—"I say, then you know, we may try the truth of this same old song."

"May we? But I never sing. Well, I wish you a good journey. I dine with Miss Tilney today, and must now be going home."

"Nay, but there is no such confounded hurry. Who knows when we may be together again? Not but that I shall be down again by the end of a fortnight, and a devilish long fortnight it will appear to me."

"Then why do you stay away so long?" replied Catherine—finding that he waited for an answer.

"That is kind of you, however—kind and good-natured. I shall not forget it in a hurry. But you have more good nature and all that, than anybody living, I believe. A monstrous deal of good nature, and it is not only good nature, but you have so much, so much of everything; and then you have such— upon my soul, I do not know anybody like you."

"Oh! dear, there are a great many people like me, I dare say, only a great deal better. Good morning to you."

"But I say, Miss Morland, I shall come and pay my respects at Fullerton before it is long, if not disagreeable."

"Pray do. My father and mother will be very glad to see you."

"And I hope—I hope, Miss Morland, you will not be sorry to see me."

"Oh! dear, not at all. There are very few people I am sorry to see. Company is always cheerful."

"That is just my way of thinking. Give me but a little cheerful company, let me only have the company of the people I love, let me only be where I like and with whom I like, and the devil take the rest, say I. And I am heartily glad to hear you say the same. But I have a notion, Miss Morland, you and I think pretty much alike upon most matters."

"Perhaps we may; but it is more than I ever thought of. And as to most matters, to say the truth, there are not many that I know my own mind about."

"By Jove, no more do I. It is not my way to bother my brains with what does not concern me. My notion of things is simple enough. Let me only have the girl I like, say I, with a comfortable house over my head, and what care I for all the rest? Fortune is nothing. I am sure of a good income of my own; and if she had not a penny, why, so much the better."

"Very true. I think like you there. If there is a good fortune on one side, there can be no occasion for any on the other. No matter which has it, so that there is enough. I hate the idea of one great fortune looking out for another. And to marry for money I think the wickedest thing in existence. Good day. We shall be very glad to see you at Fullerton, whenever it is convenient." And away she went. It was not in the power of all his gallantry to detain her longer. With such news to communicate, and such a visit to prepare for, her departure was not to be delayed by anything in his nature to urge; and she hurried away, leaving him to the undivided consciousness of his own happy address, and her explicit encouragement.

The agitation which she had herself experienced on first learning her brother's engagement made her expect to raise no inconsiderable emotion in Mr. and Mrs. Allen, by the communication of the wonderful event. How great was her disappointment! The important affair, which many words of preparation ushered in, had been foreseen by them both ever since her brother's arrival; and all that they felt on the occasion was comprehended in a wish for the young people's happiness, with a remark, on the gentleman's side, in favour of Isabella's beauty, and on the lady's, of her great good luck. It was to Catherine the most surprising insensibility. The disclosure, however, of the great secret of James's going to Fullerton the day before, did raise some emotion in Mrs. Allen. She could not listen to that with perfect calmness, but repeatedly regretted the necessity of its concealment, wished she could have known his intention, wished she could have seen him before he went, as she should certainly have troubled him with her best regards to his father and mother, and her kind compliments to all the Skinners.

CHAPTER XVI

CATHERINE's expectations of pleasure from her visit in Milsom Street were so very high that disappointment was inevitable; and accordingly, though she was most politely received by General Tilney, and kindly welcomed by his daughter, though Henry was at home, and no one else of the party, she found, on her return, without spending many hours in the examination of her feelings, that she had gone to her appointment preparing for happiness which it had not afforded. Instead of finding herself improved in acquaintance with Miss Tilney, from the intercourse of the day, she seemed hardly so intimate with her as before; instead of seeing Henry Tilney to greater advantage than ever, in the ease of a family party, he had never said so little, nor been so little agreeable; and, in spite of their father's great civilities to her—in spite of his thanks, invitations, and compliments—it had been a release to get away from him. It puzzled her to account for all this. It could not be General Tilney's fault. That he was perfectly agreeable and good-natured, and altogether a very charming man, did not admit of a doubt, for he was tall and handsome, and Henry's father. *He* could not be accountable for his children's want of spirits, or for her want of enjoyment in his company. The former she hoped at last might have been accidental, and the latter she could only attribute to her own stupidity. Isabella, on hearing the particulars of the visit, gave a different explanation: "It was all pride, pride, insufferable haughtiness and pride! She had long suspected the family to be very high, and this made it certain. Such insolence of behavior as Miss Tilney's she had never heard of in her life! Not to do the honours of her house with common good breeding! To behave to her guest with such superciliousness! Hardly even to speak to her!"

"But it was not so bad as that, Isabella; there was no superciliousness; she was very civil."

"Oh! Don't defend her! And then the brother, he, who had appeared so attached to you! Good heavens! Well, some people's feelings are incomprehensible. And so he hardly looked once at you the whole day?"

"I do not say so; but he did not seem in good spirits."

"How contemptible! Of all things in the world inconstancy is my aversion. Let me entreat you never to think of him again, my dear Catherine; indeed he is unworthy of you."

"Unworthy! I do not suppose he ever thinks of me."

"That is exactly what I say; he never thinks of you. Such fickleness! Oh! How different to your brother and to mine! I really believe John has the most constant heart."

"But as for General Tilney, I assure you it would be impossible for anybody to behave to me with greater civility and attention; it seemed to be his only care to entertain and make me happy."

"Oh! I know no harm of him; I do not suspect him of pride. I believe he is a very gentleman-like man. John thinks very well of him, and John's judgment——"

"Well, I shall see how they behave to me this evening; we shall meet them at the rooms."

"And must I go?"

"Do not you intend it? I thought it was all settled."

"Nay, since you make such a point of it, I can refuse you nothing. But do not insist upon my being very agreeable, for my heart, you know, will be some forty miles off. And as for dancing, do not mention it; I beg; *that* is quite out of the question. Charles Hodges will plague me to death, I dare say; but I shall cut him very short. Ten to one but he guesses the reason, and that is exactly what I want to avoid, so I shall insist on his keeping his conjecture to himself."

Isabella's opinion of the Tilneys did not influence her friend; she was sure there had been no insolence in the manners either of brother or sister; and she did not credit there being any pride in their hearts. The evening rewarded her confidence; she was met by one with the same kindness, and by the other with the same attention, as heretofore: Miss Tilney took pains to be near her, and Henry asked her to dance.

Having heard the day before in Milsom Street that their elder brother, Captain Tilney, was expected almost every hour, she was at no loss for the name of a very fashionable-

looking, handsome young man, whom she had never seen
before, and who now evidently belonged to their party. She
looked at him with great admiration, and even supposed it
possible that some people might think him handsomer than
his brother, though, in her eyes, his air was more assuming,
and his countenance less prepossessing. His taste and manners were beyond a doubt decidedly inferior; for, within her
hearing, he not only protested against every thought of dancing himself, but even laughed openly at Henry for finding it
possible. From the latter circumstance it may be presumed
that, whatever might be our heroine's opinion of him, his admiration of her was not of a very dangerous kind; not likely
to produce animosities between the brothers, nor persecutions to the lady. *He* cannot be the instigator of the three villains in horsemen's greatcoats, by whom she will hereafter
be forced into a travelling-chaise and four, which will drive
off with incredible speed. Catherine, meanwhile, undisturbed
by presentiments of such an evil, or of any evil at all, except
that of having but a short set to dance down, enjoyed her
usual happiness with Henry Tilney, listening with sparkling
eyes to everything he said; and, in finding him irresistible,
becoming so herself.

At the end of the first dance, Captain Tilney came towards
them again, and, much to Catherine's dissatisfaction, pulled
his brother away. They retired whispering together; and,
though her delicate sensibility did not take immediate alarm,
and lay it down as fact, that Captain Tilney must have heard
some malevolent misrepresentation of her, which he now
hastened to communicate to his brother, in the hope of separating them forever, she could not have her partner conveyed from her sight without very uneasy sensations. Her
suspense was of full five minutes' duration; and she was beginning to think it a very long quarter of an hour, when they
both returned, and an explanation was given, by Henry's requesting to know if she thought her friend, Miss Thorpe,
would have any objection to dancing, as his brother would
be most happy to be introduced to her. Catherine, without
hesitation, replied that she was very sure Miss Thorpe did
not mean to dance at all. The cruel reply was passed on to
the other, and he immediately walked away.

"Your brother will not mind it, I know," said she, "because I heard him say before that he hated dancing; but it
was very good-natured in him to think of it. I suppose he

saw Isabella sitting down, and fancied she might wish for a partner; but he is quite mistaken, for she would not dance upon any account in the world."

Henry smiled, and said, "How very little trouble it can give you to understand the motive of other people's actions."

"Why? What do you mean?"

"With you, it is not, How is such a one likely to be influenced, What is the inducement most likely to act upon such a person's feelings, age, situation, and probable habits of life considered—but, How should *I* be influenced, What would be *my* inducement in acting so and so?"

"I do not understand you."

"Then we are on very unequal terms, for I understand you perfectly well."

"Me? Yes; I cannot speak well enough to be unintelligible."

"Bravo! An excellent satire on modern language."

"But pray tell me what you mean."

"Shall I indeed? Do you really desire it? But you are not aware of the consequences; it will involve you in a very cruel embarrassment, and certainly bring on a disagreement between us."

"No, no; it shall not do either; I am not afraid."

"Well, then, I only meant that your attributing my brother's wish of dancing with Miss Thorpe to good nature alone convinced me of your being superior in good nature yourself to all the rest of the world."

Catherine blushed and disclaimed, and the gentleman's predictions were verified. There was a something, however, in his words which repaid her for the pain of confusion; and that something occupied her mind so much that she drew back for some time, forgetting to speak or to listen, and almost forgetting where she was; till, roused by the voice of Isabella, she looked up and saw her with Captain Tilney preparing to give them hands across.

Isabella shrugged her shoulders and smiled, the only explanation of this extraordinary change which could at that time be given; but as it was not quite enough for Catherine's comprehension, she spoke her astonishment in very plain terms to her partner.

"I cannot think how it could happen! Isabella was so determined not to dance."

"And did Isabella never change her mind before?"

"Oh! But, because— And your brother! After what you told him from me, how could he think of going to ask her?"

"I cannot take surprise to myself on that head. You bid me be surprised on your friend's account, and therefore I am; but as for my brother, his conduct in the business, I must own, has been no more than I believed him perfectly equal to. The fairness of your friend was an open attraction; her firmness, you know, could only be understood by yourself."

"You are laughing; but, I assure you, Isabella is very firm in general."

"It is as much as should be said of anyone. To be always firm must be to be often obstinate. When properly to relax is the trial of judgment; and, without reference to my brother, I really think Miss Thorpe has by no means chosen ill in fixing on the present hour."

The friends were not able to get together for any confidential discourse till all the dancing was over; but then, as they walked about the room arm in arm, Isabella thus explained herself: "I do not wonder at your surprise; and I am really fatigued to death. He is such a rattle! Amusing enough, if my mind had been disengaged; but I would have given the world to sit still."

"Then why did not you?"

"Oh! My dear! It would have looked so particular; and you know how I abhor doing that. I refused him as long as I possibly could, but he would take no denial. You have no idea how he pressed me. I begged him to excuse me, and get some other partner—but no, not he; after aspiring to my hand, there was nobody else in the room he could bear to think of; and it was not that he wanted merely to dance, he wanted to be with *me*. Oh! Such nonsense! I told him he had taken a very unlikely way to prevail upon me; for, of all things in the world, I hated fine speeches and compliments; and so—and so then I found there would be no peace if I did not stand up. Besides, I thought Mrs. Hughes, who introduced him, might take it ill if I did not: and your dear brother, I am sure he would have been miserable if I had sat down the whole evening. I am so glad it is over! My spirits are quite jaded with listening to his nonsense: and then, being such a smart young fellow, I saw every eye was upon us."

"He is very handsome indeed."

"Handsome! Yes, I suppose he may. I dare say people

would admire him in general; but he is not at all in my style of beauty. I hate a florid complexion and dark eyes in a man. However, he is very well. Amazingly conceited, I am sure. I took him down several times, you know, in my way."

When the young ladies next met, they had a far more interesting subject to discuss. James Morland's second letter was then received, and the kind intentions of his father fully explained. A living, of which Mr. Morland was himself patron and incumbent, of about four hundred pounds yearly value, was to be resigned to his son as soon as he should be old enough to take it; no trifling deduction from the family income, no niggardly assignment to one of ten children. An estate of at least equal value, moreover, was assured as his future inheritance.

James expressed himself on the occasion with becoming gratitude; and the necessity of waiting between two and three years before they could marry, being, however unwelcome, no more than he had expected, was borne by him without discontent. Catherine, whose expectations had been as unfixed as her ideas of her father's income, and whose judgment was now entirely led by her brother, felt equally well satisfied, and heartily congratulated Isabella on having everything so pleasantly settled.

"It is very charming indeed," said Isabella, with a grave face. "Mr. Morland has behaved vastly handsome indeed," said the gentle Mrs. Thorpe, looking anxiously at her daughter. "I only wish I could do as much. One could not expect more from him, you know. If he finds he *can* do more by and by, I dare say he will, for I am sure he must be an excellent good-hearted man. Four hundred is but a small income to begin on indeed, but your wishes, my dear Isabella, are so moderate, you do not consider how little you ever want, my dear."

"It is not on my own account I wish for more; but I cannot bear to be the means of injuring my dear Morland, making him sit down upon an income hardly enough to find one in the common necessaries of life. For myself, it is nothing; I never think of myself."

"I know you never do, my dear; and you will always find your reward in the affection it makes everybody feel for you. There never was a young woman so beloved as you are by everybody that knows you; and I dare say when Mr. Morland sees you, my dear child—but do not let us distress our dear Catherine by talking of such things. Mr. Morland has behaved so very handsome, you know. I always heard he was a most excellent man; and you know, my dear, we are not to suppose but what, if you had had a suitable fortune, he would have come down with something more, for I am sure he must be a most liberal-minded man."

"Nobody can think better of Mr. Morland than I do, I am sure. But everybody has their failing, you know, and everybody has a right to do what they like with their own money." Catherine was hurt by these insinuations. "I am very sure," said she, "that my father has promised to do as much as he can afford."

Isabella recollected herself. "As to that, my sweet Catherine, there cannot be a doubt, and you know me well enough to be sure that a much smaller income would satisfy me. It is not the want of money that makes me just at present a little out of spirits; I hate money; and if our union could take place now upon only fifty pounds a year, I should not have a wish unsatisfied. Ah! my Catherine, you have found me out. There's the sting. The long, long, endless two years and half that are to pass before your brother can hold the living."

"Yes, yes, my darling Isabella," said Mrs. Thorpe, "we perfectly see into your heart. You have no disguise. We perfectly understand the present vexation; and everybody must love you the better for such a noble honest affection."

Catherine's uncomfortable feelings began to lessen. She endeavoured to believe that the delay of the marriage was the only source of Isabella's regret; and when she saw her at their next interview as cheerful and amiable as ever, endeavoured to forget that she had for a minute thought otherwise. James soon followed his letter, and was received with the most gratifying kindness.

CHAPTER XVII

THE Allens had now entered on the sixth week of their stay in Bath; and whether it should be the last was for some time a question, to which Catherine listened with a beating heart. To have her acquaintance with the Tilneys end so soon was an evil which nothing could counterbalance. Her whole happiness seemed at stake, while the affair was in suspense, and everything secured when it was determined that the lodgings should be taken for another fortnight. What this additional fortnight was to produce to her beyond the pleasure of sometimes seeing Henry Tilney made but a small part of Catherine's speculation. Once or twice indeed, since James's engagement had taught her what *could* be done, she had got so far as to indulge in a secret "perhaps," but in general the felicity of being with him for the present bounded her views: the present was now comprised in another three weeks, and her happiness being certain for that period, the rest of her life was at such a distance as to excite but little interest. In the course of the morning which saw this business arranged, she visited Miss Tilney, and poured forth her joyful feelings. It was doomed to be a day of trial. No sooner had she expressed her delight in Mr. Allen's lengthened stay than Miss Tilney told her of her father's having just determined upon quitting Bath by the end of another week. Here was a blow! The past suspense of the morning had been ease and quiet to the present disappointment. Catherine's countenance fell, and in a voice of most sincere concern she echoed Miss Tilney's concluding words, "By the end of another week!"

"Yes, my father can seldom be prevailed on to give the waters what I think a fair trial. He had been disappointed of some friends' arrival whom he expected to meet here, and as he is now pretty well, is in a hurry to get home."

"I am very sorry for it," said Catherine dejectedly; "if I had known this before—"

"Perhaps," said Miss Tilney in an embarrassed manner, "you would be so good—it would make me very happy if——"

The entrance of her father put a stop to the civility, which Catherine was beginning to hope might introduce a desire of their corresponding. After addressing her with his usual politeness, he turned to his daughter and said, "Well, Eleanor, may I congratulate you on being successful in your application to your fair friend?"

"I was just beginning to make the request, sir, as you came in."

"Well, proceed by all means. I know how much your heart is in it. My daughter, Miss Morland," he continued, without leaving his daughter time to speak, "has been forming a very bold wish. We leave Bath, as she has perhaps told you, on Saturday se'nnight. A letter from my steward tells me that my presence is wanted at home; and being disappointed in my hope of seeing the Marquis of Longtown and General Courteney here, some of my very old friends, there is nothing to detain me longer in Bath. And could we carry our selfish point with you, we should leave it without a single regret. Can you, in short, be prevailed on to quit this scene of public triumph and oblige your friend Eleanor with your company in Gloucestershire? I am almost ashamed to make the request, though its presumption would certainly appear greater to every creature in Bath than yourself. Modesty such as yours—but not for the world would I pain it by open praise. If you can be induced to honour us with a visit, you will make us happy beyond expression. 'Tis true, we can offer you nothing like the gaieties of this lively place; we can tempt you neither by amusement nor splendour, for our mode of living, as you see, is plain and unpretending; yet no endeavours shall be wanting on our side to make Northanger Abbey not wholly disagreeable."

Northanger Abbey! These were thrilling words, and wound up Catherine's feelings to the highest point of ecstasy. Her grateful and gratified heart could hardly restrain its expressions within the language of tolerable calmness. To receive so flattering an invitation! To have her company so warmly solicited! Everything honourable and soothing, every present enjoyment, and every future hope was contained in it; and her acceptance, with only the saving clause of Papa and Mamma's approbation, was eagerly given. "I will write home directly," said she, "and if they do not object, as I dare say they will not—"

General Tilney was not less sanguine, having already waited on her excellent friends in Pulteney Street, and obtained their sanction of his wishes. "Since they can consent to part with you," said he, "we may expect philosophy from all the world."

Miss Tilney was earnest, though gentle, in her secondary civilities, and the affair became in a few minutes as nearly settled as this necessary reference to Fullerton would allow.

The circumstances of the morning had led Catherine's feelings through the varieties of suspense, security, and disappointment; but they were now safely lodged in perfect bliss; and with spirits elated to rapture, with Henry at her heart, and Northanger Abbey on her lips, she hurried home to write her letter. Mr. and Mrs. Morland, relying on the discretion of the friends to whom they had already entrusted their daughter, felt no doubt of the propriety of an acquaintance which had been formed under their eye, and sent therefore by return of post their ready consent to her visit in Gloucestershire. This indulgence, though not more than Catherine had hoped for, completed her conviction of being favoured beyond every other human creature, in friends and fortune, circumstance and chance. Everything seemed to co-operate for her advantage. By the kindness of her first friends, the Allens, she had been introduced into scenes where pleasures of every kind had met her. Her feelings, her preferences, had each known the happiness of a return. Wherever she felt attachment, she had been able to create it. The affection of Isabella was to be secured to her in a sister. The Tilneys, they, by whom, above all, she desired to be favourably thought of, outstripped even her wishes in the flattering measures by which their intimacy was to be continued. She was to be their chosen visitor, she was to be for weeks under the same roof with the person whose society she mostly prized—and, in addition to all the rest, this roof was to be the roof of an abbey! Her passion for ancient edifices was next in degree to her passion for Henry Tilney—and castles and abbeys made usually the charm of those reveries which his image did not fill. To see and explore either the ramparts and keep of the one, or the cloisters of the other, had been for many weeks a darling wish, though to be more than the visitor of an hour had seemed too nearly impossible for desire. And yet, this was to happen. With all the chances against her of house, hall, place, park, court, and cottage, Northanger turned up an abbey, and she was to be its inhabitant. Its long, damp passages, its narrow cells and ruined chapel, were to be within her daily reach, and she could not entirely subdue the hope of some traditional legends, some awful memorials of an injured and ill-fated nun.

It was wonderful that her friends should seem so little elated by the possession of such a home, that the consciousness of it should be so meekly borne. The power of early habit only could account for it. A distinction to which they had been born gave no pride. Their superiority of abode was no more to them than their superiority of person.

Many were the inquiries she was eager to make of Miss Tilney; but so active were her thoughts, that when these inquiries were answered, she was hardly more assured than before, of Northanger Abbey having been a richly endowed convent at the time of the Reformation, of its having fallen into the hands of an ancestor of the Tilneys on its dissolution, of a large portion of the ancient building still making a part of the present dwelling although the rest was decayed, or of its standing low in a valley, sheltered from the north and east by rising woods of oak.

CHAPTER XVIII

With a mind thus full of happiness, Catherine was hardly aware that two or three days had passed away, without her seeing Isabella for more than a few minutes together. She began first to be sensible of this, and to sigh for her conversation, as she walked along the pump-room one morning, by Mrs. Allen's side, without anything to say or to hear; and scarcely had she felt a five minutes' longing of friendship, before the object of it appeared, and inviting her to a secret conference, led the way to a seat. "This is my favourite place," said she as they sat down on a bench between the doors, which commanded a tolerable view of everybody entering at either; "it is so out of the way."

Catherine, observing that Isabella's eyes were continually bent towards one door or the other, as in eager expectation, and remembering how often she had been falsely accused of being arch, thought the present a fine opportunity for being really so; and therefore gaily said, "Do not be uneasy, Isabella. James will soon be here."

"Psha! My dear creature," she replied, "do not think me such a simpleton as to be always wanting to confine him to my elbow. It would be hideous to be always together; we should be the jest of the place. And so you are going to Northanger! I am amazingly glad of it. It is one of the finest old places in England, I understand. I shall depend upon a most particular description of it."

"You shall certainly have the best in my power to give. But who are you looking for? Are your sisters coming?"

"I am not looking for anybody. One's eyes must be somewhere, and you know what a foolish trick I have of fixing mine, when my thoughts are a hundred miles off. I am amazingly absent; I believe I am the most absent creature in the world. Tilney says it is always the case with minds of a certain stamp."

"But I thought, Isabella, you had something in particular to tell me?"

"Oh! Yes, and so I have. But here is a proof of what I was saying. My poor head! I had quite forgot it. Well, the thing is this: I have just had a letter from John; you can guess the contents."

"No, indeed, I cannot."

"My sweet love, do not be abominably affected. What can he write about, but yourself? You know he is over head and ears in love with you."

"With *me*, dear Isabella!"

"Nay, my sweetest Catherine, this is being quite absurd! Modesty, and all that, is very well in its way, but really a little common honesty is sometimes quite as becoming. I have no idea of being so overstrained! It is fishing for compliments. His attentions were such as a child must have noticed. And it was but half an hour before he left Bath that you gave him the most positive encouragement. He says so in this letter, says that he as good as made you an offer, and that you received his advances in the kindest way; and now he wants me to urge his suit, and say all manner of pretty things to you. So it is in vain to affect ignorance."

Catherine, with all the earnestness of truth, expressed her astonishment at such a charge, protesting her innocence of every thought of Mr. Thorpe's being in love with her, and the consequent impossibility of her having ever intended to encourage him. "As to any attentions on his side, I do declare, upon my honour, I never was sensible of them for a moment—except just his asking me to dance the first day of his coming. And as to making me an offer, or anything like it, there must be some unaccountable mistake. I could not have misunderstood a thing of that kind, you know! And, as I ever wish to be believed, I solemnly protest that no syllable of such a nature ever passed between us. The last half hour before he went away! It must be all and completely a mistake—for I did not see him once that whole morning."

"But *that* you certainly did, for you spent the whole morning in Edgar's Buildings—it was the day your father's consent came—and I am pretty sure that you and John were alone in the parlour some time before you left the house."

"Are you? Well, if you say it, it was so, I dare say—but for the life of me, I cannot recollect it. I *do* remember now being with you, and seeing him as well as the rest—but that we were ever alone for five minutes— However, it is not worth arguing about, for whatever might pass on his side, you must be convinced, by my having no recollection of it, that I never thought, nor expected, nor wished for anything of the kind from him. I am excessively concerned that he should have any regard for me—but indeed it has been quite unintentional on my side; I never had the smallest idea of it. Pray undeceive him as soon as you can, and tell him I beg his pardon—that is—I do not know what I ought to say—but make him understand what I mean, in the properest way. I would not speak disrespectfully of a brother of yours, Isabella, I am sure; but you know very well that if I could think of one man more than another—*he* is not the person." Isabella was silent. "My dear friend, you must not be angry with me. I cannot suppose your brother cares so very much about me. And, you know, we shall still be sisters."

"Yes, yes" (with a blush), "there are more ways than one of our being sisters. But where am I wandering to? Well, my dear Catherine, the case seems to be that you are determined against poor John—is not it so?"

"I certainly cannot return his affection, and as certainly never meant to encourage it."

"Since that is the case, I am sure I shall not tease you any further. John desired me to speak to you on the subject, and therefore I have. But I confess, as soon as I read his letter, I thought it a very foolish, imprudent business, and not likely to promote the good of either; for what were you to live upon, supposing you came together? You have both of you something, to be sure, but it is not a trifle that will support a family nowadays; and after all that romancers may say, there is no doing without money. I only wonder John could think of it; he could not have received my last."

"You *do* acquit me, then, of anything wrong? You are convinced that I never meant to deceive your brother, never suspected him of liking me till this moment?"

"Oh! As to that," answered Isabella laughingly, "I do not pretend to determine what your thoughts and designs in time past may have been. All that is best known to yourself. A little harmless flirtation or so will occur, and one is often drawn on to give more encouragement than one wishes to stand by. But you may be assured that I am the last person in the world to judge you severely. All those things should be allowed for in youth and high spirits. What one means one day, you know, one may not mean the next. Circumstances change, opinions alter."

"But my opinion of your brother never did alter; it was always the same. You are describing what never happened."

"My dearest Catherine," continued the other without at all listening to her, "I would not for all the world be the means of hurrying you into an engagement before you knew what you were about. I do not think anything would justify me in wishing you to sacrifice all your happiness merely to oblige my brother, because he is my brother, and who perhaps after all, you know, might be just as happy without you, for people seldom know what they would be at, young men especially, they are so amazingly changeable and inconstant. What I say is, why should a brother's happiness be dearer to me than a friend's? You know I carry my notions of friendship pretty high. But, above all things, my dear Catherine, do not be in a hurry. Take my word for it, that if you are in too great a hurry, you will certainly live to repent it. Tilney says there is nothing people are so often deceived in as the state of their own affections, and I believe he is very right. Ah! Here he comes; never mind, he will not see us, I am sure."

Catherine, looking up, perceived Captain Tilney; and Isabella, earnestly fixing her eye on him as she spoke, soon caught his notice. He approached immediately, and took the seat to which her movements invited him. His first address made Catherine start. Though spoken low, she could distinguish, "What! Always to be watched, in person or by proxy!"

"Psha, nonsense!" was Isabella's answer in the same half whisper. "Why do you put such things into my head? If I could believe it—my spirit, you know, is pretty independent."

"I wish your heart were independent. That would be enough for me."

"My heart, indeed! What can you have to do with hearts? You men have none of you any hearts."

"If we have not hearts, we have eyes; and they give us torment enough."

"Do they? I am sorry for it; I am sorry they find anything so disagreeable in me. I will look another way. I hope this pleases you" (turning her back on him); "I hope your eyes are not tormented now."

"Never more so; for the edge of a blooming cheek is still in view—at once too much and too little."

Catherine heard all this, and quite out of countenance, could listen no longer. Amazed that Isabella could endure it, and jealous for her brother, she rose up, and saying she should join Mrs. Allen, proposed their walking. But for this Isabella showed no inclination. She was so amazingly tired, and it was so odious to parade about the pump-room; and if she moved from her seat she should miss her sisters; she was expecting her sisters every moment; so that her dearest Catherine must excuse her, and must sit quietly down again. But Catherine could be stubborn too; and Mrs. Allen just then coming up to propose their returning home, she joined her and walked out of the pump-room, leaving Isabella still sitting with Captain Tilney. With much uneasiness did she thus leave them. It seemed to her that Captain Tilney was falling in love with Isabella, and Isabella unconsciously encouraging him; unconsciously it must be, for Isabella's attachment to James was as certain and well acknowledged as her engagement. To doubt her truth or good intentions was impossible; and yet, during the whole of their conversation her manner had been odd. She wished Isabella had talked more like her usual self, and not so much about money, and had not looked so well pleased at the sight of Captain Tilney. How strange that she should not perceive his admiration! Catherine longed to give her a hint of it, to put her on her guard, and prevent all the pain which her too lively behaviour might otherwise create both for him and her brother.

The compliment of John Thorpe's affection did not make amends for this thoughtlessness in his sister. She was almost as far from believing as from wishing it to be sincere; for she had not forgotten that he could mistake, and his assertion of the offer and of her encouragement convinced her that his mistakes could sometimes be very egregious. In vanity, therefore, she gained but little; her chief profit was in wonder. That he should think it worth his while to fancy himself in love with her was a matter of lively astonishment. Isabella talked of his attentions; *she* had never been sensible of any; but Isabella had said many things which she hoped had been spoken in haste, and would never be said again; and upon this she was glad to rest altogether for present ease and comfort.

CHAPTER XIX

A few days passed away, and Catherine, though not allowing herself to suspect her friend, could not help watching her closely. The result of her observations was not agreeable. Isabella seemed an altered creature. When she saw her, indeed, surrounded only by their immediate friends in Edgar's Buildings or Pulteney Street, her change of manners was so trifling that, had it gone no farther, it might have passed unnoticed. A something of languid indifference, or of that boasted absence of mind which Catherine had never heard of before, would occasionally come across her; but had nothing worse appeared, *that* might only have spread a new grace and inspired a warmer interest. But when Catherine saw her in public, admitting Captain Tilney's attentions as readily as they were offered, and allowing him almost an equal share with James in her notice and smiles, the alteration became too positive to be passed over. What could be meant by such unsteady conduct, what her friend could be at, was beyond her comprehension. Isabella could not be aware of the pain she was inflicting; but it was a degree of wilful thoughtlessness which Catherine could not but resent. James was the sufferer. She saw him grave and uneasy; and however careless of his present comfort the woman might be who had given him her heart, to *her* it was always an object. For poor Captain Tilney too she was greatly concerned. Though his looks did not please her, his name was a passport to her goodwill, and she thought with sincere compassion of his approaching disappointment; for, in spite of what she had believed herself to overhear in the pump-room, his behavior was so incompatible with a knowledge of Isabella's engagement that she could not, upon reflection, imagine him aware of it. He might be jealous of her brother as a rival, but if more had seemed implied, the fault must have been in her misapprehension. She wished, by a gentle remonstrance, to remind Isabella of her situation, and make her aware of this double unkindness; but for remonstrance, either opportunity or comprehension was always against her. If able to suggest a hint, Isabella could never understand it. In this distress, the intended departure of the Tilney family became her chief consolation; their journey into Gloucestershire was to take place within a few days, and Captain Tilney's removal would at least restore peace to every heart but his own. But Captain Tilney had at present no intention of removing; he was not to be of the party to Northanger; he was to continue at Bath. When Catherine knew this, her resolution was directly made. She spoke to Henry Tilney on the subject, regretting his brother's evident partiality for Miss Thorpe, and entreating him to make known her prior engagement.

"My brother does know it," was Henry's answer.

"Does he? Then why does he stay here?"

He made no reply, and was beginning to talk of something else; but she eagerly continued, "Why do not you persuade him to go away? The longer he stays, the worse it will be for him at last. Pray advise him for his own sake, and for everybody's sake, to leave Bath directly. Absence will in time make him comfortable again; but he can have no hope here, and it is only staying to be miserable." Henry smiled and said, "I am sure my brother would not wish to do that."

"Then you will persuade him to go away?"

"Persuasion is not at command; but pardon me, if I cannot even endeavour to persuade him. I have myself told him that Miss Thorpe is engaged. He knows what he is about, and must be his own master."

"No, he does not know what he is about," cried Catherine; "he does not know the pain he is giving my brother. Not that James has ever told me so, but I am sure he is very uncomfortable."

"And are you sure it is my brother's doing?"

"Yes, very sure."

"Is it my brother's attentions to Miss Thorpe, or Miss Thorpe's admission of them, that gives the pain?"

"Is not it the same thing?"

"I think Mr. Morland would acknowledge a difference. No man is offended by another man's admiration of the woman he loves; it is the woman only who can make it a torment."

Catherine blushed for her friend, and said, "Isabella is wrong. But I am sure she cannot mean to torment, for she is very much attached to my brother. She has been in love with him ever since they first met, and while my father's consent was uncertain, she fretted herself almost into a fever. You know she must be attached to him."

"I understand: she is in love with James, and flirts with Frederick."

"Oh! no, not flirts. A woman in love with one man cannot flirt with another."

"It is probable that she will neither love so well, nor flirt so well, as she might do either singly. The gentlemen must each give up a little."

After a short pause, Catherine resumed with, "Then you do not believe Isabella so very much attached to my brother?"

"I can have no opinion on that subject."

"But what can your brother mean? If he knows her engagement, what can he mean by his behavior?"

"You are a very close questioner."

"Am I? I only ask what I want to be told."

"But do you only ask what I can be expected to tell?"

"Yes, I think so; for you must know your brother's heart."

"My brother's heart, as you term it, on the present occasion, I assure you I can only guess at."

"Well?"

"Well! Nay, if it is to be guesswork, let us all guess for ourselves. To be guided by second-hand conjecture is pitiful. The premises are before you. My brother is a lively and perhaps sometimes a thoughtless young man; he has had about a week's acquaintance with your friend, and he has known her engagement almost as long as he has known her."

"Well," said Catherine, after some moments' consideration, "*you* may be able to guess at your brother's intentions from all this; but I am sure I cannot. But is not your father uncomfortable about it? Does not he want Captain Tilney to go away? Sure, if your father were to speak to him, he would go."

"My dear Miss Morland," said Henry, "in this amiable solicitude for your brother's comfort, may you not be a little mistaken? Are you not carried a little too far? Would he thank you, either on his own account or Miss Thorpe's, for supposing that her affection, or at least her good behaviour, is only to be secured by her seeing nothing of Captain Tilney? Is he safe only in solitude? Or is her heart constant to him only when unsolicited by anyone else? He cannot think this—and you may be sure that he would not have you think it. I will not say, 'Do not be uneasy,' because I know that you are so, at this moment; but be as little uneasy as you can. You have no doubt of the mutual attachment of your brother and your friend; depend upon it, therefore, that real jealousy never can exist between them; depend upon it that no disagreement between them can be of any duration. Their hearts are open to each other, as neither heart can be to you; they know exactly what is required and what can be borne; and you may be certain that one will never tease the other beyond what is known to be pleasant."

Perceiving her still to look doubtful and grave, he added, "Though Frederick does not leave Bath with us, he will probably remain but a very short time, perhaps only a few days behind us. His leave of absence will soon expire, and he must return to his regiment. And what will then be their acquaintance? The mess-room will drink Isabella Thorpe for a fortnight, and she will laugh with your brother over poor Tilney's passion for a month."

Catherine would contend no longer against comfort. She had resisted its approaches during the whole length of a speech, but it now carried her captive. Henry Tilney must know best. She blamed herself for the extent of her fears, and resolved never to think so seriously on the subject again.

Her resolution was supported by Isabella's behaviour in their parting interview. The Thorpes spent the last evening of Catherine's stay in Pulteney Street, and nothing passed between the lovers to excite her uneasiness, or make her quit them in apprehension. James was in excellent spirits, and Isabella most engagingly placid. Her tenderness for her friend seemed rather the first feeling of her heart; but that at such a moment was allowable; and once she gave her lover a flat contradiction, and once she drew back her hand; but Catherine remembered Henry's instructions, and placed it all to judicious affection. The embraces, tears, and promises of the parting fair ones may be fancied.

CHAPTER XX

Mr. and Mrs. Allen were sorry to lose their young friend, whose good humour and cheerfulness had made her a valuable companion, and in the promotion of whose enjoyment their own had been gently increased. Her happiness in going with Miss Tilney, however, prevented their wishing it otherwise; and, as they were to remain only one more week in Bath themselves, her quitting them now would not long be felt. Mr. Allen attended her to Milsom Street, where she was to breakfast, and saw her seated with the kindest welcome among her new friends; but so great was her agitation in finding herself as one of the family, and so fearful was she of not doing exactly what was right, and of not being able to preserve their good opinion, that, in the embarrassment of the first five minutes, she could almost have wished to return with him to Pulteney Street.

Miss Tilney's manners and Henry's smile soon did away some of her unpleasant feelings; but still she was far from being at ease; nor could the incessant attentions of the general himself entirely reassure her. Nay, perverse as it seemed, she doubted whether she might not have felt less, had she been less attended to. His anxiety for her comfort—his continual solicitations that she would eat, and his often-expressed fears of her seeing nothing to her taste—though never in her life before had she beheld half such variety on a breakfast-table—made it impossible for her to forget for a moment that she was a visitor. She felt utterly unworthy of such respect, and knew not how to reply to it. Her tranquillity was not improved by the general's impatience for the appearance of his eldest son, nor by the displeasure he expressed at his laziness when Captain Tilney at last came down. She was quite pained by the severity of his father's reproof, which seemed disproportionate to the offence; and much was her concern increased when she found herself the principal cause of the lecture, and that his tardiness was chiefly resented from being disrespectful to her. This was placing her in a very uncomfortable situation, and she felt great compassion for Captain Tilney, without being able to hope for his goodwill.

He listened to his father in silence, and attempted not any defence, which confirmed her in fearing that the inquietude of his mind, on Isabella's account, might, by keeping him long sleepless, have been the real cause of his rising late. It was the first time of her being decidedly in his company, and she had hoped to be now able to form her opinion of him; but she scarcely heard his voice while his father remained in the room; and even afterwards, so much were his spirits affected, she could distinguish nothing but these words, in a whisper to Eleanor, "How glad I shall be when you are all off."

The bustle of going was not pleasant. The clock struck ten while the trunks were carrying down, and the general had fixed to be out of Milsom Street by that hour. His greatcoat, instead of being brought for him to put on directly, was spread out in the curricle in which he was to accompany his son. The middle seat of the chaise was not drawn out, though there were three people to go in it, and his daughter's maid had so crowded it with parcels that Miss Morland would not have room to sit; and, so much was he influenced by this apprehension when he handed her in, that she had some difficulty in saving her own new writing-desk from being thrown out into the street. At last, however, the door was closed upon the three females, and they set off at the sober pace in which the handsome, highly fed four horses of a gentleman usually perform a journey of thirty miles: such was the distance of Northanger from Bath, to be now divided into two equal stages. Catherine's spirits revived as they drove from the door; for with Miss Tilney she felt no restraint; and, with the interest of a road entirely new to her, of an abbey before, and a curricle behind, she caught the last view of Bath without any regret, and met with every milestone before she expected it. The tediousness of a two hours' wait at Petty France, in which there was nothing to be done but to eat without being hungry, and loiter about without anything to see, next followed—and her admiration of the style in which they travelled, of the fashionable chaise and four—postilions handsomely liveried, rising so regularly in their stirrups, and numerous outriders properly mounted, sunk a little under this consequent inconvenience. Had their party been perfectly agreeable, the delay would have been nothing; but General Tilney, though so charming a man, seemed always a check upon his children's spirits, and scarcely anything was said but by himself; the observation of which, with his discontent at whatever the inn afforded, and his angry impatience at the waiters, made Catherine grow every moment more in awe of him, and appeared to lengthen the two hours into four. At last, however, the order of release was given; and much was Catherine then surprised by the general's proposal of her taking his place in his son's curricle for the rest of the journey: "the day was fine, and he was anxious for her seeing as much of the country as possible."

The remembrance of Mr. Allen's opinion, respecting young men's open carriages, made her blush at the mention of such a plan, and her first thought was to decline it; but her second was of greater deference for General Tilney's judgment; he could not propose anything improper for her; and, in the course of a few minutes, she found herself with Henry in the curricle, as happy a being as ever existed. A very short trial convinced her that a curricle was the prettiest equipage in the world; the chaise and four wheeled off with some grandeur, to be sure, but it was a heavy and troublesome business, and she could not easily forget its having stopped two hours at Petty France. Half the time would have been enough for the curricle, and so nimbly were the light horses disposed to move, that, had not the general chosen to have his own carriage lead the way, they could have passed it with ease in half a minute. But the merit of the curricle did not all belong to the horses; Henry drove so well—so quietly—without making any disturbance, without parading to her, or swearing at them: so different from the only gentleman-coachman whom it was in her power to compare him with! And then his hat sat so well, and the innumerable capes of his greatcoat looked so becomingly important! To be driven by him, next to being dancing with him, was certainly the greatest happiness in the world. In addition to every other delight, she had now that of listening to her own praise; of being thanked at least, on his sister's account, for her kindness in thus becoming her visitor; of hearing it ranked as real friendship, and described as creating real gratitude. His sister, he said, was uncomfortably circumstanced—she had no female companion—and, in the frequent absence of her father, was sometimes without any companion at all.

"But how can that be?" said Catherine. "Are not you with her?"

"Northanger is not more than half my home; I have an establishment at my own house in Woodston, which is nearly twenty miles from my father's, and some of my time is necessarily spent there."

"How sorry you must be for that!"

"I am always sorry to leave Eleanor."

"Yes; but besides your affection for her, you must be so fond of the abbey! After being used to such a home as the abbey, an ordinary parsonage-house must be very disagreeable."

He smiled, and said, "You have formed a very favourable idea of the abbey."

"To be sure, I have. Is not it a fine old place, just like what one reads about?"

"And are you prepared to encounter all the horrors that a building such as 'what one reads about' may produce? Have you a stout heart? Nerves fit for sliding panels and tapestry?"

"Oh! yes—I do not think I should be easily frightened, because there would be so many people in the house—and besides, it has never been uninhabited and left deserted for years, and then the family come back to it unawares, without giving any notice, as generally happens."

"No, certainly. We shall not have to explore our way into a hall dimly lighted by the expiring embers of a wood fire—nor be obliged to spread our beds on the floor of a room without windows, doors, or furniture. But you must be aware that when a young lady is (by whatever means) introduced into a dwelling of this kind, she is always lodged apart from the rest of the family. While they snugly repair to their own end of the house, she is formally conducted by Dorothy, the ancient housekeeper, up a different staircase, and along many gloomy passages, into an apartment never used since some cousin or kin died in it about twenty years before. Can you stand such a ceremony as this? Will not your mind misgive you when you find yourself in this gloomy chamber—too lofty and extensive for you, with only the feeble rays of a single lamp to take in its size—its walls hung with tapestry exhibiting figures as large as life, and the bed, of dark green stuff or purple velvet, presenting even a funereal appearance? Will not your heart sink within you?"

"Oh! But this will not happen to me, I am sure."

"How fearfully will you examine the furniture of your apartment! And what will you discern? Not tables, toilettes, wardrobes, or drawers, but on one side perhaps the remains of a broken lute, on the other a ponderous chest which no efforts can open, and over the fireplace the portrait of some handsome warrior, whose features will so incomprehensibly strike you, that you will not be able to withdraw your eyes from it. Dorothy, meanwhile, no less struck by your appearance, gazes on you in great agitation, and drops a few unintelligible hints. To raise your spirits, moreover, she gives you reason to suppose that the part of the abbey you inhabit is undoubtedly haunted, and informs you that you will not have a single domestic within call. With this parting cordial she curtsies off—you listen to the sound of her receding footsteps as long as the last echo can reach you—and when, with fainting spirits, you attempt to fasten your door, you discover, with increased alarm, that it has no lock."

"Oh! Mr. Tilney, how frightful! This is just like a book! But it cannot really happen to me. I am sure your housekeeper is not really Dorothy. Well, what then?"

"Nothing further to alarm perhaps may occur the first night. After surmounting your *unconquerable* horror of the bed, you will retire to rest, and get a few hours' unquiet slumber. But on the second, or at farthest the *third* night after your arrival, you will probably have a violent storm. Peals of thunder so loud as to seem to shake the edifice to its foundation will roll round the neighbouring mountains—and during the frightful gusts of wind which accompany it, you will probably think you discern (for your lamp is not extinguished) one part of the hanging more violently agitated than the rest. Unable of course to repress your curiosity in so favourable a moment for indulging it, you will instantly arise, and throwing your dressing-gown around you, proceed to examine this mystery. After a very short search, you will discover a division in the tapestry so artfully constructed as to defy the minutest inspection, and on opening it, a door will immediately appear—which door, being only secured by massy bars and a padlock, you will, after a few efforts, succeed in opening—and, with your lamp in your hand, will pass through it into a small vaulted room."

"No, indeed; I should be too much frightened to do any such thing."

"What! Not when Dorothy has given you to understand that there is a secret subterraneous communication between your apartment and the chapel of St. Anthony, scarcely two miles off? Could you shrink from so simple an adventure? No, no, you will proceed into this small vaulted room, and through this into several others, without perceiving anything very remarkable in either. In one perhaps there may be a dagger, in another a few drops of blood, and in a third the remains of some instruments of torture; but there being nothing in all this out of the common way, and your lamp being nearly exhausted, you will return towards your own apartment. In repassing through the small vaulted room, however, your eyes will be attracted towards a large, old-fashioned cabinet of ebony and gold, which, though narrowly examining the furniture before, you had passed unnoticed. Impelled by an irresistible presentiment, you will eagerly advance to it, unlock its folding doors, and search into every drawer— but for some time without discovering anything of importance—perhaps nothing but a considerable hoard of diamonds. At last, however, by touching a secret spring, an inner compartment will open—a roll of paper appears—you seize it—it contains many sheets of manuscript—you hasten with the precious treasure into your own chamber, but scarcely have you been able to decipher 'Oh! Thou— whomsoever thou mayst be, into whose hands these memoirs of the wretched Matilda may fall'—when your lamp suddenly expires in the socket, and leaves you in total darkness."

"Oh! No, no—do not say so. Well, go on."

But Henry was too much amused by the interest he had raised to be able to carry it farther; he could no longer command solemnity either of subject or voice, and was obliged to entreat her to use her own fancy in the perusal of Matilda's woes. Catherine, recollecting herself, grew ashamed of her eagerness, and began earnestly to assure him that her attention had been fixed without the smallest apprehension of really meeting with what he related. "Miss Tilney, she was sure, would never put her into such a chamber as he had described! She was not at all afraid."

As they drew near the end of their journey, her impatience for a sight of the abbey—for some time suspended by his conversation on subjects very different—returned in full force, and every bend in the road was expected with solemn awe to afford a glimpse of its massy walls of grey stone, rising amidst a grove of ancient oaks, with the last beams of the sun playing in beautiful splendour on its high Gothic windows. But so low did the building stand, that she found herself passing through the great gates of the lodge into the very grounds of Northanger, without having discerned even an antique chimney.

She knew not that she had any right to be surprised, but there was a something in this mode of approach which she certainly had not expected. To pass between lodges of a modern appearance, to find herself with such ease in the very precincts of the abbey, and driven so rapidly along a smooth, level road of fine gravel, without obstacle, alarm, or solemnity of any kind, struck her as odd and inconsistent. She was not long at leisure, however, for such considerations. A sudden scud of rain, driving full in her face, made it impossible for her to observe anything further, and fixed all her thoughts on the welfare of her new straw bonnet; and she was actually under the abbey walls, was springing, with Henry's assistance, from the carriage, was beneath the shelter of the old porch, and had even passed on to the hall, where her friend and the general were waiting to welcome her, without feeling one awful foreboding of future misery to herself, or one moment's suspicion of any past scenes of horror being acted within the solemn edifice. The breeze had not seemed to waft the sighs of the murdered to her; it had wafted nothing worse than a thick mizzling rain; and having given a good shake to her habit, she was ready to be shown into the common drawing-room, and capable of considering where she was.

An abbey! Yes, it was delightful to be really in an abbey! But she doubted, as she looked round the room, whether anything within her observation would have given her the consciousness. The furniture was in all the profusion and elegance of modern taste. The fireplace, where she had expected the ample width and ponderous carving of former times, was contracted to a Rumford, with slabs of plain though handsome marble, and ornaments over it of the prettiest English china. The windows, to which she looked with peculiar dependence, from having heard the general talk of his preserving them in their Gothic form with reverential care, were yet less what her fancy had portrayed. To be sure, the pointed arch was preserved—the form of them was Gothic—they might be even casements—but every pane was so large, so clear, so light! To an imagination which had hoped for the smallest divisions, and the heaviest stone-work, for painted glass, dirt, and cobwebs, the difference was very distressing.

The general, perceiving how her eye was employed, began to talk of the smallness of the room and simplicity of the furniture, where everything, being for daily use, pretended only to comfort, etc.; flattering himself, however, that there were some apartments in the Abbey not unworthy her notice—and was proceeding to mention the costly gilding of one in particular, when, taking out his watch, he stopped short to pronounce it with surprise within twenty minutes of five! This seemed the word of separation, and Catherine found herself hurried away by Miss Tilney in such a manner as convinced her that the strictest punctuality to the family hours would be expected at Northanger.

Returning through the large and lofty hall, they ascended a broad staircase of shining oak, which, after many flights and many landing-places, brought them upon a long, wide gallery. On one side it had a range of doors, and it was lighted on the other by windows which Catherine had only time to discover looked into a quadrangle, before Miss Tilney led the way into a chamber, and scarcely staying to hope she would find it comfortable, left her with an anxious entreaty that she would make as little alteration as possible in her dress.

CHAPTER XXI

A moment's glance was enough to satisfy Catherine that her apartment was very unlike the one which Henry had endeavoured to alarm her by the description of it. It was by no means unreasonably large, and contained neither tapestry nor velvet. The walls were papered, the floor was carpeted; the windows were neither less perfect nor more dim than those of the drawing-room below; the furniture, though not of the latest fashion, was handsome and comfortable, and the air of the room altogether far from uncheerful. Her heart instantaneously at ease on this point, she resolved to lose no time in particular examination of anything, as she greatly dreaded disobliging the general by any delay. Her habit therefore was thrown off with all possible haste, and she was preparing to unpin the linen package, which the chaise-seat had conveyed for her immediate accommodation, when her eye suddenly fell on a large high chest, standing back in a deep recess on one side of the fireplace. The sight of it made her start; and, forgetting everything else, she stood gazing on it in motionless wonder, while these thoughts crossed her:

"This is strange indeed! I did not expect such a sight as this! An immense heavy chest! What can it hold? Why should it be placed here? Pushed back too, as if meant to be out of sight! I will look into it—cost me what it may, I will look into it—and directly too—by daylight. If I stay till evening my candle may go out." She advanced and examined it closely: it was of cedar, curiously inlaid with some darker wood, and raised, about a foot from the ground, on a carved stand of the same. The lock was silver, though tarnished from age; at each end were the imperfect remains of handles also of silver, broken perhaps prematurely by some strange violence; and, on the centre of the lid, was a mysterious cipher, in the same metal. Catherine bent over it intently, but without being able to distinguish anything with certainty.

She could not, in whatever direction she took it, believe the last letter to be a *T;* and yet that it should be anything else in that house was a circumstance to raise no common degree of astonishment. If not originally theirs, by what strange events could it have fallen into the Tilney family?

Her fearful curiosity was every moment growing greater; and seizing, with trembling hands, the hasp of the lock, she resolved at all hazards to satisfy herself at least as to its contents. With difficulty, for something seemed to resist her efforts, she raised the lid a few inches; but at that moment a sudden knocking at the door of the room made her, starting, quit her hold, and the lid closed with alarming violence. This ill-timed intruder was Miss Tilney's maid, sent by her mistress to be of use to Miss Morland; and though Catherine immediately dismissed her, it recalled her to the sense of what she ought to be doing, and forced her, in spite of her anxious desire to penetrate this mystery, to proceed in her dressing without further delay. Her progress was not quick, for her thoughts and her eyes were still bent on the object so well calculated to interest and alarm; and though she dared not waste a moment upon a second attempt, she could not remain many paces from the chest. At length, however, having slipped one arm into her gown, her toilette seemed so nearly finished that the impatience of her curiosity might safely be indulged. One moment surely might be spared; and, so desperate should be the exertion of her strength, that, unless secured by supernatural means, the lid in one moment should be thrown back. With this spirit she sprang forward, and her confidence did not deceive her. Her resolute effort threw back the lid, and gave to her astonished eyes the view of a white cotton counterpane, properly folded, reposing at one end of the chest in undisputed possession!

She was gazing on it with the first blush of surprise when Miss Tilney, anxious for her friend's being ready, entered the room, and to the rising shame of having harboured for some minutes an absurd expectation, was then added the shame of being caught in so idle a search. "That is a curious old chest, is not it?" said Miss Tilney, as Catherine hastily closed it and turned away to the glass. "It is impossible to say how many generations it has been here. How it came to be first put in this room I know not, but I have not had it moved, because I thought it might sometimes be of use in holding hats and bonnets. The worst of it is that its weight makes it difficult to open. In that corner, however, it is at least out of the way."

Catherine had no leisure for speech, being at once blushing, tying her gown, and forming wise resolutions with the most violent dispatch. Miss Tilney gently hinted her fear of being late; and in half a minute they ran downstairs together, in an alarm not wholly unfounded, for General Tilney was pacing the drawing-room, his watch in his hand, and having, on the very instant of their entering, pulled the bell with violence, ordered "Dinner to be on the table *directly!*"

Catherine trembled at the emphasis with which he spoke, and sat pale and breathless, in a most humble mood, concerned for his children, and detesting old chests; and the general, recovering his politeness as he looked at her, spent the rest of his time in scolding his daughter for so foolishly hurrying her fair friend, who was absolutely out of breath from haste, when there was not the least occasion for hurry in the world: but Catherine could not at all get over the double distress of having involved her friend in a lecture and been a great simpleton herself, till they were happily seated at the dinner-table, when the general's complacent smiles, and a good appetite of her own, restored her to peace. The dining-parlour was a noble room, suitable in its dimensions to a much larger drawing-room than the one in common use, and fitted up in a style of luxury and expense which was almost lost on the unpractised eye of Catherine, who saw little more than its spaciousness and the number of their attendants. Of the former, she spoke aloud her admiration; and the general, with a very gracious countenance, acknowledged that it was by no means an ill-sized room, and further confessed that, though as careless on such subjects as most people, he did look upon a tolerably large eating-room as one of the necessaries of life; he supposed, however, "that she must have been used to much better-sized apartments at Mr. Allen's?"

"No, indeed," was Catherine's honest assurance; "Mr. Allen's dining-parlour was not more than half as large," and she had never seen so large a room as this in her life. The general's good humour increased. Why, as he *had* such rooms, he thought it would be simple not to make use of them; but, upon his honour, he believed there might be more comfort in rooms of only half their size. Mr. Allen's house, he was sure, must be exactly of the true size for rational happiness.

The evening passed without any further disturbance, and, in the occasional absence of General Tilney, with much positive cheerfulness. It was only in his presence that Catherine felt the smallest fatigue from her journey; and even then, even in moments of languor or restraint, a sense of general happiness preponderated, and she could think of her friends in Bath without one wish of being with them.

The night was stormy; the wind had been rising at intervals the whole afternoon; and by the time the party broke up, it blew and rained violently. Catherine, as she crossed the hall, listened to the tempest with sensations of awe; and, when she heard it rage round a corner of the ancient building and close with sudden fury a distant door, felt for the first time that she was really in an abbey. Yes, these were characteristic sounds; they brought to her recollection a countless variety of dreadful situations and horrid scenes, which such buildings had witnessed, and such storms ushered in; and most heartily did she rejoice in the happier circumstances attending her entrance within walls so solemn! *She* had nothing to dread from midnight assassins or drunken gallants. Henry had certainly been only in jest in what he had told her that morning. In a house so furnished, and so guarded, she could have nothing to explore or to suffer, and might go to her bedroom as securely as if it had been her own chamber at Fullerton. Thus wisely fortifying her mind, as she proceeded upstairs, she was enabled, especially on perceiving that Miss Tilney slept only two doors from her, to enter her room with a tolerably stout heart; and her spirits were immediately assisted by the cheerful blaze of a wood fire. "How much better is this," said she, as she walked to the fenders—"how much better to find a fire ready lit, than to have to wait shivering in the cold till all the family are in bed, as so many poor girls have been obliged to do, and then to have a faithful old servant frightening one by coming in with a faggot! How glad I am that Northanger is what it is! If it had been like some other places, I do not know that, in such a night as this, I could have answered for my courage: but now, to be sure, there is nothing to alarm one."

She looked round the room. The window curtains seemed in motion. It could be nothing but the violence of the wind penetrating through the divisions of the shutters; and she stepped boldly forward, carelessly humming a tune, to assure herself of its being so, peeped courageously behind each curtain, saw nothing on either low window seat to scare her, and on placing a hand against the shutter, felt the strongest conviction of the wind's force. A glance at the old chest, as she turned away from this examination, was not without its use; she scorned the causeless fears of an idle fancy, and began with a most happy indifference to prepare herself for bed. "She should take her time; she should not hurry herself; she did not care if she were the last person up in the house. But she would not make up her fire; *that* would seem cowardly, as if she wished for the protection of light after she were in bed." The fire therefore died away, and Catherine, having spent the best part of an hour in her arrangements, was beginning to think of stepping into bed, when, on giving a parting glance round the room, she was struck by the appearance of a high, old-fashioned black cabinet, which, though in a situation conspicuous enough, had never caught her notice before. Henry's words, his description of the ebony cabinet which was to escape her observation at first, immediately rushed across her; and though there could be nothing really in it, there was something whimsical, it was certainly a very remarkable coincidence! She took her candle and looked closely at the cabinet. It was not absolutely ebony and gold; but it was japan, black and yellow japan of the handsomest kind; and as she held her candle, the yellow had very much the effect of gold. The key was in the door, and she had a strange fancy to look into it; not, however, with the smallest expectation of finding anything, but it was so very odd, after what Henry had said. In short, she could not sleep till she had examined it. So, placing the candle with great caution on a chair, she seized the key with a very tremulous hand and tried to turn it; but it resisted her utmost strength. Alarmed, but not discouraged, she tried it another way; a bolt flew, and she believed herself successful; but how strangely mysterious! The door was still immovable. She paused a moment in breathless wonder. The wind roared down the chimney, the rain beat in torrents against the windows, and everything seemed to speak the awfulness of her situation. To retire to bed, however, unsatisfied on such a point, would be vain, since sleep must be impossible with the consciousness of a cabinet so mysteriously closed in her immediate vicinity. Again, therefore, she applied herself to the key, and after moving it in every possible way for some instants with the determined celerity of hope's last effort, the door suddenly yielded to her hand: her heart leaped with exultation at such a victory, and having thrown open each folding door, the second being secured only by bolts of less wonderful construction than the lock, though in that her eyes could not discern anything unusual, a double range of small drawers appeared in view, with some larger drawers above and below them; and in the centre, a small door, closed also with a lock and key, secured in all probability a cavity of importance.

Catherine's heart beat quick, but her courage did not fail her. With a cheek flushed by hope, and an eye straining with curiosity, her fingers grasped the handle of a drawer and drew it forth. It was entirely empty. With less alarm and greater eagerness she seized a second, a third, a fourth; each was equally empty. Not one was left unsearched, and in not one was anything found. Well read in the art of concealing a treasure, the possibility of false linings to the drawers did not escape her, and she felt round each with anxious acuteness in vain. The place in the middle alone remained now unexplored; and though she had "never from the first had the smallest idea of finding anything in any part of the cabinet, and was not in the least disappointed at her ill success thus far, it would be foolish not to examine it thoroughly while she was about it." It was some time however before she could unfasten the door, the same difficulty occurring in the management of this inner lock as of the outer; but at length it did open; and not vain, as hitherto, was her search; her quick eyes directly fell on a roll of paper pushed back into the further part of the cavity, apparently for concealment, and her feelings at that moment were indescribable. Her heart fluttered, her knees trembled, and her cheeks grew pale. She seized, with an unsteady hand, the precious manuscript, for half a glance sufficed to ascertain written characters; and while she acknowledged with awful sensations this striking exemplification of what Henry had foretold, resolved instantly to peruse every line before she attempted to rest.

The dimness of the light her candle emitted made her turn to it with alarm; but there was no danger of its sudden extinction; it had yet some hours to burn; and that she might not have any greater difficulty in distinguishing the writing than what its ancient date might occasion, she hastily snuffed it. Alas! It was snuffed and extinguished in one. A lamp could not have expired with more awful effect. Catherine, for a few moments, was motionless with horror. It was done completely; not a remnant of light in the wick could give hope to the rekindling breath. Darkness impenetrable and immovable filled the room. A violent gust of wind, rising with sudden fury, added fresh horror to the moment. Catherine trembled from head to foot. In the pause which succeeded, a sound like receding footsteps and the closing of a distant door struck on her affrighted ear. Human nature could support no more. A cold sweat stood on her forehead, the manuscript fell from her hand, and groping her way to the bed, she jumped hastily in, and sought some suspension of agony by creeping far underneath the clothes. To close her eyes in sleep that night, she felt must be entirely out of the question. With a curiosity so justly awakened, and feelings in every way so agitated, repose must be absolutely impossible. The storm too abroad so dreadful! She had not been used to feel alarm from wind, but now every blast seemed fraught with awful intelligence. The manuscript so wonderfully found, so wonderfully accomplishing the morning's prediction, how was it to be accounted for? What could it contain? To whom could it relate? By what means could it have been so long concealed? And how singularly strange that it should fall to her lot to discover it! Till she had made herself mistress of its contents, however, she could have neither repose nor comfort; and with the sun's first rays she was determined to peruse it. But many were the tedious hours which must yet intervene. She shuddered, tossed about in her bed, and envied every quiet sleeper. The storm still raged, and various were the noises, more terrific even than the wind, which struck at intervals on her startled ear. The very curtains of her bed seemed at one moment in motion, and at another the lock of her door was agitated, as if by the attempt of somebody to enter. Hollow murmurs seemed to creep along the gallery, and more than once her blood was chilled by the sound of distant moans. Hour after hour passed away, and the wearied Catherine had heard three proclaimed by all the clocks in the house before the tempest subsided or she unknowingly fell fast asleep.

CHAPTER XXII

THE housemaid's folding back her window-shutters at eight o'clock the next day was the sound which first roused Catherine; and she opened her eyes, wondering that they could ever have been closed, on objects of cheerfulness; her fire was already burning, and a bright morning had succeeded the tempest of the night. Instantaneously, with the consciousness of existence, returned her recollection of the manuscript; and springing from the bed in the very moment of the maid's going away, she eagerly collected every scattered sheet which had burst from the roll on its falling to the ground, and flew back to enjoy the luxury of their perusal on her pillow. She now plainly saw that she must not expect a manuscript of equal length with the generality of what she had shuddered over in books, for the roll, seeming to consist entirely of small disjointed sheets, was altogether but of trifling size, and much less than she had supposed it to be at first.

Her greedy eye glanced rapidly over a page. She started at its import. Could it be possible, or did not her senses play her false? An inventory of linen, in coarse and modern characters, seemed all that was before her! If the evidence of sight might be trusted, she held a washing-bill in her hand. She seized another sheet, and saw the same articles with little variation; a third, a fourth, and a fifth presented nothing new. Shirts, stockings, cravats, and waistcoats faced her in each. Two others, penned by the same hand, marked an expenditure scarcely more interesting, in letters, hair-powder, shoe-string, and breeches-ball. And the larger sheet, which had enclosed the rest, seemed by its first cramp line, "To poultice chestnut mare"—a farrier's bill! Such was the collection of papers (left perhaps, as she could then suppose, by the negligence of a servant in the place whence she had taken them) which had filled her with expectation and alarm, and robbed her of half her night's rest! She felt humbled to the dust. Could not the adventure of the chest have taught her wisdom? A corner of it, catching her eye as she lay, seemed to rise up in judgment against her. Nothing could now be clearer than the absurdity of her recent fancies. To suppose that a manuscript of many generations back could have remained undiscovered in a room such as that, so modern, so habitable!—or that she should be the first to possess the skill of unlocking a cabinet, the key of which was open to all!

How could she have so imposed on herself? Heaven forbid that Henry Tilney should ever know her folly! And it was in a great measure his own doing, for had not the cabinet appeared so exactly to agree with his description of her adventures, she should never have felt the smallest curiosity about it. This was the only comfort that occurred. Impatient to get rid of those hateful evidences of her folly, those detestable papers then scattered over the bed, she rose directly, and folding them up as nearly as possible in the same shape as before, returned them to the same spot within the cabinet, with a very hearty wish that no untoward accident might ever bring them forward again, to disgrace her even with herself.

Why the locks should have been so difficult to open, however, was still something remarkable, for she could now manage them with perfect ease. In this there was surely something mysterious, and she indulged in the flattering suggestion for half a minute, till the possibility of the door's having been at first unlocked, and of being herself its fastener, darted into her head, and cost her another blush.

She got away as soon as she could from a room in which her conduct produced such unpleasant reflections, and found her way with all speed to the breakfast-parlour, as it had been pointed out to her by Miss Tilney the evening before. Henry was alone in it; and his immediate hope of her having been undisturbed by the tempest, with an arch reference to the character of the building they inhabited, was rather distressing. For the world would she not have her weakness suspected, and yet, unequal to an absolute falsehood, was constrained to acknowledge that the wind had kept her awake a little. "But we have a charming morning after it," she added, desiring to get rid of the subject; "and storms and sleeplessness are nothing when they are over. What beautiful hyacinths! I have just learnt to love a hyacinth."

"And how might you learn? By accident or argument?"

"Your sister taught me; I cannot tell how. Mrs. Allen used to take pains, year after year, to make me like them; but I never could, till I saw them the other day in Milsom Street; I am naturally indifferent about flowers."

"But now you love a hyacinth. So much the better. You have gained a new source of enjoyment, and it is well to have as many holds upon happiness as possible. Besides, a taste for flowers is always desirable in your sex, as a means of getting you out of doors, and tempting you to more frequent exercise than you would otherwise take. And though the love of a hyacinth may be rather domestic, who can tell, the sentiment once raised, but you may in time come to love a rose?"

"But I do not want any such pursuit to get me out of doors. The pleasure of walking and breathing fresh air is enough for me, and in fine weather I am out more than half my time. Mamma says I am never within."

"At any rate, however, I am pleased that you have learnt to love a hyacinth. The mere habit of learning to love is the thing; and a teachableness of disposition in a young lady is a great blessing. Has my sister a pleasant mode of instruction?"

Catherine was saved the embarrassment of attempting an answer by the entrance of the general, whose smiling compliments announced a happy state of mind, but whose gentle hint of sympathetic early rising did not advance her composure.

The elegance of the breakfast set forced itself on Catherine's notice when they were seated at table; and, luckily, it had been the general's choice. He was enchanted by her approbation of his taste, confessed it to be neat and simple, thought it right to encourage the manufacture of his country; and for his part, to his uncritical palate, the tea was as well flavoured from the clay of Staffordshire, as from that of Dresden or Sêve. But this was quite an old set, purchased two years ago. The manufacture was much improved since that time; he had seen some beautiful specimens when last in town, and had he not been perfectly without vanity of that kind, might have been tempted to order a new set. He trusted, however, that an opportunity might ere long occur of selecting one—though not for himself. Catherine was probably the only one of the party who did not understand him.

Shortly after breakfast Henry left them for Woodston, where business required and would keep him two or three days. They all attended in the hall to see him mount his horse, and immediately on re-entering the breakfast-room, Catherine walked to a window in the hope of catching another glimpse of his figure. "This is a somewhat heavy call upon your brother's fortitude," observed the general to Eleanor. "Woodston will make but a sombre appearance today."

"Is it a pretty place?" asked Catherine.

"What say you, Eleanor? Speak your opinion, for ladies can best tell the taste of ladies in regard to places as well as men. I think it would be acknowledged by the most impartial eye to have many recommendations. The house stands among fine meadows facing the south-east, with an excellent kitchen-garden in the same aspect; the walls surrounding which I built and stocked myself about ten years ago, for the benefit of my son. It is a family living, Miss Morland; and the property in the place being chiefly my own, you may believe I take care that it shall not be a bad one. Did Henry's income depend solely on this living, he would not be ill-provided for. Perhaps it may seem odd, that with only two younger children, I should think any profession necessary for him; and certainly there are moments when we could all wish him disengaged from every tie of business. But though I may not exactly make converts of you young ladies, I am sure your father, Miss Morland, would agree with me in thinking it expedient to give every young man some employment. The money is nothing, it is not an object, but employment is the thing. Even Frederick, my eldest son, you see, who will perhaps inherit as considerable a landed property as any private man in the county, has his profession."

The imposing effect of this last argument was equal to his wishes. The silence of the lady proved it to be unanswerable.

Something had been said the evening before of her being shown over the house, and he now offered himself as her conductor; and though Catherine had hoped to explore it accompanied only by his daughter, it was a proposal of too much happiness in itself, under any circumstances, not to be gladly accepted; for she had been already eighteen hours in the abbey, and had seen only a few of its rooms. The

netting-box, just leisurely drawn forth, was closed with joyful haste, and she was ready to attend him in a moment.
"And when they had gone over the house, he promised himself moreover the pleasure of accompanying her into the
shrubberies and garden." She curtsied her acquiescence.
"But perhaps it might be more agreeable to her to make
those her first object. The weather was at present favourable,
and at this time of year, the uncertainty was very great of its
continuing so. Which would she prefer? He was equally at
her service. Which did his daughter think would most accord
with her fair friend's wishes? But he thought he could discern. Yes, he certainly read in Miss Morland's eyes a judicious desire of making use of the present smiling weather.
But when did she judge amiss? The abbey would be always
safe and dry. He yielded implicitly, and would fetch his hat
and attend them in a moment." He left the room, and Catherine, with a disappointed, anxious face, began to speak of
her unwillingness that he should be taking them out of doors
against his own inclination, under a mistaken idea of pleasing her; but she was stopped by Miss Tilney's saying, with
a little confusion, "I believe it will be wisest to take the
morning while it is so fine; and do not be uneasy on my father's account; he always walks out at this time of day."

Catherine did not exactly know how this was to be understood. Why was Miss Tilney embarrassed? Could there be
any unwillingness on the general's side to show her over the
abbey? The proposal was his own. And was not it odd that
he should *always* take his walk so early? Neither her father
nor Mr. Allen did so. It was certainly very provoking. She
was all impatience to see the house, and had scarcely any
curiosity about the grounds. If Henry had been with them indeed! But now she should not know what was picturesque
when she saw it. Such were her thoughts, but she kept them
to herself, and put on her bonnet in patient discontent.

She was struck, however, beyond her expectation, by the
grandeur of the abbey, as she saw it for the first time from
the lawn. The whole building enclosed a large court; and
two sides of the quadrangle, rich in Gothic ornaments, stood
forward for admiration. The remainder was shut off by
knolls of old trees, or luxuriant plantations, and the steep
woody hills rising behind, to give it shelter, were beautiful
even in the leafless month of March. Catherine had seen
nothing to compare with it; and her feelings of delight were

so strong, that without waiting for any better authority, she boldly burst forth in wonder and praise. The general listened with assenting gratitude; and it seemed as if his own estimation of Northanger had waited unfixed till that hour.

The kitchen-garden was to be next admired, and he led the way to it across a small portion of the park.

The number of acres contained in this garden was such as Catherine could not listen to without dismay, being more than double the extent of all Mr. Allen's, as well her father's, including church-yard and orchard. The walls seemed countless in number, endless in length; a village of hot-houses seemed to arise among them, and a whole parish to be at work within the enclosure. The general was flattered by her looks of surprise, which told him almost as plainly, as he soon forced her to tell him in words, that she had never seen any gardens at all equal to them before; and he then modestly owned that, "without any ambition of that sort himself—without any solicitude about it—he did believe them to be unrivalled in the kingdom. If he had a hobby-horse, it was *that*. He loved a garden. Though careless enough in most matters of eating, he loved good fruit—or if he did not, his friends and children did. There were great vexations, however, attending such a garden as his. The utmost care could not always secure the most valuable fruits. The pinery had yielded only one hundred in the last year. Mr. Allen, he supposed, must feel these inconveniences as well as himself."

"No, not at all. Mr. Allen did not care about the garden, and never went into it."

With a triumphant smile of self-satisfaction, the general wished he could do the same, for he never entered his, without being vexed in some way or other, by its falling short of his plan.

"How were Mr. Allen's succession-houses worked?" describing the nature of his own as they entered them.

"Mr. Allen had only one small hot-house, which Mrs. Allen had the use of for her plants in winter, and there was a fire in it now and then."

"He is a happy man!" said the general, with a look of very happy contempt.

Having taken her into every division, and led her under every wall, till she was heartily weary of seeing and wondering, he suffered the girls at last to seize the advantage of an outer door, and then expressing his wish to examine the effect of some recent alterations about the tea-house, proposed it as no unpleasant extension of their walk, if Miss Morland were not tired. "But where are you going, Eleanor? Why do you choose that cold, damp path to it? Miss Morland will get wet. Our best way is across the park."

"This is so favourite a walk of mine," said Miss Tilney, "that I always think it the best and nearest way. But perhaps it may be damp."

It was a narrow winding path through a thick grove of old Scotch firs; and Catherine, struck by its gloomy aspect, and eager to enter it, could not, even by the general's disapprobation, be kept from stepping forward. He perceived her inclination, and having again urged the plea of health in vain, was too polite to make further opposition. He excused himself, however, from attending them: "The rays of the sun were not too cheerful for him, and he would meet them by another course." He turned away; and Catherine was shocked to find how much her spirits were relieved by the separation. The shock, however, being less real than the relief, offered it no injury; and she began to talk with easy gaiety of the delightful melancholy which such a grove inspired.

"I am particularly fond of this spot," said her companion, with a sigh. "It was my mother's favourite walk."

Catherine had never heard Mrs. Tilney mentioned in the family before, and the interest excited by this tender remembrance showed itself directly in her altered countenance, and in the attentive pause with which she waited for something more.

"I used to walk here so often with her!" added Eleanor; "though I never loved it then, as I have loved it since. At that time indeed I used to wonder at her choice. But her memory endears it now."

"And ought it not," reflected Catherine, "to endear it to her husband? Yet the general would not enter it." Miss Tilney continuing silent, she ventured to say, "Her death must have been a great affliction!"

"A great and increasing one," replied the other, in a low voice. "I was only thirteen when it happened; and though I felt my loss perhaps as strongly as one so young could feel it, I did not, I could not, then know what a loss it was." She stopped for a moment, and then added, with great firmness,

"I have no sister, you know—and though Henry—though my brothers are very affectionate, and Henry is a great deal here, which I am most thankful for, it is impossible for me not to be often solitary."

"To be sure you must miss him very much."

"A mother would have been always present. A mother would have been a constant friend; her influence would have been beyond all other."

"Was she a very charming woman? Was she handsome? Was there any picture of her in the abbey? And why had she been so partial to that grove? Was it from dejection of spirits?"—were questions now eagerly poured forth; the first three received a ready affirmative, the two others were passed by; and Catherine's interest in the deceased Mrs. Tilney augmented with every question, whether answered or not. Of her unhappiness in marriage, she felt persuaded. The general certainly had been an unkind husband. He did not love her walk: could he therefore have loved her? And besides, handsome as he was, there was a something in the turn of his features which spoke his not having behaved well to her.

"Her picture, I suppose," blushing at the consummate art of her own question, "hangs in your father's room?"

"No; it was intended for the drawing-room; but my father was dissatisfied with the painting, and for some time it had no place. Soon after her death I obtained it for my own, and hung it in my bed-chamber—where I shall be happy to show it you; it is very like." Here was another proof. A portrait—very like—of a departed wife, not valued by the husband! He must have been dreadfully cruel to her!

Catherine attempted no longer to hide from herself the nature of the feelings which, in spite of all his attentions, he had previously excited; and what had been terror and dislike before, was now absolute aversion. Yes, aversion! His cruelty to such a charming woman made him odious to her. She had often read of such characters, characters which Mr. Allen had been used to call unnatural and overdrawn; but here was proof positive of the contrary.

She had just settled this point when the end of the path brought them directly upon the general; and in spite of all her virtuous indignation, she found herself again obliged to walk with him, listen to him, and even to smile when he smiled. Being no longer able, however, to receive pleasure from the surrounding objects, she soon began to walk with lassitude; the general perceived it, and with a concern for her health, which seemed to reproach her for her opinion of him, was most urgent for returning with his daughter to the house. He would follow them in a quarter of an hour. Again they parted—but Eleanor was called back in half a minute to receive a strict charge against taking her friend round the abbey till his return. This second instance of his anxiety to delay what she so much wished for struck Catherine as very remarkable.

CHAPTER XXIII

AN hour passed away before the general came in, spent, on the part of his young guest, in no very favourable consideration of his character. "This lengthened absence, these solitary rambles, did not speak a mind at ease, or a conscience void of reproach." At length he appeared; and, whatever might have been the gloom of his meditations, he could still smile with *them*. Miss Tilney, understanding in part her friend's curiosity to see the house, soon revived the subject; and her father being, contrary to Catherine's expectations, unprovided with any pretence for further delay, beyond that of stopping five minutes to order refreshments to be in the room by their return, was at last ready to escort them.

They set forward; and, with a grandeur of air, a dignified step, which caught the eye, but could not shake the doubts of the well-read Catherine, he led the way across the hall, through the common drawing-room and one useless antechamber, into a room magnificent both in size and furniture—the real drawing-room, used only with company of consequence. It was very noble—very grand—very charming!—was all that Catherine had to say, for her indiscriminating eye scarcely discerned the colour of the satin; and all minuteness of praise, all praise that had much meaning, was supplied by the general: the costliness or elegance of any room's fitting-up could be nothing to her; she cared for no furniture of a more modern date than the fifteenth century. When the general had satisfied his own curiosity, in a close examination of every well-known ornament, they proceeded into the library, an apartment, in its way, of equal magnificence, exhibiting a collection of books, on which an humble man might have looked with pride. Catherine heard, admired, and wondered with more genuine feeling than before—gathered all that she could from this storehouse of knowledge, by running over the titles of half a shelf, and

was ready to proceed. But suites of apartments did not
spring up with her wishes. Large as was the building, she
had already visited the greatest part; though, on being told
that, with the addition of the kitchen, the six or seven rooms
she had now seen surrounded three sides of the court, she
could scarcely believe it, or overcome the suspicion of there
being many chambers secreted. It was some relief, however,
that they were to return to the rooms in common use, by
passing through a few of less importance, looking into the
court, which, with occasional passages, not wholly unintri-
cate, connected the different sides; and she was further
soothed in her progress by being told that she was treading
what had once been a cloister, having traces of cells pointed
out, and observing several doors that were neither opened
nor explained to her—by finding herself successively in a
billiard-room, and in the general's private apartment, without comprehending their connection, or being able to turn
aright when she left them; and lastly, by passing through a
dark little room, owning Henry's authority, and strewed with
his litter of books, guns, and greatcoats.

From the dining-room, of which, though already seen, and
always to be seen at five o'clock, the general could not forgo
the pleasure of pacing out the length, for the more certain information of Miss Morland, as to what she neither doubted
nor cared for, they proceeded by quick communication to the
kitchen—the ancient kitchen of the convent, rich in the
massy walls and smoke of former days, and in the stoves
and hot closets of the present. The general's improving hand
had not loitered here: every modern invention to facilitate
the labour of the cooks had been adopted within this, their
spacious theatre; and, when the genius of others had failed,
his own had often produced the perfection wanted. His endowments of this spot alone might at any time have placed
him high among the benefactors of the convent.

With the walls of the kitchen ended all the antiquity of the
abbey; the fourth side of the quadrangle having, on account
of its decaying state, been removed by the general's father,
and the present erected in its place. All that was venerable
ceased here. The new building was not only new, but declared itself to be so; intended only for offices, and enclosed
behind by stable-yards, no uniformity of architecture had
been thought necessary. Catherine could have raved at the
hand which had swept away what must have been beyond

the value of all the rest, for the purposes of mere domestic economy; and would willingly have been spared the mortification of a walk through scenes so fallen, had the general allowed it; but if he had a vanity, it was in the arrangement of his offices; and as he was convinced that, to a mind like Miss Morland's, a view of the accommodations and comforts, by which the labours of her inferiors were softened, must always be gratifying, he should make no apology for leading her on. They took a slight survey of all; and Catherine was impressed, beyond her expectation, by their multiplicity and their convenience. The purposes for which a few shapeless pantries and a comfortless scullery were deemed sufficient at Fullerton, were here carried on in appropriate divisions, commodious and roomy. The number of servants continually appearing did not strike her less than the number of their offices. Wherever they went, some pattened girl stopped to curtsy, or some footman in dishabille sneaked off. Yet this was an abbey! How inexpressibly different in these domestic arrangements from such as she had read about— from abbeys and castles, in which, though certainly larger than Northanger, all the dirty work of the house was to be done by two pair of female hands at the utmost. How they could get through it all had often amazed Mrs. Allen; and, when Catherine saw what was necessary here, she began to be amazed herself.

They returned to the hall, that the chief staircase might be ascended, and the beauty of its wood, and ornaments of rich carving might be pointed out: having gained the top, they turned in an opposite direction from the gallery in which her room lay, and shortly entered one on the same plan, but superior in length and breadth. She was here shown successively into three large bed-chambers, with their dressing-rooms, most completely and handsomely fitted up; everything that money and taste could do, to give comfort and elegance to apartments, had been bestowed on these; and, being furnished within the last five years, they were perfect in all that would be generally pleasing, and wanting in all that could give pleasure to Catherine. As they were surveying the last, the general, after slightly naming a few of the distinguished characters by whom they had at times been honoured, turned with a smiling countenance to Catherine, and ventured to hope that henceforward some of their earliest tenants might be "our friends from Fullerton." She felt the unexpected compliment, and deeply regretted the impossibility of thinking well of a man so kindly disposed towards herself, and so full of civility to all her family.

The gallery was terminated by folding doors, which Miss Tilney, advancing, had thrown open, and passed through, and seemed on the point of doing the same by the first door to the left, in another long reach of gallery, when the general, coming forwards, called her hastily, and, as Catherine thought, rather angrily back, demanding whither she were going?—And what was there more to be seen?—Had not Miss Morland already seen all that could be worth her notice?—And did she not suppose her friend might be glad of some refreshment after so much exercise? Miss Tilney drew back directly, and the heavy doors were closed upon the mortified Catherine, who, having seen, in a momentary glance beyond them, a narrower passage, more numerous openings, and symptoms of a winding staircase, believed herself at last within the reach of something worth her notice; and felt, as she unwillingly paced back the gallery, that she would rather be allowed to examine that end of the house than see all the finery of all the rest. The general's evident desire of preventing such an examination was an additional stimulant. Something was certainly to be concealed; her fancy, though it had trespassed lately once or twice, could not mislead her here; and what that something was, a short sentence of Miss Tilney's, as they followed the general at some distance downstairs, seemed to point out: "I was going to take you into what was my mother's room—the room in which she died—" were all her words; but few as they were, they conveyed pages of intelligence to Catherine. It was no wonder that the general should shrink from the sight of such objects as that room must contain; a room in all probability never entered by him since the dreadful scene had passed, which released his suffering wife, and left him to the stings of conscience.

She ventured, when next alone with Eleanor, to express her wish of being permitted to see it, as well as all the rest of that side of the house; and Eleanor promised to attend her there, whenever they should have a convenient hour. Catherine understood her: the general must be watched from home, before that room could be entered. "It remains as it was, I suppose?" said she, in a tone of feeling.

"Yes, entirely."

"And how long ago may it be that your mother died?"

"She has been dead these nine years." And nine years, Catherine knew, was a trifle of time, compared with what generally elapsed after the death of an injured wife, before her room was put to rights.

"You were with her, I suppose, to the last?"

"No," said Miss Tilney, sighing; "I was unfortunately from home. Her illness was sudden and short; and, before I arrived it was all over."

Catherine's blood ran cold with the horrid suggestions which naturally sprang from these words. Could it be possible? Could Henry's father—? And yet how many were the examples to justify even the blackest suspicions! And, when she saw him in the evening, while she worked with her friend, slowly pacing the drawing-room for an hour together in silent thoughtfulness, with downcast eyes and contracted brow, she felt secure from all possibility of wronging him. It was the air and attitude of a Montoni! What could more plainly speak the gloomy workings of a mind not wholly dead to every sense of humanity, in its fearful review of past scenes of guilt? Unhappy man! And the anxiousness of her spirits directed her eyes towards his figure so repeatedly, as to catch Miss Tilney's notice. "My father," she whispered, "often walks about the room in this way; it is nothing unusual."

"So much the worse!" thought Catherine; such ill-timed exercise was of a piece with the strange unseasonableness of his morning walks, and boded nothing good.

After an evening, the little variety and seeming length of which made her peculiarly sensible of Henry's importance among them, she was heartily glad to be dismissed; though it was a look from the general not designed for her observation which sent his daughter to the bell. When the butler would have lit his master's candle, however, he was forbidden. The latter was not going to retire. "I have many pamphlets to finish," said he to Catherine, "before I can close my eyes, and perhaps may be poring over the affairs of the nation for hours after you are asleep. Can either of us be more meetly employed? *My* eyes will be blinding for the good of others, and *yours* preparing by rest for future mischief."

But neither the business alleged, nor the magnificent compliment, could win Catherine from thinking that some very different object must occasion so serious a delay of proper repose. To be kept up for hours, after the family were in bed, by stupid pamphlets was not very likely. There must be some deeper cause: something was to be done which could be done only while the household slept; and the probability that Mrs. Tilney yet lived, shut up for causes unknown, and receiving from the pitiless hands of her husband a nightly supply of coarse food, was the conclusion which necessarily followed. Shocking as was the idea, it was at least better than a death unfairly hastened, as, in the natural course of things, she must ere long be released. The suddenness of her reputed illness, the absence of her daughter, and probably of her other children, at the time—all favoured the supposition of her imprisonment. Its origin—jealousy perhaps, or wanton cruelty—was yet to be unravelled.

In revolving these matters, while she undressed, it suddenly struck her as not unlikely that she might that morning have passed near the very spot of this unfortunate woman's confinement—might have been within a few paces of the cell in which she languished out her days; for what part of the abbey could be more fitted for the purpose than that which yet bore the traces of monastic division? In the high-arched passage, paved with stone, which already she had trodden with peculiar awe, she well remembered the doors of which the general had given no account. To what might not those doors lead? In support of the plausibility of this conjecture, it further occurred to her that the forbidden gallery, in which lay the apartments of the unfortunate Mrs. Tilney, must be, as certainly as her memory could guide her, exactly over this suspected range of cells, and the staircase by the side of those apartments of which she had caught a transient glimpse, communicating by some secret means with those cells, might well have favoured the barbarous proceedings of her husband. Down that staircase she had perhaps been conveyed in a state of well-prepared insensibility!

Catherine sometimes started at the boldness of her own surmises, and sometimes hoped or feared that she had gone too far; but they were supported by such appearances as made their dismissal impossible.

The side of the quadrangle, in which she supposed the guilty scene to be acting, being, according to her belief, just opposite her own, it struck her that, if judiciously watched, some rays of light from the general's lamp might glimmer through the lower windows, as he passed to the prison of his wife; and, twice before she stepped into bed, she stole gently from her room to the corresponding window in the gallery, to see if it appeared; but all abroad was dark, and it must yet be too early. The various ascending noises convinced her that the servants must still be up. Till midnight, she supposed it would be in vain to watch; but then, when the clock had struck twelve, and all was quiet, she would, if not quite appalled by darkness, steal out and look once more. The clock struck twelve—and Catherine had been half an hour asleep.

CHAPTER XXIV

THE next day afforded no opportunity for the proposed examination of the mysterious apartments. It was Sunday, and the whole time between morning and afternoon service was required by the general in exercise abroad or eating cold meat at home; and great as was Catherine's curiosity, her courage was not equal to a wish of exploring them after dinner, either by the fading light of the sky between six and seven o'clock, or by the yet more partial though stronger illumination of a treacherous lamp. The day was unmarked therefore by anything to interest her imagination beyond the sight of a very elegant monument to the memory of Mrs. Tilney, which immediately fronted the family pew. By that her eye was instantly caught and long retained; and the perusal of the highly strained epitaph, in which every virtue was ascribed to her by the inconsolable husband, who must have been in some way or other her destroyer, affected her even to tears.

That the general, having erected such a monument, should be able to face it, was not perhaps very strange, and yet that he could sit so boldly collected within its view, maintain so elevated an air, look so fearlessly around, nay, that he should even enter the church, seemed wonderful to Catherine. Not, however, that many instances of beings equally hardened in guilt might not be produced. She could remember dozens who had persevered in every possible vice, going on from crime to crime, murdering whomsoever they chose, without any feeling of humanity or remorse; till a violent death or a religious retirement closed their black career. The erection of the monument itself could not in the smallest degree affect her doubts of Mrs. Tilney's actual decease. Were she even to descend into the family vault where her ashes were supposed to slumber, were she to behold the coffin in which they were said to be enclosed—what could it avail in such a case?

Catherine had read too much not to be perfectly aware of the ease with which a waxen figure might be introduced, and a supposititious funeral carried on.

The succeeding morning promised something better. The general's early walk, ill-timed as it was in every other view, was favourable here; and when she knew him to be out of the house, she directly proposed to Miss Tilney the accomplishment of her promise. Eleanor was ready to oblige her; and Catherine reminding her as they went of another promise, their first visit in consequence was to the portrait in her bed-chamber. It represented a very lovely woman, with a mild and pensive countenance, justifying, so far, the expectations of its new observer; but they were not in every respect answered, for Catherine had depended upon meeting with features, hair, complexion, that should be the very counterpart, the very image, if not of Henry's, of Eleanor's—the only portraits of which she had been in the habit of thinking, bearing always an equal resemblance of mother and child. A face once taken was taken for generations. But here she was obliged to look and consider and study for a likeness. She contemplated it, however, in spite of this drawback, with much emotion, and, but for a yet stronger interest, would have left it unwillingly.

Her agitation as they entered the great gallery was too much for any endeavour at discourse; she could only look at her companion. Eleanor's countenance was dejected, yet sedate; and its composure spoke her inured to all the gloomy objects to which they were advancing. Again she passed through the folding doors, again her hand was upon the important lock, and Catherine, hardly able to breathe, was turning to close the former with fearful caution, when the figure, the dreaded figure of the general himself at the further end of the gallery, stood before her! The name of "Eleanor" at the same moment, in his loudest tone, resounded through the building, giving to his daughter the first intimation of his presence, and to Catherine terror upon terror. An attempt at concealment had been her first instinctive movement on perceiving him, yet she could scarcely hope to have escaped his eye; and when her friend, who with an apologizing look darted hastily by her, had joined and disappeared with him, she ran for safety to her own room, and, locking herself in, believed that she should never have courage to go down again. She remained there at least an hour, in the greatest agitation, deeply commiserating the state of her poor friend, and expecting a summons herself from the angry general to attend him in his own apartment. No summons, however, arrived; and at last, on seeing a carriage drive up to the abbey, she was emboldened to descend and meet him under the protection of visitors. The breakfast-room was gay with company; and she was named to them by the general as the friend of his daughter, in a complimentary style, which so well concealed his resentful ire, as to make her feel secure at least of life for the present. And Eleanor, with a command of countenance which did honour to her concern for his character, taking an early occasion of saying to her, "My father only wanted me to answer a note," she began to hope that she had either been unseen by the general, or that from some consideration of policy she should be allowed to suppose herself so. Upon this trust she dared still to remain in his presence, after the company left them, and nothing occurred to disturb it.

In the course of this morning's reflections, she came to a resolution of making her next attempt on the forbidden door alone. It would be much better in every respect that Eleanor should know nothing of the matter. To involve her in the danger of a second detection, to court her into an apartment which must wring her heart, could not be the office of a friend. The general's utmost anger could not be to herself what it might be to a daughter; and, besides, she thought the examination itself would be more satisfactory if made without any companion. It would be impossible to explain to Eleanor the suspicions, from which the other had, in all likelihood, been hitherto happily exempt; nor could she therefore, in *her* presence, search for those proofs of the general's cruelty, which however they might yet have escaped discovery, she felt confident of somewhere drawing forth, in the shape of some fragmented journal, continued to the last gasp. Of the way to the apartment she was now perfectly mistress; and as she wished to get it over before Henry's return, who was expected on the morrow, there was no time to be lost. The day was bright, her courage high; at four o'clock, the sun was now two hours above the horizon, and it would be only her retiring to dress half an hour earlier than usual.

It was done; and Catherine found herself alone in the gallery before the clocks had ceased to strike. It was no time for thought; she hurried on, slipped with the least possible noise through the folding doors, and without stopping to look or breathe, rushed forward to the one in question. The lock yielded to her hand, and, luckily, with no sullen sound that could alarm a human being. On tiptoe she entered; the room was before her; but it was some minutes before she could advance another step. She beheld what fixed her to the spot and agitated every feature. She saw a large, well-proportioned apartment, an handsome dimity bed, arranged as unoccupied with an housemaid's care, a bright Bath stove, mahogany wardrobes, and neatly painted chairs, on which the warm beams of a western sun gaily poured through two sash windows! Catherine had expected to have her feelings worked, and worked they were. Astonishment and doubt first seized them; and a shortly succeeding ray of common sense added some bitter emotions of shame. She could not be mistaken as to the room; but how grossly mistaken in everything else!—in Miss Tilney's meaning, in her own calculation! This apartment, to which she had given a date so ancient, a position so awful, proved to be one end of what the general's father had built. There were two other doors in the chamber, leading probably into dressing-closets; but she had no inclination to open either. Would the veil in which Mrs. Tilney had last walked, or the volume in which she had last read, remain to tell what nothing else was allowed to whisper? No: whatever might have been the general's crimes, he had certainly too much wit to let them sue for detection. She was sick of exploring, and desired but to be safe in her own room, with her own heart only privy to its folly; and she was on the point of retreating as softly as she had entered, when the sound of footsteps, she could hardly tell where, made her pause and tremble. To be found there, even by a servant, would be unpleasant; but by the general (and he seemed always at hand when least wanted), much worse! She listened—the sound had ceased; and resolving not to lose a moment, she passed through and closed the door. At that instant a door underneath was hastily opened; someone seemed with swift steps to ascend the stairs, by the head of which she had yet to pass before she could gain the gallery. She had no power to move. With a feeling of terror not very definable, she fixed her eyes on the staircase, and in a few moments it gave Henry to her view. "Mr. Tilney!" she exclaimed in a voice of more than common astonishment. He looked astonished too. "Good God!" she continued, not attending to his address. "How came you here? How came you up that staircase?"

"How came I up that staircase!" he replied, greatly surprised. "Because it is my nearest way from the stable-yard to my own chamber; and why should I not come up it?"

Catherine recollected herself, blushed deeply, and could say no more. He seemed to be looking in her countenance for that explanation which her lips did not afford. She moved on towards the gallery. "And may I not, in my turn," said he, as he pushed back the folding doors, "ask how *you* came here? This passage is at least as extraordinary a road from the breakfast-parlour to your apartment, as that staircase can be from the stables to mine."

"I have been," said Catherine, looking down, "to see your mother's room."

"My mother's room! Is there anything extraordinary to be seen there?"

"No, nothing at all. I thought you did not mean to come back till tomorrow."

"I did not expect to be able to return sooner, when I went away; but three hours ago I had the pleasure of finding nothing to detain me. You look pale. I am afraid I alarmed you by running so fast up those stairs. Perhaps you did not know—you were not aware of their leading from the offices in common use?"

"No, I was not. You have had a very fine day for your ride."

"Very; and does Eleanor leave you to find your way into all the rooms in the house by yourself?"

"Oh! No; she showed me over the greatest part on Saturday—and we were coming here to these rooms—but only"—dropping her voice—"your father was with us."

"And that prevented you," said Henry, earnestly regarding her. "Have you looked into all the rooms in that passage?"

"No, I only wanted to see— Is not it very late? I must go and dress."

"It is only a quarter past four"—showing his watch—"and you are not now in Bath. No theatre, no rooms to prepare for. Half an hour at Northanger must be enough."

She could not contradict it, and therefore suffered herself to be detained, though her dread of further questions made her, for the first time in their acquaintance, wish to leave him. They walked slowly up the gallery. "Have you had any letter from Bath since I saw you?"

"No, and I am very much surprised. Isabella promised so faithfully to write directly."

"Promised so faithfully! A faithful promise! That puzzles me. I have heard of a faithful performance. But a faithful promise—the fidelity of promising! It is a power little worth knowing, however, since it can deceive and pain you. My mother's room is very commodious, is it not? Large and cheerful-looking, and the dressing-closets so well disposed! It always strikes me as the most comfortable apartment in the house, and I rather wonder that Eleanor should not take it for her own. She sent you to look at it, I suppose?"

"No."

"It has been your own doing entirely?" Catherine said nothing. After a short silence, during which he had closely observed her, he added, "As there is nothing in the room in itself to raise curiosity, this must have proceeded from a sentiment of respect for my mother's character, as described by Eleanor, which does honour to her memory. The world, I believe, never saw a better woman. But it is not often that virtue can boast an interest such as this. The domestic, unpretending merits of a person never known do not often create that kind of fervent, venerating tenderness which would prompt a visit like yours. Eleanor, I suppose, has talked of her a great deal?"

"Yes, a great deal. That is—not, not much, but what she did say was very interesting. Her dying so suddenly" (slowly, and with hesitation it was spoken), "and you—none of you being at home—and your father, I thought—perhaps had not been very fond of her."

"And from these circumstances," he replied (his quick eye fixed on hers), "you infer perhaps the probability of some negligence—some"—(involuntarily she shook her head)—"or it may be—of something still less pardonable." She raised her eyes towards him more fully than she had ever done before. "My mother's illness," he continued, "the seizure which ended in her death, *was* sudden. The malady itself, one from which she had often suffered, a bilious fever—its cause therefore constitutional. On the third day, in short, as soon as she could be prevailed on, a physician attended her, a very respectable man, and one in whom she had always placed great confidence. Upon his opinion of her danger, two others were called in the next day, and remained in almost constant attendance for four and twenty hours. On the fifth day she died. During the progress of her disorder, Frederick and I (*we* were both at home) saw her repeatedly; and from our own observation can bear witness to her having received every possible attention which could spring from the affection of those about her, or which her situation in life could command. Poor Eleanor *was* absent, and at such a distance as to return only to see her mother in her coffin."

"But your father," said Catherine, "was *he* afflicted?"

"For a time, greatly so. You have erred in supposing him not attached to her. He loved her, I am persuaded, as well as it was possible for him to—we have not all, you know, the same tenderness of disposition—and I will not pretend to say that while she lived, she might not often have had much to bear, but though his temper injured her, his judgment never did. His value of her was sincere; and, if not permanently, he was truly afflicted by her death."

"I am very glad of it," said Catherine; "it would have been very shocking!"

"If I understand you rightly, you have formed a surmise of such horror as I have hardly words to— Dear Miss Morland, consider the dreadful nature of the suspicions you have entertained. What have you been judging from? Remember the country and the age in which we live. Remember that we are English, that we are Christians. Consult your own understanding, your own sense of the probable, your own observation of what is passing around you. Does our education prepare us for such atrocities? Do our laws connive at them? Could they be perpetrated without being known, in a country like this, where social and literary intercourse is on such a footing, where every man is surrounded by a neighbourhood of voluntary spies, and where roads and newspapers lay everything open? Dearest Miss Morland, what ideas have you been admitting?"

They had reached the end of the gallery, and with tears of shame she ran off to her own room.

CHAPTER XXV

THE visions of romance were over. Catherine was completely awakened. Henry's address, short as it had been, had more thoroughly opened her eyes to the extravagance of her late fancies than all their several disappointments had done. Most grievously was she humbled. Most bitterly did she cry. It was not only with herself that she was sunk—but with Henry. Her folly, which now seemed even criminal, was all exposed to him, and he must despise her forever. The liberty which her imagination had dared to take with the character of his father—could he ever forgive it? The absurdity of her curiosity and her fears—could they ever be forgotten? She hated herself more than she could express. He had—she thought he had, once or twice before this fatal morning, shown something like affection for her. But now—in short, she made herself as miserable as possible for about half an hour, went down when the clock struck five, with a broken heart, and could scarcely give an intelligible answer to Eleanor's inquiry if she was well. The formidable Henry soon followed her into the room, and the only difference in his behaviour to her was that he paid her rather more attention than usual. Catherine had never wanted comfort more, and he looked as if he were aware of it.

The evening wore away with no abatement of this soothing politeness; and her spirits were gradually raised to a modest tranquillity. She did not learn either to forget or defend the past; but she learned to hope that it would never transpire farther, and that it might not cost her Henry's entire regard. Her thoughts being still chiefly fixed on what she had with such causeless terror felt and done, nothing could shortly be clearer than that it had been all a voluntary, self-created delusion, each trifling circumstance receiving importance from an imagination resolved on alarm, and everything forced to bend to one purpose by a mind which, before she entered the abbey, had been craving to be frightened. She remembered with what feelings she had prepared for a knowledge of Northanger. She saw that the infatuation had been created, the mischief settled, long before her quitting Bath, and it seemed as if the whole might be traced to the influence of that sort of reading which she had there indulged.

Charming as were all Mrs. Radcliffe's works, and charming even as were the works of all her imitators, it was not in them perhaps that human nature, at least in the Midland counties of England, was to be looked for. Of the Alps and Pyrenees, with their pine forests and their vices, they might give a faithful delineation; and Italy, Switzerland, and the south of France might be as fruitful in horrors as they were there represented. Catherine dared not doubt beyond her own country, and even of that, if hard pressed, would have yielded the northern and western extremities. But in the central part of England there was surely some security for the existence even of a wife not beloved, in the laws of the land, and the manners of the age. Murder was not tolerated, servants were not slaves, and neither poison nor sleeping potions to be procured, like rhubarb, from every druggist. Among the Alps and Pyrenees, perhaps, there were no mixed characters. There, such as were not as spotless as an angel might have the dispositions of a fiend. But in England it was not so; among the English, she believed, in their hearts and habits, there was a general though unequal mixture of good and bad. Upon this conviction, she would not be surprised if even in Henry and Eleanor Tilney, some slight imperfection might hereafter appear; and upon this conviction she need not fear to acknowledge some actual specks in the character of their father, who, though cleared from the grossly injurious suspicions which she must ever blush to have entertained, she did believe, upon serious consideration, to be not perfectly amiable.

Her mind made up on these several points, and her resolution formed, of always judging and acting in future with the greatest good sense, she had nothing to do but to forgive herself and be happier than ever; and the lenient hand of time did much for her by insensible gradations in the course of another day. Henry's astonishing generosity and nobleness of conduct, in never alluding in the slightest way to what had passed, was of the greatest assistance to her; and sooner than she could have supposed it possible in the beginning of her distress, her spirits became absolutely comfortable, and capable, as heretofore, of continual improvement by anything he said. There were still some subjects, indeed, under which she believed they must always tremble—the mention of a chest or a cabinet, for instance—and she did not love the sight of japan in any shape: but even *she* could allow that an occasional memento of past folly, however painful, might not be without use.

The anxieties of common life began soon to succeed to the alarms of romance. Her desire of hearing from Isabella grew every day greater. She was quite impatient to know how the Bath world went on, and how the rooms were attended; and especially was she anxious to be assured of Isabella's having matched some fine netting-cotton, on which she had left her intent; and of her continuing on the best terms with James. Her only dependence for information of any kind was on Isabella. James had protested against writing to her till his return to Oxford; and Mrs. Allen had given her no hopes of a letter till she had got back to Fullerton. But Isabella had promised and promised again; and when she promised a thing, she was so scrupulous in performing it! This made it so particularly strange!

For nine successive mornings, Catherine wondered over the repetition of a disappointment, which each morning became more severe: but, on the tenth, when she entered the breakfast-room, her first object was a letter, held out by Henry's willing hand. She thanked him as heartily as if he had written it himself. " 'Tis only from James, however," as she looked at the direction. She opened it; it was from Oxford; and to this purpose:

Dear Catherine,

Though, God knows, with little inclination for writing, I think it my duty to tell you that everything is at an end between Miss Thorpe and me. I shall not enter into particulars—they would only pain you more. You will soon hear enough from another quarter to know where lies the blame; and I hope will acquit your brother of everything but the folly of too easily thinking his affection returned. Thank God! I am undeceived in time! But it is a heavy blow! After my father's consent had been so kindly given—but no more of this. She has made me miserable forever! Let me soon hear from you, dear Cather-

ine; you are my only friend; *your* love I do build upon. I
wish your visit at Northanger may be over before Captain
Tilney makes his engagement known, or you will be uncomfortably circumstanced. Poor Thorpe is in town: I
dread the sight of him; his honest heart would feel so
much. I have written to him and my father. Her duplicity
hurts me more than all; till the very last, if I reasoned
with her, she declared herself as much attached to me as
ever, and laughed at my fears. I am ashamed to think how
long I bore with it; but if ever man had reason to believe
himself loved, I was that man. I cannot understand even
now what she would be at, for there could be no need of
my being played off to make her secure of Tilney. We
parted at last by mutual consent—happy for me had we
never met! I can never expect to know such another
woman! Dearest Catherine, beware how you give your
heart.

                                        Believe me, etc.

Catherine had not read three lines before her sudden
change of countenance, and short exclamations of sorrowing
wonder, declared her to be receiving unpleasant news; and
Henry, earnestly watching her through the whole letter, saw
plainly that it ended no better than it began. He was prevented, however, from even looking his surprise by his father's entrance. They went to breakfast directly; but
Catherine could hardly eat anything. Tears filled her eyes,
and even ran down her cheeks as she sat. The letter was one
moment in her hand, then in her lap, and then in her pocket;
and she looked as if she knew not what she did. The general,
between his cocoa and his newspaper, had luckily no leisure
for noticing her; but to the other two her distress was
equally visible. As soon as she dared leave the table she hurried away to her own room; but the housemaids were busy
in it, and she was obliged to come down again. She turned
into the drawing-room for privacy, but Henry and Eleanor
had likewise retreated thither, and were at that moment deep
in consultation about her. She drew back, trying to beg their
pardon, but was, with gentle violence, forced to return; and
the others withdrew, after Eleanor had affectionately expressed a wish of being of use or comfort to her.

After half an hour's free indulgence of grief and reflection, Catherine felt equal to encountering her friends; but

whether she should make her distress known to them was another consideration. Perhaps, if particularly questioned, she might just give an idea—just distantly hint at it—but not more. To expose a friend, such a friend as Isabella had been to her—and then their own brother so closely concerned in it! She believed she must waive the subject altogether. Henry and Eleanor were by themselves in the breakfast-room; and each, as she entered it, looked at her anxiously. Catherine took her place at the table, and, after a short silence, Eleanor said, "No bad news from Fullerton, I hope? Mr. and Mrs. Morland—your brothers and sisters—I hope they are none of them ill?"

"No, I thank you" (sighing as she spoke); "they are all very well. My letter was from my brother at Oxford."

Nothing further was said for a few minutes; and then speaking through her tears, she added, "I do not think I shall ever wish for a letter again!"

"I am sorry," said Henry, closing the book he had just opened; "if I had suspected the letter of containing anything unwelcome, I should have given it with very different feelings."

"It contained something worse than anybody could suppose! Poor James is so unhappy! You will soon know why."

"To have so kind-hearted, so affectionate a sister," replied Henry warmly, "must be a comfort to him under any distress."

"I have one favour to beg," said Catherine, shortly afterwards, in an agitated manner, "that, if your brother should be coming here, you will give me notice of it, that I may go away."

"Our brother! Frederick!"

"Yes; I am sure I should be very sorry to leave you so soon, but something has happened that would make it very dreadful for me to be in the same house with Captain Tilney."

Eleanor's work was suspended while she gazed with increased astonishment; but Henry began to suspect the truth, and something, in which Miss Thorpe's name was included, passed his lips.

"How quick you are!" cried Catherine: "you have guessed it, I declare! And yet, when we talked about it in Bath, you little thought of its ending so. Isabella—no wonder *now* I have not heard from her—Isabella has deserted my brother, and is to marry yours! Could you have believed there had been such inconstancy and fickleness, and everything that is bad in the world?"

"I hope, so far as concerns my brother, you are misinformed. I hope he has not had any material share in bringing on Mr. Morland's disappointment. His marrying Miss Thorpe is not probable. I think you must be deceived so far. I am very sorry for Mr. Morland—sorry that anyone you love should be unhappy; but my surprise would be greater at Frederick's marrying her than at any other part of the story."

"It is very true, however; you shall read James's letter yourself. Stay— There is one part—" recollecting with a blush the last line.

"Will you take the trouble of reading to us the passages which concern my brother?"

"No, read it yourself," cried Catherine, whose second thoughts were clearer. "I do not know what I was thinking of" (blushing again that she had blushed before); "James only means to give me good advice."

He gladly received the letter, and, having read it through, with close attention, returned it saying, "Well, if it is to be so, I can only say that I am sorry for it. Frederick will not be the first man who has chosen a wife with less sense than his family expected. I do not envy his situation, either as a lover or a son."

Miss Tilney, at Catherine's invitation, now read the letter likewise, and, having expressed also her concern and surprise, began to inquire into Miss Thorpe's connections and fortune.

"Her mother is a very good sort of woman," was Catherine's answer.

"What was her father?"

"A lawyer, I believe. They live at Putney."

"Are they a wealthy family?"

"No, not very. I do not believe Isabella has any fortune at all: but that will not signify in your family. Your father is so very liberal! He told me the other day that he only valued money as it allowed him to promote the happiness of his children." The brother and sister looked at each other. "But," said Eleanor, after a short pause, "would it be to promote his happiness, to enable him to marry such a girl? She must be an unprincipled one, or she could not have used your brother so. And how strange an infatuation on Frederick's side! A

girl who, before his eyes, is violating an engagement voluntarily entered into with another man! Is not it inconceivable,
Henry? Frederick too, who always wore his heart so
proudly! Who found no woman good enough to be loved!"

"That is the most unpromising circumstance, the strongest
presumption against him. When I think of his past declarations, I give him up. Moreover, I have too good an opinion
of Miss Thorpe's prudence to suppose that she would part
with one gentleman before the other was secured. It is all
over with Frederick indeed! He is a deceased man—defunct
in understanding. Prepare for your sister-in-law, Eleanor, and
such a sister-in-law as you must delight in! Open, candid,
artless, guileless, with affections strong but simple, forming
no pretensions, and knowing no disguise."

"Such a sister-in-law, Henry, I should delight in," said
Eleanor with a smile.

"But perhaps," observed Catherine, "though she has behaved so ill by our family, she may behave better by yours.
Now she has really got the man she likes, she may be constant."

"Indeed I am afraid she will," replied Henry; "I am afraid
she will be very constant, unless a baronet should come in
her way; that is Frederick's only chance. I will get the Bath
paper, and look over the arrivals."

"You think it is all for ambition, then? And, upon my
word, there are some things that seem very like it. I cannot
forget that, when she first knew what my father would do for
them, she seemed quite disappointed that it was not more. I
never was so deceived in anyone's character in my life before."

"Among all the great variety that you have known and
studied."

"My own disappointment and loss in her is very great;
but, as for poor James, I suppose he will hardly ever recover
it."

"Your brother is certainly very much to be pitied at present; but we must not, in our concern for his sufferings, un-
dervalue yours. You feel, I suppose, that in losing Isabella,
you lose half yourself: you feel a void in your heart which
nothing else can occupy. Society is becoming irksome; and
as for the amusements in which you were wont to share at
Bath, the very idea of them without her is abhorrent. You
would not, for instance, now go to a ball for the world. You

feel that you have no longer any friend to whom you can speak with unreserve, on whose regard you can place dependence, or whose counsel, in any difficulty, you could rely on. You feel all this?"

"No," said Catherine, after a few moments' reflection, "I do not—ought I? To say the truth, though I am hurt and grieved, that I cannot still love her, that I am never to hear from her, perhaps never to see her again, I do not feel so very, very much afflicted as one would have thought."

"You feel, as you always do, what is most to the credit of human nature. Such feelings ought to be investigated, that they may know themselves."

Catherine, by some chance or other, found her spirits so very much relieved by this conversation that she could not regret her being led on, though so unaccountably, to mention the circumstance which had produced it.

CHAPTER XXVI

FROM this time, the subject was frequently canvassed by the three young people; and Catherine found, with some surprise, that her two young friends were perfectly agreed in considering Isabella's want of consequence and fortune as likely to throw great difficulties in the way of her marrying their brother. Their persuasion that the general would, upon this ground alone, independent of the objection that might be raised against her character, oppose the connection, turned her feelings moreover with some alarm towards herself. She was as insignificant, and perhaps as portionless, as Isabella; and if the heir of the Tilney property had not grandeur and wealth enough in himself, at what point of interest were the demands of his younger brother to rest? The very painful reflections to which this thought led could only be dispersed by a dependence on the effect of that particular partiality, which, as she was given to understand by his words as well as his actions, she had from the first been so fortunate as to excite in the general; and by a recollection of some most generous and disinterested sentiments on the subject of money, which she had more than once heard him utter, and which tempted her to think his disposition in such matters misunderstood by his children.

They were so fully convinced, however, that their brother would not have the courage to apply in person for his father's consent, and so repeatedly assured her that he had never in his life been less likely to come to Northanger than at the present time, that she suffered her mind to be at ease as to the necessity of any sudden removal of her own. But as it was not to be supposed that Captain Tilney, whenever he made his application, would give his father any just idea of Isabella's conduct, it occurred to her as highly expedient that Henry should lay the whole business before him as it really was, enabling the general by that means to form a cool and impartial opinion, and prepare his objections on a fairer ground than inequality of situations, She proposed it to him accordingly; but he did not catch at the measure so eagerly as she had expected. "No," said he, "my father's hands need not be strengthened, and Frederick's confession of folly need not be forestalled. He must tell his own story."

"But he will tell only half of it."

"A quarter would be enough."

A day or two passed away and brought no tidings of Captain Tilney. His brother and sister knew not what to think. Sometimes it appeared to them as if his silence would be the natural result of the suspected engagement, and at others that it was wholly incompatible with it. The general, meanwhile, though offended every morning by Frederick's remissness in writing, was free from any real anxiety about him, and had no more pressing solicitude than that of making Miss Morland's time at Northanger pass pleasantly. He often expressed his uneasiness on this head, feared the sameness of every day's society and employments would disgust her with the place, wished the Lady Frasers had been in the country, talked every now and then of having a large party to dinner, and once or twice began even to calculate the number of young dancing people in the neighbourhood. But then it was such a dead time of year, no wild-fowl, no game, and the Lady Frasers were not in the country. And it all ended, at last, in his telling Henry one morning that when he next went to Woodston, they would take him by surprise there some day or other, and eat their mutton with him. Henry was greatly honoured and very happy, and Catherine was quite delighted with the scheme. "And when do you think, sir, I may look forward to this pleasure? I must be at Woodston on Monday to attend the parish meeting, and shall probably be obliged to stay two or three days."

"Well, well, we will take our chance some one of those days. There is no need to fix. You are not to put yourself at all out of your way. Whatever you may happen to have in the house will be enough. I think I can answer for the young ladies making allowance for a bachelor's table. Let me see; Monday will be a busy day with you, we will not come on Monday; and Tuesday will be a busy one with me. I expect my surveyor from Brockham with his report in the morning; and afterwards I cannot in decency fail attending the club. I really could not face my acquaintance if I stayed away now;

for, as I am known to be in the country, it would be taken exceedingly amiss; and it is a rule with me, Miss Morland, never to give offence to any of my neighbours, if a small sacrifice of time and attention can prevent it. They are a set of very worthy men. They have half a buck from Northanger twice a year; and I dine with them whenever I can. Tuesday, therefore, we may say is out of the question. But on Wednesday, I think, Henry, you may expect us; and we shall be with you early, that we may have time to look about us. Two hours and three quarters will carry us to Woodston, I suppose; we shall be in the carriage by ten; so, about a quarter before one on Wednesday, you may look for us."

A ball itself could not have been more welcome to Catherine than this little excursion, so strong was her desire to be acquainted with Woodston; and her heart was still bounding with joy when Henry, about an hour afterwards, came booted and greatcoated into the room where she and Eleanor were sitting, and said, "I am come, young ladies, in a very moralizing strain, to observe that our pleasures in this world are always to be paid for, and that we often purchase them at a great disadvantage, giving ready-monied actual happiness for a draft on the future, that may not be honoured. Witness myself, at this present hour. Because I am to hope for the satisfaction of seeing you at Woodston on Wednesday, which bad weather, or twenty other causes, may prevent, I must go away directly, two days before I intended it."

"Go away!" said Catherine, with a very long face. "And why?"

"Why! How can you ask the question? Because no time is to be lost in frightening my old housekeeper out of her wits, because I must go and prepare a dinner for you, to be sure."

"Oh! Not seriously!"

"Aye, and sadly too—for I had much rather stay."

"But how can you think of such a thing, after what the general said? When he so particularly desired you not to give yourself any trouble, because *anything* would do."

Henry only smiled. "I am sure it is quite unnecessary upon your sister's account and mine. You must know it to be so; and the general made such a point of your providing nothing extraordinary: besides, if he had not said half so much as he did, he has always such an excellent dinner at home, that sitting down to a middling one for one day could not signify."

"I wish I could reason like you, for his sake and my own. Good-bye. As tomorrow is Sunday, Eleanor, I shall not return."

He went; and, it being at any time a much simpler operation to Catherine to doubt her own judgment than Henry's, she was very soon obliged to give him credit for being right, however disagreeable to her his going. But the inexplicability of the general's conduct dwelt much on her thoughts. That he was very particular in his eating, she had, by her own unassisted observation, already discovered; but why he should say one thing so positively, and mean another all the while, was most unaccountable! How were people, at that rate, to be understood? Who but Henry could have been aware of what his father was at?

From Saturday to Wednesday, however, they were now to be without Henry. This was the sad finale of every reflection: and Captain Tilney's letter would certainly come in his absence; and Wednesday she was very sure would be wet. The past, present, and future were all equally in gloom. Her brother so unhappy, and her loss in Isabella so great; and Eleanor's spirits always affected by Henry's absence! What was there to interest or amuse her? She was tired of the woods and the shrubberies—always so smooth and so dry; and the abbey in itself was no more to her now than any other house. The painful remembrance of the folly it had helped to nourish and perfect was the only emotion which could spring from a consideration of the building. What a revolution in her ideas! She, who had so longed to be in an abbey! Now, there was nothing so charming to her imagination as the unpretending comfort of a well-connected parsonage, something like Fullerton, but better: Fullerton had its faults, but Woodston probably had none. If Wednesday should ever come!

It did come, and exactly when it might be reasonably looked for. It came—it was fine—and Catherine trod on air. By ten o'clock, the chaise and four conveyed the two from the abbey; and, after an agreeable drive of almost twenty miles, they entered Woodston, a large and populous village, in a situation not unpleasant. Catherine was ashamed to say how pretty she thought it, as the general seemed to think an apology necessary for the flatness of the country, and the size of the village; but in her heart she preferred it to any place she had ever been at, and looked with great admiration at every neat house above the rank of a cottage, and at all the little chandler's shops which they passed. At the further end of the village, and tolerably disengaged from the rest of it, stood the parsonage, a new-built substantial stone house, with its semicircular sweep and green gates; and, as they drove up to the door, Henry, with the friends of his solitude, a large Newfoundland puppy and two or three terriers, was ready to receive and make much of them.

Catherine's mind was too full, as she entered the house, for her either to observe or to say a great deal; and, till called on by the general for her opinion of it, she had very little idea of the room in which she was sitting. Upon looking round it then, she perceived in a moment that it was the most comfortable room in the world; but she was too guarded to say so, and the coldness of her praise disappointed him.

"We are not calling it a good house," said he. "We are not comparing it with Fullerton and Northanger—we are considering it as a mere parsonage, small and confined, we allow, but decent, perhaps, and habitable; and altogether not inferior to the generality; or, in other words, I believe there are few country parsonages in England half so good. It may admit of improvement, however. Far be it from me to say otherwise; and anything in reason—a bow thrown out, perhaps—though, between ourselves, if there is one thing more than another my aversion, it is a patched-on bow."

Catherine did not hear enough of this speech to understand or be pained by it; and other subjects being studiously brought forward and supported by Henry, at the same time that a tray full of refreshments was introduced by his servant, the general was shortly restored to his complacency, and Catherine to all her usual ease of spirits.

The room in question was of a commodious, well-proportioned size, and handsomely fitted up as a dining-parlour; and on their quitting it to walk round the grounds, she was shown, first into a smaller apartment, belonging peculiarly to the master of the house, and made unusually tidy on the occasion; and afterwards into what was to be the drawing-room, with the appearance of which, though unfurnished, Catherine was delighted enough even to satisfy the general. It was a prettily shaped room, the windows reaching to the ground, and the view from them pleasant, though only over green meadows; and she expressed her admiration at the moment with all the honest simplicity with which she felt it. "Oh! Why do not you fit up this room, Mr. Tilney? What a pity not to have it fitted up! It is the prettiest room I ever saw; it is the prettiest room in the world!"

"I trust," said the general, with a most satisfied smile, "that it will very speedily be furnished: it waits only for a lady's taste!"

"Well, if it was my house, I should never sit anywhere else. Oh! What a sweet little cottage there is among the trees—apple trees, too! It is the prettiest cottage!"

"You like it—you approve it as an object—it is enough. Henry, remember that Robinson is spoken to about it. The cottage remains."

Such a compliment recalled all Catherine's consciousness, and silenced her directly; and, though pointedly applied to by the general for her choice of the prevailing colour of the paper and hangings, nothing like an opinion on the subject could be drawn from her. The influence of fresh objects and fresh air, however, was of great use in dissipating these embarrassing associations; and, having reached the ornamental part of the premises, consisting of a walk round two sides of a meadow, on which Henry's genius had begun to act about half a year ago, she was sufficiently recovered to think it prettier than any pleasure-ground she had ever been in before, though there was not a shrub in it higher than the green bench in the corner.

A saunter into other meadows, and through part of the village, with a visit to the stables to examine some improvements, and a charming game of play with a litter of puppies just able to roll about, brought them to four o'clock, when Catherine scarcely thought it could be three. At four they were to dine, and at six to set off on their return. Never had any day passed so quickly!

She could not but observe that the abundance of the dinner did not seem to create the smallest astonishment in the general; nay, that he was even looking at the side-table for cold meat which was not there. His son and daughter's observations were of a different kind. They had seldom seen him eat so heartily at any table but his own, and never before known him so little disconcerted by the melted butter's being oiled.

At six o'clock, the general having taken his coffee, the carriage again received them; and so gratifying had been the tenor of his conduct throughout the whole visit, so well assured was her mind on the subject of his expectations, that, could she have felt equally confident of the wishes of his son, Catherine would have quitted Woodston with little anxiety as to the How or the When she might return to it.

CHAPTER XXVII

THE next morning brought the following very unexpected letter from Isabella:

Bath, April—

My dearest Catherine,

I received your two kind letters with the greatest delight, and have a thousand apologies to make for not answering them sooner. I really am quite ashamed of my idleness; but in this horrid place one can find time for nothing. I have had my pen in my hand to begin a letter to you almost every day since you left Bath, but have always been prevented by some silly trifler or other. Pray write to me soon, and direct to my own home. Thank God, we leave this vile place tomorrow. Since you went away, I have had no pleasure in it—the dust is beyond anything; and everybody one cares for is gone. I believe if I could see you I should not mind the rest, for you are dearer to me than anybody can conceive. I am quite uneasy about your dear brother, not having heard from him since he went to Oxford; and am fearful of some misunderstanding. Your kind offices will set all right: he is the only man I ever did or could love, and I trust you will convince him of it. The spring fashions are partly down; and the hats the most frightful you can imagine. I hope you spend your time pleasantly, but am afraid you never think of me. I will not say all that I could of the family you are with, because I would not be ungenerous, or set you against those you esteem; but it is very difficult to know whom to trust, and young men never know their minds two days together. I rejoice to say that the young man whom, of all others, I particularly abhor, has left Bath. You will know, from this description, I must mean Captain Tilney, who, as you may remember, was amazingly disposed to follow and tease me, before you went away. Afterwards he got worse, and became quite my shadow. Many girls might have been taken in, for never were such attentions; but I know the fickle sex too well. He went away to his regiment two days ago, and I trust I shall never be plagued with him again. He is the greatest coxcomb I ever saw, and amazingly disagreeable. The last two days he was always by the side of Charlotte Davis: I pitied his taste, but took no notice of him. The last time we met was in Bath Street, and I turned directly into a shop that he might not speak to me; I would not even look at him. He went into the pump-room afterwards; but I would not have followed him for all the world. Such a contrast between him and your brother! Pray send me some news of the latter—I am quite unhappy about him; he seemed so uncomfortable when he went away, with a cold, or something that affected his spirits. I would write to him myself, but have mislaid his direction; and, as I hinted above, am afraid he took something in my conduct amiss. Pray explain everything to his satisfaction; or, if he still harbours any doubt, a line from himself to me, or a call at Putney when next in town, might set all to rights. I have not been to the rooms this age, nor to the play, except going in last night with the Hodges, for a frolic, at half price: they teased me into it; and I was determined they should not say I shut myself up because Tilney was gone. We happened to sit by the Mitchells, and they pretended to be quite surprised to see me out. I knew their spite: at one time they could not be civil to me, but now they are all friendship; but I am not such a fool as to be taken in by them. You know I have a pretty good spirit of my own. Anne Mitchell had tried to put on a turban like mine, as I wore it the week before at the concert, but made wretched work of it—it happened to become my odd face, I believe, at least Tilney told me so at the time, and said every eye was upon me; but he is the last man whose word I would take. I wear nothing but purple now: I know I look hideous in it, but no matter—it is your brother's favourite colour. Lose no time, my dearest, sweetest Catherine, in writing to him and to me,

Who ever am, etc.

Such a strain of shallow artifice could not impose even upon Catherine. Its inconsistencies, contradictions, and falsehood struck her from the very first. She was ashamed of Isabella, and ashamed of having ever loved her. Her professions of attachment were now as disgusting as her excuses were empty, and her demands impudent. "Write to James on her behalf! No, James should never hear Isabella's name mentioned by her again."

On Henry's arrival from Woodston, she made known to him and Eleanor their brother's safety, congratulating them with sincerity on it, and reading aloud the most material passages of her letter with strong indignation. When she had finished it—"So much for Isabella," she cried, "and for all our intimacy! She must think me an idiot, or she could not have written so; but perhaps this has served to make her character better known to me than mine is to her. I see what she has been about. She is a vain coquette, and her tricks have not answered. I do not believe she had ever any regard either for James or for me, and I wish I had never known her."

"It will soon be as if you never had," said Henry.

"There is but one thing that I cannot understand. I see that she has had designs on Captain Tilney, which have not succeeded; but I do not understand what Captain Tilney has been about all this time. Why should he pay her such attentions as to make her quarrel with my brother, and then fly off himself?"

"I have very little to say for Frederick's motives, such as I believe them to have been. He has his vanities as well as Miss Thorpe, and the chief difference is, that, having a stronger head, they have not yet injured himself. If the *effect* of his behaviour does not justify him with you, we had better not seek after the cause."

"Then you do not suppose he ever really cared about her?"

"I am persuaded that he never did."

"And only made believe to do so for mischief's sake?"

Henry bowed his assent.

"Well, then, I must say that I do not like him at all. Though it has turned out so well for us, I do not like him at all. As it happens, there is no great harm done, because I do not think Isabella has any heart to lose. But, suppose he had made her very much in love with him?"

"But we must first suppose Isabella to have had a heart to lose—consequently to have been a very different creature; and, in that case, she would have met with very different treatment."

"It is very right that you should stand by your brother."

"And if you would stand by *yours,* you would not be much distressed by the disappointment of Miss Thorpe. But your mind is warped by an innate principle of general integrity, and therefore not accessible to the cool reasonings of family partiality, or a desire of revenge."

Catherine was complimented out of further bitterness. Frederick could not be unpardonably guilty, while Henry made himself so agreeable. She resolved on not answering Isabella's letter, and tried to think no more of it.

CHAPTER XXVIII

SOON after this, the general found himself obliged to go to London for a week; and he left Northanger earnestly regretting that any necessity should rob him even for an hour of Miss Morland's company, and anxiously recommending the study of her comfort and amusement to his children as their chief object in his absence. His departure gave Catherine the first experimental conviction that a loss may be sometimes a gain. The happiness with which their time now passed, every employment voluntary, every laugh indulged, every meal a scene of ease and good humour, walking where they liked and when they liked, their hours, pleasures, and fatigues at their own command, made her thoroughly sensible of the restraint which the general's presence had imposed, and most thankfully feel their present release from it. Such ease and such delights made her love the place and the people more and more every day; and had it not been for a dread of its soon becoming expedient to leave the one, and an apprehension of not being equally beloved by the other, she would at each moment of each day have been perfectly happy; but she was now in the fourth week of her visit; before the general came home, the fourth week would be turned, and perhaps it might seem an intrusion if she stayed much longer. This was a painful consideration whenever it occurred; and eager to get rid of such a weight on her mind, she very soon resolved to speak to Eleanor about it at once, propose going away, and be guided in her conduct by the manner in which her proposal might be taken.

Aware that if she gave herself much time, she might feel it difficult to bring forward so unpleasant a subject, she took the first opportunity of being suddenly alone with Eleanor, and of Eleanor's being in the middle of a speech about something very different, to start forth her obligation of going away very soon. Eleanor looked and declared herself much concerned. She had "hoped for the pleasure of her company for a much longer time—had been misled (perhaps by her wishes) to suppose that a much longer visit had been promised—and could not but think that if Mr. and Mrs. Morland were aware of the pleasure it was to her to have her there, they would be too generous to hasten her return." Catherine explained: "Oh! As to *that,* Papa and Mamma were in no hurry at all. As long as she was happy, they would always be satisfied."

"Then why, might she ask, in such a hurry herself to leave them?"

"Oh! Because she had been there so long."

"Nay, if you can use such a word, I can urge you no farther. If you think it long——"

"Oh! No, I do not indeed. For my own pleasure, I could stay with you as long again." And it was directly settled that, till she had, her leaving them was not even to be thought of. In having this cause of uneasiness so pleasantly removed, the force of the other was likewise weakened. The kindness, the earnestness of Eleanor's manner in pressing her to stay, and Henry's gratified look on being told that her stay was determined, were such sweet proofs of her importance with them, as left her only just so much solicitude as the human mind can never do comfortably without. She did—almost always—believe that Henry loved her, and quite always that his father and sister loved and even wished her to belong to them; and believing so far, her doubts and anxieties were merely sportive irritations.

Henry was not able to obey his father's injunction of remaining wholly at Northanger in attendance on the ladies, during his absence in London, the engagements of his curate at Woodston obliging him to leave them on Saturday for a couple of nights. His loss was not now what it had been while the general was at home; it lessened their gaiety, but did not ruin their comfort; and the two girls agreeing in occupation, and improving in intimacy, found themselves so well sufficient for the time to themselves, that it was eleven o'clock, rather a late hour at the abbey, before they quitted the supper-room on the day of Henry's departure. They had just reached the head of the stairs when it seemed, as far as the thickness of the walls would allow them to judge, that a carriage was driving up to the door, and the next moment confirmed the idea by the loud noise of the house-bell. After the first perturbation of surprise had passed away, in a "Good heaven! What can be the matter?" it was quickly decided by Eleanor to be her eldest brother, whose arrival was often as sudden, if not quite so unseasonable, and accordingly she hurried down to welcome him.

Catherine walked on to her chamber, making up her mind as well as she could, to a further acquaintance with Captain Tilney, and comforting herself under the unpleasant impression his conduct had given her, and the persuasion of his being by far too fine a gentleman to approve of her, that at least they should not meet under such circumstances as would make their meeting materially painful. She trusted he would never speak of Miss Thorpe; and indeed, as he must by this time be ashamed of the part he had acted, there could be no danger of it; and as long as all mention of Bath scenes were avoided, she thought she could behave to him very civilly. In such considerations time passed away, and it was certainly in his favour that Eleanor should be so glad to see him, and have so much to say, for half an hour was almost gone since his arrival, and Eleanor did not come up.

At that moment Catherine thought she heard her step in the gallery, and listened for its continuance; but all was silent. Scarcely, however, had she convicted her fancy of error, when the noise of something moving close to her door made her start; it seemed as if someone was touching the very doorway—and in another moment a slight motion of the lock proved that some hand must be on it. She trembled a little at the idea of anyone's approaching so cautiously; but resolving not to be again overcome by trivial appearances of alarm, or misled by a raised imagination, she stepped quietly forward, and opened the door. Eleanor, and only Eleanor, stood there. Catherine's spirits, however, were tranquilized but for an instant, for Eleanor's cheeks were pale, and her manner greatly agitated. Though evidently intending to come in, it seemed an effort to enter the room, and a still greater to speak when there. Catherine, supposing some uneasiness on Captain Tilney's account, could only express her concern by silent attention, obliged her to be seated, rubbed her temples with lavender-water, and hung over her with affectionate solicitude. "My dear Catherine, you must not— you must not indeed—" were Eleanor's first connected words. "I am quite well. This kindness distracts me—I cannot bear it—I come to you on such an errand!"

"Errand! To me!"

"How shall I tell you! Oh! How shall I tell you!"

A new idea now darted into Catherine's mind, and turning as pale as her friend, she exclaimed, " 'Tis a messenger from Woodston!"

"You are mistaken, indeed," returned Eleanor, looking at her most compassionately; "It is no one from Woodston. It is my father himself." Her voice faltered, and her eyes were turned to the ground as she mentioned his name. His unlooked-for return was enough in itself to make Catherine's heart sink, and for a few moments she hardly supposed there were anything worse to be told. She said nothing; and Eleanor, endeavouring to collect herself and speak with firmness, but with eyes still cast down, soon went on. "You are too good, I am sure, to think the worse of me for the part I am obliged to perform. I am indeed a most unwilling messenger. After what has so lately passed, so lately been settled between us—how joyfully, how thankfully on my side!—as to your continuing here as I hoped for many, many weeks longer, how can I tell you that your kindness is not to be accepted—and that the happiness your company has hitherto given us is to be repaid by—But I must not trust myself with words. My dear Catherine, we are to part. My father has recollected an engagement that takes our whole family away on Monday. We are going to Lord Longtown's, near Hereford, for a fortnight. Explanation and apology are equally impossible. I cannot attempt either."

"My dear Eleanor," cried Catherine, suppressing her feelings as well as she could, "do not be so distressed. A second engagement must give way to a first. I am very, very sorry we are to part—so soon, and so suddenly too; but I am not offended, indeed I am not. I can finish my visit here, you know, at any time; or I hope you will come to me. Can you, when you return from this lord's, come to Fullerton?"

"It will not be in my power, Catherine."

"Come when you can, then."

Eleanor made no answer; and Catherine's thoughts recurring to something more directly interesting, she added, thinking aloud, "Monday—so soon as Monday; and you all go. Well, I am certain of—I shall be able to take leave, however. I need not go till just before you do, you know. Do not be distressed, Eleanor, I can go on Monday very well. My father and mother's having no notice of it is of very little consequence. The general will send a servant with me, I dare say, half the way—and then I shall soon be at Salisbury, and then I am only nine miles from home."

"Ah, Catherine! Were it settled so, it would be somewhat less intolerable, though in such common attentions you would have received but half what you ought. But—how can I tell you?—tomorrow morning is fixed for your leaving us, and not even the hour is left to your choice; the very carriage is ordered, and will be here at seven o'clock, and no servant will be offered you."

Catherine sat down, breathless and speechless. "I could hardly believe my senses, when I heard it; and no displeasure, no resentment that you can feel at this moment, however justly great, can be more than I myself—but I must not talk of what I felt. Oh! That I could suggest anything in extenuation! Good God! What will your father and mother say! After courting you from the protection of real friends to this—almost double distance from your home, to have you driven out of the house, without the considerations even of decent civility! Dear, dear Catherine, in being the bearer of such a message, I seem guilty myself of all its insult; yet, I trust you will acquit me, for you must have been long enough in this house to see that I am but a nominal mistress of it, that my real power is nothing."

"Have I offended the general?" said Catherine in a faltering voice.

"Alas! For my feelings as a daughter, all that I know, all that I answer for, is that you can have given him no just cause of offence. He certainly is greatly, very greatly discomposed; I have seldom seen him more so. His temper is not happy, and something has now occurred to ruffle it in an uncommon degree; some disappointment, some vexation, which just at this moment seems important, but which I can hardly suppose you to have any concern in, for how is it possible?"

It was with pain that Catherine could speak at all; and it was only for Eleanor's sake that she attempted it, "I am sure," said she, "I am very sorry if I have offended him. It was the last thing I would willingly have done. But do not be unhappy, Eleanor. An engagement, you know, must be kept. I am only sorry it was not recollected sooner, that I might have written home. But it is of very little consequence."

"I hope, I earnestly hope, that to your real safety it will be of none; but to everything else it is of the greatest consequence: to comfort, appearance, propriety, to your family, to the world. Were your friends, the Allens, still in Bath, you might go to them with comparative ease; a few hours would take you there; but a journey of seventy miles, to be taken post by you, at your age, alone, unattended!"

"Oh, the journey is nothing. Do not think about that. And if we are to part, a few hours sooner or later, you know, makes no difference. I can be ready by seven. Let me be called in time." Eleanor saw that she wished to be alone; and believing it better for each that they should avoid any further conversation, now left her with, "I shall see you in the morning."

Catherine's swelling heart needed relief. In Eleanor's presence friendship and pride had equally restrained her tears, but no sooner was she gone than they burst forth in torrents. Turned from the house, and in such a way! Without any reason that could justify, any apology that could atone for the abruptness, the rudeness, nay, the insolence of it. Henry at a distance—not able even to bid him farewell. Every hope, every expectation from him suspended, at least, and who could say how long? Who could say when they might meet again? And all this by such a man as General Tilney, so polite, so well-bred, and heretofore so particularly fond of her! It was as incomprehensible as it was mortifying and grievous. From what it could arise, and where it would end, were considerations of equal perplexity and alarm. The manner in which it was done so grossly uncivil, hurrying her away without any reference to her own convenience, or allowing her even the appearance of choice as to the time or mode of her traveling; of two days, the earliest fixed on, and of that almost the earliest hour, as if resolved to have her gone before he was stirring in the morning, that he might not be obliged even to see her. What could all this mean but an intentional affront? By some means or other she must have had the misfortune to offend him. Eleanor had wished to spare her from so painful a notion, but Catherine could not believe it possible that any injury or any misfortune could provoke such ill will against a person not connected, or, at least, not supposed to be connected with it.

Heavily passed the night. Sleep, or repose that deserved the name of sleep, was out of the question. That room, in

which her disturbed imagination had tormented her on her
first arrival, was again the scene of agitated spirits and unquiet slumbers. Yet how different now the source of her inquietude from what it had been then—how mournfully
superior in reality and substance! Her anxiety had foundation in fact, her fears in probability; and with a mind so occupied in the contemplation of actual and natural evil, the
solitude of her situation, the darkness of her chamber, the
antiquity of the building, were felt and considered without
the smallest emotion; and though the wind was high, and often produced strange and sudden noises throughout the
house, she heard it all as she lay awake, hour after hour,
without curiosity or terror.

Soon after six Eleanor entered her room, eager to show attention or give assistance where it was possible; but very little remained to be done. Catherine had not loitered; she was
almost dressed, and her packing almost finished. The possibility of some conciliatory message from the general occurred to her as his daughter appeared. What so natural, as
that anger should pass away and repentance succeed it? And,
she only wanted to know how far, after what had passed, an
apology might properly be received by her. But the knowledge would have been useless here; it was not called for;
neither clemency nor dignity was put to the trial—Eleanor
brought no message. Very little passed between them on
meeting; each found her greatest safety in silence, and few
and trivial were the sentences exchanged while they remained upstairs, Catherine in busy agitation completing her
dress, and Eleanor with more goodwill than experience intent upon filling the trunk. When everything was done they
left the room, Catherine lingering only half a minute behind
her friend to throw a parting glance on every well-known,
cherished object, and went down to the breakfast-parlour,
where breakfast was prepared. She tried to eat, as well to
save herself the pain of being urged as to make her friend
comfortable; but she had no appetite, and could not swallow
many mouthfuls. The contrast between this and her last
breakfast in that room gave her fresh misery, and strengthened her distaste for everything before her. It was not four
and twenty hours ago since they had met there to the same
repast, but in circumstances how different! With what cheerful ease, what happy, though false, security, had she then
looked around her, enjoying everything present, and fearing

little in future, beyond Henry's going to Woodston for a day! Happy, happy breakfast! For Henry had been there; Henry had sat by her and helped her. These reflections were long indulged undisturbed by any address from her companion, who sat as deep in thought as herself; and the appearance of the carriage was the first thing to startle and recall them to the present moment. Catherine's colour rose at the sight of it; and the indignity with which she was treated, striking at that instant on her mind with peculiar force, made her for a short time sensible only of resentment. Eleanor seemed now impelled into resolution and speech.

"You *must* write to me, Catherine," she cried; "you *must* let me hear from you as soon as possible. Till I know you to be safe at home, I shall not have an hour's comfort. For *one* letter, at all risks, all hazards, I must entreat. Let me have the satisfaction of knowing that you are safe at Fullerton, and have found your family well, and then, till I can ask for your correspondence as I ought to do, I will not expect more. Direct to me at Lord Longtown's, and, I must ask it, under cover to Alice."

"No, Eleanor, if you are not allowed to receive a letter from me, I am sure I had better not write. There can be no doubt of my getting home safe."

Eleanor only replied, "I cannot wonder at your feelings. I will not importune you. I will trust to your own kindness of heart when I am at a distance from you." But this, with the look of sorrow accompanying it, was enough to melt Catherine's pride in a moment, and she instantly said, "Oh, Eleanor, I *will* write to you indeed."

There was yet another point which Miss Tilney was anxious to settle, though somewhat embarrassed in speaking of. It had occurred to her that after so long an absence from home, Catherine might not be provided with money enough for the expenses of her journey, and, upon suggesting it to her with most affectionate offers of accommodation, it proved to be exactly the case. Catherine had never thought on the subject till that moment, but, upon examining her purse, was convinced that but for this kindness of her friend, she might have been turned from the house without even the means of getting home; and the distress in which she must have been thereby involved filling the minds of both, scarcely another word was said by either during the time of their remaining together. Short, however, was that time. The carriage was soon announced to be ready; and Catherine, instantly rising, a long and affectionate embrace supplied the place of language in bidding each other adieu; and, as they entered the hall, unable to leave the house without some mention of one whose name had not yet been spoken by either, she paused a moment, and with quivering lips just made it intelligible that she left "her kind remembrance for her absent friend." But with this approach to his name ended all possibility of restraining her feelings; and, hiding her face as well as she could with her handkerchief, she darted across the hall, jumped into the chaise, and in a moment was driven from the door.

CHAPTER XXIX

CATHERINE was too wretched to be fearful. The journey in itself had no terrors for her; and she began it without either dreading its length or feeling its solitariness. Leaning back in one corner of the carriage, in a violent burst of tears, she was conveyed some miles beyond the walls of the abbey before she raised her head; and the highest point of ground within the park was almost closed from her view before she was capable of turning her eyes towards it. Unfortunately, the road she now travelled was the same which only ten days ago she had so happily passed along in going to and from Woodston; and, for fourteen miles, every bitter feeling was rendered more severe by the review of objects on which she had first looked under impressions so different. Every mile, as it brought her nearer Woodston, added to her sufferings, and when within the distance of five, she passed the turning which led to it, and thought of Henry, so near, yet so unconscious, her grief and agitation were excessive.

The day which she had spent at that place had been one of the happiest of her life. It was there, it was on that day, that the general had made use of such expressions with regard to Henry and herself, had so spoken and so looked as to give her the most positive conviction of his actually wishing their marriage. Yes, only ten days ago had he elated her by his pointed regard—had he even confused her by his too significant reference! And now—what had she done, or what had she omitted to do, to merit such a change?

The only offence against him of which she could accuse herself had been such as was scarcely possible to reach his knowledge. Henry and her own heart only were privy to the shocking suspicions which she had so idly entertained; and equally safe did she believe her secret with each. Designedly, at least, Henry could not have betrayed her. If indeed, by any strange mischance his father should have gained in-

telligence of what she had dared to think and look for, of her
causeless fancies and injurious examinations, she could not
wonder at any degree of his indignation. If aware of her having viewed him as a murderer, she could not wonder at his
even turning her from his house. But a justification so full of
torture to herself, she trusted, would not be in his power.

Anxious as were all her conjectures on this point, it was
not, however, the one on which she dwelt most. There was
a thought yet nearer, a more prevailing, more impetuous
concern. How Henry would think, and feel, and look, when
he returned on the morrow to Northanger and heard of her
being gone, was a question of force and interest to rise over
every other, to be never ceasing, alternately irritating and
soothing; it sometimes suggested the dread of his calm acquiescence, and at others was answered by the sweetest confidence in his regret and resentment. To the general, of
course, he would not dare to speak; but to Eleanor—what
might he not say to Eleanor about her?

In this unceasing recurrence of doubts and inquiries, on
any one article of which her mind was incapable of more
than momentary repose, the hours passed away, and her journey advanced much faster than she looked for. The pressing
anxieties of thought, which prevented her from noticing anything before her, when once beyond the neighbourhood of
Woodston, saved her at the same time from watching her
progress; and though no object on the road could engage a
moment's attention, she found no stage of it tedious. From
this, she was preserved too by another cause, by feeling no
eagerness for her journey's conclusion; for to return in such
a manner to Fullerton was almost to destroy the pleasure of
a meeting with those she loved best, even after an absence
such as hers—an eleven weeks' absence. What had she to
say that would not humble herself and pain her family, that
would not increase her own grief by the confession of it, extend an useless resentment, and perhaps involve the innocent
with the guilty in undistinguishing ill will? She could never
do justice to Henry and Eleanor's merit; she felt it too
strongly for expression; and should a dislike be taken
against them, should they be thought of unfavourably, on
their father's account, it would cut her to the heart.

With these feelings, she rather dreaded than sought for the
first view of that well-known spire which would announce
her within twenty miles of home. Salisbury she had known

to be her point on leaving Northanger; but after the first stage she had been indebted to the postmasters for the names of the places which were then to conduct her to it; so great had been her ignorance of her route. She met with nothing, however, to distress or frighten her. Her youth, civil manners, and liberal pay procured her all the attention that a traveller like herself could require; and stopping only to change horses, she travelled on for about eleven hours without accident or alarm, and between six and seven o'clock in the evening found herself entering Fullerton.

A heroine returning, at the close of her career, to her native village, in all the triumph of recovered reputation, and all the dignity of a countess, with a long train of noble relations in their several phaetons, and three waiting-maids in a travelling chaise and four, behind her, is an event on which the pen of the contriver may well delight to dwell; it gives credit to every conclusion, and the author must share in the glory she so liberally bestows. But my affair is widely different; I bring back my heroine to her home in solitude and disgrace; and no sweet elation of spirits can lead me into minuteness. A heroine in a hack post-chaise is such a blow upon sentiment, as no attempt at grandeur or pathos can withstand. Swiftly therefore shall her post-boy drive through the village, amid the gaze of Sunday groups, and speedy shall be her descent from it.

But, whatever might be the distress of Catherine's mind, as she thus advanced towards the parsonage, and whatever the humiliation of her biographer in relating it, she was preparing enjoyment of no everyday nature for those to whom she went; first, in the appearance of her carriage—and secondly, in herself. The chaise of a traveller being a rare sight in Fullerton, the whole family were immediately at the window; and to have it stop at the sweep-gate was a pleasure to brighten every eye and occupy every fancy—a pleasure quite unlooked for by all but the two youngest children, a boy and girl of six and four years old, who expected a brother or sister in every carriage. Happy the glance that first distinguished Catherine! Happy the voice that proclaimed the discovery! But whether such happiness were the lawful property of George or Harriet could never be exactly understood.

Her father, mother, Sarah, George, and Harriet, all assembled at the door to welcome her with affectionate eagerness, was a sight to awaken the best feelings of Catherine's heart; and in the embrace of each, as she stepped from the carriage, she found herself soothed beyond anything that she had believed possible. So surrounded, so caressed, she was even happy! In the joyfulness of family love everything for a short time was subdued, and the pleasure of seeing her, leaving them at first little leisure for calm curiosity, they were all seated round the tea-table, which Mrs. Morland had hurried for the comfort of the poor traveller, whose pale and jaded looks soon caught her notice, before any inquiry so direct as to demand a positive answer was addressed to her.

Reluctantly, and with much hesitation, did she then begin what might perhaps, at the end of half an hour, be termed, by the courtesy of her hearers, an explanation; but scarcely, within that time, could they at all discover the cause, or collect the particulars, of her sudden return. They were far from being an irritable race; far from any quickness in catching, or bitterness in resenting, affronts: but here, when the whole was unfolded, was an insult not to be overlooked, nor, for the first half hour, to be easily pardoned. Without suffering any romantic alarm, in the consideration of their daughter's long and lonely journey, Mr. and Mrs. Morland could not but feel that it might have been productive of much unpleasantness to her; that it was what they could never have voluntarily suffered; and that, in forcing her on such a measure, General Tilney had acted neither honourably nor feelingly— neither as a gentleman nor as a parent. Why he had done it, what could have provoked him to such a breach of hospitality, and so suddenly turned all his partial regard for their daughter into actual ill will, was a matter which they were at least as far from divining as Catherine herself; but it did not oppress them by any means so long; and, after a due course of useless conjecture, that "it was a strange business, and that he must be a very strange man," grew enough for all their indignation and wonder; though Sarah indeed still indulged in the sweets of incomprehensibility, exclaiming and conjecturing with youthful ardour. "My dear, you give yourself a great deal of needless trouble," said her mother at last; "depend upon it, it is something not at all worth understanding."

"I can allow for his wishing Catherine away, when he recollected this engagement," said Sarah, "but why not do it civilly?"

"I am sorry for the young people," returned Mrs. Morland; "they must have a sad time of it; but as for anything else, it is no matter now; Catherine is safe at home, and our comfort does not depend upon General Tilney." Catherine sighed. "Well," continued her philosophic mother, "I am glad I did not know of your journey at the time; but now it is all over, perhaps there is no great harm done. It is always good for young people to be put upon exerting themselves; and you know, my dear Catherine, you always were a sad little shatter-brained creature; but now you must have been forced to have your wits about you, with so much changing of chaises and so forth; and I hope it will appear that you have not left anything behind you in any of the pockets."

Catherine hoped so too, and tried to feel an interest in her own amendment, but her spirits were quite worn down; and, to be silent and alone becoming soon her only wish, she readily agreed to her mother's next counsel of going early to bed. Her parents, seeing nothing in her ill looks and agitation but the natural consequence of mortified feelings, and of the unusual exertion and fatigue of such a journey, parted from her without any doubt of their being soon slept away; and though, when they all met the next morning, her recovery was not equal to their hopes, they were still perfectly unsuspicious of there being any deeper evil. They never once thought of her heart, which, for the parents of a young lady of seventeen, just returned from her first excursion from home, was odd enough!

As soon as breakfast was over, she sat down to fulfil her promise to Miss Tilney, whose trust in the effect of time and distance on her friend's disposition was already justified, for already did Catherine reproach herself with having parted from Eleanor coldly, with having never enough valued her merits or kindness, and never enough commiserated her for what she had been yesterday left to endure. The strength of these feelings, however, was far from assisting her pen; and never had it been harder for her to write than in addressing Eleanor Tilney. To compose a letter which might at once do justice to her sentiments and her situation, convey gratitude without servile regret, be guarded without coldness, and honest without resentment—a letter which Eleanor might not be pained by the perusal of—and, above all, which she might not blush herself, if Henry should chance to see, was an undertaking to frighten away all her powers of performance; and, after long thought and much perplexity, to be very brief was all that she could determine on with any confidence of safety. The money therefore which Eleanor had advanced was enclosed with little more than grateful thanks, and the thousand good wishes of a most affectionate heart.

"This has been a strange acquaintance," observed Mrs. Morland, as the letter was finished; "soon made and soon ended. I am sorry it happens so, for Mrs. Allen thought them very pretty kind of young people; and you were sadly out of luck too in your Isabella. Ah! Poor James! Well, we must live and learn; and the next new friends you make I hope will be better worth keeping."

Catherine coloured as she warmly answered, "No friend can be better worth keeping than Eleanor."

"If so, my dear, I dare say you will meet again some time or other; do not be uneasy. It is ten to one but you are thrown together again in the course of a few years; and then what a pleasure it will be!"

Mrs. Morland was not happy in her attempt at consolation. The hope of meeting again in the course of a few years could only put into Catherine's head what might happen within that time to make a meeting dreadful to her. She could never forget Henry Tilney, or think of him with less tenderness than she did at that moment; but he might forget her; and in that case, to meet—! Her eyes filled with tears as she pictured her acquaintance so renewed; and her mother, perceiving her comfortable suggestions to have had no good effect, proposed, as another expedient for restoring her spirits, that they should call on Mrs. Allen.

The two houses were only a quarter of a mile apart; and, as they walked, Mrs. Morland quickly dispatched all that she felt on the score of James's disappointment. "We are sorry for him," said she; "but otherwise there is no harm done in the match going off; for it could not be a desirable thing to have him engaged to a girl whom we had not the smallest acquaintance with, and who was so entirely without fortune; and now, after such behaviour, we cannot think at all well of her. Just at present it comes hard to poor James; but that will not last forever; and I dare say he will be a discreeter man all his life, for the foolishness of his first choice."

This was just such a summary view of the affair as Catherine could listen to; another sentence might have endangered her complaisance, and made her reply less rational; for soon were all her thinking powers swallowed up in the reflection of her own change of feelings and spirits since last she had trodden that well-known road. It was not three months ago since, wild with joyful expectation, she had there run backwards and forwards some ten times a day, with an heart light, gay, and independent; looking forward to pleasures untasted and unalloyed, and free from the apprehension of evil as from the knowledge of it. Three months ago had seen her all this; and now, how altered a being did she return! She was received by the Allens with all the kindness which her unlooked-for appearance, acting on a steady affection, would naturally call forth; and great was their surprise, and warm their displeasure, on hearing how she had been treated—though Mrs. Morland's account of it was no inflated representation, no studied appeal to their passions. "Catherine took us quite by surprise yesterday evening," said she. "She travelled all the way post by herself, and knew nothing of coming till Saturday night; for General Tilney, from some odd fancy or other, all of a sudden grew tired of having her there, and almost turned her out of the house. Very unfriendly, certainly; and he must be a very odd man; but we are so glad to have her amongst us again! And it is a great comfort to find that she is not a poor helpless creature, but can shift very well for herself."

Mr. Allen expressed himself on the occasion with the reasonable resentment of a sensible friend; and Mrs. Allen thought his expressions quite good enough to be immediately made use of again by herself. His wonder, his conjectures, and his explanations became in succession hers, with the addition of this single remark—"I really have not patience with the general"—to fill up every accidental pause. And, "I really have not patience with the general," was uttered twice after Mr. Allen left the room, without any relaxation of anger, or any material digression of thought. A more considerable degree of wandering attended the third repetition; and, after completing the fourth, she immediately added, "Only think, my dear, of my having got that frightful great rent in my best Mechlin so charmingly mended, before I left Bath, that one can hardly see where it was. I must show it you some day or other. Bath is a nice place, Catherine, after all. I assure you I did not above half like coming away. Mrs. Thorpe's being there was such a comfort to us, was not it? You know, you and I were quite forlorn at first."

"Yes, but *that* did not last long," said Catherine, her eyes brightening at the recollection of what had first given spirit to her existence there.

"Very true: we soon met with Mrs. Thorpe, and then we wanted for nothing. My dear, do not you think these silk gloves wear very well? I put them on new the first time of our going to the Lower Rooms, you know, and I have worn them a great deal since. Do you remember that evening?"

"Do I! Oh! Perfectly."

"It was very agreeable, was not it? Mr. Tilney drank tea with us, and I always thought him a great addition, he is so very agreeable. I have a notion you danced with him, but am not quite sure. I remember I had my favourite gown on."

Catherine could not answer; and, after a short trial of other subjects, Mrs. Allen again returned to—"I really have not patience with the general! Such an agreeable, worthy man as he seemed to be! I do not suppose, Mrs. Morland, you ever saw a better-bred man in your life. His lodgings were taken the very day after he left them, Catherine. But no wonder; Milsom Street, you know."

As they walked home again, Mrs. Morland endeavoured to impress on her daughter's mind the happiness of having such steady well-wishers as Mr. and Mrs. Allen, and the very little consideration which the neglect or unkindness of slight acquaintance like the Tilneys ought to have with her, while she could preserve the good opinion and affection of her earliest friends. There was a great deal of good sense in all this; but there are some situations of the human mind in which good sense has very little power; and Catherine's feelings contradicted almost every position her mother advanced. It was upon the behaviour of these very slight acquaintance that all her present happiness depended; and while Mrs. Morland was successfully confirming her own opinions by the justness of her own representations, Catherine was silently reflecting that *now* Henry must have arrived at Northanger; *now* he must have heard of her departure; and *now,* perhaps, they were all setting off for Hereford.

CHAPTER XXX

CATHERINE's disposition was not naturally sedentary, nor had her habits been ever very industrious; but whatever might hitherto have been her defects of that sort, her mother could not but perceive them now to be greatly increased. She could neither sit still nor employ herself for ten minutes together, walking round the garden and orchard again and again, as if nothing but motion was voluntary; and it seemed as if she could even walk about the house rather than remain fixed for any time in the parlour. Her loss of spirits was a yet greater alteration. In her rambling and her idleness she might only be a caricature of herself; but in her silence and sadness she was the very reverse of all that she had been before.

For two days Mrs. Morland allowed it to pass even without a hint; but when a third night's rest had neither restored her cheerfulness, improved her in useful activity, nor given her a greater inclination for needlework, she could no longer refrain from the gentle reproof of, "'My dear Catherine, I am afraid you are growing quite a fine lady. I do not know when poor Richard's cravats would be done, if he had no friend but you. Your head runs too much upon Bath; but there is a time for everything—a time for balls and plays, and a time for work. You have had a long run of amusement, and now you must try to be useful."

Catherine took up her work directly, saying, in a dejected voice, that "her head did not run upon Bath—much."

"Then you are fretting about General Tilney, and that is very simple of you; for ten to one whether you ever see him again. You should never fret about trifles." After a short silence—"I hope, my Catherine, you are not getting out of humour with home because it is not so grand as Northanger. That would be turning your visit into an evil indeed. Wherever you are you should always be contented, but especially at home, because there you must spend the most of your time. I did not quite like, at breakfast, to hear you talk so much about the French bread at Northanger."

"I am sure I do not care about the bread. It is all the same to me what I eat."

"There is a very clever essay in one of the books upstairs upon much such a subject, about young girls that have been spoilt for home by great acquaintance—*The Mirror*, I think. I will look it out for you some day or other, because I am sure it will do you good."

Catherine said no more, and, with an endeavour to do right, applied to her work; but, after a few minutes, sunk again, without knowing it herself, into languor and listlessness, moving herself in her chair, from the irritation of weariness, much oftener than she moved her needle. Mrs. Morland watched the progress of this relapse; and seeing, in her daughter's absent and dissatisfied look, the full proof of that repining spirit to which she had now begun to attribute her want of cheerfulness, hastily left the room to fetch the book in question, anxious to lose no time in attacking so dreadful a malady. It was some time before she could find what she looked for; and other family matters occurring to detain her, a quarter of an hour had elapsed ere she returned downstairs with the volume from which so much was hoped. Her avocations above having shut out all noise but what she created herself, she knew not that a visitor had arrived within the last few minutes, till, on entering the room, the first object she beheld was a young man whom she had never seen before. With a look of much respect, he immediately rose, and being introduced to her by her conscious daughter as "Mr. Henry Tilney," with the embarrassment of real sensibility began to apologize for his appearance there, acknowledging that after what had passed he had little right to expect a welcome at Fullerton, and stating his impatience to be assured of Miss Morland's having reached her home in safety, as the cause of his intrusion. He did not address himself to an uncandid judge or a resentful heart. Far from comprehending him or his sister in their father's misconduct, Mrs. Morland had been always kindly disposed towards each, and instantly, pleased by his appearance, received him with the simple professions of unaffected benevolence; thanking him for such an attention to her daughter, assuring him that the friends of her children were always welcome there, and entreating him to say not another word of the past.

He was not ill-inclined to obey this request, for, though his heart was greatly relieved by such unlooked-for mildness, it was not just at that moment in his power to say anything to the purpose. Returning in silence to his seat, therefore, he remained for some minutes most civilly answering all Mrs. Morland's common remarks about the weather and roads. Catherine meanwhile—the anxious, agitated, happy, feverish Catherine—said not a word; but her glowing cheek and brightened eye made her mother trust that this good-natured visit would at least set her heart at ease for a time, and gladly therefore did she lay aside the first volume of *The Mirror* for a future hour.

Desirous of Mr. Morland's assistance, as well in giving encouragement, as in finding conversation for her guest, whose embarrassment on his father's account she earnestly pitied, Mrs. Morland had very early dispatched one of the children to summon him; but Mr. Morland was from home—and being thus without any support, at the end of a quarter of an hour she had nothing to say. After a couple of minutes' unbroken silence, Henry, turning to Catherine for the first time since her mother's entrance, asked her, with sudden alacrity, if Mr. and Mrs. Allen were now at Fullerton? And on developing, from amidst all her perplexity of words in reply, the meaning, which one short syllable would have given, immediately expressed his intention of paying his respects to them, and, with a rising colour, asked her if she would have the goodness to show him the way. "You may see the house from this window, sir," was information on Sarah's side, which produced only a bow of acknowledgment from the gentleman, and a silencing nod from her mother; for Mrs. Morland, thinking it probable, as a secondary consideration in his wish of waiting on their worthy neighbours, that he might have some explanation to give of his father's behaviour, which it must be more pleasant for him to communicate only to Catherine, would not on any account prevent her accompanying him. They began their walk, and Mrs. Morland was not entirely mistaken in his object in wishing it. Some explanation on his father's account he had to give; but his first purpose was to explain himself, and before they reached Mr. Allen's grounds he had done it so well that Catherine did not think it could ever be repeated too often. She was assured of his affection; and that heart in return was solicited, which, perhaps, they pretty equally knew was already entirely his own; for, though Henry was now sincerely attached to her, though he felt and delighted in all the excellencies of her character and truly loved her society, I must confess that his affection originated in nothing better than gratitude, or, in other words, that a persuasion of her partiality for him had been the only cause of giving her a serious thought. It is a new circumstance in romance, I acknowledge, and dreadfully derogatory of an heroine's dignity; but if it be as new in common life, the credit of a wild imagination will at least be all my own.

A very short visit to Mrs. Allen, in which Henry talked at random, without sense or connection, and Catherine rapt in the contemplation of her own unutterable happiness, scarcely opened her lips, dismissed them to the ecstasies of another tête-à-tête; and before it was suffered to close, she was enabled to judge how far he was sanctioned by parental authority in his present application. On his return from Woodston, two days before, he had been met near the abbey by his impatient father, hastily informed in angry terms of Miss Morland's departure, and ordered to think of her no more.

Such was the permission upon which he had now offered her his hand. The affrighted Catherine, amidst all the terrors of expectation, as she listened to this account, could not but rejoice in the kind caution with which Henry had saved her from the necessity of a conscientious rejection, by engaging her faith before he mentioned the subject; and as he proceeded to give the particulars, and explain the motives of his father's conduct, her feelings soon hardened into even a triumphant delight. The general had had nothing to accuse her of, nothing to lay to her charge, but her being the involuntary, unconscious object of a deception which his pride could not pardon, and which a better pride would have been ashamed to own. She was guilty only of being less rich than he had supposed her to be. Under a mistaken persuasion of her possessions and claims, he had courted her acquaintance in Bath, solicited her company at Northanger, and designed her for his daughter-in-law. On discovering his error, to turn her from the house seemed the best, though to his feelings an inadequate proof of his resentment towards herself, and his contempt of her family.

John Thorpe had first misled him. The general, perceiving his son one night at the theatre to be paying considerable attention to Miss Morland, had accidentally inquired of Thorpe if he knew more of her than her name. Thorpe, most happy to be on speaking terms with a man of General Tilney's importance, had been joyfully and proudly communicative; and being at that time not only in daily expectation of Morland's engaging Isabella, but likewise pretty well resolved upon marrying Catherine himself, his vanity induced him to represent the family as yet more wealthy than his vanity and avarice had made him believe them. With whomsoever he was, or was likely to be connected, his own consequence always required that theirs should be great, and as his intimacy with any acquaintance grew, so regularly grew their fortune. The expectations of his friend Morland, therefore, from the first overrated, had ever since his introduction to Isabella been gradually increasing; and by merely adding twice as much for the grandeur of the moment, by doubling what he chose to think the amount of Mr. Morland's preferment, trebling his private fortune, bestowing a rich aunt, and sinking half the children, he was able to represent the whole family to the general in a most respectable light. For Catherine, however, the peculiar object of the general's curiosity, and his own speculations, he had yet something more in reserve, and the ten or fifteen thousand pounds which her father could give her would be a pretty addition to Mr. Allen's estate. Her intimacy there had made him seriously determine on her being handsomely legacied hereafter; and to speak of her therefore as the almost acknowledged future heiress of Fullerton naturally followed. Upon such intelligence the general had proceeded; for never had it occurred to him to doubt its authority. Thorpe's interest in the family, by his sister's approaching connection with one of its members, and his own views on another (circumstances of which he boasted with almost equal openness), seemed sufficient vouchers for his truth; and to these were added the absolute facts of the Allens being wealthy and childless, of Miss Morland's being under their care, and—as soon as his acquaintance allowed him to judge—of their treating her with parental kindness. His resolution was soon formed. Already had he discerned a liking towards Miss Morland in the countenance of his son; and thankful for Mr. Thorpe's communication, he almost instantly determined to spare no pains in

weakening his boasted interest and ruining his dearest hopes.
Catherine herself could not be more ignorant at the time of
all this, than his own children. Henry and Eleanor, perceiving nothing in her situation likely to engage their father's
particular respect, had seen with astonishment the suddenness, continuance, and extent of his attention; and though
latterly, from some hints which had accompanied an almost
positive command to his son of doing everything in his
power to attach her, Henry was convinced of his father's believing it to be an advantageous connection, it was not till
the late explanation at Northanger that they had the smallest
idea of the false calculations which had hurried him on. That
they were false, the general had learnt from the very person
who had suggested them, from Thorpe himself, whom he
had chanced to meet again in town, and who, under the influence of exactly opposite feelings, irritated by Catherine's
refusal, and yet more by the failure of a very recent endeavour to accomplish a reconciliation between Morland and Isabella, convinced that they were separated forever, and
spurning a friendship which could be no longer serviceable,
hastened to contradict all that he had said before to the advantage of the Morlands—confessed himself to have been
totally mistaken in his opinion of their circumstances and
character, misled by the rhodomontade of his friend to believe his father a man of substance and credit, whereas the
transactions of the two or three last weeks proved him to be
neither; for after coming eagerly forward on the first over-
ture of a marriage between the families, with the most liberal proposals, he had, on being brought to the point by the
shrewdness of the relator, been constrained to acknowledge
himself incapable of giving the young people even a decent
support. They were, in fact, a necessitous family; numerous,
too, almost beyond example; by no means respected in their
own neighbourhood, as he had lately had particular opportunities of discovering; aiming at a style of life which their
fortune could not warrant; seeking to better themselves by
wealthy connections; a forward, bragging, scheming race.

The terrified general pronounced the name of Allen with
an inquiring look; and here too Thorpe had learnt his error.
The Allens, he believed, had lived near them too long, and
he knew the young man on whom the Fullerton estate must
devolve. The general needed no more. Enraged with almost

everybody in the world but himself, he set out the next day for the abbey, where his performances have been seen.

I leave it to my reader's sagacity to determine how much of all this it was possible for Henry to communicate at this time to Catherine, how much of it he could have learnt from his father, in what points his own conjectures might assist him, and what portion must yet remain to be told in a letter from James. I have united for their ease what they must divide for mine. Catherine, at any rate, heard enough to feel that in suspecting General Tilney of either murdering or shutting up his wife, she had scarcely sinned against his character, or magnified his cruelty.

Henry, in having such things to relate of his father, was almost as pitiable as in their first avowal to himself. He blushed for the narrow-minded counsel which he was obliged to expose. The conversation between them at Northanger had been of the most unfriendly kind. Henry's indignation on hearing how Catherine had been treated, on comprehending his father's views, and being ordered to acquiesce in them, had been open and bold. The general, accustomed on every ordinary occasion to give the law in his family, prepared for no reluctance but of feeling, no opposing desire that should dare to clothe itself in words, could ill brook the opposition of his son, steady as the sanction of reason and the dictate of conscience could make it. But, in such a cause, his anger, though it must shock, could not intimidate Henry, who was sustained in his purpose by a conviction of its justice. He felt himself bound as much in honour as in affection to Miss Morland, and believing that heart to be his own which he had been directed to gain, no unworthy retraction of a tacit consent, no reversing decree of unjustifiable anger, could shake his fidelity, or influence the resolutions it prompted.

He steadily refused to accompany his father into Herefordshire, an engagement formed almost at the moment to promote the dismissal of Catherine, and as steadily declared his intention of offering her his hand. The general was furious in his anger, and they parted in dreadful disagreement. Henry, in an agitation of mind which many solitary hours were required to compose, had returned almost instantly to Woodston, and, on the afternoon of the following day, had begun his journey to Fullerton.

CHAPTER XXXI

MR. and Mrs. Morland's surprise on being applied to by Mr. Tilney for their consent to his marrying their daughter was, for a few minutes, considerable, it having never entered their heads to suspect an attachment on either side; but as nothing, after all, could be more natural than Catherine's being beloved, they soon learnt to consider it with only the happy agitation of gratified pride, and, as far as they alone were concerned, had not a single objection to start. His pleasing manners and good sense were self-evident recommendations; and having never heard evil of him, it was not their way to suppose any evil could be told. Goodwill supplying the place of experience, his character needed no attestation. "Catherine would make a sad, heedless young housekeeper to be sure," was her mother's foreboding remark; but quick was the consolation of there being nothing like practice.

There was but one obstacle, in short, to be mentioned; but till that one was removed, it must be impossible for them to sanction the engagement. Their tempers were mild, but their principles were steady, and while his parent so expressly forbade the connection, they could not allow themselves to encourage it. That the general should come forward to solicit the alliance, or that he should even very heartily approve it, they were not refined enough to make any parading stipulation; but the decent appearance of consent must be yielded, and that once obtained—and their own hearts made them trust that it could not be very long denied—their willing approbation was instantly to follow. His *consent* was all that they wished for. They were no more inclined than entitled to demand his *money*. Of a very considerable fortune, his son was, by marriage settlements, eventually secure; his present income was an income of independence and comfort, and under every pecuniary view, it was a match beyond the claims of their daughter.

The young people could not be surprised at a decision like this. They felt and they deplored—but they could not resent it; and they parted, endeavouring to hope that such a change in the general, as each believed almost impossible, might speedily take place, to unite them again in the fulness of privileged affection. Henry returned to what was now his only home, to watch over his young plantations, and extend his improvements for her sake, to whose share in them he looked anxiously forward; and Catherine remained at Fullerton to cry. Whether the torments of absence were softened by a clandestine correspondence, let us not inquire. Mr. and Mrs. Morland never did—they had been too kind to exact any promise; and whenever Catherine received a letter, as, at that time, happened pretty often, they always looked another way.

The anxiety, which in this state of their attachment must be the portion of Henry and Catherine, and of all who loved either, as to its final event, can hardly extend, I fear, to the bosom of my readers, who will see in the tell-tale compression of the pages before them, that we are all hastening together to perfect felicity. The means by which their early marriage was effected can be the only doubt: what probable circumstance could work upon a temper like the general's? The circumstance which chiefly availed was the marriage of his daughter with a man of fortune and consequence, which took place in the course of the summer—an accession of dignity that threw him into a fit of good humour, from which he did not recover till after Eleanor had obtained his forgiveness of Henry, and his permission for him "to be a fool if he liked it!"

The marriage of Eleanor Tilney, her removal from all the evils of such a home as Northanger had been made by Henry's banishment, to the home of her choice and the man of her choice, is an event which I expect to give general satisfaction among all her acquaintance. My own joy on the occasion is very sincere. I know no one more entitled, by unpretending merit, or better prepared by habitual suffering, to receive and enjoy felicity. Her partiality for this gentleman was not of recent origin; and he had been long withheld only by inferiority of situation from addressing her. His unexpected accession to title and fortune had removed all his difficulties; and never had the general loved his daughter so well in all her hours of companionship, utility, and patient endurance as when he first hailed her "Your Ladyship!" Her husband was really deserving of her; independent of his peerage, his wealth, and his attachment, being to a precision the most charming young man in the world. Any further definition of his merits must be unnecessary; the most charming young man in the world is instantly before the imagination of us all. Concerning the one in question, therefore, I have only to add—aware that the rules of composition forbid the introduction of a character not connected with my fable— that this was the very gentleman whose negligent servant left behind him the collection of washing-bills, resulting from a long visit at Northanger, by which my heroine was involved in one of her most alarming adventures.

The influence of the viscount and viscountess in their brother's behalf was assisted by that right understanding of Mr. Morland's circumstances which, as soon as the general would allow himself to be informed, they were qualified to give. It taught him that he had been scarcely more misled by Thorpe's first boast of the family wealth than by his subsequent malicious overthrow of it; that in no sense of the word were they necessitous or poor, and that Catherine would have three thousand pounds. This was so material an amendment of his late expectations that it greatly contributed to smooth the descent of his pride; and by no means without its effect was the private intelligence, which he was at some pains to procure, that the Fullerton estate, being entirely at the disposal of its present proprietor, was consequently open to every greedy speculation.

On the strength of this, the general, soon after Eleanor's marriage, permitted his son to return to Northanger, and thence made him the bearer of his consent, very courteously worded in a page full of empty professions to Mr. Morland. The event which it authorized soon followed: Henry and Catherine were married, the bells rang, and everybody smiled; and, as this took place within a twelvemonth from the first day of their meeting, it will not appear, after all the dreadful delays occasioned by the general's cruelty, that they were essentially hurt by it. To begin perfect happiness at the respective ages of twenty-six and eighteen is to do pretty well; and professing myself moreover convinced that the general's unjust interference, so far from being really injurious to their felicity, was perhaps rather conducive to it, by improving their knowledge of each other, and adding strength to their attachment, I leave it to be settled, by whomsoever it may concern, whether the tendency of this work be altogether to recommend parental tyranny, or reward filial disobedience.

A Select Bibliography
of Writings about Ann Radcliffe

Arnaud, Pierre. *Ann Radcliffe et le fantastique; Essai de psychobiographie.* Paris: Aubier Montaigne, 1976.

Conger, Syndy M. "Sensibility Restored: Radcliffe's Answer to Lewis's *The Monk.*" *Gothic Fictions: Prohibition/Transgression.* Ed. Kenneth W. Graham. NY: AMS, 1989. 113–49.

Durant, David Sedgwick, Jr. *Ann Radcliffe's Novels: Experiments in Setting.* NY: Arno Press, 1980.

Ellis, Kate Ferguson. *The Contested Castle: Gothic Novels and the Subversion of Domestic Ideology.* Urbana and Chicago: U of Illinois P, 1989.

Garber, Frederick. "Meaning and Mode in Gothic Fiction." *Studies in Eighteenth Century Culture* 3 (1973): 155–69.

Garrett, John. *Gothic Strains and Bourgeois Sentiments in the Novels of Mrs. Ann Radcliffe and Her Imitators.* NY: Arno Press, 1980.

Grant, Aline. *Ann Radcliffe: A Biography.* Denver: Alan Swallow, 1951.

Greenfield, Susan C. "Veiled Desire: Mother-Daughter Love and Sexual Imagery in Ann Radcliffe's *The Italian.*" *The Critical Response to Ann Radcliffe.* Ed. Deborah D. Rogers. London and Westport, CT: Greenwood Press, 1994. 57–70.

Heller, Lynne Epstein. *Ann Radcliffe's Gothic Landscape of Fiction and the Various Influences upon It.* NY: Arno Press, 1980.

Howells, Coral Ann. "The Pleasure of the Woman's Text: Ann Radcliffe's Subtle Transgressions in *The Mysteries of Udolpho* and *The Italian.*" *Gothic Fictions: Prohibition/*

Transgression. Ed. Kenneth W. Graham. NY: AMS, 1989. 151–62.

MacAndrew, Elizabeth. *The Gothic Tradition in Fiction*. NY: Columbia UP, 1979.

McIntyre, Clara Frances. *Ann Radcliffe in Relation to Her Time*. New Haven: Yale UP, 1920.

Miles, Robert. *Gothic Writing 1750–1820*. London and NY: Routledge, 1993.

Murray, E. B. *Ann Radcliffe*. NY: Twayne, 1972.

Napier, Elizabeth R. *The Failure of Gothic: Problems of Disjunction in an Eighteenth-Century Literary Form*. Oxford: Clarendon Press, 1987.

Punter, David. *The Literature of Terror: A History of Gothic Fictions from 1765 to the Present Day*. NY: Longman, 1980.

Rogers, Deborah D. *Ann Radcliffe: A Bio-Bibliography*. London and Westport, CT: Greenwood Press, 1995.

———, ed. *The Critical Response to Ann Radcliffe*. London and Westport, CT: Greenwood Press, 1994.

Sedgwick, Eve Kosofsky. "The Character in the Veil: Imagery of the Surface in the Gothic Novel." *PMLA* 96 (1981): 255–70.

Sherman, Leona F. *Ann Radcliffe and the Gothic Romance: A Psychoanalytic Approach*. NY: Arno Press, 1980.

Smith, Nelson Charles. *The Art of Gothic: Ann Radcliffe's Major Novels*. NY: Arno Press, 1980.

Spacks, Patricia Meyer. *Desire and Truth: Functions of Plot in Eighteenth-Century English Novels*. Chicago: U of Chicago P, 1990.

Stoler, John Andrew. *Ann Radcliffe: The Novel of Suspense and Terror*. NY: Arno Press, 1980.

Swigart, Ford Harris, Jr. *A Study of the Imagery in the Gothic Romances of Ann Radcliffe*. NY: Arno Press, 1980.

Todd, Janet. "Posture and Imposture: The Gothic Manservant in Ann Radcliffe's *The Italian*." In *Men by Women*. Ed. Janet

Todd. NY and London: Holmes and Meier, 1981 (ns 2 of *Women and Literature*): 25–38.

Tompkins, J.M.S. *Ann Radcliffe and Her Influence on Later Writers.* NY: Arno Press, 1980.

Varma, Devendra P. *The Gothic Flame.* London: A. Barker, 1957.

Wieten, Alida Alberdina Sibbellina. *Mrs. Radcliffe—Her Relation towards Romanticism.* Amsterdam: H.J. Paris, 1926.

Wilt, Judith. *Ghosts of the Gothic.* Princeton: Princeton UP, 1980.

Wolstenholme, Susan. *Gothic (Re)visions: Writing Women as Readers.* Albany: State U of New York P, 1993.

A Select Bibliography
of Writings about Jane Austen

Babb, Howard S. *Jane Austen's Novels: The Fabric of Dialogue*. Columbus: Ohio State UP, 1962.

Bradbrook, Frank. *Jane Austen and Her Predecessors*. Cambridge: Cambridge UP, 1966.

Brown, Julia Prewitt. *Jane Austen's Novels*. Cambridge: Harvard UP, 1979.

Butler, Marilyn. *Jane Austen and the War of Ideas*. Oxford: Clarendon Press, 1975.

Cecil, Lord David. *A Portrait of Jane Austen*. London: Constable, 1978.

Chapman, R.W. *Jane Austen: Facts and Problems*. Oxford: Clarendon Press, 1948.

Cottom, David. *The Civilized Imagination: A Study of Ann Radcliffe, Jane Austen, and Sir Walter Scott*. Cambridge: Cambridge UP, 1985.

Gilbert, Sandra and Susan Gubar. *The Madwoman in the Attic: The Woman Writer and the Nineteenth-Century Imagination*. New Haven: Yale UP, 1979.

Harding, D. W. "Regulated Hatred." *Scrutiny* (1940).

Halperin, John. *The Life of Jane Austen*. Baltimore: The Johns Hopkins UP, 1984.

Honan, Park. *Jane Austen: Her Life*. NY: St. Martin's Press, 1987.

Kirkham, Margaret. *Jane Austen, Feminism and Fiction*. Brighton, England: Harvester Press and Totowa, NJ: Barnes and Noble, 1983.

Lascelles, Mary. *Jane Austen and Her Art*. Oxford: Clarendon Press, 1939.

Leavis, F.R. *The Great Tradition*. NY: G.W. Stewart and London: Chatto and Windus, 1948.

Litz, A. Walton. *Jane Austen: A Study of Her Artistic Development*. London: Chatto and Windus, 1965.

Mudrick, Marvin. *Jane Austen: Irony as Defense and Discovery*. Princeton: Princeton UP, 1952.

Southam, B.C. *Jane Austen: The Critical Heritage*. London: Routledge and Kegan Paul, 1968.

Sulloway, Alison. *Jane Austen and the Province of Womanhood*. Philadelphia: U of Pennsylvania P, 1989.

Thompson, James. *Between Self and World: The Novels of Jane Austen*. University Park and London: Pennsylvania State UP, 1988.